BURNING NIGHT

BURNING NIGHT

ALAN SMALE

CAEZIK
SF & FANTASY
ARC MANOR
ROCKVILLE, MARYLAND

✴

SHAHID MAHMUD
PUBLISHER

www.caeziksf.com

This is a work of fiction.

Cover art by Christina P. Myrvold; artstation.com/christinapm

Interior illustrations by Udimamedova Leylya; facebook.com/lkiudlkiud

ISBN: 978-1-64710-166-4

First Edition. First Printing November 2025.
1 2 3 4 5 6 7 8 9 10

An imprint of Arc Manor LLC

www.CaezikSF.com

CONTENTS

Schematics 1

Part One: L5
May-July 1983 7

Part Two: Venus
September-November 1983 105

Part Three: Mars
March-May 1984 181

Part Four: Space
September-November 1984 245

Part Five: Moon
February-June 1985 343

Acknowledgements 539

Dramatis Personae 541

Technical and Political Background 543

Bibliography 547

SOYUZ SPACECRAFT

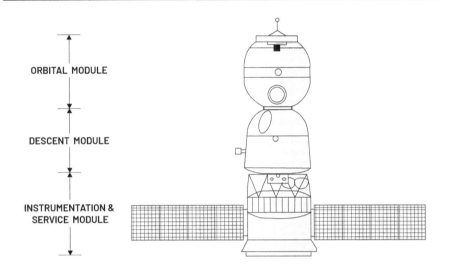

ORBITAL MODULE

DESCENT MODULE

INSTRUMENTATION &
SERVICE MODULE

LK LANDER

LEK LANDER

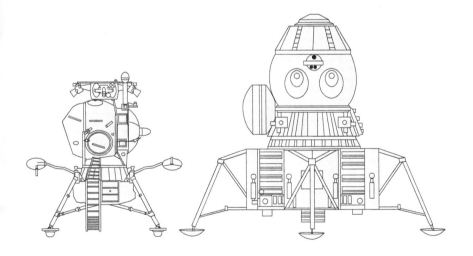

1

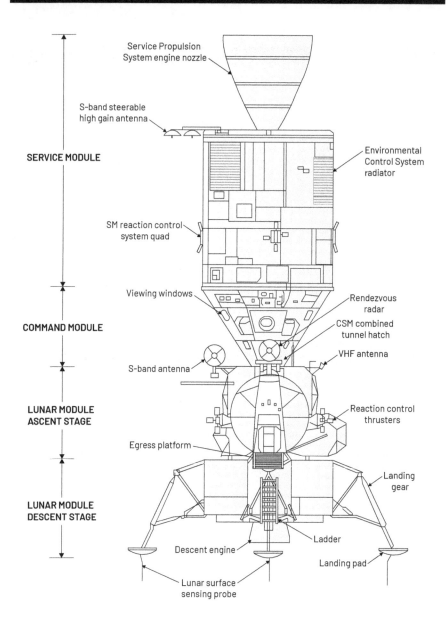

Service Propulsion System engine nozzle

S-band steerable high gain antenna

SERVICE MODULE

Environmental Control System radiator

SM reaction control system quad

Viewing windows

COMMAND MODULE

Rendezvous radar

CSM combined tunnel hatch

VHF antenna

S-band antenna

LUNAR MODULE ASCENT STAGE

Reaction control thrusters

Egress platform

Landing gear

LUNAR MODULE DESCENT STAGE

Ladder

Descent engine

Landing pad

Lunar surface sensing probe

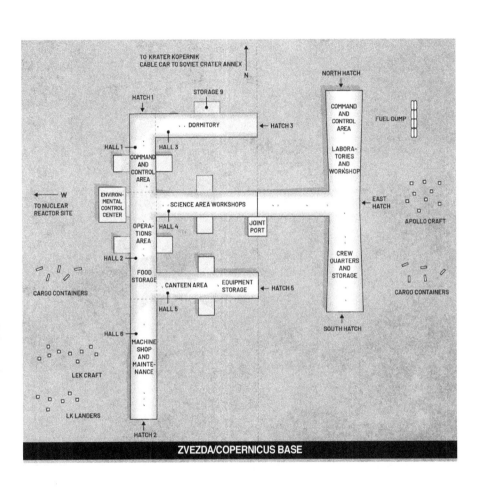

ZVEZDA/COPERNICUS BASE

TO KRATER KOPERNIK
CABLE CAR TO SOVIET CRATER ANNEX
N

NORTH HATCH

STORAGE 9

HATCH 1

COMMAND
AND
CONTROL
AREA

FUEL DUMP

DORMITORY — HATCH 3

HALL 1   HALL 3

LABORA-
TORIES
AND
WORKSHOP

COMMAND
AND
CONTROL
AREA

W
TO NUCLEAR
REACTOR SITE

ENVIRON-
MENTAL
CONTROL
CENTER

SCIENCE AREA WORKSHOPS

EAST
HATCH

APOLLO CRAFT

OPERA-
TIONS
AREA

HALL 4

JOINT
PORT

HALL 2

CREW
QUARTERS
AND
STORAGE

FOOD
STORAGE

CARGO CONTAINERS

CANTEEN AREA   EQUIPMENT
STORAGE   — HATCH 5

CARGO CONTAINERS

HALL 5

HALL 6

SOUTH HATCH

MACHINE
SHOP
AND
MAINTE-
NANCE

LEK CRAFT

LK LANDERS

HATCH 2

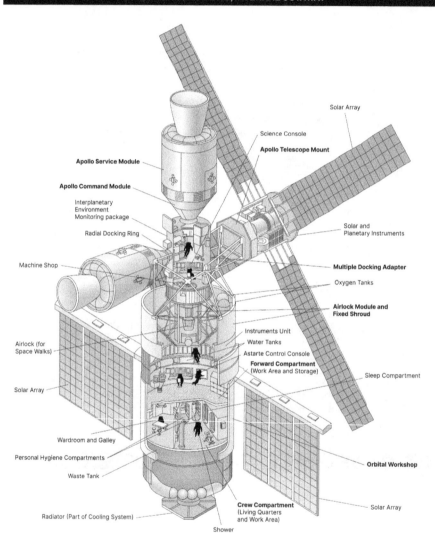

Solar Array

Science Console

Apollo Telescope Mount

Apollo Service Module

Apollo Command Module

Interplanetary
Environment
Monitoring package

Radial Docking Ring

Solar and
Planetary Instruments

Machine Shop

Multiple Docking Adapter

Oxygen Tanks

**Airlock Module and
Fixed Shroud**

Instruments Unit

Airlock (for
Space Walks)

Water Tanks

Astarte Control Console

Forward Compartment
(Work Area and Storage)

Sleep Compartment

Solar Array

Wardroom and Galley

Personal Hygiene Compartments

Orbital Workshop

Waste Tank

Radiator (Part of Cooling System)

Crew Compartment
(Living Quarters
and Work Area)

Solar Array

Shower

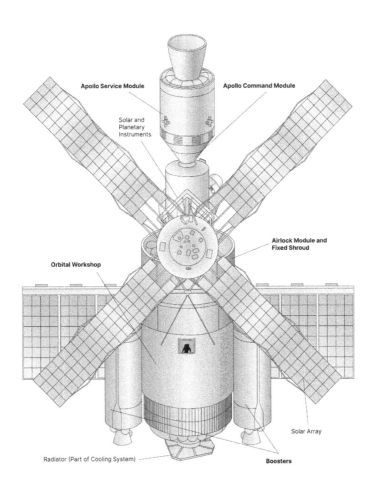

Apollo Service Module

Apollo Command Module

Solar and
Planetary
Instruments

Airlock Module and
Fixed Shroud

Orbital Workshop

Solar Array

Radiator (Part of Cooling System)

Boosters

PART ONE: L5

May-July 1983

CHAPTER 1

WHEN the going gets tough, the tough use duct tape.

Spacesuited, well-tethered, and in free fall outside the far aft section of Apollo Venus Astarte, Vivian Carter put the finishing touches to her latest quick fix. A thick ribbon of unused black sticky tape still twisted in hard vacuum beside her like a living thing, threatening to adhere randomly to her suit glove and everything else around it. She parked it safely on the elbow of her suit instead, turned her attention back to her makeshift stent, and eyed it suspiciously as if it might all unfurl again and drift away right in front of her. It wouldn't be the first time.

So far, so good. She pulled a small toggle clamp out of the tool bag strapped to her thigh—taking care not to let the rest of the contents drift out into space—and applied it gingerly to her stent-and-tape creation to hold it firm. If she bent the thin metal pipe or the clamp slid off, she'd need to start the whole process again from scratch and then epoxy it all, but that would just complicate everything later on, when the welding crew came out to do the job properly.

She poked at it. Gave it little tugs in two different directions. It remained in place.

"Looks okay," she said. "Probably is okay."

"Until it's not," said Marco Dardenas, her EVA buddy from about twenty feet away, and sure enough, her CAPCOM Ellis Carter said the same thing two and a half seconds later from Mission Control in Houston, delayed by the signal travel time.

"Jeez, you guys. If you're this predictable now, what's it going to be like for the next two years?" She shook her head.

"Hell on Earth," said Dardenas, and Vivian waited patiently for him to add: "Or, *not* on Earth."

"Honestly, I could just replace you with a Chatty Cathy doll. It'd eat less too."

She peered up at him. He was wielding a wrench with some glee, tightening a bolt on the solar array panel. As he did so, his whole body swung the other way. Equal and opposite reaction, naturally. "Dammit," he said, sotto voce.

"Okay, Marco? Need another pair of hands?"

"Um." He looked again at what he was doing. "What I really need is not to be flapping in the breeze. How 'bout you anchor my legs?"

They'd already equipped a number of high-traffic regions around the outside hull of the Astarte Skylab with the EVA foot restraints the astronauts called "shoes," which they could slip their boot-tips into to brace themselves. Naturally, there were none within ten feet of the solar array. That seemed like an oversight.

"Sure thing." She floated up and pulled herself orthogonal to him. Jamming her boots against the metal beam bounding the array, she grabbed a rail with her left glove and wrapped her right arm around his knees. "How's this?"

She felt him twist and pushed back the other way to keep him in place. Past his shoulders, she glimpsed the wrench turning smoothly in his gloved hand. "Aces," he said. "Much easier."

Vivian Carter, veteran astronaut and moonwalker, was holding a crewman steady against an opposing torque while he tightened a loose bolt, staring at his spacesuit-padded butt and sweating like a pig. Also, she was starving. "Ah, the glamor of spaceflight."

"You know it."

Her shoulders already ached. They'd been outside working through a seemingly endless list of fixes and adjustments for the past six hours. And after she and Marco were done patching up the outside of the

Astarte, they'd need to go indoors and do two hours of *organized* exercise, riding the stationary bike a couple dozen miles and "lifting weights" using resistance bands until their arms and legs felt deadened by the pain. Living permanently in microgravity required them to exercise constantly to maintain bone and muscle mass and preserve their cardiovascular health. And they'd need to keep doing that for the next two years. Hard labor, day in and day out, no matter what.

Or maybe they'd need to take a few days on either side of their Venus and Mars encounters off from the exercise regime. Those days would be brutal in a different way. They'd be busy off their asses taking photos and grabbing all the science data they could, and likely not get through everything on their schedule however hard they tried.

Betweentimes, they'd likely need to do a bunch of contingency spacewalks to fix issues like these during the mission, as they trekked on their long looping journey past Venus and Mars to arrive back at Earth two years from now. During those EVAs they wouldn't have the recognizable disks of Earth and Moon in their local sky at all. They and the other planets would appear as bright stars at best. What would *that* be like?

Maybe quite hairy. Even if whatever maintenance task they were doing that particular day was straightforward, they'd still be millions of miles from home and safety, millions of miles from a hospital, millions of miles from even a hyperbaric chamber if one of them had problems with decompression. And often *tens* of millions of miles.

Vivian snorted. *Sure. Fine. Safety nets are for the weak, am I right?*

"Okay, that's it," Dardenas said. "Phew. Good grief. That was work."

"Cool." Vivian shoved off from his legs and drifted back down to where she'd been before, swinging her arms as best she could in the bulky suit to work the stiffness out. "Hey Josh, this is Viv. Flow coolant?"

"Roger that," came Josh Rawlings's Texas twang in their headsets from Astarte. "Here goes nothin'."

Vivian saw her duct tape patch quiver just a little, as liquid surged through the metal tube it was holding in place. "Maybe not a hundred percent on the seal," she had to admit. "Looks like it's holding for now, but we'll stay here in position a bit longer before declaring victory. EVA team is taking five."

She checked her tether for possibly the hundredth time, then pushed herself gently backward and allowed herself to pivot slowly through a hundred and eighty degrees until her PLSS life support backpack nudged gently against the Astarte's hull. She was now upside down relative to her previous position, looking outward.

Working on the Apollo Venus Astarte Skylab in the merry month of May, 1983, Vivian and her new crew were getting through a whole lot of duct tape, epoxy, and drill bits, because a *lot* of things kept breaking. Two months until launch, and they were still clawing their way up the learning curve of which subsystems and components they could rely upon to work as specified, and which they couldn't, and every quirk and anomaly and adjustment helped to push them further behind schedule.

Ideally, Vivian would have preferred to take another six months to work out the kinks in the system, but they didn't have that kind of time. Celestial mechanics waited for no one. This July 4th marked the opening of their optimum mission window for the flight to Venus, and the flyby that would also serve as a gravitational slingshot to propel them on their way to Mars.

For that matter she would have liked another year just to work with her crew, to train and bond with them and ensure compatibility, and forge them all into a single well-organized and trusting machine. That was NASA's tried-and-tested interval between crew assignment and flight for an expeditionary mission. But she wouldn't be getting that, either.

Venus. Then Mars. It still didn't seem real. Vivian could pick out Venus readily enough in the radiant sky around her, but Mars? She had no idea which direction to look, and there were plenty of bright reddish stars out there in the ecliptic to choose from.

She focused her gaze closer to home.

The US complex at L5 had grown considerably over the seven weeks that Vivian had been here. Its most obvious features were the two complete Skylabs. The first, called L5 Prime, would form the nucleus of the permanent space station that NASA was establishing here at the fifth Earth-Moon Lagrange point. The second was Vivian's Apollo Venus Astarte craft, of course: bound for death or glory in the inner solar system.

Both Skylabs were currently bolted onto the same side of a stout support truss, sixty feet long with a ten-foot square cross-section, that they called the Common Connector. Mounted on the opposite side of the Connector were two spent and empty Apollo S-IVB third stages; "wet workshops" that would someday hold the prototype lunar ore processing and component manufacturing plant. Packets of compressed lunar regolith would be shot out to L5 using the Bright Driver railgun at Daedalus Base, on the Moon's far side. These would—in theory—be captured at a secondary L5 facility called a "catcher station" located at a safe distance from L5 Prime, and brought into the central facility to be refined, processed, and cast into flat panels. Ultimately, these building blocks would be used to expand the L5 station to what its Project Scientist, Gerard O'Neill, hoped and dreamed would be a heroic size.

But all that was in the future. For the past six months, and for the next forty days, NASA's resources and crew at L5 would be entirely focused on preparing Apollo Venus Astarte for launch. Two Cargo Carriers had arrived since Vivian had taken command here at the beginning of April, with a third and maybe even fourth delivery vessel scheduled for the coming weeks.

Alongside the third stages were two Command Modules, one of the new NASA Big Geminis with eight seats, and the two Cargo Carriers. In addition to the Common Connector that held them rigidly in place—the two Skylabs—the empty third stages and the Big Gem were also linked by inflated docking tunnels, flexible and expandable. As Vivian watched, the tunnel linking Prime and the third stage oscillated back and forth as one of the crew passed between the two craft, bouncing back and forth off the walls as he went.

From the outside, the two Skylabs looked identical. The Astarte Skylab had a larger high-gain antenna dish, to support S- and X-band communications during the mission, but that was the only significant difference visible from outside.

Internally, it was a different story. For one thing, Prime was getting lighter and Astarte a lot heavier, because in addition to meticulously loading and logging supplies, Vivian's crew were cannibalizing the Prime electronics and structural components to ensure that Astarte was in as good a shape as it could be for its mission. Prime could be restocked, after all; its harried and long-suffering commander had a standing "shopping list" for replacements and resupplies for future Cargo Carrier runs from Earth. Apollo Venus Astarte would be limited to whatever it left L5 with. There could be no restocking for them during the long flight, no replacement parts shipped in, no food parcels from home or fuel top-ups or new boosters or … anything. Whatever the Astarte had on board on July 4th, 1983, was what its crew would have to make do with until they arrived back in Earth orbit in May 1985.

That alone was daunting, leaving aside everything *else* that had to go right during those years.

They'd be taking a *lot* of duct tape. And superglue, WD-40, Scotch tape, and Shoe Goo, in addition to a complete stock of more space-age adhesives, epoxies, fastenings and screws and bolts and lubricants: the full range of high-and low-tech Band-Aids to hopefully cover anything that might ail any of the varied components of Astarte. They also had a compact but fully equipped machine shop, of course.

Vivian glanced down at the Omega Speedmaster watch wrapped around the wrist of her suit. In fact, rather longer than five minutes had gone by while she'd been woolgathering and staring out at the wonders of the fifth Lagrange point.

Above her, Vivian could see Dardenas looking at the schedule on the cuff of his spacesuit and fidgeting. He said: "Josh, Ellis, this is Marco; is the rest of this essential to get done today? Because if not, I'd like to get my ass indoors for a snack before I have to exercise and do my maintenance checks on the air filtration system."

"I think you're good to go," Rawlings said absently, obviously busy with something else.

"Sure," Ellis said. "Nothing that won't keep for the next EVA. Call it a wrap for today."

Vivian knew as well as the rest of them that they'd only done two-thirds of the items on that checklist, but out here in real space these fixes always took longer than the Houston backroom expected. And Ellis, always with his eye on safety, didn't want them getting too tired out here. Tired astronauts made mistakes.

"Music to our ears. Go Team." Vivian swung herself around to study the stent again. It still looked okay. "Y'all inside: are the readings still good? Flow rate nominal, no significant coolant loss? I hope?"

"Good enough, until we can weld a real covering over that pig's ear," said Rawlings, who could see it through Vivian's helmet cam.

Vivian took no offense. It was a kludge, and it looked like a kludge, and it would stay a kludge until they had time to fix it properly. "Roger that. Close out Anomaly 506."

"506 closed, roger. And Anomaly 720 added, for when you come back out with the hot-weld crew."

"Gah." Vivian sighed. "Okay. I'll do a quick visual inspection of the ship before we terminate. Then we'll head in. Am I good to go with that?" She'd hate for them to have left a maintenance panel open, or some other dumb oversight.

"Tether check," Ellis said immediately, ever cautious.

"Sure thing, Dad," she said, but gave her tether a good strong pull and eyeballed the connection anyway, before pushing off and drifting away from the Astarte's outer skin. "Tether check A-OK. Going walkabout."

The combined craft they called Apollo Venus Astarte was not sleek, to put it kindly. It was a patchwork quilt of several different vehicles and components, all originally designed for different missions and bolted together to make a Frankenstein of an interplanetary spaceship.

First up, the Astarte Skylab itself, which in size and layout was largely identical to the very first Skylab flown; the one in Earth orbit that had been visited by three crews between May 1973 and February 1974 for missions of between one and three months. It even had a similar solar observatory aboard, plus additional instrumentation for the planetary flybys, all bundled into the Apollo Telescope Mount. Two large solar panels spread out from each side of Astarte's lower hull, with another four narrower solar panels splayed out like an X atop the ATM.

Astarte Skylab had its own thrusters for small maneuvers, in addition to sophisticated control-moment gyroscopes for attitude control, but for serious propulsion it would rely upon the two Centaur-G boosters already attached to its sides. The pair could provide them with variable amounts of thrust, and each was capable of multiple restarts.

The driver's seat for this unwieldy bus? The Apollo Command and Service Module combination, CSM-1—docked at the Astarte's axial port, on the fore tip past the ATM—would serve as their primary piloting area. They would fly the whole ship from there—where "they" really meant Dave Horn, with capable help from Joshua Rawlings and Marco Dardenas, all veteran Command Module pilots and orbital mechanics specialists.

And, because they needed redundancy in everything, they had a second complete Command and Service Module, CSM-2, docked at one of the two radial ports. This gave them a full backup for command and control, plus a second lifeboat in case of dire need.

The sizes of all these components were mismatched, adding to Astarte's awkward appearance. The body of the Skylab was eighty-two feet long and some twenty-two in diameter, not counting the outthrust of the Apollo Telescope Mount, which locally added nearly fifteen feet, or the two solar panels that extended out thirty-four feet on either side. The Centaur-G boosters each measured thirty feet long and fourteen feet in diameter. And each of the CSM combinations were thirty-five and a half feet long by almost thirteen feet wide, which meant the one sticking out from the radial port on the Docking Adapter on the opposite side to the ATM gave the appearance of severely unbalancing the combined craft. Apollo Venus Astarte was asymmetric on every axis, giving the impression that it might topple over at any moment.

But this was how they'd fly to Venus and beyond, in the ungainly format Vivian was looking at right now.

"Josh, this is Viv. Looks okay. Not seeing any surprises."

From inside the ship, Josh just grunted.

"You doing all right in there, sport?"

"Oh, sure. CO_2 level is just creeping up a bit."

Meaning that Vivian would get a literal headache as soon as she got inside, until they got the carbon dioxide partial pressure down again. "Great. Just what we need."

"I did *tell* you I needed to get inside and service the filtration," Marco said, rather peevishly.

"I'm bleeding some off to Prime in the meantime, but it'll take a few minutes," Josh said.

Vivian pulled herself hand-over-hand along Astarte, heading for the Docking Adapter. Stretched across Astarte's hull was a sunshade of aluminized Mylar fabric, treated with a zinc oxide coating to max-imize reflectivity. During their long voyage, the bright searchlight of the Sun would be permanently trained upon Astarte, and reflecting away as much of that heat as possible would be a priority. So, Vivian took care not to abrade it as she went by. "Look on the bright side. At least everything's breaking now. That'll save time later."

"Yup," said Rawlings. "Glad we're getting this nonsense out of the way up-front, so we won't have to worry about it when we're on the road."

Another ongoing joke. *Once we get on our way nothing will go wrong, because we've already fixed everything that could possibly break.*

"Sure," Vivian said. "Because that's *exactly* how that works."

Marco had already disappeared into the airlock, but with stale air awaiting her inside Astarte, Vivian wasn't in a particular hurry. Instead, she pulled herself around and up onto the ATM and threaded her way between its X-shape of solar panels to glance over the multitude of telescope tubes and detectors. From this angle, she hadn't a clue which instrument was which. Fortunately, she had three scientists who did.

Everything looked to be in good order as far as she could see. Nothing was flapping around, at any rate. Metal and glass gleamed. The ATM solar panels looked fine as well. Nice and shiny.

She looked beyond them. *Hmm.*

She held position and pushed a button on her chest radio unit, to change frequency. "Hey, Dave?"

"Carter? Horn," he said crisply into her headset.

"Stand easy, crewman. I was just thinking about that second empty third stage on the Connector, is all."

"What about it?"

"How about we take it with us?"

Horn paused. "With us where?"

"Uh, where do you think?"

"You want to take another S-four-B with us to *Venus?*"

"Why not? The L5 team has plans for it, prototyping the manufacturing facility and all, but … not yet. They already have one to be going along with, and they're behind on refitting it. We need the second one more than they do. Using part of it for storage would free up some of the tightness in Astarte, and we could sure use the extra volume for our mental and physical well-being. Exercise, and contingency space. And a bunch of other reasons I haven't thought of yet. What the hell—they can replace it next month or the month after. Probably be another one showing up next week, unless they have more of those Centaur-G's than I've seen on the provisioning manifest."

Horn still didn't respond. Vivian waited for a few moments, then prodded. "So, how about it? How would the extra mass affect your propulsion math? Would we be back to the drawing board?"

17

"Still thinking," Horn said. "We'd likely have to move CSM-1 to the second radial port and attach the new third stage to the axial. But there's no deal-killing gotcha that immediately jumps out at me. We factored in a sizeable mass margin right from the start."

"Of course you did." Vivian had the numbers memorized, and she was betting Horn did as well. "Sooo, a CSM loaded with fuel is something like sixty-three thousand six hundred pounds, yes? The Skylab, we're talking about another hundred-sixty-eight thousand, seven hundred, by the current book. Plus two fully-gassed-up Centaur-G's at thirty-seven thousand three hundred apiece, so that's … a whole lot of pounds. Okay, so wait a moment …. Damn." She held position in space and gestured in front of her, as if writing on a chalkboard. "Switching to tons, it's easier. I make it a hundred eighty-five tons and change, total, for the current Apollo Venus Astarte configuration."

"Heavier than that, fully loaded. But that's close enough for Government work."

"An empty third stage is maybe twenty-nine seven … call that fifteen tons. So we'd be adding a measly fifteen tons to bring the total mass up to two hundred tons. It's a nice round figure, anyway. What d'you think?"

"Big change late in the game," Ellis said dubiously from Houston.

"Oh hi, you're still there? Okay. But we're making bigger changes every day."

"Slight exaggeration," he said.

"Not by much. Dave?"

"Oh, I'm already drafting a message to the mission manager powers-that-be about it," he said. "May as well get it onto their teletype in writing."

"Plan B, if they say no: take along some inflatable extra space instead? Or as well?"

"Either way, we could only have it with us until Venus," Horn said. "The close-approach math is bad enough with just the main Astarte. At our closest altitude—our peri-Venus, periapsis, whatever—its atmosphere will be way attenuated, detectable but with not too much drag … but I don't think we want what little there is to be tugging on another catty-corner CSM combo."

"Fine, so we jettison it before Venus. That still means we have a nice big play-space for the first four-plus months. That's not nothing."

Over the airwaves Vivian could hear Dave scribbling on a pad. "Got it. Leave it with me, Commander."

18

"Roger that, Pilot."

"You guys," Ellis said, sighing.

"Oh, that's nothing," Vivian said. "Wait till you hear what I come up with tomorrow."

"Jeez. This is going to be a *long* mission, isn't it?"

"You know it, Houston. Okay, I'm climbing into the airlock now. Viv out."

Vivian entered the domed area in Astarte's forward compartment to a hive of activity. Some of the support crew were tossing crates of equipment in a human chain down into the crew compartment, while others threaded the needle back the other way, bumping into wall cupboards and even control panels as they passed. It put Vivian's teeth on edge. Were those crates even going in the right direction? She couldn't even tell without stopping the work to doublecheck the codes on the crates against today's version of the manifest. She'd need to take inventory at the end of the day. Again.

Dardenas and Rawlings were huddled together at the Astarte Skylab command station, frowning over the dials and muttering to each other in monosyllables, oblivious to everything going on around them. She admired their ability to concentrate at the epicenter of all this chaos.

Inside, Astarte had 12,700 cubic feet of "work volume" or pressurized area. For the eight prime crew this came to 1,587 cubic feet per person, or a cube eleven feet six inches on a side. This was either a lot, compared to the crew space in a Command Module (two hundred and ten cubic feet in total, just seventy cubic feet for each of the three crew members), or not very much, considering that it would be their sole living volume for nearly two years. Plus, of course, they were rapidly filling up that pressurized space with instrumentation, spacesuits, liquid oxygen cylinders, water tanks, food, recreational supplies, medical equipment and drugs for every conceivable malady, tools, spare parts for their various mechanical and electrical systems, and manuals and procedure lists for everything. The closer they got to the launch, the more packed and constricted the internal volume of Astarte became.

Vivian both loved and hated this air of rushing, hurrying—of only having half the time they needed. The schedules were makeshift.

Inevitably, people made mistakes. In her first two weeks here, Vivian had found herself spending an extra three or even four hours a day checking up on other people's tasks, until she was able to appoint one of the L5 Prime astronauts to the doublechecking and cross-checking and sanity-checking … at which point she was galled to discover she was making as many mistakes as anyone else on her crew.

Still, the work got done. And then redone. Last week's decisions about where and how their copious provisions would be packed and organized would inevitably be overruled this week. And in the process, they would likely recognize an even more logical and efficient way of organizing and repack next week. Plus, it seemed like every day they were making additions to their manifest and then trimming back in other areas to save mass. They were learning by experience, and on a brutally short timescale.

But that wasn't even what worried Vivian the most.

Pulling herself up beside Josh and Marco at the Astarte command station, Vivian scanned her current master checklist: five pages of densely packed action items, with various people's initials and dates against some small fraction of the lines. Yeah, it hadn't miraculously improved while she'd been outside.

"How's the air now?" she said.

"Normalizing," Josh said. "Soon, anyway."

"Then: conference, guys," she said. "Dave's office."

Command Module One was crowded with four people, but it was workable. Dave Horn and Marco Dardenas shoved themselves back into the lower equipment bay, beneath where the couches would be if they were all folded out, with Horn naturally taking the spot by the Guidance and Navigation computer. Josh floated where the right-hand couch would be, leaving the left-hand commander's position for Vivian.

Vivian saw no reason to beat about the bush. "Guys, I'm not happy about all these anomalies."

Dardenas and Rawlings glanced at each other, but said nothing.

"Well, what?" she demanded.

"We had a ten-spot riding on whether you'd read us the riot act today or tomorrow," Josh said.

"Then it's as obvious to you as to me that this isn't exactly going great. We're spending more than a third of our time fixing crap that breaks, plus the time taken to requisition the extra materials we need to do those fixes. We can't afford that kind of overhead, with everything else we have to do in the next two months."

At her tone, Josh pulled himself slightly straighter, as if bringing himself to attention. "They're just teething troubles, Vivian. We factored in a ton of schedule buffer for this sort of thing."

"And we're using that whole buffer, and more. This always happen with a new Skylab?"

"Perhaps not to this degree," Josh admitted.

"Exactly my point. Guys, this mission was sold to me—and to Congress, and the Space and Appropriations Committee—as established technology. Tried and tested vehicles, legacy hardware and software, with all the teething troubles ironed out. That's not what I'm seeing. What I'm seeing is a lot of the same problems the original Skylab astronauts had to deal with in the nineteen-seventies. Thermal issues. Comms issues. The goddamned plumbing. So … did we just get a lemon from McDonnell Douglas? Given the constraints on this mission—and how far we'll be from any help whatever, for most of it—I was sure hoping for their very best Skylab."

"And this is it," said Josh. "Guaranteed. Look, all that time you were on the Moon, where do you think I was? I was spending more than half that time in St. Louis, Missouri, on the factory floor at McDonnell, kicking ass and taking names. I had my head in every part of this bird, the whole time they were building it. And Marco was there spelling me and backing me up for a lot of it."

"Okay. And?"

"And you really think I'd agree to fly off to freaking *Venus* in a ship I'm not a hundred percent confident in?"

Vivian's hands were already up. "Look, I'm not accusing you of anything. Not saying anyone did a shit job or was asleep at the wheel. I'm just not getting the warm fuzzy feeling about this Astarte vehicle that I was hoping for."

"It's frustrating, for sure," Josh said. "But I don't think it's surprising. For one thing, the thermal profile at L5 is completely different from how it is around the Earth or in lunar orbit. We're not going from day to night every ninety minutes or every two hours, depending where you are."

"In other words: the same conditions as we'll be facing all the way to Venus," she said.

"Exactly, which is why we're holding this shake-down cruise here at L5 to get the bugs out, rather than in Earth orbit."

"Bugs," Vivian said.

Marco cleared his throat. "None of this stuff is serious, Vivian. Honestly."

"But there's a lot of it."

"Sure, right now there is."

"And a fair fraction requires outside work. I really don't think we want to be doing deep-space EVAs on a daily or even weekly basis for the next two years."

"And we won't need to," Josh said. "I'm guessing two more weeks and all that will smooth out."

Vivian pursed her lips. "So, fine. What if all this 'little stuff'—which, let me tell you, doesn't look so minor from where I'm sitting—is just the tip of the iceberg? What if they're warning signs, indications of serious deficiencies in design and engineering that'll smack us in the face six months or a year from now?"

"They're not," Josh said. "You want to know how often we had to do EVA fixes on Columbia Station once we'd gotten the place booted up and settled into equilibrium in lunar orbit? Almost never."

Vivian stared him down. "So. You can tell me, right now, with a hundred percent confidence, that all along the line McDonnell Douglas stuck to their development timetable for this machine? That they never cut corners on testing or quality control?"

"This bird wasn't rushed," Josh said, simply. "Vivian, trust me. This is the third Skylab I've seen through its entire development cycle. Astarte is fine."

Marco, ever the diplomat, raised his hand again. "Josh, let me try. Vivian, here's the thing. Yes, it's tried and true technology, sure. But all along the way there have been changes, necessary changes, because of the nature of our mission. You know that. For some systems we've added redundancy—hell, no Skylab has even had two complete waste management compartments before."

"So our problem is that we have *too much* redundancy?"

"Hear him out," Josh said. "Jeez, Vivian."

She took a deep breath. "Sorry. I haven't had much sleep in the last six months, and I'm a bit cranky. And a little less CO_2 in the air would be nice. Go ahead, Marco."

Dardenas soldiered on. "We're carrying three times as many water tanks as the other Skylabs, and additional food racks in the galley area. Larger refrigeration units for all that food. Added redundancy in our water purification systems. Additional clothing and other personal supplies. Even a washing machine for those clothes, which no other Skylab has had. All that puts different stresses on the superstructure and requires more truss support. Plus, like we said to begin with, we have a vastly different thermal profile. We'll be inside the orbit of Venus for an extended period, facing twice the solar irradiance we're getting here. That requires extra shielding, extra radiator area, additional coolant pipes inside and out … as you know. The cooling subsystem you were fixing today didn't even exist on Columbia Station."

Josh took over. "And on top of all that we have planetary science instrumentation that's never flown in space before. We have boosters attached to us in places we've never attached anything before. At the component level, sure, we're flying systems designed for reduced maintenance, because we'll be so far from supplies, but—"

"Reduced maintenance," Vivian said. "Again, the whole advantage of using a Skylab was that it was mature technology. We've spent ten years ironing the kinks out of Skylabs, and now they're all back again."

"No. These are new kinks."

"You're not reassuring me, Josh."

He sighed. "Different constraints. We're using a space station as a spaceship. That makes sense on paper, but the devil's in the details, like always. Some of those details are biting us in the rear end, right now. But let's just say that none of them really surprise me."

Vivian rubbed her eyes. "Yeah. Despite the legacy components, Astarte is a one-of-a-kind ship. I mean, I get that, of course."

"Yes. In that sense, Astarte right now is a less mature system, with a few new problems that are still hiding from us. Will we have surprises? Stuff to fix? Always, on a Skylab. Are we running a significant risk of a Criticality One component failure between Venus and Mars? No. I can say with high confidence that we are not."

They all fell silent, and Vivian paused to take a breath. A Criticality One component failure would cause the loss of the spacecraft … meaning that they would all die.

Neither Marco nor Josh wanted to perish in deep space. And Vivian didn't doubt that they'd worked their tails off over the past years.

But maybe they were too close to the problem? Maybe they'd just gotten used to a higher tolerance for "bugs"?

No. Like Josh said, this wasn't their first Skylab. And they were both brilliant guys. Smart enough not to get suckered into complacency, or just worn down by the litany of problems to the point that they couldn't be objective. And, deep down, Vivian knew that. "All right," she said.

Horn stirred. "For what it's worth, I concur with their assessment. In the areas of propulsion and guidance, we're clean as a whistle. Environmental controls, we're mostly clean, even if the second waste management system, the new one, is causing us some grief. Today's carbon dioxide excess is mostly because of all the extra bodies in here today slinging supplies around. And our eggheads are happy as three peas in a pod, most of their gear is humming along just fine, though they're still working overtime to calibrate some of it. These guys here, Josh and Marco, are the experts on Skylab systems, and they say we're within reasonable limits. All this thermal work, all those little weird gotchas in, well, every system with fluids … sure, they're a pain in our asses, but I think it'll be okay."

From Dave Horn, *I think it'll be okay* was hardly a rousing *Hurrah* for the technical excellence of Venus Astarte. But it would have to do.

Besides, what choice did they have? The alternative was a complete end-to-end review of the whole system: spacecraft, connectors, booster stages, plus the manufacturing processes and management procedures that had led up to this point. A full-up honest to God zero-based review. But that wasn't on the cards. They didn't have time. Even the minutes taken for this extra conversation were pushing all four of them behind schedule in other areas.

Better, of course, would have been if Vivian herself could have been on the mission from day one. Looking over everyone's shoulder, kicking every tire and reading every memo. But that was why she had Josh and Marco, plus the rest of the NASA mission team at Johnson, Marshall, Kennedy, and NASA HQ.

"Okay," she said. "Good. Thank you for your candor, and for letting me sanity-check for a moment."

"No problem," Josh said, with some relief, as both Dave and Marco surreptitiously checked their watches.

But, she thought, *if we get to launch day and I still have major concerns, don't think for one minute that I won't pull the plug on this thing.*

"Meanwhile," she said, "let's put another task on the backup crew's plate, with assistance from Mission Control. Review the locations of shoes and handrails; see whether they really correlate with were we're seeing the most outside traffic. I mean, the solar arrays? How come we didn't have shoes there from the start?"

"Let's just put in a shoe where I needed one today," Dardenas said.

"No, let's do this properly and see where else we need one. How about near the high gain antenna? At the corners of the micrometeorite shield, in case that starts peeling away again? Let's get this crap done *now*, and by someone else. It's hardly something that the prime crew needs to be doing."

Marco looked wry. "Would it make any difference if I said, 'they're not going to like it?'"

"None whatsoever," Vivian said.

Sure, the backup crew and the rest of the L5 support team had crammed schedules and never-ending task lists as well. Vivian didn't care. Those guys could rest on July 5th and spend the next two years badmouthing her from the beach on Maui.

"Okay. Thanks. You're all the best. Thanks for letting me vent. Let's get back out there and ..." Vivian shook her head.

"Try to catch up with the freaking schedule?" Dave Horn offered.

"Yeah. That."

Could they bring in more help? Not likely. Vivian knew the drill. At any moment there were four heavy-lift Saturn V's being stacked for flight in the Vertical Assembly Building at Kennedy Space Center on Merritt Island, and the three launch pads at Launch Complex 39, labeled A though C, were in continuous rotation. Vivian herself had launched three times from Pad 39B. Meanwhile, the ELVs—the uncrewed Expendable Launch Vehicles; the Atlas, Deltas, and Delta Heavies—went up from the newly-refurbished Pad 37, and the occasional Saturn 1B or 1B-Heavy from Pad 34, both of which were on Cape Canaveral, separated from Merritt Island by the Banana River. The Air Force maintained Launch Complex 19 on Cape Canaveral and still launched from there on occasion, but their main facility was at Vandenberg Air Force Base in California. At Vandenberg the Air Force had separate Space Launch Complexes for their Titans,

Atlases, and other launchers, though Complex 4 and Complex 6 saw most of the action. Smaller NASA satellite and experimental and commercial payloads could be launched from Wallops Flight Facility in Virginia.

That sounded like a lot of launch capacity. But these days, supporting the lunar community as well as the stations in Earth and lunar orbit, the logistics of keeping everyone supplied were horrendous.

So they couldn't just solve every problem by throwing more people at it. They'd already brought in three additional techs earlier in May, raising the number of astronauts bunking aboard L5 Prime to an uncomfortable eleven, for a total of 19 souls at L5. Vivian and her crew were naturally all sleeping aboard Astarte.

The space business had expanded rapidly over the past ten years, and the trend looked set to continue. But even with this impressive infrastructure there was a limit on how fast the US could pump people and machines into space.

NASA was stretched to its limit. They were pushing the hairy edge of the budget envelope to just get to where they were right now. They couldn't expect any more hands on deck, this close to July 4th.

Vivian would just have to make do with the folks she had and … get it all done. Somehow.

"So, we're wondering what all that was about."

Changed into shorts and a tank top and about to get onto the exercise bike for an hour of torment, Vivian looked around, distracted. "Hi, Amy. All what?"

Amy Benson, crew doctor, perched on a crate of oxygen cylinders next to Vivian and glanced around casually. Nobody else was within earshot. The noise level inside a Skylab was pretty high at the best of times, between all the fans and pumps, the hum of electronics, and the occasional thermal creaking and flexing. "All that with our four bona fide astronauts huddling in Module One."

Vivian managed not to sigh. "Okay. How about you do some of my daily med stuff while we're talking, to save time later?"

Amy half-grinned. "Sure." She pushed off to the med cabinet and came back with a blood pressure cuff and a paper-wrapped syringe and test tube combination. She took Vivian's BP, which was surprisingly normal, then stripped off the paper cover to put the disposable needle onto the syringe. "Go ahead. I can multitask and … you've had plenty of time to think about your answer."

"Didn't need the time." Vivian saw no reason not to be honest. "I was concerned about the number of engineering contingencies we're dealing with over the past couple weeks. The guys put my mind at rest, for now. But we still have a whole list of issues I'll be keeping my eye on in the run-up to launch."

Amy stuck the needle into Vivian's arm and eased the plunger out. The tube began to fill with Vivian's blood. "Friendly advice?"

"Buy low, sell high?"

"Vivian …"

"Uh, sure. You're the doctor. Go ahead."

Amy paused to make and hold eye contact. She'd probably been trained to do that, to engage the person she was talking to and make sure she had their complete attention. Vivian suppressed the urge to stick out her tongue.

Amy said: "Don't shut the rest of us out when you have discussions like that. It's our asses on the line too, you know."

Vivian sighed inwardly. "It was a technical discussion. With my Skylab astronauts."

"Sure. But the last thing we want on this mission is some kind of us-and-them scenario, where it's always us four scientists bullshitting about our stuff over here while you four veteran astronauts have your Serious Mission Talks over there."

Vivian could certainly hear that capitalization. "We all have our specialties, Amy. I'm not about to insert myself into your science conversations, for example."

"But, if it's mission safety we're talking about … plus, it's good for bonding if we all get to piss and moan together." Amy grinned. "Just from a mental health perspective. We're one crew, right?"

Vivian grinned back. She did like Amy, despite her shrink training. "One crew, totally. I hear you."

Amy unclipped the blood vial and stoppered it, then pulled a thin-tipped Sharpie out from behind her ear to scribble Vivian's name and the date onto the label. "But, do you agree with me?"

"Sure I do. Sort of."

"I guess that'll have to do. Think about it, anyway."

"Will do." It was past time for a subject change. "Ellis tells me you've padlocked all the medical supply chests and cabinets."

Amy's expression tightened. "Too bloody right, I have. Every time I opened one up, all my pills and potions and critical equipment had been moved around. The mission team was making changes without telling me, and then I'd have to chase them down to find what the variance was, *and* then double-check everything. From now on, every goddamned change to medical supplies goes through me and I make the change."

"Okay," Vivian said.

"Nobody touches my medical supplies without me being right there staring at them. Nobody adds, no one subtracts. I spend half my time just standing there with my back to the medical cupboards with a machete in my hand to beat off the foe."

Vivian looked at her sideways. "Machete?"

Amy shrugged. "Metaphorical."

"I mean … it wouldn't be the first time someone's bought an unauthorized weapon on one of my missions."

"Seriously, Viv, if we have a medical emergency you do *not* want me having to ransack my entire pharmacy cabinet or medical supplies storage looking for what I need."

"Right. I don't."

"Which means you concur?"

"Totally."

"Okay, great. Thanks." Amy gave her a quick grin and pushed off, arrowing through the hexagonal hatch into the crew quarters without touching the sides.

Vivian had been on board seven weeks, and in that time Amy had come to "chat" to her, what, four times? Amy and Vivian had gotten on like a house on fire straight out of the gate, whereas she was still getting to know the other three scientists. So, Amy had clearly been voted their representative for such "chats."

Great.

It was already obvious that managing eight people with very different backgrounds was going to be much more difficult than managing a three-person Apollo crew, or even a six-person combined astronaut and cosmonaut crew.

And they hadn't even left L5 yet.

CHAPTER 2

Lunar South Pole: Terri Brock
May 23, 1983

"**ANOTHER** day, another chilly-assed crater," said Terri Brock to Pope and Doyle.

Doyle grinned dutifully, but didn't respond. His attention was laser-focused on watching geologists Evans and Vasquez out of the MOLAB side window as they hammered in the pitons for the safety lines and attached themselves to those lines, prior to going over the crater rim and down into the darkness. Kevin Pope didn't even grin. He was frowning at their guidance computer, in between glancing back and forth between his plasticky Texas Instruments calculator and a medium-resolution photograph of the region around them, taken from MOL-B in its highly eccentric lunar orbit far above.

Brock didn't like the look on Pope's face, so she poked him. They were basically almost on top of each other anyway in the confined space of the MOLAB, stuffed as it was with the samples that the NASA geologists insisted on bringing in after every stop, plus all the military and tech gear they'd need in the event of a positive detection. "Problem, man?"

"No. Except, yes. This is the wrong crater."

"Oh, for crying out loud. Seriously?"

"Yeah. Look." Pope gestured at the photo. "This curve? Is supposed to be that curve." He pointed out of the window. "And it isn't. The darned crater's the wrong shape, because we're actually parked *here*, by *this* crater." He pointed again at the photo.

Terri squinted. Even with her extensive lunar experience she could barely tell the difference. "You sure? The shadows are completely different in the photograph."

Pope sighed. "Exactly. We need to be two hundred meters west of where we are."

She looked out the window. "West."

He pointed forward towards the MOLAB's cab, and a little to the right. "Thataway."

"Gah."

As last, Pope grinned. "You sound like Vivian when you do that."

Brock was already pressing buttons to get in touch with the EVA crew. "Hey, Christian, guess what? This isn't the place. We need to be at the next-crater-but-one over, on the MOLAB's two o'clock. *That's* the place."

"Well, shit," said Christian Vasquez, out on regolith in his Apollo Moon suit, his upper body turned as he looked around to the right and left. His new geologist partner, Jon Evans, just sighed and kept hammering.

"Sooo, guys? Maybe pick up sticks and take a walk?"

Vasquez glanced back at the MOLAB, then down at Evans. "Well, since we're already here and in place ..."

Doyle rolled his eyes. Pope glanced at Brock. "You knew that was coming."

"Yeah. I did." Brock pushed-to-talk. "Sure, sure, rockheads; take your damned samples of bolus or talus or whatever, but hurry it up, okay? We don't have all day."

"Roger that, ma'am," Vasquez said dutifully.

"Ha," said Pope. They did, in fact, have a very long period of lunar day still ahead of them. At this precise point, so close to the South Pole, it barely got dark at all.

"Don't you start." Brock looked out at Vasquez, who was now passing out line to Evans as he backed across the crest of the rim and out of Brock's sight. He'd likely go a good forty or fifty feet down before taking his samples and, given the cautious way they had to proceed under these conditions, they were likely looking at a good thirty-minute schedule variance before they could roll over to the right crater and start this again. Brock checked her watch. "Guess I'll go hit the head while these bozos are—"

Vasquez broke in, his voice suddenly tense through the loudspeaker. "Break-break. Paydirt."

"What?" Terri's heart started pounding. She glanced quickly out of each window, then swung forward to check the ground radar. Meanwhile, Doyle leaped up and ran for his spacesuit at the rear of the MOLAB.

Pope blinked owlishly and pushed-to-talk. "Well? Report!"

"Large structure, down below us. Man-made. Looks like a hab. Wholly in shadow. No lights, no sign of activity."

"Holy living *crap*." Terri leaned across Pope. "Get your asses out of there, pronto," she said into the microphone, but through the window she could already see Evans and Vasquez high-tailing it back up over the crater rim and bounding across the lunar surface to the protection of the MOLAB. To Pope, she said: "And let's get Peter on the horn."

"Already on it," Pope said, as Terri hustled to the back of the truck to put on her Night Corps exosuit and grab her weapons.

Kevin Pope shook his head and added. "Well, so much for information science."

Four months ago, the Lunar Geological Survey 1 mission led by Vivian Carter had come under attack near the lunar South Pole. It was still an open question whether their attackers had been Soviet or Red Chinese, and whether they'd made the long and difficult trek overland all the way from the Marius Hills to attack LGS-1, or had come a much shorter distance from a separate South Polar base. Night Corps had been tasked with trying to resolve the issue using a combination of orbital surveillance and ground level investigations. Pope and Brock were leading the ground segment, while back at Marius, their partner Jose Rodriguez was still conducting a deep forensic investigation of the cryptonaut base there.

The Air Force backroom boffins had apparently used game theory to assess which craters the Night Corps group should eyeball in person, and in what order. Terri had only the vaguest idea what game theory was, but, as best she could tell, it involved estimating the probability of each crater bearing fruit by multiplying together a whole bunch of factors with various weights—size, illumination, inner wall gradient, rockiness of external terrain, ground distance from the attack on

Vivian's LGS-1 (not too near, not too far), and … who knew what else. Plus, it was odds-on that the hostiles would choose a site at a spot where the Earth wasn't visible, to prevent even the chance of an Earthbound telescope picking up visual, infrared, or radio clues to its existence. Anyway, the eggheads had racked and stacked the results and then strung together those best-guesses into a route that optimized the high priority targets without too many twists and turns and go-backs, which allowed their Night Corps South Pole unit to traverse it in the minimum amount of time.

At least, that was what they'd been told by a very self-important Air Force information scientist, but to Terri Brock this sure felt like a random walk between a bunch of very similar and very boring craters.

That route had been their mission for the past ten days and, frankly, it was getting old. The method repeatedly and notoriously threw out the craters Brock herself might have wanted to visit. The "famous" ones like Shackleton had either been studied already or were too sheer to serve as a hiding place for a giant lunar transport like the cryptonauts had used. And the more geologically interesting shallow craters weren't in perennial darkness, meaning an observation from on high by USAF MOL-B would already have detected any enemy activity in those.

And ironically, despite all that USAF analysis effort, and however the hell much it had cost, it looked like they'd just located the hostile base by happy accident.

At least, Brock hoped it would be happy.

The structure was obvious, just from shining a powerful flashlight into the crater. It wasn't hidden, and no one had attempted to cover or disguise it. It was in deep permanent shadow, and until today that had been more than good enough. Its flat roof was covered with regolith, and its walls were irregularly shaped, so God only knew what orbital radar would have made of it, but looking down at it from obliquely it was very obviously a human habitat. A habitat likely capable of housing twenty or even thirty people, if the cryptonauts had stuffed it to the population density of the Marius Hills habitation.

It was actually two habs, stuck together. One part looked like a re-purposed Cargo Container, and the other was an inflatable annex, now sagging and crumpled and literally out of gas. It closely resembled the hab cluster found in the Marius lava tube four months earlier, with all kinds of crap strewn around outside it, plus a bunch of gnarly looking holes in the steeper north wall of the crater where its inhabitants had been … mining?

Neither the habs nor any items in the surrounding area showed up in the infrared. That meant it was all at ambient temperature, the same as the crater rubble around it, so it must have been deserted for a while. The site was as dead-ass cold as everything else in the shadows, which meant no one was there. There was no conceivable way of obscuring a human-livable presence against a minus-two-hundred-Celsius background temperature.

The crater surrounding it was about four hundred feet across, and maybe fifty feet deep. The far side of the crater was a mess of chunky boulders, some of them head high. Terri knew from geology briefings that all that blocky stuff was likely the remains of the secondary hit that had created this crater they were standing in.

Boulders. Fascinating from a lunar geology perspective. From a security viewpoint, the last things that Night Corps wanted to see inside a crater that contained a hostile base.

It was unlikely that there was still an enemy cosmonaut—or taikonaut—hiding behind any of those chunks. But it wasn't impossible, and it was going to complicate the task of scoping this crater out.

Pope was describing the scene to Sandoval. "No signs of movement. No thermal signature. Which also means no active nuclear reactor. I'm thinking it's long deserted."

"Don't assume anything," Sandoval said over the loop from USAF Mission Control in Cheyenne Mountain, the tension clear in his voice.

"Oh, we won't."

Terri grunted. Nope, they wouldn't be taking any chances. For their exploratory EVA, the NASA geologists had been wearing their customary Apollo Moon suits, but to approach the cryptonaut base the Night Corps team would be going in in their sleek-but-sinister gray battle suits with full body armor and power-augmented boots, and bristling with weapons. Because you never knew what tricks the enemy might have up their sleeves. For all the thermal deadness of the site, there *could* still be hostiles around, somewhere outside the base in the sunlight, or shielded behind a ridge or boulder. Or under the soil: nobody had forgotten that the first blast in the attack on Carter's Convoy had come from the other sort of mine, an explosive device placed just under the regolith in the path that the hostiles had known their victims would take. Bill Dobbs had been very lucky to survive that blast.

They'd deployed out of the MOLAB at full speed, but after that the Night Corps squad moved into this anonymous crater *slowly.*

First, they dispersed around the crater rim, getting eyes in there from several different vantage points, scanning the region thoroughly and taking photographs. In the process, they identified an area a few hundred yards around the crater where its inner slope was much less rocky and steep, providing a route in and out that didn't require pitons and ropes. Judging by the footprints in the area, this looked like the route the cryptonauts themselves had most often taken to enter and exit the crater.

After an hour of this surveillance and documentation, they gingerly began to move in.

They walked in single file with Doyle out in front, followed by Pope and then Brock, with Krantzen fifty feet back, bringing up the rear. Preceding them all was the radio-controlled rover they called Sniffer Dog; not only would its weight trigger any anti-personnel mine that the cryptonauts happened to have left behind them, but with luck would detect one even before rolling over it. The instrument rack that extended out in front of Sniffer Dog included a metal detector and a ground-penetrating radar device, while its "nose" also monitored for suspicious volatiles in the regolith or the presence of scant gases in the space above. In addition, the mechanical beast carried three cameras, providing a dog's-eye-view of what it was seeing ahead and on either side. Geologists Evans and Vasquez, back aboard the MOLAB, were watching the readouts from these instruments, while Doyle kept a close eye on the screen on his handset, steering the Dog with a lever on the same handset.

Back in Cheyenne Mission Control, Peter Sandoval and his team would also be monitoring that feed, plus the feeds from the cameras mounted on each of the Night Corps helmets. Every now and then, Peter would come in with a terse question, or demand that they halt and shine their flashlights in a particular direction. Not that they were hurting for illumination anymore: Vasquez had driven the MOLAB up to the crater's edge, to maintain radio contact and also bring the MOLAB's powerful and steerable headlights to bear on the scene.

On they went, slowly and deliberately. One step at a time, following forty feet behind Sniffer Dog. Krantzen was keeping a constant eye out on their left flank, Terri to their right, and the geologists in the MOLAB were guarding their six and keeping a weather eye out over the whole area, including monitoring the skies with their radar.

Terri shivered involuntarily when they went into full shadow, even though her war suit geared up its heating automatically and effortlessly to compensate for it.

"Really does look a lot like the Marius hab," said Doyle.

"Made in China," said Pope. "Stamp 'em out with cookie-cutters."

"Whatever." Brock shook her head. The two of them had given up arguing about the cryptonauts' country of origin weeks ago. "Kinda makes me happy they had a second base, though. Makes much more sense."

"I'm still amazed we found the damned thing," Pope added.

Terri nodded. They'd come perilously close to missing it. Whereupon they'd have spent the next six weeks futilely peering into one empty crater after another, until they ran low on supplies and had to sprint north to Vaporum Base. "Yeah. Sure glad we haven't been pounding regolith down here for the last twenty days for nothing."

"Guys," Sandoval broke in. "Less unnecessary chatter."

"Roger," said Brock, and they all took another step forward.

Everything around them *glinted*, the glare of their many lights scattering back to them from the lunar soil.

"Still no signs of a reactor," said Doyle. "I don't get that."

The cryptonauts would certainly have needed one, to survive inside a cold-trap of this intensity. Terri's suit fans were whirring in overtime, though she was perfectly comfortable. "Shipped it out with them, when they left?"

"Meaning we should have found two at Marius?" They'd only found one, deep in the lava tube.

"It'd be heavy," came Peter's voice over the airwaves. "They're not going to just sling it over their shoulders and hike out."

"Huh," Terri said. "Please tell me there isn't *another* base, somewhere else."

Pope shook his head. "I can't imagine how much energy it must have taken to power all this, in perpetual shadow. It's at like minus two hundred degrees."

"The habs in the Marius cave were also in perpetual shadow," Krantzen said from the rear.

"Yes," Terri said patiently. "But that was inside a lava tube. Ambient temperature below ground in a tube holds at a constant fifty degrees Fahrenheit. It's actually a very benign thermal environment. Here, not so much."

At about forty feet out from the habs, Doyle stopped, bringing Sniffer Dog to a halt too. "We're coming up on something. Garbage pit?"

They spent ten minutes moving around it before confirming that, yes, they'd found where the hostiles had taken out the trash.

"Mark any debris you can clearly associate with US-Copernicus or Zvezda Bases," said Sandoval in their ears.

Terri looked around. "You really want us to hold up here?"

"Recommend we continue on to the habs, get a complete picture," Pope said.

Sandoval considered that a moment. "Concur. The garbage can wait."

Terri nodded, relieved. She was sure they'd just find the same mix of Cyrillic and Chinese-character information they'd found at Marius. With luck, a follow-up forensics team could futz with that kind of deep diagnostic work at a later date.

On they went.

"They must have winched heavy shit in and out of here. This slope's a *lot*."

"Did they really bring a transport down here? What's the biggest incline it could handle?"

"That's a question for Rod," said Pope. The original cryptonaut transport was still at Marius.

"The Marius transport has a regolith weave over the top, as well as the track-redaction capability," Doyle reminded them. "If they were real careful, they could just leave the transport at the crater rim and use a winch to help get stuff up and down."

"Okay," Sandoval said. "So here's what we need to know, first up: the probable number of occupants, likely duration of stay, time since they left. Plus, whether they left anything behind we can scavenge."

The on-site Night Corps team glanced wryly at one another. They all knew that, of course. Those had been the mission goals from the start. Sandoval was doing his level best to stay relevant. Wanted to be involved and, sure, was still their commanding officer, although Pope technically held the field command, and the four of them had all this well in hand.

Though, in all fairness, Terri thought, *it must suck to be grounded.*

An hour later they'd circled the habs, raking up and bagging forensic regolith samples along the way, and had relaxed just a little.

"Going to take the weight off for a moment." Terri leaned to her left, deployed the extensible support stick mounted into the left leg of her suit, and rested against it. "I don't mind telling you, boss, it's kind of spooky. It really feels like they left ten minutes ago."

Sandoval's tone tightened. "Based on what? Any reason to assume they really did? That they're still there?"

"Negatory, nothing like that. Just that nothing ever changes on the Moon. I don't see how we're going to be able to tell when they packed out of here, unless they helpfully left a calendar hanging on the wall in one of the habs, or we find a teletype printout or something else with an obvious date on it."

"It would be *really* useful to know whether there were people there at the same time as the Marius occupation, or only before," Sandoval said.

"Roger that," Pope said. "We've got this, boss, okay?"

They sent Sniffer Dog on ahead into the hab, but the mechanical pupper had seen very little of interest. Dormitories, Marius-style. Deserted corridors. Trash everywhere. The whole place was open to space and showed no signs of recent occupation.

"Okay," said Pope. "Let's get boots in there. Krantzen, you're with me."

Something niggled at Terri, some weird sixth sense. "Hey, Kevin? Let me come in with you."

"No, you two hold position out here."

Okay, so it made good operational sense to not have both ranking officers inside, but still ….

"Take your time," Sandoval warned. "We're in no hurry. Get footage of everything, whether it looks important or not. We'll be doing a lot of forensics on this."

Pope paused. "Want me to start taking samples on this pass?"

"No, don't get distracted," Sandoval said. "Big picture first. See what we've got, what they were up to. Count beds. Look for anything obvious the Dog can't see from his level. Meanwhile, Brock and Doyle: can you get me the rough outside dimensions of the habs, distance from the crater rim, and so on?"

"Sure thing." Brock didn't have a measuring tape, but she had a coil of rope, and knew how tall she was in the suit, and how long her boot was, so she could bootstrap that into a barnyard-math estimate.

She monitored the guys inside with half an ear while she did her measurements. She regularly paused to eyeball the crater rim, and Doyle did too, but everything was just as empty as it had been previously. By now the sharply defined shadows had moved, almost imperceptibly, but enough for Brock to note the difference.

She wouldn't be sorry to get out of this place and back into the MOLAB. It still gave her the creeps down here.

"We're looking at twenty-four bunks," Pope said from inside the hab. "Still with sheets and blankets on them. Food trash just left everywhere. Some clothes on the floor. A lot of clutter. Kind of dirty and dusty. Real Marie Celeste vibe."

"Coffee's still hot in the cups?" Doyle said.

"Not exactly. The whole place is still cryogenic."

"No calendars," Krantzen said. "Mess everywhere, but none of it is papers."

"Wait, though," Pope said. "I'm entering what might be a command and control area. Desks, not bunks. And here's a bookshelf."

"Show me," Sandoval demanded over the loop.

"Okay, here you go." Pope was evidently training his helmet-cam more squarely on whatever he was looking at. "Yeah, it sure looks to me like …. Whoa, damn."

They heard a scuffling sound, and a fraction of a second later Terri glanced up to see a blinding flash of light—a sudden flare from within the hostile hab reflected off its shiny, plasticky corridor walls.

The ground shook beneath her feet. A plume of smoke erupted through the hab roof, and debris flew.

As rocks pummeled her, Terri instinctively dropped forward onto one knee, turning away and raising her arms to cover her helmet. "Kevin!"

Through her radio headset she'd caught the faintest hint of a cry of pain. Almost a whimper, over so quickly she might have imagined it.

The bright light vanished. And into the sudden and uncanny silence came Sandoval's urgent voice, seconds too late: "Pope, hold up! Freeze! Tripwire!"

Terri chilled to the bone. *Oh, sweet baby Jesus .... Please, God, no.*

"Shit!" Krantzen screamed through the radio, deafening Brock to the point where she instinctively raised a hand to hit her volume dial. And then, so laconically that it might have been a different person speaking, he said: "Man down."

From her left, Brock saw Doyle loping in from the boonies, power-assisted boots shunting him six feet above the ground with every leaping step, but she was still frozen in place. "Kevin?"

Sandoval: "Pope! Report!"

"Oh, he's gone," said Krantzen, still in that stunned monotone.

That freed her. Brock shoved up the lever on her rifle that served as a safety, and ran full tilt into the hab, not stopping to think whether that was a smart thing to do.

Sandoval's voice boomed in her ear again. "What's happening! Report!"

"Shut the hell *up*, Peter," she said, pounding through the hab. Open area to her right, presumably for supplies and suiting up. The dormitory crammed with bunks to her left. And, sure enough, that command and control center with desks and chairs dead ahead.

Krantzen cleared his throat, perhaps trying not to gag. "Pope just bought the farm. Booby-trap. A tripwire of some sort, at waist level."

Brock had to shove Krantzen aside to get through the door, and as soon as she had, she wished she hadn't.

If you were wearing a Night Corps war suit and took enemy fire, there were only two possible outcomes. You were fine, though maybe a bit battered around. Or you were dead. A one or a zero, and it was as simple as that.

No doubt at all which number Pope had drawn today.

Kevin Pope was all the way dead, his legs and hips blown away, the lower half of his exosuit turned to slag. The parts of his abdomen Terri could glimpse were darkened, already burned and flash-frozen, his blood boiled away. His helmet looked oddly pristine, although Terri absolutely didn't want to look in through the visor to see what Kevin's face had become.

Booby-trap. Explosive device. IED.

The goddamned stupid frigging Dog had gone right under it. Leaving it in place for when Pope had come through.

God damn it.

"Out, out, out!" she shouted. "Krantzen? Out!"

"We can't leave him here," Krantzen said dully, the delayed shock clear in his voice. "We never leave a man behind."

"Straight out, soldier. Touch nothing, walk out. Exactly the way you came in. Keep your light on the ground but your eyes peeled. There may be other traps in here." She pushed at him. "*Now.* That's an order."

"Yes, ma'am," Krantzen said, and turned away dutifully.

Terri trained her light and helmet camera on the floor again, sweeping slowly across the wreckage that had been Kevin Pope. Just for the record. Being careful not to point that light anywhere else.

"God, have mercy on his soul," she said.

"You too, Brock," Peter said. "Out. Right now. Do it."

"Yessir. Exiting now," she said, and left.

"Idiot! Idiot!" And worse words, flowing out of Terri's mouth as if someone else were screaming them, and Krantzen took four steps backward away from her rage and fell over a low row of boxes, flailing.

"For God's sake! I should have gone in with him! I knew! I *knew!*" She hadn't known, of course. She'd just felt ... something. "Shit!" Heedless of the potential danger, she kicked out at the boxes Krantzen had just toppled over.

"Terri, Terri ... Brock! Stand down! Take a breath, for God's sake." Sandoval, from Cheyenne. She didn't reply—just stood still, tilted her head back.

Stars bright above her. Frigid shadow all around.

"Damn you, Kevin," she said.

She began to run. Fired up her boots instinctively, her lopes taking her higher and higher as she ran across the bowl of the crater, covering hundreds of feet. Still running, harder and harder and faster. Up the other side of the crater to the rim and then she was in sudden free fall, seeming to take an age to arc back down to the lunar surface.

She scanned the horizon. No one to kill. She fired anyway, three short bursts on full automatic, just to feel the bullets fly out of the gun, feel herself shoved backward by the reaction.

She stopped, turned, panted. Sandoval was shouting something at her on her main A channel, but she ignored him.

No one to take revenge on. No one to kill.

At least, not yet.

"Bastards. Bastards. Bastards."

Terri Brock paced back and forth, a relentless coiled spring of energy. Back in the MOLAB and out of her exosuit, her blood had turned cold, but still she had that raw restlessness that wouldn't let her sit.

Doyle looked up, his face gaunt, eyes glistening. "Terri. We're all hurting here. Maybe take a seat and shut the hell up, just for a moment?"

Brock punched the wall instead. "Fine. Sure. You do realize that Kevin is just the latest in a long line of dead guys in spacesuits I've had to deal with, right? Norton. Klein. Ibarra. Some I didn't even know, after the Marius assault. All buried in regolith. And then Gerry Lin. And the guys that went down at the Marius conflict."

The first of those were no longer buried, she realized even as she spoke: their bodies had been vaporized in the Hadley blast. *That* didn't help her feel any better.

Krantzen had his eyes closed, his hands over his face. "Ma'am. Please."

Brock turned to the TV screen. "And, you! Why the hell weren't you here? You should have been here. Your place was here!"

Sandoval blinked. "Uh, how could I have been?"

"Why did you have to be such a fricking boy scout that you got yourself exiled to Earth?"

His voice hardened once he understood her drift. "Because I had to tell the truth, and not put anyone else in danger ..." He stopped.

"Not put anyone else in danger?" She gestured toward the crater. "And how did that turn out?"

Doyle glared over at her. "Terri. This is not Peter's fault. It's the fault of the cryptonaut who set a tripwire in an abandoned facility on the off-chance of killing an American astronaut."

"Oh, trust me, they're not off the hook either. When I lay my hands on them ..."

"Yes," came Sandoval's voice from Earth. "We'll find them. And, God willing, with luck I'll help you kill them."

Brock nodded, her eyes bleak. "Roger that."

"Please," said Doyle, now drumming his hands on the console, tense with stress and anger. "*Please* just sit down. Can you do that?"

Terri stopped, choked up. "I'm sorry, guys. I'll be right back." She walked into the hygiene facility, closed the door as calmly as she could.

"Wow," said Krantzen to no one in particular.

"She'll be okay," said the image of Sandoval on their TV screen, soon after.

"Think again," said the voice of Terri Brock from behind the bathroom door.

"None of us will be fine," said Doyle.

Peter Sandoval raised his head, his own eyes haunted. "Yeah. I know."

CHAPTER 3

L5: Vivian Carter
May 24, 1983
Launch Clock: T-41 days and counting

"FOR this mission, the Apollo Telescope Mount is gimballed on a two-axis pointing system so that we can point the science instruments much more accurately at the Sun, Venus, and Mars when they're far away. The CMGs—our control moment gyroscopes—only give us coarse attitude control, and our thrusters give us even less attitude precision."

Rudy Frank, their solar physics mission specialist, looked back and forth between Vivian and Marco, and they both nodded dutifully.

Vivian knew all this. She also knew that the CMG wheels each weighed around two hundred and forty pounds, were almost two feet in diameter, spun at nine thousand revs per minute, and were located in spheres positioned around three sides of the ATM.

From Marco's expression, he knew it too. But training was training, and no knowledge could be assumed. Plus, Marco had been busier with the other areas on Astarte than Vivian had, and was even further behind on science training than she was. She reminded herself that at least half the time she'd spent in Navy and NASA classrooms and enduring other types of training, she'd already been expert on the topics she was supposedly being trained on. In some cases, she could have led the class. That was just how all this worked.

But it was galling to be lectured by a member of her own crew, when she had about a hundred times more space experience than he did.

"For most of our mission we'll be in Sun-stable attitude, or solar inertial, meaning both that our solar arrays are pointed directly at the Sun, and so are our instruments. Once we start making observations of Venus as we approach it, we'll use the CMGs to turn Astarte into roughly the right attitude and then pivot the instrument pallet for pinpoint accuracy. Just like a ground-based optical observatory."

He grinned and nodded, confident that neither of them had spent time at a ground-based optical observatory. Unfortunately, he was right.

"The two-axis pointing system, or TAPS, only has a range of plus-minus ten degrees, and we'll be trying to keep it away from the extremes. It's not like the whole array can swing ninety degrees. If we did that, we'd bash the smaller ATM mount solar panels into the main body of Astarte."

"I think you can safely move on to the individual science instruments," Marco said. "That's the area we need to focus on. Me, anyway."

"Well, sure, but first take a lookee here. This is the part of the panel with the TAPS controls, and these are the readouts …"

Vivian also already knew that when they pivoted the array, the whole Skylab creaked and shivered. Even though the ATM was a small fraction of the total mass of the Astarte, cranking it around had a noticeable effect on the ship. Privately, she wasn't convinced that the TAPS was robust enough to survive the two-year mission. But that wasn't her area of expertise, and for the all-important Venus and Mars flybys they'd be so close to the planets that the TAPS attitude fine-tuning would likely be overkill. If it broke down, they'd manage.

As for the rest … Vivian knew the basics, which was all she really needed for right now..

While Rudy continued his briefing, she allowed her eyes to flicker across the console: here were the controls for the two X-ray telescopes, one imaging and one spectroscopic; there were the trio of confusingly-named ultraviolet telescopes and spectrographs that she'd probably never be able to tell apart; and then further around the board she could pick out the screens and controls for the visible light coronagraph and the two hydrogen-alpha telescopes they'd used to point the ATM instruments and obtain TV and photographs of the solar disk. She also knew these instruments were surprisingly large and bulky, considering how bright and near their target was: many of them were around ten feet long, and quite heavy.

A third of the science console space in front of her was shinier and looked newer, but all the screens there were blank and the lights were out, the circuit breaker at the top of the space clearly in the Off position. Those were the controls for the instruments that would study the two planets, and were more clearly labeled than the solar experiments: the terrain camera, a multispectral photographic camera, an infrared spectrometer, a multispectral scanner, and a microwave radiometer.

Phew, Vivian thought. *Hardcore. No wonder we need to take three whole scientists for all this.*

Aside from all this observing-at-a-distance, Venus Astarte was also carrying three small probes that they'd release into Venus's atmosphere in passing, and one for Mars, which had been better studied in the past.

While Rudy continued to pontificate, Vivian glanced casually around the Multiple Docking Adaptor. Columbia Station, the Skylab that she'd been most familiar with prior to arriving on Astarte, had had an array of materials processing equipment here in the MDA, along with the solar science station. On Astarte, that same space was their machine-shop area, occupied by a workbench and tool racks. It was cramped in here with the three of them, though during normal operations it would be rare to have more than one or two of them up here in the MDA at a time.

Vivian had the uncomfortable feeling that she needed experience with the machine shop tools much more than she needed to know how the solar instruments worked. She looked at her watch. "We do probably need to move on. I have a date with a bike in half an hour."

Rudy almost raised his eyes to heaven, but restrained himself manfully. The main chair at the console had stirrups and was on a hinge, to make it easier for the operator to swing back and forth across the whole width of the board without sailing off through the air. He swung it now, so that he could reach the far side of the board. "Roger that. So, in our last twenty minutes let's focus on the H-alpha spotting scopes …"

Sweat flew. Vivian's thighs, ankles, and shoulders all ached even worse than they had before. She gritted her teeth, kept up the cadence. *Cycling to nowhere. Or, if you like, cycling to Venus.*

It sure *felt* like she was cycling to Venus. She pedaled harder, upped her cadence even more. Maybe if she really worked at it, she could get them there quicker. Ha.

The exercise bike was set up in the crew compartment, which was located beneath the larger volume of the forward compartment. This crew area was divided into four: the wardroom and galley, for meals and informal meetings; the sleep area, where they each had bunks and locker space; the waste management and personal hygiene areas, with two separate toilets and a fully enclosed shower facility; and the ops zone where the bike, rowing machine, and resistance bands were set up. On the regular Skylabs like Columbia Station and Eagle Station, this area was quite spacious. Here on Astarte it was crammed with boxes and crates full of equipment and supplies, stacked three layers deep and held in place with thick rubber bungie cords. Vivian barely had room to flex her elbows, and the sweat and humidity built up on the crew deck quite quickly. They would need to do something about that, perhaps by making more efficient use of the storage area beneath her, or by strapping another layer of containers over the forward compartment or something, but that was a problem they hadn't gotten around to addressing, and frankly might have to wait until they were on their outbound cruise and really had time to get everything organized logically. Just another item on the increasing list of jobs they'd be postponing into the post-launch phase.

Vivian exerted so much during her regular days on Astarte that she doubted an additional dedicated exercise session on the bike was necessary. But the docs said it was, and Amy was taking notes, and so that was what Vivian had to do.

She'd try to get it out of the way as quickly as possible, though, and that was one reason why she was pounding quite so hard on the pedals. That, and to try to shift some of the pent-up stress off her shoulders and brain.

Horn poked his head through the hexagonal hatch above her head. "Wow, Viv, holy shit. Don't break that thing before we even leave L5."

Come to think of it, the exercise bike was one of the few pieces of apparatus that had worked flawlessly so far. Of course. Damned torture machine.

She slowed her relentless pace. "I'll go easy on the damned thing. What's up?"

"Night Corps is on the line. Peter Sandoval needs to speak to you. Priority."

Her left foot slid off its pedal and she rocked sideways. "Shit."

Horn eyed her with some amusement. "Peter wanting to talk to you is bad?"

Vivian stopped pedaling altogether, unhooked the elastic tether that was holding her down on the bike seat, and allowed herself to drift upward while she toweled her face and neck and reached out to snag the globs of sweat in freefall around her. "Night Corps on a priority line is *always* bad. They tend to grab me and take me places I don't want to go."

"Not this time."

"You hope."

"Well, let's put it this way: over my dead body."

"Don't tempt fate, Pilot."

Vivian's mind was racing. Was there anything so important that she'd be willing to give up Apollo Astarte? Something only she could do?

Willing? They could *order* Vivian to give up her command. Reassign her. Mission reassignments happened all the time.

She shook her head violently, sending more sweat droplets flying. *Maybe don't panic just yet. Maybe wait and see what Peter wants. And then panic.* "He's on a maximally secure line?"

"Yeah, so take it in CM-2. Hatch closed and all, so none of us regular joes can hear your state secrets."

"He's waiting on the line, or I'm supposed to call him back?"

"Waiting."

"Okay." It figured, though. Even after all this time, Vivian had no idea how to *call Night Corps back.* That was still above her pay grade. She tossed her damp towel into a zip bag to deal with later and ran her fingers through her hair. "How do I look?"

"Sweaty mess, to be honest."

"Thanks. Thought so." Couldn't be helped. Priority meant Right Now. No time to make herself look more appealing.

"Oh, hey, look who it is," she said, as casually as she could manage. "Long time no see."

"Yes." She could see him peering at the screen. "Are you okay? You look a bit … ?"

"Disheveled, yeah. You pulled me away from a session of mandatory cardio. And I'm trying to break the bike. What's up?"

Sandoval nodded, paused a moment. Vivian found that encouraging. *Well, at least this isn't one of those calls where every second counts.* But there was still something bothering him, she could tell.

Eventually, he said: "So, you're going planet-hopping?"

She grinned and felt a surge of relief flood her. "They finally told you, huh?"

He nodded his head, then shook it in disbelief. "That is one *hell* of a big thing that you couldn't tell me, Captain Carter."

"Need-to-know is a bitch, Colonel. But you already know that. I'm happy they told you now, though."

He looked slightly ticked at this. "The NASA powers-that-be decided maybe Night Corps needed to be looped in, in case we were hearing any Soviet chatter about it that we needed to interpret. They should have told us sooner. It's imperative for us to be informed about all major US assets operating in space, especially if they might be vulnerable to … attack, or sabotage."

He'd said that oddly. "And are we?" she demanded.

"Not as far as I know. We've intercepted no intel about your operation. Zero evidence of a credible threat."

"Well, that's good, then."

Two and a half seconds later, Sandoval looked wry. "But, heck, Vivian …. Do I wish you could have told me yourself? Yes. Do I understand why you couldn't? Of course. Do I wish we could have a proper goodbye before you go gallivanting off around the Sun on your nutty inner-Solar-System grand tour? Also, yes. Do I wish it didn't take so damned long to loop around two planets and get home again? Yes, I really do. You weren't kidding when you said it might be a while."

"No. And me too, by the way. To all of that."

He looked perplexed. "NASA didn't use to keep its missions secret."

"I know, right? And I'm not a fan of that. Then again, the Soviets keep their missions secret, sometimes from even from their own people. And they're the ones we're competing with, when we're not collaborating with them. It's complicated."

Vivian was surprised at her own bitterness. Sometimes she needed to say something out loud to realize how she truly felt about it.

Plus, Peter hadn't dropped any bombshells on her yet, so maybe this was going to be okay. Night Corps super-secure line notwithstanding, he'd get around to telling her why he was really calling in his own sweet time. For now, it was just nice to be able to chat with him again like a normal person. If this counted as a normal conversation, that is.

"Anyway, Peter ... The superpowers always love their pissing contests, but all that makes is trouble. Distrust. I'd rather work with the Soviets than be doing all this behind their backs."

"With the Soviets?" He looked dour. "You would?"

Her radar twitched again. "Okay. What's going on?"

"Well, first of all, the last time I saw you, we'd just finished leading an assault force on the Soviets."

"Or the Chinese," she said.

Peter didn't take the bait. "And now you'll be gone two years? Two whole damn years. So before we move on, is there anything you need me to do for you, while you're away?"

This conversation really wasn't going the way Vivian had feared. She found herself beginning to relax. "You could go feed my cat. He's likely getting pretty hungry after all this time." She laughed at Sandoval's look of alarm. "Just kidding. No cat." She thought for a moment. "Do your best to get back in the air? Not that I have to tell you that."

"No, you sure don't."

"Sorry. I honestly can't imagine you Earthbound."

"Well, I'm not. Not completely." At her quizzical look, Sandoval clarified. "I'm only grounded from military flying. But you can bet I'm doing some flying as a private citizen, doctor's orders be damned."

"Okay, good." Not that Vivian could really imagine Peter Sandoval puttering around in a Cessna. "Then: maybe check in on my other friends at Copernicus, from time to time? Casey Buchanan, Starman, and all. I know you're not exactly close with them, and there's all that jockeying between the NASA folks and Air Force folks besides, but ... maybe stay in touch? Frankly, I'm still worried Casey might be in danger."

"Me, too. Okay, will do."

"And obviously, I know you'll watch Terri's back."

Sandoval visibly flinched. "Much as I'm able, stuck here on Earth."

She looked at him more closely. "Peter. Terri's okay, yes?"

"Sure. Terri's fine." He took a deep breath. "But Kevin isn't. Kevin Pope."

"Kevin? Shit, what's happened to Kevin?"

"My team was involved in an ... action, on the lunar surface." Sandoval seemed to consider, and then the words came out in a rush. "Okay, so they were on a mission to survey the likely South Pole craters to see whether the Soviets had a covert base down there. One they'd attacked you from."

"And I'm guessing they found it? Come on, Peter ... just tell me."

"Yes. Long deserted, but ... booby-trapped. In their initial scan, Kevin tripped a wire and triggered an explosive device. It blew him up, Vivian. He must have died instantly."

"Oh my God." Vivian rocked backward, physically buffeted by the news, and came adrift from her handhold. She allowed herself to float away from the screen until she fetched up across the other side of the Command Module and banged into the cabinets inside the hull there. "Oh, my *God*."

Vivian had liked Kevin Pope within moments of meeting him. She'd enjoyed their long Blue Gemini trip out to MOL-B. And they'd kept eyes on each other during the Marius battle, as well as they could.

Vivian hadn't known Pope all that long, but she hadn't needed to. She knew a great guy when she saw one. A good man, a solid buddy, and steady in action.

"Bastards," she said.

Sandoval nodded. "You and Brock. That's her favorite word right now."

"And Terri's really okay?"

"Sort of. She's in a hole, emotionally, but she's uninjured. So she's okay enough, I guess." Sandoval paused. "Listen, if you could talk to her sometime? I think that would be good for her. I can set it up. She's not taking it well. At all."

"I can imagine." Vivian remembered to breathe. "And how about you?"

He sighed, letting his official façade completely drop. "Yeah, frankly I'm not doing great either."

"Understandable." A long silence fell. Eventually, Vivian cleared her throat. "Um. So, is there anything else?"

The shock on Peter's face rocked her back again. "Jesus, Vivian. Isn't that enough?"

"Of course, I … look, I only meant, is there any other really godawful news you're still waiting to tell me?"

"No. That's it. Sorry." He sighed. "And sorry for not telling you right away, up front, and then springing it on you. I just wanted a few minutes of something like normality, before I hit you with it."

"Sure. That was fine. Thanks." She peered at him; he'd looked away, biting his lip. "Peter, what?"

"It's my fault."

Vivian shook her head. "What is? Why?"

"Kevin buying the farm, of course. If I'd been there, maybe I'd have seen the tripwire with my own eyes and been able to warn my crew in real time."

"Maybe. Or maybe you'd have missed it, like they did. You'd likely have insisted on going in first, boy scout. And then maybe you'd have bought it instead of Pope."

Another long silence. Eventually, Sandoval said: "You know, I'd have been okay with that."

"Peter …"

"Seriously. Did you ever meet Kevin's wife and kids?"

Vivian swallowed. "No. No, I never did."

"Well, if you had … they were a hell of a family. Super devoted to each other."

Vivian took a breath. "Sure, Peter. It's awful that Kevin was a family guy, and he's leaving behind a wife and kids who loved him. But blaming yourself and wishing you'd died in his place …. that doesn't seem too healthy."

"So I'm told."

"And is also kind of upsetting, to be honest."

"Sorry." He closed his eyes, opened them again. "Yes, I get that, of course. Sorry. Oh, and by the way: Brock thinks I'm blaming her. And meanwhile Brock is blaming herself and also Krantzen, who was right there on the scene. Everyone's a mess. A firefight, some kind of battle, a real action: anything would be better than *this*. It was just too sudden. And they're still out there, of course—my crew. At the Pole, and getting in each other's hair."

"Good grief. Peter. I don't know the details, but I'm very sure it's not your fault, and not Terri's, or Krantzen's, or Kevin's. It's the fault of whoever set the goddamn booby-trap. Right?"

"Oh, yes." Vivian saw Peter's jaw set. "We're all definitely blaming *them*."

Well, so much for healthy. "Okay. This will have to sit with me for a while. You should take a break, too. But can we talk again, soon? Now you know what's going on? Or are you still sequestered away in Cheyenne?"

He frowned. "How do you know I'm in Cheyenne?"

"Credit me with some smarts, Mr. Intelligence Guy," she said. "That backdrop behind you is nowhere in your house."

His lips quirked, though his eyes were still dark. "All right. How's your schedule looking for tomorrow, the next day, and the day after that?"

"Like absolute crap," she said.

"Then I guess we'll need to work on it. I can patch through to you on the NASA friends-and-family channel? I mean, for a more regular conversation."

"Of course. You have the internal number to talk to the scheduler. And, you can get me patched in with Terri sometime? I'd really like to talk to her as well."

"Leave that with me. Non-trivial, given where she is. But I'm sure the shrinks will be on board with it. I'll figure it out and get back to you."

"Roger that."

Yet another of those soul-crushing silences fell. Vivian felt like she should say something personal, something intimate. Something loving. But the big blast-crater that Kevin's death had left in their conversation was hard to cross.

So instead, she just grinned as best she could. Putting on a brave face, literally. "Well, then. We'll talk soon, under happier circumstances, I hope."

He nodded and met her gaze. "Good luck, Captain."

She saluted. "Over and out, Colonel."

A little ironically, he saluted back.

Vivian blinked, and just stared at his face, letting it settle into her memory.

Peter Sandoval appeared to be doing the same. Many more seconds of silence passed before they broke the connection.

Well, okay then.

Vivian was done with the bike for today. She didn't want to be held down anymore, didn't want to feel constrained. But she was still bursting with restless energy—and some anger.

Okay, at least she knew where to go to let some of *that* out.

Even though Vivian came in here on a semi-regular basis, it was still startling to find herself floating inside a giant empty fuel tank. It looked kind of like a Skylab with everything stripped out of it down to the rivets, but of course it was the reverse: an Apollo third stage that had never been kitted out as a space station.

An empty S-IVB tank was the largest single pressurized volume in space. Fifty feet long inside, and twenty feet in diameter, its overall shape was obviously identical to that of a Skylab but—of course— much emptier. Completely empty, in fact, aside from the long propellant utilization tube along one side that had not been removed, and a few helium tanks the size of basketballs mounted onto the inner walls that had once served for propellant pressurization, plus a new gear locker at the entrance end for athletic equipment and towels. The tank insides still had a musty smell; this was not due to residual propellant, which had merely been liquid hydrogen and liquid oxygen with very little odor, but from the fiberglass that lined the interior.

The end of the tank Vivian had just entered had once held 66,770 gallons of liquid hydrogen, weighing 40,000 pounds. The area aft, ahead of her right now, had held 19,360 gallons of liquid oxygen that weighed in at a further 192,200 pounds. The mutual bulkhead between those two tanks had been removed, and the spent Rocketdyne J-2 engine out in space beyond the base of the oxygen tank would never fire again.

Inside a Skylab, you could launch yourself from the very lowest part of the living space up through the crew compartment and forward compartment, and up through the airlock adapter and Multiple Docking Adaptor into the Command Module beyond in a single swoop. But you had to practice to make sure you set off in a dead-straight line, or be uncannily lucky, or you'd bang into the sides of the hatches you were hoping to float through. This space was much less encumbered and much more relaxing.

Vivian was glad to find she had the place to herself: this was a popular recreational space. Fortunately, it appeared she was the only one currently free to recreate. She set herself to do a serious workout, with spins and flips, pushing herself across the space as fast as was physically safe—she hardly needed to sprain a wrist or twist an ankle this close to the launch of Astarte, but she needed to burn off her restless energy and frustration somehow.

Twenty minutes later, Dave Horn floated into the open expanse to find Vivian doing laps, propelling herself from one end to the other, absorbing the impact with her arms and quickly folding into a racing turn, swimmer-style, to shove off back in the opposite direction with her legs, her face screwed up in concentration. "Oh, here's where you ended up. You okay?"

Vivian hadn't realized he was there until he spoke. She considered briefly: tell Horn about Pope's death, or not?

Not. Or, at least, not now. The two men had never met, as far as Vivian was aware, and Pope had been Night Corps into the bargain. She'd only given Dave a brief, sanitized outline of her activities in those long weeks between her abrupt "reassignment" to Night Corps on the boom outside Eagle Station, and her arrival weeks later back at Eagle to transfer to L5 for the Astarte mission.

For all she knew, the hostile base at the South Pole and Pope's death there—maybe even Pope's existence—were classified. Peter hadn't said so, but he hadn't said they weren't, either.

Besides, Vivian wasn't in the mood for baring her soul. "Everyone's asking me that today." She turned, pushed off a little less fiercely, and drifted again toward the base of the S-IVB tank. "Anyway, hi. What's up?"

"Ironic that you're in here. I just heard back from the mission managers. Our motion was denied."

"Our what? Sorry, too much going on. What did we do, again?"

"This." Horn gestured around them. "Our pitch to take this third stage with us, as an extra happy space. No one's in favor. Half of the management voted no because they want to keep it here for the real L5 space factory activities. It sets back their schedule by several weeks if they lose this one to Astarte and need to bring in another third stage and go through the whole cleaning, passivation, and neutralization process again before they can start using it."

"They haven't been exactly rushing to fill this one up with ore processing machinery," Vivian said.

"No. But still. And the other half just don't want the complication and added risk of flying this on Astarte. The Administrator went with their vote. This S-four-B stays put at L5."

"Added risk? But they're perfectly fine with the risk of having it *here*."

"Well, sure, but that's not the same. Here, we're within a few days of Earth. The risk matrix is completely different once Astarte is weeks and months away. And we can't afford to slip if this causes a complication."

"Well, the launch wouldn't slip, because this wouldn't have been a critical-path item."

"Yes, but … knock-on schedule effects? We know how easily those happen. Anyway, the decision is made. Done deal."

"Yeah." Vivian exhaled. "Okay, never mind. That's fair. Disappointing, but fair. So I'm guessing this means we won't get any extra inflatable volume either?"

"Correct. That was also judged to be too much of a risk. Too much chance of a micrometeorite deflation or some other complication. There's a non-zero puncturing risk at the speeds we'll be going, with a lack of ability to recover."

"Okay, but maybe we should consider taking it as, you know, emergency space? Not for the nominal mission, but for contingency use?"

Horn grinned. "They're too smart to fall for that one."

"Well, crap." Vivian looked around her. "It would have been nice. But, whatever. I guess we'll just have to enjoy it while we can."

And, she thought suddenly, *it's also important to enjoy your friends while you've got them.*

Not exactly profound. But also, not exactly the way Vivian was used to thinking. And maybe that was a mistake. If she'd known Kevin Pope would be gone so quickly …

She pushed off at what used to be the rocket-motor end of the third stage and drifted "up" toward him. "So, you got a few minutes to goof off? Jump around, maybe grab a ball and play some catch? I mean, help get your cardio requirement checked off and slow your muscle loss? It's billable. Amy'll give you a check mark for it."

"Thought you'd never ask," Horn said, and propelled himself to the gear locker to get his glove.

CHAPTER 4

Lunar South Pole: Terri Brock
May 24, 1983

TERRI Brock couldn't sleep. Which maybe wasn't surprising, having seen a good friend get blown to pieces by an IED, but that wasn't all that was keeping her up.

This crater bothered the hell out of her. They'd missed something. Something important.

Eventually, she couldn't stand it anymore. Everyone else was dead to the world, so to speak. Aside from Vasquez, the rest of the crew slept far more deeply than Brock did, even at the best of times. Tonight they were all exhausted, and even Vasquez had taken a Seconal. And, sure, Brock was exhausted too, but … this couldn't wait.

Should she wake someone up to buddy her? Nope. If she woke up one person she'd end up waking everyone, and none of them would thank her for that.

Call Peter? That, too, was a definite no, at least for now.

Peter Sandoval was always big on the buddy system. No one went out on surface alone on his watch. But Sandoval wasn't here, so it wasn't his watch, and with Pope out of the picture, Terri had just gotten an unwelcome field promotion. So she got to decide, right? No point wasting time and energy trying to talk Peter into letting her do something she was going to do anyway.

She climbed down from her bunk. No one else moved. She used the head, came out, and still no one had moved. So she walked through the accordion-pleated connecting tunnel into the radiation-shielded Pod that served as their trailer, eased the door closed, and began to suit up slowly and carefully, since she had no one spotting her and the beginnings of a tiredness headache lurking behind her eyes.

Was this a dumb thing to do? Probably. Was she going to do it anyway? Hell, yes. If only to put some space between her and her crew-mates for a while, but mainly to satisfy her curiosity.

Vivian Carter wasn't the only maverick astronaut in the bunch. Not anymore.

As Terri opened the outer airlock door and stepped down onto the lunar surface, rifle in hand, she took a strange comfort in that. Because going out by herself on a hunch and walking down into a permanently dark and possibly still booby-trapped crater in the middle of a sleep period: that did feel like a very *Vivian* thing to be doing.

She had to see. And if she was right about what she'd seen, she wanted the chance to … process it quietly, with no one else around.

She didn't use the guide rope as she loped down into the still-unnamed crater toward the hostile habitat. No big deal if she took a tumble: her Night Corps suit wouldn't even get a scratch, though with its greater mass it would be harder to get back up onto her feet again than it was in an Apollo suit. Terri did stick to the beaten track though, following their own footprints over well-trodden ground, at least for now.

Down here by herself, and without the MOLAB's headlights illuminating the area, the abandoned habitat looked even spookier. Her suit headlight sent sinister shadows dancing across its walls and the ground just beyond. Terri was glad that she'd brought the rifle with her, from the rack in the Pod. Not that she was expecting to be attacked by hostiles down here after all—not after the care they'd taken surveying the area the previous day—but it was comforting to know she could blow one away if she did.

That would be nice. For all her faith in God, Terri would be quite happy to have an enemy to kill, right now. Catharsis by bullet. That might help her mental state quite a bit.

Hey, now. Take a breath, girl.

She stopped walking and took a moment to tilt her head back to look at the stars, which were easily visible from within the permanent darkness of the crater. None were twinkling, of course, with no atmosphere to create that effect. Equally obviously, she saw no clouds or haze above her. The star fields were constant, harsh, and very, very clear. Vivian could likely see them even better at L5.

Terri snorted. L5? What a joke. Why the hell Vivian had agreed to go *there* of all places, Terri would never understand. A more useless location was hard to imagine. Given the choice between going back to Earth and a posting to L5, Terri wouldn't even hesitate.

Terri did miss Vivian, though. Being the only chick on the team was fine … most of the time. Like any woman in the astronaut corps, and even more especially in Night Corps, Terri was comfortable in male company. But many of the best, worst, and most memorable times Brock had spent on the Moon, or in orbit nearby, had been with Vivian Carter.

Anyway. She needed to get on with this. At any moment, one of her crew might wake up, find her missing, and sound the alarm. So Terri walked past the hab, giving it a wide berth in case of stray mines that Doyle had somehow missed in his external sweep—however unlikely *that* was—and headed out through the boulder field, toward the much steeper, craggy crater face opposite.

Even before Terri got there, she was nodding. The crystalline shards in the regolith always scattered her headlight beam back under conditions like these, but the sparkles she was looking at right now were very different and unlike anything else she'd seen on the Moon.

From inside the hinged panel in the calf of her suit, she tugged out a geologist's hammer and a baggie. Channeling Vivian again, she thought wryly; most Night Corps astronauts didn't go out prepped for mineral sampling. Then she took a fierce whack at the wall in front of her and grabbed a couple of the larger chunks as they drifted slowly down toward the ground.

She held them up and squinted. Turned them around in the glare of her headlight. Watched how the light scattered off her samples … and *through* them.

Her heart started thumping again, but this time it wasn't fear. *Could it be?*

If so, this beat even the rare earth elements that Vivian had been looking for with LGS-1.

She whacked the wall again. Took some more samples. Grabbed herself about a pound of rock in all, bundled it up in the baggie, shoved the baggie and hammer back into that calf pocket, and headed up and out of the crater's far side.

Back in sunlight, she deployed her suit's "kickstand" so she could sit comfortably. Pulled one of her samples out of the baggie again, and stared intently at it, occasionally tilting it in her hands.

Holy living shit.

Terri Brock had been the first U.S. woman to put boot prints on the Moon. But this? This might be bigger.

And she couldn't help her next mischievous thought. *Vivian is going to be* so *ticked off that I found this, and not her.*

She turned the sample clumsily in her gloved fingers. Watched how the sunlight played on it. Nope, there really wasn't any doubt.

I found water on the Moon.

Technically, of course, the cryptonauts had found it first. But screw *them.*

"E.T., phone home," she said out loud, turned on her suit telemetry, and toggled her radio to Transmit. She glanced across the width of the crater at the roof of the MOLAB, where their main high-gain antenna was situated, steadily tracking whichever NAVSTAR or Night Corps orbiting asset was nearest, and saw the green light flicker on at its base and the dish begin to turn.

"Cheyenne Mission Control, this is Brock, Night Corps SP. You copy?"

Immediate response, modulo the signal travel time. "Night Corps South Pole, this is Cheyenne. Go ahead, Brock."

"I need to speak to Colonel Sandoval. Priority."

"Colonel Sandoval is off duty."

"But bunking in the mountain, right? He'll want to hear this. Guaranteed."

"Brock? Sandoval. Report."

She could hear the grogginess in his voice. "Sorry for having you woken, sir. It's not bad news. But I thought you'd want to be the first to know."

"Uh. Okay." He paused. "Wait. Telemetry is showing you out on surface? And you're *alone.* What the hell?"

Terri looked back into the darkness of the crater. "Honestly, if the Moon has taught me anything, it's that buddies aren't worth a damn."

She paused. "I don't mean that like it sounds. Crewmates, colleagues, a helping hand; sure. But out here on the lunar surface, if anything goes wrong, really no one can help you. Vivian spent weeks out on the surface alone. Even at Hadley Base, astronauts were always going out solo. Seriously, the buddy system may be fine for deep sea diving, but on the Moon? Whatever."

"When Vivian's suit failed out on surface, Okhotina's action saved her goddamned *life*," Sandoval pointed out, a little testily.

"Fair point. But that was a combat situation. Tonight, I didn't want to disturb my buddies' beauty sleep. Because, dear God, they all need it."

Sandoval's voice acquired that familiar edge of irritation. "Brock, get to the point. What the hell are you doing out there?"

"Figuring out one of the reasons the cryptonauts were based here. The appeal of this particular crater."

"Which is?"

Again, Terri held up her chunk of the "rock" and watched again how the rays of sunlight scattered through it. "Well, I'd need to lick it to be sure, or at least melt or sublime it, but ... I'm damned sure they were mining deep-frozen water from the crater walls. Quite a high concentration, mixed in with a rocky aggregate."

Silence on comms. Then: "Say again?"

"Water. Our commie friends found water at the South Pole, and from the gashes on the inner crater wall, they took somewhere between a shit-ton and a shit-ton-and-a-half of it with them when they left."

After a long silence, Sandoval just said: "*Amazing.*"

Yes. It truly was. For a moment, Terri felt dizzy. Then, she refocused. "Okay. What do you want me to do next?"

"Back room is telling me: look around more. Since you're already on site, take twenty minutes to get it all on camera. Take some more samples, try and guesstimate the width and height of the deposit. And then get your ass back into that MOLAB before your crew wakes up, so that no one panics and thinks you've taken a walk. None of them needs that stress—not today."

"Uh, sir? I *have* taken a walk."

"I meant a short walk off a long pier. Your team—they've suffered enough."

Kevin Pope. Terri winced, involuntarily. For just a few moments, she'd managed to ... not forget, exactly, but to put the shock of his death to the side of her mind. "Roger. Will do. Except, sir: that would be a long walk off a short pier."

A pause. "Right."

"Have you gotten any sleep at *all*? Sir?"

"Sure."

She switched her tone from military to friendly. "Peter? Be straight with me."

"I'm fine."

Which didn't answer the question, and wasn't true, but whatever. "Okay. Good." Suddenly, Terri yawned. *Oh, great.* Now *I'm sleepy?* Naturally, her next thought was to check her oxygen supply, just in case, but her O_2 was nominal.

"Brock ... stay alert. Don't get comfortable. And keep looking down."

"I certainly will." She swallowed. "To tell the truth, I'll probably be looking out for tripwires for the rest of my life."

He paused. "Understood."

As soon as Sandoval broke the connection, a moment of intense sorrow washed over her. *Sure wish Kevin was still around to see this.* For all her flak on buddies, she would love to have him standing beside her on the lunar surface right now. He'd be taking this with a combination of awe and his usual gentle wisecracks.

She was just finishing up her brief estimate of the deposit's size, which was considerable, when her radio crackled again. "Terri? Christian here. Where are you? What's going on?"

"I'm safe. Just doing a bit of prospecting."

"Huh?"

Glancing across at the MOLAB window she could see Jon Evans looking out at her, with Vasquez standing next to him, still rubbing sleep out of his eyes. "Did I wake you?" she said, reviewing in her head whether any of her on-surface activities could have pinged an alarm inside the MOLAB.

"No. Sandoval did."

"Of course he did."

"Everything okay out there?"

"Sure." She grinned. "Did he tell you what I have in my hand?"

"No. Terri ..."

"Water," she said.

A very long silence, during which Vasquez and Evans in the MO-LAB window did an almost comical double take, then stared at each other for a few moments and then back out at her. More than anything else that had happened so far, their stunned reaction helped to drive it home to her just what a big deal this was.

"Water?" Vasquez said eventually. "You're absolutely sure?"

"Pretty damned sure. Water ice. In the crater, out back. We'll need to test it, but it sure as hell *looks* like ice, and when you hold it in sunlight it sublimates off steadily just like water would. But hey, you're the geologists—you tell me."

"Okay, then," and she could hear the excitement in his voice. "So bring some in, sealed in a baggie and shielded from light, and we can confirm it lickety-split."

"Roger that." Terri stowed her kickstand and began to walk around the crater rim back to the MOLAB. "Worth waking up for, right?"

"To be honest," Vasquez said, "I feel like I'm still dreaming."

CHAPTER 5

Zvezda Base: Svetlana Belyakova
June 1, 1983

"**MAJOR-GENERAL** Belyakova." Starman stood. "Thank you for coming."

She gave a slight formal bow and stepped into his office. "Commander Jones. How are you?"

"Swell, thanks for asking," Svetlana had no difficulty picking up the slight edge in his voice that gave the lie to his words. "Please, take a seat. We have a lot to talk about."

She thought about the report she had read that morning. "Yes. There is the good news, and there is the bad news."

"And more of each than you probably know."

Belyakova raised her eyebrows. "Then I look forward to learning more of these matters. Shall we begin with the water?"

"Water on the Moon," he said, studying her face. "In a permanently shadowed crater near the South Pole. And it's surely not just that one crater. Quite a thing. Who'd have thought it?"

Belyakova met his eye. "It has been speculated for some time, but I certainly knew nothing of it being discovered. Or of the South Pole habitations that your Night Corps team found, until the news came through." *The news* had been a formal complaint lodged by the US against the USSR. The Americans missed no opportunity to try to make political capital. Svetlana found this very tiring.

Starman grinned thinly, skeptically. "Because it's Chinese?"

"Yes. Must we again repeat that same conversation? It would be a better use of our time to talk of what we will do about it, now that it has been discovered."

Starman regarded her for a long moment, and then sat forward, opened a thin file, and pushed it across the table toward her. "Sure. Let's do that. I've been cleared to make you an offer. In the spirit of international cooperation, NASA would like to propose that we exploit this find together and add it to our list of joint collaborations. They'd like us to assemble a joint geological team and send it south to investigate the limits of the deposit, and have our technical people figure out how best to proceed. Do we ship some of the water-bearing ore up here to Zvezda-Copernicus to extract and purify the water, or set up a small extraction plant down there *in situ?* We don't know yet which would be the most efficient. We *do* know that having a ready source of water on the Moon will greatly simplify our supply chain, and yours. I'm sure you wouldn't disagree."

"Very fair, and very cooperative all of a sudden. Why?"

"Tensions are high," Starman said simply. "On Earth as well as up here. We'd like to take them down a notch. The more collaborating we can do, the better. Right? Plus, this will likely be a major operation. It'll take quite a few resources."

She grinned. "You cannot afford it?"

"Oh, we can afford it. And I'm sure the investment will pay off in the end. But we'd make much quicker progress together than separately. Why set up two operations where one will do?"

Belyakova considered. The Americans could, perhaps, afford it. On the other hand, she knew all too well that the Soviet space efforts were already stretched thin. It was surely in American interests to have the Soviets spend their limited resources on water mining rather than, say, bringing in further troops to defend themselves in case of a future conflict.

That was the cynical view. But Svetlana knew that if Vivian were here, she would also be pushing passionately for cooperation over competition.

There was no reason why both motivations could not be true at the same time, of course.

Perhaps Starman misinterpreted her pause for thought. "If that was a *Soviet* base down there, then I guess the Soviets would have first dibs on the water. But since you deny Soviet involvement, then it's up for grabs and we may as well join forces on it. Right?"

Svetlana did not rise to the bait. "I would agree, if it were up to me alone. To collaborate on extracting this water ice, and on refining the water for our joint use. Of course, I will need to consult my superiors."

"Naturally. When you do, point out that it'll look better for both of us in a legal sense, and avoid any potential hassles down the line."

"Legal?"

"The Outer Space Treaty of 1967 prohibits the appropriation of the Moon's resources. Mining is sort of a grey area ... so why not just sidestep that rights thing altogether, say the water's for everyone, and agree to play nice?"

"How quaint that you still quote from that treaty," Belyakova said. "Given your country's construction of the Dark Driver, which blatantly contravenes it."

"And your country's detonation of a nuclear device, annihilating the US base I worked so hard to establish." Starman shook his head. "We could trade barbs all day, Svetlana. But let's not. Let's just talk about the next steps instead. It's water. We could all use it. And NASA is damned if it wants to go to war with you over water rights, of all things." His lip quirked. "We have enough trouble with that in our own states, back home."

She looked quizzical. "'NASA would like to propose? NASA is damned?'"

"Of course. Because NASA is a civilian organization, and this is a NASA base. And our two countries now have a several-year history of collaborating up here on various projects of mutual interest."

Belyakova shook her head. "But it is such a fiction, is it not?"

"I don't understand."

"That our interests on the Moon are not military. I do not point the finger at you, Commander Jones. Not this time. I mean both our sides: Soviet interests, and also your American interests. Night Corps has its bases at Vaporum and Kepler and Marius, and now at the South Pole. And where else, I wonder?"

He nodded. "And we also both know that covert Soviet forces have recently established at least one new military base, south of us at Hortensius Crater. And I also wonder: where else?"

"I dislike the militarization of the Moon as much as you do," Belyakova said soberly. "Perhaps more. You may believe me when I say this."

Starman relented. "I do, at least in this. Vivian trusts you, at least up to a point, and that counts for a lot with me."

Or says she does, Belyakova thought. *When it is in her interests.* Out loud she said: "Back to the water. The American half, you will also share it with Night Corps?"

"Yet again: NASA has no formal connection with Night Corps," Jones said. "Separate organizations. Separate supply chains. The Air Force and NASA have pursued their own separate goals in space, and on the Moon, for coming up on a decade and a half. That history must be well-known, even in the Kremlin. That stove-piping is often irritating; hell, NASA collaborates more with you than we do with the Air Force. In other words, Night Corps can go get their own water, or negotiate with NASA for it, or whatever. Above my pay grade."

Belyakova inclined her head. "As you say."

"So, what about it, Svetlana? Are you game? What could we do to strengthen this water-collaboration proposal, for when you take it to your superiors in the Kremlin?"

Starman looked earnest. Perhaps he was, at last.

"Very well," she said. "Let us consider practicalities. Will it be worth the expense of carrying this water-bearing rock all the way here from the South Pole? We Soviets do not have the vehicles to carry such weight such long distances, and so NASA would need to contribute that capability, at least for now. Later on, I imagine that a new base at the South Pole must be the most efficient method. We must establish a base down there, to mine the water ore. If we extract the water there, it is merely that water we must carry back up here to Zvezda."

"I think that depends on how much of it there is, and where. If there's a huge amount all in one place, then sure. If we've got to scout around noodling out small amounts of rock from a crater here, a crater there, then maybe having a dedicated facility down there becomes less attractive. Better to stay mobile, in that case."

"Speaking geologically, it seems unlikely that the water is in just one crater. Or that it is in deposits so small."

"That's my bias too, but we'd need to go prove it."

"Daedalus Base will want water as well," Belyakova pointed out. "If we were to build a refining center here at Zvezda, is it worth then taking water all the way around the Moon? Or will Daedalus need its own separate refining plant? I do not even know how large such a plant must be."

"Me neither." Starman shrugged. "None of this is my field. And we really don't know yet, right? We need to do some more exploration, and some math, and then have folks on Earth with mining experience chime in with recommendations. But it sure seems like math we *should* be doing. It would be a big step to becoming self-sufficient up here."

"I agree." Finally, Belyakova grinned. "Very well, then, Commander Jones. I accept your offer. Let us put together a joint prospecting team to go and sample the waters of the South Pole, while we still can. And so let us begin immediately, why not? Rather than ask, I will *tell* my superiors that we are putting together an exploratory team, within our existing resources, and request confirmation to proceed. That will mean they have to take action to prevent us from doing so."

"Wow," he said. "Bold."

"And, perhaps we should go ourselves?"

Starman raised his eyebrows. "Us? You mean, you and I? To the Lunar South Pole?"

"With our teams, yes. Why not? Let us each see more of the Moon, and," she prodded the stack in his inbox, "do less paperwork."

"Jeepers." Starman sat back.

"After all, where have you been on the Moon for the last years, besides here? Where have I been? Vivian Carter gets to go everywhere while we stay buried here, counting our bottles of air and bottles of water and having our arguments. Perhaps we, too, should travel. Do you not want to?"

"You would do that, on your own initiative?"

"I would try," she said. "What do I have to lose?"

"Well. I appreciate that, Svetlana. I really do. I'm flattered that you would consider such a trip, given our checkered history. But that sorta brings me to my next topic."

Belyakova raised a perfect eyebrow. "Already, this does not sound like good news."

"That depends on where you sit. For my wife, it's great news. I'm leaving the Moon next week. Forever."

Belyakova's jaw dropped open in genuine surprise. "Forever? No …"

"Yes. No kidding. Svetlana, I've been here a long time. I do have a life at home, and I want to get back to it. I'm so fried I'm crispy."

"Fried?"

"It means I'm worn out. Here's an open secret: I never wanted this job in the first place. I took it because I couldn't see anyone around me who I thought could do it better, and I didn't want it to get screwed up. Hubris, I guess, and a sense of duty. But I've wanted to leave all this behind for a long while now, and I've stuck it out longer than I intended." He grinned. "So there it is. I'm finally getting off this rock and going home. I'm still working the logistics with Houston, so my flight time is not yet confirmed, but I sure hope that by this time next week I'm in a Command Module, cruising back to Earth. And once I get back, you can be darned-tooting sure that I'm never sitting on top of another rocket to get blasted back here."

"That will be a great loss," Belyakova said. "I am serious. And who will take over as Commander of US-Copernicus, once you leave us?"

"That would be Daniel Grant, my number two. It was always NASA's plan for him to rotate into my slot when I left."

"*Yoh moyoh,*" Belyakova said abruptly.

"Sorry?"

"I think there is not a good translation that I should use in English. But I am not happy to hear this." Belyakova looked around thoughtfully. "Commander Jones … Starman. Can I speak freely in here? Or do the walls have ears?"

"If they have ears, it's because your people put them there. We Americans aren't in the habit of spying on each other."

"You are so sure of that?"

"Yes," he said. "Yes, I am."

"Then: Grant is an idiot. I do not trust him, and he is difficult and impolite to my people, and rude and offensive to me besides. You know this from the many meetings we have all had together. No?"

"Yes," Starman said. "And, candidly, I think you're right to be concerned. Just between us chickens, Grant wouldn't have been my first choice either. But you'll still have Casey Buchanan. *He* isn't going anywhere. Maybe he can help you smooth things over."

"Hmm," she said.

"And that's why I wanted to leave on a strong note, by getting the water collaboration started up before, well, anything else can happen. Don't think I'm not tempted but … it's just too late for me to be setting out on a major lunar road trip."

She leaned forward and fixed him with her Svetlana gaze. "Commander Jones, I truly believe you should reconsider and stay on the Moon longer."

"Thanks for the vote of confidence, but I have a family waiting for me, and other things to do with my life. US-Copernicus can't be my problem forever."

Belyakova shook her head. "I think this will not go well."

"I'm sure you'll make it work. Anyway, how 'bout you? You've been on the Moon this time for quite the extended stay. Weren't you supposed to be taking turns with Yelena Rudenko?"

"Indeed, Comrade Rudenko will be returning within the next few days, but it is not the plan for me to leave. Rudenko will become my deputy, and I badly need her help."

"And how does Comrade Rudenko feel about that little demotion?"

"She will do her duty without complaint, as will we all. And as Zvezda has grown in numbers, she will become the deputy of a larger base than she commanded in the past. We work well together."

"Sure, but Yelena was boss first. How come she doesn't get to give you orders?" His eyes twinkled.

"Rudenko is excellent, but her English is not. And since none of you will learn Russian …"

"Oh, some of us do a little, now. I don't, though. Nor does Daniel. Wasn't part of the plan for either of us to become diplomats."

"That," Belyakova said, "is very clear. I, myself, of course …"

"No diplomat either. With all due respect."

They both grinned. It was truly a shame that the ice between them was breaking so late in the game.

Casually, she asked: "And Vivian Carter? What is she doing? Have you heard anything from her, recently?"

"Not really. She's at L5. Been there a while now."

"When she told me that she would be going, it was a great surprise. I cannot imagine that Vivian would find such a mission interesting. Or that she would prefer L5 to the Moon."

"I think the Moon wore out its welcome, toward the end there. She told me as much. After all, she went through a lot, here."

Svetlana was watching him carefully. "And yet, it was not a mission that she had trained for. She was never on the L5 team, at Daedalus or on Earth."

"She's a quick study, and she has good command skills." Starman shrugged. "More often than not, we just go where we're told. We're spread thinner than we'd like in several areas."

"I have always felt that when Vivian Carter wants something, she gets it. If this is what Vivian has got, it is because she wanted it."

"I guess someone made her an offer she couldn't refuse."

"It does not ring true." She studied him. "Why do I feel that, once again, the United States is doing something in space that is being kept secret from us?"

"Well, if so, it's being kept secret from me, too." Starman paused. "I don't mean to sound flippant, but ... aren't you being a bit paranoid? We both know Vivian. Even if there was some secret military effort going on in deep space, she'd want nothing to do with it. And frankly, I doubt whether our military people would want her anywhere near it either."

Belyakova considered, and then nodded. "That does make sense."

And thus, she thought, *there is only one other possibility that I can think of.*

She smiled and stood. "Well, then. Good morning, Commander Jones, and I suppose I must congratulate you on your successful time here."

"Well, thank *you.*"

"I trust we will meet again before you depart?"

"Count on it," Starman said. "We should likely toast with some awful lunar vodka, or something."

"Or perhaps I can find something a little better."

He raised his eyebrows. "Really? I always suspected you were keeping something up your sleeve."

Belyakova just smiled.

The LEK fell toward the lunar surface in silence, fired its retrorockets at the last minute, and eased itself down to the ground. To Svetlana, the Soviet landings always looked more alarming from outside than they seemed from inside the cabin. Then again, the American LM landings were so slow and cautious that they must surely seem boring to their astronaut crews.

A few minutes after the dust settled, two of the LEK's occupants crawled out and down the ladder, spent a few moments looking around them, and then made their way across to Zvezda Hatch 2. The third, the pilot, would be still busy at work on his shutdown checklist.

Watching out of the periscope, Belyakova smiled. Rudenko was a seasoned lunar professional, easy to identify from confident gait on the surface as well as her slightly smaller spacesuit with the command stripe on its upper arm. The other individual crossing the regolith was obviously a man, with all the uncertainty of a lunar novice.

As Rudenko unlatched her helmet and lifted it carefully away from her long black hair, Belyakova slapped her companionably on the arm. "Yelena Dubovna, it is good to see you again."

"Major-General," Rudenko said crisply, and saluted her.

Belatedly, Belyakova returned the salute and looked warily at the man standing next to her.

"May I introduce Colonel Konstantin Keretsky?"

Despite his lower rank, Keretsky did not salute, merely made an effort to click his space-booted heels together and gave a bow so small that it was almost a head-nod.

Belyakova immediately understood and saluted Keretsky anyway.

Zampolit. She had no doubt at all. The man exuded "political commissar" from every pore on his face, every muscle of his body.

Technically, Belyakova outranked him. In real life, the power rested with him, and his authority would be total.

And yet he was nothing like Yashin, the nominal zampolit from the attack force against the Americans that Belyakova had helped pilot, several years before. Keretsky was no KGB goon, not a soldier in commissar's clothing. Even at first sight, Belyakova knew his type: a born-and-bred paper-pusher, a seedy little bureaucrat who had made it into the cosmonaut corps on the purity of his political virtues rather than any military prowess.

Despite that, Keretsky had piercing, intelligent eyes. Svetlana was sure that those eyes would not miss anything. The reverse, in fact: she might legitimately be concerned that those eyes might see things that were not there.

Given her history and mixed reputation, Svetlana Belyakova would need to be very careful how she behaved around Colonel Konstantin Keretsky. Very careful indeed.

As if to confirm her fears, his next words were: "Major-General Belyakova. We must talk, as a matter of urgency." He glanced at the clock over the doorway. "I must remove this spacesuit," he glanced down at it with what appeared to be mild distaste, "and make myself presentable. Shall we say, fifteen minutes?"

"Yes, sir." She turned to Rudenko. "And you will join us, I presume?"

Rudenko's eyes met hers, and the other woman gave her a fleeting, and perhaps apologetic, half-grin before saying: "That would be ideal."

"There are, perhaps, issues that I should be aware of?"

"There are." Keretsky, now dressed in a neat black suit, sat with one knee crossed over the other behind her desk and gazed across it at her. "I must inform you that concerns have been raised against you, by the other occupants of this base."

"And what concerns are these?"

"That you have not pursued your command here with the expected rigor. That your decisions have been adversely affected by ... fraternization with the imperialists."

Belyakova kept her expression stony. "I regret that you have been misinformed. Such accusations are baseless. I have acted with correctness, along with all due diplomacy. Where I have ... not 'fraternized', but 'interacted' ... with individual Americans it has been for the purpose of soliciting information and intelligence. I have fully reported all such contacts, as you must surely know."

"Ryan Jones. Vivian Carter. Casey Buchanan."

"The base commander. A suspected intelligence officer. And a confirmed intelligence officer."

"Nonetheless. Going forward, I will need to know where you are at all times. I will also require you to complete a written report at the end of each day describing your actions, and the reasons behind them."

In the space of a few seconds, Belyakova's hope of going on a water-seeking expedition to the South Pole had evaporated. And it could be even worse than that. Much worse.

She bristled. "Am I under suspicion, Comrade Keretsky? Do you question my loyalty?"

"I? These are not my decisions. I am merely following my orders. As you must, also. My only goal is to assure that you are free from taint, having spent so long fraternizing with the Americans."

She shook her head, almost unbearably frustrated. "Being in close quarters is not the same as fraternizing. Strategic discussions are not fraternization. Collaborations approved by both the Soviet and American leadership are not fraternization."

"But, undue friendship with particular Americans: *that* is fraternization."

Belyakova glanced briefly at Rudenko, who looked back impassively. The writing was already on the wall, here. If she gave Keretsky the slightest excuse he would remove her from command of Zvezda Base and replace her with Rudenko. She was on shaky ground indeed.

"I am curious, comrade. Is Daedalus Base also to receive a zampolit?"

"That is considered unnecessary. The Soviet contingent at Daedalus Base is already under much stricter military supervision than here at Zvezda." He paused, but Belyakova did not rise to the bait, did not even blink at the implied insult. He continued: "There, we shall be adopting a different solution."

"Very well," she said. "I accept this judgment, of course. I am sure that it will not take me long to dispel any such adverse notions that you may have."

That shark-like tight grin again. "I hope so, Commander. I do certainly hope so."

CHAPTER 6

L5: Vivian Carter
June 20, 1983
Launch Clock: T-14 days and counting

IN their infinite wisdom, the White House, NASA HQ, and NASA Public Affairs decided to go public with the news of Apollo Astarte's historic trip two weeks before its scheduled July 4th launch date.

In some ways it was a prudent decision. Switching to a two-week public lead-up, rather than announcing the mission on its launch date, allowed them to maximize the publicity with a big song and dance. Following so closely after the discovery of water at the lunar South Pole (which was presented to the public as a serendipitous American discovery, with all associated military details redacted), NASA was hoping to capitalize on an upswell in public interest and attention in the US space program. Given how Congress ran hot and cold on NASA funding, it was a shrewd move.

Which was all very well, but it hurled a gigantic monkey wrench into Vivian's carefully constructed prelaunch schedule. All of a sudden, and with little warning, she and her crew now had to weave interviews and press events among and between their final preparations and system checks. NASA sent along three more astronauts to "help" with the final preparations, but they were a mixed blessing; Vivian felt as if she spent as much time briefing them on what she wanted them to do as it would have taken to do it herself. In addition, one of the guys had been a front-runner for a slot on the Astarte mission, and Vivian had shit-canned him for various reasons during the final selection. Despite his helpfulness and professionalism, he was finding it hard to disguise his resentment at not making the prime crew, yet still being hauled in so close to the finish line to help them with the final scut-work.

Unlike during the Gemini and Apollo eras, the Astarte backup team members had no expectation of being assigned to a future mission. The Astarte flybys of Venus and Mars would be a single-shot, one-off mission (some would say "stunt"), not the beginning of a new era of inner-Solar-System exploration.

Almost as bad as the workload: most of Vivian's friends and colleagues were also now finding out about her mission for the first time and either wanting to talk to her about it, talk her out of it, or wrap up unfinished business before she disappeared into the deep black yonder. It became a very trying time for the Astarte crew and their colleagues at L5, and tempers were getting short.

Perhaps "shorter" would be more accurate. Even within the cone of silence that had surrounded the mission prior to the news release, Vivian's popularity within the NASA team had already taken a hit. A month earlier, she had insisted on spinning up two independent tiger teams. The first, engineering-based, was to perform an end-to-end review of Astarte's EECOM system—Environment, Electrical and Consumables, to resolve as many final issues as possible, and try to identify and root out any unpleasant surprises before they left L5. The second, to be conducted back at Johnson Space Center, was a tabletop audit of all the anomalies reported and fixed during Astarte's construction, commissioning, and pre-mission checkout, cross-correlating them with similar anomaly lists for the other eight Earth-orbiting and Moon-orbiting Skylabs and looking for trends. Both of these teams, of course, had to function in parallel with NASA's usual progression of Mission and Flight Readiness Reviews leading up to their inflexible July launch date.

One call Vivian did agree to take, though, was from Svetlana Belyakova.

"Well hi, fellow spacewoman," Vivian said. "Good to see you. Hope everything's going great at home. Though I guess you have something to tell me. Or ask me."

Belyakova glanced off to her right and said, "*Raz-raz-raz-dva,*", one-one-one-two, presumably confirming her voice was being picked up by the microphone. Then she turned back to the camera. "Ah. Now I see you. Hello, Vivian. I wished to convey to you my congratulations. A journey to the inner planets—it is very ambitious. I hope that it all goes smoothly." Belyakova might have been talking about a vacation to the Adirondacks, her tone was so matter of fact.

"Thanks," Vivian said. "It's really quite a daunting prospect, just between the two of us. But we'll give it our best shot."

"I am sure your best will be more than enough." Belyakova smiled that typical smile, the one that made some men start stammering but always made Vivian want to count her fingers afterward. "And I was not surprised at all to learn that your ambitions reached much further than the L5 Lagrange point."

Vivian cocked her head. "As it happens, I'm curious about that. Did you already know about Venus Astarte, ahead of the announcement? I'm wondering whether one of the reasons NASA went public early is because the Soviets had gotten wind of it and were about to blow our big surprise."

"I am sure that the United States propaganda machine would hate to be scooped," Belyakova said wryly. "For myself, I admit that I have had my doubts for a long time, and have not been silent about them. I could scarcely believe that Vivian Carter had suddenly become obsessed about visiting a patch of empty space. I told Nikolai of my suspicions that you had become involved in another secret activity. Whether this led to anything, whether my people had gained hard evidence of your intentions, I do not know. But it is a large thing to hide."

Now, Svetlana actually looked wistful: "I must say it aloud: I wish I was coming with you."

Vivian grinned. "Even with me as mission commander?"

"Yes, even so. That would have provided an … interesting extra challenge."

"You know what? I wish you could have come too. And as a matter of fact, I *did* question NASA's decision to keep this as an all-American mission. For the record, I'd have supported opening this up to Soviet participation. But that wasn't on the cards."

For once, the two-and-a-half second time lag was proving useful. It allowed Vivian a little time to second-guess herself about whether she should be raising such topics, and then choose the most diplomatic words.

It looked very much like Belyakova was taking the same care about her words. Eventually, she nodded. "Your Lunar Geological Survey team included Soviets. That was a true collaboration. And we should have more of those, even if sometimes they are not easy."

As she said this, Belyakova sounded almost defiant. Talking to the walls? Vivian started to speak, but Belyakova evidently wasn't finished yet. "This is a difficult time, here on the Moon. Whatever we can do to focus on studies and tasks we do together, rather than the ones that push us apart and force us to compete … those are things we should be doing." She gave what looked like a distracted half-smile. "And so once again I find myself out of agreement with my superior officers."

Vivian nodded and adopted an expression of commiseration. Zvezda-Copernicus certainly wasn't easy. Nor were the bipartisan efforts at Daedalus Base on Bright Driver and the real L5 project, where literal fistfights occasionally broke out between groups of army guys from the opposing superpowers. "LGS-1 was very smooth. All six of us, American and Soviet: we gelled as a team right from the start and just kept on like that through the whole mission."

"You were lucky," said Belyakova.

"Sure, but we made smart choices and worked hard at it. Couldn't happen this time, though. And to be fair it would have made crew selection an absolute bear, no pun intended. Time was against us all the way, and by 'us' I'm including the people working Apollo Venus Astarte before I even knew it existed. But hey, we can dream. Maybe next time." The time delay encouraged everyone to speak in paragraphs, and by now Vivian felt like she was rambling, so she shut up and waited.

All Belyakova said in return was, "Yes, we can dream."

"So, go back to what you just said? What are you out of agreement with your bosses on now? Or can't you tell me?"

The Soviet's pause was wafer-thin, but Vivian still picked up on it. "The water," Belyakova said.

"Ah, yes," Vivian said. "The lunar water, of course."

"You know of this, perhaps? Commander Jones suggested that we collaborate on an expedition to the South Pole to assess the extent of the water and start deciding how best to extract it. I agreed and proposed that he and I should jointly lead it—go ourselves, in person. He turned me down. And then I asked my superiors to send me anyway, as part of a joint team. They said no. They wish to wait. For what? Perhaps for the Americans to perform the first study of the feasibility, before the Soviets agree to spend resources on it. I am unclear. But anyway, it means that I must stay here."

The frustration Belyakova's voice was plain. "Sorry. That sucks. Anything else going on there, at Zvezda-Copernicus, that I should know about? Anything fun?"

"Fun?" Belyakova raised an eyebrow, spent a moment in thought, and then said: "Not really."

Vivian frowned. It was hard to read between the lines when those lines were so short. "Okay, then. Well, good luck for the rest of your stay there. I hope you can *make* some fun. Get out and about." What a weird conversation this was, she thought. Sympathizing with the first woman on the Moon about her not getting out much. "Are there other matters we should be discussing, while we're both on the line?"

"Not for now, I think. But, perhaps, if your superiors continue to permit it, we might talk again, during your mission?"

"Uh, sure." Vivian blinked. "I think that should be okay. My bosses haven't shown any concern about us talking in the past." Of course, that had been because Vivian's bosses were interested in whatever intelligence she could wrangle out of her relationship with Belyakova. Just as Belyakova's bosses might well be interested in ... what, at this point? Science details from Venus Flyby?

Or maybe this was just a genuine call between friends. Maybe all this was above board, and a bid for Vivian's continued friendship?

When it came right down to it, Svetlana Belyakova had very few peers, and likely even fewer she could talk to candidly. Assuming that Belyakova had ever been honest with Vivian at all, that is.

But, as Belyakova herself had just said: *We can dream.*

"Okay, sure. I can trade you Venusian traveler's tales for Copernicus scuttlebutt."

The pause was even longer than the signal travel time for that one, as Belyakova clearly tried valiantly to interpret it. She probably had to take "scuttlebutt" on faith. Then she nodded. "That sounds like a good deal."

They seemed to have run out of things to say. "Right then," Vivian said. "I should probably get going. My schedule is insane right now, and I'm double-booked for the next hour as it is. Goodbye for now ... and if I say 'watch your back,' I mean that as serious friendly advice, and not as a threat. You understand me, right?"

Belyakova favored her with another thin smile. "I understand you very well, Vivian Carter. I will watch my back. And you will watch yours, also? Space can be very unforgiving."

That was the understatement of the week. "I sure will."

"Farewell for now, and .... Godspeed, you say? Godspeed, Vivian Carter."

"Thanks. Hang in there."

Svetlana inclined her head and put her hand up to her brow in a gesture that was half acknowledgment, half salute. Then she broke the connection.

That last "Godspeed" had put a lump into Vivian's throat. *Wow. Are Blond Svet and I really ... friends, now?*

Didn't see that coming, I've got to say. I guess absence really does make the heart, well, do funny things. It was a change of perspective, at the very least.

Their final Cargo Carrier had arrived just a few hours beforehand, so Vivian left CSM-2 to discover the now-familiar hive of activity in the Astarte fore and crew compartments, and to be handed a clipboard with the full delivery manifest by Laura Simmons, Vivian's Mission Scientist for Planetary Science (Mars) ... along with a small package. "Oh, and there's this, addressed to you. A care package?"

"A what?"

Laura glanced down at the brown paper packaging. "From a Terri Brock, apparently?" Now her jaw dropped open. "The ... first woman on the Moon?"

"That's the one." Vivian took the package. It was surprisingly "heavy"—even in weightlessness, she could tell by rocking it from side to side that it contained more mass than its volume would indicate. "Okay, then. Thanks."

"You *know* Terri Brock?" Laura persisted.

"Uh. Yes?" Vivian couldn't exactly complain or mock. She had been just as starry-eyed about the original crop of Moon landers, the men of the early Apollo missions.

"Wow."

Frustratingly, Vivian had to spend the next two hours going through the delivery manifest confirming and doublechecking everything. But finally she was able to take a twenty-minute lunch break. She grabbed a tube of something from the galley and headed off for the crew compartment.

Although the outer layer of brown paper bore Terri's name as sender, the first thing Vivian found when she got the package back to her sleeping quarters for privacy and tore the paper off the box was a note from Peter.

Hi Vivian,

Kevin often talked about your impromptu astronomy session on board his Blue Gem, so I know he would have wanted you to have these. Likely, he'd have sent them himself if he'd had time. They may come in handy if you get bored or want to double-check that your mission ops folks aren't sending you to the wrong planet.

Godspeed Apollo Venus Astarte!

Another Godspeed, her second today. And they'd all signed it: Peter, Terri, and Jose Rodriguez. Because those were the only three left.

Twice in the last few years, Peter had lost one of his core four-person team to enemy fire. That sucked. Vivian took a moment to internalize that, wondering what it would be like if she'd lost, say, Dave Horn one year and Katya Okhotina a couple of years later. Sure, she'd been horrified by Lin's death herself, and she was certainly rocked now by Kevin Pope's. The deaths of several of her friends at Hadley Base had come as a shock, when she'd finally found out about them. But surely none of that was anywhere near as rough as how Peter and his team had had it.

Then the logical part of her brain that was still working in the background joined the dots, and she realized what must be inside the parcel: "Oh," she said out loud. "Really?"

She tore the paper off. Sure enough.

It was Kevin's sextant. And a book.

She pulled out the sextant, held it for a moment. It really was a thing of beauty. Technically, both of her Command Modules had their own "sextants", but those were pieces of modern-day high tech that performed the same function. There was nothing like a good old-fashioned honest-to-God brass naval sextant, and Vivian had always wanted one. It was compact and portable, too: eight inches by eight, and about four inches thick at the widest point.

But … to get it this way was far more bitter than sweet.

She released the instrument and let it float next to her, and pulled out the dog-eared copy of *Tinker, Tailor, Soldier, Spy*. Sure enough, it had Kevin Pope's name hand-scrawled inside the front cover.

Shit. That hit her harder than she'd expected. She tried to blink away the tears, ended up having to brush at her eyes. Crying never worked well in zero G.

Then she closed her eyes, set her jaw. *Damn it. Damn it. This is a bit too much*. But she wasn't going to bawl. No, sir. Not her style.

God damn it, though. A good man had died.

Maybe she'd get around to reading the Le Carré, once the mission got off and running. Kevin had said that it was one of his favorite books, after all. And she should be scheduling herself *some* downtime during this pleasure cruise.

Anything else? Just one thing—a message on the brown paper that had covered the back of the gift, that Vivian hadn't noticed before.

And in Terri's recognizable but difficult scrawl, a message: *Gimme a call before you leave known space, yah? We'll want it secure. TB xx.*

And beneath it, a frequency—in the Night Corps bandpass, Vivian noted—and a short sequence of letters and numbers that could only be some kind of secure key.

Vivian grinned. "Sure thing, babe," she said out loud.

Terri would have to wait another day, though. Vivian had to gear up for yet another EVA, to ride herd on a bunch of guys spot-welding a long list of items on Astarte's hull.

Which would hopefully be the last hardcore welding jobs she'd need to insist on before launch, if there was any justice at all.

"You sly old fox."

"Terri! Hi."

"Slinking off like that after the battle at Marius, all 'woe is me, shit to do, off to L5, ho hum, whatever pays the bills,' and the whole time you were scheming to go to fricking *Venus?* And you didn't even tell me? *Dang*, that was cold."

"Need-to-know, babe," Vivian said straight-faced. "You know how that shit goes."

"I do." Terri broke into a grin. "Anyway. Congratu-fricking-lations, girlfriend. Hope you have a ball."

"Me too," she said. "Long road, though. I hear space is pretty empty."

"Got yourself a good crew, looks like. I read the bios."

"Of course you did." Terri always scrupulously read her briefings. "I guess they're okay. Best I could do at short notice." Vivian grinned. "No, seriously, they're very solid, smart and dedicated, and I'm going to need all that. I'm not looking forward to the parts of the journey where the time lag is going to rule out fast-paced chats like this with you all at home, though."

"Hey, I'll still babble away at you and, big plus, you won't be able to interrupt." Terri paused. "Hey. Straight talk, Vivian. Are you really doing okay?"

"Not gonna lie, I'm a bit tired. I'm building this mission on a foundation of complete exhaustion. Which is not great, but at least no one is shooting at me."

"Not yet," Terri said.

"Oh, thanks." Vivian peered at her, wishing her screen was larger. It was sometimes hard to read people's expressions. "Sooo, Terri. The same, back at you. Are *you* all right?"

Brock blew out a breath. "I'm working on it. Pope buying the farm, and all. It's been a lot."

"For sure. I'm gutted about that, too. I'm really sorry. He was a great guy. Easy-going, funny. Sharing a Gemini for a day and a half with a guy you've only just met? That could easily have been freaking awkward. With Kevin, it went just fine. It turned out that after all the stuff I'd been though, leading up to that point, a few hours with Kevin was just what I needed."

"Sure," Brock said. "I can imagine. And I served with him for months. Crossed the Moon with him, front to back, in a MOLAB, after the Hadley nuking. Then served with him in a MOL in Earth space and lunar space. We trained squaddies together." Terri shook her head. "He was a good man. And *funny*. The dude had no downsides at all."

A short, respectful silence. Instinctively, Vivian reached out and put her fingertips on the edge of the camera screen, without blocking the camera's view of her face. After a few moments' pause, Terri did the same. Fingers touching on a screen, with only a quarter million miles between them. It almost felt comforting.

Vivian cleared her throat, which suddenly felt two sizes too small. "So, where do we stand with finding the bastards that killed him?"

"Oh, we've got nothing."

"That's not what I hoped you'd say."

"But it's what you expected."

"Yes. If we don't know any more by now, we likely never will." Vivian paused. "Are you still there? At wherever it is that Kevin … passed?"

"No, we're off on our travels again. Believe it or not, we're continuing the damned mission, peering into adjacent holes in the ground in case come across some *other* goddamned bases. We're certainly being more careful, given the potential for more … surprises. But if we uncover anything else, this time we'll be sending an actual bomb disposal squad in ahead of us in even thicker armor."

"Oh, what fun."

"Yeah. Anyway, before we left the, uh, scene of the crime, we did find two mines buried out back of the hab, in between it and the rock face where they mined out the water. Fortunately, I managed not to put my big feet on them. We disabled both without any further loss of life. We also found a sintered block and some debris in an area where they must have had a small nuclear reactor on site for power, though there was no sign of the reactor itself. They must have hauled that out somehow, which is significant, right? Presumably. But otherwise, same deal as their Marius base. A midden full of trash in several languages. Extremely confined living quarters. So, like the most miserable camping trip ever."

"Any sign of a second big transport thing?"

"No."

"No tracks, I guess." Vivian thought about that for a moment. "But, no sign that there *wasn't* one, either?"

Terri grinned tightly. "Still thinking like a spook, I see. You really should have transferred over to Night Corps with me. Correct: we discovered no other vehicles, and to take that reactor *out* again, they must have had a large transport of some kind, whether or not it was the same as the Marius transport."

"Still mysteries, then."

"Always mysteries." Terri Brock nodded. "Nothing is ever quite resolved on the Moon, is it?"

"Apparently not," Vivian said. "Always unfinished business."

"And, US-Copernicus: you never found out who the mole was?"

Vivian sighed. "Sometimes, I just don't want to know who the bad guy is."

"You want to *not* know?"

"I want to move on. Right now, I just want to tackle the next problem. I want to look ahead and leave the bad stuff behind."

"Must be nice," Terri said. "To be able to leave the bad stuff behind."

"Oh, I just have new bad stuff. You should see my dance card for the next forty-eight hours."

Terri cleared her throat. "But, Vivian, I've got to say: I don't know how come you still want to work with the Soviets, after all they've done."

"Do I?"

Terri studied her from afar. "The inside scoop is that you pitched for some Soviet crew members for Astarte?"

"Sure. I still think it would have been a great idea. They just need to be the right Soviets."

"But, murdering Kevin Pope? Not giving a shit about the body count at Hadley or Marius? Trying to kill us, personally, several times over? Vivian, you can try as hard as you want to be some kind of … idealist international collaborator, but when it comes down to it, anything we do with the Soviets just *enables* them."

"Not all Soviets are the same, Terri. Hell, not all Americans are the same."

"You're sure? Or are some of them just smarter and more opportunistic, and better at working both sides of the street?"

Vivian shook her head. "By that logic, you and I are complicit with the US interventions in Latin America, all the deaths in Guatemala and El Salvador, Nicaragua, wherever. Hell, we're complicit with Hiroshima. And SDI."

"Aren't we, though? Just a bit? That's the side we're fighting on, Viv. You want to pick the other side? Didn't think so. We're better than that, but we're not going to be perfect. We just have to take the bad with the good and just say, yeah, that's how it is."

"Fighting?" Vivian blew out a breath. "See, right there. Maybe let's not be fighting with the Soviets. How about trying that?"

Terri stared. "Vivian … I love you, but sometimes I swear to God you're an idiot."

Vivian winced. "Thanks, girlfriend."

"I'm serious. This is bullshit. And deep down inside, you must know it. Look, I pulled Norton's corpse into a crater and covered it up with regolith. We both saw Gerry Lin's body. I saw Kevin Pope, torn apart. *This is war*, Vivian, whether we're officially calling it that or not. And you of all people need to treat it that way."

"Mmm-kay," Vivian said. "You do remember I'm heading out of town for a while, right? No Soviets where I'm going. So maybe we don't need to talk about this right now."

"Okay. Except that you talked to Svetlana Belyakova the day before yesterday, and arranged to talk again, downstream."

"Jesus Christ. You guys are *spying* on me?"

"For God's sake, Vivian, don't be naïve. This is exactly what I'm talking about."

"Okay," Vivian said. "Fine. Then, being a good spook yourself, you should realize that any avenue we can use to get intel on the enemy is a good thing. Right?"

"Sure, if we could ever trust a single thing Belyakova says. You know what, Vivian? Screw the Soviets. Yeah, fine, I know a couple of them are your friends. And Nikolai Makarov was a decent guy, I guess. I mean, there's always got to be one, right? But he's the only Soviet who I don't want to kill right now."

"Terri … Svetlana didn't kill Kevin."

"Her people did. Belyakova's a good Red soldier. Her hands aren't clean."

"Well. That's one way of looking at it."

"It's the *only* way. Vivian, I know you want us all to be brothers and sisters in space, but that's not how the real world works. We're in a competition, here, at best. And a war at worst. A war that could break out at literally any second. On the Moon, the situation is getting worse and worse by the day. It's a tinderbox, and it could go up at any moment. I'll be really surprised if it *doesn't* go up."

"I know. It's part of our job to stop that."

"Nope," Brock said. "That's not part of *my* job. My job is to preserve US lives, material, and strategic dominance in space. In Earth orbit, lunar orbit, or the lunar surface. Wherever I'm sent. That's my job now. And if shooting breaks out again, I know for damned sure which way my gun will be pointing."

Vivian just nodded and waited.

Terri stopped, breathed, sat back. "Okay. I'm sorry. I'm still on the Moon, and you're not, and I'm screwed up about Kevin, and Peter isn't here, and you'll be away for *years*. And, I don't know; there are probably some other shitty parts of all this that I'm forgetting. And I have way too many dead friends already."

"I hear that. Sorry."

They paused in silence for a moment.

Then Vivian said: "Okay, so hear me out for a moment. There's one thing you might want to consider, if you haven't already. Belyakova told me that her masters had nixed the idea of her, or any other Soviet team from Zvezda, participating in a joint exploratory expedition to assess the water situation at the South Pole."

Terri looked dour. "I guess I'm not the only one leery of these joint programs."

"That's not my point. My point is: maybe Belyakova's masters are holding her back from going to the Pole on a water exploiting run because they *already* have another covert team down there, maybe mining water somewhere else."

"Oh." Terri thought about that for a while. "Crap."

"So you could have more company down there than you know about. Or maybe not. But it's worth keeping in mind and maybe passing up the line to Peter."

"Will do. And, on that note ... Vivian, a word to the wise. You need to know that Peter is also taking Pope's death pretty damned hard, and he's going to be on an even shorter fuse than me about your whole making-deals-with-Soviets bullshit. So you might want to tread carefully there."

"I already got that memo." Vivian took a deep breath and counted to five. "Terri, I'm not responsible for how Peter feels. Or you, or anyone else. I mean, I'm sorry I'm not there for him, or for you, but ..."

"You sure as hell aren't."

"Well, shit." Vivian looked away. "Hey, maybe this conversation is over."

"No, no, wait." Terri leaned back in her chair, stared at the ceiling for a moment, then rubbed her eyes. "Stay there. Sorry. I just needed to get all that out, but I'm being a jerk. Peter isn't mad at you; he's too much of a straight arrow. *I'm* mad at you—sure I am—but I'm mad at every single person in the world right now, because I'm a bitch. Can't help it. I guess I got some of that old-fashioned stand-by-your-man thing from my mother. And Tammy Wynette."

"Tammy who?"

Terri blinked. "Seriously? The country singer?"

"That would explain it. Never heard of her."

" 'D-I-V-O-R-C-E'? 'The Ways to Love Your Man'?"

"Those are song titles? Tammy Wynette sounds like a laugh riot."

"She sure is." At last, Terri grinned. "Hey, Vivian. I'm sorry, okay? I just needed to blow off some steam, with someone I trust. Someone I'm not serving with. With *you*. Are we good?"

"Sure," Vivian said reluctantly, because she had to. And then pulled herself together. Terri was a friend too good to lose over … whatever all this had been. Friends could disappear out of your life at any time. They both knew that now. "Sure, babe. We're good."

"I'm going to be here for you, on your trip. One hundred percent. Talk again? I mean, if you can spare time from talking to *Svetlana* …"

"Terri."

"Sorry, just can't leave that one alone. But hey, yeah, I want to live this super Venus and Mars jaunt vicariously through you, and I'm guessing you might need a friend to vent at now and then, when the going gets rough. Even with your awesome Grade A crew."

Vivian grinned back. "Sounds great. After all, we have a book to write."

"In what spare time, exactly?"

"Tell me about it." Vivian glanced up at the console clock. She couldn't spare much more time for this particular call. Couldn't spare much more time for anything. "Hey, Ter'? Got to go. But, take care. Live through it, okay?"

"I pray to God we do," Terri said, very seriously.

Terri didn't often talk about her faith. Vivian knew about it, and didn't share it, and Terri knew that. But right now was not the time to bring that up again.

"I pray you're right," Vivian said. "We'll talk again soon. Keep your head down."

"You too. Or, up. Whatever."

They grinned at each other, and both reached for the comms switch at the same time, modulo the time delay.

It was going to be okay.

CHAPTER 7

L5: Vivian Carter
July 4, 1983
Launch Clock: T-10 minutes and counting

LAUNCH Day saw Vivian sharing an Apollo Command Module with Dave Horn, just like old times. Horn was in the left-hand seat, since he was in charge of the upcoming maneuvers. And Vivian herself had very little to do during the run-up to the burn which, as always, gave her the itch. She would prefer to be intensely busy than sit on her hands and watch other people work.

If Ellis Mayer had been in the center couch it would have been perfect. As it was, with Ellis on the loop at Mission Control as CAPCOM, it was … still damned near perfect.

As the chief pilot for the mission, Dave Horn would be controlling their "launch", more technically their trans-Venus injection burn. Vivian would back him up, doing his cross-checks and reading out any numbers he might need. Not that Dave would need much help. For all its significance, this would be a very straightforward process.

In CM-2, the Command Module docked in the radial port, was Marco Dardenas, with Amy Benson riding shotgun. Even more redundancy, though if they hit a snag that required them to transfer control from CM-1 to CM-2 right at the beginning of the mission, they already had more trouble than they needed.

Meanwhile, Josh Rawlings was in the main body of Astarte, monitoring the stresses and strains on the Skylab. Those torques had been measured and modeled a dozen different ways, but it still paid to keep an active watch on all systems, all the time. The three remaining crew were also inside Astarte, strapped in various places. As scientists and mission specialists they had no role in the piloting, which also meant they would get the best view of all this through Astarte's bigger windows.

Approaching the four-minute mark, the Flight Director at Mission Control in Houston ran through the launch status checks. "Okay, flight controllers coming up on auto-sequence. Booster, how you?"

"Go, Flight."

"Retro?" Responsible for abort procedures. Such as they were.

"Go, Flight."

"FIDO?" Flight dynamics.

As FIDO acknowledged, Vivian checked her comms light was off and leaned over toward Dave. "We're pushing that damned go-button whatever they say, right?"

Dave Horn, continuously scanning all the greens on his console and running his fingers over the switch settings for about the twentieth time, spared Vivian half a glance. "Sometimes not even I'm sure whether you're joking."

"Neither am I."

Houston: "Surgeon?"

"Surgeon is Go."

"Flight Surgeon?"

From CM-2 they heard Amy Benson's voice. "Astarte Flight Surgeon: we are Go, Houston."

Now, Horn grinned. "She loved that. Being on the control loop on the big day?"

Vivian nodded. "You betcha."

"EECOM?" Checking the cryo levels for the fuel cells, the electrical distribution systems, and a dozen other Skylab systems that Josh Rawlings and Marco Dardenas had checked themselves just minutes beforehand.

"Electrical, Environmental, and Consumables is a solid Go at this time."

"Wow." Vivian grimaced. "Wordy." Though they were probably just making a point, after all the grief Vivian had given them during the tiger team investigation.

"GNC?" Guidance, navigation, and control.

"GNC is Go for TVI burn."

On it went. Telemetry. Flight control. Comms. Eventually they got back around to the Astarte crew again. "Astarte, Houston. Mission Control is Go. How do you read?"

"Reading you five by five, Houston," Vivian said.

"Astarte Command and Control?"

"CM-1 is Go," said Horn, and a second later they heard Dardenas: "CM-2 is Go."

"Commander?"

For a few milliseconds Vivian felt a surge of, what? Nerves? Stage fright? And then it was over and she heard herself saying: "Houston, Apollo Venus Astarte is Go."

"We know it'll be a good flight."

"That's the plan, Houston."

"Astarte, you have the comm at T minus three minutes and counting."

This was where Dave and Vivian took over. They'd call the shots during the burn itself. Ellis Mayer at the CAPCOM desk and the other folks in Mission Control would follow along, confirming telemetry and relay information as best they could, but that two-point-five second time delay in communications between Earth and L-5 was two and a half seconds too many. Any contingencies during the burn would require an immediate astronaut response.

"Firing command coming online now," said Horn.

Vivian nodded. "On automatic sequence and approaching the two-minute mark. Two minutes and counting, and we're still green across the boards."

"Roger, Astarte," said Ellis.

She glanced at Dave. "Verify DSKY."

"Verified."

They ran the final abort checks, and all at once they were on the automatic sequence leading up to the burn.

"Ignition in ten."

Right now, at almost the moment when her greatest adventure would begin, Vivian experienced another disorienting moment of déjà vu. The last time she'd been in a Command Module attached to a Sky-lab and anticipating a serious delta-V maneuver, she'd been in a crazy orbit around the Moon with three of the same people who were on her crew today: Josh, Marco, and Dave. Along with Nikolai Makarov, Svetlana Belyakova, and a whole cast of others.

Today was July 4th, 1983. Then, it had been February 17th, 1980. Or perhaps the day before or after; Vivian wasn't sure anymore. Anyway: three years and going on for five months.

And what had happened during those years? Everything. It seemed like a very long time ago.

Horn didn't count down to zero, and no one else did either. No need for such drama. They watched the seconds tick off on the timer instead.

"Okay to proceed?" Horn said, almost lazily.

"Proceed," Vivian said, and Horn pushed the button.

A faint judder rippled through the walls. They experienced a fleeting sense of compression, and a slight yaw, but it was all within limits. The Astarte spacecraft combination was a lot bigger and less rigid than a lone Command and Service Module. It would inevitably wave around a bit, but the computers would correct for any shimmies or slight offsets in the center of gravity of the stack, and Horn's fingers were hovering over the DSKY keyboard in case they didn't.

For Vivian and Dave, this burn was eyeballs-out. The bulk of the Astarte Skylab was right there in front of them, filling the windows of their Command Module, and the Centaur-G stage that was gently powering them on their way was mounted toward the opposite, aft, end of Astarte, and firing in the other direction. So this burn was pulling them out of their seats and against their strap restraints, rather than pushing them into their couches.

Fortunately, it was a very gentle burn, because it was *long*. Given the mass of the combined Apollo Astarte craft, it would take them a while to build up speed. The burn would last for just over nine minutes, which made it the longest burn Vivian had experienced since the plane-change burn around the Moon prior to their landing at Hadley Base.

How would this feel to Marco and Amy? The second Command Module was docked at one of the radial ports. The structural loads in the docking interfaces had been calculated and tested rigorously, but CM-2 must surely have flexed in an alarming way as the burn began. "CM-2, Vivian. All okay in there?"

"Affirmative," said Dardenas. "Shimmy and shear are in bounds."

"Gravity sure is weird, though," Amy said.

Right. Because for them the G-forces were shoving them *downward*, toward their feet. Neither eyeballs-in or eyeballs-out, but pulling them laterally in their couches. But neither of them had sounded alarmed or even concerned.

The acceleration steadied. And just like that, they were slipping the surly bonds of, well, the fifth Lagrangian Point, and were heading for Venus. Or, more accurately, traveling along a curving path toward that point in space where Venus would be in November.

Right now, they only had one possible abort mode, and it would expire a mere forty-five minutes after the beginning of the burn. That abort would require them to fire both Centaur-G boosters at right angles to their current trajectory for several minutes, deflecting their current Venus-bound elliptical orbit into a hyperbolic trajectory. Then, almost immediately, they would need to abandon Astarte for the Apollo Command and Service Modules, and rely on their SPS rocket motors to bend them the rest of the way around into cislunar space and head for lunar orbit. Given the momentum they'd already achieved, the abort would be a five-or six-day hell-trip, with four astronauts in each of the three-person Command Modules.

That would be quite the feat, and an ignominious end to the mission, after all this. Truly a last resort.

But they weren't going to need it. Dave Horn and Ellis Mayer were quietly trading vectors and instrument readings, settings, and angles, but Vivian barely needed to listen at this point. She could tell from their tones of voice and frequent agreements that their trajectory was nominal and their residuals—errors and uncertainties in their course—were smaller than they'd anticipated. Marco, in CM-2, confirmed, and Josh Rawlings would occasionally chime in to let them know that all the systems in the Astarte Skylab were nominal, and none of the torques and stresses were out of bounds.

In short: everything was just fine, everything was copacetic, and they really were on their way. Vivian could afford the luxury of being absorbed in her own thoughts, and with so much trust in Dave Horn, Ellis Mayer, NASA, and the sheer inevitability of math, as applied to orbital mechanics.

Astonishing. Who was Vivian Carter now, anyway?

Who were any of them?

Vivian had a feeling they were about to spend the next two years finding out.

The burn cut off exactly when it was supposed to, and they were back in free fall.

"Burn nominal." Horn paused, perhaps wondering whether he ought to say something more stirring, but settled for: "We're off, then, I guess."

Vivian eye-rolled him, then said: "Houston, this is Apollo Astarte, off and running on our long journey to the planets Venus and Mars, and in the fullness of time, all the way back around to good old planet Earth."

"Preliminary trajectory is looking good," Ellis said. "You're in the groove."

Dave nodded. "Just another day in the office, Houston."

"Y'all come back soon now."

"Will do," Vivian said.

The Flight Director came back on the line. "Astarte, Houston. The launch team and entire ground crew wish you good luck, Godspeed, and smooth sailing."

Three Godspeeds in all, for luck, from three very different people. Svetlana, her Night Corps friends, and now Mission Control. "Thanks very much, Houston. We appreciate it. And thanks for all your work, today and over the past few … years." She'd been about to say *months*. Caught herself just in time.

And that was it for ceremony, at least for now. Later on, there would be the inevitable dog and pony show for the evening news. The words of congratulations, with everyone reading from their prepared notes and printouts while trying to make it sound spontaneous. After Apollo 32, her regular broadcasts throughout LGS-1, plus her earthly participation as CAPCOM or PR cheerleader for several other NASA missions, Vivian could pretty much phone all that in. Literally, this time.

Despite everyone's calmness, this was a big deal. They'd completed the critical burn at last, and they were committed. Apollo Venus Astarte was now in a heliocentric orbit. It was the first time human beings had ever been in one. Already, they were making history.

There could be no going back, short of a major and almost immediate disaster. They'd cut the cord with Earth and were already well outside cislunar space and moving on into the blackness.

As a result, Vivian Carter, three of her closest friends, and four other people she was still getting to know, would spend the next almost-two-years in these three small pressurized vehicles that made up Apollo Astarte. Before they saw any other human again in the flesh, they'd have traveled several hundred *million* miles and scooted within just a couple hundred miles of two goddamned *planets*. From Earth, with the naked eye, Venus and Mars just looked like points of light. For Vivian and her crew, those planets would be *right there*, in front of their windows, as close as the Earth appeared from low Earth orbit.

It seemed almost too wild for words. Vivian couldn't wait. But, of course, she'd have to.

She scanned the boards, a knee-jerk reaction at this point. Everything was still fine. It made a nice change to have achieved a major success, with no crises.

"Okay, then." She turned off the comms and looked sideways at Horn. "Well. Here we go. The final frontier, or one of them."

Dave responded with an atrocious William Shatner impersonation. "Boldly going … where no man … has gone before."

"No *man?* Go wash your mouth out with soap."

"Aye aye, Commander." As always, Horn's eyes were scanning all his instruments, reading and rereading all the gauges, while his fingers automatically tapped the guidance computer keys, replaying the numbers. Given that they'd received two thumbs up from Houston on the burn, this went way beyond triple-checking, but it was the obsessive caution and attention to detail of men like Dave Horn—and Ellis Mayer, and Feye Gisemba—that kept crews alive and safe, and had helped put Vivian where she was now.

Vivian's own obsession and hard work had played a role in that too, of course.

Because it was good form, she waited in Command Module One until Ellis in Mission Control confirmed that Astarte was no-go for the abort-to-lunar option. By this time, even Dave was spending more time looking out the window than at his boards, though he'd likely stay in the hot seat for another hour or so, until Houston had piled up enough range-rate data to confirm their trajectory.

They hadn't spoken for the past twenty minutes, beyond confirming the status checks with Houston. Already, the Earth and Moon were visibly shrinking behind them. And, as Vivian unbuckled and shoved off for the CM's top hatch, all she said was: "Well, then. Guess I'll see you later."

Horn grinned. "Yep. I guess you will."

In addition to the galley area, which had the usual four chairs with no space for more, the interior of Astarte had eight seats with straps at the various instrument stations and in front of the window. During their Venus and Mars slingshot encounters it would be more comfortable to be held in place. Aside from that, if all went as planned there would only be a few very brief engine burns for course corrections during this entire mission. Which was amazing in itself, right? Gravity, orbital mechanics, and a great deal of hardcore and preprogrammed calculus would be doing the lion's share of the work from now on.

Josh was still working the main status board for the Astarte Skylab, the Astarte command console in the forward compartment, and as Vivian came in through the Multiple Docking Adapter hatch he glanced up at her and gave her a quick thumbs-up. Marco would still be in CM-2, but Amy Benson had returned to Astarte and pulled herself to a seat in front of the window to look back at the Earth receding behind them. Rudy Frank was up at the science station; Vivian had passed him on her way down. He wasn't taking data right now, but would get back to his solar observations just as soon as Dave and Marco stabilized the Astarte's Sun-inertial attitude. As Josh's backup today, Laura Simmons was alternating her gaze between the status boards and the window, blinking rapidly, while Greg Heinz wore a slight frown and an otherwise glazed expression, staring into his own internal space rather than out into the real expanse of interplanetary space that would surround them for months to come.

Vivian thought of addressing her crew, attempting a rousing speech to cut the obvious tension, but decided against it. She would allow them the luxury of their own thoughts for a while longer. The pace of shipboard life would crank up soon enough, and once they got onto a real timeline, calm introspective intervals might be hard to come by.

Dave Horn, Josh Rawlings, and Marco Dardenas were known quantities, of course. Josh had been in the same astronaut class as Vivian, and they'd enjoyed the same highs and endured similar lows during that training. She hadn't met Marco until her first visit to Columbia Station, orbiting the Moon just before the Hadley Conflict, but had spent much longer with him in the aftermath of that conflict as part of their mixed US and Soviet crew back aboard Columbia, awaiting rescue from their bizarre lunar orbit. Josh and Marco were solid career astronauts, cut from the same cloth, and they knew the Skylab and Command Module systems inside and out.

Horn's major preoccupation throughout this entire flight would be to oversee their trajectory and their navigation around Venus, then around Mars, and all the way back to Earth through a couple of complete orbits of the inner solar system. Currently on a free-return trajectory around Venus, he would soon amend that to the classic flyby that would hurl them away from Venus on a course for Mars. He would want to make as few burns as possible and at the most effective times, both for the sake of his own pride and (more importantly) to conserve as much fuel as possible.

Vivian wasn't supposed to play favorites, but after her NASA astronaut guys, her preferred crew member was their doctor, Amy Benson. Amy was two inches taller than Vivian, and a little leaner and more muscular. With her army background and page-boy-cropped hair, Benson reminded Vivian a tiny bit of Terri Brock, which she took to be a good omen.

As crew, Amy was smart, quick-learning, and no-nonsense. She had the astronaut banter down almost to a fault, but whenever she switched into one of her many roles as their combined doctor, dentist, nurse, EMT, and psych specialist, her demeanor changed completely. Prior to launch, Amy had worked with each crew member to establish their medical baseline and work through every detail of their medical history. Which, among other things, also meant that Amy was now Vivian's OB/GYN. But, no big deal: Amy had taken that in stride and shifted to become the competent but also empathic and very human medical professional that Vivian needed.

97

On this trip, Amy had her work cut out for her. She would give the crew frequent electrocardiograms, and take detailed measurements of heartbeat volume, venous pressure, and vascular tone in various parts of their bodies. She would also give them regular breathing capacity tests, to make sure their lungs were not suffering effects from their long-term microgravity environment.

Even more important, she'd study them for signs of muscle atrophy, bone marrow loss, and any reduction in the number of T-lymphocytes in their blood. NASA had plenty of data on medium-term zero-G space habitation of a few months or so from their Skylabs orbiting Earth and the Moon. But Astarte's voyage around the inner solar system would multiply that total in-space duration by almost a factor of ten.

That was a lot of crew interaction, much of it unpleasant by its nature, and so they'd needed exactly the right person.

It helped that Vivian had trusted Amy on sight. And, although this was her own strictly unscientific prejudice, she had really wanted their mission doctor to be a woman. The male doctors in the Agency tended to support the men over than the women, and to not take women's issues as seriously. If matters on the Astarte mission did go sideways, Vivian needed above all to be able to trust her doctor to tell her the truth. Space travel in close quarters would always be weird, and Astarte would be even more taxing than usual, and Vivian and Dave had spent more time interviewing the candidates for Astarte's medical officer than they had for the other three scientists combined.

Those other three? Rudy Frank, their solar physicist, was blond with almost surfer-dude good looks but about the geekiest conversational style that Vivian could imagine. As an academic and scientific instrument builder at various Earthbound solar observatories, Rudy had a stellar background for his mission specialist position, pun most definitely intended. Yet he could talk about solar prominences and sunspots and coronal mass ejection events with both the passion of a true aficionado and the skills of a professional educator—meaning he could dumb heliophysics down to the point where even Vivian could understand it.

This skill would be important on the journey, when he'd be helping to prepare lectures and lessons and other education and public outreach activities, in addition to taking the lion's share of the observations with the eight separate solar experiments on the Apollo Telescope Mount.

Wrapping up the team were mission specialists and planetary scientists Greg Heinz, their Venus expert, and Laura Simmons, who would take point for their Mars encounter. Greg was quiet, hard-working, and unassuming, a natural team player, in addition to knowing more about Venus and the other planets in the solar system than was possibly healthy. As an obsessive herself, Vivian naturally recognized and respected obsession in others, but Greg seemed to love every planet in the solar system equally, even those he would never get much closer to than he was right now. Which seemed a *little* strange. But who was Vivian to judge?

Laura's was the only other name that Vivian had a mental asterisk against. Laura was extremely knowledgeable about Mars, and about Earth science as well. She was good-natured, but tended to talk about herself just a bit too much. Vivian had a feeling that Laura's conversational style might begin to grate on her, and quite likely on the others, before long.

As commander, it was Vivian's duty to be alert to anything that might disturb the delicate balance of her crew. And so Vivian did wonder how the interpersonal relations would play out over the course of two years in their very small tin can zooming around the inner solar system.

She'd already discussed this, of course, with both Dave Horn and Amy Benson; Amy because she was the psych expert and it was part of her job, and Dave because he was a friend.

"We'll all have to give and take. Tolerate each other's faults." Horn glanced at her. "You know that, of course. More than anyone. Having to crew with me, and all."

"See, that's it in a nutshell," Vivian said. "That's the kind of self-deprecating comment that Laura would never make."

"She's good. And you helped choose her. It'll be fine. You have a good team. Don't second-guess yourself."

Vivian nodded. Sure, they'd had other choices, but Laura had been far and away the best, in every category except those minor personality nits.

Dave was right. Second-guessing herself now was pointless. And at least this way her crew had a five-three gender split. Their other options would have given them a six-man, two-woman crew. So this configuration was healthier, considered as a whole. Right?

Whatever. Vivian had other issues she needed to focus on. So she pulled her attention back to where it should be.

"Okay," she said. "Apollo Venus Astarte crew: congratulations on beginning the long haul. This is the end of the beginning. You've all worked damned hard to get here. Be proud of that."

Now the hard work really begins, Vivian thought, but instead said: "Now we get to kick back a little and get into our routine. Which means, right now, two hours of clean-up and shakedown, then we get our first meal of the voyage together. Then two of us get to play on the exercise machines while Amy and Rudy get some shuteye and the other four of us hit the books for some cross-training. So, let's get to it, people."

They already knew this, naturally. Vivian was willing to bet that they all had the first week's rota memorized, and maybe the second and third weeks too. Her crew were lightning-quick studies with great memories, and likely any of them could recite the upcoming rosters and who they'd be on duty and off duty with for an indefinite number of weeks into the future. But Vivian needed to mark the occasion. She had to say *something*.

And, it was true: right away, there was housekeeping to do. Any burn followed by a return to weightlessness shook loose a variety of screws, washers, dirt, fluff, stray food items, and even occasional socks. This happened even in the best and most carefully tended spacecraft, and likely double for a space station that had been pressed into service as a vehicle. They spent the next two hours clearing the crap out of the air, tidying up and reconfiguring the ship for cruise mode, and then, blessedly, they finally got to eat.

Vivian well remembered how cavernous Columbia Station had seemed when she'd first arrived in lunar orbit, prior to the very first conflict with the Soviets. After being in her Apollo 32 Command Module for three days with Ellis Mayer and Dave Horn, the sheer volume of the domed forward compartment of the Skylab had been dizzying.

Astarte was structurally a carbon copy of Columbia. Vivian had spent plenty of time inside the Astarte Skylab over the last couple of months, but she'd also had the big empty third-stage play-space, and various other spaces. Today, Astarte felt cramped.

The reason for that wasn't hard to find. *It's because this is all we have.* Aside from the two CMs bolted on like barnacles, this Astarte space would be Vivian's world, her eight-person crew's entire habitable universe, for close to two years. It was a sobering thought.

They were making good time. Just twenty-four hours after leaving L5, Astarte had already traveled almost a quarter of a million miles, doubling its distance from the Earth and Moon. Both objects were visibly much smaller behind them. Very soon, the crew stopped looking back at them—or at least stopped mentioning it. What was there to say? "Yep. Earth is still shrinking. Looks like a little blue peanut right now."

They were heading into the unknown, but at least they'd always know where they were. They'd be tracked almost continuously in their travels by the Deep Space Network, NASA's array of giant radio antennas at Goldstone in California, near Madrid in Spain, and near Canberra in Australia. As the Earth rotated, Astarte would always be in view of at least one of those sites. Over the Astarte's mission, the Doppler range-rate measurements the DSN performed using Astarte's radio transmissions would be able to pinpoint their position to within a few kilometers and measure their speed to an accuracy of a few centimeters per second.

The crew on board would also be taking optical sightings, and combining them with the data in their IMU—inertial measurement unit. Their efforts would be less accurate than the DSN's impressive number-crunching but—if they absolutely had to—good enough to keep the mission alive if they lost contact with the Earth.

Despite the massive emptiness of the universe around them, Vivian found it comforting that those they'd left back on Earth could tell them their position and speed with such precision. It didn't stop her playing with her sextant every chance she got, though. And the numbers she got out of it, after a bit of practice, were surprisingly good.

"Next up, weeks of monotony," said Laura. "Whee."

"Weeks of *training*," Vivian said. "Trust me, I'll make sure you're not bored."

Rudy grinned. "Busy doesn't necessarily mean not bored."

Even as Commander—and especially as a Commander-come-lately—Vivian herself still had a great deal of training to do. She had a lot of new science and tech to study up on, and a whole bunch of mission sims and procedures to run, especially now, while they were still near enough to the Earth that the communications travel time wouldn't be prohibitive. And once the Earth had faded even further into the background, Vivian would be running encounter sims onboard with her crew, refining and repeating the sequences of actions they'd need to perform until they could all do everything in their sleep. They'd only get one shot at each planet, after all. There'd be no going back, no do-overs.

Then, in addition to the core science of their mission, they had all the housekeeping: a whole complex ship and its instruments to clean and maintain, with those two hours of heavy physical exercise also shoehorned into each and every day just to stay fit and prevent bone and muscle loss.

Food to eat. Even laundry to do, which was a rare experience; even on the longer-term lunar missions items of clothing were worn for three to seven days and then discarded. In cislunar space the water to clean them would be heavier, and thus more expensive, than the thin fabric of the clothing. Here on Apollo Venus Astarte, the longest of long-duration missions, the math worked out slightly differently. They washed clothes in reclaimed water, dried the clothes, then reclaimed that water as well. And in the small and doubtless expensive laundry unit, the clothes *almost* got clean.

And then in the evenings, or what passed for the evening "downtime" for each of them, they had reports and journals to write. At varying levels, they had friends and family to stay in touch with. They also had a whole lot of movies to watch and books to read, but so far there'd been precious little time for those.

And none of the above included the contingencies, on fixing stuff that broke, or trying to keep up with whatever Mission Control wanted right now, or what was going on at home, in politics and in their family lives.

Aside from the Venus and Mars encounters themselves, the crew had a metric ton of science to do on the way. UV and IR measurements looking back at the Earth, now they could see it as a single point and get the integrated whole-Earth spectrum. Solar astronomy in the

UV, X-ray, and IR. Radar measurements of the surfaces of Venus and Mercury. X-ray astronomy. Measurements of their local interplanetary environment: radiation, magnetic fields, and so on.

It turned out that a couple of weeks after the Venus flyby Mercury would be in alignment, only three-tenths of an astronomical unit away—meaning, about a third of the Earth-Sun distance, a mere twenty-eight million miles—and so now they were tasked with taking Mercury data as well. Their telemetry stream back to Earth would be constantly full of science data.

They'd do shifts, changing partners regularly so they wouldn't get stale. Feye Gisemba might not have been on the trip, but he was there in spirit, helping out from his desk in Houston. Scheduling was totally his thing, and he was between missions right now; waiting for a posting to US-Copernicus that never quite came through, and willing to help.

No one would be twiddling their thumbs on this journey. Vivian hoped it would help to make the time pass quicker.

Hard to complain, given the extraordinary opportunity they'd all been given, the astonishing privilege and excitement of being the first humans to pass close to Venus and Mars, the first to orbit the Sun in a separate spacecraft, in its own heliocentric orbit, and all the rest of it.

Of course, being human, they complained anyway.

And that was just the first few days. Then came the next few days … and the days after those, as the Earth dwindled away behind them with teeth-gritting slowness.

After a while, the realization sank in. Intellectually, they'd known it all along, but now it became very real to them.

Venus was a *long* way away.

PART TWO: VENUS

September-November 1983

8

Zvezda Base: Svetlana Belyakova
September 2, 1983

SVETLANA Belyakova stalked into the US-Copernicus Commander's office with bad grace, and dipped her head in perfunctory acknowledgment of its seated occupant. "Commander Grant." She glanced to her left and right at the two U.S. marines who had escorted her through the corridors on the American side of the base. "This military escort, is it really required?"

"I thought perhaps you would feel more comfortable walking among our people with a little protection," he said.

"I was unaware that I needed it."

"These days, you never can tell," Grant waved the marines out, and they closed the door as they left. "Please, sit."

Svetlana did so, looking around her. "I believe your office is smaller now?"

"Yup. Space has become a premium again. Pressurized space, I mean. We've been moving a lot of walls around since the new kids joined us."

"As have we." She paused. "And how do your well-trained and very dangerous group of Night Corps soldiers like to be called 'new kids'?"

"What makes you think they're Night Corps?"

"Please. It is very easy to tell."

107

Grant shrugged. "I don't make the crew assignments. But if they were Night Corps, it would only go a small way toward balancing the number of Red Army goons your country has been shipping up here. Both right here, and to the south at Hortensius Crater."

"Of course. As we, too, are aware of the buildup of your troops at your military bases in the Marius Hills, Kepler Crater, and Mare Vaporum."

Grant snorted. "I'm afraid you're mistaken. At Marius and Vaporum, the added scientific staff are there to perform geological investigations. Any 'troops', as you call them, are just there for their protection."

"Huh."

"As always, you and any non-military geologists you may have available are free to join us there. We welcome the participation of Soviet science teams, in the spirit of international cooperation. Lots of good rockhounding to be done in both places."

"But not at Kepler."

"No, ma'am. Not at Kepler, I regret to say. That is indeed entirely an Air Force facility, and I have no insight to what little flyboy games they might be playing there."

She shook her head. "The lies come so easily to you."

He grinned tightly. "Listen, lady: I was a Marine, and now I'm NASA. Trust me, I go out of my way to avoid talking to the Air Force. Not my circus, not my monkeys, and definitely not my concern. And probably not yours, either."

"This escalation is bad for both of us. Our escalation, and your escalation; nothing good can come of it."

"Well." That infuriating thin grin again. "Major Belyakova, you of all people are very aware of recent history. Capture of US facilities. Theft of US property. The killing, attempted killing, and kidnap of US astronauts. I'm not in the Night Corps chain of command, but I'm guessing our friends to the west are just there to ensure nothing like that ever happens again. That y'all behave, and stick to the Lunar Accord like you're supposed to."

Svetlana studied him. "They train you well."

'Unfortunately." For a moment, Grant looked dour. "They forced me to go through media training and negotiation school before they gave me this command. Pain in the ass. If they wanted Starman or Vivian Carter or one of the other accommodationists in this position, they should just have assigned one of their asses into this chair and spared me that crap."

"Ah, here is the Daniel Grant that I recognize."

"At least you didn't bring your tame spy with you this time. I'm glad."

"You have no need for concern. Since we are being so candid today: Comrade Keretsky is not spying on you. He is spying on me."

"I know that." Grant studied her. "And you're happy living inside a repressive system that treats you that way? I can't fathom why."

Belyakova favored him with a thin smile. "You are so confident you are not being spied upon by your own people, in return? At least I am aware of whose eyes are upon me."

"Oh, I'm sure there are many pairs of eyes on you."

And there it was. Always, Grant would find a way to make unwelcome and degenerate remarks based on her appearance. At least he no longer called her "blondie" or "honey." That, at least, had been trained out of him by "all that crap" he had been forced to endure.

Belyakova ignored it and moved on. Grant had, in fact, sent for her, but she had no intention of ceding the initiative to him. "Perhaps. But let us concentrate on your country's newest incursion on lunar soil, without the official notification required by the Lunar Accord. Our Salyut stations in lunar orbit are telling us that two new craft have arrived from Earth and landed together behind the Jura Mountains."

"I'll take your word for it. These days I don't keep track of the exploratory Apollos. That's a whole different office."

"Also, there was a Cargo Container drop in the same location, just prior to their arrival."

"Well, well. Your *Almaz* stations do seem to be paying close attention to us, Major-General."

"I am sure you cannot blame us, given the history of US secret operations on the Moon."

Grant shook his head. "Okay, fine, you win. Let me see." He dug around on his desk, opened a folder, and riffled through its pages. "Ah. Here you go." He passed a flimsy sheet over to her. "The press release for this particular pair of Apollos, sent out to the world media a month ago. So, perhaps not so secret?"

"A press release that does not mention a Cargo Container. And your exploratory Apollo missions are usually scheduled out a year in advance, or even two. This one appears to have jumped the queue."

"Oh, look back at the record, Major-General. It's hardly the first time we've reorganized the program on the fly. And it's still nothing like the USSR's policy of keeping the details of its launches secret from even your own people, let alone us, until after the fact."

Daniel Grant sat back and studied her. It always seemed that he enjoyed the view this gave him, despite his guarded speech and frosty tone. Long used to enduring male appraisal, Belyakova stared him down patiently, until he said, "I'm sure I don't know what your point is. Maybe you're about to tell me."

"In the past, as you must already know, Cargo Carriers have been used by NASA only at Hadley Base and here at Zvezda-Copernicus. Night Corps, too, uses those or similar containers only at sites of extended operations. And I could see from your reaction that you believe this to be interesting as well."

"But not really my concern." At the look on her face, he added: "Sure, I guess I'm mildly curious why they'd need extra supplies. Our exploratory missions are generally just a couple of weeks, done and gone by nightfall. Perhaps the experiments here will last through lunar night and need the extra power. I can inquire, if it would put your mind at rest. Anything to keep the peace. But I honestly have no idea."

"I am certainly curious to know what NASA will claim. And have that claim clearly stated for the record, for later."

Grant shrugged. "Okay, sure."

"And your masters might not even tell you what you want to know. Which would, in itself, be interesting, would it not?"

"I guess." He glanced at the clock and rocked his chair forward again. "But listen, none of this is why I called you here. It's about Casey Buchanan."

Belyakova's mouth went dry, but she did not even blink. "And what about him?"

"He's very sick. Even sicker than usual. Svetlana … the docs are saying he doesn't have long left."

"Oh." She dropped her gaze. "I am very sorry to hear that."

Unlike most American men, Casey had always been straight with her. Vivian Carter and Casey Buchanan were the closest Belyakova had come to having American friends.

No; Casey *was* a friend. Vivian might have become a true friend, if she had been able to stop making her constant snide remarks, from needling Svetlana every chance she got. It did not take a psychologist to interpret Vivian's behavior: once Sergei Yashin was dead, Vivian had transferred all her anger about her capture and torture at Zvezda onto Svetlana's shoulders. Sometimes she seemed to put that aside and become amenable, but she could slide back to being prickly and irritating on the turn of a dime.

Svetlana did not quite trust Vivian, and she was sure the feeling was mutual. With Casey, on the other hand, the question of trust never arose. They were just … friends.

And now, apparently, she was about to lose that friend.

Once Keretsky arrived, her casual one-on-one meetings with Casey had been curtailed. Belyakova had keenly felt that loss, but had hoped it would be temporary. Now, it appeared that her new zampolit had robbed her of the last chances to sit, relax, and just "shoot the breeze" with Casey Buchanan.

"Sorry to hear that," she repeated, into the silence.

Grant cleared his throat. "So, do you want to know the real reason my office is smaller?"

Belyakova shook her head. The subject change was incongruous.

He gestured to his right. "There's a door in that wall. It leads straight into Casey's new sick room. I've chosen to keep him close by. Which means that anyone who visits me can also visit him without anyone else knowing." He held her gaze.

Grant, of all people, had really thought that far ahead? "Then … well, yes, I should like to see him. If that is truly what you are offering."

He cocked his head, affecting confusion. "Oh, but wait. Don't you need to run and get permission from your minder, before you 'fraternize' with him?"

"I believe I shall not ask." Belyakova fixed him with a stare. "And I believe *you* will not tell Comrade Keretsky of your … unusual humanitarian gesture. It is possible he would misunderstand. Are we agreed?"

Grant mimed zippering his mouth. "Oh, my lips are sealed, I assure you. Despite what you choose to think of me, I would do anything for my people. That's what makes a good leader, not all the other B.S." He gestured again at the wall to his right. "Casey Buchanan has given a lot for his country. As far as I'm concerned, what Casey wants, Casey gets, for whatever time he has left on this Earth. I mean, here."

He grinned at her expression and stood up to slide his fingers into a crack beneath a lunar map. The hidden door swung open. "Maybe I'm not the monster you think I am."

"I believe I will be the judge of that," Belyakova said, but smiled as she said it, then paused in the doorway. "But … thank you."

The room smelled of sweat and decay, and the figure on the bed was gaunt. Casey Buchanan seemed to have shriveled. His bald head appeared to have shrunk, his papery skin hanging loose on his face.

He blinked up at her, and for a moment she was not sure that he recognized her. Then his lips parted in a tired smile. "Ah. Comrade Svetlana. You came to … rescue me from all this?" "Comrade Casey." For once, she found herself lost for banter.

Grant shook his head. "You two crack me up. Well, I'll leave you to it." He closed the door behind them.

She perched awkwardly on the edge of a chair. "I regret that you do not look well."

"A … typical Russian understatement."

"You know well that I am Ukrainian." She leaned forward to put her hand over his and allowed her fingers to curl around his wrist. His pulse was beating as fast as a bird's and his skin was hot with fever. His fingernails had a bluish tinge to them. "How do you feel?"

"About as well as can be expected."

"Ah, so like a … 'piece of shit,' then, you are saying?"

He grinned again. "You got it, comrade."

"But it 'beats the alternative'?"

"I'm not …" Pain creased him, and she could see beads of sweat popping out of his forehead. "You know, Svetlana, this time … I'm not sure it does."

Once, Casey had been the only American man who could raise Svetlana's mood, let alone make her laugh. She did not think she would be laughing today.

Over the past months he had so often been the peacemaker between her and Grant. Only two weeks ago he had been walking around, talking, joking; not healthy, of course, he was never healthy, but his sudden decline came as a shock. "I am so sorry," she said.

"Not as sorry as me." He turned his arm over and squeezed her fingers. "But, while I can still think, I need to …" His voice came back, a little stronger, and for a moment the old Casey came back, the one who flirted harmlessly and made her laugh. "Would you like to see my bedsores?"

"You tempt me," she said. "But perhaps later."

"Now may be all the time we have," he said. He released her hand and tried to sit up, but the effort was too much. He coughed weakly and fell back.

Svetlana stood up. "Comrade Casey, you should rest. Conserve your strength."

"For what?" He kicked his right leg weakly, and the bedding slipped partly off his foot. "Major-General Belyakova, do me one favor: please look at the back of my right calf and tell me what you see."

Now his voice was stronger again. Casey seemed to be oscillating in strength on a very rapid timescale. Belyakova had no idea what that meant, but she could tell from his tone that he was serious.

Without further ado, she peeled the bedclothes back from Buchanan's feet. "Excuse me," she said, and reached tentatively for his knee.

"Oh, be my guest." He coughed again.

She raised his knee to bend his leg so that she could see the back of his calf. She saw only a red pimple, bright and angry against the tired blue and grey wattling of his skin, surrounded by a ring of soreness. "This concerns you?"

"It should concern you too. Sit me up. Come on, love, sit me up—you won't break me any worse. It helps my throat and lungs to drain. Do you know what pulmonary edema is?"

"I have no idea."

"I hope you never do. Sit me up."

She did so, even though she could tell she was hurting him. By the time he was sitting with pillows holding him half upright, Casey was clutching his chest and wheezing. Mucus bubbled at the edge of his lips, and without comment Svetlana took a tissue from her pocket and wiped it away.

"Thank you." He gave out a deep wracking cough that sounded too loud to come from such a wasted and damaged body, and pain again twisted his face. "How many days since I last saw you? Eight, perhaps ten? And since then I have been down to the Annex and back. And now, here I am. The docs say I'm looking at respiratory failure in days.

That's if something else doesn't kill me first. Liver, kidneys, nervous system collapse. Good grief. After a while, I stopped listening."

Belyakova nodded. It was amazing that Buchanan had survived this long, given the amount of radiation poisoning he'd suffered and the possibilities of opportunistic infections over the years. She knew he'd been bedridden for days on several previous occasions and come out of it. And if now the end was to come suddenly, perhaps that was for the best …

Casey was staring at her intently, and for a moment she thought he'd died right there in front of her. Then he blinked, and rasped: "You're missing something. I thought you were smart?"

"Smarter than you, old man," she said automatically.

"Don't make me call you Major-General again."

"Oh." Suddenly, Belyakova understood. She bent and placed her hand on his ankle, again turning his leg until she could see the red mark. "When did this happen?"

He nodded. "Ah, there she is. The ice queen with the sharp mind, unfazed by mere death and putrefaction. Two days ago."

"And where were you?"

"Passing through Joint Port after my trip back from Zvezda Annex."

"And you felt a sudden pain."

"I did."

"After removing your spacesuit, I think. Not while you were still wearing it."

His eyes glittered. Or perhaps those were merely tears from fighting the pain. "Correct."

"And …" She blinked.

"Probably nothing, though." He was watching her intently. "Perhaps a bee sting. Or a random cosmic ray hit. Who could say? So much wrong with me already."

"Who was near you at the time?"

"Near? No one."

But Belyakova knew the current Zvezda-Copernicus protocols intimately. "You had been escorted back by two American astronauts, or one American and one cosmonaut. Two suit technicians would also have been there. And perhaps …" She raised her eyebrows.

"Naturally the scene was supervised, to ensure that no inappropriate fraternization occurred."

"I don't believe it," she said flatly.

That weak smile again. "And yet?"

"Why?" She sat again and leaned forward. "Casey. Why *now*? And why tell me?"

"Oh, please," he said. "Ask better questions."

"Very well." Belyakova thought it through. "Does Commander Grant know?"

"Yes."

"Do the doctors know?"

"No. Not much good as doctors, are they? Then again, they've been predicting my imminent death for years. Probably just happy to be right for once."

"Casey. *Who else knows?*"

"Just the three of us. And we need to keep it that way."

"I agree." Svetlana nodded slowly. "Is there anything else I need to know?"

Casey put his hand on hers again, leaned back into his pillow, and said nothing.

"All right. Then: what else do you need?"

He stared at her sadly, and perhaps tried to squeeze her hand, although the pressure was fleeting. "Just sit with me a little longer? If you can? And don't make me talk too much more, there's a dear."

"Of course," she said.

He shook his head sadly. "Just call me Georgi, eh?"

She was momentarily startled. "That is my husband's name."

Casey grinned in brief delight, the old glint again flickering in his eye. "Then, just call me Georgi all the more ... but, no, sorry. I didn't mean him."

Belyakova nodded. She understood, of course. Casey had meant Georgi Markov, a prominent Bulgarian dissident and traitor, who had been assassinated in September 1978 by the Bulgarian secret police with the probable involvement of the KGB. He had been poisoned by a pellet that had been shot into the back of his right thigh using, of all things, an umbrella containing a compressed gas cavity.

That pellet had been laced with ricin, a potent toxin. He had died four days later. Belyakova was no medic, and did not remember the details—but Buchanan's meaning was very clear.

Casey Buchanan was not dying from the inevitable degradation of his body by radiation. Apparently, the many cancers he was suffering were not killing him quickly enough. The KGB—Belyakova's own people—had decided that Casey must die sooner.

"I am very sorry," she said. "Although, coming from me, that might not be a comfort."

"Coming from you, it is a very great comfort." He coughed, weakly. "I'll likely fall asleep on you any moment now."

"Then I will be here when you do."

"Thank you ... but listen. I ... wanted you to know. You'll do what you will with the information ..."

"Oh, I shall," she said grimly.

"But it would be best, I think, if your people did not know that *we* know. That the Americans are aware of what is killing me. You understand?"

Belyakova nodded. "You may trust me."

Casey's lip quirked. "Would Vivian agree?"

"I doubt it," she said. "But I know Vivian will be sorry she was not here, to spend time with you, here at the end."

"Yeah." Buchanan gave a dry grunt, that would probably have been a laugh if he'd had the strength. "She'd give me all kinds of hell for dying, I'm sure."

"Yes, I am sure she would."

Svetlana reached out reflexively and covered his hand with her own. It felt bony, his skin paper-thin, as if she might rip it and draw blood if she pulled away too sharply. "Comrade Casey?"

"Yes?"

"I am sorry that you never got to go home."

Almost in a whisper, he said, "I am home."

Less than five minutes later, he was asleep and snoring gently. From the expression on his face, it was not a gentle sleep.

Belyakova stayed with him fifteen minutes longer, watching as he slept, and then knocked on the door that led back into Grant's office.

Grant looked up from his paperwork and raised his eyebrows.

"He is sleeping."

"Good. He had enough strength to tell you all of it?"

"Yes."

"And I hope he impressed upon you the need for discretion?"

Without being invited, Belyakova sank into the chair opposite him and said nothing.

"Major-General Belyakova … Svetlana. It must be clear to you what would happen if my guys in US-Copernicus were to find out that *your* people are murdering Casey Buchanan?" He leaned in. "Of course you do. I can see it in your face. Casey is well loved here. My people would go crazy, and rightfully so. They would run wild, and they would attack *your* people with extreme prejudice and every justification. That would be the final end of this …" Grant gestured around him, "this misguided experiment in superpower cooperation. And I would prefer my first major off-world command to *not* end in a bloodbath."

"You are a fine leader," she said bitterly. "You have told me so, your-self. Would you not be able to stop them?"

"Negative," he said. "Not even me. Not against this. Everyone has a line, and out there everyone's line would be crossed at the same time. And as you yourself have pointed out—a whole lot of highly trained killing machines have arrived at US-Copernicus, just recently."

"And it took this to make you admit it," she said.

"Except that this conversation never happened."

Belyakova rubbed her eyes. For a moment she felt as tired as Casey Buchanan. But just for a moment, because after that her resolve came back in full force, and all of a sudden she had to get out of this unbear-able situation and back into Zvezda Base.

"What conversation?" She stood. "Thank you for the briefing, Com-mander Grant, and your clarity on many issues. I am grateful to you."

He grunted. "Must be a first."

"As a matter of fact, it is. But, do not worry. I will continue to press you about the Jura Mountains, and your country's insane military buildup. Perhaps even more, now."

"Of course you will." He grinned. "And I'll look forward to it."

Belyakova nodded to him and left.

Standing with her hands clasped behind her back and staring forward, Belyakova said: "I must brief you on an event that happened earlier today. It will be in my nightly report, but you might prefer to hear about it now."

Keretsky looked at her with those fishlike eyes. "Yes?"

Belyakova took a deep breath. "Casey Buchanan asked me to sit with him. As I believe you must be aware, he is very sick and not expected to live much longer."

"And you did so?"

"Of course I did. It is hard to refuse a man's dying wish, whoever that man may be." She gave Keretsky a chilly grin. "It appears Buchanan has developed some affection for me, for whatever reason."

Keretsky openly eyed her body and smiled. "For whatever reason."

Oh, you scum. Belyakova swallowed. Grant and Keretsky, two peas in a pod. To hell with them both.

She persevered. "I chose to do so because it was the compassionate thing to do, but also because who knows what Buchanan might have let slip in his weakness? We well know that Buchanan was CIA, and privy to information that those around him on the Moon did not have. Plus, this kindly act may have eared me some credit with Daniel Grant, which may make him more reasonable in future."

Keretsky grunted. "Buchanan is an imperialist, and one of the worst of them. By rights all imperialists should die alone and in pain."

Belyakova nodded dutifully. "As you say."

"And so: what did you learn?"

"Unfortunately, very little." She looked down now and held his gaze. "Comrade Keretsky, I owe you an apology. It appears that I have underestimated you."

He examined her face. "Oh? How so?"

"I will admit it: I assumed you were a mere bureaucrat. I failed to recognize that you are also a man of action. Decisive action." She looked at the walls, at the ceiling. "Are we overheard, do you think?"

"We are not. I have ways of ensuring it."

"And even if we were: your superiors undoubtedly already know that you have the killer instinct. You would hardly have acted without orders in this matter."

"I?"

She held his eyes again, unblinking. "You. You, who have eliminated Casey Buchanan."

Keretsky half-smiled. "A drink, perhaps?"

"A toast? I will not say no."

The zampolit reached into his desk drawer and pulled out a small bottle of cognac. An actual glass bottle, which meant it had come all the way from Earth. Belyakova did not manage to conceal her surprise adequately, because Keretsky smiled again. "For you, today, the best. Please, sit."

She inclined her head in thanks and did so. He poured each of them a small tot. "And yet, Buchanan was a very sick man. This is well known. I suspect that nature needed little help from us."

"I disagree. Buchanan was strong, despite his ailments." Belyakova took another sip of Keretsky's admittedly excellent cognac. "He had lived this long. Perhaps he would have outlived us all. But it appears that was not in our interests."

"The poison of the imperialist system must have given him some kind of perverse strength."

Belyakova nodded. "I always thought so. I spent a great deal of time with Buchanan. Which I know has been misinterpreted by you, and by others. But I was always aware that the American Commander Jones had tasked Buchanan with trying to flush out the Soviet mole in the US-Copernicus system. It was in our interests to know how close he was getting."

"Too close. It was not pleasant." Keretsky sighed. "When one has to remove dissident youths, strong and fierce, at least one can take comfort that the damage they will inflict on the Soviet system has been harmlessly drained away into the sewer. Removing a sick old man? It did not feel so noble."

"I am sure." Svetlana sipped at her glass, resisting the urge to fling the contents in Keretsky's smug face. Breathed out, as if she were just about to fire a weapon, to still any possible tremors in her voice. "And it appears that you were undetected. Buchanan did not even mention you being present in the Joint Port area." This was a lie, but a useful one.

"I have ways of remaining unseen." Keretsky smiled. "No, there is no magic. I was merely at some distance. There is a long line of sight from Zvezda into Joint Port. Designed that way from the beginning, of course."

Belyakova put a thoughtful expression on her face. "And we are sure that Buchanan has not been able to convey his suspicions to anyone else? Not to Grant, or back to NASA, or to Vivian Carter? He spoke regularly with all of them."

"His quarters were bugged. The so-called 'Family Area', where the American astronauts talk to their loved ones on Earth—that is also bugged. The only place where the Americans can speak securely is from one of their MOLABs, or from Commander Grant's office, and we are on the verge of cracking the American secure radio in those areas also."

Grant's office, not bugged? Belyakova breathed an internal sigh of relief. Also, Keretsky seemed unaware that Casey had been moved to his new location. "Excellent. Our people have been working hard. At last."

"At last?"

Belyakova took a deep breath, thinking: *As the Americans say: here goes nothing.* Out loud, she said: "The so-called Chinese operation. The cryptonauts. That was unbearably sloppy. The Americans know we were behind it."

"They may know, but can they prove it?" Keretsky poured her another small glass of cognac. "I concur. If patriots of the quality of you and I had been in charge, I am sure we could have concocted a more ironclad scheme."

"Oh, without doubt."

He paused to admire her, yet again. She gritted her teeth. "I like you, Svetlana Antonovna. I confess it. I feel that perhaps we should consider working together … far more closely."

From his facial expression, and the way his hands lingered on the glass, his meaning was clear.

Svetlana remained calm. She had been propositioned many times over the years by other cosmonauts and had extensive experience in turning such men down kindly, without incurring their hostility. This of course, was different. It was rare that a proposition was so unwelcome, or that the consequences of rejecting it might be so drastic. And from this weasel of a man? Who had just calmly confessed to murdering Casey Buchanan?

Plus, damn him. He had also just casually confirmed that the Soviet Union had been behind the cryptonaut attacks, and the Marius base.

That was something Svetlana Belyakova had very much wanted not to believe. And now she had no choice.

She had trusted her superiors. It appeared she had been merely a useful fool, all along.

Even with Belyakova's stern control of herself, all of this made it difficult for her to react normally to this KGB viper. She swallowed hard and did her best to don a neutral smile. "I look forward to a constructive partnership here on the Moon. As far as other matters are concerned: it is possible I misread you, but you must be aware that I have a husband. I would not wish there to be any unfortunate misunderstandings on that issue."

"A husband *on Earth*," he said. "Obviously, I would never attempt to come between a woman and her husband. On Earth."

She forced herself to hold his eye. "I am sure you would not be encouraging any moral weakness, Konstantin Borisovich." It was tough to keep the sneer out of her voice.

"Nothing could be further from my thoughts," he said, unblinking.

"I have much to lose, you understand, if any impropriety were to become well-known. I must protect myself at all times, or?" She shrugged. "No one else will do it for me. But, by all means, it would be pleasant to get to know each other a little better."

Coldly calculating, Svetlana nonetheless forced herself to give him an appraising look in return. Her eyes narrowed, but playfully, and she even momentarily allowed her nostrils to flare. She saw his reaction immediately.

You bastard, she thought. *I could play you like a violin, if I chose.*

Keretsky was a weak fool, a man who thought himself strong. He really thought she would be attracted to him, because he held death at his fingertips? Because he was powerful enough to kill a sick old man? This cowardly apparatchik who could only kill furtively, from a distance, with a spy's tools?

The cognac in her stomach roiled, and for a moment she thought she might be sick.

No. I will not. He does not have that power over me.

Keretsky had killed Casey. And was now making advances on her. Disrespecting her. And, her bosses had lied to her, repeatedly, about the cryptonauts.

It all stuck in her craw.

And all of a sudden, Svetlana Belyakova found that she could not play these stupid games anymore. Could not even smile at this reptile and be tactful with him for one minute longer.

"But," she said, and now that steel arrived in her tone, with a vengeance. "This will never happen again, comrade. You killed an American. In my base. Without my authority. For as long as I am in command here, you will do nothing like this without briefing me first. Is it understood?"

He raised his eyebrows.

"And, if I must report to you every day, then you must report to me promptly and honestly, whenever any matter that concerns the security of this base is concerned."

"I must?"

"Yes." She stood abruptly. "Thank you for the drink. And I am glad that matters are now clear between us."

"For as long as you are in command, you say." Keretsky appeared to find that amusing. He leaned in. "Then, enjoy your next forty-eight hours of triumph, Svetlana Antonovna."

All Belyakova could do was give him a curt nod and leave.

Stalking back to her quarters, Svetlana's thoughts returned to Apollo Venus Astarte. Millions of miles away, Vivian Carter would even now be preparing for her encounter with Venus. Pure science and exploration, technical challenges, and camaraderie, far away from power politics, military buildups, and corrosive relationships with both the Americans and some of her fellow Soviets.

Svetlana envied Vivian her life's simplicity.

CHAPTER 9

Interplanetary Space: Vivian Carter
September 9, 1983
Mission Elapsed Time: 67 days

THE first thought in Vivian's mind on awakening was: *Oh, hey. Today's the day. Halfway to Venus.*

Shame that means it's just the same as any other day, and there are as many days ahead of us as there are in the rearview mirror.

And that was just to get to the first destination. The cruise to Venus was the shortest leg of this marathon trip.

Her second thought was, *Christ, my neck hurts again.*

On that first item, Vivian didn't know whether anyone else on the ship had been doing the math. Certainly no one had mentioned it. Vivian herself was trying not to think about it. She was working very hard at treating this mission as an experience in itself, with every day its own reward rather than merely counting down the days before the first of its two fleeting climaxes, but she just couldn't help it.

The numbers were daunting. Earth to Venus: 133 days. Venus to Mars: 190 days. Mars back around to Earth: 259 days, for a grand total mission elapsed time of 582 days. Meaning that today's milestone marked only … eleven percent of the journey.

No, Vivian really shouldn't be dwelling on those numbers. Before the mission, its duration had seemed almost abstract, and a big adventure. Now, it felt very, very concrete.

On her second thought: some people loved sleeping in weightlessness, but Vivian wasn't among them. For her, sleeping in zero G always sucked, and somehow it seemed to suck even worse in Astarte than it did in a Command Module, or even a Blue Gemini.

Vivian's neck ached, and her back ached, and she had a permanent stuffy head and mild sinus headache. Last night she'd tucked her hands into the straps in front of her sleeping bag to anchor herself in position more effectively, and this morning her left elbow was stiff as well.

Some of these problems were due to the ventilation. The environmental control system kept a steady flow of air moving through the sleeping quarters. This was to keep them all alive: without a forced airflow a globe of carbon dioxide would accumulate around her head and she would suffocate in her own exhalations. But the flow rate wasn't adjustable and always felt a bit fierce. All that coolish air flowing across her neck made it ache, and exacerbated the nasal stuffiness and facial bloat that always came with zero G.

Just the usual space stuff. But it made her grumpy first thing in the morning.

She unhooked the light band she wore around her temples to keep her head anchored in one place—without that her neck would be even stiffer in the mornings. Unzipping from her sleeping bag, she rolled around in the empty space in front of it, allowing herself to bump back and forth between the walls as she stretched and twisted to work out the kinks. Then she pulled on shorts and a T-shirt and headed for the hygiene facility.

One plus was that Vivian never seemed to need as much sleep in a weightless environment as she did in gravity, so she was generally up ahead of the others on her shift. Or maybe it was her puritan work ethic that poked her awake each day ahead of her alarm clock, her instinctive feeling that the commander should be visibly working harder and longer hours than everyone else. Leading by example. Ha.

As she pulled herself across from the hygiene cubicle to the wardroom, she heard Amy's voice drifting through the triangular gridded floor that separated Vivian from the forward compartment. "Scalpel," she said. "Forceps." And then she laughed, and Vivian heard Greg laugh too.

That sure didn't sound like a medical emergency, but Vivian poked her head up through the hexagonal hatch anyway. "Everything okay? Oh."

Amy and Greg were floating sideways-on to Vivian, their socked feet slid under one of the "shoe" rails to stabilize themselves. Amy was wielding scissors and a comb and trimming Greg's hair at the back. "Okay," she said. "Suction," and Greg duly passed her the small hand-held dry-vac so she could suck away all the stray hairs that were now floating in the air between them.

Amy peered down at Vivian. "Fear not, my captain. Only minor surgery."

"Unless she cuts my throat," Greg said.

"Oh, trust me, that could *never* happen." Amy winked at Vivian.

"Looking very dapper," Vivian said. "Okay, carry on." She pulled herself back down and shoved off, gliding gently into the galley area for some coffee.

Once out of their sightline, she grimaced. Despite Amy's best efforts, half of that loose hair was bound to end up in the air vent traps later that day. But, on the bright side: at least Greg was getting his hair cut. Unlike Rudy, who was beginning to look even more like a hippie surfer guy than he did before.

Laura's long hair irritated Vivian even more. When Laura wore it loose, weightlessness pushed it out into a huge blond aura around her head. When tied back, which was more usual, it was nominally more under control but still inherently risky. Laura's natural movements were often jerky and birdlike, meaning that at the dinner table she might inadvertently send her bunched ponytail-hair whipping across someone else's cheek.

Vivian sucked down some coffee and then took a sip of orange juice to freshen her mouth again. She opened the breakfast locker and slid out the rack. From the series of packages within, all stuck down with tape to stop them floating out in the usual free-fall jack-in-the-box style, she selected the three small containers dated for today with the purple tabs that indicated they were hers.

Oatmeal with brown sugar, "scrambled eggs," and a sweet roll. Could be worse, and it often was. She often wished she could send a message back to Past Vivian and tell her not to rush her meal planning, that after a few months it would really matter what she found in her meal tray, and that after being in zero G for this long her taste buds would be craving spicier food than usual. *Should have upgraded to the huevos rancheros. Ah, well. I'll get it right on my next mission. Hahaha.*

She drifted backward far enough to reach the hot and cold water spigots and rehydrate her food, then floated back the other way. Glancing out of the wardroom window she saw … stars. Just lots and lots of stars, bright enough to be visible in the low light setting that they used in the wardroom during breakfast shifts. Brighter lighting was for dinnertimes. To remind them what meal it was, Greg always joked.

"Morning, boss." Josh Rawlings sailed into the wardroom, just as Vivian got her feet hooked under the rail at the table. As her mouth was full of oatmeal, she just waved to him.

She mentally reviewed. Her shift crew today would be Josh, Dave, and Laura. Those going off shift, who would eat dinner after the breakfast crew had cleared out of the galley: Marco and Rudy, who were presumably up in the Multiple Docking Adapter taking data from either the Sun or Venus, and Amy and Greg, who she'd just seen, technically already into their downtime period but using it to take care of personal grooming. The shift assignments moved around every three or four days, mixing and matching the various crew members in rotation to ensure that no one spent too long with the same other people. Apparently, there was some elaborate social science or game theory behind it, but the rota sure looked random to Vivian.

She did like it when she ended up having morning quality time with one of her original astronaut buddies, though. It happened less often than she might like.

Josh had pulled the rack out to study the packaging with the green tabs, and grimaced. "Hey. You know what today is, right?"

"Pancakes and sausage?"

"I mean mission-wise."

"My turn to scrape the black gunk out of the water filtration system?"

"Vivian. We're halfway to Venus."

She nodded and swapped in a mouthful of scrambled eggs to cut the overly sweet and chewy monotony of the oatmeal. Around it, she said, "And I thought maybe I was the only one counting."

"Glass is half full, now."

"Or half empty. And it's just the first of three glasses."

They grinned at each other, and Josh applied himself heartily to whatever rehydrated mush was on his menu for the morning.

Eventually, he raised his eyes again. "What? You've got that look."

126

"What look?" He just waited, so Vivian gave in. "Okay. As it happens, there's something I've been meaning to ask you for the last, I don't know, couple of million miles."

"Fire away," he said.

"Didn't you once mention feeling claustrophobic on Columbia Station? Long time ago, before the first Soyuz attack. And that was even before you were held captive on Columbia for an extra ..." She tried to do the math and failed. "I don't know, what was it? Two and a half months, or more? God knows. Anyway. Claustrophobia?"

"Oh, I got over that."

She pierced him with a look. "Tinkerbell waved her magic wand? Come on, it's just us here. Tell me."

"No, seriously. I was half-joking anyway. It wasn't actual claustrophobia, not like a panic attack or anything." He was watching her as he said this, his eyes apologetic, but Vivian carefully didn't react. "The thing about Columbia was that we weren't going anywhere. We were just flying around and around the goddamn Moon again, and again, and again. It was like, I don't know ... just covering the same ground all the time. It felt like I was stuck in a holding pattern. This isn't that. On Astarte, we're actually going somewhere. it's different."

"It's really that different? Even though it's the same-sized space, or less, and with two extra bodies?"

"It is, somehow. I can't explain it. Plus ... and don't take this the wrong way ..." He hesitated.

"Josh. This is me you're talking to."

"I know." He met her eye again. "It's because this time three of you are women, and that helps. It feels like a more normal environment, more relaxed. Don't ask me to say why, exactly. It just makes this feel more like a ..."

"Community?"

"I guess." He studied her, clearly curious. "So, how does it feel to you?"

"If I was the only woman on this tour, it would've gotten old real fast. Been there, done that. Nothing against you, or any of the other guys. I've spent a lot of time around men. I *like* men. I've never been a girl's girl. But on a trip like this, for *years?*" She shook her head. "You're right. This is healthier."

"Anyway, bottom line: I'm a lot of things, but I'm not claustrophobic. I'm fine."

"Okay," she said. "Just needed to check. Need to look after my people."

He eyed her quizzically. "So, the psych people on the ground didn't put you up to this?"

"No, they did not. Otherwise, it would have been Amy asking you all this."

"Yeah, I guess."

"And besides, I would never have told the psych folks about that conversation." She glanced over his shoulder. "Uh-oh. Incoming."

Josh half-nodded, as Laura pulled herself into the wardroom. Her hair was loose again and seemed to fill up the doorway. Vivian sighed inside, but smiled at her Mars specialist. "Gooood morning, sunshine."

"Is it?" Laura grimaced and, like any sane person, made a beeline for the coffee, while Josh tried to suppress a smirk. He could still read Vivian like a book, it seemed. Vivian flicked her eyes upward in a brief God-help-us sort of way.

Laura took a long pull at her bulb of coffee. "Man, that's disgusting."

Josh nodded sagely. "Hey, today's coffee used to be yesterday's coffee."

"And is going to be tomorrow's coffee." Laura took another chug.

Another recurring joke. Once Vivian had heard it fifteen times it had passed beyond unfunny to become mildly irritating. But the same jokes, repeated, seemed to comfort the rest of her crew.

Different strokes for different folks. In all likelihood, Vivian herself had a bunch of stock phrases or verbal tics that she didn't even know about, that pissed her crew off a dozen times a day.

In fact, their water recovery system was a thing of beauty. It recycled everything, their washing water as well as their urine, in a snazzy distillation unit that spun around its axis to compensate for the lack of gravity. More filtering and catalysis, and they had themselves water that tasted just as good as anything that came out of a faucet in a moderate-sized city on Earth. Mystery black gunk notwithstanding. That was in the mechanism, not the water itself.

Having used the Skylab showers aboard Columbia and Eagle at the end of the Hadley Conflict several years ago, Vivian still wasn't sure they were worth the space they took up and the hassle they would inevitably become, at some point in the mission. The thing was just too awkward to clean up afterwards. It was messy, and a pain in the neck, and none of them had that kind of time.

But that was a side issue. Josh had been right, back at L5. Now they were past shakedown and on the mission itself water management was nominal. But they were still all nervous about what might happen if it went off kilter. They had a backup system and plenty of spare parts for the critical parts of the unit, but no one was keen on needing to try them out.

Conversation lapsed, as they applied themselves diligently to their breakfast. But eventually Laura released her lap strap, unhooked her toes from the rail, and allowed herself to drift upward. "Okay, well, let's go see what we can screw up today."

Vivian didn't react right away. She did understand the sentiment; they were still behind schedule in lots of areas, particularly training, through no fault of anyone's. It was the schedule's fault. To say the least, it was success-oriented.

On the other hand, it was a depressing note to start the day on.

So, she just smiled. "Or? Kick ass, take names, and get shit done."

Vivian Carter, currently the best motivational speaker inside the orbit of Venus.

"Sure thing." Laura nodded and sailed out of the wardroom to go work a shift at the science station.

"Okay, what's my first?" Vivian grabbed up a clipboard from a rack on the wall by the table. "Oh, yay. Scrubbing the walls in the ops area with disinfectant. My favorite."

"Rank has its privileges," Josh said.

Vivian grinned, flipped him the bird, and set off on her way.

"Can we chat?"

"Sure." Vivian looked up at Amy's expression. "Oh. That kind of chat." She glanced at the status board in front of her. "Looks like CM-2 is free."

As she floated into the second Command Module ahead of Amy, Vivian instinctively scanned all the boards. Nothing out of the ordinary. "Should I fold down one of the couches?"

"You know I'm not a real shrink, right?"

"Really? You fake it well."

"Uh, thank you?"

Vivian folded down a seat anyway, and loosely strapped in. "Okay. I'm braced. Hit me with it."

"Way back there on Planet Earth, the genuine mission shrinks are worried about you."

"Crap." Vivian immediately flashed on Peter's woes. The psych folks couldn't exactly ground Vivian, not now ... but they could certainly complicate her life. Which was the last thing she needed. "What did I do now?"

"You're not taking advantage of the friends-and-family connections as much as the other crew. Not calling home. They're concerned that maybe you're losing touch with the home planet a little too quickly. Getting mentally isolated."

"What? I talk to people."

"Not people on Earth. You're talking to us."

"And that's a problem?"

"Vivian, we're not exactly friends-and-family."

"You haven't met my family."

"Well, no ..."

"Frankly, if you had, you'd understand. I mean, they're not bad people, but it's not like we're chatty. When I became an astronaut, they ... well, my parents were a bit weird about it all. I mean, they were proud of me and everything: 'Great job Vivian, and that's very impressive! And so, so surprising!' 'Thanks Mom.' But on the other hand, they were absolutely against me going into space. My mom was humiliated to think I'd be floating around in confined spaces with guys I wasn't married to. And my dad was peeved that I'd outrank him, like I was doing it deliberately to one-up him. So, they acted like I thought I was too good to talk to them, even though I didn't think that, and I'm pretty sure that wasn't the vibe I was giving off ..."

Vivian shook her head. Too much heart-on-sleeve stuff. This was the most she'd ever talked about her family to another astronaut, aside from Peter Sandoval, who was in his own separate category. Besides, it wasn't Amy she needed to convince. Amy was just following orders, same as everyone else. *Get Vivian Carter back on the same page as everyone else, okay? If she flames out, we're in big trouble.*

Which meant she'd have to start checking some more friends-and-family boxes, to make them go away, damn it. She stalled. "I get on great with my Gran, but she likes the real-life touch, doesn't even like talking on the phone, so you can imagine how well she'd do with the long transmission pauses we have to put up with here. And I

130

do talk to Ellis now and then, offline and aside from whatever CAP-COM shifts he's pulling."

"And that's okay with his wife?"

"Sure. As far as I know. Judy's great. But Ellis and I were crew. We went to the Moon together. That's a bond that endures."

Amy studied her. "Right."

"I'm no threat to his marriage. And there's so much of what we go through that only other astronauts can understand."

"You really believe that?"

"Sure. Don't you? I mean, you're an actual astronaut. That doesn't ring true to you?"

"This isn't about me."

"Wow." Vivian grinned. "You really aced those psych classes, I bet."

"I studied hard in all my classes. Okay, fine. I've done my duty." Amy gave her a wry grin and tossed her clipboard aside. Naturally, it floated across the compartment, bounced off one of the lockers, and went into a spin. They both watched it with amusement.

"So, you're off duty now?"

Amy snagged the clipboard and stuck it to a Velcro patch. "Sure. And no, I've got no concerns about you and Ellis. They made me ask that. Dipshits."

"Then perhaps we could talk about something else?"

Amy tented her fingers, leaned forward. "Fire away."

"Don't do that. You look like a shrink again."

"Sorry."

Vivian took a breath. "Honestly, I'm surprised you're not more worried about Rudy?"

"Why would I be worried about Rudy?" Amy said neutrally.

"Uh, we've talked about this before."

A faint smile crossed Amy's face. "Not officially."

It was growing increasingly hard to prise Rudy away from his solar observing duties. Just a month out from Earth, just after he'd finished training them all on how to operate the solar instruments, he'd started cutting deals with the various crew members to take their turn at the solar observing in exchange for other chores.

Which actually worked out okay, logistically speaking. The career astronauts found the repetitive nature of the solar observations tedious and were quite happy to trade their stints for other duties. Vivian had done the same a couple of times, but for different reasons: she liked taking measurements of the Sun as much or as little as many of her other duties, but the Multiple Docking Adapter area was noisier than other areas on the ship. The computers, fans, extractors, and water system took the noise level up to around sixty decibels, not in the realm of causing permanent hearing loss but notably louder than the forty-five to fifty decibels in the Forward Compartment and crew quarters. Plus, they were annoying decibels: lots of irregular bangs and whirls, nothing like white noise.

The science station was also right next to their small machine shop workbench. This meant that Vivian was either in the MDA all by herself for hours at a stretch, or sharing it with someone who was fixing a broken mechanism or machining a new part for some subsystem or other, and inevitably swearing a lot in the process, neither of which helped with the ambient noise situation.

And then, and *then*: Rudy would then inevitably drop by partway through her shift to see for himself how the solar prominences or sunspots or spectra or whatever were looking, and explain to her exactly how interesting they were and how she wasn't quite taking the right data or writing up the logbook correctly, before she pulled rank and chased him away.

In short, the prevailing opinion among the crew was that if Rudy wanted the Sun, he could have it. But Vivian was still concerned. "So, he doesn't seem a trifle … obsessed, to you?"

Amy cocked an eye at her. "Coming from you?"

"Shut *up*. We're talking about Rudy now."

"Seriously: I wouldn't worry about it," Amy said. "Having something to fret about takes his mind off all the other crap. And one day he'll get a bunch of lead-authored papers out of it and make faculty at some snazzy Ivy League university and be happy as a clam for the rest of his life."

Vivian frowned. "Which other crap?"

"Oh, being tens of millions of miles away from humanity. The fallibility of all the systems keeping us alive. Missing his family. All the usual things that weigh on people's minds."

"Ah." Vivian was quite happy being millions of miles from home, at least most of the time, and she trusted the spacecraft systems to keep her alive. When those systems had their hiccups and minor crises, she had faith in herself and the people around her to fix them. And if they couldn't, it was hardly worth worrying about until it happened.

"Scientists are different," Amy added helpfully, looking at her face.

"You bet," said Vivian.

"Everyone here's doing fine. Seriously. Better than fine. Boredom is an issue, obviously, and we all have our bad days, but we don't take it out on each other. We get cranky with *things*, not people. We get annoyed and we deal with it."

"Yes, because we're all fricking grown-ups," Vivian said.

"Because we all have to live together in this tin can, and we're smart enough to know it. We all just need to have a bit of give and take."

"Oh." Vivian sighed. By now she knew Amy well enough to see the subtext. "Fine. What am I doing wrong now?"

"Nobody's doing anything wrong. But maybe we could all ease up on the schedule just a little? You're the commander, but maybe we don't all want to hear what time it is and what we're supposed to be doing ten minutes from now, quite as often as we do."

"Uh, how? These days, we're always behind."

"And if we haven't caught up yet, we're never going to. So, just maybe, we should be allowed to say 'screw it' a little more often than we do."

Oh." Vivian received a daily Execute Package from Houston on the teletype. Many of the items on it were time-critical, and they needed to be folded into the training program and the routine maintenance, and Vivian herself carried the can for making sure all of that got done.

It was true: every day, they got further and further behind schedule and then had to readjust, reschedule, and reprioritize, and that always led to arguments with Houston. They'd figure out how to renormalize the schedule, and everything in the garden would come up roses for a couple days. Then several of them would trade roles—since they were required to cross-train extensively—and, boom. That would inevitably nudge them back behind schedule again. It was maddening.

Everything took twice as long as Houston thought it should, and that wasn't new. The very first Skylab crews, a decade ago, had learned the same thing. For the first weeks at least, every job was just harder and slower than anticipated. Future Skylabs had flown with eased schedules, and on its around-the-Moon mission the Columbia Station crew had had it relatively cushy, but for Apollo Venus Astarte the mission schedulers had ramped everything up again, because the stakes were high and there was *so much* to do to maximize mission success.

Surely, everyone must know this by now. All Vivian could find to say was: "It's not quite that easy."

"Look at it this way: anything you can let go of, takes a layer of stress of you as well."

"I guess. Let me internalize that for a few days."

Amy grinned. "Learning the lingo, I see."

"Always pays to stay on the right side of the medics."

"Now you're talking." Amy reclaimed her clipboard and glanced at it. "I think we're all done here. At least until I come after your blood and urine in six hours."

"Excellent. Can't wait. I'll cross my legs especially for you and make sure you get *lots*."

"You do always like to overachieve."

"Yes, yes, I do."

"So," Amy said casually, as if it had just occurred to her. "How are things between you and Peter, anyway?"

Vivian sighed. "Damn it, Amy … I'll call him and let you know."

As it happened, Vivian had talked to Peter Sandoval only a couple of times during these first two months of the cruise phase to Venus.

Part of this was logistical. For more than half of his time Peter was simply unreachable, either on duty in Cheyenne Mountain doing whatever Night Corps ground support people did there, or out somewhere training recruits. For way more than half of Vivian's time, she was busy on Astarte, asleep, or at minimum preoccupied with planning whatever she was about to be busy with next. And like everyone else on Astarte, the hours of Vivian's duty shift progressed steadily around the clock, meaning she was often awake when everyone on US Mountain Time was asleep.

Given all that, it was hard to find times to talk. Plus, Vivian found it tricky figuring out what to say. It wasn't like they were an established couple with a shared history and an easy conversational rhythm. Peter couldn't tell her much about what he was doing, and most of Vivian's daily grind didn't make for scintillating conversation. Neither of them talked politics or sport a whole lot, and Vivian hated small talk.

On top of all that, there was the elephant in the room: Vivian was in space, living the dream, and Peter was still grounded.

And so, after some awkward silences that lasted even longer than the ever-increasing time delay, they'd agreed that their whatever-this-relationship-is was on hold until Vivian got back. In the meantime, they'd settle for typed messages, basically I'm-still-fine status updates, every few days, sent over the secure network.

The other crew members, especially those with kids, scheduled family time daily or nearly so. Those without a spouse or kids seemed to find random friends to talk to without difficulty. But the simple truth was that Vivian didn't need a whole lot of cozy-friend-time. She never had. Two of her best astronaut friends were aboard this vessel, in Dave Horn and Josh Rawlings. Plus, she had a growing rapport with Amy Benson herself that seemed reasonable enough to Vivian, given her spotty record of friendships with people of her own gender, and she got on passably well with her other crew members.

If Vivian could have set up conversations with Terri Brock, Katya Okhotina, Svetlana Belyakova or even Nikolai Makarov, she would absolutely have done that. But the frequency and code that Terri had given her only worked that one time. Since then, Terri's schedule had seemed permanently orthogonal to Vivian's, and Vivian obviously couldn't make personal calls to the Soviet Union. Her attempts to make contact with Svetlana at Zvezda Base had been stymied, for reasons that weren't entirely clear.

Vivian had her mission, and that was enough. More than she could handle, at times. But sure, whatever: she'd call Peter again this week, and try to jam some more damned friends-and-family time ... somewhere into her impossible schedule.

"We're still heading for Venus, then?" Vivian pulled herself all the way into CM-1 and, as always, scanned the boards.

"Halfway there," Horn said. "And it looks like the residuals are small enough that we won't need a course correction burn for another few weeks."

"Well, that's good to ..." Vivian paused, raised her hands in front of her face and sneezed. "Goddamn dust."

"Bless you." Horn shook his head in sympathy. Dust didn't settle out in weightlessness, and by now there was a lot of it in circulation. Calling it "dust" was a euphemism, of course. Some of it might be genuine dust, but by now the largest part by far must be coming from the crew themselves: from epidermal flaking and dandruff, with additional contributions from hair and whiskers. The air circulated regularly and went through extensive filtering to extract such tiny debris, and likely removed a high percentage of it. But not a hundred percent.

"I mean, I knew interplanetary travel would be slow, but … good grief. We're *crawling*."

Horn grinned. "We're not crawling."

Intellectually Vivian knew that, but it was certainly hard to see. In fact, it was hard to see *anything* of interest. Venus Astarte was oriented so that its solar panels gained maximum power advantage from the Sun and the solar experiments worked most effectively. That meant that from the crew's perspective the Earth was "below" the Skylab, beyond the aft compartments, which were currently storage and would increasingly fill with trash as the mission progressed. CM-1, where Vivian and Horn spent half an hour or so together when their schedules lined up, "checking their course," which mostly meant just chatting, was in the axial port, and so Earth had quickly become occulted behind the bulk of the Skylab. For most of the time the only good view of the Earth was from CM-2.

A couple of times a week they changed the spacecraft attitude specifically to look back toward Earth and take photographs and make measurements with the science array in the Apollo Telescope Mount and then realign once again to look ahead to Venus—still just a radiant speck in the sky ahead—and snag some data from there as well. These were the week's high points for Greg and Laura, the planetary specialists, though Rudy chafed at any time spent pointing the science instrument package anywhere but at the Sun.

He'd need to get used to that. In just a couple of weeks they'd start ramping up the time they spent observing Venus. The orientation plan for Astarte would become much more complex then, to optimize science while also maintaining their battery levels from the Sun's light and making sure various areas of the spacecraft didn't overheat. But during the cruise phase, the goal was just to cover the distance. To get closer to Venus.

Vivian hadn't expected to spend quite *this* much effort on the schedule. As it turned out, that first couple of weeks had been a honeymoon, and by now the honeymoon was long over.

In principle, they should be working eight-hour days, not including food preparation and cleanup, and taking downtime at the weekends. But those daily eight-hour schedules had no contingency time, and in real life, just about every task took longer than expected. And then there were the gotchas: the spills and breakages, the spaceship quirks, the unscheduled system diagnostics. And then there were the many, many times when one of them would go to a particular cupboard or panel or chest for a specific tool or other piece of equipment … that wasn't there. Which, since the Astarte was a closed system, meant that it had to be somewhere else, and would need to be tracked down.

Their constant refrain: "We spent sooo much time making lists of where everything was. And correcting them when we repacked, to make the more vital stuff easier to find. Lists, lists, and more lists, and we still can't find anything worth a damn."

Decluttering the crew level at the expense of the forward compartment had been a big part of that. They'd loaded up oxygen, food, water, and other supplies and then basically moved most of it somewhere else. They'd taken tools from *up here* to *down there* when it was clear they'd need them *down there* more often than expected.

Even Amy, who was in sole control of all the medical supplies, swore that the contents of her medical chest moved around from one week to the next.

"Gremlins," Dardenas said. "Every Skylab has 'em. They just all moved over from L5 Prime to here so now we have double gremlins."

Vivian blamed their backup crew for at least part of it. Sure, none of them would have deliberately screwed with either the supplies or the records, but it was only human nature: if this wasn't *your* mission, you had less of a laser focus on ensuring all the records were correct. And a lapse in concentration at the wrong time ….

None of which, of course, explained the items that magically moved from one week to the next, long after they'd left L5.

"A stowaway, perhaps." Rudy looked around mock-suspiciously. "Come out, come out, wherever you are."

It all took time away from training, from exercising, and most of all, from their relaxation periods. Every eight-hour day inched longer, sometimes all the way to twelve hours. They'd go to sleep exhausted, and overnight even more items would move around and be found in non-intuitive places for the following week.

It was Greg who finally gave in and announced he'd be doing a four-hour shift on Saturday mornings "just to play catch-up," specifically with his own training chores. That, of course, meant other people had to join him.

Long before they got anywhere near Venus, the planned differences between the days of the week evaporated altogether. At that point they agreed to move to a different philosophy: they'd only work a half-day the day before an EVA, to make sure everyone was fresh, and those who had actually worked the EVA would take more rest time the day after.

However, since EVAs were only necessary once every three or four weeks, their total activity level remained high.

Then, just a few weeks before Venus encounter, they got word from Mission Control. News big enough for the whole crew to assemble for it.

Geology news, as it turned out, from one of Vivian's old friends.

Bill Dobbs and Christian Vasquez had been Vivian's geology team on her Lunar Geological Survey mission back in March, but Dobbs had suffered a head wound during a hostile attack on LGS-1, and had been medevaced home. To everyone's relief, he had made a full recovery. Unfortunately, due to the severity of his brain injury, FAA and NASA regulations mandated a five-year recovery period and subsequent testing before he could be considered for further spaceflight opportunities. So Bill was rattling around the Lunar Sample Office Facility at Johnson Space Center, biding his time and providing glum but excellent support in the detailed analysis of the LGS-1 geology samples, while Jon Evans took his place as Vasquez's partner, having all the fun on the Moon.

Now, though, it looked like Dobbs might be having some fun of his own. His voice almost dripped with enthusiasm and excitement as it came across the airwaves from Houston.

"We haven't yet completed a full area map from the LGS-1 data. All this takes time. The wheels of science run slow. But we're finally beginning to uncover some interesting results. We were always hoping to find rare earth elements, right? So that's been our focus. And, though it's early days yet …"

"Jesus, Bill, cut to the chase," Josh Rawlings murmured.

Dobbs continued blithely; he wouldn't hear Josh's comment for several more minutes. "As best we can tell so far, the area on the Near-side with the highest detected thorium and other rare elements is …" He pointed at the lunar map behind him, and looked at the camera. "Drumroll, please? Right here. The highland area around and between these craters, Mairan and, uh, Bouguer? Named after French scientists, I guess. Or mimes. One or the other, I forget."

"Man," said Vivian. "Dobbs has turned into a real comedian since he nearly died."

"He should definitely hit the club circuit," Rawlings said.

Dobbs continued. "You might recall that Mare Imbrium has this extension, this circular bay-like area to its northwest called Sinus Iridum. Bay of Rainbows, though, funny thing, I don't remember seeing any rainbows when we passed through. Anyways, it's a basaltic lava plain surrounded by the Montes Jura range, at about forty-five north, thirty-ish west. You can see this-here bunch of big craters, which are the Mairan series, the Sharp series, Bianchini, Bouguer? That's where the REE's aren't. But *this* whole highland area at Jura bounded by Mare Imbrium to the east, Oceanus Procellarum to the west and Mare Frigoris, the Sea of Cold, named after my wife … I kid, I kid. But all that area at sixty degrees north looks like a goldmine of rare earth elements. Not in the craters, presumably because the REE's were created when the Moon first formed, whereas the craters are much newer, and threw other materials around when they did. Pausing now for you to take notes. And drink coffee." Dobbs picked up his mug and stared thoughtfully at his big wall map of the Moon while he drank.

"My God," Vivian said. "That's freaking terrific. And on this side of the Moon. My money was on the South Pole-Aitken Basin."

"Entirely reasonable, based on what we knew at the time," Greg said.

Vivian allowed herself a moment of smugness. "So, some background. It always seemed to us like the geology backroom was obsessed with craters. They always wanted us to get more crater data. But on LGS-1 we insisted on taking samples from everywhere, even those areas that looked dull. And, see? Boring is where we'll be mining the REEs, right there in the Jura Mountains.

"And, not to brag, and who's counting? Certainly not me—but I'm damned sure I took most of those samples. I was on point for the first half of that area, after we rounded Promontorium Heraclides and went up into those highlands …"

"Sure," Rawlings said dutifully, and Vivian checked herself. No one cared about her lunar reminiscences right now. And the collecting of the samples had really been a team effort. "So: how far is this from US-Copernicus?"

"As the lunar crow flies, that whole area is between seven hundred miles and eight-hundred-forty miles from US-Copernicus," she said. "A serious journey, but these days not a huge one."

Not a huge one, she thought. *Ha. Sure, Vivian, that's only like a tenth to an eighth of the lunar circumference. So blasé, I've become.*

"Anyway," she added, "it's better than having to drive all the way round to the Aitken Basin to stake a claim."

Rawlings was still looking at the maps on the screen. "Interesting to note that the Mairan area has volcanic domes, just like Marius. Mairan, Marius: similar in names, and similar in terrain. A complete coincidence, obviously."

"The Moon does like to confuse," Vivian said.

"So. Where there are domes there are also lava tubes?"

"Probably. I don't think they've been found at Mairan yet, though I'm not sure whether they've done a thorough search. Right now, everything will be about the nifty silver metals."

"Anyway," Dobbs said from Houston, continuing his spiel. "The next step is to send out prospecting teams, which is exactly what we're doing …"

There was a lot more to the presentation, and for once Vivian and the scientists were enthralled.

"Vivian, I just got terrible news." Josh's face was grim.

"Crap. What's broken now?"

"No, the ship is fine. News from earth."

Vivian sighed in frustration. "God damn it, do we always have to get a downer after every upper?"

"I guess that's our world."

She took a deep breath. "Okay, let me have it. Tell me your terrible news."

"Casey Buchanan has passed away."

"Shit." Vivian rolled backward.

Casey, gone at last. Hardly a surprise, but sad nonetheless.

"Yeah."

Vivian suffered a moment of weird and inappropriate jealousy. "And ... you found out about it before I did?"

"Sure. We were crew."

"When?" She thought back. "Oh. Of course." Way back when in what felt like the dim and distant past but was in fact only January 1979, Apollo 21, crewed by Norton and Buchanan, had landed near Hadley Rille to become the first contingent of the new Hadley Base. Josh Rawlings had been their Command Module Pilot and transferred at the same time into the new Columbia Station in lunar orbit.

If Ellis Mayer had died, Vivian certainly expected to be informed before anyone else. The same logic held with Josh Rawlings.

"Sorry, man. I'm such an idiot sometimes. Or maybe all the time."

"No, you're fine."

"And what's ..." Vivian took another breath. "Well, what's next? Where's he going to be interred?"

"The disposal plan?" Rawlings grinned. "Hey, that's what Casey used to call it. Matter of fact to a fault. His will asked for him to be cremated and his ashes spread on the lunar surface. No specific location, just wherever he happened to be at the time. He wasn't sentimental about it, but he did want his ashes to become moondust."

"That seems appropriate." She looked at Josh sideways. "And that's what's going to happen, right? No stuffed shirt is going to stop them contaminating the lunar surface with human remains? I mean, it wouldn't be the first time."

"Oh, it's already done. Grant made sure Casey got his dying wish before anyone could raise red flags. Said he was more inclined to ask for forgiveness than permission."

"Good. Good." Vivian's impression of Grant went up a notch. The idea of Casey Buchanan's ashes resting forever on the lunar surface was oddly comforting. "I'm glad the old dude gets what he wanted."

Rawlings nodded, then hesitated. "There's another thing. Just as an FYI. Much less significant, but you'll probably be interested."

"Okay, sure."

"It seems that less than a day after Casey died, Svetlana Belyakova got shit-canned."

"She ... what?"

"Got the axe. Got removed from her command and sent home from the Moon. She launched out less than twelve hours after they said the last rites over Casey. The Soviets claim it was all just routine—time for her to cycle out and be replaced by Rudenko, who was already on site to be swapped in. Grant's not buying that, though. Apparently Belyakova never stopped by to say goodbye to him, and he's getting the sense that it came as a shock to the other Soviets at Zvezda. Sent home in disgrace, is his best bet."

"Okay." Vivian's mind ticked over. "Did she attend the service, or whatever, for Casey? The two of them got on well."

"So Grant told me. No, she was apparently forbidden from attending. Not by NASA, not by Grant. Her own people nixed it."

"Huh." Vivian thought about that for a moment. "That would really piss her off. But surely not enough to leave? Or for her own powers-that-be to fire her ass?" On the other hand, Belyakova did have a temper. But ... on the *other* other hand, Belyakova was the Zvezda Base commander. "None of this makes sense to me, Josh."

He shrugged. "Well, that's all I know. Okay, I've got to get back to work. Uh, if you want to talk about Casey sometime, over a fruit juice or whatever? Once the shock has worn off. I wouldn't mind having our own little private memorial out here in the middle of nowhere, when time permits."

"Absolutely. We will absolutely do that." Vivian shook her head. "Casey Buchanan, damn. What a legend. I hope his passing was easy."

Josh squeezed her shoulder as he exited the Command Module. "After all this time? And all the pain and other shit Casey went through? I'm sure it was."

Their flyby was scheduled for November 14, 1983. By November 1, Venus was visibly a naked-eye disk. Even five million miles out it subtended about five arcminutes, a sixth of the diameter of the full Moon as seen from Earth. And it was *bright*, very bright, outshining everything else aside from the Sun; a searchlight in the sky that appeared to be trained squarely on Apollo Venus Astarte.

In just a few days more, it became a *planet* with a differentiated atmosphere, a changing color scheme, and a phase that slowly changed as they approached.

In the reality of cold, hard relative velocities, they were approaching Venus at much the same speed as they'd departed from the Earth's vicinity. But in the final weeks of their approach it sure looked like the Evening Star—now the Evening Planet—was rushing toward them. Perhaps because Vivian and her crew knew all too well how much work remained to be done before their arrival, and especially how much of a sustained panic the week before and after flyby were going to be.

Vivian and Dave had planned to run at least three flyby simulations, with the whole crew going through the motions of what they'd be doing during those days. In reality, that had been much too hard to manage given their other mission responsibilities. They'd managed one sim, alternating sim days with regular days and conducting lessons-learned between each day, and they'd run some of the closest-approach sequences several times. Many of the science measurements would be pre-programmed and semi-automated, but others would require the human touch. This meant that the four hours around the flyby itself would be a complex dance of aligning instruments, taking measurements, taking photographs and replacing film cartridges, and a dozen other activities.

They'd drilled hard during those sims. They'd gone mostly okay. And Vivian and Dave would have to be content with that, because they'd done all that was realistically possible.

The rest of the crew seemed comfortable with their level of training, even the most meticulous of the scientists. They felt ready. They felt good.

But Vivian herself still felt that they were all terribly unprepared for the reality of the Venus flyby.

CHAPTER 10

Venus Inbound: Vivian Carter
November 14, 1983
Mission Elapsed Time: 133 days

IN that final week they all became Venus obsessives. The approach of the White Planet was the one source of rapid change in their otherwise static universe. The excitement built among the planetary mission specialists first, but quickly spread to the rest of the crew. Even Vivian started trading sleep for time at the windows or up at the science station, and the Multiple Docking Adapter was often crowded with three or four of the crew at a time, studying the planet as it came into clearer focus in the optical, infrared, and ultraviolet. Tantalizing details began to emerge.

Optically, Venus was a bright pearl suspended against black velvet, the side facing the Sun an almost impossible white but with a delicate yellow tint. They were coming at the planet from behind and slightly inside its orbit, so for these last days of the approach the left half of Venus was in bright sunlight while its right side was night-dark. They would skim the inner, sunward side, using the planet's gravity assist to throw them out past the orbit of Earth again and on to Mars.

By now, Venus seemed more real to Vivian than her own home planet, or even the Moon. After all, Venus was right here, growing rapidly in front of their eyes. Ethereal yet solid, shiny-clean in appearance and yet ridiculously toxic: Earth's evil sibling.

This was the world of Amtor, in the Edgar Rice Burroughs novels some of her crew seemed fixated on. The Perelandra of C.S. Lewis. The swamp world, desert world, and ocean world of various other pulp novels. And, for once, even Vivian found herself dwelling on the fictional representations of Venus. How different would this mission be, and how would it be to look down on the planet from just a couple hundred miles aloft, if this had really been the Venus that people in the past had imagined?

Of course, the reality was likely to be even more spectacular.

From the orbit of Venus, the Sun was noticeably larger and twice as bright. Plus, and unexpectedly, Earth shone brightly in their skies and was hard to miss.

"Well, of course," Greg had said, when Marco brought it up. "The Earth as seen from Venus is about three times as bright as Venus ever is, when seen from the Earth."

"Um." Marco frowned. "Didn't you tell us that Venus's albedo is over twice the Earth's? And the two planets are almost the same size."

"Yes, both true. But the important thing is that from the Earth we don't see the fully illuminated Venus when it's on the same side of the solar system as us, only when it's on the far side of the Sun, and so much further away. Now, Astarte is well inside Earth's orbit, so that Earth is almost always fully illuminated, and it's close to being in conjunction."

"That'll be a lot different once we get to Mars," said Josh.

"Exactly. Mars has a low albedo and is smaller, so it won't blind us like Venus does. And from there the Earth will look a lot dimmer."

"Going to the dark side," said Dave Horn, and everyone looked at Vivian.

She raised her eyes to heaven, at least for her current bodily orientation. "Star Wars. The Sith. Yes, guys: by now I get the reference."

"There's one. There's two. And the third. And … bombs away!" Marco Dardenas cackled, cracked his knuckles, then unhitched his lap strap and drifted up from his seat at the Astarte command console.

"Copy that," Vivian said, still frowning at the board. Sure, their three Venus probes had been deployed from their tubes—using about the clunkiest spring-loaded ejection mechanism she could imagine—but their baby propulsion systems still had to fire up on cue, and those probes and engines had been sitting inert in those tubes a long time and suffered through a number of extreme heating and cooling cycles.

"I have a visual on Probe One," said Laura, from the big window, her nose almost pressed up against it as she squinted up and sideways.

"That means she can see it," Rudy said, amused.

Laura ignored him. "We have a thruster plume! It's separating. It's off. Go-go-go, you pretty thing. Go! And there: number two has fired as well."

Through the loudspeaker came Greg Heinz's voice, from his post at the science station. "I have clean telemetry from all three. Confirming engine starts."

"And ... there," Laura said with satisfaction. "Probe Three has fired up and is on its way." She clapped, and Rudy and Marco joined her in this smattering of applause.

Venus dominated their windows and their thoughts. They were twenty-four hours from periapsis, meaning their closest approach to the planet during flyby, and the pace of their activities aboard Astarte was ramping up steeply.

"Houston, Astarte," Vivian said into her headset. "We confirm Venus Probes One through Three are deployed and beginning their long descent into hell. Which you'll already know, because the signals from the probes have beaten my voice back to you by a few seconds. Anyway, it's all looking good from here, from both instrumentation and crew visuals."

And with that, she took the headset off, already thinking ahead to the next item on their flyby checklist.

The probes, each a spherical pressure vessel weighing two hundred pounds, had been ejected mechanically from their sterilized containers atop the fore end of the Multiple Docking Adapter, and their rocket motors had all fired perfectly. From now on they would make their own way to Venus. They'd enter the planet's atmosphere at around twenty-five thousand miles an hour but be rapidly slowed by the density of its air, and take about an hour to drift down through the searing and polluted atmospheric muck. Each carried a neutral mass spectrometer, a solar flux radiometer, a gas chromatograph, an infrared radiometer, and a cloud particle size radiometer, in addition to more conventional devices to measure temperature, pressure, and acceleration.

Down they'd would go, their little instrument covers and gate valves cranking open automatically at the fifty-mile-altitude mark to measure temperature, radiative energy, wind speed and turbulence in the atmosphere. Their entries into that atmosphere would be staggered: Probe One would enter Venus's atmosphere on the "early day" side at a latitude of around sixty degrees north, Probe Two further around and into the southern hemisphere, and Probe Three would plunge into the "night" side. If the experimenters were lucky, one or more of them might even survive all the way down to the planet's surface.

All thrilling stuff for the scientists, but Vivian's attention was back on more immediate matters: constantly monitoring that everyone knew what they were supposed to be doing every second of the day and that their preparations for closest approach stayed on schedule, whether her crew hated her for it or not; ensuring that they all continued to eat and sleep at least a safe minimum amount; rather neurotically triple-checking that all their cameras had film; and (more mundanely) making sure that they didn't neglect the obvious stuff like air filtration, water purification, and power management in their excitement, and thus jeopardize their own safety.

"Shouldn't you be on the exercise bike right now?" For once it was Amy's turn to play bad cop, while Vivian just floated in the background.

"Well, yeah, but ..." Greg waved at the spectrograph. "Surely this takes precedence? I still have a lot to do. Even this far out, we're already seeing the circulation structure in the cloud top region. It'll take analysis to figure out the wind velocities and radiances and scattering properties ..."

"Analysis that doesn't need to be done immediately."

"Well, no, it can't be, because—"

"So what you mean is, everything's under control right now."

"So far, yes, great. So maybe I'll just catch up on the torture machine after the encounter, okay?"

Amy put her hands on her hips and frowned, which was less imposing when she was drifting upward on a diagonal. "Or maybe you should stick with the program, and take care of your health? The data will still come in whether you're here or not, and Viv is scheduled to ride herd on it for the next couple hours anyway."

Greg looked past Amy at Vivian. "Is that an order?"

Amy didn't blink. "I give the medical direction aboard this ship. Look, man: it'll be easier to maintain your schedule now than try to regain ground after sloughing off for a few days. And once you get out of the rhythm, it'll be too tempting for you to never get back into it. Trust me. And, good grief, you're just obsessively calibrating and reca-librating that thing anyway. I see you."

"I'll get back into it." Greg huffed out a breath, perhaps making an effort to remain tactful. "Look. Two and a half hours of exercise a day, including the changing and cleanup and all? I just don't have that kind of time right now." He looked past Amy at Vivian again. "Venus is coming. It's nearly here. And I'm sure the commander has better things to do right now than watch this board. I'm doing us both a favor."

"Plus," Amy said, remorseless. "you'll sleep better tonight if you exert today, and you absolutely *need* to be rested and on top form tomorrow."

Vivian bit down on her own exasperation. *Venus is coming.* She herself had been the first to use that phrase, when futilely trying to convince her crew to do just one more end-to-end training sim the previous week. She had failed, and for good reason: other maintenance had to take precedence. But since then, every single one of her crew had used it straight back in her face whenever they didn't like whatever they were being asked to do.

Greg looked back at Amy. "Split the difference. One hour. Okay?"

"God damn it." Amy sighed. "Okay. But only if you do three hours on Tuesday or Wednesday. And I *will* be checking up on you."

He frowned. "What day is it today?"

"Sunday," she said.

"Deal," he said promptly, got up, and shoved himself off feetfirst past Vivian and through into the forward compartment. She only just managed to avoid him as he went by.

Amy pulled herself into the science console chair. "He's right. You have better things to do than this. I've got it."

"You're supposed to be on break."

"And this is how I choose to relax. I need to get away from all those bozos for a while, anyway. Seriously."

"You're kidding." Vivian was half irritated and half amused. "So it's fine for you to reinvent your schedule on the fly, but not Greg?"

"Take the win," Amy said absently, skimming through the spectrograph log and flipping a couple of switches to check the display. "Go clean the windows again, or get ahead on something else, or just see if everyone apart from me is where they're supposed to be. Or take a power nap, because you know you could use one. Dealer's choice."

Vivian gave it up. If Greg wanted to lose his muscle tone and have the nutrients leak out of his bones, or whatever, that was on him. And if Amy wanted to blow her miniscule downtime staring at spectra that were coming in automatically, far be it from Vivian to get in her face about it.

So maybe it *would* be better for her to spend this bonus time stepping back to review and sanity-check. "You got it," she said. "Thanks."

After all, Venus *was* coming. And fast.

It would have been nice to saunter around Venus, maybe stay a while. Spend some time in the neighborhood, stop to smell the sulfurous roses. But the harsh reality of orbital mechanics meant that wasn't going to happen.

Crunching the numbers for their closest approach was fascinating. They'd be approaching the White Planet at a little over fifteen and a half thousand miles per hour, and they'd leave at that same velocity. Those were speeds relative to Venus, of course, but as the planet itself was sprinting around its orbit at eighty thousand miles an hour, the Astarte would benefit from an impressive gravitational slingshot to send it powering on toward Mars.

At fifteen and a half thousand miles an hour, they'd be traveling a distance equivalent to one Venus diameter every fourteen minutes. Meaning that right here and now, a little under twenty-four hours and three hundred seventy thousand miles from periapsis, Venus appeared over a degree across, twice as wide as the full Moon, and was growing in front of them in real time.

From fifteen hours before the encounter until fifteen hours after, they'd be closer to Venus than the Moon was to the Earth. At the twelve-hour mark, Venus would be two degrees across, as large in their sky as the Earth appeared from the lunar surface. Four hours out, seven degrees across. Two hours, fourteen degrees. And then in that final hour, as they rocketed past, not far above the very cloud tops of Venus, it would grow from thirty degrees across to fill half the sky for those precious minutes of closest approach.

By now they'd altered the attitude of Apollo Astarte so that all the science instruments on the Apollo Telescope Mount pallet were constantly focused on the planet, which also meant that—by design, of course—Venus was always visible through their big picture window in the forward compartment, as well as the window in the wardroom and one of the portholes in the Multiple Docking Adapter. Even this far out and waning gibbous, Venus was so bright that it dazzled if you stared at it for too long.

It was for the best that everyone on the crew was either a scientist or had undergone rigorous scientific and technical training, and that they trusted instruments and math, because it sure looked like they were on course to collide with the bright planet. Vivian had even come across her three scientists engaged in a very cerebral discussion over lunch about would happen if the Astarte did plow straight into the central disk of Venus. Opinions differed on how long Astarte would survive before breaking up in a fireball, but none of the possibilities would get them anywhere near the surface—heat ablation and structural stresses would doom the craft at many tens of miles of altitude. Death, they all agreed, would come quickly.

They weren't going to crash into Venus. They all knew that. But it still required a certain nerve to stay the course, and everyone—including Vivian—was feeling a little jittery as the White Planet grew in front of them.

It helped that they were ridiculously busy. Between accumulating and checking scientific data, taking what seemed like ten thousand photographs, and doing regular reports for the scientists back home, plus filming news segments for the public, there was little time for chit-chat.

The additional broadcasts notwithstanding: to say that they felt remote from the rest of humanity would be an understatement. This was a sight that no other humans had ever seen. And the Earth was, right now, seventy million miles away. Two hundred and eighty times the Earth-Moon distance. Even at Mars, they would not be as far from the Earth as they were right now. And this separation drew them closer together.

This was it: the big one. Boldly going where no humans had gone before.

Vivian drifted through the hatch from the Multiple Docking Adapter into the main body of Astarte. She was only getting in the scientists' way up there anyway. Josh was swinging back and forth in his chair at the Astarte control console, punching buttons. "Okay?" she said.

"Sure. Thermal stresses a little … unusual." He glanced up, spared her a grin. "It's fine. No problems. Really."

"Great," she said. "Because this would be a really lousy time for an emergency EVA."

He mock-shuddered. "Don't even."

She pulled herself closer to the big window. In ten minutes she'd go check in with Dave, and then loop pack to the science station, but for right now she could at least take a few moments to feast her eyes on the approaching planet.

"Hoo, boy," she said. "Looks like a scorcher down there. Even from here."

That wasn't the half of it. Ironically for a planet named for the goddess of beauty and love, Venus was no paradise. Its surface was a literal hellscape. The temperature at ground level was nine hundred degrees Fahrenheit, hot enough to melt lead, but no one would survive long enough to burn to death because the atmospheric surface pressure was ninety-two times that of the Earth. Plus, that atmosphere was ninety-five percent carbon dioxide, and Venus's skies were permanently obscured by yellow-grey clouds of sulfuric acid, ludicrously unbreathable and toxic. That sulfuric acid often condensed out into a burning drizzle, a rain that evaporated before it reached the surface.

Although Vivian couldn't see the surface through the thick cloud, she knew that the ground topography was mostly flat, wrinkled volcanic plains, with two broad highland areas: Ishtar Terra in the north, and Aphrodite Terra in the south. Venus also had its share of different types of terrain with a variety of nomenclatures even more obscure than the lunar naming systems: tesserae and tholi, plana and planitiae, regiones and rupes, lineae and labyrinthi … which basically boiled down to plateaus, mountains, valleys, scarps, rilles and creases and cuts.

Oh, and volcanos. Lots and lots of volcanoes—many of them still active. And none of which she could see right now. Bummer.

It took almost two hundred and twenty-five days for Venus to orbit the Sun, but a day on Venus lasted even longer: two hundred and forty-three Earth days. Its rotation was retrograde, meaning that it spun backwards relative to the other planets in the solar system, an effect presumably caused by the drag of that monstrous atmosphere, which meant that if you could somehow find a way to hang out on the surface for the one hundred seventeen days between sunrises, you'd see the Sun rising in the west and setting in the east.

Not that you'd see much of the Sun from the surface, through the clouds.

Then there were the winds. Venus had a massively powerful jet stream, with winds of four hundred kilometers per hour high up in its atmosphere. These super-rotational winds at the cloud tops passed all the way around Venus every four to five Earth days, meaning that they traveled sixty times faster than the surface was rotating. The cause of these excessive winds was … obscure.

To Vivian's eye it was a ridiculous excuse for a planet, a boiling, seething mess of a world, hostile to human life in every possible way. It was the exact opposite of the static, sterile Moon that Vivian was much more familiar with. But, because of that, Venus harbored a multitude of scientific mysteries: about its atmospheric dynamics and chemical composition, its surface vulcanism and its mineralogy. And Vivian sure hoped that, even in the short time that Apollo Astarte would be in the vicinity of the White Planet, they could take data that might make *some* kind of dent in those mysteries. Greg and Laura, of course, were counting on it.

And talking of Greg and Laura … She sighed. Time to go back up there and force Laura to take her scheduled break from the science console. She was sure *that* would be a joy. She'd bite that bullet first, and *then* go see Dave.

In those final hours, crew activities elevated to a white heat.

But it was a *good* heat. This was what they'd come to do. This was why they were here. Any small peeves and antagonisms were swept aside, and the eight of them operated quickly and competently like the well-oiled machine Vivian had trained them to be, on top of the months of training they'd been through before Vivian had arrived onboard.

During periapsis, the time of closest approach Venus filled the window, just as the Earth dominated the sky from low Earth orbit. But unlike the Earth, Venus was ... alien.

Completely alien. The planet was the furthest thing from being inviting. Venus looked dour, toxic, and bilious, with those high, yellow, nasty clouds that obscured the surface. Hideous. Vivian could almost smell the sulfuric acid from here.

This close, they could see the planet seethe, the clouds shifting, parting and rejoining, and the tendrils of fog reaching out from them. It was hypnotic. And from time to time they glimpsed the jagged pulses of lightning, in cloud-to-ionosphere discharges. Venus was a cauldron world.

Vivian and her crew all had clearly defined roles during the flyby. Planetary scientists Greg and Laura were on point at the Apollo Telescope Mount science console—Experiment Control Station, up in the Multiple Docking Adapter. As the Venus guru Greg would lead the activities here, with Laura providing support and backup, and at Mars the positions would be reversed. With the number of instruments they had and the range of observing modes, most of the observation sequence was preplanned, but Greg and Laura would watch the incoming data with eagle eyes, ready to tweak parameters or override the whole sequence if they glimpsed something of more compelling scientific interest.

With his solar observations on hold, Rudy was on call to take close-up photographs of any particular area the planetary scientists directed him to photograph. Otherwise, he'd help out with documenting the instrument setup, managing the logging, and backing up data where possible, plus taking pictures of the scientists themselves in action, for the historical record.

Dave Horn would be at his customary position in CM-1, watching their trajectory as they swung around Venus and preparing to make any correction burns that he deemed necessary to adjust their onward course. He'd be continuously eyeballing all the numbers, recomputing their position, course, and delta-V, and making sure nothing could go wrong. Beside him would be Marco Dardenas, to provide extra hands, eyes, ears, measurements, or programming help as needed. Over the past few months the two of them had been running this encounter in sims almost as obsessively as Rudy had been taking solar measurements, including throwing anomalies at each other and then working their way out of them. Vivian doubted very much that they'd left any stone unturned.

As the unquestioned expert on the Astarte's subsystems, Josh Rawlings would be at the main command board in the Forward Compartment, checking the stresses and strains on their weird composite vehicle as it passed by Venus. During this time he'd be in constant communications with the guys in CM-1, Vivian, and the science team, and would advise Mission Control back in Houston of their progress.

Amy Benson was taking photographs, out at the planet Venus through the picture window of Apollo Astarte as it approached and they sailed past it, and of the crew themselves. She was a competent photographer with an excellent eye, and had already come up with a steady stream of candid—and yet not embarrassing—pictures of the crew, on the voyage so far. This flyby was one for the history books, and Amy would document the history, while also being on call for any medical issue that might arise during this crucial time.

Vivian, as Commander, would be monitoring everyone's activities, coordinating as necessary, and being on hand to lead them through any emergencies that might crop up with the Venus Astarte spacecraft guidance, its onboard systems, the science acquisition, or the people doing all that work.

Which basically meant that Vivian's main job was to make that everyone else was doing their jobs and that it was all proceeding Just Fine.

Normally, having no major and specific task to perform gave Vivian the vapors. However, in this particular case, she was quite happy to make sure that the scientists were getting the data they needed, that Astarte would not spin off into some new and bizarre heliocentric orbit that would prohibit them from returning home, and to otherwise just watch and marvel. She would also snap a few photos of Amy along the way, to make sure their mission doctor was as well represented in the historical record as everyone else.

This encounter was planned and rehearsed to a T. They'd trained for months for it. Which meant that obviously something was bound to break or go seriously wrong. Right?

Except: that wasn't what happened at all.

All the observations went off as scheduled. Horn's burn induced some swearing from Greg and Laura at the vibrations it induced in the Apollo Telescope Mount, but that couldn't be helped. And Amy presumably got some great shots of them all doing their work.

They did have a few tense moments, because that was inevitable. Times when the computers rebooted for no apparent reason. Moments when the creaking and stresses and strains on Astarte caused some rapid-fire discussion of shear and moments of inertia and some anxious monitoring of gauges. And, overall, even without those small moments of crisis, their babbling on the loops for that extended eight-hour period took all of their strength. By the time they were done, Greg, Laura, and Josh were all hoarse. It was exhausting, it was tense, it was exhilarating, and by the end of it they all definitely needed showers.

But, fundamentally, it all went to plan. Which, loosely translated, meant that Venus Encounter was a magnificent success, for Vivian, Vivian's team, NASA, the United States, and humanity in general.

Plus, they had some unexpected excitement. In a good way.

It was over almost before they were ready. For Vivian, Venus went from being dead ahead to being in the rear-view mirror almost in the blink of an eye.

And now they were past Venus and it was shrinking away behind them. Vivian, exhausted and famished, had taken just a couple minutes to swing by the wardroom and rehydrate some food to shove into her mouth. Even while she was chewing, she had no idea what she was eating. She was still spellbound by the sight of Venus retreating behind them, its sides now switched from how they'd been previously: nighttime on the left of its disk, daytime on the right.

"Boss, you'll want to get up here, right away. Trust me." Greg's voice sounded tinny through the loudspeaker.

Vivian lunged for the comms panel and pushed-to-talk, tossing her tube of food back over her shoulder. "Trouble?"

"No. Something wonderful."

Well, that sure makes a change, was Vivian's first thought, and then she was off, bouncing off the sleep-area doorway and streaking up through the hatch into the forward compartment. A quick glancing shove to a thermal blanket on the inner hull in passing sent her arrowing up toward the MDA hatch with practiced ease. She adroitly dodged Rudy Frank, who was leaving the Multiple Docking Adapter in the opposite direction, to find Greg Heinz snapping photographs out of the window with a Hasselblad while Laura stabbed at switches on the science console. The main lights were out in the MDA, leaving it lit eerily by Venus-light, the glow of green and amber lights from the console, and the flare from its several screens.

"What's up?" she said.

"Look at Venus," is all Greg said.

Vivian pulled herself up beside him, taking care not to bump him and spoil his camera shots or knock away the film magazine that was floating above his head, and looked out at the White Planet.

As she'd seen from the wardroom, Venus now appeared as a waxing crescent approaching first quarter, its dark side dominating but with that bright sickle-shape of the day side still iridescent. The faint night-glow from atmospheric particles formed a light rim around the limb on the dark side. It was beautiful, just as ethereal as before. "Sure, fine. What am I supposed to be looking for?"

Laura passed her up a piece of cardboard. "Hold this up to your eyes, block out the bright part. Screen your eyes as much as you can from reflected light. Look closely at the night side of Venus."

"Okay." Vivian did so.

"It'll take a moment," Greg said. "Let your eyes adapt. But then you'll see a shape. Maybe. Tell me when you do."

Vivian blinked again. "Sort of? A square-ish patch, uh, rounded at the corners? With a part that looks brighter and extends over quite an area. Some kind of big cloud, maybe?"

"In which hemisphere?" he demanded.

"Northern, at about the sixty-degree latitude."

Greg nodded. "You got it quicker than I did. Even with your naked eye. Be proud of your vision. Now, try it with this."

He reached above himself, and Vivian realized that what she'd taken for a film magazine was really a box of filters. He let go of the camera briefly to tug out a dark red square of polymer-coated glass and hand it to her, leaving the box rotating slowly in space next to her shoulder. "Broadband infrared filter. If that doesn't work, try a lower wavelength filter, different people have different sensitivity at eight hundred nanometers—"

"Holy crap," she said. The shapes she was looking at on the darker side of Venus had jumped into sharp relief, and now she could see … "*Structure*? What the hell is *that*?"

Was she dreaming? No clouds she'd seen on the screen in the infrared or ultraviolet were that clearcut. Not with the immense, turbulent and shearing winds of Venus's atmosphere. "*Do not* tell me that I'm seeing the surface of Venus right now."

"Guess what?" Greg said, still clicking pictures. "You nailed it in one. Surface of Venus."

"It can't be."

Laura giggled, her face almost ecstatic, but her words were clear and precise, still scientific. "You're seeing thermal emission. The surface temperature on Venus is about eight-sixty-seven Fahrenheit, day or night, because its atmosphere is so thick. Meaning that even on the nightside the surface of Venus is so hot it glows faintly in the very-near infrared. It's at the edge of what the human eye can see, which is why that filter helps by taking out the shorter wavelengths. The lighter areas you're seeing are hotter, the dark areas cooler."

Greg interrupted. "You're looking at Ishtar Terra, the big highland region in the northern Venusian hemisphere. Specifically the Lakshmi Planum."

"Five kilometers higher than the lowland regions that surround it."

"And therefore cooler, which is why it looks darker to you."

"Look at the radar image of the same area," Laura said. "No, down here. Compare and contrast. Ishtar Terra has mountain ranges and deep rift valleys, and you can even see hints of those with the naked eye. They come out clearer on this other screen here, where I can adjust the contrast. Which reminds me: switch."

Laura reached out to reset an event timer clock and shoved herself up from the seat. Greg left the camera floating in the air and switched places with her to sit at the console. He looked quickly across the boards and reached out to adjust a vernier by a few percent. Vivian glanced down to see the clock counting backwards. Her mission specialists were trading position every five minutes, so they'd get equal time viewing Venus with their own eyes, while still maintaining efficient control over the rest of the observations. All their previous snipping and combativeness had fallen away in the heat of the moment, and they were working together as a smooth team.

Vivian looked again at the radar map, and then at the other screens that Greg was now indicating. "Sure enough," she said. "Wow. Holy cow."

"Volcano," Greg said suddenly. "There. That bright white dot northeast of center. Holy crap, that must be a volcanic eruption. Laura, you see it?"

"Hang on." Laura released the Hasselblad, grabbed the monocular, and cautiously focused it on the planet through the window. "Yes, I think so." She traded it back for the camera and took three fast pictures. "Happening right in front of us, in real time." It sounded like Laura was having trouble breathing.

"Really?" Vivian pulled herself up beside Laura, blinked a couple times to rid herself of the afterimages from the console, and within a few seconds she could see it too. A mere white fleck in the grey-bright region, but now it was visibly swelling to become a dot, and then a smear. A giant eruption, growing and swelling, and *fast*? A big lava flow, maybe, several hundred degrees hotter than the surface around it? "Good *grief*. How the hell big is that?"

Neither of them answered her. At the science station, Greg's hands were dancing across the boards, adjusting switches and checking monitors and sensor gauges, before peering back up through the window. Meanwhile, Laura was busy with the camera.

Which left Vivian free to stare at the surface of Venus, in silence. At *the surface of frigging Venus*, changing right in front of her eyes as a volcano resurfaced what had to be a non-trivial area of Ishtar Terra.

Wow, what a trip. What a trip.

"This is bonkers," she said.

Laura bumped shoulders with her companionably. "Amen."

Vivian had never expected to see the surface of Venus with her naked eye, however faintly. None of them had. She took the filter away, and her makeshift cardboard light-screen, and looked at the whole of Venus again, that bright jewel. The globe of the White Planet was already perceptibly smaller than when she'd come up here to the science station.

She put the cardboard and filter up again and blinked away the afterimage of that bright crescent and then stared down through the atmosphere of Venus once more. The surface of Venus, seen through a glass darkly. After another couple of minutes, she dropped the filter to gaze upon it again with her naked eye. Just astonishing.

"Switch."

Her mission specialists traded places again, babbling at each other in acronyms, wavelengths, and exposure times. Greg had to swerve around Vivian to grab the Hasselblad, and spun himself laterally so that they could share the small window more readily.

Vivian ought to go down to the big picture window on the fore-deck and leave the science station to the scientists. Space up here was at a premium, and her planetary scientists took priority. "I'll get out of your hair. Okay if I take the filter with me? I can bring it back soon."

"Sure. No worries. We have a dozen of them."

Which meant, Vivian realized, that Greg had suspected all along—or just hoped—that they might get a visual glimpse of the surface of Venus on the night side. He'd kept it to himself all this time, in case he was wrong. Fair enough. It would have been a particularly rough anticlimax if they'd all been waiting for it, and it hadn't been possible.

"Thanks," she said. "And thanks for being awesome and giving us even more Venus than we expected. Oh. We should tell the others, damn it. I should have thought of that sooner …"

"Rudy's already on it," Greg said. "He was going to look in on Dave Horn as well, just in case the dude has any brain cells to spare from staring at his guidance computer."

"Good," Vivian said. She didn't want to lose any time she could be spending just staring at Venus …

Two hours later, the weary crew was debriefing on the foredeck.

"That was fricking awesome."

High fives sent them flying away from each other.

"Hugs?" Amy asked. "Doctor-approved."

They all took turns impetuously hugging one another.

Laura cried, unashamedly, as Venus grew smaller behind them. No one thought any the worse of her for it. Some of the men may have discreetly wiped away a tear or two as well. Or maybe it was just all the dust suspended in Astarte's atmosphere? Yes, that must have been it.

Dave Horn emerged from the fore hatch and drifted slowly down toward them, his weariness evident, but a small grin of satisfaction on his face.

Rawlings eyed him. "So, no big deal, but how's our course?"

"Ma wee burn went fine," said Horn, in an unexpected and not very convincing Scottish accent.

Vivian blinked. Such was her confidence level, it hadn't even occurred to her to check in with her pilot. "So everything was nominal?"

"Smooth as a whistle. Residuals on the delta-V from the assist are smaller in X and Y than I expected, to be honest. Z-axis, we're heading very slightly up out of the plane, but we'll maybe pull that back with a tiny nudge-burn in forty-eight hours or seventy-two, however long it takes FIDO to crunch the numbers." The Flight Dynamics Officer and his team, way back at Mission Control.

"So, we're all set for Mars?" Laura prompted him.

"All set. And honestly Marco and I could take the next two months off and we'd still be just fine."

Vivian grinned. "Take a few hours, at least. And then I'm sure there's some greasy surface that needs disinfecting, or some mold growing somewhere we don't need it."

"Wow, Viv. Way to crush the mood."

"Just keeping it real." She paused. "Thanks, Dave. You're really rocking this."

"Thanks," was all he said, but she could hear his pleased satisfaction.

She turned to the scientists next. "And, aside from that parting surprise … the rest of the data is good?"

"Yes, oh yes." Greg's eyes were shining. "From the reflected light, the ordinary white light, we can see what's going on in the cloud tops, at the seventy-kilometer altitudes. In the near-infrared we can see features from lower cloud levels, like fifty to sixty kilometers. The features on the day side are similar to what we saw with Mariner 10. But on the night side, further into the infrared, we're seeing narrow ribbon-like clouds, dark streaks and some curved features, probably connected with mesoscale vortices—relatively small, less than a thousand kilometers across. We don't see those on the day side."

"Less than a thousand klicks is small?" Vivian asked.

"When you're talking Venus? Yes."

Rawlings stirred. "And all that means what, exactly? In layman's terms?"

"Differences in cloud properties. We also see evidence for standing gravity waves in the UV on the day side, but not the night side."

Laura sighed. "But, since we weren't observing for very long, who knows what that really means. People will be digging into all these data for years. All we can say with confidence right now is that the vertical structure of the Venusian clouds is very complicated, and the day and night hemispheres are *very* different. There's a lot of complex chemistry in there."

"Sounds like we can also say with confidence that this mission is already a huge success." Vivian said.

"We sure can." Laura glanced sideways, over at Greg. "Even before we get to Mars, and make it even *more* of a success."

Ah, the needling has begun again, Vivian thought. *It was nice while it lasted. While we were all one big Venus Encounter family.*

Greg nodded, unfazed. "Given that we're a flyby mission and not an orbiter, our science haul has been damned impressive. Anyone who had doubts about what this mission could achieve can just shut the hell up now."

"Okay," Vivian said, amused now. "Good to know."

"So, straight talk. Did you know beforehand we had a chance of seeing right though, down to the surface, with our own eyes?"

Three hours later, the disk of Venus had dwindled to a mere tenth of a degree across. The crew of Astarte were still all awake, all watching as the white-and-black pearl shrank back into the dark, but by now they were all beginning to calm down. Rudy was shouldering the data-taking duties at the science station, but the other seven crew members were assembled in front of the big window on the fore deck, some of them eating. No one was supposed to consume food outside the wardroom, but today of all days neither Vivian nor Josh seemed inclined to enforce the rule.

"I'd hoped," Greg confessed. "But I didn't want to mention it and get everyone's hopes up. I thought I saw glimmers of structure while we were still inbound, but I wasn't sure and didn't have time to do any computer cleanup processing. We can do a deep dive into the data later, now we know what we're looking for. On the way out, though, it just jumped out at me."

"With hindsight ... luckily for us, the atmospheric opacity is at a minimum at the short-wavelength end of the near infrared." Suddenly, Laura yawned. "Jesus, what time is it?"

"Look between one point five and two point five microns, and all you'll see is the cloud patterns," Greg added. "We know that from observations with large telescopes on Earth. That's further into the IR than humans can see, though."

"So there's this one little window in the wavelength range, just where we needed it." Laura blinked at the real window in front of her, then looked across at Greg. "I'm beat. Are we good for now?"

"Before you go, there's more good news," Dardenas said. "We heard back from Houston just before this confab. All three probes made it down to the surface. The one on the southern Brightside lasted seventeen minutes, the others fried sooner, but all the instruments worked just fine. So we have good *in situ* data from three separate areas of the Venusian atmosphere and surface."

"And simultaneous with our own observations," Laura said, grinning at Greg. "Triple threat!"

Greg smiled back at her. "Neat. Can't wait to see the data."

Rawlings looked from one to the other. "Y'all going to be busy little bees, aren't you?"

"We sure are," Greg said. "For the next decade or so."

Laura prodded him. "So, about sleep?"

"We're good to go. Now I've grabbed a bite I'll go up and spell Rudy for a while in ..." He yawned himself. "About twenty minutes, and after that ... uh. Boss, what then?"

Rawlings was nearest to the master clipboard, so Vivian let him answer. "You and Amy are due to ride herd on the science station for the next three hours. And I'm on the darned exercise bike and resistance bands for the next two hours. Lord, have mercy." He turned the page. "Marco and Vivian are on downtime now and then hit the sack. Lucky stiffs. Hey, Viv, want to trade?"

Vivian grinned. "No, I absolutely do not." She'd been up for nearly twenty-four hours. Longer than Laura, as it happened, but Laura and Greg had been busier than her and done great work today, and she was happy to cut them any slack they seemed to need. Speaking of which: "Laura, you heard him. Just go to bed."

"Oh, and surprise, surprise." Now, Josh was checking the teleprinter. "In the not-so-good column: Houston wants a complete briefing. NASA PR needs to start up the press machine and get some releases out about all this, pronto."

"Huh," Vivian said. "Earth still exists, doesn't it?"

"Apparently."

"Oh, crap," Laura said.

"Jesus, woman, just go," Amy said. "Listen to your body."

"Except?" Laura gestured at Josh.

Greg raised his hand. "Suggestion? I spend ten minutes summarizing for Houston so that their press gurus and science writers and all know what to prepare for. Then we ask for twelve or fifteen hours to put together the best visuals we can from the data we have up here. This is big, so we should take whatever time we need to get it right. Same with the words. And it's only fair to include Laura in all that. In eight hours, once she's rested."

"Sounds good." More than good, since Venus was nominally Greg's baby and he could technically have pulled rank and done it alone. Vivian looked up at Josh. "Can do?"

"Sure. Whatever works." Josh started typing.

"Which means, Greg, you should sack out soon as well. Maybe Rudy can pull a couple extra hours to cover, he's only been up fifteen hours. I'll come up with you and talk to him about it."

"No, I've got it," Amy said. "I'm going that way anyway. And, not to nag, but it's my job: it's not just Josh who's getting on that exercise bike Real Soon Now."

"Fine." Vivian took another long gaze at Venus out of the window. It had shrunk by another twenty percent since this conversation had begun. "I'll do a mini-workout right here with resistance bands, work out some aches and soreness, and then crash. We'll caucus next shift, me and Marco on the encounter, burn, and spacecraft systems, and Greg and Laura on Venus observations, and put together a full report package for the folks back home. And after that we'll all catch up on our proper exercise."

"Okay, then." Amy pushed off toward the MDA, and Laura drifted in the opposite direction, through to the sleep quarters.

Vivian looked around at the rest. A lot of tired faces looked back at her. But everyone was happy, or at least quietly content, and they were all on the same page. A red-letter day.

All Vivian could find to say was, "Great job, everybody."

They all split, in different directions.

Over an unusual group breakfast the following morning, the crew belatedly got to see the footage taken by the Venus probes during their long descents toward the surface. Fluffy yellow clouds below, featureless cloudbank above.

Below about twenty-five miles the parachutes became pointless; the atmosphere of Venus was so dense that the probe would sink slowly from here to the planet's surface, more like sliding down through water than plummeting through air. The color of the light was changing steadily, into a deeper and more sickly orange, and now they could see a rough rocky plain coming into view beneath the probe. A reddish-brown surface, cracked and fractured. As they watched in silence, Vivian saw an impact crater here, a smaller one over there, not a patch on the Moon's cratering, but still recognizable. She saw scouring that must have been formed by wind action, and boulders, lots of rocks. The visibility was maybe a quarter-mile, if she could even trust her sense of perspective on such an alien landscape.

Greg cleared his throat. "Data from the probes indicated that between about ten and fifty kilometers there's almost no convection in the atmosphere of Venus. Below a haze layer at about thirty kilometers, the atmosphere is relatively clear.

"In addition, below an altitude of fifty kilometers the temperatures reported from the probes indicated very few differences even though their entry sites were separated by thousands of kilometers."

"That's all good?" Vivian hazarded.

"It's all good science."

"Not a great place to raise your kids," said Amy Benson, still looking at the surface of Venus on the monitor.

"I'm thinking not," Rudy said.

"That's Mars," said Greg. "Elton John's 'Rocket Man' ..."

"Yeah, yeah," Amy said patiently. "We know."

Vivian turned to stare back at the real disk of Venus. She could always watch the Probe footage on reruns, but Venus itself would be dwindling away to nothing before they were ready. It had all happened so fast. "Shame no one is ever going to colonize that place."

"Well, actually, we could," said Greg. "As it turns out, Venus is a perfect place for balloons. If you float a superpressure balloon at an altitude of somewhere between fifty to seventy-five kilometers, just above the cloud layer, the pressure would be about one bar, same as on Earth, and the temperature would be somewhere similar to Earth's as well. Say sixty-five kilometers, so you're in the clear. Hang a gondola off that, and you'd have a perfect sightseeing platform. Just a bit of that upper-atmosphere haze."

Rudy gazed back at Venus. "Sightseeing."

"And round and round the planet you'd go. Probably doing a great radar survey of the surface and doing all kinds of other cool atmospheric science. Dropping a probe down through the atmosphere every now and then. It would be terrific."

"Nothing to breathe, though."

"Fierce winds, sure. Corrosive atmosphere, also for sure. But it would be *very* cool."

"Until the sulfuric acid corroded your balloon and gondola to hell."

Heinz shook his head. "Tungsten is inert to sulfuric acid, so that's what you make the outer shell of the gondola from. Insulate the important electronics with aerogels or seal them in ceramics. And a balloon of bilaminated Mylar with a Teflon sheath would be pretty resistant to the sulfuric acid."

" 'Pretty resistant'," Laura said. "That's comforting. But if your balloon pops, then down you go. Scarily slowly, because the atmosphere is so dense it would be more like sinking down into the sea than falling. Plenty of time to enjoy boiling to death on the way down."

Vivian looked at the clock and clapped her hands. "Okay, guys. This is all very fun and educational and all, and I'm sorry to always be the bad guy, but ... it's time to spruce up and put on a show. Or a dozen shows."

She was met with a good-natured chorus of groans, but some grins as well.

In the forty-eight hours that followed, they did a succession of TV broadcasts summarizing what they'd seen.

They talked to President Reagan. They talked to queens, kings, other presidents, and prime ministers of other nations, and addressed massed gatherings of employees at various NASA centers, plus Boeing, Rockwell, Grumman, McDonnell Douglas, IBM, Honeywell, and more other organizations than they could count, and actually enjoyed it. Most of it, anyway.

The time gap helped, of course. It was basically their show, and no one could interrupt them.

After all the long-distance glad-handing and dog and pony shows were finally over, Vivian overrode Houston and called an eighteen-hour hiatus of all activities other than eating, sleeping, celebrating, and relaxing. Her crew had definitely deserved it.

"And exercising, of course. Sorry, guys; got to keep those bones and muscles healthy. But after that eighteen hours is up, we'll go to a low-impact schedule across the board for the following week, and then, on …" Vivian realized she'd lost track of the calendar again. "And then on the seventh day we'll start picking up the pieces and put a proper schedule together for the eighth. Sound okay?"

No one cheered, and in fact no one reacted at all for a couple of seconds. It took Vivian herself a moment to realize that her crew were in shock at their unexpected liberty.

"That sounds great," said Amy at last. "We could all do with some R&R and everyone definitely needs sleep. And I'm available as usual, for anything you might need."

"Thanks, Amy."

"I might just spend a bit of time at the science station," Rudy said. "No pressure on anyone else, though."

"Me too," Greg said. "In a calm, relaxed sort of way."

"Sure." Vivian grinned. "Whatever floats your boat."

"Good job, everyone," said Rawlings. "We did NASA proud."

"Yep." Greg Heinz, of all people, started clapping. "Round of applause for everyone. That was unforgettable, and we came through, as a team. And especially for Vivian, for bringing us through it all."

That was a bit uncomfortable, but of course everyone else then had to start clapping too.

"Okay, okay," Vivian said. "Thanks, all. Class dismissed." And, with some determination, she headed toward her sleep quarters, just to close her eyes for a moment before she changed and tidied herself up a bit, and went onto the night shift, to watch over Apollo Venus Astarte while those on her crew who'd been doing the *real* work got some well-deserved shut-eye.

Just to be in a space, however small, where there were no other people.

They'd been a great team. Absolutely outstanding. Venus flyby had been an absolute and total success. But, Gods, she was tired. And she could feel it already building behind her eyes: the crashing feeling of ... not anticlimax, exactly, but sadness that their long-awaited encounter was over so soon.

Such an astonishing experience, and it had literally flown by. And such a mix of conflicting emotions: the objective knowledge that by any sane measure Venus was a hell-world, daunting, toxic, and inimical to life ... and yet, it had its undeniable majesty and beauty.

The wonder of being up-close and personal to a whole new world ... coupled with the knowledge of how long they would have to wait for the next mission high, and her clear-eyed understanding of just how fleeting that high would be.

Ah, well. Time to take the notch on her belt, and start preparing for the next phase. A change was as good as a rest, right?

She started a request up through channels, to talk to Peter Sandoval. Only to find out that he'd been attempting to contact her for the past three days, blocked by NASA at the highest levels.

Wow.

Peter Sandoval, blocked? That ... surely wasn't good.

She got Ellis on the case, set the wheels in motion, and managed to set up a call.

CHAPTER 11

Interplanetary Space: Vivian Carter
November 15, 1983
Mission Elapsed Time: 134 days

"CONGRATULATIONS," said Colonel Peter Sandoval on her TV screen, then peered into his camera and hesitated. Vivian was only now hearing words that he'd spoken nine minutes ago and a hundred million miles away, and Peter looked self-conscious and uncomfortable with the delay. For Vivian, it had become natural weeks ago to be speaking her own original words *now* while also responding to comments from Mission Control and others from several minutes back *then*, knowing she would wait an equivalent amount of time to hear Ellis's responses. It was a little schizophrenic, and sometimes confusing, especially when they were juggling a list of topics, but managing it had become second nature to her.

She gave a big grin. "Hi, Peter, great to see you," she said, hoping to put him at ease as soon as possible. Even though she was allegedly on break, she couldn't spend forever on this conversation; she had reports to write up and logs to update, before grabbing a snack and recording a news segment for CBS, taking a science shift in the MDA, and finally exposing her arm and leg muscles to some serious exertion. Even Vivian had skimped on some of her exercise sessions during the hectic aftermath of Venus flyby. She'd need to do extra today to get back in Amy's good graces.

"It'll be great to see your face in a few moments," he said, obviously unaware that he was repeating what she had just said. "From what I'm hearing, your Venus encounter was a great success. I saw some of the photos and they looked, well, weird but spellbinding. It's a very different planet, and you're *there*. I can look up into the sky and see it like a little point, and for you it's a real place you've just been."

"Weird but spellbinding," she said. "That's about right. I don't know whether it comes across in the photos, but Venus looks really … sinister. Unfriendly, inhospitable. I don't think any of us were ready for it to look quite that hostile. But, yes, it was pretty wild, and we got great data."

Peter had started speaking again while she was still talking. She was following along with what he was saying while completing her own sentences on automatic pilot. "Listen, I'm going to just sit and wait till I get confirmation that we've established contact. No point in me just talking into the abyss, if the abyss isn't talking back. If you see what I mean."

Sandoval was frowning a little, distracted, ill at ease. *Sure, I'm the one isolated in deep space and I have to comfort him?* "Now I'm the abyss? So flattering." She grinned again to remove any sting. "But, I get it. Sure. Of course, by the time you hear this, you'll know the abyss is talking back."

She paused. What did she really want to get across to him? Since he wasn't used to this, she didn't want to overload him with things to respond to.

Plus, *he'd* called *her*. His office had set up the call with her through Mission Control, and insisted on secure radio and isolation, so Vivian was taking this call from CM-1. She looked out of its windows at the eternal backdrop of the looming Multiple Docking Adapter, with a border of stars around the outside. Peter obviously had something to tell her, and she hoped it wasn't anything bad.

Nine minutes would be a long time to wait to find out.

"Okay, so in a minute I'm just going to shut up too, till I hear what's up, but I'll just say that I'm fine and healthy, and so is everyone else in the crew. Venus Encounter was successful but also predictably rough. We got a lot done in a small space of time. Everything we really needed to. Did it go perfectly? Not really. But well enough." She grinned again. Best not get into the details. He likely wouldn't care anyway.

"We're all taking it easy this week, resting up and trying to get our strength back for the next part of this long haul." She paused, realizing this next truth. "And I'd love it if you and I could talk more often. I'm told it's a long way to Mars from here."

Maybe he's calling to break up with me, she thought suddenly. To tell me he's found someone new. Which would be entirely Peter's right, and she clearly couldn't blame him if he did. Would he want her to know as soon as possible? Yes. He was just exactly that type of boy scout. Would he do it on secure radio? Yes, again, because he wouldn't want the paparazzi getting hold of it, splashing it across the newspapers. *Venus Astronaut Jilted.* The papers would have a field day, especially coming right after the Encounter.

So maybe I'll hold off on the lovey-dovey stuff for a bit, she thought.

She glanced at the clock. "Man, this time lag sucks out loud, am I right? I'm just going to scribble some things down while I wait." She bent her head and started typing industriously into her log file.

Eventually, Sandoval visibly reacted and said: "Hey, there you are. Good to see you." He paused, blinking. "Inhospitable. Yeah. I guess it must be. Looking forward to the high-rez pictures." He straightened. "Listen, Vivian, there's been a lot happening over the last couple weeks back here on Earth. Matters of natural security. I've been directed to give you a full …" He reacted again to her delayed words—grinned. "No, you're not exactly an abyss. Far from it. Nope. You're just *in* one. Uh, so: I'm directed to give you a full briefing. This will include classified information, above top secret, highest-level stuff, so you'll have to treat that appropriately. But the folks here consider it important for you to know, for reasons that will become apparent. Okay?"

Well, none of that sounded promising, but at least Vivian hadn't been jilted yet. "Okay. Awaiting the briefing."

"I'll assume you just said yes, and proceed," he said.

"Now you're getting the hang of this," she said.

Sandoval was already off and running. "The incidents I'm about to brief you on have been happening over the last couple weeks, but the decision was made here to keep them from you and your crew, so that you wouldn't get distracted during your all-important Venus flyby. And it's a lot, so hang onto your hat."

This was sounding worse and worse. Colonel Peter Sandoval was in full clipped, official, just-the-facts-Ma'am mode.

Vivian picked up a pencil and got ready to take notes.

"I'm going to give you all the information in time-order, so's you can keep it all straight, okay?" He paused. "Just to reassure you, here's the bottom line: the world is not at war. No ICBMs are flying. But superpower tensions are kind of maxed out and, quite honestly, anything could happen. It's anyone's guess how all this will develop later today, tomorrow, next month, next year. Things are getting really dicey here."

"Really dicey?" she said. "Got it. If you see me looking down some more, it's because I'm taking notes. Notes I'll keep private."

"Okay, so today is November 15th, 1983." He grinned briefly. "Tuesday. The first event in the sequence happened a while ago and was publicly known, and that was the shooting down of KAL 007 …"

"The Korean airliner, roger," she said, largely so that Peter would be able to keep track of where she was in the briefing and put any of her subsequent comments in context.

"… the Korean Air Lines commercial flight that was shot down by the Soviets on September 1st, en route to Seoul. The Soviets claim the jet had infringed their airspace, but how they could treat a loaded 747 like a spy plane beats me. Anyway, they shot it down into the sea to the west of Sakhalin Island, and 269 people died. That caused a major international incident, obviously. It didn't help that the Soviets denied shooting the plane down for almost a week, never apologized, and blamed the CIA for the whole thing.

"Okay, that was bad, but it was just the beginning."

"KAL 007 is just the beginning, affirmative," Vivian said.

"We're not supposed to know the next one ever happened. But the US has a couple of moles deep inside the Kremlin and in the Soviet Army, so here's what we know: an all-out nuclear war nearly started on September 26th. By accident. No kidding."

"Whoa," said Vivian. What had she and her crew been doing on the twenty-sixth of September? Six weeks before Venus closest approach? They'd been working their tails off, as usual. Well, if their entire planet had been destroyed it would certainly have cast those weeks into a different perspective.

"It appears that the Soviet Early Warning System satellites erroneously reported that the US had launched five ICBMs, and that they were headed toward the Soviet Union. Such a detection was supposed to initiate an automatic retaliatory nuclear strike against the US and

NATO allies. And the only reason that didn't happen is because one of the engineers—one single low-level guy on duty at the command center, by the name of Stanislav Petrov—suspected it was a false alarm and held off on sending the information up the chain of command. If that one single member of the Soviet Air Defense Forces had acted differently, we could well have experienced a full-scale nuclear conflict in the hours that followed. The Reds would have launched, and we'd have launched, and …" He just shook his head.

"Full-scale nuclear conflict," Vivian repeated. "One man prevented Armageddon?" *What a crazy system*, she thought, *where that could happen.*

"It's actually amazing that a level head prevailed," Sandoval continued. "The backstory is that Yuri Andropov and his Minister of Defense, Dmitry Ustinov, have been concerned for some time that Reagan will launch a preemptive nuclear strike on the Soviet Union. They're clearly for real about this, not kidding at all. To them, this looks feasible and logical."

"Great. Thanks, Ronnie."

" … After all, we're going ahead with the Strategic Defense Initiative, plus Reagan is about to put a hundred-plus Pershing II medium range nuclear missiles into Western Europe, capable of hitting targets in the USSR within ten minutes … and *then* when you toss in the unusually big naval exercise the US did this spring near the Soviet Aleutian Islands, you can kind of see why. They're on a hair trigger, and it was a miracle that this false detection didn't just start the whole apocalypse rolling.

"Okay, so that was incident number two. Onto number three."

Vivian paused from scribbling notes, shook her head, stretched her hand. "Jeez. Number three coming up, copy that. I hope it involves puppies and flowers."

Sandoval paused, took a drink of water, looked at his notes again. "Fast forward to October 23rd, when the US Marine barracks in Beirut, Lebanon was attacked by two truck bombs. Suicide bombers. Three hundred and seven members of the military peacekeeping force were killed, about two hundred and forty of them American, and with another hundred and twenty-eight US injured. The Islamic Jihad claimed responsibility, blaming the attack on US and French support for Iraq."

"Man, we have lots of friends around the world." Vivian's wise-cracks were almost automatic, her way of covering up her mounting dread at these successive waves of awful news.

"Incident number four coming up. Two days later, and unconnected to anything else: the US and its allies invaded Grenada, toppling the Grenadian People's Revolutionary Government there. Reagan claims he did it in part to protect six hundred US medical students who were there, but it seems self-evident that overturning a Soviet-supported regime was his main objective." He took another drink of water. "Okay, so that's already a lot, right?"

"Holy shit," Vivian said. "There's *more?*"

"So by this point, tensions between the superpowers had ramped up really high. But the worst is yet to come. Two more incidents, and then I'll get into analysis."

Holy moly. But Vivian resisted the urge to interject any more cracks or comments out loud. This was all grim stuff, and she didn't want to derail Peter nine minutes from now with her succession of smart-assed comments.

Sandoval's face went wry. "I was thinking of starting this briefing by saying: 'So, funny story: the world nearly went nuclear six weeks ago, and then again last week.' I decided that wasn't a great way to start. But, hey, your sense of humor has always been dark. Would have at least gotten your attention, right?"

"There's dark and *dark*, man," she said. "Seriously."

"So now we come to the biggie: Able Archer 83 is a full-up US military exercise which is actually part of Autumn Forge 1983, yet another major months-long series of NATO maneuvers and wargames. We do one of these exercises every year, but this year's was a beast; the US and allies airlifted something like nineteen thousand troops and over a thousand tons of materiel, simulating a conventional war, and the Able Archer part then simulated and exercised the transition from conventional to nuclear war.

"I don't know how much you know about these exercises, but they aren't restricted to neutral turf. We had US Navy aircraft probing twenty miles inside Soviet airspace … wait, you were a naval aviator, so you may know that already. But Able Archer 1983 had a whole bunch of new stuff: radio-silent air lifts, shifts of the command structure from 'permanent' to 'alternate' war headquarters, new nuclear release procedures, the works. And this year, for extra kicks, they involved high-level officials all the way up to the Secretary of Defense and the Chairman of the Joint Chiefs of Staff. They even had cameos by Reagan and Vice President Bush to make it look even more realistic and high-profile. Able Archer exercised a conflict escalation going all the way up to a simulated DEFCON 1 nuclear attack. With all that going on, if you were the Soviet Union, you might sit up and pay attention, right?"

"Damn. That's … somewhere between hardcore and completely ridiculous."

Sandoval answered his own question, his face grim. "Right. The Soviet Politburo became convinced that this was a major buildup under the flimsy pretext of an exercise. They concluded that the US and its allies were genuinely gearing up to launch a nuclear first strike, followed by an invasion by NATO ground forces. And so, guess what? The Soviets started readying their own nuclear arsenal, and the Warsaw Pact countries started mobilizing in response. Soviet fighters were put on alert in East Germany and Poland, loaded with nukes. The entire Soviet Bloc got ready to let fly with everything they had, at short notice. Are we having fun yet?"

Vivian refrained from comment.

Sandoval took a breath. "Another relevant fact about the timing of all this: the Able Archer exercise just happens to line up with October Revolution Day, which is a national holiday in the USSR. The Reds go on drinking binges, and as we all know, a lot of their major politicians poison themselves regularly with vodka at the best of times. So, you might naively think this is not a swell date to be poking the Soviet bear, and you'd be right.

"Anyway. This time, the cooler heads that prevailed were on our side. The Chiefs of Staff of the US Air Forces in Europe decided all this was getting a bit too on the nose. They terminated Able Archer and started pulling everyone back on November 11th.

"To repeat, all of this is classified. Hush-hush, Top Secret. You won't be hearing it in your regular news bulletins. But you need to know, to provide context for anything that might happen around these parts on short notice. I'll pause now to let you process that." Sandoval sat back for a moment, took a big chug of his water, and scanned through his notes.

Context for anything that might happen ... meaning the US and USSR might still collapse into a nuclear war any time now? That Earth might just go dark and stop communicating with them? After all, they'd dodged nuclear Armageddon twice, maybe the third time would be the charm.

But we don't think like that.

"Probably a good thing," Vivian said. "For me to be briefed on it all, for context. And thanks for pushing for that. Not sure I'll be sleeping any easier for knowing it all, but it's the right thing to do."

Sandoval nodded, almost as if he'd heard her. "Okay, last item. If all that superpower nuclear brinksmanship wasn't enough for you, there's a more local postscript. We've had a homegrown terrorism incident. The *very same day* as the Able Archer alert was at its maximum intensity, which was November 7th, the U.S. Congress ... got bombed."

"*What?*" Vivian said out loud. The world was going to hell when this was only the *sixth* most important piece of news Peter Sandoval had to tell her. "Jesus Christ, that's a goddamn *local postscript*? What the hell was the body count there?"

Sandoval was still talking, reading from his notes, and just by chance, answered her right away. "Nobody was killed, mercifully. The Senate was supposed to be working late into the night, but they'd somehow managed to wrap up early."

"Somehow," Vivian said. She couldn't just shut up and listen anymore, in the face of this deluge of awful news. She had to speak up or explode herself. All this was just *insane.*

"The politicos were all gone by mid-evening. The bomb went off just before eleven p.m., causing a huge explosion in the Capitol's north wing. Doors got blown off, and lots of windows blown out. Lots of damage to furniture and such. The building structure still seems sound, though."

"Oh my God. Even so ..."

"Turns out they'd hidden the bomb under a bench just outside the Senate chamber, so it did substantial damage to the various nearby public areas. If that chamber had been full of senators and aides and whoever, like it often is at that time of night, the death toll might have been horrendous."

"So, who the hell did *that?*" Vivian said. "Sorry, I know I'm talking to the future, but I can't help it. Peter, this is awful."

175

Sandoval, of course, was already answering this. "A few minutes before the bomb detonated, the Capitol switchboard got a call from the, uh, 'Armed Resistance Unit.' He put his notes down and looked into the camera. "And the CIA knows exactly who that is. It's an ultra-left-wing group, Marxist-Leninist. They also go by two other names: Resistance Conspiracy, and the May 19th Communist Organization, or M19CO, but it's all the same people. Apparently right now they're pissed off about our peacekeepers in Lebanon, and our recent military actions in Grenada, so taking their own little military action against us.

"The same bunch bombed Fort McNair back in April, maybe as a trial run. Kind of a warm-up act. They're apparently, and I quote, aiming their attacks against 'the institutions of imperialist rule rather than at individual members of the ruling class and government.' We believe a lot of their leaders used to be members of the Weather Underground. Remember them? The Weathermen? Far-left Marxist group from the mid-seventies. Days of Rage? Opposing the Vietnam War? They bombed the Capitol, the Pentagon, Department of State. I was away fighting for my country, and they were making pipe bombs and fighting *against* my country." Sandoval shook his head, disgusted. "Bastards, all of them. And, perhaps of interest, many of their current leaders just happen to be women."

"Yeah," Vivian said. "Newsflash, women can be assholes too."

"And in case you're wondering why I'm telling you so much about this, guess what: it's because this latest bunch, the so-called Armed Resistance Unit, have also put calls into NPR and the Washington Post ranting about 'imperialism in space', and Star Wars, and their opposition to the—and I'm quoting again—'militarization of the sky.' By which they mean space, clearly. They mean *us*. So NASA and the Air Force are keeping an eye on that. Though, I'd kind of like to see them try anything against the Air Force or Night Corps. We'd squish them like bugs."

Peter checked his watch. "Okay, that was a lot. I'm going to take a break from talking at you now, and wait for any questions you may have, and answer them as best I can.

"But here's the bottom line, Viv. Sad to say, the world could go to war at any time. There's no way to really prepare for it, too many variables in play. But," he grinned, almost painfully, "it was decided that you needed to know. Just you, though. Not the rest of your crew unless it's absolutely necessary."

Vivian could decipher that easily enough. If a major nuclear conflict did break out, or even if there was a smaller but still catastrophic terrorist attack on NASA, Vivian would need to know why communications with Earth had been cut off. And it was only under those circumstances that she was cleared to share the information with her crew.

What a terrible day *that* would be.

"Okay," she said. "Collecting my questions now."

After the conversation, Vivian stared out into space for a while, trying to get all her thoughts under control. And then she called in her chief pilot.

The hell with *just you*: Vivian had requested permission to brief Dave Horn on all the news from Earth. Begged, really: Vivian needed someone to talk all this over with in real time, without gaping conversational holes. And if Apollo Astarte did get cut off from Earth, she'd be relying heavily on Dave to help the mission overcome it and keep Astarte on course back to Earth without Houston's assistance. Best to forewarn him so they could come up with some kind of contingency plan.

Sandoval had grudgingly agreed, but insisted that it stopped there: Dave Horn and no one else, unless the worst happened and Astarte lost contact with Earth. "In which case, use your discretion. But maybe even then, give as few details as possible, and especially about the Stanislav Petrov incident, that second one on my list about the false alarm that could have annihilated the planet. If word gets back to the Soviets that we know about that, especially the guy's name, it'll give them valuable clues as to who our assets are in their organization. We don't want to put those assets lives at risk *or* lose the valuable intelligence they might be able to give us in the future."

"Fair enough, on keeping the Petrov details off the table," she'd said. Vivian hardly needed any more blood on her hands.

So, she spent the next fifteen minutes bringing Dave up to speed. He took the news in stride with a surprising lack of emotion, a steely-eyed missile man through and through.

"It turns out May 19th is significant to this Armed Resistance Unit because it's the birthday of both Malcolm X and Ho Che Minh. Nice heroes to commemorate, right?"

Horn just nodded as if that had been obvious. "And they're sure these jerks aren't being bankrolled by the USSR? Because that would seem like the obvious conclusion. Encouraging homegrown sedition is right up there, front and center in the Communist playbook."

"I asked the same thing. Yeah, they're communists, or are mouthing off like they are, but the FBI or CIA or NSA or whoever haven't established any direct link to the Kremlin. Turns out that students with nothing better to do are quite capable of self-delusion without being pushed into it. But either way, Andropov and his KGB buddies must be watching this closely. Even if they're not directly inciting Americans to make war on their own Government—and NASA—it might be in their interests to, you know, help out later wherever they can. With money, or materials, or whatever."

Horn looked sour. "We found out during 'Nam that some of our own kids were our worst enemies. I'd guess that at least a few of them have links to Soviets, or that they're being subtly 'encouraged' by the Kremlin. Either way, hardly matters, does it?"

Vivian shook her head. "All the craziness happening right there on Earth, and our terrorist faction are all up in arms about what NASA is doing on the Moon?"

"They want to keep it pure," Horn said. "Untouched by human hand. There were terrorist threats against NASA as long ago as Apollo 15. Though this current lot is more worried about Death from the Skies. Smart pebbles, Rods of God, all that Strategic Defense Initiative stuff."

Vivian sat back and looked out at the stars. "My Lord. Too much politics for one day."

Horn nodded and blew out a long breath. "Well, that's sure a lot of cheery news from Colonel Peter Sandoval. And to think that all this time I thought Poland was the country we'd be needing to worry about."

Vivian shook her head. "Poland?"

"Sure. Lech Walesa? Solidarnosc?"

"Ah, rings a bell," Vivian said, disingenuously.

Horn gave Vivian the disbelieving look that people always aimed her way when she missed a pop culture or political reference, the one that said, *Jeez, Viv, how can you be that oblivious?*

To which Vivian's answer would always be clear: *Because I'm busy all the goddamn time, is why …*

Instead, she said: "Okay, fine. If it's relevant, I guess you should fill me in."

"You were still on Earth for a lot of it. Lots of labor unrest back in 1980, strikes and factory occupations, especially in the Lenin Shipyard in Gdansk. Led by this guy called Lech Walesa. The shipworkers formed Solidarity, a national labor union in September of 1980, and started pitching for a more open society. You don't recall?"

"I do remember being a bit preoccupied in 1980."

"The Soviets have been threatening military intervention ever since, but so far they've kept their powder dry. They came very close when Solidarity called for workers in other Eastern Bloc countries to join them in late 1981. That was a bit much for everyone, and the Polish government had a big internal crackdown. The First Secretary, Jaruzelski, declared martial law. Tanks on the streets, curfews, censorship, the works. They lifted it, the martial law, this last July, just a couple weeks after we launched, but who knows when it's all going to blow up again? And if it does, I'm damned sure that this time the Soviets aren't just going to patiently sit by and hope for the best."

"Great," she said. "And there was me, thinking we left Earth to get away from politics."

"We did? If so, we made a terrible job of that."

"But it chases us, anyway." Vivian checked her watch. "Guess what? I need to go and work out. All this stress and non-activity has my muscles screaming."

The heck with the terrorists. Earth might really step forward into a worldwide nuclear holocaust, while Apollo Astarte was a bajillion miles away?

Vivian could barely visualize such a war. Hundreds of ICBMs, hundreds of nuclear blasts ... and hundreds of millions killed? Her imagination shied away from it.

And if that happened, the Astarte would be well and truly cut off. On a fool's errand to Mars to collect data no one would ever look at, and take another year and a half to crawl back to a wrecked Planet Earth.

Hoo, boy.

"Yeah," she said. "Definitely time to go and exercise."

Horn was staring moodily out the window. Now he shook himself and scanned the boards in front of him out of long habit. "You know, if you wouldn't mind the company, maybe I'll come and do the same."

PART THREE: MARS

March-May 1984

CHAPTER 12

"**HEY,** girl. You doing okay?"

Vivian peered out of her sleep compartment. From anyone other than Amy Benson, Vivian wouldn't have taken a greeting that informal aboard her own ship. But Amy was different. They role-switched on a regular basis. "Sure. I guess so. Just taking five before I plunge back into the fray."

Amy grinned. "At least the schedule pressure has relaxed a bit."

"Sure has." Considerably, in fact. In many ways, Venus flyby had been a splendid dry run for Mars flyby, and so the preparation for Mars would be much less. Plus, by this point in the mission, her entire crew were all trained up to the point where they could often achieve forty-five-minute routine tasks in around twenty minutes. Especially if they skimped a bit, which they all did. Including Vivian. She'd finally come to agree that sanity was more important than a hundred percent germfree environment.

She peered upward through the grid floor that separated the crew area from the forward compartment. Down here she could never tell if anyone was near enough to overhear. Right now Dave would be in CM-1 and Marco in CM-2, doing routine diagnostics and course refinement. Considering how repetitive their tasks were, it was a miracle both men hadn't already gone mad. Then again …

Anyway. She had no real idea where the rest of the crew were, right now, which was also a change. By now she knew she could either trust them to get on with whatever they were supposed to be doing, or trade tasks so someone else would do it for them.

She looked back at Amy. "Why do I get the feeling you showed up for one of your 'chats'?"

"I'm guessing it's your amazing perceptiveness and uncanny telepathic ability."

"Or just nearly a year of mission experience." Vivian backed up. "Well, it'll be a bit of a squeeze, but come in, I guess."

In Vivian's sleep quarters the maximum separation the two women could achieve was about two and a half feet. Then again, everyone's sense of appropriate personal space had evolved since launch.

"You exaggerate," Amy said. "It's only been nine months."

"Plus a couple prior to launch. And, I was actually trying not to do the math." Vivian latched the folding door. This was about as private as they could get, short of locking themselves in one of the Command Modules or the Multiple Docking Adapter. She pulled herself back into the corner of her bed, while Amy propped herself into the opposite corner between the door and Vivian's narrow locker. "Okay, shoot. Who are we worried about today?"

"Oh, no one. Just checking in."

"Me, then. Jeez, Amy. Honestly, I'm fine."

"No, not you." Amy considered. "Though you do seem to have gotten over that tense phase you went through after Venus."

Tense phase? Possibly an understatement, after all the world politics Sandoval had saddled her with. Stuff she could only talk to Dave Horn about, and Dave really didn't want to talk about it. But, hey, seventeen weeks had gone by since then (but who was counting?), and the world hadn't blown up yet, so Vivian had definitely relaxed a bit.

"It's really everyone else I'm worried about. Everyone's so much quieter and spending more time on their own. Even you, sneaking a visit to your bunk in the middle of the day. We're all a bit … off. A little depressed, I think, although no one's admitting it. We're bored and restless."

"We're hunkered down for the long haul," Vivian said. "A bit of introspection can't be that surprising."

Amy sighed. "I'm hoping people start sleeping better once we get nearer Mars. If not, we're likely to run out of Seconal before the mission ends."

"Yup," Vivian said, and chose not to add that she was hoarding tablets herself, so that some nights she could take a double dose.

Her doctor hesitated. "Let me ask you a question about something a bit abstract that still seems weird to me. On the L5-to-Venus leg of the trip, everyone knew where we were all the time, relative to the Earth and the other planets, and how long we had until the next burn, or until Venus itself. Now, no one knows any of that. Ask even Laura where Mars is and I doubt she could point to it. We've all … as a crew, we've lost our bearings, somehow. It's hard to explain."

"I'm sure Dave and Marco haven't. That's the important thing. For the rest of us, we're just hanging loose."

"Hmm."

Vivian herself couldn't have pointed out the direction to any of the planets by this point, without going to one of the windows and checking constellations. Venus had still been behind them until just a short while ago, but Astarte had been arcing around while Venus continued on its orbit, and as for the Earth, it hardly mattered, right? All she knew was that they were in a Sun-inertial attitude, which meant …

No, Vivian couldn't be bothered to work it out either. "Does it matter? Doesn't it just mean we're all relaxing into this and not fretting?"

"That would be nice. But, no, Vivian. I'm thinking it's definitely isolation-induced anxiety and depression."

"Then why aren't I suffering from it? I'm not depressed or anxious. Seriously. Wasn't I the one you were worried about earlier?"

"You're different," Amy said, ironically. "Or so it seems."

"I do get fed up occasionally," Vivian said. "I mean, who wouldn't? Some things weigh on my mind a bit. But, depression? Nothing like the depression I felt after Apollo 32, of being back on Earth. I mean, I'm in space, right? This is where I want to be."

"And that's the difference, I guess."

Vivian looked at her. "And how about you, Amy? Are *you* doing okay? Who looks after you while you're looking after us?"

"You all do," Amy said. "Despite everything I've said, this is still a very supportive crew. Every single one of you checks in with me quietly from time to time to make sure I'm all right. Overall, I'm impressed." She sighed. "I have the same sleep disturbance pattern as everyone else, I guess, and I do get a little anxious occasionally when stuff breaks down. But I don't feel angry."

Vivian paused, noting that word choice. "Wait—who's angry?"

Amy blinked and her lip puckered. "Uh. No one."

"Come on. Doctor-patient confidentiality is fine back in civilization. Here, if someone's on a short fuse, I need to know about it."

"No, you don't," Amy said.

"Seriously?"

"Seriously. I'm not about to suspend confidentiality just to satisfy your curiosity."

"Whoa." Vivian sat back, as much as she could in such a confined space.

Amy looked ... peeved. "Vivian, don't blow this out of proportion. If I thought there was a risk to the mission, I would tell you."

"And you get to decide that? The buck stops with *me* on this mission ..."

"Yes," Amy said. "I get to decide. Drop it, Viv. It just kind of slipped out. It's just yet another obvious but occasional symptom among people dealing with isolation."

Vivian grimaced. "And if I don't drop it, you're going to say it's because I'm angry or anxious? I can't win this, can I?"

"No." Amy put her hand on Vivian's arm. "You can't. So stop trying."

Vivian stifled the urge to knock Amy's hand away. And swallowed and took a breath. Because that *was* an abnormal reaction for her.

"Everyone here is a rational adult, Vivian. And they're all kind of introspective, and super-smart. They'll figure out their own ways of coping."

Vivian shook her head. "Amy. You came in here specifically because you were worried, and now you're trying to convince me there's nothing to worry about."

Amy considered and then shrugged. "True."

"So, okay. Let's just decide we're all fine and move on." It was obvious Vivian wasn't going to get any more out of Amy about her crew's potential anger issues, but at least now she knew to be more alert for the warning signs.

"Sure." Amy took a breath and looked relieved. "No worries. We're all good."

Vivian nodded. "Thanks, doc. I don't know if any of us say it often enough, but … thanks."

Finally, Vivian got that big smile from Amy. It was a long time since she'd seen that. "You're welcome, Viv."

After Amy was gone, Vivian stared at the wall for a few moments. What the hell was that all about? Was Amy really worried about everyone else, or about Vivian herself? Who was angry? And did any of this really matter, or was it all too easy to start fixating on stupid stuff when people were—yes—this isolated?

Vivian was happy enough to be in space. But she'd have needed to be superhuman not to be in a state of borderline irritation with just about every member of her crew.

There was Greg's obsessive scientific accuracy of language; how he couldn't just let a hand-wavy approximation go by but just had to gently correct whoever had just said it. The man was just too literal and precise for words.

Rudy was the exact opposite. He was just too offhand and dismissive, about everything except the Sun. And then there was Laura, who split her time between being a downer and almost manically excited about the upcoming Mars encounter. Then, of course, there was Amy herself: her clinical worldview, and the way she was always scrutinizing everyone else while pretending not to …

Her military guys all spoke in clipped military tones, and often with a fast back-and-forth: the characteristically efficient astronaut-speak that went back to Gemini and probably even further. Sometimes the scientists emulated that, and at other times—often when they were all caught up in a topic they cared about—they would talk in goddamned paragraphs, and they just had to finish each and every sentence. Sometimes, Vivian had to wait two minutes to get a word in edgewise.

Suddenly, Vivian grinned at herself and shook her head.

This was all super-minor. None of it was dangerous. None of it was even more than low-level irritating. In books and on TV shows, astronaut crews on long missions usually got into shouting matches, or even fist fights, and everything got crazy. All of Vivian's crew were much too buttoned down, too professional to do anything like that. They all understood the mission, and knew they needed to work together. Everything was safely tucked away under the surface, and not on anyone's sleeve.

That reminded her of something Dave Horn had said a couple of weeks ago, specifically about Laura and Greg. "They might be passive-aggressive, but look on the bright side: that means they're passive, rather than actually aggressive."

"Hooray," she'd said.

Dave had peered over at her. "I'm just saying, it could be worse."

And, of course, it very much could.

But still. God, it was tiring having to deal with her crew, in this little tin can, day after day after day after goddamned day … and just wait for Mars to come and save them.

And then, to euphemize, there was the hygiene situation.

They'd spent a *lot* of time studying how the toilets worked. They were almost more concerned with the Skylab's plumbing than their own.

And even when the system was working well, it apparently wasn't working well enough.

Marco's forehead was creased, his concern clearly visible. "We were supposed to be recovering over eighty percent of the water from our urine, but … oh, man." He shook his head.

Pee. Great. Vivian's number one favorite topic. Well, her second favorite topic, after Number Twos.

Ah, fecal humor. Another of the crew's favorites. She suppressed a sigh. "What's the problem this time?"

"Too much calcium. The bone density loss that we're seeing, spending so long in zero G, means our pee has too much calcium and potassium in it. And that's gumming up the works. Bottom line: we can really only recover sixty or seventy percent safely."

Amy was nodding, so Vivian took their word for it. But still: "Amy, you're not concerned that we're all losing so much calcium?"

"It's no more than I expected, and perhaps a bit less. Seems to be more than the water system designers had in mind, though."

"But that's not too bad, right? Considering how much water we have, and how easy it is to make more?"

Marco refused to be mollified. "Seriously, Vivian, our urine is a big deal."

Vivian grinned. "I can't believe you just said that with a straight face."

Marco cracked a reluctant smile. "Okay, yes, when you put it like that ..."

Astarte was not carrying all the air and water the crew would need for a two-year mission. The weight cost of that would be prohibitive. Instead, they had several highly sophisticated ways of generating them.

First, they were reclaiming and recycling as much water as they could. Their urine needed to be preprocessed separately using a centrifuge and a low-pressure gas distillation process, but after that it combined with the wastewater, and water vapor reacquired from their local atmosphere through condensation over cold plates followed by adsorption, to pass back through filter beds and a catalytic reactor ... and then, around it all came again. And there ended Vivian's knowledge of the Water Processing Unit, because she didn't want to think about it too much.

In addition, they were creating more water, and by several different redundant processes. The carbon dioxide they exhaled was removed from the air using a four-bed molecular sieve, whatever that was. Their Sabatier reactor then combined this CO_2 with hydrogen to produce methane and water. They could extract oxygen from this water by electrolysis, which went back into their air supply, and rotate some of the hydrogen back through the Sabatier on the next cycle. As a backup, since removing the carbon dioxide from their air was essential to their survival, they also had a separate amine scrubber ... whatever *that* might be. Anyway, it was all much more sophisticated than the toxic lithium hydroxide canisters formerly in use on Apollo missions. Having nearly been killed by LiOH while out on the lunar surface during her Trek of Death, Vivian had been delighted to discover that method was now obsolete, at least for spacecraft.

Some of this was newish technology, and despite having been rigorously tested on the Moon, it verged a little close to the experimental for Vivian's taste. By contrast, they had two arrays of alkali fuel cells aboard, one in each CSM, as a backup for the six solar arrays. Fuel cells had been used extensively throughout the Gemini and Apollo missions and were very well understood. They acted like a battery by combining hydrogen and oxygen to create impressive amounts of electrical power, and they provided water good enough to drink as a by-product.

The fuel cell system required a lot of maintenance—the oxygen needed to be purged daily and the hydrogen every two days—but Vivian could hardly complain about that from a resource standpoint.

The paradoxical result of all this high tech was that they had way more oxygen than they needed, and almost as much water, and were using the original water they'd loaded aboard at the beginning of the mission at a *much* lower rate than predicted.

This meant that their life support calculations and discussions were focused less on survival, or even on conserving scarce resources, and more on how to balance the inputs and outputs of these various processes. Methane was the sole end product of any non-trivial volume that they routinely vented overboard, and Dardenas even complained about this: there were apparently processes for "cracking the methane to recover the hydrogen molecules" that he had been championing, about which the planetary scientists nodded sagely, but the mission planners had considered this an unnecessary frill to add to an already complex set of systems.

So Vivian was needing to try real hard to get worried enough about today's apparent urine processing crisis. "Marco. What's the worst case, if it breaks down completely and none of our pee-water gets reclaimed?"

"It increases the risk that we might get close to redlining."

Vivian looked skeptical. "Redlining? No way."

He sighed. "Look. We're all peeing about twenty fluid ounces a day. Multiply that by eight and it comes to about twenty pounds of water that we're losing. Factor in everything else, and sure, technically we still have enough water in our energy budget to see us through. But it means we're only one more breakdown away from disaster. And, if the fuel cells were to have an anomaly as well ..." He shook his head. "That would be a *real* bad day."

"Okay," Vivian conceded. "That's fair." They didn't want to give up any redundancy they didn't have to, not with this much of the mission still ahead of them.

"Man." Laura's face looked as if she'd bitten into a lemon. "That is a *lot* of pee."

"Pretty sure I rack up more than forty ounces a day," Josh Rawlings said, very seriously.

"And I didn't need to know *that*, either," Laura said.

Vivian sighed. "Boy oh boy. This mission is just one damned thing after another. Okay, fine. Drag out the manuals for the processing unit, Marco, and let's get to grips with this."

While saying this, she resisted the urge to look at her watch. For a mission with "nothing to do" until they reached Mars, she sure seemed short on downtime.

Rudy drifted up into the forward compartment, his clothes soaked, Water globules followed him through the hatch. "Uh, guys. Really sorry, but … I might need a bit of help with the shower again."

Laura raised her eyes to heaven. "Great."

By now, everyone but Rudy had agreed that the shower was more trouble than it was worth. The women were down to showering once every two or three weeks, and the other men had given up on it altogether. The water flow was paltry at the best of times, and gathering up all the wastewater and wiping the walls down to clean up afterward was a pain, even in a closed system. A sponge bath with germicidal wipes worked out just fine and used much less water.

Vivian could wash her hair well enough using about eight ounces of water from a squirt bottle, combing it gradually through their hair and then applying no-rinse shampoo and brushing it out with a little more water. Some water globules always made a break for it, and sometimes the women paired up for hair washing, to effectively chase the stray drops down. And by now Laura had mercifully given up on her long tresses and had allowed Amy to cut it back to shoulder length.

Of course, it figured that the one guy who really wanted to have showers was the one with the least technical expertise in fixing it when it went wrong.

Finally, Vivian got back to her crew compartment. She looked around. Even without Amy in it, this place was kind of small. Why hadn't that really bothered her until today?

Well, time to do something constructive to relieve this stress. She headed up to the Multiple Docking Adapter.

Vivian had to dig right to the bottom of their massive handy-dandy machine-shop chest to find what she was looking for and then could only find two of them. Three would be better; in fact, three was the minimum.

Wait. She went to the opposite end of the ship to scrutinize the backup garbage compactor—the one backup they'd never needed to press into service, even temporarily. "Bingo." It had three springs mounted across the bottom of the unit, to act as shock absorbers. Just what she needed. She grabbed a ratchet spanner and got to work removing one, then fastened a memo card in its place so that it would be clear what she'd done, if anyone else came looking.

A hard vinyl bag stuffed with shredded clothing and Vivian was set. She mounted her three springs onto the bag and then latched the other ends of the springs across the inner doorway of her sleep quarters with brackets, nuts and bolts, and … hey presto.

She poked at it, and it quivered appealingly. So, she lined up, anchored her feet with her exercise straps … and punched it, left and right, then punched it again a few more times.

Sure, that'll work.

She'd need to rig up something better in the way of gloves so she wouldn't abrade her knuckles, but that would be easy enough. The bag would be better if she had some sand to mix in with the clothing scraps, but she was a bajillion miles away from a beach, so this would have to do.

Vivian Carter had an honest-to-God punchbag to take out her frustrations on. And thumping it didn't make a whole lot of noise, what with the usual fans and pumps and creaks and groans of the Astarte Skylab, so with a bit of luck she would never need to 'fess up to anyone else that she was taking out her frustrations by hitting something.

Cool.

"Hey, guess what?" Marco said. "The Chinese are in space."

Horn looked wry. "Is that a fact?"

"For real this time, and officially. They have three astronauts in orbit, two men and a woman."

"Taikonauts," Vivian said.

"Yuhangyuan, actually," said Greg.

"Bless you," Marco said. "They're planning several more launches, and aiming to have a small space station called Shuangong in Earth orbit by year's end, as well as fast-tracking a lunar landing program. They aim to join the Soviet Union and the United States in peaceful exploration of Earth's satellite, for the glory of People's Republic of China."

"I heard they were encountering obstacles along the way," Greg said. "Both the US and Soviets reached out to them, offering technical assistance, but the Chinese said Boo to that."

Amy's lip quirked. "Boo?"

"It's Chinese for No," Greg said, and Vivian could tell he was delighted to be able to share that snippet with them.

"Chinese is all very dependent on tone and inflection, though," Rudy said. "If you don't get the inflection exactly right, you might be saying 'Tuning fork' or 'ham sandwich' or something instead."

Mercifully, Marco got them back on track. "We really offered assistance to Red China?"

"My enemy's enemy ..." Amy murmured.

"Exactly," Rudy said. "Relations between the Soviets and the Chinese have been rough for a while. And we did send Nixon to China."

Naturally, Greg submitted a correction. "Nixon sent himself. He was talking about it way before he even became President."

"Right. But we'd rather have decent détente with China and have them leaning toward us and away from the Soviets, than have the two of them getting into bed together and ganging up on us."

"Anything we can do to turn down the heat on the Cold War works for me," Vivian said. "Hey, Pilot. Are you planning on finishing that chocolate pudding?"

Horn floated the half-full tube over to her. "Have at it. I can barely taste it."

"Me neither," Vivian said. "But I can tell it has sugar in it. By now, that's all I need."

Amy pretended to write a note in the air. "Tooth decay."

"Anyway, the more the merrier,' Vivian said. "The Chinese, I mean."

Marco looked at her. "Not the response I was expecting."

"Well, at least if China puts real Chinese on the Moon, it'll be harder for the Soviets to put fake Chinese there."

Greg grimaced. "They weren't exactly 'fake Chinese.'"

"Okay, okay. Whatever." Vivian turned back to Marco. "What does 'fast-tracking' mean to them? When can we expect to see them making their own Great Leap Forward for all mankind?"

Rudy was shaking his head. "All you guys are just so *cynical*."

"Sure, hippie guy. So, when?"

"Their goal is to get Chinese boots on the Moon within the next couple of years."

"Okay, great." Vivian grinned. "I look forward to meeting them. Under somewhat better circumstances than last time."

From here, the conversation veered into a discussion of European politics. Vivian tried to look interested. Amy Benson was always keen for them all to discuss Earth-issues; apparently their level of engagement with affairs on their home planet was a positive factor in their mental health, and Vivian didn't want to get another sleeping-quarters visit from her doctor. Especially not now she had a punchbag mounted in there.

Also: after hearing Sandoval's litany of woes about how the world had nearly gotten vaporized in a nuclear apocalypse the previous fall, Vivian was a little more sensitive to international politics. After all, the geopolitical situation on Earth might still become of critical interest to the crew of Apollo Mars Astarte.

"Oh, nobody wants Germany to re-unify," Greg Heinz was saying. "No one in Europe, on either side. It's a pipe dream."

Rudy looked at him sideways. "Really? Nobody?"

"Really. Having been through the Second World War, no one in Europe wants a strong Germany. It's only the neo-Nazis who have any kind of appetite for it, which obviously makes everyone else want to run the other way.

"The West German Chancellor, Helmut Kohl, is absolutely against it. Plenty of Ostpolitik going on, which is apparently German for 'talking,' normalizing relationships… But you can bet that Kohl doesn't want to be responsible for East Germany as well as West Germany. And no one else in Europe is keen on a reunified Germany. Mitterrand is against it. Craxi and Andreotti—they're opposed as well."

Vivian glanced at Horn, who said, "Bettino Craxi is the Italian Prime Minister, Giulio Andreotti is the premier."

"Man, you must have a lot of free time up there in CM-1," she said.

"Thatcher's against it, too. So is Gorbachev."

"Okay. Germany not unifying, got it. Thanks."

None of them had mentioned SS-20s or Pershing 2 missiles, so maybe in some ways Vivian was better informed than they were. She didn't mention that.

Plus, if Sandoval was right, Germany had a much higher chance of vaporizing in a series of nuclear blasts than getting back together as one happy family. Vivian decided not to bring that up either.

Rather than get lectured by Greg Heinz, she asked Rawlings and Dardenas quietly, while they were taking their shift making solar observations at the science console. "So, who the hell is Gorbachev anyway?"

"Good question," said Dardenas. He flipped a switch to archive a data file. "Mikhail Gorbachev. He's quite new. In his early fifties, just a kid by Politburo standards. Which makes him a toddler by Soviet leadership standards."

Rawlings looked around. "Don't let Amy know you're skipping your news-watching. She says that it's psychologically essential to maintain mental and emotional contact with what's happening on the home planet."

"Yeah, tell me about it. Sooo … why do we care about Gorbachev? Andropov's still in the hot seat, right?"

"Oh, sure. In fact, Andropov is stronger than ever. For a while, he had health issues but maybe he's laying off the vodka a bit. Which is good, since he's only a few inches from the nuclear codes. Him, plus his little cadre of hardliners of the old guard: Andrei Gromyko, Dmitri Ustinov, couple others."

Vivian's mind swerved away from nuclear codes. Gromyko, she had heard of. Ustinov, not so much. Or, had Peter mentioned him? Maybe so.

Dardenas pulled out a logbook and started jotting down the times and measurements he'd just made. Rawlings took over the job of educating Vivian on Kremlin politics. "Why do we care? Well, Gorbachev is the pleasant face, the young—youngish—guy with the energy and the smile. The one you believe you can do business with. Breath of fresh air, and all."

"Putting a more amenable face on the Communist Bloc?"

"Maybe, but he's not just a pretty face—he's a hard worker too. He became a Secretary of the Central Committee back in 1978. Joined the Politburo as a candidate member in '79, full member in '80. Youngest member. After Brezhnev got shuffled aside, Andropov made sure that Gorbachev succeeded him as General Secretary of the Communist Party."

Dardenas resurfaced, pressed another button to start an automated sequence of imaging and spectral exposures, and put his feet up. "And how do we know? 'Cause Gorby's been on delegations to Western European countries for years, and the news shows lap him up. He went to Canada last year and wowed Pierre Trudeau there. Later on in the year he was in Britain, meeting with Margaret Thatcher. He's selling himself as a reformer, but that isn't going down too well at home."

"It's a bit of a headscratcher," Rawlings said. "He's a protégé of Andropov's—there's no way he'd have gotten to where he is now without Andropov's patronage—but he's actually on the opposite side to Andropov on a lot of issues."

Dardenas nodded. "People are all hopeful that if his red star keeps ascending, he might be able to ease the Soviets toward reform."

"Or he might just mysteriously disappear in the night," said Rawlings. "That's my bet. It would hardly be the first time."

"Okay," Vivian said. "Good enough ..."

Gorbachev. Whatever. Vivian was pretty sure the new boss would be the same as the old boss. Even if the old boss ever stepped down.

The Soviet Union was still a very long way away, and Vivian still found it very difficult to maintain interest in the conversation.

Of course, she could have no way of knowing that Soviet politics and ambitions were about to take a turn that would affect their entire mission.

CHAPTER 13

Mars Inbound: Vivian Carter
April 20, 1984
Mission Elapsed Time: 291 days

ON the small TV screen mounted in the instrument panel of CM-2, Ellis Mayer's expression was somber. "So, Vivian, Dave: hi. I'm afraid I have good news and bad news. I'll give you the bad news first."

Dave Horn, screwdriver in hand, did not even look up from his work in the lower equipment bay. "More bad news? Shock me again."

The heating system in CM-2 was on the fritz, and Marco Dardenas had been up in the machine shop for the past hour, working on the lathe to make some small but critical replacement component. In the meantime, Dave was taking the opportunity to dig into the rest of the system and clean it out by hand. Vivian, bundled up against the chill and anchoring herself on the left-hand couch, gave an exasperated sigh. Why the hell did Amy and the psych people insist on them calling home so often, when the tidings from the home planet were so frequently dire?

"Well, fire away," she said ironically to the screen. It would be many minutes before Ellis heard their words, but she spoke them anyway to preserve the fiction that this was actually a conversation.

"The Soviets are going to Mars," Ellis said, and peered into his own camera as if he could magically see Vivian's reaction through it.

That reaction was oddly understated. "Huh?" she said, and blinked. She'd heard Ellis's words, but had no way of interpreting what they might mean. Going to Mars when? How?

Ellis, of course, hurried to explain. "In fact they launched on March 17th, departing from lunar orbit, but are only now publicizing the mission. Knowing the Soviets, they wanted to ensure that the burns were successful and that the trajectory was guaranteed to get them to Mars before they went public, so they wouldn't have egg on their faces if the mission failed."

"Cowards," said Horn, still busy with his screwdriver. Vivian was just staring at the screen, unable to think clearly.

"Their TMK-Mars has nuclear propulsion, so that might have been one big reason for their caution …"

"Jesus *Christ*," Vivian said. "The bastards can't be aiming to beat us to Mars?"

"No way," Horn said. "Nuclear motors aren't magic."

"… and as yet we're unable to track them effectively, but according to Soviet news sources, TASS and Pravda and all, they're aiming to arrive in Martian orbit in early September …"

Horn nodded. "See? Long after us." Apollo Astarte was scheduled to fly by Mars on May 22, 1984, in just over a month's time.

"Martian *orbit*," Vivian repeated for emphasis. And at last Horn paused and frowned up at the screen.

"And, guess who's commanding the mission? Nikolai Makarov. We thought he'd retired from active space duty. Turns out that was incorrect. So, yeah." Mayer grimaced. "Your old friend Nikolai Makarov plans to steal a march on you at the Red Planet."

" 'Friend' might be overstating it," Horn said.

"Dave. Quiet."

Ellis was still talking. "… crew of just four in total, all experienced cosmonauts. The other three are Igor Kaleri, Vitaliy Petrushenko, and Fyodor Terekhin. Only that last one has any science background. He's their token planetologist. Like this is actually a science mission and not a pissing contest. They aren't aiming to go down to the surface, of course. Their goal is to rendezvous with the Martian moon, Deimos, and make a landing on it."

Horns eyebrows went up. "Deimos? Neat."

"Meaning that they can claim they're walking Martian soil, or as close to Mars as makes no difference." Mayer raised his hands. "That's going to be an impressive scoop on their part. Sorry to say it, guys. Pausing for a moment while you digest all that."

"Okay, I guess?" Vivian examined her emotions and shook her head. In truth, now her initial surprise had worn off, she wasn't sure she really cared. It was hardly a scoop, to her eyes: the US would fly past Mars, and then four whole months later the Soviets would do a Deimos photo op? In crass Space Race terms, that would maybe diminish Apollo Astarte's achievement by a hair. But Vivian and her crew would still get to see the Red Planet close up and personal well before Nikolai, and their flight was still epic and groundbreaking.

And Nikolai, of all people, deserved to have some fun. Let him have his moment of glory, walking around on his orbiting rubble pile.

Horn shook his head, bemused. "That Makarov. Never misses a trick."

"Makes perfect sense," Vivian said. "Even now he's still one of the best orbital mechanics guys they have. Only guy I know who's even in the same league as you."

"Oh, please."

"Bet his wife's pissed with him, though ..."

From tens of millions of miles away, Mayer looked up from his sheet of paper and started speaking again. "And because of all this, people at the White House and at NASA have been talking."

"Uh-oh," Vivian said. "That's never good."

"The orbital mechanics folks have been working overtime on the math. As you know, you have plenty of fuel, with contingency thrust two or three times over what you'll ever realistically need—"

"Oh, crap," Vivian said.

"—and so the thinking here is that maybe Apollo Astarte should hold at Mars—"

"Hold at *Mars*? What, don't even—"

"Vivian." Now it was Dave's turn to hold up his hands, staring at the screen. "Hush."

"—with a view to maybe rendezvousing with Phobos. Sure, let the Reds have Deimos. We won't encroach on the territory they plan to stake out, because that would be petty, right?"

"And we would never be petty," Vivian couldn't help interjecting. Horn just gave her a look.

"No, you'll go to the *other* moon of Mars, so that we and the Soviets survey both between us, and maximize the science yield of the two missions, which benefits everyone. And, well, it just so happens that you'll arrive first."

"Uh, sure .... But at the cost of a *massively* increased risk. Wasn't the whole point of Astarte to minimize risk? Isn't NASA supposed to be the cautious agency, and the Soviets the reckless ones? Holy *shit*, Ellis. I can't believe you're seriously suggesting this."

As if he'd heard her, Ellis said: "We're looking carefully at the risk matrix, but we think it's manageable. Thrust, consumables for the extra mission duration: all close, but within bounds. By now we've gained confidence in the Centaur-G boosters, and you really only need one of the pair to work to give you the thrust you'll need to break orbit and get home. And we already have a Plan C in the works, in case for some crazy, unforeseen reason *both* Centaurs were to have anomalies while you're in Martian orbit."

Horn was nodding. "The necessary thrust and delta-V's aren't as great as you might think, Viv. Remember we'd just be in orbit, not deep in the gravity well."

While they were in Martian orbit. But alarm bells were already ringing in Vivian's mind. "For the love of God, don't be sending me a NERVA."

Ellis half-grinned. "You're not going to be thrilled. Sorry."

"You're going to send us a goddamned NERVA, Ellis. Just spit it out."

"We're sending you a NERVA," Ellis continued, oblivious. "And, not that we're prejudging the issue, but it's already on the launch pad. If we're going to do this at all, we need to take advantage of the same Mars window that the Soviet are using for TMK, and it's closing rapidly. So we're just going to send it, so that it'll arrive just a couple of months after you get there."

"Not at all prejudging the issue," she said. "Obviously."

Even Dave Horn was looking startled by now. "A couple of *months*, you say?"

"So, to recap." Ellis threw up a graphic on the screen, which neither of them really needed. "If the final decision, here, puts you into orbit around Mars in May, we can either schedule your trans-Earth injection burn earlier, because the earlier you leave the shorter your return trip will be. Or later, with the NERVA, which gives you greater thrust. If the decision is made that you won't wait for the NERVA, or this new mission profile is scrubbed and you continue on with the flyby as scheduled, we'll just leave it there in Martian orbit in preparation for the *next* US mission to Mars—because, guess what: you know there's going to be another one. Now the ball is rolling, you can bet that both we and the Soviets will be taking advantage of the next Mars launch window, right? So, in all likelihood, this is actually *good* news for the Agency. The NERVA advantage is that they have a longer shelf-life for a parking orbit, so it should still be good as new in a few years. We can't really say the same for chemical-only rocket motors."

"They sure didn't use to have a longer shelf-life," Horn said, mostly to himself. "That was one of the issues. Guess they've licked that somehow in the meantime."

Vivian was still trying to process it all. A NERVA would be coming to Mars: an Apollo third stage containing a Nuclear Engine for Rocket Vehicle Application. A *nuclear* thermal rocket of the specific type that Vivian had been *extremely clear* about ruling out for Apollo Astarte when she was only a few days into her command.

"So, that's the story, guys." Ellis looked at his watch. "We don't expect an answer right away. You're going to want to talk about this among yourselves and with the rest of your crew."

"No shit, Ellis. Yeah, we might need a little chat."

"Dave, we've prepared a full briefing to get you up to speed. We know you're likely to have a lot of questions about the maneuvers involved, and how we plan to arrange the trajectory to minimize the effect of the Martian gravity on the approach instead of maximizing it … so we'd like to show you all the math upfront. It's a recording about an hour long, and it's right now transferring into your video buffer. Y'all take a look, think it over, and get back to us when you're ready with opinions, questions, concerns. Within twenty-four hours, if possible? Even sooner? That way we'll all know how to plan with confidence. Listen, Vivian, Dave I'd love to be able to stick around for your immediate reaction—"

"I just bet you would," she said. "You love it when smoke comes out of my ears."

"—but it's already been a long day, and I have," he looked embarrassed, "my kid's dance recital to go to. I know, I'm a walking cliché.

I'll be back on console tomorrow morning. Good luck with the, uh, crew conversation."

"Yeah, thanks, man."

"Astarte, CAPCOM out."

" 'Bye, good buddy."

The image blanked, and Vivian undid her lapstrap and let herself float up into the Command Module space, turning slowly. Gently bumped into the closed hatch above her, and let herself float back downward, relaxing her pent-up muscles as best she could.

Despite Ellis's glib assurances, going into orbit around Mars must surely require a lot of thrust. A lot of delta-V? Oh, no worries, because NASA had a *fricking NERVA* on the way in case they used too much juice. "Christ on a pony."

Horn was still frowning at the blank screen, not blinking much, which meant that he was deep in thought. Vivian said nothing more, just waited for him to be ready.

They watched the technical briefing together, mostly in silence—Vivian wanted to see the nitty-gritty details just as badly as her pilot did—and then they sat back and stared into space again, literally: one at each window.

From CM-2, mounted in the radial port and extending outward from the axis of Astarte, Vivian realized she could glimpse the pale red beacon of Mars. "You weren't even surprised."

Horn shook his head. "No. The possibility's been in my mind ever since we launched."

"For real?"

"Yep. I mean, why not?"

She gaped. "Why *not*?"

"I mean, aside from lengthening our mission by a few more months and adding several long critical burns, plus the added risk of the Phobos spacewalks."

A few more months. "With this crew?"

"You had some other folks in mind? This is a great crew, all things considered. We can make it work."

Dave Horn presumably wasn't the one with anger issues. He likely didn't even have a punchbag in his sleeping compartment. "Dave, this isn't just a theoretical exercise. They want us to actually *do* this. Commit to Mars's gravitational field and hope we can break free of it when we need to and get back on track for Earth. With *this* ship, and our actual bodies and lives."

He blinked at her. "Yes. I know. I get that."

"Okay."

"Well, just consider: you, Vivian Carter, could be the first person ever to walk on a planetary body outside the Earth-Moon system."

"Huh." Somehow, this had never sunk in. "I guess so. Hadn't occurred to me."

"Really?"

"Too startled at my entire mission profile being upended on the fly, I guess."

"It would be quite the thing. Even though you're already famous, and all." He studied her. "Be honest. It's the NERVA that freaks you out the most."

Horn and Ellis knew her too well. "I'm not fond of nukes."

"This isn't a nuke. It's a rocket. We trust it."

"*You* trust it. Because everything that comes out of Los Alamos is awesome?"

Horn shook his head. "It's a Westinghouse reactor powering a thermal Aerojet engine."

"I heard the briefing, Dave. I know what it is."

"And we don't necessarily have to use it. But, frankly, if we do go into Martian orbit, I'd prefer to stick around until we can grab it. It would reduce the admittedly-small chances of a poor Centaur burn getting us into trouble."

"Stay in Martian orbit for *months*?"

"That's what the man said. That's what we're talking about. Yes."

She studied his face. "So, you're up for this?"

Horn looked down at the pad of paper in front of him, dense with the notes he'd taken during the briefing. "Well, I'm sure as hell not signing off on it right away. We'll need to go through all of this in detail, run some equations on the guidance computer—generally let it all sink in. I'd like a day or two to do that. I definitely have questions and reservations. But I'm not dismissing the idea out of hand."

"Okay. Sure. And if you're a Go, I guess we then have to run it by the rest of the crew." Vivian almost shuddered. "That'll be a blast."

"I don't think we should wait. Let's tell them today and let them be mulling it over while I do the math. And that way we can get Josh and

Marco's eyes on the maneuver math as well. We shouldn't be keeping something this huge to ourselves any longer than we have to."

"I know. I know. I was just hoping for more time to think it through myself ..." She sighed. "Fine. We'll go tell 'em right away. We're coming up on shift overlap, everyone should be awake."

For the first time, Horn broke out in a big grin. "And if they're not awake when you start speaking, they sure will be by the time you're two minutes in."

CHAPTER 14

Mars Inbound: Nikolai Makarov
April 20, 1984

NIKOLAI Makarov sat at the aft window of his Salyut spacecraft and looked out at the cosmos before him. And at one particular point of light. A very *red*-looking star, that wasn't a star at all.

For this trip, orbital mechanics were not on Nikolai's side. It was counterintuitive, but the way Vivian was going to Mars, using Venus as a steppingstone, was a much more reasonable path in terms of mission duration.

One-way trips to Mars were well understood, and both NASA and the Soviets had sent robotic missions into Mars orbit and down to its surface for over a decade. Round-trip missions were a little more complicated. For the faster and more efficient outbound trajectory, by the time they arrived at Mars the Earth was then in an unfavorable alignment for the return trip.

There were two ways of dealing with this: the short-stay or "opposition-class" missions and the long-stay or "conjunction-class." The "opposition" missions involved one short leg, either outbound to Mars or inbound on the return, and one longer leg. The longer leg involved a perihelion passage inside the orbit of Venus, and a large total energy requirement. "Conjunction" missions required a 900-day total mission, with a 500-day stay at Mars while the astronauts waited for the two planets to be ideally aligned.

The alternative to both was just to burn an unconscionable amount of fuel. This was, of course, the approach the Soviets were adopting for TMK-Mars.

Nikolai and his crew would be coming back on a nonoptimal return trajectory. Brute forcing their way home. Which was, as they all said, "very Russian."

Thus, the TMK-Mars mission would last a much more modest fourteen months. None of the heroic posturing all across the inner solar system that NASA and Vivian Carter were performing. The USSR's missions were more focused, and its achievements all the more impressive as a result. Clean, simple missions, leading to clear and straightforward achievements that the people of the Soviet Republics and the world could easily understand and applaud. Nikolai Makarov approved.

Conceptually, the TMK-Mars spacecraft bore similarities to Vivian's Apollo Astarte. A straight copying of the idea, common lineage, or just the most sensible design for a quick-start interplanetary mission cobbled together from tried-and-true technologies and already-existing craft? Probably a bit of each. Makarov didn't know. His job was just to pilot the thing.

The combined Soviet Tyazhely Mezhplanetny Korabi—Heavy Interplanetary Vessel—Mars craft consisted of a standard Salyut space station, mated in series with one of the latest Soyuz craft docked on one end, and a standard off-the-shelf LEK Lunar Lander on the other. Beyond the Soyuz, a stout main booster provided the motive power needed: a nuclear thermal rocket engine, RD-0410, developed by the Chemical Automatics Design Bureau in Voronezh in southwestern Russia.

Superficially, the combination appeared sleeker than Vivian's Apollo Astarte spacecraft; at least for TMK-Mars all the components were lined up in a row, rather than having some components jutting out from the sides in an ungainly fashion. Makarov was aware that his TMK-Mars ship had much less redundancy than the American craft, but he had a strong faith in Soviet engineering, and each of the vehicles that made up TMK-Mars had an established heritage.

And, the bloated eight-person roster of Apollo Astarte? His TMK-Mars had a crew of just four, and much less mission complexity in terms of telescopes and experiments and probes and all the rest of it. If Makarov had one word to apply to the Astarte mission, it was "overdesigned."

TMK-Mars had a tight team and a manageable list of mission objectives: Get to Mars. Achieve orbit. Take photos—lots and lots of photos. Rendezvous with Mars's moon, Deimos, and station-keep nearby. Use the LEK to land on it, plant the Soviet flag, and then utilize a converted Lunokhod Rover with spiked wheels to drive around on it effectively. They would pay four multi-day visits to Deimos in all, with varying combinations of crew, and explore it thoroughly: take rock samples, and search for the loosely bound water that these samples may contain (up to twenty percent of the total mass, by some estimates).

And, most importantly, at least for the Rodina: they would declare a resounding propaganda success that would again resonate around the world and keep the US down in its perennial position as the second-best spacefaring power.

Nikolai himself had a compact list of personal objectives: survive through this experience, make the Rodina look good once again on the world stage, and be the first man to set foot on a planetary body outside of the Earth-Moon system. "First man to walk on Deimos" would be a fine achievement to add to "second man to walk on the Moon," and likely earn him his third Order of the Soviet Union. Assuming he managed to come home again at the end of this adventure, of course. It would be a shame if it were awarded posthumously.

The nuclear rocket engine was the wild card. Any sane man would have his doubts, especially at the high thrust levels TMK-Mars would demand of it. But Makarov had spent a great deal of time studying the specifications of this engine and working with the engineers at the Chemical Automatics Design Bureau. This rigorous study had convinced him that the RD-0410 not only had a higher performance and likely greater reliability than the superficially similar US NERVA engine, and a much more compactly designed reactor core. It was as reliable as it could possibly be, and he felt confident about it. He would not have accepted command of the mission if he did not.

Did he feel similarly confident about his crew? That had been the second wild card. Here was a difference from the American system that Makarov admired a little less: his crew assignments were all made for him, with little to no input from him, and it seemed this crew had been chosen as much for its political appeal as technical.

Thus, the crew of TMK-Mars consisted of the following: Nikolai Makarov, commander. Vitaliy Petrushenko, flight engineer. Igor Kaleri, flight engineer. Fyodor Terekhin, cosmonaut-scientist. Nikolai himself, plus three other men, all slim and dark-haired, all of Great Russian stock, all of similar military and aerospace backgrounds. It had been decreed from the start that this would be an all-male crew: much safer, personality-wise, for a long-haul mission.

When they'd been assigned, Makarov had at least recognized them all from Star City, the cosmonaut training center twenty-five miles northeast of Moscow, but had known none of them well, and prior to their crew assignment had never even eaten a meal or drunk vodka or cognac with any of them. All possessed considerable spaceflight experience but none had ever flown together before—not that you could tell that now: their four weeks of training together in Earth orbit had already turned them into a smooth and cooperative team before they'd even lit the candle that would send them to Mars. Their destination might be so far distant that it was sometimes difficult to pick out of the bright starscape that surrounded them, but journeying there just took the same skills they already had, but for a longer time.

Kaleri was the joker—calmer and more relaxed than the other men, and funnier as well. Petrushenko was quietly competent with a quite remarkable memory: he never needed to be told anything twice. Fyodor Terekhin was serious and earnest to a fault, as befitted the lone scientist in a crew of career cosmonauts, and without complaint he worked the extra hours necessary to train himself on those Salyut systems he was less familiar with. Makarov fitted into this group as smoothly as if they had been brothers in arms for many years. He was quite satisfied with the men assigned to his command.

They were at least taciturn individuals. He would not have liked to share a fourteen-month journey in an interior space as small as the combined Salyut-Soyuz-LEK pressurized volume with anyone garrulous. But at least his small four-person crew meant that there was ample scope for withdrawing, where necessary.

It was bittersweet that his mission goal was to trump Vivian Carter's flyby of Mars and thus diminish what would otherwise have been one of the crowning achievements of her life. He genuinely liked the American woman and, left to his own devices, would have been quite happy to concede her this little victory. Or, had matters gone differently, he might have preferred the first voyage to another planet to be a collaborative venture, but the Americans had made that impossible with their underhand plans to steal a march on the Soviets by going it alone.

But he had been given his orders and would carry them out, and he was quietly excited at the prospect of seeing the Red Planet, and of landing on Deimos.

He had, in fact, barely thought of Vivian Carter in the meantime. He had admired her LGS-1 journey around the Moon's surface without being particularly moved by it. To him, it had seemed a bit of a gimmick, but he had been glad that two of his young proteges had been able to participate. He had noted that a kind of personality cult was forming around Vivian Carter in the corrupt United States press, which always tended toward hero-worship to a sometimes-sickening degree.

But, let politics be politics, at least for now.

Nikolai Makarov had a mission to run.

CHAPTER 15

Mars Inbound: Vivian Carter
April 20, 1984
Mission Elapsed Time: 291 days

"**... AND** that's what Houston and the White House are proposing. They want us to give it our thorough consideration, and provide them with feedback, to assist with the final decision."

Vivian's crew just looked at one another, shell-shocked.

"I understand," Vivian said. "It's a lot to take in."

"It's insane, is what it is," Amy said.

"I'll admit, that was my first reaction too."

"Really?" Laura Simmons' eyes were wide as she looked around each of them in turn. "We *have* to do this. I mean, fine, let's talk through it all and make sure it's technically feasible, but ... come on, everybody! Go into orbit around *Mars*? Walk on *Phobos*? Hell, yeah!"

"And, already, we've covered both ends of the possible responses," Vivian said sardonically. "Good job, people."

Rudy was frowning. "This ship doesn't even have a lander. How the hell do we *land* on Phobos?"

"It'll be less of a landing and more of a docking," Horn said. "Phobos is pretty darned small. The real trick will be not getting flung off it by accident."

"Oh, fabulous." Amy Benson looked away.

"I'm being a little facetious," Horn said quickly.

"That's not going to happen," Laura said. "Being thrown off. Though it might be good for us to drill into it to tether ourselves. Stabilize the ship so that nothing gets out of hand. Right?"

"Uh, sure," Vivian said, and Dave Horn nodded.

Laura was still looking at Vivian. "Permission to give the crew a quick refresher on Phobos? I think we all need a clear understanding of what we're talking about, here."

Vivian ignored Greg's sigh. "Yes. Please go ahead."

Laura nodded. "Okay, so the two Martian moons are Phobos and Deimos, right? As far as we can tell they're superficially similar, but we don't know how they were formed. They might have coalesced into moons at the same time Mars became a planet—basically just accreted into their current orbits. Or, they could be asteroids that got captured and then circularized through tides or atmospheric drag. Me, I like that second idea, because their orbits aren't exactly normal ..."

"Good grief." Vivian waved. "Speed it up, Laura, okay?"

"Okay. But the point is, they're not spherical. They're both basically potato-shaped, and teeny-tiny compared to the Earth or the Moon. Deimos is nine and a half miles by seven and a half, by almost seven. Phobos is a bit larger, at something like sixteen miles by thirteen by ten." She looked at Vivian. "Hey, we could even circumnavigate it. You could add another moon grand tour to your collection. And quite quickly. It would only be thirty to fifty miles."

Noting the impatient looks she was getting, Laura hurried on. "Phobos orbits so close to Mars that it goes around the planet more quickly than the Martian rotation itself. Meaning, it orbits about twice a Martian day. If you were standing on the surface of Mars, Phobos would rise in the west, whip across the sky in, like, four hours, and then set in the east."

Rudy raised his hand. "Could you even see it from the surface? You just said it's pretty small."

"Yeah, but it's also low. I'd have to check the math, but I want to say that if you were on the equator watching it go over, it'd subtend around point two of a degree ... so maybe a third the size of the Moon, seen from Earth. Deimos trucks around relatively sedately by comparison."

"Does that matter?" Greg demanded.

"Well, it's cool," Dardenas said. "So what does that make Phobos's gravitational field, compared to the Earth's? Effectively zero?"

"About a thousandth," Laura said. "And, yes, it is so absolutely cool. We have to go."

"Go?" Greg shook his head. "I can't believe we're even discussing this."

Laura also shook her head in disbelief. "Seriously, you'd pass up *Phobos*?"

"I'd pass up *dying*."

"You'd be quite fine going back to Earth and saying, 'Yeah, we could have gone and landed on Phobos while we were there—landed on a freaking *Moon of Mars*—but we didn't have the balls, so we gave it a miss?' After coming all this way?"

Vivian opened her mouth to speak, but Rawlings beat her to it. "Uh, Laura? Maybe tone it down a bit?"

Laura took a deep breath. "I'm sorry. Let me rephrase."

"You don't need to, we get it." Rudy looked around them all, up and down and across at his crewmates. "Guys, come *on*. We're not going to Phobos. We're not going into orbit around anything and risking getting stuck there until we run out of food and oxygen and just … die. It's not going to happen."

"You're right," Laura said. "We're not going to die. Because we're going to be careful. Dave has just told us we have enough power to put ourselves in orbit around Mars and rendezvous with Phobos. And the rendezvous technically isn't a problem for a guy of his skills, plus Marco's skills and Josh's skills, and *backed up by the whole of NASA*. And we have enough supplies for the extra stay, if we're careful."

Vivian raised her hand, even though this was her own meeting. "Remember, if we decide to go ahead with this: we'll be resupplied. Along with the NERVA, NASA can send us a whole Cargo Carrier of extra goodies."

"Which will arrive a couple of months after we do, but that's fine," Dave said.

"A couple of months." Greg Heinz rolled his eyes.

Laura glared at him. "This is not hard. The NERVA and supplies are just backup, because NASA loves multiple redundancy. Even without it, we can get home with the rocket power we still have. And we'll be fine with the food and oxygen we have as well. None of this is a problem. It's going to be okay. This is a no-brainer."

"You mean, it makes sense to someone with no brain?" Heinz shot back.

"Hey, easy," Vivian interjected. "Let's keep this civil, okay? Just to make a change."

Laura was uncowed. "You remember how awesome it was to be so close to Venus for a couple hours? We can be that close to Mars for *months*."

"Sure," said Greg. "And maybe forever."

Rawlings raised a hand next. "If the Soviets really are aiming to go to a Martian moon, we should get to one first, if we can. And it turns out that we *can*. I say we do it."

Heinz looked frustrated. "Why does space exploration always have to be such a goddamned pissing contest?"

"Because it's a race," Horn said patiently.

"Because it's nationalistic … horn-trumpeting."

Rawlings shrugged. "Okay, yeah. It is. But, so what? Competition is good, it's healthy—"

"Not if it kills us all," Greg said.

Rawlings eyed him but kept going. "As I was saying, competition gets us all to be our best selves, to solve problems, push the envelope. And it frees up money in Congress. You've got to face it: nobody in the House of Representatives gives a damn about the march of science. What they *do* care about is national prestige and beating the Russkies. Okay, fine: they get what they want, you eggheads get what you want, and we all get to pull off something really impressive."

Vivian nodded. The thought had crossed her mind as well. The longer the Space Race kept going, the closer the Soviets stayed to the Americans' achievement level and vice versa, the longer Congress would keep paying the bills to keep NASA afloat.

She cleared her throat. "Any of you remember that feeling of colossal anticlimax we all felt after Venus? That feeling of 'Is that all we get?' We won't be feeling that if we go into orbit around Mars, visit one of its moons, and bring back samples. I'm just saying. Mostly I want to hear you talk, but give some thought to how we'll feel after we shoot past Mars at however-many miles per hour, knowing that we could have stayed a while." She gestured. "Okay. Back over to the rest of you."

"Shooting *past* Mars is what we signed up for in the first place," Rudy pointed out.

"Yes, it is. But now we can have *more*."

213

Laura raised her hand. "Hi. The Mars scientist is still right here. And the *more* we can get is colossal. If we're in orbit around Mars for a hundred and twenty-five days, long enough to pick up the NERVA and the extra supplies, we'll get to survey its entire equatorial surface, again and again, in all kinds of lighting and Martian weather conditions. That'll be incredibly valuable information for the future, when NASA is preparing to land humans on the surface for real."

"Sure," said Greg. "And that kind of surveying can be done by an unmanned satellite just as easily and less dangerously. Put it into a higher inclination orbit and you get to see even more of the globe, after enough passes. That's the right way to do it."

"After years of delay." Laura eyed him balefully. "Let me check I've got this right: you don't want us to orbit Mars because you didn't get to orbit Venus?"

He stared at her. "It's a little more complicated than that, Laura." "Is it?"

"We're scientists," Laura protested. "You're a planetary scientist yourself, for God's sake. It's Mars. How can you *not* want to do it?"

"Because it's a whole new level of risk that, with all due respect, I'm not sure that NASA down there or our folks here have had time to accurately assess. People spent months, years even, planning this mission in its current form. The flyby idea has been in the works for twenty years or so, right? And we're now planning to throw that out the window and do something completely different, based on a few days of analysis?"

Horn raised his hand. "If I may? First of all, NASA has been studying missions to Mars for a *long* time. They've been producing whole books of tables on how to do interplanetary missions since the early 1960s—no exaggeration. We've already put unmanned probes into orbit around Mars and other planets. This is a well-understood problem. But even so: if we do decide to go this route, we'll be putting in a ton more analysis to make sure we have all the burn parameters right, and we'll be as rigorous with the measurements and calculations as any mortal humans could possibly be. We have buildings full of computers at Langley, and Cray supercomputers at Ames, should we need that amount of computing power … which we don't, but if we did, we have it. I guarantee we will absolutely have these burn parameters and orbital solutions figured out to five nines or better by the end of next week, and refining it even more after that."

Rawlings grunted. "I'll just remind you that we canceled two planned course corrections on the way to Venus because we didn't need them, and looped around the planet on exactly the curve we predicted, in the groove all the way."

"What about the unknowns?" Rudy looked at the pilots in turn. "You're telling me there are no unknowns?"

"Of course not," Rawlings said. "Mars has mascons, mass concentrations, just like the Moon does, connected with the impact basins. Tharsis, in particular. Plus, the gravitational field around Phobos will be … small, very small—not scary, but also very uneven. We'll need to take care. But these are things we can deal with.

"We have confidence in the engines. Lots of confidence, plus the possibility of a new engine coming to join us. Will the NERVA and the Cargo Carrier end up in the right orbit? Probably, but not guaranteed. But we'll be taking no undue risks to acquire them, and they're not critical to our survival."

Horn drifted backward, spread out his arms. "I know this is a lot to take in. And we'll need to work hard, and for longer. But if we agree to do it, we *can* do it, with a high probability of success."

Laura looked around them all. "These guys have gotten us this far. I'm betting they can get us to Mars orbit and then to Phobos."

Greg gave her a jaundiced look. "You say that because you want to believe it."

"No, I say that because all the evidence suggests it's true."

It was Amy's turn to raise her hand. "Look, people, we're in the second year of the mission and we're already fried. You're fried. I'm fried. Already several of us are not thinking straight. Regardless of whatever particular perils Mars holds—and there are a ton of those: the orbital insertion, the spacewalks, even the goddamn NERVA drive we'll have to hitch onto ourselves and carry with us, how do you think that gets bolted on? By us. Just attaching the NERVA alone will take *days* of spacewalks."

They waited. Eventually Vivian prompted: "But regardless of all that?"

"Right. See? Case in point. I just lost my train of thought. That's me not thinking straight, right there. I was going to say: regardless of all that, we're talking about adding *months* to the mission. The clock will be at two and a half fricking *years* by the time we get home. Something like this time next year? So, another full year in space, from right now. Are we all ready for that? I'm not so sure.

"So: I'd vote to skip it. Stick to the plan, take the slingshot, head for home. Guys, this mission is still an immense achievement just as it is. We already made history. We're just piling up the risks, and I'm not interested in that. Also?" She scanned the compartment. "I'm the one responsible for everyone's health on this goddamn ship, and I cannot guarantee this is in the interests of everyone's mental health. We're eight people in a tin can hundreds of millions of miles from Earth, and every one of us is hanging out on the hairy edge of weirdness. No offense."

Laura shook her head. "Damn. I happen to think that actually visiting the Martian system rather than just flying by it would be *excellent* for our mental health. I still absolutely vote that we do it."

"And I vote we don't," Rudy said.

"Except that this isn't a democracy," Horn said, and then stopped when Vivian shot him a glance. *Damn it, Dave had to go say the quiet part out loud.*

"Because ultimately *she'll* make the decision." Greg nodded. "Got it."

Vivian didn't love the tone of that *she*, but chose not to rise to the bait. "That's correct. As mission commander, the decision will be mine, and NASA's. My responsibility, and I'll be the one held accountable for it."

"And there you have it," Rudy said. "What we think doesn't ultimately matter anyway."

"Of course it does," Vivian said patiently. "I'm asking for opinions. Right now. That's why we're having this conversation."

"Or maybe it's to give us the illusion that we were involved in the decision."

"Rudy." Laura reached out and put her hand on his arm. "Not a helpful comment."

Rudy just shrugged. "Sue me."

Vivian pushed herself forward, allowed herself to float across the middle of the forward compartment, meeting each of their eyes in turn. "Okay, listen up. Yes, Dave's right. I'll make the decision, and the ultimate responsibility will be mine. But before I make that decision, I absolutely want to hear all viewpoints, and I haven't heard everyone's, yet.

"So, okay, straw poll, non-binding, just among ourselves so we know where everyone stands. I'll go around the room based on where people are located right now, starting at the forward end. So. Josh?"

"I vote Aye." He grinned. "For once I won't be the guy who just gets to orbit or fly past things and never land on 'em."

"Greg?"

"Nay. As must be obvious right now."

"Marco?"

"Sure. Aye. Why not?"

"Why not?" Rudy Frank raised his eyes to heaven. "God protect us from gung-ho astronauts."

Marco frowned. "In case you haven't noticed, man, it's us protecting you. You science types would already be dead six times over if we weren't here."

"Break," Vivian said. "Cut it out. So, Rudy, you're a Nay? For the record?"

Rudy looked around them all, meeting their eyes where he could. "Well, since it looks like no one else wants to say this, I guess I will. I'm ready to go home to my family. Let's finish what we set out to do and then go back and live the rest of our lives. This new ... thing? This is what the engineers call requirements creep, right? Always trying to take that one step too far? You bet your ass I vote Nay."

"Okay, thanks. Dave?"

"I can sure as hell argue." Laura's chin was out. "Rudy has gotten years of great solar data. He's just fine. He's already gotten what he needs from this trip. The rest of us, me and—yes—Greg, though he's not seeing it right now? We need Mars. And by 'we,' I mean the entire planetary science community."

Greg didn't respond. He seemed to be thinking.

Dave Horn leaned into the silence. "If I may, again? I didn't get to walk on the Moon, and never really cared about that ... but Phobos? And getting to orbit Mars for the first time? Plus, cool maneuvers no one has done before. I'm in."

"Amy?"

Amy Benson was already shaking her head. "No. In terms of crew health and safety, I can't in good conscience sign off on this right now. Sorry."

Rudy pointed at her triumphantly, turned to Vivian. "That kills the idea, right? Shouldn't the medic get the final say?"

Amy raised her hands. "No, no—hold on. I'm not pulling any kind of rank here. Vivian told us this discussion was off the record, right? Straw poll. All I'm doing is expressing my personal opinion. Would I like to stare at Mars up close and personal for good long time, and maybe even walk on Phobos? I … guess so? But I'm nervous about it, sure I am. It worries the shit out of me, though, because, and I mean this in the most loving way possible: we're all a bit flakey already."

"To the point of being crispy," Rudy said.

"If we go to Phobos, we all get to walk on Phobos, unless we're prevented by some technical issue," Vivian said, and looked at Laura sardonically. "Aaand, Laura, for the record?"

"Hey, guess what, I'm a Yes vote."

"And you?" Horn said to Vivian.

She might as well say it out loud. "A tentative Aye, in that we should go ahead and give this further thought."

"Ha." Rudy nodded and looked around at the others.

"That doesn't mean the decision is made," Vivian added. "We still have a lot of thinking and talking left to do."

"I will just point out," Amy said carefully, "that all the career astronauts plus the Mars chick are in favor, and the rest of us aren't. You astronauts all come from test pilot backgrounds aside from Viv, who's still a hotshot military pilot. Right? So it's possible that you have a different perception of what 'acceptable risk' is."

"Sure," Vivian said. She could hardly deny it.

"But one still based on facts and logic," Rawlings added.

"Uh-huh," said Greg.

"Okay," Amy said. "While we're at it, let's just sanity-check another item on the laundry list of issues with this idea. The engines. The NERVA they're planning to send us." She looked at Horn, Rawlings, and Vivian. "Someone tell us a bit more about the technical feasibility. And a little more about just how insane it is to be attaching a nuclear engine to our spacecraft."

"I'll confess that I was extremely happy when that option was taken off the table," said Greg. "By our glorious leaders, who are sitting right here. And for very good reasons."

"Yes," said Horn. "That was our decision—then—because chemical power could do the original mission just fine. And the strong odds are that it still can, even under these new expanded mission parameters. I'm ninety-eight percent sure the Centaurs are enough, that they'll do the job of getting us into the orbit we need and getting us to Phobos, and then performing a trans-Earth injection burn to break us out of Martian orbit. But it's always good to have a backup plan. One gets you ten that we bolt on the NERVA and never need it. But we'd be stupid to turn it down."

Rudy shook his head. " 'Expanded mission parameters?'" That's quite the euphemism you've got there, Kemosabe."

Vivian said: "To be fair, the NERVA also has more thrust, giving us the option of getting back more quickly, and shaving some time off our return. Which would be nice, if we want to light that candle." She shuffled her feet, even though they weren't in contact with anything. "And, sure, I have my own list of doubts and concerns. I have my own long-standing issues with nuclear stuff that we don't need to get into here, and I don't love the idea of being attached to a rocket that's powered by enriched uranium, whether we fire it or not."

Horn raised his hand. "Everyone should note that I need to check the numbers on that. We'll be heavier with the NERVA, so ... well, leave it with me, but assume for now that we can make it work with just the Centaurs. Then again, if y'all really want to bolt the most advanced rocket motor in existence onto our caravan and then *not* use it, and take much longer on the return as a result, that's certainly an option."

"I'd sure prefer to not need to fire it," said Amy.

"Which will be tomorrow's issue," Vivian said. "They'll send it anyway. What we do with it is up to us." She looked around them all. "Maybe this is a good time to break. Dave and I need to get with Houston, do a full risk-reward analysis. We all need more information than we currently have." She glanced at Laura Simmons. "Even you."

"Roger that," Laura said, readily enough.

"Okay. Then if we're done here?" Rudy shoved off, headed down toward the hatch. "I think I need to get on the horn and tell my wife I might be late home for dinner."

"Not until the decision is made and approved, and we're cleared to discuss it," Vivian said. "Until then, we don't discuss it outside this vessel."

Instant uproar. "We can't even discuss this with our families?"

Amy gave her a warning look, and Vivian backtracked. Maybe that wasn't smart. Just because she herself didn't have a family member she'd need to discuss this with ... "Okay, sorry. Hold that thought for a while. Let me check with Houston and get back to you."

Rudy put his hands up to his temples. "Remind me why I ever signed up for this cruise?"

"For the love of science," Amy said drily.

"Oh yeah," he said. "That."

Horn drifted over to her. "Interesting how you argued against it when you were talking to me, and for it when we were broaching it with the scientists."

"I'm still thinking it through," she said.

"Don't make the decision just to piss them off," said Horn. "Make the right decision."

"Obviously."

"Sorry. I know you've got this."

Vivian shook her head in frustration. "I can sure see now why you didn't want to command this mission."

"Right? Being the boss *sucks*. I'll never understand why people want that kind of responsibility for other people's lives."

"Me neither." Vivian sighed. "Okay, let's take ten, and then I'll join you in CM-1 and we'll phone home."

He grinned. "You got it. See you there."

Laura tagged her. "Vivian? One last thing, thirty seconds, and it's kind of facetious."

Vivian wasn't sure she felt facetious right now, but there was probably no escaping it. "Fine. Hit me with it."

"Okay, so you haven't read Edgar Rice Burroughs but you know about him, right? In addition to the Tarzan stuff, he also wrote a series about John Carter of Mars. Now, you would get to be Vivian Carter of

Mars. Honestly, it's so perfect that we have to do it just for that. NASA Public Affairs will have a field day with it."

Vivian smiled as diplomatically as she knew how. "I'm sure they would."

Laura wasn't fooled. "Okay. I can see you hate it. But you might have to get used to it."

"I guess I've gotten used to worse …"

As Vivian unhooked the folding curtain to her sleeping compartment, Amy Benson floated through the hatchway from the forward compartment. "Hey, boss. You okay?"

"Hey, doc. Sure. Why wouldn't I be?"

"Well, this is kind of a big spanner in the works, and it's all on you."

"Sure is." Vivian nodded, kept going. "Good talk."

Amy side-eyed her, amused. "Tell me you don't want to be the first person to step onto the soil of a world beyond the Earth-Moon system."

"Jeez, you and Dave. Calling Phobos a *world* …"

"Even if it is a rubble pile, it's still a *moon of Mars*. And, yes, it has such a weedy little gravity that you'll have to work hard to actually step on it and walk on it. But either way, I think you want this."

"I don't know what I want any more." Vivian admitted. "I want to make a couple of calls first."

"Who to? Peter?"

"Uh …" That hadn't occurred to her. Sure, she'd be staying away from Earth even longer, now. "No, actually, I kind of want to talk to Terri Brock."

Amy nodded. "Right. First American woman on the Moon."

"And always a useful sanity-check. No offense, you're great, but …"

"I don't replace your other friends. And wouldn't want to." Benson considered. "And ideally you'd quite like to talk to Svetlana as well."

Vivian frowned. "Get out of my head, psych-lady."

Amy nodded, unfazed. "But that's not on the cards, given that Makarov is already on his way to Mars, and Soviets can't play any part in your decision-making."

"Affirmative. Plus no one even knows where Belyakova is right now. Why is all this always so complicated?"

Benson pulled herself up onto the exercise bike, began to strap herself in. "First American woman on the Moon. First Soviet woman on the Moon. Does it ever occur to you that it's really something that you have both those ladies in your personal Rolodex?"

"As it happens, I think about that a lot."

"I think that's kind of your answer, then."

"What?" Sorry, I don't get it."

"Well, that's obviously why you want to talk to those two in particular. And their legacy … you'd kind of be joining them on the pedestal of female achievement in space."

Exasperated, Vivian shook her head. "I'm not thinking about this the way you all seem to think I am. Honestly."

"Okay. But if you ever want to talk about it with your shrink, my rates are very reasonable. As you know."

"Got it. And thank you. But right now, I need to just stop talking and close my eyes for a moment."

Amy gestured upward, toward the forward compartment. "You know that out here the talking doesn't stop when you leave, right?"

"I'm counting on it." Vivian slid into her sleep quarters. "Happy trails."

Amy started pedaling. "Sweet dreams."

"Yeah," Vivian said. "That'll be the day."

CHAPTER 16

Phobos: Vivian Carter
April 22-May 25, 1984
Mission Elapsed Time: 293-326 days

APRIL 22 was Easter Sunday, and Vivian and Marco Dardenas had celebrated the holiday by taking an impromptu spacewalk outside Astarte to repair and reposition the micrometeorite shield. The work had left them exhausted and pouring with sweat, and Marco had gone to nap for an hour while Vivian took a long and luxurious shower, her first for months. With her hair wet and much of her body still damp under her jumpsuit she pulled herself into the wardroom for a very late and well-deserved lunch, to be greeted by Josh Rawlings. "Well, we're approved for the mission extension. No caveats."

Mission extension had to be about the most mundane possible way of putting it, but sure, Vivian could be a laconic steely-eyed missile man as well. "Roger that. Good to know."

Horn was next in, swinging himself through the hatch. He pulled out the food drawer and studied his yellow-tagged foil packages before glancing across at Vivian. "You okay?"

"Sure," she said. "I have a shower every Easter, whether I need one or not."

"That EVA looked like a bear."

"It definitely was."

"And you heard about Phobos? Approved."

"Yeah. Guess we're really doing it, huh?"

"Yep." He grinned. "And, not to be a downer, but they've launched the NERVA. On the plus side, it's attached to a giant Cargo Carrier full of food, more books and movies than we'll possibly get through on the cruise home, a bunch of replacement clothes, and the list of tools and engineering spares we wanted. And—not that I think this has occurred to anyone at Houston—but I'm seeing no reason why we can't keep the Cargo Carrier itself in the second radial port as additional playspace for the trip home."

Vivian raised her eyebrows. "Oh! Okay."

Greg poked his head round the door. "Did I hear right that we're approved for Mars? And Phobos?"

Rawlings gave him a thumbs-up. "All systems go."

"F.A.B.! I'll go spread the word." Greg's head retreated.

Vivian looked at the other two guys. "What does that mean?"

Dave Horn finished rehydrating his food and pulled himself over to sit at the table. "I have no idea. At least we're all on the same page."

Vivian nodded and stuffed more food into her face. Her voice rather muffled, she said, "Great. Wonder how long that'll last."

Despite their spirited exchange of views when the Mars orbit and Phobos rendezvous were first raised, it had taken the crew a surprisingly small amount of time to reach consensus.

Laura had caucused with the scientists, literally locking themselves in the Multiple Docking Adapter for several hours of discussion, skipping routine maintenance and exercise sessions to do so. Meanwhile, Vivian's three Command Module pilots and navigators, Rawlings, Horn, and Dardenas, had gone into a similar huddle by the command console, and later in CM-1, for a detailed discussion of the propulsion, maneuvering, and orbital mechanics issues involved.

Within forty-eight hours it had gone from a fractious controversy to a done deal. Both Greg's wife and Laura had managed to persuade him that a sojourn at Mars was not to be missed, and he'd regret it for the rest of his life if he passed it up. And, despite his original grumpiness about the idea, once Rudy had been clued in on the sheer volume of Martian science accessible from orbit and the scope for making major discoveries—and his chance to get coauthorship on dozens of academic papers—he'd quickly come around. With the passion of true converts, Greg and Rudy now spent literally all their downtime discussing their upcoming Mars observations with Laura. And once Amy Benson had seen the positive energy surging through the entire crew at the prospect of going into Mars orbit, her concerns about the crew's health had evaporated. She was now looking forward to Mars with the same excitement as everyone else.

And then, after all that, they'd needed to wait for the formal final go-ahead from NASA HQ and the White House. The hours had ticked away with agonizing slowness, and Vivian and Amy had begun quiet conversations about how they'd handle it if the approval didn't come through, and they needed to return to the original timeline. The sudden need for the micrometeorite shield EVA had come as a welcome distraction.

And now the word was in, and it was official. NASA Public Affairs was even on the verge of renaming the mission Apollo Mars Astarte.

Those long months ago, way back in November, Venus had looked poisonous and severe. Colored a sickly yellow-tinged white, it had appeared unhealthy and diseased. It had also looked *huge* to Vivian and her crew as they'd approached it. The mantle of toxic gases that shrouded it had generally blocked their view of the planet below and also made it feel *bigger*—bigger even than Earth, though in fact it was just slightly smaller.

By comparison, the approaching disk of Mars appeared neither huge nor noxious. If anything, the planet seemed fragile and welcoming. A delicate rose color, its ground features were subtle but very visible. It appeared to glow from within, the solar system's nightlight, although that was clearly an optical illusion.

Out here, close to the orbit of Mars, the whole sky felt different. From the Earth, the Sun's diameter subtended an angle of about half a degree, or thirty arcminutes. From near Venus, the Sun appeared half again as large—three quarters of a degree, forty-five arcminutes—and this greater size was very evident and felt threatening. But here in the Martian environs the Sun looked only point three of a degree across, twenty arcminutes, which felt much saner and more manageable. This calmer, more distant Sun allowed the stars and other heavenly bodies in the sky to appear brighter. To Vivian, at least, it felt like a much more "balanced" view of the cosmos.

Gods, now that she could see Mars clearly with her own eyes, Vivian wanted to go down there. To actually land on the Red Planet. She wanted that, a lot.

But she also knew that wouldn't be feasible for years, maybe a decade or more, so she put it out of her mind. Phobos was the target, and glory enough in itself. Three thousand seven hundred miles above the surface of Mars: that would have to do.

As they passed through Mars's shadow just before initiating the orbital injection burn, it was the first time in two years that Astarte had not been in direct sunlight. The effect was immediate, with loud ticks giving way to alarming cracking sounds.

At the Astarte command console Rawlings said calmly, "Amy, by me, if you would."

She arrowed across the space to join him at the console, arresting her forward motion using the seat back and Josh's shoulder.

"We're fine so far," Rawlings added. "Amy, watch temperatures and pressures. I'll watch stresses and strains." She nodded, her gaze flitting back and forth as she scanned the gauges and readouts almost as adeptly as Josh himself.

Another loud crack from the hull. "Still fine," Amy said, almost conversationally.

For this maneuver Horn was in CM-1, with Dardenas in CM-2. Despite the momentous nature of what they were about to attempt, the orbital injection burn itself was straightforward and required little from the pilots in real time.

This time, Vivian would leave them to it. That allowed her to be with the rest of her crew during a burn for a change, and to watch the view through the big window in Astarte's forward compartment. No reason why the scientists should get to hog all the sightseeing.

She did do a sanity check at T minus two minutes, though, to ensure that her crew were all strapped in before the burn began.

The burn took … a while. It seemed to go on forever, and the thrust was greater than Vivian had been anticipating.

Then it cut off, and she was weightless again. No one said anything. She blinked, and waited.

"Okay," Horn said at last, his voice coming in loud and clear through the loudspeaker. "My board is showing all green and all nines. Stable orbit. Ladies and gentlemen, Apollo Astarte is in orbit around the planet Mars."

Amy blew out a deep breath. "Well, that was satisfyingly anticlimactic."

"Makes a change," said Greg. "Hey, check out Laura."

Laura Simmons was staring, rapt, at the surface of the Red Planet beneath them, mouth open, almost unblinking, hands up to her chin as if praying.

"I think 'anticlimactic' might be the wrong word," Rudy said. "Someone fetch Laura a towel."

"Hey, give her a break," Vivian said. "It is pretty spectacular."

Perhaps not as spectacular as it might have been for the brief minutes of flyby. Their current altitude of three thousand seven hundred miles was much further away than the couple hundred miles of their closest approach on their previous mission profile.

But still, but still … at this height the disk of Mars filled forty-five degrees of arc. Which still made it damned big, and red, and impressive, and nothing at all like the Earth.

Mars was *beautiful*.

"Wow," said Vivian, inadequately.

Their current orbit was mildly eccentric. Horn would circularize it later, once he took a few more measurements. He, Vivian, and the other two CMPs had discussed this strategy at great length. By now, Vivian would have been confident in their ability to wing it; between Dave Horn's meticulous care and the massive computing power of his sidekick, the Cray-1 at NASA Ames, she'd have been fine with them attempting a single burn to put them into a circular, Phobos-height orbit. Horn disagreed, insisting on this initial orbital burn followed by a much more exacting circularization and Phobos-rendezvous burn once they'd accumulated the numbers from yet another bunch of star sightings, to complement and fine-tune the Deep Space Network's angle and range measurements. And if that was how Dave wanted to do it, that was how they'd do it. Either way, they'd still be landing on Phobos within the week.

Even after several weeks of preparation, *landing on Phobos* was a phrase that Vivian hadn't quite gotten used to.

In the forward compartment, the four scientists were just wrapping up a video broadcast to send back to Earth. They were doing a great job of it, and the additional exposure would help to cement their reputations for the rest of their careers. Vivian was happy for them—they were certainly earning it—and very content to get a break from being on the spot herself, to be viewed by the likely hundreds of millions of people on Earth who would see at least part of that footage. Vivian had done quite enough of that over the years.

"I listened in for the first part," Rawlings said. "Enthusiastic, confident, with all the Right Stuff." He grinned. "From the footage, you'd never guess how hard three quarters of them originally argued against doing this."

"That's how it should be," Vivian said. "Have our arguments in private. Agree on what we're doing. Then all link arms and walk forward together."

"They're a good team. I know they're pains in the ass sometimes, but I do think you're a bit too hard on them sometimes."

"I'm sure you're right," Vivian said, adding privately: *Jeez, enough people-talk.*

Anyway. Phobos. Vivian picked up the flimsies and pulled out a pencil. "Okay, so let's go over the timeline again, just once more ..."

"Butterscotch planet," Rudy said. "Caramel, maybe."

Laura turned a beatific smile on him. "Or maybe it's its own thing. Peachy-pink and beautiful."

Vivian exchanged glances with Josh Rawlings. Maybe scientists saw color differently.

And yet, it *was* beautiful.

To Vivian's eye, it was just a reddish-pink. Sometimes more red, and at others a lighter shade. If pushed, occasionally it looked ... vermillion?

But, there would be plenty of time for them to Mars-watch. Right now, she needed to focus on Phobos.

Vivian had never been close to a celestial body that looked this irregular. It very definitely resembled a potato, and not a very healthy-looking one at that, and she said so.

"Honestly, even as potatoes go, that's darned ugly," Amy said. "Not sure I'd serve it to my kids."

Docking with Phobos was much more dramatic, even nerve-wracking, than decelerating into Mars orbit insertion. Vivian, Dave, and Amy were strapped into CM-1 to watch the giant boulder approaching. Marco and Rudy were in CM-2 as backup, and were also supplying independent distance estimations, which the CM-1 crew didn't have time for. Josh was in his standard spot monitoring the Astarte systems, while Greg was manning the science station and Laura sat in Astarte by the big window, mainly operating the camera and exclaiming repeatedly at the sheer beauty of her Phobos potato. Living her dream. Vivian recognized the symptoms, and certainly understood Laura's enthusiasm, but still. "Laura, keep it down, okay? Only chime in in an emergency."

"Got it," Laura said immediately. "Sorry."

Concentration was essential, right now. Despite being a "small" moon, Phobos looked enormous from the angle they were coming in at. And, this wasn't a case where they could preprogram the burn and monitor it. Too complicated for that. This would be a realtime maneuver, and with no possible help from Houston, given the time delay.

Her whole crew was suited up, with their full spacesuits plus either PLSS backpacks or umbilicals for oxygen. This was the first and only time they'd done this, but then again, this was the only time Apollo Astarte would be coming into direct contact with something massive. They were docking with a *moon*, or maybe it was just a captured asteroid, but either way it was one gigantic hunk of rock. If Horn somehow had a brain aneurysm at exactly the wrong time and Astarte smacked into that moon and lost pressurization, today might be a really short day. For an encounter this risky, they were taking every precaution.

"Five hundred feet," Marco said, from CSM-2. "Four-fifty."

"I confirm," Amy said.

Phobos filled their windows now, and was still growing. Thank God for radar, because Vivian found it impossible to estimate range herself; she had not memorized every detail of Phobos's surface the way she had for the Moon and had no instinctive feel for its scale. If she hadn't had the range-rate estimates from Marco and Amy in her ears, she would have had no clue whether the giant rock was fifty feet away or two miles.

The Martian moon must surely be exerting a gravitational pull on the Astarte, and Horn must be aware of that, but it wasn't evident to the rest of them.

But in the end, they grazed up against Phobos, as light as a kiss.

Oh. My. God, Vivian thought, and at that same moment she heard a quickly-muted squeal over the loop that could only have been Laura.

"Everyone hang tight," Horn said, his terseness giving away his tension. "We're not stable yet."

Since the Apollo Astarte had no landing gear, their goal was to bring it right up to Phobos until it was just lying on its surface, with the Apollo Telescope Mount and all its scientific instrumentation facing upward, the window also facing upward, and its main solar panels lying parallel to the surface of Phobos. They had—infinitely slowly and carefully—transferred CSM-2 to the radial docking station ninety degrees around Astarte into the same plane, so that neither of the Command and Service Modules would make contact with the ground. For the EVAs, they would exit out of the airlock module, which would put them twelve feet above the surface.

That also meant Dave Horn had to complete this maneuver keeping the attitude of Astarte rock steady.

They felt, rather than heard, Astarte's skin scrape against Phobos's surface, and then a counter-pulse from the attitude jets, light as a feather.

"Okay," Horn said, and from the other CSM Dardenas confirmed it. "Okay, we're good. We're good."

"Seeing no variances," Amy said. "Nothing."

They'd stopped moving. The rocky terrain right outside their window was staying put, with the giant ball of Mars above them. But still, Vivian wanted confirmation. "Uh. Dave?"

"We're here," he said. "Dead stop. We're down."

"Oh," Vivian said. "Okay. Good."

Amy shook her head. "That's all you've got? Future generations are going to mock you relentlessly."

"As if," Dave said. "We'll accidentally erase the tape."

Vivian grinned. It was hard to believe. Just like that, Apollo Mars Astarte had "landed" on Phobos.

Just resting there on the surface, in reflected Mars-light. Phobos gravity was a thousand times weaker than the Earth's, but Astarte massed around a hundred eighty tons, give or take. Now that they were down and "docked," Astarte wasn't going anywhere until they fired up the engines again for the launch burn, or whatever they were going to call it, that would scooch them off the surface and back into Martian orbit.

They'd walk on the surface of Phobos, and months before the Soviets would arrive on Deimos.

Another giant leap for mankind. And, for Vivian and her crew.

Vivian pushed-to-talk. "Houston, Apollo Astarte has docked at Phobos Base." She looked at Horn. "That sounded even niftier than I was expecting. Are we stable? Soon as you're confident we're not going anywhere, we need to get out there and take an emergency sample, in case there's some reason we can't stay. You know the drill, flags and footprints and all that."

We, in this case, meant Vivian and Laura Simmons. Mars was, after all, Laura's gig and her passion. But Vivian would positively, definitely be the first one to set foot on this new world.

Another celestial body, another round of congratulatory messages and mandatory publicity events. Another "phone call" from the President, although given the time lag, Reagan sent a recorded message and Vivian and the others made a recording in response. This at least gave them the opportunity to rehearse it, a luxury they valued given how tired they all were.

Even though Laura was literally bouncing off the walls, Houston mandated a sleep period before their first Phobos EVA. Vivian completely agreed. They hardly needed to rush: the Apollo Astarte would be staying right here for the next three months, waiting for the NERVA and the optimal window for return to Earth. No reason at all why they had to rush this.

They were no longer in microgravity, after all. Milligravity? Vivian wasn't sure that was a word, but now they were down and moving around the inside of Astarte, the gravitational field of Phobos was at least noticeable. They'd discussed it at length, on the inbound journey.

"The gravity of Phobos is like a thousandth of the Earth's gravity," Laura had said. "If you weigh a hundred fifty pounds on Earth, you'll weigh two ounces on Phobos."

Vivian frowned. "For the record, I don't weigh a hundred and fifty pounds."

"Just an example. It's a round figure, close to the mean mass of everyone on board."

Greg was scribbling on his yellow pad. "So ... since I can easily jump two feet in the air when I'm on Earth, I could jump over half a mile straight up, on Phobos? I totally want to do that."

"You might get bored," Amy said, playing with the slide rule she'd recently learned how to use. "Your round trip would take something like ... twenty-six minutes?"

"Correct," Greg said. "Gosh. That really *would* be a giant leap for mankind."

"Hmm. Isn't that dangerous? What's the escape velocity of Phobos?"

"About twenty-five miles an hour," Laura said. "Not even hunky Greg is going to break free of Phobos's gravity well, even with a running start."

"I can sure as hell pitch a softball off it though," he said.

"In one of these spacesuits?" She grinned. "I'd like to see you try."

Phobos isn't a playground, the serious part of Vivian wanted to say. But what she said instead was, "Hell, I wouldn't mind throwing a rock at Mars from the surface of Phobos, and knowing it'll actually get there one day."

"Maybe." Horn looked dubious. "Even if it did, it would take a while."

"Everything's going to take a while on Phobos," Rudy said. "Even learning how to walk on something this light is going to be tough. We need to be prepared for that."

"Oh, I'm prepared." Laura grinned.

Vivian had nodded, thinking *Okay, it's going to work*. Her crew of science nerds had come all the way around and were now seriously intrigued by the weirdness and challenges of Phobos.

Getting geared up for that first step, with her Hasselblad still camera mounted on her chest, and a small Westinghouse TV camera beside it, felt just like old times. But opening the airlock door and seeing the reddish surface of Phobos lying there twelve feet below her, was like no experience Vivian had ever had before.

Moments later, she'd released her hold on the sides of the hatch-way and was allowing herself to drift down, ever so gently, onto the rubble-strewn surface.

"Touchdown," she said. "I'm ... on Phobos."

The sheer change of scale was dramatic. For the past two years, Vivian had been inside Astarte, aside from her infrequent EVAs to recover film or do minor repairs. Now, her ship was very definitely above her, and there was *land* to either side, instead of the abyss of space. She moved out from underneath it cautiously, but with determination.

As she came out of its shadow into full sunlight, her boots left the surface, putting her in a leisurely arc. "Whoa," she said.

"What?" Laura's voice from above her, still in the airlock.

Vivian was beginning to drift down again now. "Oh, nothing. Just that low gravity is really *low*."

"Well, yeah. Okay for me to come out?"

"Sure. Come and give it a try. You're the expert."

"Ha." Laura landed on the ground beside Vivian, and immediately bounced up and away.

"Bye," Vivian said ironically.

After ten minutes, including several agonizingly slow tumbles apiece, they realized that *walking*, as such, wasn't going to work. They could jump, being extremely careful about how they applied that kick-off force, and cover a lot of ground but in a very uncontrolled way, or they could locomote with an extremely slow but stable shuffle. Any attempt at a normal stride, really any movement with any upward moment whatsoever, and they'd lose control. They were going to need help with this.

"Zip guns," Vivian said.

"Yeah."

Half an hour later, they'd pressurized up a couple of zip guns, the type they used in zero G to propel themselves around. Those zip guns helped a lot in translating them where they wanted to go and keeping them upright and suitably orientated as they went there.

Even aside from the gravity, moving around on Phobos was weird. The moon was small, very small, and from even a casual glance in any direction was clearly not a sphere. Its curvature was immediately obvious, and very variable, and its "horizon" was very close.

That said, the surface area of the entire rock was around six hundred square miles, half the size of Rhode Island and a third of the size of the Grand Canyon, and only double the size of New York City. So, still plenty big enough for some intense exploring.

Phobos was knobbly, cratered, distorted in a very disorienting way, and deeply grooved. Off to their left was one such groove, which looked a couple hundred feet wide and stretched away as far as the eye could see—which of course wasn't far. From Laura's additional briefings, Vivian knew that those grooves could be up to a hundred feet deep and many miles long. But in Phobos's milligravity they didn't need to be afraid of those grooves: they could jump across them with ease, and even if they were to jump into the deepest groove they could find, they'd land softly and be able to hop right out again with very little difficulty.

And, in addition: Phobos was just the *wrong color*. After spending many months of cumulative time on the lunar surface over the past few years, Vivian was extremely familiar with the greys and blacks and occasional apparent browns of its palette. But nowhere on the Moon was anything like Phobos. The surface of Phobos was very much *not* the surface of the Moon; it was darker in color overall, but with reddish and bluish tinges to the soil in various areas. And its soil was larger-grained, quite different from the lunar regolith.

"We've got to see it all," Laura said, with that oddly combined tone of dreamy urgency that she'd been adopting ever since the start of the EVA. "Vivian, we need to go around the whole thing, sample everything, everywhere. Craters, the grooves and ridges, the whole deal. We can sample the entire moon in just a few days. We have to. You know that, right?"

She sounded like an anxious child, almost pleading. A kid in a candy store. But she hardly needed to beg. "Absolutely," Vivian said. "We absolutely have to do that."

Laura paused. "Good!"

"You really thought I'd say no?"

The Moon's rilles had been formed by ancient volcanic action. The grooves and streaks on Phobos were something of a mystery. Perhaps they'd been created by meteoroids scraping across the surface of the tiny moon, either as side effects from impacts on Mars, or prior to such impacts; others may have been due to the "splashing" of debris due to cratering on Phobos's surface. Maybe they were even caused by stresses due to tidal interactions. Resolving that issue was one of the reasons Laura wanted to perform extensive sampling.

And Vivian agreed. If her LGS-1 lunar circumnavigation mission had been able to do such a bang-up job on the Moon, with the limited sampling of the whole sphere that they'd been able to do, the results of doing a much more thorough job exploring and sampling Phobos might be even more spectacular.

"Pity we didn't bring a core drill," she said.

Laura paused. "Crap. Yeah. That would have been great. Could we rig one up?"

"Um," Vivian said. "Well. We do have a drill. Several drills, in fact. But they aren't core drills. And—"

"Anything that could get us deeper below the surface." Laura scuffed at the surface. "It doesn't look as tightly packed as the lunar surface."

"No, it certainly does not."

"Maybe we could even cut into it in slices?"

"Hey, ladies? Leave that with me for a bit," came Marco Dardenas's voice, over the radio. "We've got a lathe in here, we have tubing of various diameters, and some of it should hold a cutting edge ... let me hit the machine shop and see what I can come up with."

"Bless you," said Laura. "My hero."

Mars was directly above them at all times, and so always visible. Phobos was tidally locked to Mars, and so it would remain overhead for the entire duration of their stay on the moon's surface. So, while they were exploring Phobos they'd also be continuously studying Mars. Even now, Rudy and Greg were taking measurements of the Red Planet in their sky.

Even while walking on Phobos, it was very difficult not to be distracted by Mars.

It did not look welcoming, not exactly. It still looked barren, and cratered, and sterile. But it did not look anywhere near as poisonous and repellant as Venus. Mars would not be hell. It would merely be a challenge.

But, a good challenge. A great challenge. Even in these first few days in Martian orbit, they had clearly seen ancient valleys that must surely have been carved out by rivers, back in Mars's long-ago past. They could see floodplains and deltas. If Mars did not have canals, it at least showed what seemed like excellent evidence for flowing water ... once upon a time. Surely, the climate of Mars had once been very different.

As for what remained, it was still glorious. Every Martian cycle, Vivian would feast her eyes on Tharsis Montes, a very recognizable trio of volcanoes arranged neatly in a line, and the towering heights of Olympus Mons. And, that giant dark crack in the surface of Mars, the rift valley of Valles Marineris … Superficially, and from this altitude, Marineris resembled Arizona's Grand Canyon, except that it was much, much larger.

Mars was clearly a planet with a weather system, and terrain that looked very different from rotation to rotation. No canals— Schiaparelli and Lowell had been on the wrong track there—but from high above the surface, it was already clear that the clouds and even the exact extent of the polar ice caps changed over timescales of days.

The speed of Phobos's orbit around it was very evident. The sunlight levels and direction were changing rapidly even in the short time the two of them had been out on its surface so far. The length of a Phobos "day" was seven hours and thirty-two minutes, and this also meant that the temperature of the surface around them would gyrate rapidly, from minus four Celsius in full sunlight to minus a hundred and twelve degrees in local night.

"We're going to need a detailed plan for this," Vivian said. "This illumination phasing is going to be a pain in our asses."

They'd known ahead of time that this would be the case, but now Vivian was actually out and experiencing it … it was even worse than she had expected. But she wouldn't let it hold them back.

Now, she looked up at Astarte, at its outer hull pitted and scarred from micrometeorite impacts, the stains on its thermal fabric. "This old girl has a bunch of miles on her," she said. "It's a shame."

"Oh, she has a few million more left in her," Horn said through her headset.

"Damned well hope so," someone said, so softly in her ears that Vivian couldn't tell whether it was Greg or Rudy.

"Look on the bright side," Laura said. "No way we can get lost. Not with Mars up there like a giant … peachy night-light."

"Soon as you go over the local horizon, you'll lose radio contact," Rawlings warned.

"No big deal," said Laura.

"You hope."

"In future we'll do this in teams of three," Vivian said. "Three on surface, one monitoring the radio from Astarte, the other four on board taking downtime or classifying the samples, or …" she paused. Strictly speaking, this wasn't her circus. "Or, if Laura has a better plan, we'll do it her way."

In the weeks leading up to their arrival, the crew and the Houston backroom had identified a network of "representative regions of scientific interest," covering the surface of Phobos. Their hope was to spend several weeks here, and pace themselves in the meticulous job of sample-taking, but if this proved to be impossible for any reason, they had a shortlist of top priority sites that they needed to hit. These were: the floor of Stickney Crater, its side wall and far rim, the overturn area of the crater and the grooves, the area where the red and white soil areas overlapped with those grooves; a "young" fresh crater; and samples of the deep groove structure.

By the end of the second day, Vivian, Laura, and Greg had completed this initial assignment. After that, it was time for the rest of the crew to take their turns on the surface of this strange new world.

Stickney Crater was far and away the largest crater on the surface of Phobos. Six miles in diameter, it would have been a minor feature on the Earth's Moon. Here, Stickney felt gigantic. Most of the other craters on Phobos were likely caused by secondary impacts following the carving out of Stickney by whatever impactor had formed it. Obtaining sufficient samples to determine the age of Stickney Crater was one of their principal science goals.

Despite its superficial resemblance to a lunar crater—circular, deep, and with a rim—Stickney was very different. Its crater floor was smoother, and its interior walls showed obvious evidence for the avalanching of rocky material down its inner slopes—although in the tiny gravity of Phobos, that landslide would have been a really slow-rolling event. The rock in the southwest of the crater had a distinct bluish tinge, and Laura ensured early in the EVA that she had a fine sample of it.

Six miles across, yet they could bound across it in mere minutes, leaping in long, high arcs. The trick was achieving enough traction when they landed to slow their ridiculous momentum. Even with the zip guns to help stabilize their centers of gravity, navigating across the surface of Phobos required completely different skills from the kangaroo-hop or lope that astronauts invariably adopted in the one-sixth lunar gravity. On his first excursion, Greg Heinz had gotten himself into an end-over-end roll, involving several graceless bounces off the Phobos surface before he managed to get his feet back under him and eventually skated to a halt. The main difficulty of Phobos was just the length of time it took to change direction, and to get errors back under control. Despite the high arcs and fast covering of the ground, the very scantness of its gravity made it very hard to maneuver accurately to a designated spot and then stay there.

By the end of their first shift on the Phobos surface, Vivian and Laura had gotten their travel techniques down. Other crew members spent less time out on the surface and so took longer to get their "Phobos legs," but by the end of the first week, Phobos had turned into their playground, providing a tension release that they badly needed, along with a welcome injection of humor, after the pent-up months of traveling. They were all very glad to be here.

"Congratulations, Vivian Carter. Great achievements, both your fly-by of the planet Venus and your arrival now on Phobos, the second moon of Mars."

Vivian grinned at the face of Nikolai Makarov on her TV screen. "Why, thanks, comrade. That means a great deal to me, coming from you."

His eyes twinkled. "Of course, you will see us soon on the first moon, which we shall claim for the Soviet Union."

"The United States didn't claim this rock I'm on right now," Vivian pointed out. "We didn't even put a flag on it. It still belongs to all of us. Or to no one, depending on how you look at it."

"Ah, yes. Well." He chuckled. "You know as well as I that this is all just rhetoric. The words my country likes to use."

Words have consequences, Vivian thought. *Sometimes, enormous consequences.* It was always "rhetoric" when it was your own side, and "reckless provocation" when similar words were spoken by your enemy. But now was hardly the time for a political debate.

"Anyway: congratulations to you, as well, Nikolai Ilyich. On being the captain of the first *Soviet* interplanetary mission." Two could play at this game. It was, after all, just rhetoric, right? "And I look forward to welcoming you to Mars orbit."

"Yes, indeed." He almost saluted.

The irony that her first conversation with a reasonable time lag for many months was with a Soviet cosmonaut was not lost on her. After all these months of minutes-long delays, it felt like Makarov and his TMK-Mars ship were right next door.

Of course, soon they would be.

"I honestly never expected to see you back in space again," she said. "As far as we knew, you'd been promoted out of the active cosmonaut lineup."

"For a while, it seemed that I was." Makarov shrugged. "But my boy Piotr is in the army now. Lidia is at university, and Olga has grown tired of me hanging around the house and walking out at night to stare up into the sky. And we have a shortage of trained cosmonauts for all that we must do; this you know, of course. We agreed that this is the best solution for everyone."

"It is a shame that we have different destinations," she said soberly. "So near and yet so far, eh?"

Nikolai gave her what might have been a meaningful look and flipped switches. Raised his index finger, with an obvious message: *Wait a moment.*

Vivian waited. He frowned at his instrument panel, then nodded, apparently satisfied, and turned back to the camera.

"Vivian, perhaps you understand, this is now a personal call. Our transmitters are on tight beam facing forward, toward Mars, and yours in the opposite direction are currently at least a hundred and twenty degrees from including the Earth in your beam. I give you my word that we are not being overheard by the Kremlin, or by any on Earth."

Vivian's ears pricked up. "So, you are no longer talking to the walls, my friend?"

"No. I am talking only to you, and you alone."

"Your crew can't hear you?"

"They cannot. Yours?"

"No, I'm sealed in." Vivian glanced up at the hatch and across her comms boards, to be sure. "I confirm: no one else on Astarte is listening in. I'm the only one on this loop. And I have no recording devices in operation, I promise you."

"And nor do I, my word upon it."

"Well, then, Nikolai Ilyich. I guess it's just us chickens here, then. So, what's on your mind."

"There are several matters I must discuss." His voice was subdued,

"Okay, then shoot," she said, adding, "That's a figure of speech, by the way."

"The first," Makarov hesitated. "I am worried about Svetlana Belyakova. Very worried."

Last Vivian had heard, Belyakova had returned to Earth. "Why? What's the deal with Svetlana?"

"The deal? She has been attracting attention."

Vivian couldn't help herself. "Can't be all *that* unusual for Blond Svet."

Makarov paused. "KGB attention."

"Oh."

"She has been outspoken, about my country's activities on the Moon, and about the competition our two countries are involved in. I do not know the details, but apparently she left the Moon under high suspicion. Since then, she has submitted to voluntary reeducation."

"Submitted to ... that sounds like a contradiction in terms. What does it actually mean?"

"Training in ideology. A return to correctness." He waved about him. "Although Svetlana was always correct. More correct than I. Vivian, I have no idea what could possibly have happened, none at all. Do you?"

"Me? How would I know? No, not the slightest clue."

"You have friends on the Moon, good friends. And perhaps it was some interaction with the Americans at Zvezda ..." Makarov sighed. "Ah, well. Then I suppose we must just remain in the dark, and hope for the best."

"Uh, yes. Let me know if you hear anything. And I will too, not that I expect to."

"Very well." Makarov checked his watch and scanned something in front of him, probably his own communications board. "Then, the next topic, which I hope will be more pleasant. Vivian, I have been asked by my superiors at Mission Control Moscow, by men on the Central Committee, whether you would be willing to meet."

"Meet?"

"Rendezvous, in Martian orbit. Your Apollo Astarte and my TMK-Mars, docking somehow, for a rendezvous, for a meeting between us and our crews. In person." He half-smiled. "A Martian summit?"

Vivian found herself lost for words. "Uh ... meet? Rendezvous *here*? At Mars?"

"Very publicly. For the news media. Everything recorded. There are many tensions between our countries these days. Any that we can loosen, any signs of friendship between our countries, I think this would be a good thing."

"I ... guess."

Makarov looked surprised, and perhaps even a little irritated, at Vivian's lack of enthusiasm. "The idea was originally Gorbachev's, I feel sure. He is trying to bring change, I think, if he can."

For once, Vivian was glad that she'd been exposed to all the political chatter in Astarte over the past few months. If not for that, she wouldn't have the first clue who Mikhail Gorbachev was, and that would have been embarrassing.

Not that Vivian herself had much faith in politicians. Especially Soviet politicians.

Makarov was still talking, looking most earnest. "I believe that our countries have the chance for a new start. I do, Vivian. With your Ronald Reagan soon to leave the Presidency of the United States, his successor must surely be a more reasonable man."

Vivian knew that Reagan's Vice President, George H.W. Bush, was facing only token opposition in the Republican primaries. She also knew that Walter Mondale, currently well ahead in the Democratic primaries, was considered unlikely to prevail in the election. But there her knowledge ended: Vivian had no idea whether a President Bush would seem more reasonable in the eyes of the world than Reagan. Her only clues were that Bush had once been in charge of the CIA, and that Andropov had been in charge of the KGB. Was there really much difference between them?

"A new start in the USSR as well? With Gorbachev? Are you sure? Because the Soviet Union ... it might not be easy to make any significant changes there. Changes that mean anything to the rest of the world, anyway."

"Comrade Andropov is wearing out," Makarov said bluntly. "He is seen little in public, these days, and we hear little from him. Oh, he still has his power, that is not to be doubted—he, and Gromyko, and Ustinov, the hard men are still there. But Gorbachev, yes, I have met him. I have had dinner with him, and with his wife, Raisa. He has a different head on his shoulders. And he is young, and on his way up. Perhaps all the way up, and perhaps sooner than people think."

From what little Vivian had gleaned, Gromyko seemed like a pretty strong guy among the Soviet apparatchiks. She wondered how much Makarov really understood of what was really going on, back in his country. After all, information was tightly controlled within the Soviet Union, and being so far away from it, presumably the information Makarov received would be even more restricted.

"But wasn't Gorbachev a protégé of Andropov's?" *Listen to you, Vivian: up on all the Kremlin gossip.* She'd have to remember to thank her crew sometime for their relentless fascination with Earth politics.

He nodded. "I agree that it must be a difficult path to walk. Gorbachev owes his place to Andropov, that is certain. And yet he is a different man. A new man, a man for the future." He paused, collected himself. Looked straight into the camera. "But yes, this is being urged by Gorbachev. Vivian, if there is the chance of a peaceful rendezvous, we should take it, I think. A collaboration, a gesture of friendship, to make the Earth news not all about Poland, not all about the worst side of your country and of the Rodina, but the best."

"So, a distraction, is what you're saying?"

"A balance, perhaps. To give hope."

"Whatever. But Nikolai, you must know that I have zero power to commit to this. NASA would have to approve any rendezvous. Hell, the White House would have to approve it. Seriously, there's no way—"

Vivian stopped, because Makarov was holding up his hand. "This I know, of course, all of this. The orders must come from the top, on both sides. And I also know my people are already approaching NASA about the possibility. But before the discussions go too far, I wanted to ask you. You and I must first agree that this would be a good thing, that we are willing to do it. If you say no, then no is the answer, and I will tell my superiors to abandon this effort, and the idea ends today. You understand me, I think?"

"I do, Nikolai." Vivian took a deep breath. "Uh, just give me a moment to think? Because this would be a honking big deal. And perhaps more complicated than you realize."

He shrugged. It seemed that to Nikolai Makarov, all matters were simple and straightforward. *Just a question of doing the right thing, nyet, tovarisch?*

So simple, to figure out what the right thing was.

"Okay, look: I'll need to talk to Dave Horn," she said. "He's the boss of what we can and can't do and can advise on the feasibility of the orbital mechanics and logistics. He'd need to be willing to do it, as well. And my crew ... I can't give you an answer on the fly."

Makarov half-bowed. "I understand, of course. Do what you must, talk to whoever you need to."

"Okay. I'll let you know, soon as I can."

"And, Vivian? I hope that we can do this. It would be good to see you again. Even in such unusual circumstances."

"Yes." She smiled at him. "Agreed. It would be great to see you again, Nikolai."

He looked around him. "If for nothing else, I have been a long time, with the same people. It is a long way we have come."

"A long way," she said. "Copy that. And I feel the same. I'd ..." Kill? Perhaps not. "I'd give a lot to see a fresh face."

He nodded, sanguine. "But, for now? Farewell."

"*Do svidaniya, tovarisch,*" she said, and enjoyed his doubletake.

"Your accent has improved."

She grinned. "*Mne priyatno eto slishat'.*" *Kind of you to say so.*

He shook his head. "Vivian Carter. Always a new surprise."

"You know it, man," she said. "Anyway, I'll see you soon, just maybe. Vivian out."

She broke the connection, leaned back, and exhaled. Nikolai Makarov still had a few surprises up his own sleeve as well.

I had to go all the way to Mars to have a private conversation with Nikolai Makarov? How absurd. And yet, how typical.

Makarov had given her a lot to think about. But most of that, Vivian could do at leisure. For now, she needed to get Dave Horn in here for a chat about ... potentially rendezvousing with a Soviet spacecraft, around Mars. And after that, maybe, she'd presumably need to broach it with the rest of her crew.

Out loud, she said: "And I'm sure *that* will be a barrel of laughs."

PART FOUR: SPACE

September-November 1984

CHAPTER 17

Phobos: Vivian Carter
September 1-9, 1984
Mission Elapsed Time: 425-433 days

"SO," Vivian said casually. "Anyone feel like paying the Soviets a visit?"

All eyes turned to her.

"I mean, we're on here on Phobos, and they're over by Deimos, and that's not too far apart, right?" She grinned, having achieved the shock value she was aiming for. "Seriously, it's an idea that's being floated. But Makarov and Mission Control both want our opinion on it before they move any further on it. It's not like we're about to just show up on Makarov's doorstep unannounced." She paused. "Although ... that might have been amusing. I can just imagine the look on his face."

"Just before they opened fire on us?" Marco said, and looked around them all. "Uh, that was a joke. I think."

Laura's mouth dropped open. "We could go to *Deimos* as well?"

"The *orbit* of Deimos," Horn said. "TMK-Mars is station-keeping in a loose orbit around it. We wouldn't get to go to the surface."

"Damn," she said. "Still, even to see it up close and personal ..."

"Hang on." Amy waved her down. "Vivian ... this is being seriously proposed? A meet-up between Astarte and TMK-Mars?"

"Yes. A space summit. A gesture of cooperation and friendliness in Martian orbit. You know the kind of thing."

"Friendliness with Soviets?"

"It's been known to happen," Vivian said, deadpan. "Call it 'détente' if you prefer. You've heard about the ASTP project, right?"

Greg Heinz shook his head. "I haven't. NASA and its acronyms …"

"Apollo-Soyuz Test Project? At one point in the early 1970s, or maybe even earlier, NASA and the Soviets began negotiations about a joint Apollo-Soyuz mission—meaning a link-up in space between an Apollo and a Soyuz, a handshake in Earth orbit, some joint activities. Mostly symbolic, but a useful gesture. It ultimately didn't go anywhere because there was still too much antagonism, and too much other Space Racing going on."

Horn nodded. "Guess what one of the major stumbling blocks was? Neither side wanted to reveal the details of their docking mechanisms. Which was probably a good call, considering all the crap that's happened since."

"Right," Vivian said. "That's one of the reasons Peter Sandoval spent so much time inspecting the Soyuz craft I crashed into Columbia Station, and their Progress ship as well."

"And Night Corps took those away," said Rawlings, musing. "Very carefully. You'd left by then, prepping for your delayed Apollo 32 Marius landing. I bet they disassembled them and took them back to Earth in pieces. Or at least the important pieces."

Rudy frowned. "Would this delay our departure from Mars even further?"

"No. Neither mission can afford that. It just means we pack up here a couple days early. Both missions have the schedule slack, if we choose to use it this way."

"I'm still trying to get my head around this." Amy shoved off to arrive next to Vivian. "We'd meet up for, what? Dinner and drinks?"

"Essentially, yes. We'll figure out the details later if all this goes through. Lots more steps in the diplomatic dance before we get anywhere near doing this."

"We'd go to them? Why wouldn't they want to come to us?" Greg asked. "That way they'd get to visit both moons."

"It's just common sense, energy-wise," said Horn. "Deimos is at a much higher altitude than Phobos, about twelve and a half thousand miles, compared to our three thousand seven hundred. The further down into the gravity well they bring TMK-Mars, the further back up they have to go. Plus, matching orbits down here … Phobos moves *fast*. I made it look easy, but if I'm honest, that was the hardest maneuvering I've done in my life. I was trying to hide the sweat."

"Meaning you were concealing the true level of risk from us?" Greg asked acidly.

Horn met his eye. "I wouldn't put it quite like that."

"Anyway," Vivian said. "Them staying put reduces their risk. Discretion being the better part of valor, and all. Plus, this way allows the Soviets to play the gracious hosts. It looks better for them, politically."

"Well then," Laura said. "Their loss is our gain."

"And, before you ask," Dave added, "matching Deimos's orbit is a piece of cake compared to what I had to do with Phobos. Deimos is a meandering slowpoke by contrast. And the delta-V between the two moons is only seven hundred forty-seven meters a second for a two-burn Hoffman transfer." Horn looked at the mostly blank faces that surrounded him. "Really? Even by now none of you knows what that is?"

Rawlings grunted. "Some of us do."

Vivian grinned at the scientists. "Translation: we can do it if we want to."

Marco looked back and forth between them all. "Wait. Guys. We're really considering flying from Phobos to *Deimos*?"

Laura's eyes shone. "You bet your ass we are."

Rudy Frank cleared his throat. "Laura's going to need a towel again."

"That's what's on the table," Vivian said. "Meet up with the Soviets. Shake hands. Break bread together, the space explorers of two nations. And, trade samples with them. We give them samples from Phobos, and they give us some from Deimos."

"And we'll get to see their ship up close," Horn said. "Do a few comparisons, as you might say."

"Oh, ours is bigger." Rawlings grinned. "If this is a pissing contest."

"And it's always a pissing contest with you guys," Greg said.

"Of course."

Laura was still looking intently at Vivian. "Screw the bragging rights. We'd get to see *Deimos*. Take pictures, get samples. Even if we don't get to pick them up ourselves, we'll be able to do a direct ground-truth comparison to Phobos. That's worth a *lot* scientifically. We'll need to go out and get some more Phobos rocks, though. I don't want to give away any that we already have."

"And, oh my God, we get other people to talk to," Amy Benson said. "I mean, no offense to present company, but this would be good for all of us."

"And possibly be in a different physical space for a while." This was Rudy. "If they let us aboard TMK. Which they presumably would—I mean, that's what hosting means, right?"

"Carefully supervised trips in each direction," Vivian said. "Not that we'll all fit in their Salyut, so we'd have to visit in teams. We'd obviously never all leave Astarte at the same time anyway."

Marco looked perplexed. "And our powers-that-be are quite fine with Soviets coming aboard Astarte?"

"We'd outnumber them at all times," Vivian pointed out. "And we watch them like hawks. Makarov, at least, has spent quite a bit of time on a Skylab, and of course other Soviets had free rein on Columbia Station. There are no big secrets for them to learn in here. And it definitely helps that it's Makarov we're talking about. He's earned a lot of credibility with us. I doubt anyone at NASA HQ thinks he'd come to sabotage our ship."

"Not this time, at least," Rawlings added quietly.

"But, the others?" Marco still looked concerned. "We're sure they don't pose a threat to us?"

"I asked about that, of course," Vivian said. "The CIA has already done a deep dive on them. As far as we can tell they're straightforward veteran cosmonauts, with no hint of KGB or Spetsnaz in their backgrounds. Some of our astronauts have met Terekhin and Kaleri at the Paris Air Show, and reported that they seemed like straight-up guys. Their fourth guy's a scientist with a pages-deep publication record. And, God knows, it would look bad if something critical broke on our ship right after it received a Soviet visit."

Dardenas considered. "I guess so."

Laura was scribbling numbers on a pad, glancing intermittently at her trigonometric tables. "View's going to be completely different from Deimos. Here, Mars fills forty-five degrees of our sky. From Deimos, Mars is going to look … yeah, sixteen degrees across. So it'll appear roughly the same size as the Earth looks from geostationary orbit."

"Well, I'm all for a change of scene," said Greg.

Vivian looked around. "Strange to say, I'm not hearing any of you really opposing this."

"Well, if you're ignoring me, I guess that's true," Marco said.

"You don't seem like you're hard over against it."

"Just feeling a little more cautious about it than the rest of you."

"Which isn't unreasonable."

"We're scientists," Rudy pointed out. "Collaboration is our natural mode."

Greg nodded. "Especially collaborating with the Soviets, doing useful stuff in space together, instead of constantly butting heads. Like we should *really* have been doing all along."

Vivian looked around, bemused. Her crew had argued like hell for hours about whether or not to come to Phobos, and fought like cats and dogs over various other issues along the way, and yet here they all were, casually agreeing to fly over to Deimos to go hang out with cosmonauts.

Amy picked up on her surprise. "I think the benefits outweigh the risks. We can do something important for science and international relations, and get a bit of psychological relief ourselves, all at the same time."

"But?"

"No buts. If Dave is confident in the orbital math, and you guys and Houston are okay with the Soviet angle, I say we go for it. While also taking reasonable precautions. We assign each Soviet a buddy while they're on board. Constant surveillance. Trust but verify, and all that."

"And we keep an eye out the window at all times," Marco said. "I mean it. We need a round-the-clock watch to make sure there are no, let's say, unauthorized spacewalks on their part. No activity around the outside of Astarte that might be prejudicial to our interests."

"Agreed," Vivian said, and looked around the foredeck once more. No one seemed to have anything else to say, and everyone seemed cheerful at the prospect. "Okay. I'll go tell Houston we're up for it and let them put the wheels in motion."

As Vivian walked on the surface of Phobos for the last time, disconnecting the stout tethers that had fastened Astarte to the moon of Mars, she discovered she was sad to be leaving.

She paused to savor the moment. Some of her departures from the Moon had been abrupt, even ignominious ... but she'd then gotten to go back later, long before she'd imagined she might. But once Astarte "undocked" with Phobos, Vivian was pretty darned sure she'd never pass this way again.

And, it wasn't just Phobos. It was *Mars*, hovering in the sky, huge above her. Not for the first time, she marveled how Dave had been able to circle this tiny moon and land on its underside. The space professional in her knew that this wasn't really all that different from landing on the "top" side, the side tidally locked to face away from the Red Planet, but it certainly *felt* different, as if they'd risked falling off and plunging into the Martian atmosphere.

That couldn't possibly have happened, and it wasn't about to happen when they freed themselves from Phobos with about the gentlest delta-V maneuver she could imagine, similar to her final undocking with her Lunar Module after Apollo 32. This was the closest she would ever get to Mars.

Mars! That complicated Red Planet, with its ever-changing terrain. Even now, the orbit of Phobos was whipping them over Mars's surface with a dizzying speed. Every view was different. They'd even witnessed a major dust storm that had obscured a whole hemisphere of the planet for several days. Over the past weeks Vivian had grown accustomed to the Red Planet being so close, its vista constantly changing. The planet *Mars*, and all she'd had to do to see it was tilt her head back.

But all good things come to an end, and it was time for Vivian Carter, Maid of Mars, to travel from Thuria to Cluros. Or some shit like that.

She bent down, very gently so that her boots barely lifted off the surface of the rock, sifted some Phobos gravel between her fingers and let it drop, to fall ever so slowly onto the surface of the tiny moon.

"Vivian? Okay?"

"Roger that, Dave. Just having my last philosophical moment."

"Figured. I was leaving you to it, but, you know. Orbital ephemerides wait for no man. Or woman."

"Get my butt in there, is what you're saying?"

"No need to rush, but it would be nice to keep some contingency time up our sleeves. Besides, the terminator's on its way." He paused. "Not the Arnold Schwarzenegger version. The one that makes it get dark."

"Got it."

" 'I'll be back,'" Horn said, and even Vivian knew what that meant, because her crew had watched the dumb movie about four times during the mission so far, with their most recent viewing just a week ago. A true team-building activity, somehow.

Vivian cringed. *Jeez, why were all science fiction movies so lame?* She focused back on task. "Except we won't be back. More's the pity."

"Another day, another moon," he said. "Deimos awaits."

"Ten-four." Vivian craned her head back for another scan of Mars, loving how the light changed over the surface toward its own terminator.

She stood, intentionally bouncing high, just for the experience, and made her way over to free the last cable. Now just a single line connected Astarte to Phobos, plus the tether that joined Vivian's suit to the Astarte airlock.

"This is Vivian Carter, reporting from the surface of Phobos for the very last time. We came, we saw, we collected samples. Glad we did it."

She leaned forward and pushed off, and flew the rest of the way to the airlock hatch in a single, slow, long jump.

The transition from Phobos to Deimos was also slow, but sure.

They separated without fanfare, Dave Horn steadily backing them away from Phobos's surface with gentle pulses of the RCS system, then gradually increasing their speed. A sustained burn a few minutes long took them up into an elliptical orbit with its apoares—Dave insisted that was a word, along with "periares," but anyway, the furthest from Mars that the orbit would take them—equal to the orbital altitude of Deimos. Deimos wasn't there waiting for them, of course; it would take Dave two more burns to get them into a Deimos-like circular orbit, and then four or five orbits of Mars to make the rendezvous with the moon itself. But Dave was in his element, humming cheerfully along to some crappy Aerosmith tune while Josh Rawlings winced occasionally in the right-hand seat of CM-1.

Vivian left them to it and went to watch the changing aspect of Mars from the big foredeck window and bond with the rest of her crew. Plus, they'd all need to get through the shower and into some clean jumpsuits before they met up with the Soviets.

Now that the rush of leaving Phobos was over, Vivian was looking forward to seeing Nikolai Makarov again. It had been five years, and she had assumed that she'd never see him again, that he'd stay in the Soviet Union for the rest of his life, a place that Vivian would never visit. And now she'd get to hang out with him again, in orbit around *frigging Mars*.

So, yeah, maybe Vivian wanted her hair to be just a little less greasy than it was right at this moment.

With that rosy glow, Vivian went to shower. And spent the twenty minutes afterward, naked and dripping wet, with a wrench, hammer, and duct tape, fixing up a leak in the plumbing before the next guy could come in.

Ah, the romance of deep space.

Deimos looked very different from Phobos. Smaller and smoother, with more of a red tinge, and it was a truly ridiculous shape. From their angle of approach it appeared almost triangular. It also had way fewer craters than Phobos, a fact that Vivian didn't understand and didn't feel like asking Laura about right now. If only because Laura was watching, rapt, as Deimos grew larger and larger in the window, and kept muttering "Oh my God, oh my God," under her breath, and taking photograph after photograph.

The rest of the crew was similarly quiet and attentive, and so Vivian joined in the general reverence of their approach to the second moon of Mars.

Even from a distance, they could all see that the Soviet interplanetary Salyut was much smaller than Astarte. Their own Skylab was eighty-two feet long and a little over twenty-one feet in diameter. The TMK-Mars Salyut, by comparison, could only have been fifty-ish feet by maybe fourteen in diameter. Vivian was having trouble doing the math while also carrying on two conversations at once, with her own crew and with Nikolai, but her quick scribbles implied that TMK-Mars had only a third of the livable, pressurized volume that Astarte had, with half the number of crew.

But at least it was a *different* volume. A different layout and design, a different color palette—if that was the correct terminology to describe the dour dark green and black of Soviet military spacecraft. Different food, and different people. Even with their reservations about fraternizing with the enemy, it was clear that everyone was thrilled at the opportunity to talk to new people with whom they hadn't been in close quarters for the past months and hundreds of millions of miles.

Astarte approached Deimos slowly—almost deathly slowly. The reason why was obvious: it was a question of synchronizing their motion with the moon, and then station-keeping as close as possible to the Soviet vessel, so that they could join the craft together with a makeshift boom and set up the inflatable tunnel that would link their two craft.

Because that was the cunning plan. The Soviets and Americans both routinely used such flexible walkways to link up their vehicles in Earth or lunar orbit, or at L5, and the folks back home from both nations had figured out a way to make the Soviet system mate with the Astarte airlock with an airtight seal. Marco had spent hours on the project, swearing and soldering and sometimes banging with a hammer, and rejecting all offers of help. In principle, they'd be able to connect up to TMK-Mars and stroll between the vessels in shirtsleeves. But only if Horn, Rawlings, and Dardenas managed to rendezvous within twenty feet of the Salyut, and oriented correctly, and then they could complete the dance by bringing the craft together.

Vivian left them to it and hung out with the scientists.

"Engines full stop. Ladies and gentlemen, we have arrived in, uh—for want of a better word—what I'll call 'orbit' around Deimos. Please remain seated until we come to a complete stop, and take care when leaving the spacecraft, and be sure to take all your possessions with you. Well, not all of them. But you know what I mean."

"And tip your waiters," Rawlings added.

"Thank you," said Horn. "We'll be here all week."

"Okay, guys, okay," Vivian said. "You did a great job and all. Now, let's get Astarte anchored and linked up with TMK-Mars, so they can share their vodka with us. Nikolai, good buddy, tell me you brought some vodka?"

"Alas, I fear I did not." Makarov paused in sorrow. Rather theatrically, Vivian thought.

"Well, shit."

"However. We *may* have some Armenian cognac remaining, somewhere in our supplies. We will have to investigate this."

"I knew I could rely on you." Vivian stood, clapped her hands. "Okay, my people, jump to it. Let's do our chores and get ready to party."

"Nikolai Makarov, I presume?"

He was a little greyer at the temples, maybe a little thinner, but definitely the same guy. And his smile was genuine, and the bear-hugs he gave Vivian and the rest of her crew seemed extra-genuine.

"So, this is your new moon?" she said. "Ours was bigger."

Makarov shook his head. "Vivian, please."

The Soviet mission profile for its Deimos encounter was very different to the American plan, and more similar to a normal lunar mission. On arrival at Deimos, the TMK-Mars spaceship had gone into an irregularly shaped but quasi-stable orbit around the Martian moon. The LEK lander, carrying cosmonauts Makarov, Kaleri, and Terekhin, had then separated from the Salyut and landed on Deimos in the customary way, leaving Petrushenko to maintain the spacecraft orbit and perform observations of the Martian surface. The cosmonauts had carried out a five-day exploration of Deimos and then returned in the LEK to the Salyut. After a few days of rest and analysis the LEK had then returned to Deimos, this time with Kaleri and Petrushenko switching roles. They'd repeated the cycle for two more Deimos visits, each centered on a different part of the moon. The four landings had totaled twenty-five days on Deimos over a total span of a month and a half.

Unlike Vivian's crew, the cosmonauts had not been forced to rely on boots and zip guns to make their precarious way around on Deimos. Their LEK carried a standard Lunokhod rover, but with innovative spiked wheels to maximize its grip on the terrain under the low-gravity conditions.

The Soviet mission to Deimos that the US press had attempted to ridicule as a publicity stunt had in fact been meticulously planned and had resulted in a very effective geological survey of the Martian moon. Due largely to having the Lunokhod, they'd managed to achieve a more homogeneous sampling coverage of Deimos, even considering that their moon was smaller than Phobos. As far as the Space Race went, Vivian secretly conceded that even if the Soviets had arrived at Mars later than the Americans, they'd made a much better scientific job of their visit.

Then again, theirs had been planned as a *landing* mission from the start.

The other Soviets seemed just as nice and as straightforward as Nikolai. Perhaps, Vivian thought wryly, because if one of them had stepped out of line the other three would have killed him somewhere on the way to Mars.

Also, and she was surprised this hadn't occurred to her sooner: these four men had not seen a woman for the better part of a year. This meant that Amy, Laura, and Vivian herself were very popular in the party that followed, in the Astarte's forward compartment. The Soviets were almost comically gallant and deferential to them.

A thimbleful of cognac, and several of them were already talking too loudly and laughing even louder. Vivian restricted herself to half a thimbleful, and she noted that Horn and Rawlings only touched their mouths to their drink bulbs for appearances. She didn't miss it when Rawlings traded his full bulb for Amy's empty one, but where Horn's cognac went was a mystery. Possibly also to Amy, the way she was roaring with laughter and bumping into people and walls more clumsily than usual, but the quickness of the hand deceived the eye.

It was a great evening. An odd one, spent so far away from Earth in orbit around the Red Planet … but great.

Vivian kept a close eye on the Soviets—there were, after all, only four of them—but none of them left her sight for longer than it took for a bathroom visit, and the Soviets tactfully went back to TMK-Mars to use their own facilities rather than venturing into the Astarte crew quarters. Likely, they paid equal care to see what the Americans were doing, but obviously none of Vivian's crew made any attempt to sneak over to the Soviet craft.

The food was, well … about as good as space food ever was. The Soviet borscht was not great, and some of their other food was worse. Then again, the cuisine aboard Astarte wasn't anything to write home about either.

As far as Vivian was concerned, she'd be happy to never again suffer through a serving of NASA shrimp marengo, but it was a big hit with the Russians. After some rowdy debate, the crew of Astarte unanimously agreed to trade all their remaining stock of it to the Russians for an equal amount of their beef stroganoff, which even Vivian had to agree was really not half bad. The traditional Russian pelmeni meat dumplings, though, which several of her crew seemed to favor, were a mixed blessing, and their blini tasted like cardboard, which was hardly surprising. Prepackaged pancakes in space. Yeah.

"Well, Nikolai. Who'd have thought we'd be here."

"Not I, certainly. It is an astonishing privilege, to be the second man on the Moon, and now to be the first man on Deimos."

"Congratulations. You done good."

He nodded. "When I was growing up, a child in the Soviet Union, I could never have imagined I would leave the surface of the Earth. And now we have left the world so far behind us that it is hard to find it in the sky. For many days at a time I do not even think of the Earth."

"Amazing, isn't it?"

"I do think of my family," he said. "I think of them, every day. But they seem ..." He paused to find the word.

"Abstract?"

"Yes. Not real, in a way. I know they are still there and thinking of me, and that I will one day get back to them, but I do not think of my house, or my street, or the Earth at all." He shook his head. "It is a difficult thing for me to explain."

"Me neither," Vivian said.

Frankly, by now Vivian was having trouble picturing her home neighborhood. She'd spent so little time there, and lived in so many different places, over the years. And as for Peter ... she certainly *thought* about him ... fairly regularly, but mostly to wonder what he was doing, and to hope that he was safe.

He was just so far away. "Abstract" really was the right word.

"I completely understand," she added. "No one has ever had to explain it before, quite like we have."

"That is true." He grinned. "And now Alexei Leonov can be jealous of me, instead of the other way around."

"Ha. You know, this is going to sound odd, but I'm kinda sorry Svetlana isn't here."

He sobered. "I, too."

"I think she would have loved to see all this. To see Mars, particularly. It might thaw her chilly ice queen heart."

Nikolai's eyebrows went up. "You think Svetlana cold-hearted? I suppose I cannot blame you. Me, I think of her as fire, not ice."

Vivian considered. "A bit of both, I guess."

It was a great evening. They were all sorry when it was over. And, Vivian noticed, after the celebrating was over, even after several thimbles of cognac, each crew immediately snapped back into their careful mode of watching the other crew, and paying attention to the environmental information from the frail tunnel that linked their ships.

When they finally dogged and bolted the airlock hatches that led into the tunnel, sealing the two ships off from each other for the night, Vivian's crew all breathed a sigh of relief. And hit the sack almost immediately, aside from Dave Horn, who would stay awake to take the first watch. Marco Dardenas and Greg Heinz would relieve him in four hours.

They spent two more days linked up in orbit with the Soviet craft, doing joint press events and political meet-and greets, and various other dog and pony shows. Then they separated for the last time, with Dave Horn backing the Astarte away from the TMK-Mars ship and boosting their orbit yet again, to rendezvous with the NERVA rocket and the Cargo Carrier.

It took another three days of spacewalks and internal activity to attach the NERVA to Astarte and empty the Carrier. True to form, Vivian had pitched to keep the empty Cargo Carrier connected up to Astarte as an additional pressurized space, but this proved to be infeasible and complicate their center of mass too much. With reluctance, they jettisoned it.

Besides, Vivian no longer felt the need to escape from her crew members as often as she once had. Venus had made them a team, but Mars had made them a family.

And now it was time to leave Martian orbit, and Vivian was, frankly, terrified. Meanwhile, Dave Horn was about as calm and laconic as Vivian had ever seen him. Which meant that he, too, was feeling the pressure.

Under the circumstances, Vivian figured she would leave the piloting in Command Module One to Dave Horn and Marco Dardenas, both of whom had made a serious study of the NERVA engine. She would wait for the burn in the main body of Astarte.

It was at the same time calmer and even more terrifying than being in the Command Module.

"You want something?"

Vivian jumped. "Jeez, Amy. I thought you were looking over Josh's shoulder up at the control board."

"I was, until …" Amy looked around and then took Vivian's hand and squeezed it. "Listen. If you need a Valium or whatever, you name it. You know our drug manifest almost as well as I do … but if you say yes, nobody ever needs to know."

Vivian squeezed Amy's hand in return, lingered a moment, and then pushed it away before anyone else could notice. "I *hate* nukes, Amy. Any nukes. Even nukes that are really rocket motors."

"I know. So do I."

Vivian looked sideways at her. "Did *you* take Valium?"

"You bet your goddamn life I did. Stoned off my ass right now. Physician, heal thyself. And, uh, nobody ever needs to know that either, if you're okay with that."

"You got it." Damn it, Vivian reached out for Amy's hand again. "So, the Valium. We still have lots of it left?"

Vivian wasn't looking, but Amy's voice gave away her smile. "You never quit, do you?"

"Hello? I'm in charge of this vessel." She paused. "I don't need names."

"Aside from me, this one time, only one other person has ever asked, and I only gave them five pills … carefully, one a day. And I seriously believe they had good reason. And, Vivian? Just don't even ask, because I am never, ever going to tell you who."

"Fascinating." Vivian took a deep breath. "Honestly, I thought it might be more."

"So, do you want the pill or don't you?"

"How long to the burn, again?"

"I have no freaking idea, Viv. I'm a doctor, not a pilot."

Vivian grinned. "Okay. Maybe enough time for me to take up transcendental meditation?"

The NERVA fired up on schedule and burned for exactly as long as it needed to. Apollo Astarte powered out of Mars orbit with a truly impressive delta-V. Their trajectory back to Earth was perfect, or perfect to three nines, and they all knew that Dave Horn could pick up some more nines along the way.

A week later, Horn told Vivian himself, with no prompting: he was the guy who'd asked Amy for the Valium, during the week leading up to the trans-Earth injection burn, but that he'd been clean for the seventy-two hours prior.

Vivian just nodded and smiled, and they never mentioned it again.

CHAPTER 18

Jura Highlands: Svetlana Belyakova
October 6, 1984

THE LK Lander dropped out of the sky, sunlight glinting off its bulbous metallic upper stage and sparkling off the gold foil that wrapped the descent stage and landing pads. At the last minute, a plume of fire erupted from the base of the craft, easing its descent onto the Jura Highlands west of Sinus Iridum.

The dust quickly settled. The ship had landed in radio silence, and for a while its two-person crew busied themselves executing the shutdown checklist and performing star sightings to recalibrate their reference systems and confirm their exact location on the lunar surface. Once these items were squared away, they ate a quick meal and settled down to rest, still wearing their spacesuits but with helmets and gloves put aside.

Six hours passed before another, larger Soviet craft literally fell out of the sky. At what appeared to be *later* than the last minute, two pillars of flame erupted simultaneously from its opposite ends, pointing downward and decelerating the rectangular shape at what must have been six, maybe even seven G's.

It banged down onto the lunar surface, kicking up a massive ruckus of dust and causing everything in the LK Lander to rattle and shake. The new craft was an unreflective matt gray color, but the red hammer and sickle and "CCCP" lettering on its long side seemed to glow with an eerie radiance.

Fifteen minutes later, a second identical brick-shaped vehicle plummeted down onto the surface, once again rattling the LK and its crew. The three Soviet vessels now formed the points of an equilateral triangle, separated by only fifty feet. Soviet automation of lunar landings had improved over the past decade.

The Soviet *Kirpichi*, or Bricks, were half again as large as the Night Corps Bricks. Soviets could do *big*, and they could do *functional*, even if in the process they often had to put up with *primitive* and *clunky*.

Once the second Kirpich was safely down, the LK cosmonauts depressurized their lander and opened the hatch. The newer LKs had larger hatches for rapid egress, the Soviets having learned many years ago that a quick deployment of armed personnel was often vital.

A cosmonaut swung herself out of the hatch and stepped down the ladder with confidence, an Uzi slung across her shoulder. Moments later, Svetlana Belyakova was back on the lunar surface.

The hatch closed behind her. For the time being, her flight engineer would stay aboard the LK and monitor the situation. Which Svetlana was grateful for, because for all of Dmitri Vlasav's technical competence, he was fifteen years younger than she was and painfully starstruck, and seemed intimidated to find himself copiloting for a Soviet icon, the first woman on the Moon. Belyakova had spent half her time wanting to mentor him, the other half wanting to punch him.

As she watched, the end wall of the first Soviet Kirpich opened, and the first truck lumbered out.

The Americans had their MOLABs, those effete vehicles that cruised across the lunar surface while providing all modern conveniences to their passengers. These Soviet vehicles had been built to a different set of standards. If a MOLAB was a Lincoln Continental, these Soviet lunar trucks were Skodas. These were working-class vehicles, grungy rockhoppers.

On seeing one, an American observer might think: "Volkswagen bus." A Russian would think "Purgan," one of the no-frills UAZ-452 military vans built by the Ulyanovsk Automobile Plant that were ubiquitous throughout the Soviet Union. Both were similar in shape, build, and design, and these Soviet lunar vehicles were built on much the same lines, and in fact by the same Ulyanovsk company that made the Purgans.

These lunar Purgans were, of course, airtight and armored.

They seemed dauntingly small. Each measured a mere sixteen feet long, seven feet wide, and seven feet high, excluding the superstructure; no larger than it had to be to house a two-person crew with the absolute minimum of comfort and safety. A Purgan would have fitted into a single lane on an American highway with ease.

Each had a small machine gun mounted over the cab, and a dish antenna on the cab's front right corner. Aside from that, the tops of the craft were screened off from prying eyes in the sky by a regolith weave, with a track redaction device behind the back wheels to erase their wheel tracks and obscure any evidence of their passing.

Their small size and narrow wheelbase tended to make them unstable on the rocky lunar terrain. Thus, each Purgan also had a winch mounted on its roof, so its crew could hoist it back upright if it rolled over onto its side. Back on Earth Belyakova had seen Purgan prototypes equipped with outriggers to prevent rolls, but those were difficult to screen with the regolith weave and required a track redaction system too wide to be practical.

Belyakova had trained extensively with these vehicles over rugged terrain in the Kazakh and Ukrainian Soviet Socialist Republics, and knew that they felt even smaller on the inside than they appeared. Their interiors were efficiently designed and well organized, but there was barely room to breathe. Prospecting for rare earth elements in the Jura highlands was not a job for claustrophobics.

The second Purgan exited from the Brick soon after the first. There should be five Purgans altogether in this Kirpich, plus extra fuel, oxygen, and supplies. The vehicles would return regularly to base to restock. By that time, the end walls of the Bricks would have been extended outward using an inflatable structure—again, similar to those used in Night Corps Bricks—and extra space that would be very welcome to the Purgan crews when they came back from their prospecting runs for some brief downtime.

The third and fourth Purgans deployed. Still, neither the LK's occupants nor any of the Purgan crews broke radio silence. That would come later, once they had spread out and staked their claim to any sizeable mineral deposits. For the time being, they had their orders and no communications were necessary.

The crews of the Purgans had landed already aboard their vehicles, in order to save space and deploy quickly. Now they spread out across the surface in all directions, skittering away like bugs, bouncing and swinging around. The ride inside them must be ridiculously uncomfortable.

Once the fifth Purgan was out and away, Belyakova strode toward the second Kirpich, where her own ride awaited her. Fortunately, it would not be as cramped as a Purgan. As she approached, the wall of the second Brick hinged outward on cue to reveal it.

This was a Kharkovchanka, which literally translated as "woman of Kharkov." Appropriately enough, it had been constructed at the Kharkov Transport Engineering Plant in the Ukraine, an industrial center that Belyakova had often visited. The original Kharkovchankas were designed and built to operate in the Antarctic, and that was evident in their design: tracked wheels and a high, large rectangular cab. It was large only relative to the Purgans, with a pressurized living area of just a hundred fifty square feet.

The Antarctic model had eight bunks. The lunar version could carry only six and initially would have a crew of just two: Belyakova and Vlasav. It would, however, also serve as an ambulance or emergency vehicle, in case of need.

Internally, it was divided into several tiny functional areas: a cab, with two bunks behind the driver's seat; a separate navigation cubicle; a cramped kitchen and galley area; a personal hygiene area; and an airlock and spacesuit locker in the rear. More bunks could be folded down in the galley area and by the airlock, in between the ranks of computer equipment, communications consoles, and other electronics.

On its exterior, the Kharkovchanka had solar panels and a rack of advanced rocketry mounted on its roof, beneath a retractable regolith weave camouflage rack.

This Kharkovchanka would serve as Belyakova's mobile command and control center. From here, she would coordinate the mining Purgans that were even now spreading out across the highlands near Montes Jura.

The soldiers inside the second Brick that would guard the beachhead were already rolling out hoses to refuel the LK. Of the three vehicles that had landed, only the LK could be launched off the Moon's surface again, and it would likely be only Svetlana and whoever else she might designate who would make that trip. The other Soviet soldiers, prospectors and geologists would be staying, and for quite some time, until they could be ferried back into orbit in groups of four using the new heavy-lift LEK Taxi vehicles that were still under development back on Earth.

About a couple hundred yards out, each Purgan skidded to a halt. The back door opened and a suited cosmonaut jumped down onto the surface to take a core sample. This would be the crews' task, day in and day out, for the next week: note the location, take a surface and core sample, and then move on to the next location, covering as much ground as possible in a predetermined search pattern.

If the US discovery papers were to be believed, the rare earth elements in this area were potentially worth a fortune, both financially and strategically, and the Soviet Union wanted to claim as many of those rich seams as they could, as rapidly as possible. Which meant sampling a large area, quickly analyzing the results, and collating them onto a big main mineralogical map. Coordinating the effort and masterminding that map were Belyakova's main responsibilities on this mission.

And if this broad mineralogical survey brought them into contact with the NASA surveyors already working in this area?

Svetlana hoped that any such interactions would be cordial. Americans like Vivian Carter, Starman Jones, even Daniel Grant on his good days: with such Americans, she could hope to find middle ground. But she was unlikely to know any of the US personnel up here in the Jura region.

She would do her best to keep the peace. But, if that proved impossible: well. That was why they carried the weapons. And with the Americans arrogantly staking their claim to swaths of the Jura Mountains and surrounding craters, their need for self-defense was obvious.

19

MOL-26, Earth Orbit: Peter Sandoval
November 6-9, 1984

IN the fiftieth United States Presidential Election on Tuesday November 6, 1984, George H.W. Bush defeated Walter Mondale in a landslide victory to become President-Elect.

At dawn on Wednesday November 7, three giant contingents of Soviet troops stormed across the border into Poland in a three-pronged ground assault of tanks, artillery, and motorized infantry. With the connivance and tacit support of Polish Prime Minister Wojcieich Jaruzelski, these forces quickly swept away most organized resistance at the main strategic centers of Warsaw and Krakow.

The port city of Gdansk was a different story. For many weeks that city had been in the hands of the striking shipyard workers of Solidarnosc, led by Lech Walesa, and their allies among the mineworkers and other trades. In Gdansk, the Soviet army was forced into a street-by-street, building-by-building slog, with no end in sight.

Even while the streets of Gdansk were running with blood, additional Soviet forces had continued their motorized sweep onward to Poland's border with East Germany. As Poland was roughly four hundred road miles across, with a land area equivalent to New Mexico, they arrived within thirty-six hours.

After a brief and probably one-sided negotiation, East German leader Erich Honecker opened the border and allowed the Soviet forces to enter his country, whereupon the Red Army made all haste westward toward the country's opposite border with West Germany, presumably to face off against NATO forces on the other side of the Iron Curtain.

This sudden and unexpected blitzkrieg proved to be just the beginning of a new wave of coordinated Soviet aggression. On Friday November 9, 1984, all hell broke loose both on Earth and in space, as part of a concerted operation that the Soviets called *Goryashchaya Noch'*, and the US came to know in translation as *Burning Night*.

At the navigation desk of MOL-26 in Earth orbit, Peter Sandoval looked up from the logbook he was writing in and narrowed his eyes. "Brock?"

From the DORIAN command console on the other side of the observation deck, Terri Brock glanced over innocently. "Sir?"

"Stop mother-henning me."

"Stop … sorry, sir?"

"Watching me as if I'm about to fall over." He looked her in the eye. "Look, I'm not constantly on the verge of having some kind of … incident. Clear?"

"Crystal, sir. I'll endeavor to make my concern less obvious."

"Please do." He closed his eyes, opened them again. "Thank you, by the way. I appreciate it. But I'm fine, so maybe dial it back a notch?"

Brock busied herself with studying her workspace and checking switch settings, and peered through the binocular eyepiece at the west coast of South America rolling beneath them. "Already dialed, sir."

"You are such a bullshitter, Brock."

"Got me where I am today, sir."

He sighed. "Terri? Cut it out."

She grinned briefly. "Sorry, boss."

Sandoval studied her. "You're reporting on me, aren't you?"

Now, Brock was genuinely shocked. "Absolutely not. And no one has even asked me to."

"I don't mean to the powers that be, back in Cheyenne. I mean to … you know. Our Venusian friend."

"Vivian has a new call sign?" Terri relented. "Okay, fine. I *may*, or *may not*, be updating one of NASA's most prominent astronauts on our mission status, commensurate with security and need-to-know. I decline to be specific. I believe that falls under the heading of family privacy."

"Family? You're really pulling the family card on me, with Vivian Carter?"

Terri grinned again. "Sure. For this purpose, I certainly consider Vivian to be family. And, for what it's worth, she was delighted to hear you'd been cleared to fly again. Though I still think you should have told her your own damned self. Sir."

"I was getting around to it."

"Uh-huh."

"It's the time delay," he said. "It just doesn't work, somehow. Makes her feel even further away than she really is."

"I get that. By which I mean, I don't agree. With all due respect, and all ..."

Sandoval shook his head, bemused. "Fine. Whatever you say. Carry on."

Terri just nodded. But Sandoval found himself still smiling. Despite the uncertainty going on in the world below, even with the stakes so high and the risk of conflict so great, he found it hard not to be cheerful.

After all, he was back in space at last.

Today's Manned Orbiting Laboratories were larger than those of the late 1970s: twenty feet longer, but still only ten feet wide—the width was constrained by the size of the Titan IIIM-Centaur launch vehicle, which hadn't changed significantly. When the new Titan IVs came online they'd be able to launch a larger station, although some were claiming that by then the promised improvements in digital imaging from uncrewed satellites would make them obsolete. Sandoval didn't really think that would ever happen, but it was what the Department of Defense was hoping. The MOL program was *expensive*.

Yesterday's MOLs had been configured for a forty-five-day duty cycle. The new breed—those with designations from MOL-20 onward—were designed for a 180-day lifetime and a crew of five, with a crew rotation and a Cargo Carrier resupply at the halfway point. However, because of the worsening geopolitical situation, MOL-26 had been approved for two mission extensions and was currently in its thirteenth month of operation.

Sandoval wasn't thrilled to be commanding a space vessel that was so far past its sell-by date, but he had to admit that the station was still structurally sound and its operation mostly flawless. The water purification and personal hygiene facilities were cranky at the best, and Krantzen had—unordered—taken it as his passion project to spend his downtime tinkering with both and coaxing them into better performance. Or perhaps he was just more fastidious than the rest of the crew. But everything else seemed to be nominal.

Improvements in technology and electronics miniaturization also meant that the DORIAN optical system took up less space. In principle, the crew quarters and operational space were fifty percent larger than they'd been five years ago. This meant that everyone got their own berth and privacy door rather than bunking two to a room, which was more comfortable and less stressful, and also more appropriate given that the MOL crews now included women. Aside from that, the extra space was mostly soaked up by the increased amount of supplies they needed to carry ... plus the armory.

On Sandoval's first missions the MOLs had flown unarmed, paying lip service to the Outer Space Treaty signed in 1967 that prohibited weapons in space. All of that had been swept to the wayside by the space conflicts of the early 1980s. If the Soviet Almaz stations had their RIkhter cannons designed to shoot explosive shells, fully up to Earth-atmosphere large-bomber standards, then the Air Force MOLs damned well needed to match that capability. In addition, Sandoval's current MOL stocked half a dozen air-to-air missiles—versions equally functional in the space-to-space environment—for the Dyna-Soar craft that he and Krantzen had ridden up here in. Rodriguez, Brock, Doyle, and all their supplies had arrived more conventionally in a Big Gemini six hours later.

This was only their third week aboard the vessel, and Sandoval was still getting up to speed on all the new instrumentation. But he was damned glad to be here. Sitting around his house and his Cheyenne office had been driving him slowly insane. During those months he'd finally come to understand how Vivian Carter could feel "trapped" on Earth, a concept that in the past had probably only occurred to a tiny percentage of humanity: he'd felt frustrated, constrained, and miserable. Especially when Vivian herself was leading space missions and jetting between goddamned *planets*.

But now? Sandoval was back and he loved being up here again. The Earth's surface beneath him was like an old friend.

Plus, with everything going to hell in Europe, it was important that he be here. At last, Sandoval was able to fully use his extensive expertise for a worthwhile purpose. It was work well worth doing.

"Unknown contact, three o'clock low." Brock's voice was so calm that at first Sandoval glanced over quizzically to see if she was messing with him again. But her hands were already dancing over the control panel, killing the emergency siren before it could sound and deafen them, closing the circuit breakers to boot up MOL-26's ordnance panel, and hitting the lights. Immediately the floods went out and the lower-level contingency lighting came on, bathing the control center with an eerie red glow. Next, she hit the comms button. "Cheyenne, MOL-26, Cheyenne 26, urgent. We have a probable hostile incursion at three hundred miles and closing."

"Damn." Sandoval arrowed across the small observation deck, grabbed at her seatback to arrest himself, and scanned the board in alarm.

Through the loudspeaker came the unflappable tones of their Cheyenne CAPCOM. "26, please confirm the nature of the incursion?"

"Single vehicle," said Brock. "Velocity consistent with orbital. Approaching cross-track on an intersecting course from our three o'clock. Close to intersecting, anyway. If I'm judging this right, it'll cross our orbital plane just behind us."

Sandoval's eyes had already picked up the blip on the radar screen, but the displays on these new screens could be deceptive. "Size?"

"Unclear. Could be a Soyuz. Likely not as big as an Almaz unless they're wrapped in some serious RAM. Like, something we've never seen before."

Sandoval nodded. RAM were radar absorbing materials: paints, or dielectric coatings, or whatever. But he didn't know of anything the Soviets had that could make an Almaz look like a Soyuz, either.

Something Soyuz-sized could still mess them up pretty good, though.

The loudspeaker crackled. "26, Cheyenne. We have no friendly craft scheduled in your airspace. Nothing Air Force, nothing NASA."

"Possible debris?"

"Nothing larger than a pencil showing up in either NORAD tracking or NASA's Orbital Debris Office ephemerides. Assume hostile."

"Well, shit," Terri said. "Copy that."

Sandoval hit the button for internal comms. "Bogey incoming. Battle stations, all hands." He was half deafened as his own words came out of the Tannoy system, slightly delayed, but persevered. "Doyle, Krantzen, get up here. Rod goes to the Dyna-Soar and powers it up. Rod, be ready to separate from the MOL and fire missiles at need. Everyone: suit up as best you can once you're on station and monitoring systems. Helmets and gloves off for now but keep them within reach."

"Bogey, crew to stations, suit up to helmets and gloves, copy all," came Doyle's laconic tone, and moments later Sandoval could hear the two of them bouncing around rapidly in the crew quarters below. Doyle and Krantzen: light sleepers with quick reactions, well trained to move first and ask questions later. From Rod, all he heard was a terse "On it" in response; he'd been performing routine maintenance in the Big Gem and could hustle over to the Dyna-Soar in double-quick time.

Seconds later, two pressure suits flew up through the hatch, followed by Doyle. He moved quickly to the comms and ordnance station, and strapped in. Krantzen arrived on his heels, stationing himself behind Doyle and peering over his shoulder as best he could while donning his pressure suit.

Sandoval pulled himself into the chair beside Brock, his eyes scanning the boards. Enemy craft moving in on his Manned Orbiting Laboratory. Two of his crew roused from sleep below? Hadn't Sandoval seen this movie before? Was he about to lose another MOL?

"Déjà vu all over again." He glanced across at Brock, even as his fingers danced across switches. "Don't even think of correcting my grammar."

"No worries. I'm not Vivian. What the actual … hell is going on?"

"Damned if I know. I'm taking the DORIAN. You concentrate on the intruder trajectory."

"Except that I'm …" She'd been about to say "on duty here," or some such, but at the look on Sandoval's face she desisted. "Aye, sir. You have the board."

"I have the board. How long do we have?"

"Hang on." Terri pivoted away and started typing numbers into the guidance computer keypad.

Sandoval looked at the radar screen again, at the Soviet craft serenely closing the distance between them, then at the clock and the TV screen, which showed the Atlantic Ocean now rolling beneath them. They had time before they reached the coast of Europe. "Cheyenne, I'm prepping to reorient and surveil."

A pause, then a crackle. "Affirm. You're go to reorient. But for five minutes, max."

"Five minutes, rog." He powered up the RCS system with one hand and punched the comms button with the other. "All crew, prepare for slew."

Brock glanced over. "Taking a look-see?"

"Sure. I mean, why not use one of the largest orbiting telescopes in history to look at an object a couple hundred miles away? Here we go." MOL-26 started rolling around them. "Doyle, anything else useful from Cheyenne?"

"Not a thing." Doyle busied himself with his pressure suit, his eyes still on the board. "MOL-21 is over the Eastern Bloc right now, and that's likely taking up their time."

"And we will be, soon." Hardly a coincidence, then, that the hostile chose *right now* to show up.

MOL-26 was in low Earth orbit, traveling around the planet once every ninety minutes, at a speed of seventeen thousand six hundred miles per hour. So was the MiG spaceplane: same speed, but a different orbit. Those two orbits would intersect, that was already clear; the Soviet craft wouldn't be appearing to hold steady on their three, otherwise. But to determine what angle the MiG-105's orbit made with the MOL's, they'd need to figure out how quickly it was closing with them, and do some trigonometry.

Which was what Brock was doing now. But not quickly enough for Sandoval's taste. "Terri?"

"Wait. Still doing the math."

"Jeez, Terri, give me something. Anything."

"Okay. Give our relative speeds it looks like we have around eleven minutes before their orbit intersects ours. That horizontal velocity component means their orbit is inclined at maybe five degrees to ours."

Doyle was also frowning at his own radar screen, while tapping on his calculator. "I concur. By my numbers they pass right behind us and slightly below, in just over ten minutes."

"Projected closest approach?" Sandoval said tensely.

"Looks like the bogey will pass about five miles below us and ... yeesh, a little less than a mile away laterally." Terri shook her head.

At these velocities, that definitely counted as a near miss. "Circular orbit?"

"Eccentricity less than zero point one five, anyway."

Sandoval squinted at the verniers, goosed the ship a little further over in roll and yaw. "What *is* our relative speed?" Doing it in his head he came up with about half a mile per second, but he'd prefer to hear it from someone with a calculator.

"Two thousand two hundred feet per second," Doyle said. "Give or take."

Their eyes met briefly. That relative speed wasn't greatly dissimilar from dogfighting speeds of jet fighters over, say, Vietnam. Where a jet traveling at Mach 2.7 might launch an air-to-air missile that could travel at Mach 4.

Meaning, in round numbers, that it was by no means out of the question that this hostile could successfully launch an air-to-air missile, radar-guided or infrared-guided ... and take out Sandoval's MOL-26.

But would they?

Sandoval and his crew would see the missile on radar as soon as it launched, but at that point they'd need to react very nimbly to survive.

"Good job we have nerves of steel," Brock said.

"Sure." Doyle took quick a swig of water out of his canteen. "If you say so."

Sandoval did a quick mental scan of his body, alert for the faintest stirrings of panic, but felt nothing. His pulse was slightly elevated, but maybe that could be forgiven. All well and good, but even having to think about *not* having a panic attack was distracting. And irritating.

He nudged the MOL up in pitch, left in yaw. Peered at the TV, and then through the finder scope. "Terri, help me out here. This is hard."

Brock glanced at the blip on the radar screen and took a quick look through the binocular eyepiece. "I'm guessing you give it another five or six degrees in plus-X and then scan left to right in Y."

"Ah," Sandoval translated that mentally to roll-pitch-yaw and goosed his thrusters again.

"There it is. There! You've got it. You'll need to keep correcting in yaw to maintain it in view." She whistled. "I gotta say ... that is pretty."

"What is?"

"Pretty lethal, is what I mean." Brock fired off a series of photographs, *ka-chunk, ka-chunk, ka-chunk.*

Sandoval glanced at the finder scope and then across at the TV screen. "Holy cow …"

"Yep, it's a MiG-105," she said. "Got to be. First time anyone's seen one in space." From across the way Doyle gave a low whistle, and Brock hit the button to take more photographs. Sandoval just stared for a moment, unblinking, and then burped the RCS jets in between Brock's DORIAN exposures to bring the craft back to the center of the screen.

The Mikoyan-Gurevich MiG-105, codenamed Spiral, was part of the Soviet aerospace program known as the Experimental Passenger Orbital Aircraft, despite being a single-seater vehicle. It was the Soviet Union's first—and as far as any of them knew, only—spaceplane, flown by the Soviet Air Force. They launched it at high altitude from the back of a custom-built Tupolev supersonic transport, with a liquid fuel booster rocket attached to help it on its way into orbit.

As they could clearly see, the MiG-105 was a delta-wing craft, designed to allow for normal flight in atmosphere after reentry, along with a powered landing.

The Air Force's Boeing X-22C spaceplane—Dyna-Soar—was cool, but a little clunky, a little retro. This MiG-105 had *very* smooth lines. It was a rare object of beauty in a Soviet space program largely notable for boxy structures, sometimes onion-shaped but always a little "off." Presumably because aeronautics engineers had designed the MiG-105, not rocket guys.

Plus, the US Air Force Dyna-Soar was a two-seater and the MiG-105 was a single-pilot spaceplane, which gave it a substantial edge when it came to ferrying ordnance.

Terri whistled. "Those pods under the wings?"

"Could be anything," Sandoval said.

"Must be air-to-air missiles."

"Or could be an Earth science payload. Or a camera. Just keeping eyes on Europe, same as us."

"Or extra fuel tanks," Doyle added.

Brock peered over at Sandoval. "Except that none of us believe those are anything but missiles."

"Correct. Looks like a cannon on each side of the fuselage plus an air-to-air rocket under each wing. But if we were to take aggressive action, one of those other options will be exactly what the Soviets will claim. Be assured that they're filming us right now just as carefully as we're filming them."

This goddamned MiG was loaded for bear. It would take only one of those rockets to obliterate MOL-26.

Outside of the atmosphere, the MiG had no need to hold an aerodynamic course. This one was orbiting almost sideways on and rotating slowly, putting it in a barbecue mode relative to the Sun angle. Which at least meant its weapons weren't pointed straight at the MOL. Not yet, anyway.

"No response to hails," said Doyle.

"Shock me again," said Brock.

Doyle's brow creased. "Taunt ploy?"

"Got to be," Brock said. At the same moment, Sandoval said: "Hope so."

Krantzen looked back and forth between them. "Sirs?"

"Showing off. Daring us."

With its upturned nose and a regular-looking tail, it actually didn't look all that different from the MiG-25 interceptors that Peter Sandoval had occasionally gotten into aerial scraps with high above the killing fields of Vietnam, fifteen years before. Seeing such a beast in orbit around the Earth, was ... weird.

"They're threatening us," Sandoval said. "Showing what they could do, if they wanted. But they won't."

Krantzen blinked. "And we know this because ... why?"

"Because that would be first blood. First act of war. And they would prefer we did that. They're trying to goad us into pulling the trigger first."

Krantzen was shaking his head. "With all due respect ..."

Brock raised her hand to cut him off. "Less talk. Doesn't matter." And it didn't. They had no time to abandon the station. No time to even all suit up, if they had to take their pictures of the war zones on Earth and also keep watch on the Soviet spaceplane and be ready to respond with appropriate countermeasures if it attacked them. There was no way either Brock or Sandoval could divert their attention for that long.

"Here we are, and here we stay," Sandoval added, and looked over Doyle. "I repeat: we don't fire first."

"Roger that," Doyle said, and over the radio Rodriguez chimed in. "Affirm."

"But if they launch a missile, we launch a missile. He can't do a deorbit burn, or any other type of burn, quick enough to evade us."

None of them spoke the obvious, which was that for either craft, the odds of a direct hit at that distance was only fifty-fifty, whether the missile was IR-guided or radar-guided, given all the avoidance mechanisms available to both sides.

Ka-chunk. Ka-chunk. Ka-chunk. Without needing to be told, Brock was steadily taking pictures of the MiG as it rotated. "It's almost as if they want us to take a good look."

"I'm sure they do." Sandoval glanced at the clock, and at the Earth rolling beneath them. "And almost as if they're trying to distract us. Europe is coming up. Doyle?"

Ka-chunk. Then Doyle glanced over. "We disengage from MiG observation, and reorient for Poland and East Germany?"

Sandoval looked at the verniers, and at the Earth again. "Affirm. Do it from there? And right away? We need to get ready for Germany."

"Copy." Even as Doyle said it, they felt the different *clunk* as the thrusters fired to rotate the MOL.

"MOL-26, this is Cheyenne. Reorient for ... never mind." Their CAPCOM had obviously just seen the MOL's telemetry.

Sandoval grinned. "Way ahead of you, Cheyenne."

Krantzen was clearly perturbed. "Sirs? We're turning away? Not keeping an eye on it?"

"Soon the damned thing will be in binocular range anyway," Sandoval said. "Doyle, Krantzen, let us know immediately if you see a change in radar brightness."

"Wilco." If the Soviet craft swung to point nose-on at them, its radar echo would diminish in magnitude.

"Here we go," Brock said tensely. Closest approach ... still going ... and .... And it's past us."

Which, of course, meant the threat had just increased. A sane MiG-105 pilot wouldn't attempt to destroy a vessel he was currently flying *toward*. That would mean he'd have to pass through MOL-26's debris field, just minutes—or seconds—after the kill.

No, if he was going to fire at all, he'd send that missile in their direction right now, just seconds *after* their orbits intersected.

"Eyes peeled," Brock said to Doyle.

It was as much as Sandoval could do to ignore the radar and ready his instruments and concentration, as the green and brown of Europe swung into view in the DORIAN's sightline. "Everyone remember to breathe."

Brock grunted. "Now he tells us."

"Still betting it's a fake-out," Sandoval said. "They're pushing our buttons."

Sandoval hardly needed to explain. In atmosphere, American and Soviet forces did this shit to each other all the time. US planes routinely penetrated Soviet airspace during military exercises. Just last year during Able Archer, US military jets had flown several hundred miles into Soviet territory. Conventional Soviet MiG jets flew into Alaskan airspace on a regular basis. All part of the game.

"So far so good, anyway," Brock added.

Sandoval nodded. "Remember: if they turn to face us, wait for my command to fire."

"Hold fire until your command, affirm."

"That's a single-seater craft," Doyle said. "There's one of him and five of us. He might like those odds."

Damn it, Doyle had said the quiet part out loud. "It's not up to him," Sandoval said. "It's up to his commanding officer. He's up here for a reason."

"There may not even be a *him* in there," Brock said.

"Okay, fine. Or her."

"No, I just meant it could be unmanned."

"Huh." Sandoval shook his head. He didn't have time for speculation. The DORIAN was now pointing stably at eastern France, but he hadn't yet identified which part. French countryside was dense with little towns and villages. He glanced at the map, back into the binocular eyepiece. "Less chatter. I need to focus."

"Literally," Krantzen said, and when Doyle elbowed him, added; "Sorry."

They all fell silent, which if anything was more unnerving than the conversation.

Sandoval breathed out slowly, watching as Europe unfolded beneath him. The urge to glance back at the blip on the radar display was strong, but he resisted it. That's why he had Brock and Doyle.

Once over Germany he finally got his bearings, swung the DORIAN a couple degrees, and started taking pictures. *Ka-chunk. Ka-chunk.* "Shit," he said under his breath.

Even though he'd known from intel what he expected to see, the scene laid out beneath him on the ground was chilling. On the East German side, rows of Soviet T-55 and T-62 tanks were lined up with their big guns pointed across the border. On the West German side, a similar battalion of American M-48 and M-60 tanks had their gun barrels aimed in the opposite direction. If either side gave the order to fire, or if even one tank crew went rogue or released a shot by mistake, it would surely be mutually assured annihilation on both sides. And what would happen next?

Shades of the Berlin Crisis of 1961, when Soviet T-54s and US M-48 tanks had squared off against each other at the original Checkpoint Charlie, separated by less than two hundred feet. But in Berlin there had only been ten tanks on each side. Here on the main border between East and West, there were hundreds. Way too many for him to get dedicated pictures across the whole potential battlefield.

"This is just freaking insane," Terri Brock said next to him. She'd been looking at the pictures unrolling on the TV screen, while still monitoring the retreating MiG-105.

On Earth as in space, the big guns were lined up and ready to fire. Sandoval felt himself sweating. "You're not wrong."

He kept cranking away, using up film for as long as he could, swinging the MOL to peer back in the opposite direction once the border was behind them, and then continuing with the record shots all along the main roads of Germany and as far north into Poland as he could see from their current orbiting latitude. MOL-21, overflying earlier, would have done a better job on Poland than his MOL-26 could, but every last piece of data was worth having.

Finally, he exhaled. He'd forgotten his own admonition to keep breathing.

Beside him, Brock opened the channel back to Mission Control. "Cheyenne, MOL-26. Threat appears to have passed. Hostile is moving out of effective range."

Sandoval blinked at the radar screen. "So long, comrade MiG. We hardly knew you."

279

But he hardly felt comforted, and from the grim expressions on his crew's faces, none of the others did either.

"Cheyenne, 26. We'll need to schedule a film drop once we come back around. Please advise."

"Working it. We'll get back to you, 26." Right now, they were about to begin their pass over the Soviet Union. They couldn't drop a DRV, a Data Return Vehicle carrying the film they'd just taken, until MOL-26 was back over the Pacific or, even better, American soil, in thirty to forty-five minutes. Which meant they had to schedule it now, so that a dedicated C-130 Hercules aircraft could be on station to pluck it out of the air as it floated down under its parachute.

"They'd have been nuts to fire on us," Brock said, mostly for Krantzen's benefit. "Nuts. Start a shooting war in orbit *right now*? They shoot at a manned Air Force station, what would we do? Retaliate."

"Sure," Sandoval said. "We're very vulnerable here, to high explosive or even kinetic attack. But so are their Almaz stations. Attack us, and one thing leads to another." He knew the theory as well as she did, and the rest of the crew should, as well.

Apparently, the Soviets had seen it the same way. This time.

Brock waited, and when Sandoval tailed off, she finished the thought anyway. "Most likely end result: all our MOLs and their Almaz craft get wiped out in tit-for-tat retribution attacks, along with both sides' unmanned satellites. And then *no one* can look down at the Earth. Being blind is *not* what you want when you're dancing around the edges of World War III."

They all went quiet. If a nuclear war broke out, even a supposedly "limited" war in Europe, they'd have grandstand seats to the deaths of hundreds of millions of people, and the destruction of at least one entire continent. And the way matters stood right now, that war could easily break out before MOL-26 was able to fly over Germany again.

Sandoval felt numb. "Can you take over again for this Soviet Union pass? Doyle, assisting?"

"Sure." She swung herself into position.

"You have the board."

"I have the board." Terri lined up and started taking photographs right away, not even waiting for Doyle to arrive next to her.

"Rod, Sandoval. You can stand down and come back in."

"Already running the closeout checklist. I'll be back in the Gem in ten minutes. Uh, we're all off our timelines now. Should I do an abbreviated workout in there and take a nap, then relieve you guys on schedule for the next rotation?"

"Sounds good."

"Okay, rog." Rodriguez disconnected. Sandoval took a long drink of water and then looked over at Krantzen. "So. That was one of three things. Maybe four. Discuss."

Krantzen was used to Sandoval's "teachable moments" by now, because he responded immediately. "A threat. Probing our defenses. A taunt, as the colonel said." He indicated Brock.

Sandoval nodded. "That's one."

"Second possibility is a dry run. Ensuring that they had the accuracy to do a cross-track pass and come within firing range of us. It would also have enabled them to refine our ephemeris, I guess."

"Right, meaning we should likely file an orbit adjust burn with Cheyenne to change that ephemeris, sometime after we drop the DRV. Put it on your list. Next?"

Krantzen frowned.

"We did get a good look at them," Brock prompted, still taking pictures of strategic sites in Ukraine.

"Which means they also got a good look at us," Krantzen said. "They didn't have a DORIAN, but at that close range they don't exactly need a six-foot primary mirror to image us. So now they have footage of MOL-26, the Dyna-Soar, the Gem."

Sandoval eyed Brock. "He gets no hints for the last one."

"It could have been a planned attack," Krantzen said slowly. "That was called off at the last minute. Based on ... our obvious strength?"

"I guess that's possible," Brock said. "If they didn't expect us to have the X-22C up here as well as the MOL."

"Maybe," Sandoval said. "Or they could have called it off because it was supposed to coincide with a separate ground action that they weren't quite ready for, and they're keeping their powder dry for the main event."

"A border crossing?" Doyle said. "Damn."

"Or a nuclear preemptive strike," Brock said flatly.

Krantzen looked out of the window, down at the Earth's surface, currently now going into darkness beneath them. "I was trying not to think about that."

Sandoval looked at his watch. He was due for a meal, and so was Krantzen, but he wasn't remotely hungry. Regardless, he grinned at his crew with a show of bravado he didn't quite feel. "All part of the job, right?"

War in Europe, or war in space? Which would break out first?

Sandoval had the feeling they wouldn't need to wait long to find out.

20

Daedalus Base: Katya Okhotina
November 9, 1984

THE attackers came out of the night in both of the ways that mattered, strategically: in the middle of the long fourteen-day lunar night on Farside, and also well into Daedalus Base's main sleep period. A fleet of ten steel-armored but otherwise stripped down Soviet LEKs landed in a rough semicircle around the Daedalus habitats. Armed cosmonauts from Spetsgruppa Vympel, Soviet KGB special forces, burst forth from them almost before their landing pads met the lunar soil.

The Daedalus external night guard consisted of a half-dozen USAF astronauts and an equal number of cosmonauts from the Red Army. Confused and caught by surprise, one of the Soviets raised his rifle to shoot at the invading Vympel squad and was summarily shot by his own people, his chest exploding and suit decompressing simultaneously as a large-bore shell struck home and pulverized him.

The Air Force guards dropped too, falling prone to fire their rifles. Three perished in the next thirty seconds, the other three were spared when they tossed their weapons aside and spread their arms wide in surrender.

There was no response from inside Daedalus Base. As the US contingent learned later, the radar in the central control area had been disabled twelve hours beforehand. In the event, no one was conscious

283

anyway in that control area at the time of the attack, having already been incapacitated by a vial of fast-spreading gas. The skeletal missile launchers that sat atop a half dozen USAF MOLABs around the compound to defend it were captured by the Soviet forces without incident.

Inside Habitat Two, Katya Okhotina was awoken along with everyone else as the warning klaxon belatedly shrilled, echoing through every loudspeaker on the base. She and the other five cosmonauts in their small dormitory area jumped down from their bunks and ran out into the corridor in their sleep shirts and shorts, at first believing the integrity of the station had been breached by a puncture.

Okhotina had known nothing of the Soviet plan to take over control of Daedalus, and nor had any of her fellow cosmonauts or scientists at Bright Driver. Others clearly had: the Soviet Commander of the base, Vasili Doryagin, wearing a gasmask, had already secured and handcuffed his opposite number, the Air Force's General Johnstone. However, in the pandemonium that followed over the next twenty minutes, at least as many Soviet soldiers as American died as the incoming Spetsgruppa Vympel force attempted to secure the base.

Okhotina and others were still milling around in confusion when the Tannoy blared again: three loud emergency tones, followed by Doryagin's voice, speaking in heavily Russian-accented English. "The American staff of Daedalus Base will stand down. Kneel and remain where you are with your arms outstretched, hands empty and visible, until instructed otherwise. Daedalus Base, and Bright Driver, are now under solely Soviet authority." Doryagin switched to Russian. "Comrades, please also kneel, as the Americans are doing. Our apologies for the indignity, but we would not wish you to come to any harm due to a misunderstanding. We will complete our operation as quickly as possible, and you will cooperate by remaining still until we can identify and separate you."

Katya had already dropped forward onto her knees on hearing the proclamation in English. She had no wish to die at the hands of the KGB. Inside, her mind was whirling.

This had to be some kind of bizarre … mistake? Surely? Why on Earth would the Soviet Presidio take this giant destabilizing step? Back home, was the USSR already at war with the United States? Due to its location on Farside, Daedalus Base was only in intermittent contact with Earth …

Armed Soviet soldiers in uniform were now running through the corridors. Daedalus only had two habitat buildings, both small, and it was the work of just a few minutes to subdue both.

"Comrade Okhotina? You will come with us."

"Yes, sir," she said automatically, and glanced up. She did not know the Vympel soldier who had made the request.

Apparently, due to her good English skills and knowledge of the Americans, following her role on Vivian Carter's LGS-1 mission and her more recent experience here at Daedalus, she had been selected to act as a liaison between the new invading force and the U.S. contingent.

The Soviet scientists and cosmonauts were instructed to return to their dormitories, aside from a few of the higher-ranking officers who were sent into Central Control. The Americans were herded up and secured. With Okhotina's help, Gerard O'Neill and other senior US scientists were cut out of this herd and guided into the Central Control, which still reeked of the knockout gas but was no longer a threat to consciousness. The rest were handcuffed, ziplined, or locked into their dormitories. Later, those that wished would be escorted out to their Lunar Modules in groups of three and permitted to depart, rising off the Moon's surface to rendezvous at Eagle Station prior to their return to Earth.

Those who departed were under strict orders not to fly around the Moon and land again at Zvezda-Copernicus, and advised that their LMs would be shot out of the sky if they attempted to do so. No explanation was forthcoming of how this might be achieved, but no one seemed inclined to take the chance.

Within the hour, the Soviets were in sole charge of Bright Driver.

Okhotina joined two other Soviet women who had been roped into service to ease the relations between the Soviet military and the now forcibly detained Americans. It was almost like déjà vu. However, this time, the Soviets needed no American hostages to help them run the Base. They already knew well how all the systems at Daedalus worked.

And, for that matter, they also knew how to operate the mass driver.

21

Zvezda-Copernicus: Feye Gisemba
November 9, 1984

EVEN after a month, it felt odd to be back on the Moon and ... just staying put. Especially during lunar daylight. Back when Feye Gisemba had served as second-in-command of Vivian Carter's LGS-1 mission, they'd begun and ended their journey by night at Zvezda-Copernicus, and rested up for fourteen days at Daedalus at the halfway point. But whenever the Sun was up they'd been constantly on the road and on a tight schedule, wheels rolling and busy-busy-busy.

Right now, it was eight days past local dawn at US-Copernicus, early afternoon, with the Sun high in the sky, and Gisemba was still here. Mostly dealing with paperwork, manifests, and routine maintenance, because he had a base to command.

In principle, Gisemba would not take over as Commander of US-Copernicus until Daniel Grant launched back to Earth in a week's time. For the past four weeks he'd formally been Grant's deputy, learning the ropes and preparing to step into the role. In reality, having handled the complex and ever-changing logistics of the growing Hadley Base for several months in 1979, plus the traveling roadshow of LGS-1 just a year and a half ago, managing US-Copernicus felt like a breeze by comparison. Gisemba already knew how all this worked ... or how it *should* work. He'd landed itching to make changes, and Grant seemed content to sit back and leave him to it.

In addition, Gisemba was *much* better at dealing with their Soviet counterparts than Daniel Grant was. Grant had run out of patience with the new Zvezda Commander, General Orlov, long ago, and the two rarely spoke except through intermediaries. And it just so happened that one of those intermediaries was Andrei Lakontsev, Gisemba's former team-mate on LGS-1 and a good friend. Occasionally, when their schedules eased up, the two of them could sneak a meal or a drink together and chat about old times.

Bottom line: Gisemba was already running US-Copernicus, moving and shaking and schmoozing with the Soviets, and getting the South Pole water prospecting project back on track in his spare time, while Daniel was lame-ducking it, already on his glide path out of there. And everybody was happy with that.

Until all the alarms went off in the middle of the night.

Just minutes after the Soviet attack on Daedalus Base commenced, Gisemba's pager went off right next to his head and startled him out of a deep sleep. He hit the light and bounced up onto his feet before even taking a conscious thought, pulling on pants and a shirt and running out of his sleep cubicle less than twenty seconds after that.

Gisemba's berth was barely thirty feet from the main US-Copernicus command center, and he could already hear the rapid clacking of the teleprinter, sounding like machine gun fire in the otherwise silent room. He skidded to a halt in front of it as it stopped and tore off the paper.

It was gibberish. Just a few groups of letters and numbers in irregular blocks, plus random words that made no sense in context.

Daniel Grant appeared behind him in a similar state of hasty dress, his feet bare, and plucked the paper out of his hand. Gisemba flinched. "Jesus, what the hell?"

"Shit's hitting the fan." Grant scanned the printout briefly and then dropped it and pulled himself into the hotseat, jabbing at buttons. By now Gisemba could hear other pagers going off through the thin rooms of the sleeping quarters, and the bump and stumble of people responding with various degrees of coordination and effectiveness.

Grant slid on a headset and flipped a switch. "Alpha, this is Copernicus zero actual. Conflict Protocol One. Immediate launch."

"It's what, now?" Gisemba said.

The loudspeaker buzzed immediately. "Conflict One, confirm?"

"One, confirm. This is a direct order, highest priority. Not a drill."

"Copy your Conflict One. We're on the move."

Grant flipped more switches. As he spoke, his words came out of the loudspeaker above Gisemba's head, delayed by a fraction of a second. "All crew, on your feet. Hostile contact, Code Red. Suit up."

Gisemba blinked. "Who's Alpha? What the hell is Conflict One?"

"Hold that thought." Grant spun in his chair and pointed at the window. "Open the blind, tell me what you see."

Startled into silence at Grant's definitive resumption of command, Gisemba hurried to obey. Sunlight speared in across the room, and both men squinted. "Not a damned thing," Gisemba said. "Oh, wait. Couple cosmonauts walking north."

"Yeah, I bet." Grant unlocked a drawer next to him, pulled out a sidearm and belt, and strapped them around his waist.

Gisemba stared at him for a moment, then reached forward to grab the teleprinter paper off the floor and stare at that instead. It didn't make any more sense to him the second time around. "Care to tell me what's going on?"

Loudspeaker crackle: "Copernicus, Alpha Flight is wheels-up and inbound. Awaiting further direction."

Grant turned to Gisemba again, his face grim. "Strategic Air Command and all US lunar forces are now at DEFCON-2. We expect all US Armed Forces on Earth to follow shortly."

They were on the brink of war? Just like that? Gisemba blinked rapidly. "Oh … shit."

"Exactly." Grant turned his attention back to the board. "Oh, by the way? I'm CIA and Night Corps, and I'm assuming full command of all Nearside US space assets, effective immediately. Your days of nitpicking me and playing Commander are over. You will comply without hesitation with any orders I give you."

Gisemba took a step back in surprise.

Grant half-grinned. "Yeah. Sorry. As of now, US-Copernicus is under Night Corps jurisdiction."

"The hell it is …. That contravenes the Accord. This is a peaceful scientific station. A *NASA* station."

"Negative. The last shreds of the Lunar Accord burned to ash a few minutes ago, when the Soviets stormed Daedalus Base."

"When they—*what?*"

"Gisemba, wake up, goddamn it. Go bring me a suit and suit up yourself. That's an order, soldier." Then his eyes flickered over to the window. "Crap. Never mind, no time."

Four cosmonauts were jogging across the brief swath of regolith that separated Zvezda's Hatch 3 from US-Copernicus, armed with rifles. Half a dozen more were assembling beyond them, just north of Zvezda Hatch 1.

"Here they come." Grant checked his watch, and allowed himself a full, tight smile. "Boy, do Orlov's bastards have a surprise coming."

The loudspeaker crackled again, and suddenly they were hearing gunshots and crashes. "Sir?" It was a woman's voice, one that Gisemba couldn't identify over the cacophony. "Sir, Soviets are trying to break through Checkpoint Charlie. We're taking fire, two men down …"

"Copy that. Sons of bitches." Grant strode across the room, unholstering his pistol. "Well? Come on."

Gisemba hurried after him. "But … what the hell are we doing?"

"Sounds like our American forces at Daedalus caved at the first gunshot. We're not about to cave here." Grant shot him a fierce grin. "Can't have the Reds doubting Western resolve, now can we? This one, we have to win."

Within the US corridor leading westward to Joint Port, the sound of gunfire was deafening. However, the mass of men in full body armor and riot protection helmets ahead of Grant and Gisemba were already making way, marching forward in step. Moments after they arrived, that part of the battle was already over.

Grant had his hands over his ears, listening through his headset with some difficulty. Then it all suddenly went quiet. "Done," he said to Gisemba with some satisfaction. "They've pushed the Reds back past Charlie, put up the blockade, and immobilized Joint Port. Come with me."

Grant turned on his heel, his feet still bare, and strode back into the American sector. Gisemba jogged to keep up with him, feeling dazed. "Now what?"

"Now?" Grant's lips curled back from his teeth. "Now we bring the fight to *them*."

Astronauts were already assembling at East Hatch directly in front of them, but Grant just saluted them crisply and turned left, back through the workshop areas and past Command and Control. He closed the bulkhead behind them and locked it firm. Green lights came on above the sealed door.

Ahead, ten feet short of the North Hatch, four astronauts were ripping out ceiling tiles. They were clad in Apollo Moon suits with full PLSS life support backpacks, but with helmets and gloves doffed. Beside them, six assault rifles modified for vacuum were leaned against the wall.

Gisemba gaped. These men had deployed astonishingly quickly. Had they been *sleeping* in those suits? "What the hell …?"

Continuing to ignore him, Grant snapped more orders into his headset microphone. Anyway, as Gisemba moved in closer it became obvious: above the stripped-out tiles was another small hatchway, presumably leading outside. But that hatch was not an airlock. He turned back at Grant in disbelief. "That's not on the base plans."

Grant grinned. "And if you're surprised, imagine the look on Ivan's face. There are similar security exit hatches over the South and East airlocks, plus on our side of Joint Port."

"Jesus Christ. When were you going to tell me all this?"

"I wasn't. But your new second-in-command would have known all about it."

Great. So Gisemba would have been the US-Copernicus base commander in name, cataloging his supplies and setting his duty rosters and thinking himself all-important, like a good NASA drone, while these Night Corps bastards were really the ones in control. "That's just terrific."

"Isn't it, though? Suit up, double-quick, before we blow that thing."

Gisemba hurried to obey. He'd never pulled on a spacesuit and donned a PLSS so quickly in his life, but Grant did it even faster. Meanwhile, two soldiers unhitched part of the floor, and lifted it at one end so that it became a ramp.

Grant nodded in satisfaction. "Okay, guys. Helmets on, gloves on. Raise your hand when your suit is secure."

Gisemba's was the last hand up, but only by a few seconds.

He knew all these men, or at least he'd thought he did, but they'd clearly trained for this and were used to taking orders from Grant. Which meant that Grant had been running his own covert Night Corps cell in this *NASA* base the entire time.

Gisemba felt like this world's biggest dupe. There'd been a whole shadow layer of activity operating right under his nose since he'd arrived on the Moon, and he'd had no inkling.

His anger rose, along with his fear. Night Corps was trained for lunar combat. Gisemba was not. He'd come under fire several times, but had never even fired a rifle himself on the Moon. That was obviously about to change. American lives—all their lives—were on the line.

"Here we go, then." Grant's helmet was on, and now Gisemba now heard his voice through his helmet headset. "We are Go for corridor depressurization. Blow the hatch on my mark, and then we're up and out. Choose targets and fire at will."

"Holy *shit*," Gisemba said. The others said nothing, but snatched up their rifles and quickly lined up, ready to race up the ramp.

So Gisemba grabbed up a rifle of his own, figured out where the safety was, and stepped into line behind the fourth Night Corps grunt. Like a good little soldier.

He had only a second or two to consider how crazy this was. The men in front of him weren't wearing the usual Night Corps armored suits. They presumably hadn't had time to dig them out of … storage? If they'd even brought them to Copernicus—it was easier to hide a man's motivations and training than his goddamned exosuit. Gisemba knew the layout of US-Copernicus pretty well, or had thought he did, and he had no clue where they could even have stashed a whole bunch of them. So maybe they hadn't.

And, of course, Gisemba himself was also in a standard Apollo suit. Any concentration of fire on any part of his suit—or his helmet!— would breach it. So, it was up to him not to take those bullets, if he could possibly help it.

Plus, he still had nightmares about that day at the South Pole. When Vivian Carter had taken shrapnel or debris or bullets or whatever to her PLSS backpack, her entire environmental control system had broken down. If Gisemba ended up with a dead suit here, he would be all the way dead, almost immediately. No one else would spare the time to save him.

"Mark," said Grant.

Even as the hatch exploded outward, swinging up and away to reveal bright sunlight, the first Night Corps grunt was already leaping through it, followed quickly by the second. Out on the surface, Gisemba saw the flashes as the shooting began.

Then it was Gisemba's turn. He pounded doggedly up the ramp, fast as he could ... and then he was standing on the roof of US-Copernicus and firing his rifle on full automatic at the red-suited cosmonauts fifty feet away from him, down on the lunar surface.

Those two Reds seemed to go down fast, but Gisemba wasn't fooled. He threw himself forward to lie prone on the base roof before scanning around him to see what *else* might be going on around him.

Freaking chaos, that was what.

GIsemba quickly identified four different firefights going on, in or near the various Copernicus and Zvezda hatches. Then he glimpsed a silver shape speeding out of the sky toward him like a missile, red flame jutting from its base, and instinctively turned his visor away as it passed over him. Rolling onto his back, he followed it with his eyes, tracking it with his rifle at the same time.

Gisemba had never seen a Night Corps Lunar Module, but had no difficulty identifying it. It had the blocky insect shape of a NASA LM but with a much sleeker and heavier-looking ascent stage, and fewer protrusions. Most shocking, it also had gimballed gunner positions on either side of the ascent stage, each containing a suited and armored astronaut, just sitting the hell out there in the open behind what looked like a giant gun.

"Holy shit," he said yet again, somewhat redundantly.

All that extra weight didn't seem to be holding the LM back any, nor the other two battle LMs that were following along in its wake, strafing the cosmonauts out on surface.

Where had they come from? Given the speed at which they'd appeared, they must have been stationed in Kepler Crater. Gisemba knew that Night Corps had established a forward base there, prior to the conflict at Marius a year and a half ago ... but had had no idea that it was still staffed. He hadn't been briefed, hadn't even thought about it. Night Corps operated on need to know, and evidently Gisemba didn't have that. Which would have pissed him off if he wasn't already *extremely* pissed off, and terrified into the bargain.

He was sweating like crazy, lying out here in the full blaze of sunlight. His suit already smelled of his fear. He took a moment to stab a finger at the environmental controls on his chest to bring his temperature down a notch and rocked forward. The LMs were doing a great job of scattering the Soviets, but a poor job at neutralizing them. The cosmonauts were returning fire, and many of them were still running toward Copernicus ... and toward Gisemba and Grant and his little cell of Night Corps soldiers, up here defending the Command and Control hab. Even as Gisemba watched, an explosive shell drilled into the hab twenty feet to his left, lifting the roof beneath him and sliding him sideways.

One of those running cosmonauts might be Andrei Lakontsev, or any one of a dozen Russians Gisemba had broken bread with, eaten meals with, drunk terrible bathtub vodka with, laughed with ... but right now, he couldn't afford to think about that.

He pulled his rifle around, drew a bead, and fired two shots in quick succession, a double-tap which he hoped might have breached the Soviet's helmet. The guy spun and went down in any case.

Coldly, Gisemba chose another target.

The next half hour was a confused blur. More Soviet troops had come up from the Annex, pounding down from the rim of Copernicus Crater in a goddamned V formation and firing as they came. At the same time, Soviet LK landers had swooped out of the sky onto them, only to be faced by a new wave of Night Corps LMs from ... somewhere? Who the hell even knew? Aside from Grant, that is.

Very belatedly, Gisemba made the connection: "Alpha" had to be Night Corps' Major Alpha, whom they'd met at the South Pole after the Soviet attack way back in January '83. Apparently still playing at Action Man, here on the Moon.

Sticking with Grant and his squad, Gisemba had landed up just east of US-Copernicus as part of a line defending the parked NASA Lunar Modules and Cargo Containers. He was nervously aware that the base fuel dump was just a couple hundred feet north of his position, but right now the Soviets didn't appear to be targeting it. A valuable resource for them to capture, maybe.

And here came a Soviet LEK, dropping down out of the sky right above him. Gisemba and his buddies scattered left and right as grenades exploded around them … then a Night Corps LM came in from the west, flying low over Zvezda-Copernicus to engage the LEK.

Gisemba watched in grim fascination as the Night Corps LM twisted and turned, matching the moves of the now-fleeing LEK. It was a goddamned dogfight, is what it was, using lunar landing craft. It was one of the most horrifying sights he'd seen in his life.

The result was inevitable. The two gunners on the LM had many more degrees of freedom of movement than the Soviet gunner lying prone in the LEK hatch. And for all the heaviness of the LM's appearance it was nimbler than the LEK, tighter in its turns, almost uncanny in its ability to jump higher above the lunar surface in a single "bound," or rocket pulse, to evade incoming fire.

For a few seconds it looked like a video game, or a scene out of a Star Wars movie.

The LEK swerved, tried to bank around the Upstation pillars and put them between himself and the pursuing Night Corps LM, and presumably then flee, but … no dice. Gisemba put an instinctive hand up as the LEK spun out of control and crashed just below the crater rim, although there was no flash, no explosion. Merely the brief flare of what was probably the main engine flipping up into Gisemba's line of sight in the craft's last fraction of a second before its wreckage tumbled into the crater.

A hundred yards south of him a second LM nailed another LEK Gisemba hadn't even seen until that moment, scoring a direct hit in the center of its descent stage. This LEK spun in the air, spitting flame, a firework gone wrong, and then plummeted down to crash onto the surface. The wreckage carved a line that must have been fifty feet long, chunks of it breaking off and bouncing separately across the regolith.

From this distance Gisemba couldn't see the individual cosmonauts' bodies. He hoped they'd died instantly.

This was war. It was also awful, terrible foolishness.

"With me." Grant was already up and running. The two other surviving astronauts in Grant's group scurried after him. Feye Gisemba tore his eyes away from the wreckage of the Soviet LEK and followed. Catching up with them on the crater's edge, he could see Grant gesturing while obviously talking on a frequency Gisemba could not access.

Down in Copernicus Crater Gisemba could see the blue glow from the Zvezda Annex, and a couple of the surviving LEK and LK landers fluttering in to land there. Several LMs were still circling above them all, but Night Corps now owned the skies and faced no other aerial threats. The cable car was in motion, heading down; it looked crowded with more cosmonauts than it was designed to hold, and was swaying fiercely.

Gisemba backed up quickly as one of those cosmonauts began to fire up at them, the muzzle flashes clearly visible.

"All right. Alpha and Gamma flights, this is Copernicus zero actual. Take out Upstation. Root it out. Now."

Another voice, which sounded like Major Alpha himself: "Gamma Two, you're in first. Gamma Four supporting."

"Good grief ..." Gisemba ran forward. "For God's sake, Daniel, they're retreating. Let them go ..."

"To regroup down there and come right back up over the parapet at us? No way."

"But—"

Too late for buts. A battle LM of a type Gisemba hadn't seen yet was already swooping in, this one with a rocket mounted on either side where the gunners had been on the previous LMs.

Those rockets were air-to-ground missiles. Both launched simultaneously, their ignition punching the LM upward as they released. Both missiles scored direct hits. A second LM in pursuit, presumably Gamma Four, peeled off quickly without needing to fire its own missiles.

For a moment, Upstation was obscured behind a double detonation that produced a sheet of flame and flung massive chunks of rock high into the air. Conventional high explosives, at least, Gisemba thought. If it had been a tactical nuke rather than HE, the flash would have blinded them all.

For a moment, the structure appeared to hold. Then, Gisemba saw the main pylon that held the long heavy cable shift. It shivered sideways, and then toppled forward, shearing off near the base.

"Oh my God, oh my God." Without conscious volition, Gisemba ran forward again, toward the crater rim.

At this time of lunar day, the interior of Copernicus Crater was almost entirely illuminated. Gisemba could see every drawn-out, painful detail as the two long, long cables rippled, an undulation that turned into a whiplash as the pylon smashed into the rock of the terracing and bounced further out into the space beyond.

The cable car gondola had been less than a quarter of the way along its long journey to Downstation. Gisemba saw four cosmonauts fly out of the gondola, frantically waving their arms and legs, trying to cling to a support that was no longer there. But the six that remained, holding on to the gondola, had only a brief respite. In the Moon's low gravity, they began their deceptively slow fall moments later. Even in one-sixth gravity, none could possibly survive.

Gisemba watched in horror as the bodies dropped into the void. It seemed to take an agonizing length of time before the cosmonauts smashed into lunar rock, some on the lowest tier of the terraced cratering, some bouncing sickeningly to arc upward again, already limp and broken. The miles-long cable twisted and turned as it scoured the floor of the crater, ripping up boulders and raising clouds of dust, writhing as the many stresses and torques worked themselves out, until it, too, finally came to a halt. And all in that eerie lunar silence.

Satisfied, Grant had already turned and was striding back toward US-Copernicus, flanked by the two other astronauts.

Gisemba stared into the huge crater for a few moments more. He could now see that the massive wrench of the cables had yanked Downstation clear of its rocky foundations to lie tumbled and smashed at least a half mile from its original location. Copernicus Annex still glowed, the light blue now appearing sickly, and the final Soviet landers were now putting down next to it. From this distance, he could no longer pick out the Soviet corpses.

Sickened and suddenly aware that he was alone and exposed, Gisemba turned and followed the Night Corps commander back down the slope.

Looking down on Zvezda-Copernicus from upslope, it was very clear that the base was in terrible shape. Zvezda had been breached with multiple gaping holes along its main E-shape. The Copernicus side had also suffered explosive breaches in at least two places, on the west side of the laboratory space, and the north side of the corridor that had linked Copernicus with Zvezda. There was likely other damage that Gisemba couldn't see yet.

His command, Gisemba's command, was over before it had truly begun, wrecked and torn from him by this Cold War turned hot—again—and by the ruthless actions of Daniel Grant.

He checked his radio transmitter was off, and said out loud, just to hear himself say it: "My debrief from this action is going to be mighty interesting, Daniel. I can assure you of that." Saying it felt like a promise.

And for what? Copernicus Crater itself didn't even have any intrinsic strategic value. It wasn't like they'd needed to hold the ground. It was retaliation, pure and simple. Payback for the Soviet takeover of Daedalus Base, right around the other side of the Moon.

He knew how they'd spin it, of course. A reduction in Soviet force. Removing hostile combatants that might next go and attack Jura Base, the US mining operation to the north, which did have huge strategic importance.

Like My Lai, like everywhere else, shit like this always got covered up. Gisemba would likely get nowhere. But he was still mightily, incredibly pissed about the whole thing.

Gisemba's headset now echoed with Grant's voice, the last voice he wanted to hear by now, in what was clearly a general announcement to both sides, but primarily aimed at the Soviets.

"Be advised we have armed teams out on surface, covering all your exit hatches, and that Joint Port is barricaded and closed to Soviet foot traffic at this time. Get into Zvezda and stay there while I tell you what's going to happen next.

"You Reds are devils for laying out the ultimatums, right? Well, here's ours. Every last one of you is launching off the Moon, leaving Zvezda Base, right now. There will be an immediate and complete Soviet withdrawal. We will allow you to depart only from Hatch Two, one by one and walking twenty feet apart. You will walk directly to your Lander and enter promptly on arrival. That is the only acceptable Soviet EVA at this time. Any cosmonaut heading in any other direction will be considered an enemy combatant, and we will take appropriate measures. Congregation in any area will be taken as an aggressive move on your part, and again, we shall take appropriate action without further warning. But you will not be fired upon if you proceed exactly as directed.

"I want to see the first boots outside on the ground in ten minutes or less. Launches will be conducted in the same manner: one at a time, thirty seconds apart, and launching straight into orbit.

"Any refusal or delay will be treated as an aggressive action. Ten minutes and one second from now we will begin taking steps to permanently disable what remains of Zvezda. I will leave the details to your imagination.

"We did not want this shooting war, but be assured that now you have begun one, the United States has decisively ended it. It was always a battle you could not win. Think on that, as you leave the lunar surface."

Grant paused, and then obviously couldn't help himself. His final words:

"Enjoy your moondust, suckers."

CHAPTER 22

MOL-26, Earth orbit; Peter Sandoval, Terri Brock
interplanetary space: Vivian Carter
November 9-10, 1984
Mission Elapsed Time: 494-495 days

"OKAY, people, listen up. We have a number of situations unfolding."

Sandoval looked around each of his crew in turn. Every face was serious, but he saw a variety of different reactions. Krantzen, floating up alongside the window, immediately looked out of it as if he thought the Earth might shatter into immense shrapnel in front of his eyes. Brock instinctively leaned in to check the board Rodriguez was currently manning, making routine observations over southern China, but she'd learn nothing from that. Doyle glanced at the silent cryptographic tele-printer. Rodriguez turned to stare fixedly at Sandoval as if trying to see through his skull to the thoughts beneath, and then realized what he was doing and turned his attention back to his observations of China.

No one asked questions. The new bright orange DEFCON-2 light in the top right corner of the control board told its own story.

"Matters have come to a head very quickly on the Moon. As you can see, Strategic Air Command is now at DEFCON-2 due to the lunar situation, and we expect US ground forces to follow suit imminently.

"Here's what we know. Shortly after we had our close call with the Soviet spaceplane, the Soviets took unilateral control of Daedalus

Base. A squadron of LEK landers from who-knows-where ferried in a Spetsgruppa Vympel assault team, which quickly neutralized the external security forces. Meanwhile, inside, Doryagin and friends secured the control center using knockout gas. There are several dead and injured on both sides, but the situation on the ground is now stable. The Soviets have control of the mass driver, which they claim is merely … for safe keeping, or some shit, I didn't read that part carefully."

"Quarantine," Brock said. "Officially, they've announced a quarantine of Daedalus Base, denying American military access. They're saying that the quarantine extends only to US military equipment and personnel. All food and water supplies, clothing, and other humanitarian supplies can continue to enter Daedalus unhindered—but under strict monitoring."

Rodriguez licked dry lips. "Whatever the hell they call it … they now have the capability to launch nukes at the US from the Moon?"

"Not right away. That would require additional engineering and testing. How long that would take?" Sandoval shrugged. "Not my department, but it's a great question. The Soviets do emphasize that they have no nuclear weapons on the Moon at this time. We don't believe that for a second.

"Anyway, at close to the same time, on Nearside, a pitched battle broke out at Zvezda-Copernicus. It's unclear whether the Soviets attempted a takeover there simultaneous with their Daedalus action, or Grant initiated a preemptive strike on hearing about Daedalus. Radio communications are down, and our single MOL-B overpass since the commencement of hostilities paints a confused picture. We do know that Grant pulled in Alpha Force from Kepler, and that Alpha brought in Gamma Force from Vaporum for additional air support. I expect an update imminently."

He checked his watch and glanced at the board. "On Earth, skirmishes have broken out all along the German border. Nothing organized. Sporadic firing, conventional weapons only, but things may be on the verge of escalating.

"So now I come to our new orders. First, we're to double-team on all passes over Europe and the Soviet Union, effective immediately, and suspend all training exercises during those passes. Sorry, Krantzen. Also, we're to focus on critical and strategic targets on the European and Asian spheres only. Surveillance of secondary targets on other continents is suspended, so we conserve film and don't get overloaded, but we're to remain on high alert at all times in case of new orders or new pop-up targets, given the volatility of the situation.

"Second, and this is important: in line with DEFCON-2, our defensive posture has now been upgraded. If we're approached again by a MiG, or other confirmed Soviet space asset, we're to fire upon it without warning or further notice, on the assumption that they will initiate a strike upon us if we do not. Am I understood? Please provide visual confirmation: we fire without warning."

All hands went up. Quietly, Terri Brock said: "Automatic escalation, though?"

"I didn't make these rules," Sandoval said. "They're direct from Cheyenne. Third: following completion of the next Asia pass—the one after this, so around ninety minutes from now—I've been cleared to hold another briefing to reveal additional above-top-secret information to you all. There's no time for that now, while we're reorganizing, but trust me: you'll want to know. Thus, three of you will be delaying your next sleep period by a couple of hours. Sorry." He looked around at them all. "That's all the sunny joy I have for you, right now. Rod and Doyle, you'll reconfigure the system for a war footing. Brock and I will grab a bite to eat so we're ready for the next Europe pass. Krantzen … sorry, man, but you're on maintenance and cleanup for the next hour, then you can come help out up here later as needed. Dismissed."

As Doyle squeezed by to sit with Rodriguez, and Krantzen went below, Terri Brock coasted in from Sandoval's left. "Vivian Carter?" she murmured.

Sandoval nodded, his face a mask. "She'll get a briefing in less than an hour. It's the soonest we could line one up with NASA. Now. Let's go eat and stretch a bit. The next pass over Germany is going to be a bear."

Vivian pulled herself into CM-1 and strapped in. Dave Horn was already booting up the video connection with Mission Control. She glanced around the sky. "Where's Earth, again?"

Horn paused and blinked at the guidance computer. "Um. Give me a moment."

She grinned. "Doesn't matter, I guess. It's kind of amusing. I used to think a quarter million miles was such a long way." The distance between the Earth and Moon, or the separation of either of them from L5. Tiny, in cosmic terms. "Now we're so far from anywhere that we've stopped counting, and don't even know which direction we're going in."

Horn nodded. "Hey, it's all the same, right? Wherever you go, there you are."

By now, Vivian knew the drill. "Cultural reference?"

"Oh, right. You weren't at movie night the other night."

"Star Wars?"

"Buckaroo Banzai Across the 8th Dimension."

"Really? Huh. Sounds like a classic."

Dave considered. "You know, I think it just might be, in a quirky way. Anyway, what are we here for?"

"Don't know yet," Vivian said. "But I'm sure we're about to find out." She time-checked with the clock on the board. "Okay, our scheduled update from Ellis begins in five seconds, on my mark."

"Roger that, Commander."

"Mark."

Five seconds later, Ellis Mayer's face appeared on the TV screen in front of them. He was sitting not in his usual seat in Mission Control, but in the secure room used for critical briefings, and his expression was grim. "Apollo Mars Astarte, Mission Control. Vivian, Dave, hi. I hope you're there and ready, because I have bad news. And there's a lot of it."

Their previous good cheer evaporated immediately.

Vivian floated in the middle of the forward compartment and clapped her hands for attention. "Hey, everyone. Some updates from Earth. And the Moon."

Everybody turned to look at her and their conversations died away in moments.

"You already know that the Soviets have invaded Poland and gone through into East Germany. They're now way the hell over at the border with East Germany, confronting the NATO forces. Sporadic fighting has broken out in several places, and the latest is that an additional Soviet force is mobilizing to blockade West Berlin again. Guys …" Vivian took a deep breath. "Everything's on the hairy edge. We might be looking at a nuclear exchange at any moment. Could be a tactical battlefield exchange limited to the European theater, could be … could be total. US forces everywhere are now at DEFCON-2."

She could see them all go pale. The only audible response was a silent, almost reverential "holy shit" from Rudy Frank.

"It gets worse. There's more, much more. A Soviet force has already taken control of Daedalus Base and Bright Driver. They now have the ability—at least in principle—of peppering the US with tactical nukes."

"That's what we get for building the thing in the first place," Laura said. "*Insane.*"

"Hold the backchat. This is an emergency. In addition to the Daedalus situation, there's a full-scale battle going on right now between US and Soviet forces at Zvezda-Copernicus." She swallowed. It was tough to say the words aloud and try to remain calm and factual, especially knowing that her friend Feye Gisemba, as incoming US-Copernicus Commander, was right in the thick of it. "We don't know how it started. But we do know that … there's a body count. People on both sides are dead, and probably many more will be dead before it's over. But our number one issue right now is that Astarte may also be at risk. This ship. And us."

The scientists all stared at her as if she was speaking in tongues. Josh Rawlings, Vivian noted, had immediately pulled himself up to the Astarte command console and begun a methodical check of systems.

Greg Heinz shook his head. "*What?*"

"Even out here?" Rudy added.

"Board looks clean," Rawlings said. "All systems are nominal. Not that that means much."

"I'll suit up," Marco said.

Dave Horn nodded. "I'll buddy him. Unless you want me to check the Command Module systems, Viv?"

"Outside first," Vivian said. "Go over the entire exterior with a fine-tooth comb looking for anything out of the ordinary. Anything at all."

Dardenas and Horn were already unhooking suits from the grid floor and beginning to don them. Rudy Frank was just staring at Vivian, his mouth wide. Laura looked back and forth between them all. "I … don't understand."

Vivian spelled it out for them. "Simultaneous military actions on the Earth and the Moon. Both are operations that must have been a long time in the planning. And we're fresh from a rendezvous with the Soviets."

"You seriously think that—"

"I don't think anything, Laura. But it's possible that we've been sabotaged, even that an explosive device has been placed somewhere on the Astarte."

Laura blinked rapidly. "You're kidding. When would Makarov's crew even have had time to do that?"

"We were watching them at all times," Greg said. "Even while we were partying. *Specifically* for security reasons …"

"They wouldn't do that to us," Laura protested. "Nikolai wouldn't. None of them."

Josh didn't turn from the board. "Move now, people. Speculate later."

"Got it." Rudy Frank pushed off toward the suits, talking as he went. "Permission to join the outside crew, Vivian? I know the science package better than anyone. If any of the Reds have been messing around with it, or there's anything nestled among the instruments that shouldn't be there, I'll spot it right away."

Vivian glanced up at Dave Horn, who nodded. "Makes sense. Do it. Three to EVA, as soon as possible. Laura, go wake up Amy. Then, Greg and Laura support the EVAs from inside, while Amy and Josh go over the inside of Astarte. Everywhere a cosmonaut went, anything a cosmonaut could have touched. No, scratch that. Just go *everywhere*. Check everything."

Laura dived down toward the hatch into the crew compartment. Over her shoulder, she said, "I *hate* thinking Nikolai or any of the others would do something bad to us."

I hate it too, sister, Vivian thought. *But I live in the real world.*

Out loud, she said: "We'd be fools to discount the possibility. Execute the plan, get going."

"Where will you be?" Marco Dardenas was already latching his PLSS to his back, rolling gently in free fall.

"Me, I'll check back with Houston and see if they've answered any of my questions, find out if there's anything else we absolutely need to know right now. I'll also get the ground team to look through all our telemetry, both current and retrospective, for the full duration of our contact with the Soviets, if they're not doing that already. Then I'll switch to helping Amy and Josh with the interior check." She paused.

"If any of you have other ideas for what we should be doing, speak up. Let's turn over every rock, people. But, EVA crew, listen up: don't skimp on your safety checks in your rush. Be like Ellis Mayer, not like Vivian Carter." The career astronauts, at least, knew what she meant by that. *Take all the right precautions. Be methodical. Don't be like me, on my bad days.* "Stay out there as long as it takes, commensurate with crew safety. Anything you find, report to me and Josh immediately."

She didn't need to say any more. Her crew were already moving just as fast as they could.

"How's Europe?" Doyle asked as he floated back up onto the Observation Deck.

"Bad," Brock said. "The Red Army has West Berlin encircled. It's now quarantined, just like Daedalus."

"They like that word."

"It's more politically neutral than 'surrounded.' Or 'under siege.' Occasional artillery shells explode near the American, British, and French military bases, and Soviet jets are flying low over the city, causing disruption, shattering windows, and such. Classic intimidation tactics. And, elsewhere, two Soviet divisions have breached the West German border. They're not advancing—they appear to be just proving the point that they *could* keep rolling if they choose to." She sighed in frustration. "There must be a political component to this that we haven't been briefed about."

"Always is," said Sandoval, while scanning through a densely packed teleprinter printout. "I figure they're trying to force the American hand, make them start rolling the Pershings back."

"And so what are we going to do about it?" Doyle asked.

"The usual, probably," Sandoval said. "Publicly, threaten escalation, while making an offer for resolution. While also making private, behind-the-scenes offers. Standard playbook."

"While quietly preparing hundreds of bombers on the ground," Brock added.

"The North Atlantic Council is in emergency session. That's representatives of all the NATO countries. All the Warsaw Pact forces are on alert, but none of them are moving yet. If they mobilize, if they make any serious attempt to enter Western Europe … and that includes Berlin. If they try to steamroll their way into Berlin and occupy it—well, then it's war."

Doyle shook his head. "But not to invade means backing down. Loss of face."

"And the Moon?" Rodriguez said.

"Looks like we came out ahead at Zvezda-Copernicus, though it was a bit of a Pyrrhic victory. The base—what's left of it—is in US hands. Some Soviets have been captured and will be required to leave the Moon imminently, while others apparently managed to escape, including their base commander, Orlov. The situation appears unchanged at Daedalus. We'll get into the details of all this when we have more time."

"They escaped to where, exactly?" Brock asked.

"Unknown, but presumably Hortensius. We're leaving their Spetsgruppa base there alone. Too tough a nut to crack." Sandoval put his printout aside and looked at his watch. "Where's Krantzen? … ah, okay." Even as he'd spoken the words, Krantzen had floated through the hatch. He made his way to the comms board and held position there.

"All right." Peter glanced again at the printout, then around at them all. "Good work over the past few hours, by the way. We're in good shape. So, as best we can tell right now, we're looking at a superpower confrontation limited to the European theater. At least, we sure as hell hope it stays limited to Europe. But it's even more clear now that this is all one single operation, playing out on several fronts at the same time. The signs are that the Politburo has had enough and decided that now is the time to act. Time to stamp out the rising insurgency in the Eastern Bloc satellite countries. Time to force the West to withdraw its Pershing II missiles from the border between East and West Germany. Time to reassert its dominance in space. All at once.

"Publicly, our people are trying to unlink the issues. Bush is saying that Berlin is not part of the Americas, and so the Berlin crisis should be resolved by European powers, whereas Daedalus is clearly American territory. The Soviets need to allow us back into Daedalus, whatever happens in Europe. The bottom line is that we're not trading West Berlin for the Moon, or anything on it.

"But our prime concern here at MOL-26 is, obviously, what happens on Earth. Which brings me to the current briefing. Several months ago, a highly placed Soviet defector passed us photographs of a document that's pretty terrifying. This document is titled 'Seven Days to the River Rhine' and describes their scenario for a limited nuclear conflict in Europe."

"Holy cow," said Krantzen involuntarily, and when everyone looked at him, added "Sorry."

Sandoval continued. "It's complicated, but here's the punchline: in this scenario, the Soviet Union and Warsaw Pact countries plan to bomb a whole bunch of European cities." He lifted the printout and read from it. "Hold onto your hats. Here goes: Vienna in Austria; Vicenza, Verona, and Padua in Italy, plus a bunch of military bases there. In West Germany, they'd take out Stuttgart, Munich, and Nuremberg. Then Roskilde and Esbjerg in Denmark. Their land armies would sweep through and add West Germany, Belgium, Holland, Denmark and most of Italy to the Soviet Bloc. Everything up to the River Rhine. Nice, huh?"

"You're joking." Terri was shaking her head. "That ... Peter, are we sure that's real?"

"Oh, it's real. It's a genuine exercise. We've got no doubts about its veracity. I note again that there's no confirmation that they plan to do anything like this *right now* ... but we don't know. It might come to this, in a week or a month, and if so, that's what we need to be prepared to deal with."

Terri persisted. "And the Soviets seriously think the US would stand for that?"

"That's part of the complication. The scenario is written in terms of a Soviet response to a US nuclear first strike on Poland and Czechoslovakia, meaning that the Soviets wouldn't be the first country to press the button. So it reads like a defensive document. But we know from both signal intelligence and the human side that there are hawks at the highest level of the Kremlin who are itching to do this unilaterally, as a first strike. To get the jump on us before we get the jump on them, and stake everything on the hope that the US would blink, wouldn't escalate further and start retaliating against Eastern Bloc countries, or even the Soviet Union itself."

"Mad." Brock was still shaking her head. "Pun not intended. But as soon as any US retaliatory bombs started landing even close to Soviet soil, you can bet they'd let loose their full arsenal against the mainland US, and then we'd actually have the Mutually Assured Destruction that everyone agrees would be insane."

"Maybe. Maybe not." Sandoval indicated the paper in his hand. "I'll let you all read this at some point. But the bottom line is: the US gave up Vietnam, and the Soviets and Chinese between them now dominate southeast Asia. The Soviets also still occupy Afghanistan, and Pakistan is ideologically leaning closer and closer to the Soviet bloc. And now the Red Army has invaded Poland to reestablish Soviet control there, and is threatening Berlin and the rest of West Germany.

"Bush has personally briefed the British Prime Minister, the President of France, and the Chancellor of West Germany. Ambassadors to other allies are receiving a written brief. He's announcing that for the time being the US will adopt a policy of patience and restraint. That we won't prematurely risk the costs of a worldwide nuclear exchange. That we're giving the Soviets the possibility of dialing back this provocation, but that our patience won't last forever."

"And when we run out of patience?" Brock demanded. "How much do we have, anyway?"

Sandoval shrugged. "Unclear."

"France and the UK have nuclear weapons as well," Rodriguez pointed out.

"Sure. But are France and the UK going to wage war unilaterally against the Warsaw Pact countries? I don't think so. This isn't 1939."

"This is a very depressing conversation." That was Doyle, stating the obvious.

"Isn't it just?" Sandoval grinned tightly, with no humor. "Welcome to my world. Now let's run some scenarios of our own. If nuclear war really does break out in Europe, the Soviets will likely try to hit this station. So we need to be ready to strike back and/or evacuate at a moment's notice. But we also need to plan for how we're going to cover the devastation if we remain operational while this scenario goes live. The MOL-21 crew is doing the same, and we'll put our heads together with Cheyenne during our next Pacific pass. So, buckle up and let's get into the weeds of all that …"

"Hey, Nikolai, old friend. How are you doing?"

On the screen, Makarov frowned at her. Her tone was jocular, but her expression was extremely serious. "All is well, here," he said cautiously. "And you?"

"Is this a private call? Are you overheard?"

Makarov glanced to left and right and then gave her what she chose to interpret as a warning look, which likely meant: *As private as one would expect.*

"Okay, well. We just did a thorough search of the Apollo Mars Astarte vehicle, inside and out. And guess what we found?"

He shook his head. "I do not know. What did you find?"

She studied his face. "Absolutely nothing."

He raised his eyebrows. "Nothing?"

If that was an act, it was a good one. "Nikolai … we've been led to believe that you, or one of your crew, might have sabotaged us, somehow. Even placed a bomb aboard, who knows?"

He just stared at her.

"But if you did, we haven't found it yet."

"Because we did not. Vivian … how could you think this of us?"

"Well, because of Burning Night. *Goryashchaya Noch'.*"

By now, Makarov was looking helpless. "What is that? Vivian, all of this does not make sense to me."

"On the Moon, the Soviets have taken over Dark Driver. I mean Bright Driver, though I guess … anyway. There has also been a battle between Soviet and American forces at Zvezda-Copernicus. Did you know about that?"

"No! A battle? No, no, I did not."

"Nikolai … I suppose you *do* know that the Soviet Union has invaded two of its own satellite states in the Eastern Bloc, and is poised to attack West Germany?"

By now Makarov was staring back at her in utter shock and horror. "That cannot be true, Vivian. It cannot be."

"Oh, it's all true, comrade. Trust me."

Makarov swore, a Russian curse-word she had never heard out of his lips before.

Vivian glanced at the clock. She didn't have time to give a cosmonaut an extended briefing on the actions of his own government right now. "All of those things add up to a major offensive. Everything's going to hell. And not long before it all happened, we met up with you. So, all in all, we had cause for concern. But, like I said, we found nothing."

"Because we did nothing. I am sure of my crew."

"Well, that's good. Because I would really like an assurance that there isn't something we missed, some threat to me and *my* crew."

"If I knew," he said fervently, "I would tell you. I swear it!"

"Okay." She leaned back again and nodded. "Okay. Okay."

"This is terrible," he said. "Zvezda? And Germany?"

"I guess your Mr. Gorbachev isn't doing so well with that break with the past you were talking about," she said.

Maybe that had been a cheap shot. Makarov already looked poleaxed. "Vivian. I can assure you, give you every promise, that I did nothing to your ship. And none of my men did … I would know. I am sure I would know."

"It's okay, man," Vivian said. "I believe you."

Really, she had to. She didn't have much choice. After all, just like Laura, Vivian could not really believe—could not possibly fathom—that *Nikolai Makarov* of all people would do something as cowardly as sabotaging their spacecraft. He'd saved Vivian's life once, or likely more than once if she counted the confused mess on Columbia Station when they'd all been fighting for their lives against Sergei Yashin and his thugs.

No. Nikolai was just too much of a boy scout. Although she hated to think of it in those terms, Nikolai was even more of a boy scout than Peter Sandoval, who would certainly take out innocent cosmonauts with explosives if it was in his mission brief.

"Thanks," she said. "Look, I've got to get back to my crew. But let's talk later, okay?"

"Yes, please," he said. "And maybe you can tell me more about … all of this? The Moon, and the Earth?"

"Uh, I guess. Sure." Weird, that she might be briefing a Soviet on Soviet aggression.

"So, what, in twenty-four hours? We try to talk again exactly a day from now?"

"If I can," he said. "Please be safe, Vivian."

"I will absolutely give that my best shot."

He gave her a wry salute and broke the connection.

Vivian stared at the blank screen for a moment. *Crazy world*, she thought. *Crazy solar system. Crazy universe.*

But they're the only ones we've got.

Then she opened the hatch back into Astarte and rejoined her crew.

They were all still jittery, so just to be safe, they performed another complete sweep of Astarte, inside and out. This time Vivian, Greg

Heinz, and Josh Rawlings went out on EVA while the previous EVA team took the lead on searching inside the ship. After all that they convened in the crew quarters for a meal, with some of them squeezed into the wardroom and the others just outside it, many of them rubbing their eyes to try and stay awake.

Eventually, Amy said, "Uh, so any news from the Moon?"

"Oh," Vivian said. "Right. I never told you the full story about that, did I?"

She didn't really have the energy to get into it now, but her crew deserved to know. So she quickly brought them up to speed on everything she knew about the surprise attack at Daedalus that had left the base in Soviet hands and sketched out a broad-brush description of the events at Zvezda-Copernicus. They just blinked at her. Most of them stopped eating, their food drifting away unnoticed.

Honestly, she was getting a bit tired of the disbelieving looks these folks kept leveling at her.

Eventually, Rawlings said: "Grant ... destroyed the cable car into Copernicus?"

"I'm told there's video," Vivian said. "It's apparently quite a sight as it goes over."

"But, were there any Soviets on it at the time?"

"I wasn't told explicitly, but I'm guessing so. The ride up and down takes a while. But we *do* know that the Soviets down at the Annex are now trapped there, pinned down. Night Corps set up artillery at the top to fire on any Soviet landers that tried to enter the crater. When the folks up top started taking fire from the Reds down in the Annex, Grant sent down a few missiles of his own. Shots to warn, not to destroy, although the Annex sustained some damage, possibly even fatalities. He also blew up one of their supply containers. But there's still activity down there, so we suspect that most of them are still alive."

"Grant's just keeping them pinned down and not letting them leave?"

"Bargaining chips," Vivian said. "Any damage to the US population of Daedalus and, well, apparently Grant has his orders."

Amy was staring at her, mouth still agape. "For God's sake. This has all gone to hell."

"Night Corps," Laura said. "Those *bastards*."

Rawlings and Horn both carefully looked away from Vivian. "Not much glory in this for anyone," she said levelly.

"Okay," Horn said, after a brief pause. "So what about the US mining presence in the Jura Mountains?"

"Good question. Turns out that the Jura site has had some Night Corps protection from the start, so it would be a tougher nut to crack. So far, the Soviets haven't made a move on it. Likely, saving their own people at Zvezda-Copernicus is their main preoccupation at the moment. But, let's just say that another military action up there wouldn't surprise anyone. The NASA scientific presence at Marius is also being rapidly discontinued. Everyone's shipping out." Which hurt a bit, on a personal level, but she was happy that everyone there was safe. If there'd been a massacre at Marius it might have been more than Vivian's heart could take.

Laura raised her hand. "Uh. Is there more, or can I ask a more general question?"

Vivian waved. "Ask it."

"How the hell did we get here?" Laura asked. "How?"

Greg side-eyed her. "Pershings? And Poland?"

"Well, sure. But why right *now*?"

"Not keeping up with the news, then?"

Vivian cleared her throat. "Greg. Not helpful. Everyone's been preoccupied. Laura more than most."

Laura nodded. "With all the Mars data we've had to process, you bet I'm skipping the newscasts. I'm barely even talking to my family right now."

Rudy Frank raised his hand. "On the *why right now* question, I can tackle that, if I may? No polemics, I swear."

"Go ahead." Vivian knew the basics, but given Rudy's fascination with politics she had no doubt that he would know more, and get the story right first time with no go-backs. Besides, Vivian was tired of talking, and especially to Laura.

"The real trigger was Poland," Rudy said. "And since then, things have happened very quickly. You remember the murder of Jerzy Popiel …"

He glanced at Heinz, who helpfully said, "Popieluszko."

"A Roman Catholic priest, associated with the Solidarity movement?" Rudy scanned their faces. Greg Heinz clearly knew what he was talking about. Horn and Rawlings wore the attentive expressions of men pretending they knew what he was talking about. "He vocally opposed the Communist regime and spoke up for the Solidarity movement. Opposed the Polish government, big-time."

Greg nodded. "And by 'vocally', Rudy means his sermons were broadcast by Radio Free Europe. He was a hard man to ignore and a thorn in their sides for quite a while."

"And they killed him for it. He was kidnapped and murdered on October 19 by three members of the Security Force. They beat the crap out of him and then tossed his body into a reservoir, weighted down with rocks."

"Oh, Jesus," said Laura.

"When his body was eventually found on October 30, it provoked massive protests. Massive. Greater than anything they'd seen since before martial law was imposed. Within days, protests were breaking out in other Eastern Bloc countries: Czechoslovakia, East Germany, and others. In Gdansk, Poland, the shipworkers and mine workers basically took over the city. Between that and the US deployment of the intermediate-range ballistic missiles near the German border, the Soviets clearly decided they'd had enough. Soviet tanks began rolling across the border, and here we are."

"And it's likely to get worse before it gets better," Dardenas added.

"This is ... *infuriating*," Laura said. "Dozens of people have died at Daedalus and Zvezda, because a priest got killed by the secret police in Poland? There's a war on the Moon, because of Soviet dissidents and stupid missiles in Germany?"

"It's a bit more complicated than that," Greg said.

"War is war," Dave Horn said. "And the Moon and the Earth are not separate places."

"World War III might literally be about to break out." Vivian hadn't meant to say that out loud. She took a deep breath. "And if it does, we might have nothing to go home to."

Really, there was nothing anyone could add to that.

But, hey, on the bright side, at least they'd had a good time with the four TMK-Mars Soviets. And those Soviets had all been nice guys ... and hadn't tried to kill them.

There was still some good in the world.

Or, not in the world.

CHAPTER 23

Jura Mountains: Svetlana Belyakova
November 18-30, 1984

THE cockroaches returned regularly now: grimy Purgans skittering back across the regolith toward the base camp where Belyakova and Vlasav held their long vigil. They came back often, sometimes one a day, sometimes two or even three, to conduct their regular ritual: empty their sample return boxes full of rocks, rake samples and core tubes, each annotated with coordinates and photographs to describe where they'd been gathered; toss their garbage out; load up again with food, water, and air; and set out again. Their sampling locations and frequency had all been preprogrammed on a grid-based search pattern and were being carefully monitored by Belyakova.

At least, this was the turnaround process as defined by the mission plan. If her prospecting cosmonauts were genuinely exhausted on their return, which they often were, she would insist they stay in the Kharkovchanka to rest and recuperate, generally for two sleep periods and a rest day in between. If too many Purgans arrived back at the central location for restocking at the same time there would not be enough bunks in the Kharkovchanka to allow this, but at least she could arrange for each cosmonaut to get some privacy for a while.

Because of this, they were not covering the ground as efficiently as their optimistic mission plan had predicted. To ameliorate this,

Svetlana and Dmitri Vlasav were also taking their own turn at prospecting. Every other day, Svetlana would take the Kharkovchanka out on a sample-taking trip, undertaking a bruising sixteen-hour working day to increase their sampling rate. Often, she reserved for herself the regions with the most challenging terrain. The Kharkovchanka could handle steep slopes and crowded boulder fields with more stability and confidence than the Purgans. On the "off" days, she would try to catch up with her backlog of mineral assaying, mapping, forward planning, and general maintenance.

It was on their return to base camp after one such expedition, shoulders aching from the core drill, legs weary, and eyes itching from the dust, that they found they had unexpected company.

Svetlana was at her desk, typing up labels and marking up her master map as best she could in the rocking, vibrating cabin, when Dmitri Vlasav jammed on the truck's brakes, bringing them to an abrupt halt and sending her papers fluttering to the floor. She swore and heard an additional muffled curse from one of the bunks back by the airlock.

"Sorry, sorry!" Vlasav called out. "But, come and look. Someone new is there."

"New?" What was the idiot talking about? Svetlana hustled up to the cab.

Their base camp was defined by the two original Kirpichi, plus the additional inflatable living and working spaces now attached to both. The first Kirpich served to garage the Purgans, unpressurized and open but roofed to shield the vehicles from the Sun, and capable of being partially insulated with thermal blankets during the nights. The second, pressurized and with an airlock leading in and out, provided sleeping space for her four mechanical support staff and returning prospectors, a mess area, and storage.

Two of the Purgans were currently parked at Base Camp. One, belonging to the two men currently resting in the Kharkovchanka, was in the garage undergoing maintenance, and the other was parked haphazardly outside Kirpich Two, its crew likely inside on break.

And indeed, partially occulted by the second Kirpich, there were two other vehicles, both larger than Purgans.

Night would be on them soon, and as usual the low Sun and light scattering off regolith made it difficult to see. But after a few moments of squinting, Svetlana said: "Ours, I think."

"But who?" Vlasav picked up binoculars. "I suppose … yes, the first does look like a Kharkovchanka, like this vehicle, but more blocky. They are not American?"

"They look like no MOLABs I have ever seen." And, as there were no additional Soviet Bricks visible, the new vehicles must have driven here. But from where?

"I did not even know there were other Kharkovchankas on the Moon."

"Nor did I." Belyakova took the proffered binoculars and adjusted the focus. "But it appears that there are. Yes, the first is a Kharkovchanka, with a different cab shape. The second, I think, was a trailer that is now disconnected from the main vehicle."

"Help? Reinforcements?"

Belyakova considered. No one had hailed them by radio, or by the limited-range walkie-talkies that her team used when close to base camp or to one another in the field, but this was not surprising: they were preserving radio silence, except in cases of accidents and emergencies. It was unlikely that the Americans were still unaware of their presence, but Belyakova's orders were to make every effort to keep a low profile.

"I have no idea," she said. "So let us go and find out. Drive on."

As if someone had heard her, the walkie-talkie hanging on a lanyard beside Vlasav crackled into life. "Major-General Belyakova. So good of you to put in an appearance."

Belyakova swore again, a much worse curse than before. Vlasav cringed. He clearly hated it when his idol used profanity. "What is it? What is the matter?"

"Keretsky," she said.

"Who?"

"An old friend," she said, with enough acid in her tone that even Vlasav could fathom her true meaning.

Belyakova had a feeling her world was about to come crashing down. Reluctantly she picked up the walkie-talkie. "Speaking. I must apologize. I was unaware that we were expecting guests."

"Report to our command vehicle," Keretsky said. "Immediately."

Suited up, Belyakova and Vlasav loped toward the newly arrived Kharkovchanka. Behind them, the two miners who'd been sleeping on the way back to Base Camp crossed over to Kirpich One to inspect their Purgan.

Belyakova's sense of foreboding increased. This new Kharkovchanka bore considerably more armor than Svetlana's. It had been designed and outfitted as a military vehicle first and foremost, rather than a mining support unit like Belyakova's. The trailer was a personnel carrier. Four armored Soviet troops were unloading supplies from it and carrying them over to Kirpich Two.

Entering the new Kharkovchanka, she found herself face to face with Keretsky. Behind him, reviewing numbers on a console, was a second man she did not recognize, balding and in his fifties, with a sour expression and a definite air of command.

She stepped forward boldly. "Colonel Keretsky. How nice to see you again. This is Lieutenant Dmitri Vlasav ..."

Keretsky waved her to silence. Vlasav was beneath his notice. "General, I would like to introduce to you Major-General Svetlana Belyakova. Comrade Belyakova, this is General Orlov. He will be taking over here as commander of Soviet forces in the field, effective immediately."

Orlov? Hadn't he succeeded Rudenko as Commander of Zvezda-Copernicus at the end of her most recent tour, a few months after Rudenko had replaced Belyakova?

The general had barely glanced at her. Belyakova did not blink. "On what authority?"

"The highest. With us is a contingent of KGB Spetsgruppa Vympel. You will agree that you have no authority over such a group. And it is in the interests of the Rodina that this operation be brought under a ..." He looked at her disdainfully. "A firmer hand."

Vympel? The elite Soviet strike force, here, even if only a few of them? This did not bode well.

"I see." Belyakova pulled herself upright to attention, stared straight ahead, and saluted. "I understand, of course. I am at your service, Comrade Orlov."

"Ah." Taking his time, Orlov turned to stare at her with barely concealed disgust. "So this is the woman responsible for the death of Sergei Yashin?"

Belyakova did not blink. "With respect, sir, that is incorrect. Comrade Yashin did not die by my hand."

"No. He died at the hands of an American astronaut you had allied with against him. Is that not so?"

"Yashin was acting on his own initiative, and behaving irrationally. I had been informed that his actions were sanctioned neither by the KGB nor the Politburo. He exceeded his orders, and his acts were publicly condemned by the Kremlin. I was merely obeying my orders."

Orlov considered. "An interesting interpretation. When, exactly, were you informed of this ... lack of sanction?"

"I forget the exact sequence of events. All of this was resolved, long ago."

He was studying her with the distaste most men reserved for something rotten they'd discovered in their refrigerator. "If you have persuaded yourself that is true, you are either a fool or a quisling."

"I am neither, Comrade Orlov."

"Your fraternization with the American agents, Vivian Carter and Casey Buchanan, is common knowledge in the higher ranks of the KGB. You—"

Belyakova raised an eyebrow and turned her iciest gaze on him. "Fraternization? In each case I was following my written orders, and to the letter. I had been commanded to seek their friendship. To play on our similarities in training and experience to put them at ease, and to thus obtain information. I briefed my superiors fully and promptly on my actions throughout—including Comrade Keretsky, here, on matters concerning Buchanan—and I received clear instruction from them on what information they wished me to reveal or withhold from the Americans. If you are well informed, you surely know this. If not, I advise you to make the relevant inquiries."

Orlov stared at her balefully. Keretsky was grinning unpleasantly. *You are loving this, you sadist*, she thought.

They had not interrupted her, which probably meant they were hoping she would hang herself by her own words. Which she was almost on the verge of doing. Instead, she said: "As to Carter and Buchanan being agents: both are merely NASA astronauts, to the limits of my knowledge. I suspected at various times that one or other had intelligence connections, but I found no proof."

"*Were*, in Buchanan's case. He has been taken care of, as you know."

"Indeed. If I may ask, General: you came here from Zvezda-Copernicus, am I correct?"

"She has not been brought up to date with current events? Proceed. I am busy." Orlov turned back to his console and frowned anew at his readouts, taking notes in a small book.

Keretsky sat, but did not invite Belyakova to do the same, so she remained standing. He said: "Matters have progressed while you have been up here, digging in the dirt. Daedalus Base and its mass driver are now under Soviet control." At this, Vlasav gave an audible gasp. Keretsky glanced at him once, as if surprised to see him still there, and turned his gaze back upon Belyakova. "In response, the Americans at Copernicus launched a cowardly attack against Zvezda. Our men resisted vigorously, but to no avail. Our fine Zvezda Base is no more."

"I am sorry to hear that." Belyakova's thoughts raced, while she attempted to keep her expression under control. Those were two gigantic news items, and it was almost criminal that she and her prospecting team had not been informed. What if the Americans had chosen to attack *them* in retaliation, following the events at Daedalus and Zvezda?

Little point in complaining. Keretsky would merely seize the opportunity to slap her down again. "Fortunate indeed that you were able to escape."

"Luckily, we received sufficient warning to evacuate from under the noses of the Americans, while they busied themselves with wanton destruction."

Meaning you ran away, Belyakova thought. *You ran, and abandoned your men. And also, you had quick access to a Kharkovchanka, or were able to get to one promptly.*

For that, at least, the logic was straightforward. The vehicle hadn't been at Zvezda, so it must have been brought up from Hortensius, along with the Vympel contingent, to pick up Orlov and Keretsky and then bring them north to the Jura Mountains. Or the two of them had retreated to Hortensius in a Lunokhod, and proceeded north from there with the Kharkovchanka.

Either way, the significance was clear: this area, the Jura Mountains, might well be the next front line in the lunar proxy war her country was waging against the Americans. Suddenly, she was in the middle of a war zone.

Parenthetically, it also meant that her people had lied to her yet again when they had told her they had no lunar capability to support a water-prospecting trip to the South Pole. But that was so long ago now as to be irrelevant.

"I am glad," she said. "And so, how are we to proceed, here?"

"At last, you ask." Keretsky reached over for a file of telepri/nter printout. "Let us begin with a number of items concerning your recent activities … but first, enlighten me. Why were those men in your vehicle?"

The switch from the massively important to the mundane was head-spinning, and it took Svetlana a moment to adjust. "The miners? They were resting. The intense schedule and cramped confines of the Purgans are driving these men to exhaustion. Once in a while, I insist they recover with a good night's sleep and some privacy before I send them out again. Although these particular men did assist with my sampling activities to the north for a few hours during our trip, given our time constraints, with sunset imminent."

Keretsky frowned. "The men can rest in Kirpich Two. That is why it is there."

"The Kirpich is almost as uncomfortable as the Purgans. Its lavatory facility is primitive, it has no shower, and it is damp and unpleasant inside."

"That is not your problem."

"I must disagree. It is certainly my problem if one of my teams makes an error through weariness, causing an accident that kills them. I am then short one crew, and must rearrange my entire schedule."

"Aha." He nodded. "Such leniency and pampering must explain why your prospecting survey has covered much less ground than anticipated, and has thus been thoroughly unsuccessful."

"It is merely one reason of many. The lunar terrain is inhospitable, and the Purgans are too small to efficiently achieve their tasks. Simply cleaning the moondust from—"

"I will hear no excuses, Svetlana Antonovna. Your men must return to the field, full-time, with only the necessary minimum of recuperation."

At least that meant that their prospecting would continue? "Yes, sir."

"More importantly, you have yet to identify any appreciable quantity of the rare earth metals that are your core mission objective."

320

"That is correct. I suspect that the seams of rare earth elements are not as widespread as we had hoped. A careful reading of the discovery paper in the American *Journal of Geophysical Research* does make this inference. My conclusion is that either the American rare earths were a lucky find, or that they are exaggerating their significance in order not to lose face—"

"An easy excuse."

Did this fool think Belyakova was somehow *deliberately* failing to find the minerals? She glared at him, her patience fading. "Then perhaps you should take over here, and show me how it is done."

Orlov looked up at this, and grunted in … amusement? Disgust? Then he returned to work.

After a brittle pause, Keretsky said: "I was led to believe that you had undergone reeducation back at Star City, after your ignominious departure from Zvezda Base last year. It appears this was ineffective."

"By no means. My reeducation was most edifying, and helped me to understand the magnitude of some of my former lapses of judgment."

Keretsky shook his head. "You believe that you are very good at this, Svetlana Antonovna. You are mistaken. Your insincerity is evident. Your act fools no one."

"And yet," Belyakova could not help saying, "those in Star City whom I worked with were entirely satisfied with my progress, and as a result I was rewarded with this new and important assignment, back on the Moon."

Keretsky looked even more sour than usual. "That is likely more to do with the undue influence wielded over the cosmonaut program by comrades Leonov and Makarov … the latter even from afar."

"Heroes of the Soviet Union, both," she said. "As am I, myself."

"Enough of this." Orlov put his pen down and turned to Keretsky. "She will continue to lead the mineralogical survey, given her lunar and geological expertise, but under our strict supervision. And tonight she will stay in the Kirpich, to reacquaint herself with its luxuries, while we make the necessary modifications to her vehicle."

"Modifications?"

He inspected her for a moment. "How close to the American claim have your prospecting vehicles approached?"

"Our search pattern takes us all around the vicinity of the American claim site, but not too close. Their military attempts to maintain a two-mile exclusion zone around the site ..."

"And you respect that exclusion zone?"

"Our explicit mission parameters require us to keep a low profile, and to avoid confrontations with United States military forces."

"And yet, the most likely area to discover these rare minerals must surely be within that exclusion zone."

"Perhaps so." She swallowed. "If you are changing my mission parameters, I will require the new orders in writing."

"You will, will you?" He glanced at Keretsky. "I see what you mean about her. For now, kindly get her out of here. We have more important matters to discuss."

"You heard the General." Keretsky stood. "Please get out of our sight, Svetlana Antonovna. You will be informed when we require your presence again. In the meantime, I am sure you have some pressing matters to attend to. Getting this mineral survey program back on schedule, for example."

"Certainly, comrade." There were indeed multiple issues which Svetlana considered more pressing than having her achievements and motivations questioned. "I will need to stop at my vehicle to pick up my—"

"Yes, yes, get what you need. And *you*," this to Vlasav, "get out of here as well. Go with her. And try to talk some sense into her."

Now, that was almost funny. But Belyakova merely saluted, and made her way back to her suit, by the rear airlock.

Kirpich Two was dank and unusually crowded, and smelled strongly of sweat, ozone from the electrical equipment, and moondust. But, out of deference to Belyakova, Orlov's Vympel squad and the members of her own prospecting crews allowed her and Vlasav a measure of space to talk quietly while they ate from their IRPs, the individual military food rations they had been issued. Belyakova's seemed to consist solely of stewed beef, barley porridge, reconstituted and tasteless vegetables, and crackers, which did not improve her mood.

Vlasav shook his head. "I cannot believe you spoke to them in such a way."

Belyakova snorted. "Those fools have little power over me. They can cause me discomfort in here for a night, but tomorrow they will need me back in our vehicle. Even tonight, I will fall behind with the assaying of the lunar samples. This is petty and not constructive. They cannot reassign me, for I received this assignment from those above their heads, and they cannot perform this survey without me. There is no one else to do this work." She paused. "Despite your own qualifications and competence, of course."

Vlasav blanched. "I understand that I do not have half the skills necessary. Nor would I want the responsibility."

"That is understandable," she said grimly. "Especially now."

Vlasav looked around. No one from Vympel was near enough to eavesdrop. "Do you think they are here to … make an attack upon the American mining base? To capture it?"

Belyakova pushed the barley porridge away. "I am sure that is under consideration."

"I wanted to ask them, but … it was not my place to speak."

"I did *not* want to ask them," she said soberly.

"If we could just locate a mineral stake of our own," he said, forlornly. "Then there would be no need …"

"That is a brilliant idea, Dima. I am surprised it has not occurred to me before now."

Vlasav retreated visibly. "I apologize. I meant no criticism, of course. Merely wishing matters were different."

"I know, I know." Belyakova gave him a tired grin. "After all, is this not the time you are supposed to be talking sense into me?"

"I doubt that anyone could," he said, very seriously. Then he realized what he had said, and his hand flew to his mouth, and finally and with some relief, Svetlana Belyakova laughed out loud.

They well knew what the American claim site looked like. Almaz craft with sophisticated optics had passed over it several times. It was challenging to obscure an open-pit mining operation from orbital surveillance, and the Americans weren't even trying.

The veins of thorium and other lanthanides reportedly formed a fine braid through a mountain slopes to the northeast of Sharp Crater, but the mining site itself looked distinctly underwhelming. A single

Brick, with an inflatable extension, provided accommodation for the mining crew. A Cargo Container had brought a large rotary drill, a backhoe, and a large MOLAB with its rear section cut away to become an open truck. The US Brick was some distance away from the mine, since the mining operation required blasting from time to time. A heavy-lift LM truck sat off to one side, with two conventional NASA Lunar Rovers, not even armored, parked nearby.

The whole area was surrounded by a metal fence. This was merely two strands of thin aluminum suspended from almost equally thin posts, about as light as it could possibly be, but it did provide a visible demarcation of the region the US claimed as its own.

The mine itself was a NASA operation, but its security was clearly Air Force. The US Government's earnest declarations that their space program had separate civil and military branches were growing more and more hollow by the day. Then again, these days Belyakova was more suspicious of her own country's proclamations than she had once been.

This Air Force presence was more impressive than the mining site itself. Two US Bricks, a MOLAB, and three Cargo Containers. Several rovers and bikes, and four fixed gun emplacements, one at each cardinal point.

Could Orlov's force of Vympel overcome the American force? Perhaps. If they were lucky, and preserved the element of surprise …

Which would be hard, if Orlov was serious about pushing Belyakova's Purgans into the American exclusion zone.

Keretsky hated the Moon, that much was clear. He would go outside when he absolutely had to, and managed to project an appropriate air of confidence while donning his suit, but otherwise he was happy to stay inside. And he sweated a great deal at the neck, chest, and elbows, even during times when the temperatures were moderate.

Belyakova had plenty of time to observe this, for Keretsky now spent most of his time in their Kharkovchanka, "supervising" her work, and he generally slept there as well. It was infuriating to have to justify her every action to him, to have him constantly looking over her shoulder. Even, constantly *looking* at her.

Alexei Leonov and Nikolai Makarov had always been gentlemen around her. With some of the younger men their admiration was tinged with hero-worship, and given her achievements, perhaps that was not surprising. Belyakova was honest enough to admit, just to herself, that she'd hero-worshiped her own share of cosmonauts her time. But the men her own age or older, who treated Svetlana as their own personal spectacle: those men she would slap down whenever she could.

Unfortunately, she had no authority to slap down Keretsky, and especially not with Orlov around. He had political power over her, and he knew it, and so made no attempt to avert his eyes.

Belyakova tried to bear it with her usual stoic patience. She hoped that Keretsky would get what was coming to him, sooner or later.

"Still nothing." Vlasav ducked his head, as if he were personally responsible for the paucity of the ore he had just analyzed. "Even half a kilometer from the American fence, there are no such lanthanide concentrations as the Americans have reported."

Under cover of darkness, two Purgans had approached much nearer the US Jura compound than Belyakova thought wise. They had come under observation, that was clear from the movement of the American vehicles, but there had been no confrontations. Perhaps because the Americans knew that the Soviet teams were on a fool's errand, having already surveyed the area themselves.

Keretsky turned to Belyakova, his eyes narrowed. "Nearly two weeks we have been here, on top of the months of your surveying, and still nothing?"

Still nothing was a phrase that they heard from Keretsky on a daily basis. Belyakova was sick of hearing it. "We may yet strike lucky. It could happen any day. As must be evident to you by this point, the detailed mineralogical analysis of an area this large is a long and careful endeavor. And it is especially difficult to do geological sampling in the dim illumination of lunar night." Seeing his expression, Belyakova frowned. "What is it? You hold me responsible for the darkness, now?"

Vlasav piped up in her support. "My belief is that the American claim is small and rarified, and that the veins of thorium and the lanthanides are not as rich, do not spread as far as we might have hoped."

"This is not good." Keretsky gazed out of the window. "General Orlov is not pleased. He warns me that we may have to take other measures."

Belyakova frowned. "What measures does he advocate, comrade?"

Keretsky did not take the bait. He merely continued to stare out of the window, in the direction of the American compound, and said: "Perhaps you can ask him yourself, Svetlana Antonovna. The General will shortly arrive here in person, whereupon you can explain your failure to him yourself."

"I hear that disapproving tone in your voice. I continue to find you deeply insubordinate." Orlov leaned in toward her, so close that she could smell aftershave. Aftershave, on the Moon? Ridiculous. Svetlana did not flinch, but continued to stare straight ahead. Anger rose within her. If Orlov touched her, he would regret it. Soviet officers of different genders on duty together were strictly prohibited from making physical contact without express permission, except to provide emergency medical care. If Orlov breached that edict Belyakova would break his fingers, and to hell with the consequences.

Of course, he did not. He kept his distance, but barely. "Do exactly what I tell you, Major-General Belyakova, and do not get in my way, and you will not get hurt."

Now, she met his gaze, and gave her insubordinate tone full rein. "Attempt to hurt me, or lower my standing with my fellow cosmonauts, and *you* will swiftly regret it … comrade."

He gave her a crocodile smile. "Spirited, at least. But I trust you have not forgotten how to obey orders?"

"I have not, sir."

"Then stay out of my way unless I call for you. Sit down over there and let the men talk about how we are going to remove the American imperialists from their illegal occupation of the Jura Mountains."

"Certainly, comrade." Belyakova sat immediately and folded her hands in her lap. Orlov and Keretsky withdrew to the cab of the Kharkovchanka—her own vehicle—and began to correspond in low tones, with Keretsky glancing over at her from time to time.

It was chillingly easy enough to see what was going on here. Given that the Soviet mineralogical survey had come up short, Orlov's brief was to drive the NASA contingent from their Montes Jura mining claim. Which meant that a heavily armed contingent of Spetsgruppa Vympel would be arriving very soon to do his bidding, if they had not already arrived somewhere else in the vicinity. Perhaps at dawn, which was a mere three days away.

The Kremlin had lost patience. And so, instead of allowing Belyakova's prospecting mission to proceed, the KGB's sword was about to be driven home against the US contingent.

It would soon be time for war. Again. And with a man like Orlov in charge, backed up by the soulless Keretsky, it would not be pretty.

As the men returned to the main cabin, Orlov said: "We must now disembark to assess the progress of our forces. Belyakova, you will tidy this place up and then sanitize everything. It stinks in here. Disgraceful."

They stepped back toward the airlock to don their spacesuits. Stone-faced, Belyakova picked up the folders and procedure binders lying on the desk, and refiled them in their correct places on the shelves.

As soon as they entered the airlock and closed the door behind them, Belyakova stood up and kicked the wall, and blew out a long, exasperated breath. Hands on hips, she stared at the ceiling, trying to calm her thoughts.

"I am sorry …"

She turned. Such was the man's lack of presence, she'd forgotten Dmitri Vlasav was still present. She merely shook her head, not trusting herself to speak.

Timidly, Vlasav stood. "If I may assist you, comrade? I can perhaps begin by cleaning up the galley. That is not work that one of your rank and … excellent reputation should be doing."

She skewered him with a glare. "I am not too grand to clean up a working surface after myself."

"I did not mean—"

"But I *do* resent that bastard telling me to do it." The hell with it. Belyakova kicked the wall again.

Vlasav allowed himself a tentative grin. "I am sure. With all due respect, I believe that Comrade Orlov is a *naturalniy zasranetz.*"

Natural shithead. Casey Buchanan would probably have said *Certified asshole.* Despite herself, Belyakova grinned. "He is. I apologize for my temper, Dima. And I thank you for your support." She looked around the interior of the Kharkovchanka. She had to admit that the place *was* a mess, but damn it, they'd been busy. "And, I would appreciate the help."

Vlasav smiled at her, more bravely this time. "Then, Major-General, let us begin."

"Yet again: my name is Svetlana, and now more than ever, I encourage you to use it."

As if this was the first time she'd ever said that to him, Dmitri gave a half-bow. "Very well … Svetlana."

Soon after they had finished holystoning the galley and operational area in their Kharkovchanka, they were summoned to Orlov's command and control vehicle. Orlov next set Belyakova to the task of typing up a report on the past forty-eight hours of her activity, no doubt so that he could check it for any duty infractions or inefficiency. Despite her once-exalted position in the cosmonaut program, Orlov was making it very clear where she stood with him.

Without warning, the Kharkovchanka shook as if by an earthquake. Belyakova flinched, glanced across her control board, and then looked outside. A new Soviet Kirpich had just made moonfall barely fifty feet away, and with no warning.

Orlov and Keretsky both broke out laughing at Belyakova's alarm, and at the geologist Dmitri Vlasav's even greater consternation: he had grabbed the table as if to dive beneath it, and was looking around in wild-eyed panic.

Belyakova eyed them coldly. "You knew this Kirpich was coming, and chose not to warn us?"

"You had no need to know," Orlov said. "And it amused me."

Belyakova gave him a curt nod and went back to her work. *Idiots*, she thought.

And dangerous idiots too. It appeared the war for Jura was about to begin.

CHAPTER 24

Jura Mountains: Svetlana Belyakova
November 30, 1984

THE next two hours were a flurry of activity in and around the Kharkovchanka. The newly arrived Soviet Brick contained thirty-six Spetsgruppa Vympel troops, plus four Lunokhod vehicles and four of the Soviet lunar dirt bikes. The Lunokhods were the collapsible versions that unfolded and locked into place, much like the American Lunar Rovers, but with additional armor shielding that could be slotted into place on the frame. Folded up, the Lunokhods and bikes thus did not take up a great deal of space, but the three dozen soldiers and their suits, weaponry, and supplies clearly did. Plus, of course, the rocket engines that had brought them out of orbit and then fired full thrust at the last minute to prevent them from becoming a gigantic bloody smear of metal and bone on the lunar surface. All in all, it was a considerable feat of compression and endurance, given that the crew of soldiers had presumably come all the way from Earth orbit in that cramped metal coffin. Belyakova didn't envy them their journey.

Anyway: all those soldiers now spilled out onto the lunar surface, performing their deployment tasks with military precision and efficiency. If they were stiff and sore from their long journey, that certainly didn't show. They were probably delighted to be freed from their confinement. And now, they were loading ordnance onto those Lunokhods.

And then came the most chilling development. The soldiers lugged out four stripped-down rockets, loaded into simple frames, that they now set about mounting on the roof of the Kharkovchanka. Rockets of a type very familiar to Svetlana Belyakova.

Orlov had now assigned Belyakova to the comms station, where she had become little better than a receptionist, passing along his orders in those rare times when he'd needed to apply direction. Now she slipped off her headset and leaned back. "Tactical nuclear weapons?" she asked, that icy tone back in her voice. She couldn't help herself.

"That is none of your concern," Orlov said.

"And how do we plan to use those none-of-my-concern missiles?"

Keretsky turned that reptilian gaze upon her again. "You are on notice, Svetlana Belyakova. You have surely enjoyed your moments of prominence in the cosmonaut corps, and the admiration for your achievements, such as they were. However, such matters mean nothing here. As far as the KGB is concerned, you are compromised. We have been directed to permit you to remain here, and we will respect that direction. However, in return you will keep quiet and obey orders, precisely, and to the letter. Do so, and maybe you can return home to your dacha, and shop in your hard-currency stores for the best whiskey and blue jeans your fame can purchase you. I will answer no more of your questions, unless there is an operational need."

She bowed her head. "Of course, Comrade."

Keretsky looked at her suspiciously. She stared back, guileless, and eventually he looked away again.

At the radar console, Dima Vlasav raised his hand. "Comrades! Two more incoming vehicles, descending toward us." He looked at Orlov. "You are expecting further reinforcements?"

Orlov jumped forward to stare at the green blips on the radar. "I am not."

"Then they must be American." Vlasav looked more closely. "They look smaller than the Kirpichi that arrived with the prospecting teams, and with General Orlov and his men. Their size is thus consistent with the Night Corps Bricks."

Belyakova's fingers moved over the comms board. "In addition, their radar and transponders are set to typical Night Corps frequencies."

Keretsky frowned. "They are using transponders? Not coming in quietly?"

She raised an eyebrow. "To land here with precision, relative to ourselves and to the rest of the US installation, and so close together? Of course they must use transponders."

Keretsky shrugged it off. Orlov waved her to silence. "Prepare the weapons. And, I shall be watching you. Be assured that I have complete understanding of this weapons systems on this vehicle. To you shall go the honor of destroying this new incoming Night Corps force. I assume this will not be a problem for you?"

Both men stared at her. How they would love it if Belyakova refused a direct order. Of course, were she to do so, Orlov could legitimately take out a pistol and shoot her for mutiny, right then and there. She did not blink. "Why would it be a problem?"

"Do not be insolent."

"My apologies." Svetlana studied the boards, flipped switches. "However, given your greater experience with this board, I would be obliged if you would double-check me. I would not wish to introduce any errors due to my rustiness in combat situations."

"We certainly would not wish that." Orlov stepped up beside her and inhaled. Was he breathing her in? Or merely thrilling at the thought of the death to come? Probably both. KGB agents were always good at multitasking.

Even as she typed in the projected coordinates of the American Bricks' landing sites and closed the circuit breakers to funnel power to the missile array on the Kharkovchanka's roof, Svetlana's mind was whirling.

These two swine did have power over her, after all. They could give her orders that she found impossible to obey. And the consequences of a refusal …

Yes. She had been too arrogant, too headstrong. Not for the first time.

But what was done, was done. Now, Svetlana Belyakova had a choice to make. Perhaps the most important choice of her life.

The Belyakova of 1979 would have fulfilled her orders without question. Back then, the imperialists had been faceless ciphers. She had been quite content to play her part in the attacks on Columbia Station and Hadley Base, and to allow Sergei Yashin to conduct his duties on Zvezda unhindered, even when those duties involved tormenting Vivian Carter …

Well. Almost content. She had done her duty without hesitation, anyway.

Now?

For the ground attacks on Hadley Base Belyakova had been in a supporting role piloting the landers, as she had been considered too valuable a propaganda asset to be risked in the dirt bike or Lunokhod assaults. As yet, she had no American blood on her hands, not directly. The only person she had killed during that entire mission was her fellow Soviet crewman, Oleg Vasiliev, when she and Makarov had helped Vivian Carter retake Columbia Station from Yashin.

Not that Belyakova was afraid to kill if she needed to. Taking lives in itself did not perturb her, if the need was there.

But: nuclear weapons on the Moon, again? Even of the smaller, tactical variety? Her blood ran cold at the thought.

Belyakova had responded viscerally, aggressively, to the idea of the American imperialists bringing nuclear weapons to the Moon. She had been equally opposed to Yashin's use of a warhead to eradicate Hadley Base, and she and Nikolai Makarov had put themselves on the line—absolutely on the line, risking their lives—in demanding that the Americans be warned and given the chance to evacuate Hadley Plain before the nuclear inferno was unleashed upon it.

How different was today?

Belyakova well understood the stakes. Two worlds were at war. The Americans had their ridiculously destructive Pershing missiles right up against the East German border, capable of reaching Moscow if fired. And despite that, the cretins in some of the Warsaw Pact countries saw fit to rebel against Soviet authority right now, with such risk at their doorstep. She had no patience with either situation. To Belyakova, the Soviet Burning Night offensive, crushing rebellion in Poland and countering the NATO threat on the German border, seemed justified. Above all else, the Union had to survive, with its allies intact. On the Moon, Daedalus had been secured by Soviet forces against Imperialist aggression, and under the circumstances the Zvezda crew would have been within their rights to eject the American Copernicus crew, had they not been preemptively annihilated by ruthless US forces, presumably Night Corps.

Men and women had died on both sides. But all those actions had been performed with conventional weaponry. Neither side had crossed the nuclear line against enemy combatants.

Now they were about to step over that line. Now, General Orlov planned to use tactical nuclear weapons to kill dozens of American Night Corps troops, without warning and before they had even deployed.

And, what then? If the Americans were to respond in kind, how long before that same line was crossed on Earth, and the European countries of NATO and the Eastern Bloc were devastated by a storm of escalating tit-for-tat nuclear attacks?

Orlov's actions here on the Moon—presumably approved by the Kremlin—might be the opening salvo in World War III, resulting in the deaths of hundreds of millions of Soviet, European, and American citizens. What began here might end with global death and devastation.

That, Svetlana Belyakova was not willing to accept.

And another irritating thought that would not leave her mind: even if the world did not go to war, even if these were the only tactical nuclear weapons ever launched? Svetlana might know some of the Americans aboard those Bricks. People who under other circumstances she might have considered … friends? *American* friends.

She had spent time on Columbia Station with Peter Sandoval and Terri Brock. She had been injured, and in terrible pain, and the two of them had helped to care for her with just as much care and thoughtfulness as her Soviet compatriots had. And if Night Corps Bricks were about to land here at Jura, it was possible that Sandoval and Brock were aboard them.

Americans were no longer just a single faceless monolith to Svetlana Belyakova. If they shot at her, she would shoot back, and to kill, but that was war. Here and now, this was not yet war. And if it was … not quite murder, it was the nearest thing to it Belyakova could imagine.

And, although the thought was irrelevant: Belyakova would not want to be at the sharp end of Vivian Carter's fury—or even her grief—if she, Svetlana Belyakova, stood by and allowed those deaths to happen. Let alone if she pressed the buttons to bring them about.

So, Vivian Carter would never have to know.

She nodded calmly. "Do you have a trajectory update on the Bricks that I should be entering into the guidance system?" She glanced over.

Vlasav was pale and physically shaking. It seemed that the idea of sharing responsibility for dozens of American deaths in a tactical-nuke inferno was not sitting comfortably on her geologist puppy's shoulders either. "Quickly, comrade," she snapped.

"No updates, ma'am."

"Tell me immediately if there are." She spun verniers, matched the numbers, glanced up at Orlov. "Am I correct?"

"Yes, correct."

Another glance to her right. She needed to know exactly where everyone was. Keretsky was seven feet away, behind her and to the right, staring up out of the window in some fascination. Orlov was scrutinizing the screen and switches in front of her, grunting terse orders on the radio to his deputy in the field, Rhyzkov, and occasionally glancing out of the windows himself.

She turned to Vlasav and winked at him. "Time until the Night Corps landings? Spit it out, man."

Vlasav's mouth dropped open at the wink, but he quickly recovered. "One minute thirty seconds, and one minute forty-five seconds, respectively."

"I see them!" Keretsky shouted, pointing upward.

"Calmly, comrade," Orlov said. "Calmly."

"My apologies, sir."

"Setting launch to automatic," Belyakova said. "Each missile is timed to fire five seconds after the Brick's landing, at the locations I designate." Two timers began counting down in front of her. She glanced at Orlov. "Is all in order? Do I have authorization to proceed?"

Orlov cast his eyes over the settings on the firing board and nodded. "Proceed."

Svetlana Belyakova pressed the PRO button to begin the firing sequence for the two tactical nuclear missiles. "Confirmed. Missiles armed and counting down."

She nodded in satisfaction, sat back and slightly away from the board, and dropped her hands into her lap.

And slid her geologist's hammer out of the pocket on her right thigh.

To her surprise, it was Keretsky who reacted first. Something about the confident way Belyakova had moved had attracted his attention, while

Orlov was still scanning the weapons board. Or perhaps Keretsky just happened to glance down at the right moment. "Look out!"

But Svetlana was already rising, her arm up, whirling around to put the full force of her shoulder and arm muscles into the blow, as she drove the hammer deep into Orlov's left eye and through to his brain.

The hammer was a foot long, with an aluminum handle and a steel head six inches across, and it weighed almost two pounds. On one side of the head was a conventional hammerhead, on the other, a pick. It was the pick that had gone through Orlov's eye, and according to Belyakova's training such a wound should immediately have been fatal. It was not. Orlov bellowed, one hand raised up to his face but the other instinctively lashing out at her.

Belyakova was quicker. She released her hold on the hammer, knowing it would likely jam in place, and stepped back. She raised her left leg to knee Orlov in the thigh and shove him away, and reached across the board to slam her fist onto the red ABORT button. The weapons panel displays blanked and then came up again, all lights green.

But even that pause had cost her valuable moments. Her sharpened screwdriver was down in her calf pocket, but she had no time to reach for it before Orlov fell forward onto her and Keretsky came leaping in.

With a speed that belied his mousy appearance, Keretsky already had his pistol in his hand. Svetlana had hoped the shock and ferocity of her attack on Orlov would delay him, or at least give him pause, but she had misjudged him. Perhaps he had anticipated her treachery.

As she and Orlov toppled backward she grabbed at the general's body, pulling it between herself and Keretsky to screen her and earn her a brief moment of extra time. Her back hit the floor, knocking the wind out of her, but by now she'd gotten that left foot up and was able to brace it against Orlov's hips, pushing his body toward Keretsky.

The screwdriver now in her hand, she rolled, just as Keretsky's gun went off. A bullet ricocheted off the floor a few inches from her right ear.

By all means, Comrade, fire a gun in a pressurized space. Obviously the act of a genius.

Damn it, everything happened too slowly on the Moon ...

Belyakova pushed herself upright and raised the screwdriver, its blade glinting green in the lights from the weapons board ... but Keretsky was already swinging his gun around, and all Belyakova could do was duck and hope that his second bullet missed as well.

And then Vlasav, meek little Dmitri Vlasav, grabbed Keretsky by the neck and yanked him backward. The zampolit tumbled back, roaring in fury.

Svetlana swung with her left hand and scored a deep red slash into the back of Keretsky's hand. His pistol tumbled to the ground.

She switched the blade into the right hand and leaped forward. "Take your hands from his throat, damn you!"

Vlasav did so just in time, shifting his hands to grab Keretsky's temples, and Belyakova's next wild swing slashed across the zampolit's neck. Another roar from Keretsky, but that slash was still not deep enough to be a killing stroke.

The whole vehicle lurched and seemed to jump to the left, in what felt like a minor earthquake. The first American Brick had landed, and by the feel of it, startlingly close to the Kharkovchanka. Really? Orlov had planned to detonate a tactical nuclear weapon that close to their own position?

Vlasav twisted and tried to bang Keretsky's head against the wall, but Keretsky was stronger than the young geologist. He pulled free and lunged at Svetlana.

None of his blows hit. Lashing out almost on instinct, Belyakova hit him twice, punching him once over the heart with her left fist and once in the throat with her right, the screwdriver still clutched in her hand, and Keretsky rocked back, gagging. Belyakova gauged distance and this time stabbed more accurately, punching the blade of the screwdriver deep into his jugular vein. She yanked the handle right, and then left, and a fountain of blood sprayed across her chest and Dima Vlasav's face, and all the fight went out of Keretsky along with it.

Belyakova dropped to her knees, panting. She released her hold on the screwdriver, which clattered onto the floor. Yanked Keretsky's jerking, dying body off Vlasav. And right then the second US Brick hit the deck, its impact again shoving the Kharkovchanka with what felt like a giant hand.

Keretsky appeared to be staring at her, eyes bulging. Svetlana wasn't sure if he could still understand her, or if he had traveled too far into his own shock and pain.

Nonetheless, she said very clearly: "That was for Casey Buchanan, who you murdered. But, most of all it is for me. Die slowly, please."

Perhaps Keretsky went to his death thinking that she was an American double agent. As Svetlana watched the life fading from his face and body with a clinical detachment, she found the idea morbidly amusing.

No. She was merely a human being who had been pushed beyond her limits. She had found her line. Again.

"General? General Orlov?" Rhyzkov's voice over the radio, probably baffled by the aborted missile launch.

Svetlana pushed-to-talk. "A power fluctuation has rendered the missile system inoperative. Stand down."

Rhyzkov's voice hardened. "General? Do we mobilize?"

"No," she said. "Prepare to retreat from the field." Then she turned off the radio. They had no time for this.

"Svetlana! Are you all right?" came Vlasav's voice. With all that blood dripping off his face, he actually looked in worse shape than the dying zampolit.

"Yes, perfectly." She pulled herself up and peered out of the window. The two Night Corps Bricks were not so close after all: they had landed over three hundred yards away, further than she had guessed. Even as she watched, the walls fell away from the first Brick, and American troops began to spill out from it.

Around them, the rest of the Soviet forces were deploying, despite her feeble attempts to stop them. Vympel soldiers were running forward from shelter, and Moon bikes were appearing. Rhyzkov ran toward the Kharkovchanka, rifle in hand, easily identifiable by the stripe on his suit, so Svetlana flipped off the circuit breaker that controlled the airlock.

"Power up the vehicle," she said. "We are leaving."

"Leaving?" Vlasav said, stupidly.

"You wish to stay?" Like all Soviet vehicles, the Kharkovchanka was adorned with the "CCCP" and hammer and sickle of the USSR. Even if it hadn't been, this truck was clearly of Soviet design and flanked by Soviet soldiers, who were already firing on the Americans. "To Night Corps, we are the enemy."

"Then tell them that we are not!" he cried. "Tell them that we want peace!"

That we want peace. Dima Vlasav really was very young. "Idiot. I am sure they will be convinced. Just before our own people start shooting at us, instead."

Why had Vlasav joined the battle on her side? Gallantry, idealism, young lust? Resentment over the disdain Orlov and Keretsky had shown him? Not wanting American blood on his hands, if only by proxy?

Belyakova had no idea, nor did she care. He'd ended up with Russian blood on his face instead, the same blood that she had on her hands and smeared across the front of her jumpsuit, but all that would have to wait.

They had to get away from here. Now. Quickly.

And go where?

Well. That would have to be a problem for later.

Vlasav still hadn't moved, in an agony of shock and indecisiveness. Damn the kid. "Never mind," she said. "I will do it myself."

As the first US bullets sprayed the Kharkovchanka, rattling off its armored hull, Belyakova was already in the cab, stabbing buttons and switches. Outside, Rhyzkov had run around the vehicle and was now looking up at her, gesturing.

Belyakova liked Rhyzkov no better than she had liked Orlov or Keretsky; another sneering KGB drone. She kicked the Kharkovchanka forward rather venomously, and its armored prow slammed into the deputy, sending him flying through space.

The next moment, they were in serious motion, weaving left and right to thread their way between the rank-and-file soldiers as they jumped out of its path, and then describing a long loop away from the battle scene. The bullets stopped; unlike Svetlana, the Americans were apparently above striking a fleeing opponent.

Vlasav arrived in the cab, pulling himself onto the bucket seat beside her. She glanced left at him. "By the way, that was very stupid. Keretsky might have killed you."

He swallowed. "Yes. But I could not let him kill a ... kill you, Ma'am. I just could not." He cleared his throat. "The first woman on the Moon? A Hero of the Soviet Union?"

Nice recovery, Belyakova thought sardonically. Vlasav had been about to say *could not let him kill a woman*, she was sure. But she'd take it. She *was* a woman, and it would be ungracious not to acknowledge gallantry. Or, in Vlasav's case, merely a major crush.

So she gave him the most winning smile she was capable of, which made him blush even redder than before. "And I thank you. I do appreciate it. Be assured that I shall never reveal your treachery to the Rodina. That will be forever our secret." She winked at him again, half-tempted to see whether she could make his cheeks explode with pleasure. An odd moment of levity during a very grim moment.

Vlasav pulled himself upright, and almost formally, said: "Thank you, ma'am."

"Now, please put on your spacesuit. You are leaving. I am afraid it will be," she checked her instruments. "Possibly a half hour walk back already. You must head due west."

His jaw dropped. "I am not coming with you?"

"Better that you do not. Besides, I do not know where I am going, or what I will do next. I doubt I will last long. There is no need for you to share my fate."

Belyakova had managed not to say *I have no idea what I am doing any more*, but surely that must be obvious even to Vlasav.

"I want to stay with you," he said stubbornly.

"Well, you cannot." At the look in his eye, she eased her tone. All too easily these days her voice grew brittle and harsh. "Dima, Dima. You have a life. Go back to it. Place all the blame upon me for the killings, report honestly to your superiors, aside from your own role, and return to that life."

"And what about you?"

Belyakova shook her head. "Forget about me."

Killing a General and a high-ranking KGB officer? Deliberately sabotaging a Soviet attack on an illegal imperialist installation on the lunar surface? And with the only people who might be even remotely inclined to help her still tens of millions of miles away, far beyond the Earth-Moon system?

Belyakova had acted correctly and honorably. But: she had also completely screwed herself beyond any hope of redemption.

Damn you, Nikolai. Damn you, Vivian. I was quite happy with who I was, until the two of you came along.

"I am dead," Belyakova said. "Yes, I am. Please do not look at me that way, Dimitri. Surely, that must be obvious. And why are you not yet in your spacesuit? Did you not hear me? You are leaving and walking back to our Soviet forces. Immediately. Bring the suit here, so you can still hear what I am saying while you don it. And bring mine as well."

She used the brief interval to marshal her thoughts. Once he returned, she said: "Good. Now listen to me. Once you are safely away from here, once this is over: you will tell Mission Control Moscow that you need to speak to Nikolai Makarov. That you have a message for him, and him alone. Yes?"

"What? They ..." Those puppy-dog eyes were wide again. Possibly the thought of him, asking to speak to yet another legend. Makarov of *Mars*?

Without doubt, he was gearing up to say, *They would not let me speak to such a great man*, or some such nonsense. She overrode him. They had no time, and she was getting further and further from Jura. She had no idea when she'd pass beyond Vlasav's walkback radius. She looked behind them and braked. Still no signs of pursuit. "They will let you speak to him, because I am Makarov's partner, and they will wish to hear my last words to him. Of course they will."

"... All right."

"Listen carefully. You must tell him that I am dead. That I am about to kill myself. This is very important. Tell him that, just like that. You will do it?"

"Kill yourself?"

"Of course. What else is there for me? But he must hear this. And also ..." She stared through the window with sightless eyes. "Tell him I am sorry for my treachery and hope that it does not rebound upon him. And tell Alexei Arkhipovich and Valentina Vladimirovna that I am sorry. And of course, Sergei Pavlovich, and the rest of the cosmonaut corps, the same. I wish them to know how badly I have let them down, after all their kindness to me. And I wish for them to hear that from him, rather than from you. Do you understand?"

"Of course."

"Yes, but—"

"You *must* tell him this. It is important to me. Repeat it back to me. And then repeat it again."

He stammered it out, twice, verbatim, and she nodded. That would have to do. "Keep saying it to yourself as you walk. Do not forget." Hating herself, she leaned in. "Do it for me, Dima. It is the last thing I will ask of you. Please?"

"Of course. I will do it."

Stopping the Kharkovchanka, she stood. "Thank you. And thank you again for saving my life."

She kissed him on the cheeks, right-left-right, in the Russian style, and thought that perhaps his heart might stop.

"Now, go," she said softly. "Put on your helmet and go. And do not forget me."

"I will not."

"Tell me again what you will tell Nikolai."

He did so, again verbatim.

"Thank you, my friend."

"Thank you," he said. "Svetlana."

He saluted her, donned his helmet, and stepped into the airlock.

That poor boy. He'd now mourn her, and would never forget that kiss, she was quite sure of it. So, with luck, he would also remember her words for Nikolai.

Perhaps Vivian Carter was right, and she *was* a cold bitch.

And, then again: perhaps Vivian was wrong.

She watched as Vlasav trudged across the lunar surface away from the vehicle, heading back west. He could not follow the Kharkovchanka's tracks in reverse, of course—it had left little trace of its passing on the regolith, except to the most experienced and attentive eye—but he would be all right. Soon he would be able to see the Jura Mountains, and the sweeping semicircle that surrounding Sinus Iridum. It would be hard for him to get lost.

"Onward," Belyakova said aloud. She glanced at where the Sun was, to orient herself, and applied full power to the wheels, and drove off across the eternal lunar surface.

And then, less than a minute later, came the explosion, likely from a missile strike: a *whump* and crunch, sending the whole Kharkovchanka tilting into a sickening long skid.

The space truck crashed down onto its left wheels again, but Belyakova was still fighting the steering when her hearing recovered enough for her to hear the high whistling hiss above the roar of the vehicle's tortured engines, and a sudden strong breeze … and then her ears popped, hard.

The Kharkovchanka hull was holed badly, somewhere behind her. The environmental control system was doing its best to compensate by rushing extra air into the cabin, but that would only briefly postpone the inevitable.

In just a few seconds, all Belyakova's oxygen would be gone.

She glanced out of the window for the merest second before jumping to grab her suit. In the skies to her west, now turning away, was an American Lunar Module with what looked like a missile mounted on the right-hand side of its cabin.

The matching missile that used to be on the left side had just destroyed her escape vehicle.

Already, she was gasping. She glanced up once … and saw the size of the hole in the back of her vehicle.

God, help me.

It was hypnotic, that hole. It was hard to tear her eyes away from it.

As Svetlana shoved her legs into her suit, moving largely on automatic pilot, the ironic thought went through her mind:

Americans. Never any gratitude.

And her next thought, half terror and half regret:

I am not going to make it.

PART FIVE: MOON

February-June 1985

CHAPTER 25

Interplanetary Space: Vivian Carter
February 2, 1985
Mission Elapsed Time: 579 days

"VIVIAN. Vivian, sorry. Wake up."

"What the hell?" Vivian found herself being shaken awake, and as she'd taken a Seconal just three hours earlier, it took a lot of shaking. "Get off me!"

"Jeez, take it easy." But Josh Rawlings shoved himself back immediately and raised his hands in apology. "Sorry, Vivian. I did almost shout at you trying to wake you before I ... anyway: Nikolai says he needs to talk to you. He says it's urgent."

"Nikolai?" She frowned. "Nikolai *Makarov?*"

"Do we know another one?"

"That can't be good." Vivian pulled herself half-out of her sleeping bag, grabbed for a sweatshirt, and pulled it over her head. "Are we okay? The Astarte, everything nominal?"

"The boards all look good. No problems. Everything's fine, and everyone's asleep, aside from us."

"And ... nothing bad from Earth? No nukes flying?"

"As far as I know."

"Okay, good. Look the other way."

"What?"

"Jeez, man." She reached up to physically turn him around, then unzipped her sleeping bag the rest of the way and pulled on shorts. "Does Mission Control know that Nikolai is calling me?"

"He asked me not to bring them into the loop. Full confidentiality, he said. I'll leave it up to you whether to honor that."

"How does he seem? What's his mood?"

"Bleak."

"Great. Okay, let's keep this quiet for now. Don't tell CAPCOM, or anyone else on the crew until I know what's going on." She rubbed her eyes. "Gah. Where am I going for this?"

"CM-1."

"On my way. No listening in, all right?"

"I do know what *confidential* means," Rawlings said, a bit sniffily.

"Course you do, sorry. Uh, Josh, I hate to ask and all, but can you grab me some coffee?"

"Sure. I'll bring you some."

"Great. I really need it. Thanks."

With that, Vivian was off, arrowing out of the sleep space and pulling herself through the hexagonal hatch into the forward cabin about as fast as she could without injuring herself.

"Hi Nikolai. Vivian here."

"Ah." He looked up toward the camera and nodded. "Thank you. We have much to discuss."

"Are you okay? Is TMK-Mars okay? Uh, is *my* ship okay?"

"Yes. All of those. As far as I know." He took the time for a deep sigh and Vivian stifled the urge to shout at him. "It is … it is Svetlana."

"What about her?"

"She has killed two Soviet military officers, and escaped across the lunar surface," Makarov said soberly.

"Svetlana is back on the *Moon*?"

He blinked. "Of course."

"And she's …. She did *what*?"

Makarov peered at her in concern. "Vivian, are you all right?"

"You just woke me from a deep sleep."

He looked haggard. How long since he'd slept? Did TMK-Mars operate on Moscow time? What time was it in Moscow, anyway?

Irrelevant, Vivian. Try to concentrate. "Nikolai. What happened on the Moon, with Svetlana?"

"There was a battle. Perhaps you already know some of this? The Americans landed additional military forces on the Moon, at their mining operation at Jura. Svetlana was with a Soviet Vympel force that was ordered to attack the Americans as they landed. Svetlana not only refused that order but killed her two commanding officers."

"I don't know any of it, Nikolai … Svetlana is *Vympel, now?* Holy *shit*."

"No, she was there as a geologist. And she has now gone into hiding."

"Where?" Vivian shook her head convulsively, trying to shake sense into herself. "Sorry, stupid question. What sort of battle? Were there casualties?" She wanted to add: *And were any of my friends involved in it?*

"There were many dead and wounded on both sides." Makarov looked into the camera, very seriously. "Vivian, it is important that you hold everything I am about to tell you in great secrecy. You will understand why. I wish to tell you keep nothing back. This means I must tell you of matters my people would not wish you to know."

Now Vivian needed a long deep breath of her own. While she was sucking in air to say *Sure, fine*, she heard a banging on the hatch. It opened, and Josh tossed her a bulb of coffee, and slammed the hatch behind him. Vivian didn't take that slam as bad temper. As the mission progressed it was getting harder and harder to close that hatch quietly and have it latch properly. She took a long pull at the coffee, burned her mouth, and swallowed anyway.

"You are alone?" Makarov said anxiously.

"Yes. Coffee delivery. This'll help. Of course, I agree, utmost secrecy. Tell me what you know."

"It was as I said. The Soviet force, including Svetlana, were gathering to assault your Jura mining station. Two Night Corps Bricks dropped down to defend it. There was a firefight. Night Corps prevailed, and the Soviet troops fell back."

Night Corps. And Peter was back on the flying roster. And Terri, of course. *Shit.*

If one of them had been injured, or even killed in the assault, how long would it take them, or NASA, to tell her? Based on past performance, they might wait until she was back on Earth. *Christ.* "Okay. And Svetlana?"

347

"Svetlana was in the Soviet Command and Control vehicle. It appears that during the assault she had an altercation with her superior officers which left them both dead."

Vivian took another gulp of coffee.

"She later freed the one survivor, a young Soviet fellow geologist. He has told us that the field commander ordered Svetlana to destroy the Night Corps Bricks using full force. Svetlana chose to ... destroy her commanding officers instead."

"Full force? Nikolai, are you saying *nuclear* force?"

"I cannot know for certain. But from the words, I think it must be so."

"Tactical nukes? They were going to *nuke* the *Bricks*?"

"But you did not hear this from me," Nikolai said. "I never used those words, and this conversation we are having, we are not having. You understand?"

"Sure, man, I get it. Svetlana refused to nuke Americans. Good for her. Except, what's happening now? Are your people hunting for her?"

"Yes, of course they are."

"Okay, I understand." By now, Vivian was well and truly awake, although her brain was still sluggish. "So she's out on the Moon, alone. Tell me she didn't escape in just a suit, because I've done that myself, and it's ... not good." Which Nikolai knew, since he'd helped her flee Zvezda back then.

How far were the Montes Jura from Zvezda? Vivian couldn't do that math right now.

Except, Svetlana couldn't go to Zvezda. Even if she could find the supplies to walk that far, Zvezda base no longer existed.

"No. Svetlana fled the battlefield in this same Command and Control vehicle—"

"Okay, how long can that vehicle keep her alive?"

"Not at all," Makarov said. "It suffered a missile strike, a conventional missile, probably American, but who can say in all this mess? This vehicle suffered loss of cabin pressure and was wrecked."

"Oh, crap." Vivian's mouth dropped open. "But didn't you just say she disappeared?"

"Yes, this this is what I am trying to tell you. Once the Soviet forces were pushed back from their attack, and were able to go and check the vehicle, Svetlana's body was not there. Nor was her suit. Svetlana must have had time to put it on before all the air escaped."

"So now she *is* out on the surface in just a suit?"

"No. She took a smaller vehicle instead and disappeared. That is all I can tell you."

"Come on, Nikolai, for God's sake: *how long can Svetlana survive out there on her own, with what she has?*"

"I do not know," Makarov said simply.

Vivian gritted her teeth. "God damn it, Nikolai. Then *tell me about the vehicles.*"

"Our Command and Control vehicle, we call it the Kharkovchanka, is similar in size to one of your MOLABs …"

"A what? A woman, of …?"

"Yes, yes, a Lady of Kharkov, but what it *is* is a Soviet Moon tank. Much heavier and better armed than one of your MOLABs. We also have a smaller type of pressurized vehicle, I suppose you would call it a … lunar van? A small truck for two people, we call them Purgans. Four such vehicles had been parked a few kilometers back from Jura while their crews participated in the assault. One of the Purgans was missing, along with a large quantity of air tanks, food, water, and other supplies. As the person leading the mineral prospecting work, Svetlana knew where they were. She went to them, filled one Purgan very full of supplies and spare equipment and drove it away."

Makarov lifted up a folder, turned a page, and twisted it so that the camera could see it. "This is a Purgan. Small, just four wheels …"

It was much smaller than Vivian had expected. Stupidly small, for lunar use. "Unbelievable. It's a *microbus*? Svetlana is fleeing from her life on the Moon in a fricking *microbus*?"

Makarov looked at the picture himself, as if seeing it for the first time. "I suppose so."

"A microbus with a machine gun on top. Nikolai, does that … Purgan thing really work on the Moon? It looks very unstable. Top-heavy, narrow wheelbase. How careful do you have to be, to not roll it?"

"I have never driven one, of course, but it has a winch to use to recover, in case of need. These are small, for prospecting, two-man vehicles. Fast to build and inexpensive, but robust. It can take the hard treatment, like many vehicles we use in my country."

Vivian struggled to process it all. Svetlana had fled off across the Moon in a *very* small truck, and now presumably had a highly-trained Vympel squad—or several—on her heels. "This is crazy."

"Yes." Nikolai shrugged again, hopelessly.

"Does this Purgan at least have that track-smearing ... what's the word, jeez. Covering its own tracks. Redaction. Does it have the track-redaction system, or can your people just follow it?"

"Yes, yes, it has the reduction, so she could not be followed."

"Redaction. Maybe that's just what my people call it." Vivian drank some more coffee.

"It also has the disguise, the camouflage, to make it hard to recognize from above."

"Regolith weave. But even so ... Nikolai, old friend. I have no clue what her chances are."

"I have been ordered to tell my own superiors immediately, if she attempts to contact me." He paused. "She has not, of course."

"And if she does? Will you tell your people?"

Yet another sigh. Those, and the tension in Nikolai's voice, betrayed the intense stress he was under. "No. Unless she specifically asks me to relay a message to my people, which I suppose is possible. Aside from that ..."

Vivian nodded. "You don't have to say it out loud."

Nikolai did anyway. "Aside from that, I plan to disobey my orders."

"Good." Vivian was had a pounding headache coming in. She tried to think around it. "That Svetlana chick sure is full of surprises."

"Her actions saved American lives. Dozens. And prevented my country from being the first to use tactical nuclear weapons on the Moon."

"Uh, sure. If you don't count the one that wiped out Hadley."

Makarov gave her what might have been the merest hint of a smile. "A matter of definition. Or, perhaps, 'splitting hairs.' The warhead used on Hadley Base was larger than tactical."

"Oh, well *that's* all right then."

"But in this case, if your other US troops on the ground at your Jura Base had responded in the same way, it would have been a disaster. And events might have escalated even further, here, and perhaps also down on Earth."

"Oh boy. Well, I hope she finds some way out of that mess."

"Perhaps she can, Vivian. With our help."

Vivian blinked at the screen. "Us? I don't know what the hell we can do about it. We're still months away from the Moon. Oh, unless you want me to tell Night Corps to go and look for her?"

"No, no. There are still moles."

"You have Soviet spies in Night Corps?"

"Yes. I know this. It is certain."

"Oh … good grief."

"So, please do not tell them, or anyone else. Really, the only American I can trust is …" He waved at the screen.

"If you mean *me*, that's a really depressing situation you're in," Vivian said.

"And yet, here we are. Who else?"

Vivian could have named many more Americans she could trust. But Makarov had no reason to share that trust.

Plus, of course: none of her trustworthy Americans would be willing to hare across the Moon, risking their lives trying to stay ahead of Soviet death squads, just to save Svetlana Belyakova.

"I have some motivation for you," he said. "If we find her, she surely cannot go home to the Soviet Union. Maybe one day, but not today. If we find her, she has only one option."

"Defection?"

"Let us not call it that … but, yes. She will have to return with you, to the United States."

Vivian hadn't thought that far ahead. "Belyakova would *hate* that."

"Yes, she would. But, do you see another choice?"

"No. I really don't. Except, that *return with me* part isn't going to happen."

"Well," Makarov said. "That is what we must discuss."

Vivian pinched the top of her nose. Sometimes that helped, with these headaches. Not so much, tonight. "Okay. How long ago did this happen?"

"Two months ago."

"*What?*" Vivian gaped at him. "Are you kidding me? Svetlana's already been out there for two months and you're only telling me now?"

"It is only now that they are telling me. I have known only a few hours. I believe they had hoped to tidy this all up quietly, softly. It is the KGB way. But since Svetlana has managed to stay away from them for so long, they are now exploring other paths to try to find her."

"Could she possibly have survived that long?"

"She is Svetlana Belyakova," Makarov said simply.

"Yes." Vivian drank more coffee. "Yes, she is."

"If any people in the world could do that, they would be you, and her."

"Well, maybe. But I guess *they* think she might have survived this long, or they wouldn't have told you. They'd just have written her off."

"Exactly so."

"But you've heard nothing from her."

"No, I have not. Not directly. But as she was escaping, the day she killed her zampolit, she gave her young colleague, a Soviet called Vlasav, a message to relay to me. Part of that was that she intended to kill herself, to atone for her shame."

"She said ... what? *No.*"

"And other things, also: that she wanted to apologize to me, and asked me to apologize on her behalf to her mentors and superiors in the cosmonaut corps, especially Leonov and Tereshkova, and Grand Designer Korolev, for letting them down so badly."

"Really?" Vivian shook her head. "I don't buy that for a second. Do you? Svetlana's not the type to off herself. She'd always be looking for an edge, some way of manipulating the situation to change the outcome. Right up till the end."

"Yes," Makarov said.

"And also: no offense to your crewmate, but ... I'm not sure Svetlana even *has* a sense of shame."

Makarov grinned.

Vivian continued. "What she does, she's always sure it's for a good reason. Svetlana does stuff, moves on, and doesn't look back."

"Exactly."

"Okay, so maybe she didn't really say those things, but the KGB or Vympel or whoever wants you to think that she did?"

"No. I believe that is exactly what she said. But I also agree that Svetlana has not killed herself. It is unthinkable."

Vivian yawned, and shook her head, then wished she hadn't. "Sorry, Nikolai. I'm lost. You're going to have to spell this out for me."

"Killing ourselves: this was our code, hers and mine. A joke that we had between us."

"You joked about *suicide?*"

"Well, not in that way. But it was what we sometimes said to each other. 'If ever I send you a message that I have killed myself, I mean that I have killed my current life. That I have run away and let others think I am dead.' You see? We used this to talk of politics, back home. For years we have lived under close scrutiny, and especially after Columbia Station, when we went home after the death of Yashin. For a while, we did not know what would happen, Svetlana and I. A bullet in the night, or poison—such things happen."

"I always wondered about that," Vivian said.

"It was concluded that we were more useful alive, I suppose. But, you see?" He spread his hands.

"Um. Well, I see that you've somehow convinced yourself Svetlana's alive *specifically* because she said she was going to kill herself. Which makes as much twisted sense as anything else you've said."

"And if Svetlana really planned to kill herself, then why did she not just do so, once she had ensured this innocent boy soldier was clear? Svetlana is always logical, she is one for the cold equations, no? She might want to die quickly, or she might want to make some gesture, do something useful in her death, but those are not what she has done. Why hide herself in death so her body would never be found?"

"No. Svetlana is *still alive*. And she wants me to go to her. To find her. I know she does. Through the boy, through that message: this was her way of asking for my help."

"But you can't," Vivian said.

"But I can," Makarov said, with quiet determination. "I can go to her, and I will go to her, and I will save her."

Vivian's head was throbbing, now. She put her hands up to her temples and breathed deep. "Nikolai, Nikolai … just listen to yourself. I know Svetlana means a lot to you. And, sure, I guess I consider her a friend, too … of sorts. If there was anything I could do for her I would, especially if it would piss off Yuri Andropov at the same time. But she's lost on the Moon, God knows where, even if she's still alive, and I'm going home. Back to Earth. There's no way around that."

Makarov just nodded, as if he'd expected her to say those very words. "Let us talk about it. May we?"

She squinted. "You've got some crazy scheme in that head of yours, haven't you?"

"Yes."

"Oh, God." Vivian glanced at the clock in the instrument panel in front of her and checked it against her watch. "Oh, what the hell. I'm never getting back to sleep after all that coffee anyway."

And, of course, after the shock of learning that Svetlana Belyakova was now a fugitive, on the run from her own people.

On the goddamned *Moon*.

Vivian grimaced. "Okay, look. I need ten or fifteen minutes, all right? I need to use the facilities, brush my hair. Make some more coffee, God help me and my stomach lining." And pop some drugs for the headache, but she didn't say that part aloud.

"The facilities?"

"Pee, Nikolai. I need to pee. All right?"

"Ah." He blinked and nodded, then waved his hand as if shooing her out of her own Command Module. "Then … please do."

Vivian floated alone in the forward compartment, turning slowly over and over in the breeze from the fan. Oddly, this made her headache better rather than worse, perhaps because her body was relaxed and her eyes were closed, and all the lights were off except for the green and yellow glows from some of the instrument panels. Those, and the starlight that came in through the big main window, provided quite enough low-level illumination for her to find her way around.

It was rare that Vivian was up here and alone, awake when everyone else was sleeping. Around her, Astarte made its usual hums and gurgles and creaks and bangs. By now, they were almost restful, just part of the mission ambience.

Soon after leaving Mars, the crew of Astarte had given up on the shift system altogether. Now they all slept at the same time, ate their meals together in the forward compartment after preparing them in the wardroom, and often worked chores in pairs instead of singly. Mars had brought them together as a crew, and they wanted to work together. It made the living spaces more crowded, but by now they hardly noticed.

By now the astronauts were confident enough about Astarte's performance, and even Rudy was content to leave the observations of the Sun to the automatic scheduler. Josh and Marco would occasionally drift around Astarte during the night to do a system check, but they'd also rigged up a system that would awaken one of them if any of the Astarte's parameters went out of range in any respect.

Josh had apparently gone back to bed while she'd been talking to Makarov. And so, for her brief breaktime, Vivian had the Astarte foredeck to herself.

She sipped coffee from the bulb in her hand and opened her eyes. As she looked out of the window at the universe, the bright pinpoints of the Earth-Moon system slowly rolled across her field of view, to be replaced by the familiar constellations. A window full of bright stars.

She would miss that sky, once the mission was over. Once she got back to Earth, she would never have a view like this again. Even on the finest night, with the darkest of skies, the stars would always twinkle.

Once she got back to Earth …

How much did Makarov know about what was happening on Earth? If he hadn't known about the original invasions of Poland and East Germany after Burning Night, he might not know about the strikes, factory occupations and massive protests that were now spreading into Czechoslovakia and Romania and the Baltic states. Soviet control over its Eastern Bloc was slipping. Vivian's crew had spent interminable hours discussing whether this volatility was "good" or "bad" for the West. But she sure wouldn't be getting into any of that with Nikolai tonight.

She checked her watch again. Her fifteen minutes was up, and the pain in her head was attenuating.

Okay, she thought eventually. *Time to go find out what aberrant schemes are flowing around the twisted mind of nutty Nikolai.*

"Nikolai, I'm not set up for a trip to the Moon. Not at all. I don't have the gear. I don't even have a lander."

"I have a lander."

Of course *he* did: the LEK bolted onto TMK-Mars that he and his crew had used to make moonfalls on Deimos. "But I don't."

"No. You land with me, of course. We meet up in space and then we land together."

There was only one way that could work. "You're expecting me to steal one of Astarte's Command and Service Modules, and come and meet you?"

Makarov's forehead creased. "They are your Modules, are they not?"

"They belong to the mission. And ..." Crossing interplanetary space by herself in a Command Module? Inserting herself into lunar orbit? Vivian was lost for words at the audacity of it.

"It can work." He waved that away. "And we both have spacesuits, of course."

"Last I noticed, it takes a little more than that to mount an expedition across the lunar surface. Especially one that would need to cover a lot of ground."

"I have the Lunokhod and supplies. Other things, we may be able to pick up along our way."

"Oh, great, so then we become cryptonauts? Stealing vital resources and equipment from our countrymen? And from where, exactly?"

He tutted. "Vivian. I am speaking of salvage, not of theft. Of using supplies that have been abandoned."

"Abandoned in place. Well, I ..." Vivian's mind stalled. "Nikolai. You're saying all this like it's straightforward, but this would be a *mind-boggling* undertaking. Plus, whatever US and Soviet forces still remain on the Moon are all armed to the teeth, and likely to shoot first and ask questions later, and we have no weapons. Well, *I* have no weapons, anyway." She grinned dourly. "Except a pencil."

Makarov knew all about her final deadly fight with Sergei Yashin in the Soyuz, by the stricken Columbia Station. "I, too, have nothing. But I do not want to shoot anyone."

"Nikolai." She leaned forward and stared intently at the screen. "You're insane. I'm not going to the Moon. And neither are you."

"Oh. Did I not mention?" He gave a little sad smile. "I am doing it already."

"No!" Vivian rocked back. "You madman. Tell me ..."

"Tell you that it is not true? But it is. I undocked from TMK-Mars twenty-four hours ago. I am now far from them, and I have already made a small burn to adjust my direction. I am on course for the Moon."

"Jesus Christ, Nikolai ..." It was impossible. Wasn't it? "You're already flying to the Moon in just a LEK? No Soyuz, no other booster?"

"I could not bring the Soyuz, of course. I could not leave my remaining crew without a lifeboat, and without a means of returning to the Earth's surface."

"Nikolai … the massive nuclear rocket booster TMK-Mars is hauling can get them into Earth orbit all by itself, and then your countrymen could just send up a new Soyuz to bring them home."

"But that would add complications and make a thief of me. Now our Deimos mission is complete this lander is redundant, and so I am taking little of value."

"Your crew … do they know?"

"Yes. Although they will pretend they did not, that my leaving was a surprise. They are good men."

"Well, I hope so, but … you're still millions of miles from the Moon, with weeks before you get there. You're going to live in that tiny tin can that whole time?'

"It is made for three men, and I have it all to myself."

"But … damn it, do you really have enough thrust—and fuel— in just a LEK to achieve lunar orbital insertion *and* a descent to the surface?"

"Before I arrive, I can discard many things. Also, I do not need the tight, careful circular orbit. If I approach in the correct parabolic curve, I can allow the Moon's gravity to slow me and pull me in toward the surface, and then brake to deorbit and land right away. By my calculations, I can probably make it to the surface."

"But not off it again. There's no way that's possible."

"That is correct. I will need to refuel there."

"Holy cow." Well, okay, yes: by now, there had to be plenty of abandoned fuel dumps on the Moon. The LEKs and the LMs used the same hypergolic propellants, Aerozine 50 and nitrogen tetroxide. Makarov would just need to park the LEK close enough to an abandoned but functional US or Soviet dump to refuel.

Just. Ha. If he really had enough fuel to land safely at all. That alone was distinctly sketchy. And on top of that, Makarov was hoping to do a pinpoint landing within reach of a gas station?

And, if he miraculously managed all that? Even if he could return to Earth orbit in the LEK, he obviously couldn't reenter the Earth's atmosphere. He had no heatshield, zero protection. The LEK would burn up in seconds.

Unless he'd transferred to an Apollo Command Module by then, of course.

"So. Nikolai, you devious bastard. Your endgame *relies* on me joining you?"

His voice held a tinge of embarrassment. "Your help would greatly increase my chances of success. Getting to the Moon, on the Moon, and afterward, once we have Svetlana. To succeed, we must pool our resources. And not just equipment, not just supplies: some parts of the information we need are already in my possession, but other parts are items that only you may know. And, very important: your experience on the lunar surface greatly exceeds my own."

"Huh," she said.

"If you cannot come, I understand, of course. Then I will just have to take my chance as best I can. The worst case, without you, at the end I will call for American help on my way to Earth … and hope to receive it."

" 'Once we have Svetlana?' You mean, once you've searched the Moon, and found a woman the entire KGB can't find?"

"Oh?" Once again, Nikolai sounded surprised. "But I believe I know where she is."

"But you said she didn't tell you. Christ, Nikolai, stop talking in … riddles … oh."

He was already nodding. "Yes. Do you see?"

"She …" Vivian shook her head yet again. Thank God the headache meds were kicking in, or by now her skull would be about to explode. "Oh. Except that she *did* tell you. That crazy, clever bitch. Yes, I see."

"Vivian." His tone was reproving.

"Sorry. But, wow."

She looked at Makarov. Makarov looked back. And smiled, tentatively.

Weeks later, when Vivian recalled their conversation, this was the part she'd remember the best. She had been blathering away, trying to convince Makarov that what he planned to do was impossible, that he should just change his course back toward Earth and throw himself on the mercy of NASA or Night Corps, get himself rescued, defect, *anything at all* except the madness he was planning. Makarov had nodded, patiently waiting for her to finish. Then, when she finally ran out of words and just stared at him, Nikolai had said: "We would need to rendezvous. Link ourselves up, somehow. You would spacewalk to me, join me in the LEK. And then we would go down to the Moon from there."

Yet again, she had shaken her head. "Nikolai, just refining Astarte's trajectory so that it'll get back to Earth on a course accurate enough to reenter at just the right speed and angle for splashdown took Mission Control and my three guys a couple weeks of effort, and a lot of time on really big computers on Earth."

He'd waved his hand dismissively. "Yes, yes. This is easier."

"How so?"

"With the fully fueled SPS engine on your Command and Service Module, we have the power to make this simpler. We do not need to choose an exact time and place for our landing, not yet, nor a specific orbit. We merely need to arrive together, in *some* orbit, and then take matters from there."

"You mean you're planning to seat-of-the-pants it." Makarov looked puzzled. Vivian clarified. "Make shit up as you go along. Design the mission while you're flying it."

"Constantly measure and correct our courses, yes. One task at a time, and first things first. Get our ships together. Then get them toward lunar orbit. Measure and define that orbit, then choose our moment for the deorbit burn that will take us where we need to go. We will have choices. And, of course, we will have time to discuss it on the way. Vivian, we can do this."

"Sooo, back up: you'd want us to rendezvous *before* going into lunar orbit?"

"Of course. So that you can use your CSM engine to insert us into that orbit and save fuel in the LEK."

Vivian blinked rapidly. "All right. I guess we *are* both going in straight lines now—well, wide parabolas. Similar courses, since our points of origin and arrival are the same. Given the time we have, figuring out an intersecting trajectory now *would* take less time and effort than us each going into separate lunar orbits and then trying to fix up how to rendezvous."

"Yes. You see? Even a small difference in the planes of our lunar orbits would make matters very difficult for us. Consuming as little fuel as possible, that must be our main priority. Vivian, I have not completed this mathematics yet, but I am sure this is the right way to go. Once you are free from Astarte I will measure your course, measure my course, and in the next few weeks I will bring us together. All the while, I will also be calculating how to get us into orbit. However, for your own safety, and your peace of mind, you should also make a backup plan: determine how to get into lunar orbit by yourself, in case I get hit by a bus."

"A bus?"

"That is the American phrase, I think?"

Vivian exhaled. "Yes, it is. Okay. Nikolai, my head's spinning, and I don't know which way is up anymore. I'll need to think about this and do some math of my own. All right? You're not really expecting an immediate reply, are you?"

He bowed. "I need to take some measurements myself now, and also I am hungry. Today has been long. We will talk again tomorrow at the same time, perhaps?"

"I'll do my best."

He raised an eyebrow. "You are not the commander? You do not decide your own schedule?"

"Chance would be a fine thing."

But that was irrelevant. Better to let Nikolai go off and take his measurements and eat his borscht. "Sorry. Disregard. I'll make it work." She gave him a half-bow in return. "Talk to you again this time tomorrow."

He nodded, waved, broke the connection.

Vivian flipped switches. Sat back and massaged her temples.

Oh my God. This is insane.

She wasn't going to do this. She absolutely was *not*. Because it was nuts.

Wearily, she hauled herself back to bed. If she couldn't sleep, at least she'd close her eyes for a while.

The next night:

"Coming down, you'd need to use the radar on your lander, right? There's certainly a chance someone else can pick up on that radar if they're in the right place. Pretty localized."

As far as Vivian knew, anyway. She certainly didn't know anything to the contrary. Her knowledge of this stuff was superficial. She'd have to take it on faith that what she'd been told was correct.

"A risk we would have to take. You have a NAVSTAR receiver on board, that you can bring?"

"Oh. No, I don't. No reason why we'd be carrying one. No NAVSTARs around Venus or Mars."

So, no access to precision navigation while they were on the Moon? Vivian put her hand up to her brow. "Crap."

This wasn't going well. It wasn't going well at all.

Vivian *did* have an honest-to-God brass sextant, and star charts, and those were certainly portable. She also had a good mental map of the Moon, based on years of memorization, but she surely shouldn't be entrusting their lives to *that*.

Wait. "TMK-Mars, you left from lunar orbit, correct? Does that mean you have charts of the Moon aboard your ship?"

"Well, one map." He paused. "It is not high resolution. Not a full briefing book, with photographs. But a map, at least."

"A map? A single map of the whole Moon?"

"A map, one big folded sheet, yes, that is what I am telling you. Nearside is on the front, and Farside on the back."

Vivian closed her eyes. "Please tell me it at least has lunar latitudes and longitudes marked on it."

"Oh, yes, of course."

Oh, yes, of course. Vivian had the sudden urge to break out in hysterical laughter. She quickly swallowed it down. Not that any of this was really funny. Which was why it was called "hysteria" in the first place. "Well, a map would be cool. Maybe don't forget to pack it."

Okay, that was something. But somehow Vivian didn't think Nikolai would be reassured at the thought of her navigating them around the Moon using only eighteenth-century technology, and a whole lot of prayer and hopeful identification and finger-crossing.

Unless that was what he was *expecting* her to do. The Soviet space program was, after all, notorious for cutting corners.

"If only we'd known ahead of time we'd be in this position, we could have planned for it a little better."

"That is certainly so," he said, gravely.

Vivian took a deep breath, let it out. "Very well, Nikolai Ilyich. Clearly, there would be a number of obstacles in our path." Jeez, now she was even beginning to talk like him. "I'll need to think this through and take some notes, then get back to you."

"It might be wise to be cautious. Given our past experiences."

Our past experiences. Was *that* a euphemism, or what? "Got that right. Okay. I'll ping you in a couple of days, all right?"

"Days?"

"Yes. I do have a job, here, you know. And I do need a good night's sleep tomorrow night. I can't keep on like this."

"Very well. Days it will have to be. Thank you, Vivian Carter."

"Hey, you're certainly welcome."

He paused. Yes, that had been entirely too flippant. Always how she responded to insane situations. "Talk to you soon, Major-General."

"You too, Colonel."

"Okay. Vivian out." She flipped the comms switch off, before he had a chance to ask.

Searching the Moon for Svetlana. With a fricking single-sheet paper map. "Holy living shit."

It was impossible. Completely bananas.

Nonetheless, she'd keep talking to Nikolai. If only to keep the guy sane. And figure out how the hell he could even survive, if Vivian refused to go along with his madcap scheme.

Which, of course, she would. Refuse, that is.

CHAPTER 26

Interplanetary Space: Vivian Carter
March 15-April 3, 1985
Mission Elapsed Time: 620-639 days

AFTER lunch a few weeks later, just before the crew all split in different directions to go monitor experiments, run diagnostics, exercise, and holystone the decks, Vivian clapped to call them to order "Okay, guys? Could I have your attention for a few minutes? I have something I need to ask you all. I've got a big decision to make, and I'd really like your input."

Greg looked up at her. "Uh-oh. Ominous?"

"Yeah." She grinned back. "A bit."

"Is everything all right?" Amy, speaking gently and wearing her usual concerned frown.

Vivian couldn't resist giving her a slightly larger smile. "Yes, Doctor. I'm quite well, and no one here is in any danger." Adding the mental caveat: *Except me, obviously. Just like always.*

"Okay." They all arranged themselves so that they could see her and waited expectantly.

Wow. This was even harder than she'd expected. Vivian prevaricated for a moment. "So, still several weeks to go, but this mission is all over bar the shouting, right?"

"Kind of," Rawlings said. "What's up, Vivian?"

She took a deep breath. "Okay. Here's what's going on. We've been a team throughout, and a great team. We've all had our ups and downs, but we've gotten a lot done, and our mission has been a complete success." She raised a hand palm-out and looked up at Greg. "And for the love of God, don't say 'almost complete.'" Heinz just grinned and nodded. Vivian went on: "There are bound to be some bobbles in a mission this complicated. But we hit all our major objectives, and all our new, extended objectives as well. We rounded Venus, and orbited Mars for several *months*. That was a triumph beyond anything we were expecting, across the board. We've learned enough about the possibility of water on Mars and its satellites to keep scientists salivating for years, and may even have turned the space program around as a result. Plus, US and Soviet missions arrived in Martian airspace in close to a dead heat and got together to drink a toast in Mars orbit. After which, we got to discover that Soviets can be our friends, and that cosmonauts and astronauts can have more in common with one another than with the politicians in our own countries."

"*Some* Soviets," Greg said.

Rawlings cocked an eye at him. "You just can't help yourself, can you?"

"Especially Nikolai," Laura said, and winked at Amy.

"And so," Vivian said. "About that. Thanks for bringing him up, because he's central to what I need to talk about."

She looked at each of them in turn. Floating there in the volume of the Astarte, or Velcroed to a patch on the wall to keep them in place, or their toes hooked easily around a restraint bar. She'd had her run-ins with each of them, but they were all fine people. Vivian no longer thought of them as *astronauts* and *scientists*. Now they were just her crew.

They were waiting calmly. By now they knew Vivian well enough to know that she wouldn't be speechifying at them unless something important was happening. Dave Horn and Josh Rawlings were impassive. Amy was studying Vivian's face carefully, as if trying to peer through her skull and into her thoughts. Dardenas was scanning the board, as he often instinctively did, as if he might glean some clues there, but she knew his attention was on her regardless. Greg, Laura, and Rudy were exchanging glances, but none of them were freaking out or demanding she spit it out, or whatever. Vivian had at least earned enough respect for them to let her do this—whatever they thought "this" was—in her own time.

Well, it *was* time to spit it out. "I shouldn't be telling you any of what I'm just about to say. It's highly critical, beyond top secret. And as you'll see, it's of international significance. I'm sorry, but you can't tell your family about it, or anyone else at home. If you do, people might die. So I'm taking a big risk by telling you, but I'm not willing to do this any other way. I'm not just going to run out on you without explaining."

By now, Laura's eyes were huge. "Run out? Out where?"

"I'm not coming back to Earth with you," Vivian said. "I'll be taking a side trip instead. I need to go to the Moon. Again."

"The Moon?" Laura's eyes lit up. "Can we come?"

"Oh, God, no," said Rudy Frank.

Vivian grinned sympathetically at Laura. "I'm afraid not. I need to do this solo."

Dave Horn was staring at her. Quite likely, he was stunned that Vivian hadn't consulted him first about this.

"Here's the story, in a nutshell," she said. "Cosmonaut Svetlana Belyakova, the first woman on the Moon, has turned against her own people. She was ordered to use tactical nuclear weapons against American Night Corps troops. She refused, and after what I can only assume was a spirited exchange of views, she killed her commanding officers and escaped. She's hiding out somewhere on the lunar surface, and I need to go find her. Me, and Nikolai Makarov. We need to meet up, go to the Moon, and track her down before the Soviets do. Rescue her, and get her back to Earth, where she really has no choice but to defect, which would of course be a honking big deal, internationally. One in the eye for Andropov, especially as she can blow the lid on all his stealth lunar operations, some of which were likely not condoned by the rest of the Politburo."

"Holy shit," Rudy said.

Amy was shaking her head. "You're mad."

Vivian grinned. "If that's your professional opinion, I can't argue with it."

Vivian had been a maverick from the start, and it looked like she was fated to stay a maverick until the bitter end. But no woman was an island, and she couldn't do this alone. Her own family might not be such great shakes in the support department, but her Astarte crew had come through for her, and for each other, again and again.

So, it was time to trust them. Vivian just couldn't keep this to herself any longer, and if she was going to go along with any part of Makarov's desperate plan, she needed their help, and their blessing.

She'd told Makarov she'd be consulting them, of course. After originally swearing to keep all this under her hat, she couldn't then turn around and tell seven other people without letting him know. Makarov hadn't been happy, but after a while he'd grudgingly conceded her logic.

Vivian knew Dave Horn, Josh Rawlings and Marco Dardenas very well, and if any of them was a Soviet mole they'd been playing an incredibly devious and obscure game for years. Josh and Marco had been Soviet captives on Columbia Station, been at huge risk, and sustained injuries. And Dave had saved all their lives, there at the end, by spearing the Station with a frigging Agena rocket and shoving them out into a different, random, ungodly orbit. As for the scientists, the idea that the Soviets had magically chosen one of them to be a deep-cover mole during their PhD studies, or afterward, just on the off-chance that they'd get roped into a jaunt around the inner solar system, was vanishingly small. All three leaned to the left politically—a lot of academics did—but there was a huge gulf between US progressive politics and Soviet-style Communism. And, having now spent two years with them in very close quarters, Vivian couldn't possibly imagine any of them were traitors.

Was Vivian prepared to risk her life on that belief? Yes, she discovered that she was. In any clear-eyed risk-reward assessment, the benefits of bringing her crew in on the decision far outweighed the risks of treachery.

Dardenas looked puzzled. "How d'you plan to find her? Just the two of you? It's a big Moon. As you know better than anyone."

Vivian grinned tightly. "We have some ideas about that. Which I won't be sharing here, for obvious reasons."

Dave Horn leaned forward. "Vivian. Just *how* do you intend to do this? You're planning to take one of our CSMs? Because there's obviously no other way."

"Yes, I am." Vivian nodded and told them all what she and Nikolai had in mind, running through the significant points of the plan, checking them off on her fingers as she went. By the time she was done, Amy and Laura had their heads in their hands, and Josh and Marco looked shell-shocked.

In the silence that followed, Greg cleared his throat. "Is … all that really possible?"

Horn, wearing a tense frown, was jotting down numbers on a pad of paper. "I guess … that none of it is completely *im*possible. Not with me to help prepare the burns and course corrections, a crash course of supplemental Command Module training for Viv, and Nikolai's navigation chops later on. But it's certainly a *lot*. And everything would need to go just right. Solidly right from beginning to end."

"But why does it have to be you?" Laura looked like she might be about to cry. "Why not just send Night Corps in to get Belyakova out, right now?"

"I can't risk it," Vivian said. "The Soviets have moles everywhere. There must have been more than one in the NASA US-Copernicus contingent, and there has to be at least one embedded in the Night Corps organization. Makarov is convinced our space forces are riddled with them. I trust Peter Sandoval and Terri Brock, but they're unreachable." She shook her head. "Plus, a full-up Night Corps search and rescue operation would almost certainly leak to the Soviets. We already know the Soviets track Night Corps activities as best they can. So they'd end up leading the bad guys straight to Belyakova.

"So, no. Once, a while back, Peter Sandoval came in on a lone wolf mission to Zvezda Base, to try to rescue me. Which he kinda did, by a rather roundabout route that could easily have killed me … but that's another story. Now, Nikolai and I have to take a leaf out of Sandoval's book."

"Uh, forgive me for asking," Amy said, "But is Belyakova really worth all this?"

"It's both of them," Vivian said. "Belyakova *and* Makarov. Because now he's going against his own people as well. And Makarov can't do it without me."

"They're worth it," Dardenas said, reluctantly. "They've helped us before. We'd all be dead—me, Vivian, Josh, maybe Dave as well—if Nikolai and Svetlana hadn't stood with us against Yashin."

"Svetlana took bullets for us," Vivian added. "She could have died."

"Yes." Greg's frown almost belied his words. "I hate to say it, honestly ... but it does sound like you should help if you could. As for whether it's possible, well, that's not my department. To me it sounds terrifying, just a completely bonkers plan, but Dave and Viv and Josh and Marco, y'all are the experts."

"Sticking it to the man," Rudy said. "The Soviet New Man."

"But you'd take one of our CSMs?" Rawlings demanded. "Just like that, you're going to take away one of our two lifeboats? What happens if we run into trouble here?"

"And that's one of the many reasons why I'm raising it with you all," Vivian said. "I'm not about to cut and run without giving you guys a say. And I'm absolutely not going to steal one of our two CSMs, that belong to all of us. If I'm going to borrow one, I need your permission."

"Borrow?" Rawlings said.

"Fine. Take. But that will only happen if you're all okay with it."

Everyone fell silent at that. Vivian had solicited their opinions before, but as mission commander she had never before asked any of them for their permission to take action.

"Even if we don't run into problems, we couldn't fit the seven of us into one Command Module for splashdown," Greg said.

"Of course not," Horn said absently, back to scribbling numbers on his notepad. "We'd need to wait in orbit for a second one to be sent up, or snag one from an Earth-orbiting Skylab, or whatever."

"That's not such a big deal," said Laura. "They'll be sending extra Command Modules to help ship down all the rocks and cores and film magazines and medical samples, and the hundred and one other things we need to transfer back to surface. And, speaking as a tourist: we went from the Earth's surface straight to L5 on the outbound. I'd be game to be one of those who waits for the second shift. I'd love to hang out and orbit Earth for a couple of weeks as a grand finale, before going back down. It's not like I'll ever get the chance again."

"But what about contingencies?" Rawlings persisted.

"I'm pretty confident in your bird," Laura said. "Even if you're not."

"It's not a question of *confidence*. It's a question of due caution and sensible risk management ..."

"Oh, it'll be fine." Laura patted the console. "Won't it, baby?"

Dardenas tried not to cringe.

"You can't just go by yourself," Amy said to Vivian. "You should at least take a Command Module pilot with you. We have spares."

Rawlings snorted. Vivian shook her head. "This is my responsibility. We have three CM pilots in the crew for a reason. The rest of you need to get safely back into Earth orbit and then through splashdown. That's where you're going to need these guys, and you'll want all of them. Being short one person will already be bad enough, in the run-up to mission end. I don't want to deprive you of another. Plus, the Command Module maneuvers I need to do are actually quite straightforward, and can mostly be preprogrammed in, and I'm the only one here with lunar surface experience, and it's my problem and not theirs. So, all things considered … no."

She glanced at Horn, Dardenas, and Rawlings. None of them seemed inclined to argue that point. They were family men, after all. They all wanted to get home, not go jaunting off to the Moon to put their lives in danger.

"I would still come with you," Laura said. "If I was invited. And help however I could."

"Thanks, but … it just can't happen. I know you'd love to go to the Moon, Laura, but not at this cost." And that had been a spunky offer on Laura's part, to put herself into harm's way to check off another celestial body on her bucket list.

"You might need a doctor," Amy said. "You and Nikolai. And someone to watch your backs, Vivian. Little as *I* want to go to the bleeding Moon …"

By now, Vivian had a lump in her throat. Not only was most of her crew apparently supporting her crazy plan, but now they were taking turns in volunteering to come with her. Vivian hadn't seen *that* coming.

"Astarte needs its doctor more," she said. "This is your mission, all of you. You need to stay here and see it through. Nikolai's Lunokhod will only take two people anyway. Supplies, fuel … no. Adding a third person to our little road trip just isn't possible."

Rudy was running his hands through his hair again and again, in that way he had when he was thinking. By now, Vivian had gotten used to it and no longer wanted to smack his hands and tell him to keep still. Now, he said: "But, Viv, come on now: there are still all kinds of problems with this. When you're no longer with us when we get back to Earth—that'll be a pretty big clue that you've jumped ship, right? If the Soviets are paying attention, they'll guess in half a second what's going on."

"Oh, it's worse than that." Rawlings said. "Starting right now, and for the next few weeks, or even longer, it means we'd have to lie to NASA as well as everyone else. We'd need to pretend she's still here, right? Which means lying to Ellis, to our families, to everyone. Vivian, we can't do this. It's insane."

"Sure we can," Heinz said. "How often do you talk about Vivian to your families anyway?"

"And what about Mission Control? Lying to NASA ends our careers."

"Speak for yourself," Greg said.

Rudy nodded. "Frankly, I'm done with space after this. Enough of a good thing, already. It's back to the real world for me."

"We don't have lie to them." Greg grinned. "We just won't tell them the truth."

Rawlings frowned at him. "Those are the same thing."

"Vivian's not always the one talking to Mission Control anyway," Rudy said. "It's more often one of us these days anyway."

"Yeah, but you know Ellis Mayer is going to ask after her if he doesn't hear from her in person for twenty-four hours. Maybe twelve."

"I can tone down my chats with him," Vivian said. "Taper them off. Tell him we'll just wait till I'm back. Or ... something. Leave that one with me."

"I have a couple of ideas about all this." Horn was still scribbling on his pad. "You all might not like them, but at least I have them."

Amy looked at her watch. "All right. Why don't we break and go about our duties, and spend a few hours to digest all this? Doctor's orders. Then we'll take an early dinner and ... talk about how we could get this done."

"So we're doing it? You've decided?" Rawlings shook his head.

Amy met his eye. "Or, you know, do a feasibility study and rack-and-stack the alternatives, like the good NASA people we are."

Again, Vivian looked around them all in some bemusement.

The scientists were on her side. Dave and Marco were taking it seriously. Josh, once one of her two closest friends on the crew, was the lone holdout.

Well, maybe she knew the reason. She'd given them Mars and earned their loyalty by not completely sucking as a leader, or at least not all the time.

Amazing.

Her crew had already taken great leaps forward for science, and for helping to motivate new missions to the Red Planet in particular. Those were already huge achievements. Maybe they now wanted to be involved in something else that was greater than themselves: pushing America forward in the Cold War, rescuing beleaguered cosmonauts and bringing them home. Who wouldn't want a piece of that?

If Vivian and Nikolai could pull this off, that is. And that was a big "if."

It was becoming real to her, at last. At some point along this mad path her thoughts had shifted. She *was* going to do this.

"Sounds like a plan," she said lightly. "And I'll spring for dinner tonight. My treat."

She grinned, and most of her crazy-bastard crew grinned back at her.

If nothing else, I found a way to alleviate the boredom of the long cruise home by posing them some extra challenges to think about.

Of course, Josh Rawlings grabbed her for a one-on-one discussion, just as soon as he could. She took him up into CM-1 so that they could talk in privacy.

Once the hatch closed, he wasted no time coming to the point. "So this is it? You're going to abandon Astarte, before its mission is done? Leave your command?"

She glanced away, unable to meet his eye. "I'm trying not to think of it like that."

"Vivian, good *grief.*"

"Commanders delegate authority all the time. I'd just be reassigning you as Commander of Astarte. You'll keep all the bases covered. I have faith in you."

"Gee, thanks."

"And Dave Horn has final authority over our Earth orbit insertion and splashdown activities anyway."

"Vivian, if you do this …"

"What? They'll fire me?"

He stared at her for a long moment. "This could be *treason.* Or, at least, it sure wouldn't be hard to spin it as treason. Going over to help the Reds?"

371

"It is not treason," she said, perhaps more forcefully than she'd intended to. "And I'm hardly 'going over.' I'm participating in a rescue mission. And maybe I'll even come home with valuable intel that we can use. This is an opportunity, not a desertion; it's not insubordination, and it's most definitely *not* treason."

"Vivian, that's a hell of a stretch."

"I've had plenty of practice."

"It's not enough."

"It'll have to do."

He pulled himself to one of the couches and sat back into it, looping a hand around the lap strap to hold him in place. Stared out the window into space, or at least at the bulk of Astarte just beyond it. "I'm mystified," he said.

"I can't blame you for that."

"The Moon is a mess right now. A complete chaotic mess. Even more like the Wild West than it ever was. Most of the genuine astronauts and cosmonauts have been withdrawn. It's mostly military now. Firefights breaking out all over the place."

"Well, maybe not *all* over. Surely most of the sound and fury is over by now."

"But still ..." He shook his head. "Where the hell will you be going, exactly?"

"I've told you all I can."

Rawlings seemed to pull himself together. "Okay, at least tell me when you need to do this."

"I'd need to leave Astarte in two weeks, maybe three, I expect. If what Nikolai and Dave are telling me about the burn math checks out."

"But ... Vivian, that means you'll be alone in the Command Module for almost a month."

"That's right," she said, patiently. She could still do arithmetic. "That's just the way the dynamics works, to use the bare minimum of SPS fuel."

"And we can't tell NASA."

"Also correct." Vivian turned to him and held his gaze. "So, damn it, Josh: are you going to help me do this, or are you just going to be a massive pain in my ass?"

"I don't know. I'm still thinking about it. What would you do if I said no, anyway? If I put my foot down and told you there was no way I'd go along with this?"

"I honestly don't know. Not exactly."

"So you'd go anyway."

"Well … I guess I couldn't. But I'd sure want to keep … negotiating with you."

"Ha."

Rawlings took a long breath and shook his head. "Vivian, Vivian …. How can you be so sure that all this is what it seems to be? What assurances to you have that you can take it all at face value?"

"Because it's Nikolai." She sighed. "I believe he's genuine. I probably can't persuade you of this, but *I* trust him."

"Okay. But even if Makarov himself is genuine … I'm sure that everything he's telling you, he believes, and is telling you in good faith. But what if he's been misinformed? Or if he's being played? Has it really not occurred to you that this might be part of a deeper game?"

"It has," she admitted. "Though I'm not sure what the point would be."

Rawlings raised his hands. "We're talking about *Soviets*. They're experts at this kind of thing. Misdirection. Laying false trails. The KGB is the largest intelligence operation in the world, and it's run by extremely smart people. Just consider the possibility that you're being played, here. That it's you they're after, and this is a way to get you."

"But why? I'm nobody."

"Hardly. You're somebody they believe is an agent. You're actually quite famous. Most of the human beings on the planet know your name, Vivian. Damaging you would damage American prestige."

She thought about that.

"See?" he said. "You have to admit it's possible, right?"

"I suppose. Sure, I guess it's possible. But I'm still going."

"Because?"

"Because sometimes you just have to trust people and try to do the right thing."

"Vivian. For this entire mission you've been telling me that you're terrible at reading people, dealing with people—literally, anything to do with people."

Vivian didn't blink. "Yeah, I know. That's also true. What's your point?" She could tell Josh was trying hard not to shout at her. She admired his restraint.

Eventually, he said: "Because, this could be really simple. Perhaps they're just waiting for you and Makarov to lead them to Belyakova? Because you clearly know something they don't?"

"Can neither confirm nor deny," she said.

"Jesus Christ." Rawlings rocked his head back, exhaled dramatically, and seemed to count to ten. "Vivian. Has it ever occurred to you that you're too cocky for your own good?"

"Often." She took a deep breath. "Look, Josh: they need me. I'm the only US astro Makarov can trust, and I'm quite likely the only one who can do this anyway. And this is not just me trying to be altruistic. If it works out, there are payoffs to the US in terms of international prestige and intel. The US would look like the good guys for a change. We could sure use that."

"*If* it all works out. *If* you can build this house of cards and then climb up on top of it without it all collapsing."

Vivian blinked. "Nice metaphor."

He gave her a searching look. "Vivian. I've known you the longest of anyone on this mission."

"That's true."

"And I feel like I know you pretty well. So, I'm asking you, as a friend: do you really *want* to do this crazy shit, Vivian? Really?"

Josh could always see through her. She sighed and looked away. "No, Josh. Of course I fricking don't."

"You don't? Then why the hell are we having this conversation?"

"Come with me," she said.

"To the Moon? No way."

"No, no … there's something I need to show you, in my sleep quarters."

Josh blinked. "Uh. Okay."

He followed her dutifully down to the crew level, and to her berth. "Here," she said, flipping something toward him that looked a bit like a very damaged tambourine. "Take this. It's no use to me any longer."

He caught it instinctively, then looked at what he'd caught. "And this is?"

"My punchbag. I made it for myself between Venus and Mars, to … well, take out some of my frustrations, and get more exercise. It was useful."

He raised it closer to one of the lights. "Holy cow, Vivian. You've punched this a lot."

"And most of the damage you see has been done over the past month and a half." She took a breath. "None of you have asked when Nikolai first raised this plan with me. It was at the beginning of February. It's taken me this long to come to terms with it."

"That does look like six weeks' worth of damage," he said.

"Quite a bit more, actually. But, Josh: I don't *want* to go to the Moon again. This isn't fun for me. I want to go home. I want to have a life again. Let me say it one more time: I don't want to do this."

"But?"

"I have to."

He just stared at her and was silent.

"I'm afraid to go back, to be honest," she said suddenly. "So many memories. So much has already happened to me on the Moon that I was lucky to survive. This is really tempting fate, for me, and I'm not … oblivious to that fact. I'm not gung-ho about it. I'm not blind. I don't want to be a hero. I just … need to do this. I really do. I have to."

"Christ. Here." Rawlings floated the destroyed punchbag back to her, the reaction twisting him slowly backward.

Eventually, he rubbed his eyes and took a breath. "Okay."

"Okay, what? At least give it a bit longer to sink in. It took me long enough to process it all. We'll be talking again at dinner—"

"No, Vivian, I meant, okay. I'm in. I'll do it. I'll help you do this … damned stupid thing."

Vivian blinked. "Um. That was quick."

Josh shrugged helplessly. "I mean, what choice do I have? I'm your friend. We're crew. I've trusted you for years, now. What else can I do?"

"Thanks," was all Vivian could find to say.

"Which doesn't mean I'm happy about it. At all." He pushed himself back around to face her. "Vivian, if you really want it straight: I'm terrified you're about to die. Like really, shit scared. And after all you've done, dying while trying to save Soviet lives would be a very dumb way to go."

"Okay. You're right. And that's candid, at least."

They just looked at each other. After she felt that had gone on long enough, Vivian said: "Well, then. I guess I have some more planning to do."

"Me too." Rawlings reached out to the doorway of Vivian's berth to arrest his roll. "Let me go check in with Dave and see how I can help."

"Thank you," she said, again.

"Don't thank me yet." He shoved himself gently up toward the hatch into the forward compartment. "Let's hope you still think this was the right thing to do, a month or two from now."

"I will."

"I wonder." Rawlings passed through the hexagonal hatch without touching the sides, and disappeared from view.

The coming weeks were daunting. Vivian was coming into all this with a keen understanding of Apollo systems in general, years of experience with jet fighters, Lunar Modules, and an array of other flying craft. However, she had never been specifically trained as a Command Module pilot, and all of her sims to support Dave Horn for Apollo 32's reentry and splashdown had been many years ago.

To make up for that, Vivian studied the boards for hours on end, for days in a row. She read the manuals and procedures end to end half a dozen times. She got briefed extensively by Dave Horn and Josh Rawlings, and Dave had run through the trans-Earth injection and Earth deorbit procedures with her in detail, effectively dry-simming them—simulating the maneuvers by pointing to the buttons and switches without actually pushing or flipping them.

Did that mean she was *ready* for this? No. None of these were substitutes for the real-life experience of *piloting* a Command Module or even doing the detailed exercises that the ground simulators provided. In fact, the Command Module systems were significantly different from those in the LMs she was used to. The boards looked superficially similar, but the way you flew the craft, the procedures for initiating its engines, and much of the jargon was different. The Command Module was an entirely different beast.

Some items were familiar, at least. The guidance computer was similar in operation, although its preloaded programs were different. The principles of navigation obviously followed the same rules and patterns in either ship. And Vivian certainly had the advantage of watching skilled people fly CMs. On her flight to L5 from lunar orbit she'd copiloted for Dave Horn and read numbers for him. But that had been a couple years ago.

Despite Vivian's extensive Apollo experience, her imminent departure from Astarte might well be the most nerve-wracking solo flight of her career. If she screwed up, even a bit, she could very easily put herself into a heliocentric orbit, missing Makarov and the Moon altogether and heading off on another loop around the Sun, but with only a fraction of the air, water, and food she'd need to survive. To avoid that fate, she would be relying on her navigation skill and equipment, which included a slide rule, a well-traveled and battered Texas Instruments calculator, and Kevin Pope's ancient brass sextant.

"Good times," she muttered.

And, after separating from Astarte, she'd be spending three weeks in that Command Module, on approach to the Moon, all on her own, and with the radio turned off except for some brief communications with Nikolai Makarov, at carefully chosen prearranged times when their signals were least likely to be picked up by anyone else.

Also worth noting: if for some reason she failed to rendezvous with Nikolai, Vivian had no way of getting down to the lunar surface by herself. She'd have to admit ignominious defeat, program her trans-Earth injection burn to free herself from the Moon's gravity, and spend another three days heading back to Earth to face the music.

She'd be toast. Disgraced. All of her achievements downplayed. And Svetlana Belyakova would still be lost on the Moon.

That was the worst case scenario. It would be unbearable.

Well, almost the worst case scenario.

Sooo, I'd better not screw up.

And Nikolai had better not screw up.

And our stars had better align just right, in addition to the planets, the moons, and our ridiculously small spacecraft.

This shit was definitely *not* for the faint of heart.

CHAPTER 27

Inbound to the Moon: Vivian Carter
April 4-May 2, 1985
Mission Elapsed Time: 640-668 days

LIKE a thief in the night.

That was all Vivian could think of, even though she had her crew's permission and assistance in taking CSM-2, and technically it wasn't even nighttime by the ship's shift clock.

Night Corps didn't know what she was doing. Ellis didn't know. No one else in Mission Control, or NASA Johnson, or NASA HQ knew. She was on her own.

Despite her valiant attempts at rationalizing this to Josh Rawlings, Vivian Carter *was* abandoning her mission, leaving her command, and disappearing. It could hardly be denied. And that was bad, perhaps unforgivable.

And yet, in the end it was oddly anticlimactic. Vivian shook hands with some of her crew and hugged others. Aside from wishing her luck and bon voyage, they all seemed muted. Amy and Laura were clearly trying not to cry. So Vivian didn't drag it out, and there were no last speeches, no real ceremony.

She floated into CM-2 and dogged the hatch.

Even now, the Command Module board was still pretty intimidating.

The gunmetal gray instrument panel that wrapped around her now contained roughly five hundred controls. Some were toggle switches, others were buttons or levers or rotary switches with click stops. Some were protected with caps or protuberances to prevent them from being activated by accident, and others weren't. Lights, meters, and other displays peppered the board. She'd spent a lot of time staring at it, trying to memorize the positions of switches and displays, just to convince herself she knew what the hell she was doing.

"Okay, Dave? I believe CM-2 is a Go for disconnect."

"Go for disconnect, confirmed."

Vivian wasn't sure whether to laugh or cry. "We're so formal."

"That's how we roll. But, yeah, everything looks good. Technically speaking, at least."

"Roger that. But, you know what? Let me just … doublecheck everything one more time. Just because I can."

"I'll do the same."

She checked a couple of star angles and ran them through her guidance computer sequences. Checked the circuit breakers. Nodded. "Okay, I'm good. Clear to proceed?"

"Fire when ready," he said.

"Then … this is CM-2, proceeding with disconnect and separation."

She flipped switches to disengage her Command Module's control system from Astarte's, fired the separation squibs to disconnect herself, and blipped the RCS jets a couple times to start moving herself away.

And that was that. Boom. Done.

"And I'm gone," she said.

"Godspeed, CM-2," Dave responded, and Vivian had to swallow down a lump in her throat.

She was drifting further and further from Astarte. She would likely never again see inside the ship that had been her home and major command for the past two years, as she'd sailed through the inner solar system, passed within spitting distance of Venus, orbited Mars, landed on Phobos, gone to take a look-see at Deimos, and in the process passed all the way around the Sun almost twice since separating from the Earth.

That life was over. Vivian had switched trains onto another track. Another hour of separation and she'd run an alignment check and then initiate a burn to tweak her trajectory toward the Moon, with Dave Horn looking over her shoulders and sanity-checking her.

At this distance from the Earth-Moon system, it would be an extremely small delta-V correction. She'd only need her RCS thrusters for it, rather than the big Service Module SPS engine. Astarte would still be in view for hours, perhaps days, before it became too small to see from CM-2's windows. She'd have plenty of time to look back over at it and try to swallow her regrets.

But she was committed now. She had to make her way alone across the void for a few million miles, meet up with Nikolai, find Svetlana, save her, and bring her back to Earth. Vivian had a new mission now. No other choice remained. No backsies, no do-overs.

Vivian Carter was going back to the Moon.

An hour later, after Dave Horn had compiled enough data on their relative position, she heard his reassuring voice crackling in her headset: "You're in the groove, Vivian. Good to go."

"Roger that, Astarte," she said, and looked around the confined space she was currently occupying. It was familiar territory, and felt like home ... and yet, completely different. Before, the bulk of Astarte had always been visible right outside the forward windows. Now, it was nowhere in sight, and she was all alone.

God damn it, but I want to go home.

Vivian wanted Earth so badly she could taste it. Just to feel the wind on her cheeks, the smell of a forest. Even a sensible gravity. It was an odd feeling, for her.

Well. No time for brooding. She ran a completely redundant system check, just to have something to do.

And after that, she realized that for the first time ever, she was traveling in a ship without a name. "CM-2" clearly wasn't appropriate to this new phase in her own personal mission.

It took her only minutes to come up with one. Really, it was the only appropriate name she could think of.

Deliverance.

The Command Module interior soon became extremely familiar to her. It was known space, and after a week or so Vivian could navigate it with her eyes closed. Some "mornings" when she woke up, that was exactly what she did. She wasn't sleeping well anyway, so keeping her eyes closed was the next best thing.

She spent a lot of time studying and rehearsing the Command Module procedures for burns, maneuvers, and reentry, because it needed to become second nature. She reread *Tinker, Tailor, Soldier, Spy* for light relief. British Earthbound spy work seemed so leisurely and sedate, when compared to Vivian's life.

And, of course, she still needed to spend several hours a day pumping and sweating and flexing, while she did her damned exercises to preserve muscle mass and prevent her bones from wasting away. No stationary bike, of course—and thank heaven for small mercies, because Vivian was really tired of that bike by now—but she did have a number of resistance bands for weight work and, once she got them adjusted just right, she could even generate quite a sweat running in place or doing jumping jacks. Vivian couldn't slack off now: she'd be needing those muscles and bones, plus her heart and lungs, in real gravity again, very soon.

She did miss her punchbag, though.

So, this was what it must have been like for Dave Horn, for all those weeks he'd spent going around and around the Moon. Running dark, just like Vivian was now, and running in place.

Inexorably, Nikolai Makarov was getting closer, but she could only tell that from her instrument readings. She still couldn't see his LEK spacecraft, out there in the black.

Every day, the Moon grew in front of her windows. Just a little bit. Too fast, in some ways. And in others, not quickly enough.

Week Three of being alone, and there it was, almost dead ahead of her: the Earth. She would pass within a hundred thousand miles of it on the way to the Moon—in fact, she was relying on its gravity to pull her closer to the position the Moon would be when she got there. Earth had been famed as a "blue marble" ever since the famous picture taken by the Apollo 17 crew, though from the view of Africa that Vivian was getting right now she could see a fair amount of green, white and brown as well. Earth: where her Astarte crew was headed, and where by rights Vivian herself should be going as well. Once Astarte was safely in Earth orbit, she would have directed the task of packaging and loading up the mission's film and data tapes in various formats, plus the carefully sealed packages of Phobos and Deimos rocks and dividing them up: two loads for their two Command Modules for the return to Earth, and other supplemental material to be ferried down later. And then she'd have climbed aboard one of those Command Modules, probably CM-1 with Dave Horn and others, to be ferried back to what would undoubtedly have been a picture-perfect splashdown in the Pacific. She'd have been hauled aboard an aircraft carrier for the usual set of speeches about how she and her crew had pushed back yet another frontier for humankind. Flashbulbs would have popped in her face. She'd have made the evening news around the world, again.

Now, she wouldn't be there for any of that, and her crew would also be short a Command Module. At least two of them would have to wait for NASA to get one into position for them, delaying their return to Earth and their families yet again. Lucky Laura, of course, and the other would necessarily have to be one of the Command Module Pilots. She wondered which one it would end up being. Josh, probably. The new captain would be the last to leave his ship.

How would NASA handle all that, once her crew finally admitted that Vivian was elsewhere? Not just the extra Command Module, but Vivian's absence? How could that possibly be explained to the general public? "Oh, Commander Carter decided to go back to the Moon. Humanitarian reasons. We can't go into it."

No, they couldn't even say that, because her destination would need to be a close-held secret.

She was sure that NASA Public Affairs was already planning a substantial events calendar for her and her crew ... none of which Vivian Carter would be attending. Vivian herself was just as happy to skip all that, even though she was also sure she'd be earning her fair share of opprobrium for dropping it all on the ground.

But that couldn't be helped. That would have to remain NASA's problem, and her crew's. They were smart people. They'd think of something. Vivian had other, more pressing issues to focus on. And since she might be dead in a few days anyway; there was no point in getting distracted by it.

Whatever Vivian did, it always came back to the Moon. However often she left, somehow she always ended up back there.

Always, the Moon was her fate. Her destiny.

Maybe this time, when she left, it would be for the last time.

Yeah. This time. That was the ticket.

Don't get ahead of yourself, Vivian. Lots to do between now and the time you leave *the Moon.*

And then one morning she woke up and realized she could see Makarov's LEK, glinting in the sunlight as it traveled slowly across the starry background beside her. It was still many miles away but drifting inexorably closer, as their almost-parallel paths toward the Moon approached their intersection. Their rendezvous would be another very slow dance.

Naturally, meeting up with Nikolai Makarov wouldn't be anywhere near as routine as the docking between a NASA Lunar Module and Command Module, The CSM and LEK docking mechanisms and hatches were incompatible. There could be no mating of the two craft, no linking the vehicles up as a single unit with easy shirtsleeves passage between the two. No handy mating tunnel between the two craft; the tube that had worked to connect Astarte and Nikolai's Salyut couldn't work for the Command Module and the LEK. Wrong hatch sizes entirely.

Combining their forces would involve a complex set of maneuvers. It would require both Vivian and Nikolai to be outside their craft at the same time, while floating between worlds. It had sounded straightforward enough when they'd discussed it beforehand, with Vivian comfortably ensconced in Astarte and Nikolai presumably equally comfortable aboard his LEK. And, objectively, it was a well-defined problem compared to what awaited them on the Moon. But even after all Vivian's EVA experience, it still felt a bit hairy to suit up, vent all the air from *Deliverance*, open the hatch, tether up, and just drift right on out into interplanetary space.

Makarov was already waiting for her, floating outside his own craft. The fifty feet that currently separated them looked like a long way, even though that was a relatively small distance compared to some of Vivian's more desperate spacewalking exploits in the past.

"Okay, Nikolai. Let's play catch."

Nikolai duly threw out a tether, weighted at the end with a camera, of all things. Which missed her by a good thirty feet.

"Okay, we'll call that your warm-up shot."

"Hmm," he said, and wound the tether back in to try again. His second cast was no better, but the third time he got lucky: Vivian caught it, unhitched the camera, and fastened the tether to the grab rail on her Command Module.

And then came the really dodgy part, as they gradually pulled their spacecraft closer and closer, hand over hand, both using zip guns where needed, with Nikolai occasionally ducking back into the LEK to use his RCS jets to help nudge the two ships together.

It was slow, careful work. The LEK had an outer skin just as delicate as that of an Apollo LM, as easy to puncture as a Coke can. It could be holed by a carelessly wielded screwdriver, so could be damaged severely if it banged into another spacecraft.

The goal was, of course, not to puncture or crumple it. Long before the two craft made their ever-so-gentle contact, Vivian had hung out an array of makeshift buffers, thick sealed bags full of soiled clothing from the Astarte's trash pit that she'd brought along for just this purpose.

"Here we go," she said. "Here we go … yes. Touching." The two craft had in fact bumped and then drifted a few inches apart, so Vivian braced and put her back into it, tugging the tether taut to hold them together while Makarov propelled himself carefully around her CSM with a steel cable, passing it through the grab rails and his LEK descent stage structure, and then cranking it firm and clamping it.

It took six hours, but by the end of it, the two spacecraft had become one. After a fashion.

Their joined craft would continue on like this to the Moon, literally lashed together with steel cable. To say it looked unprofessional would be a drastic understatement; it was about the most jury-rigged, klutzy, Heath Robinson-esque thing Vivian had ever seen. But it should work, and that cable should easily absorb the stress of the slow, steady burn from her Service Module's SPS engine that they would need to insert themselves into lunar orbit. Figuring out the center-of-mass calculation would be a bear, but that was Nikolai's department, and he'd be tweaking their attitude on the fly for the duration of that burn.

Since Vivian had a camera to hand, she took a few pictures. Why not? It was a sight no one had seen before, and likely no one would ever see again.

"Simmons?" he said quizzically, floating up beside her, holding his tether out to keep it from snarling hers.

"What?" She glanced down at the name patch on her chest. "Oh, no. My suit is quite banged up by now, and my people wanted me to take along a spare. They're all custom, and Amy is too tall. This is Laura's."

"Very well, Laura-Vivian. Shall we eat? Your place or mine?"

Lunar orbital insertion: another trial. Vivian had just a few hours to coach Nikolai in the readings she'd need him to take.

It was the first time a Soviet had ever been inside an Apollo Command Module. Yet another rule Vivian was breaking.

"It is May the First. A good omen, is it not?"

"Mayday is a good omen? Every time I've needed to say that word …"

"No, May the First—International Workers Day. It is an important holiday, back home."

"Okay. Sure. Shame you don't get to take the day off."

During the burn itself, Nikolai was about as agitated as she had ever seen him. Used to being in command of his vessel, he clearly found it almost intolerable to be merely in a support role. And yet they got through it and, at the end of it, Vivian found herself in lunar orbit, again.

"Belyakova had sure better appreciate this," she said.

"I am sure that she will."

"Svetlana would do this for me, if the tables were turned, right?" Makarov said nothing. Vivian twisted to look over at him. "She would. Right?"

"Of course," he said dutifully. "*Momentalno.*"

"Immediately? In a heartbeat? Sure."

Makarov just grinned and looked out the window again at the lunar surface rolling beneath them.

As they circled the Moon, Vivian suffered the inversion illusion. Many other Apollo astronauts had noticed this effect, but Vivian herself never had. Her brain had been reliably preprogrammed to see craters as craters, and so she hadn't seen anything else. This time under oblique illumination, the craters became domes to her eyes, the peaks became troughs, and the rilles and cracks in the lunar surface bobbled up to become ridges. She had to blink several times to get the darned landscape to go back where it should be. Vivian found this exceptionally irritating.

Now, their roles were reversed. Having transitioned into Nikolai's LEK, he was back to being the confident pilot and commander, and Vivian in turn assumed the role of the vaguely incompetent sidekick who barely knew where the important dials and displays were, and had great difficulty in reading them. Not that Nikolai needed her help.

Vivian had been in an LK Lander before, but that vehicle was tiny, and very different. The LEK had reasonably generous space for three, its internal area laid out more like a Soyuz. But Vivian always felt disconcerted by Soviet engineering; to her eye the instrument panels and gauges looked clunky, amateurish, and old fashioned.

Most unnerving of all were the sounds the LEK made. Lunar Modules had their own symphony of fans and pumps, and clicks and whirrs, naturally. But the LEKs, or at least this one, rattled in an alarming way, and even made occasional random snapping sounds, which Nikolai Makarov entirely ignored. Its thruster firings were also noisier, something Vivian dimly remembered from those moments of panic when she had fired the thrusters on a Soyuz to crash it into the Soviet Progress module attached to Columbia Station, many years before.

Overall, the noise level in the LEK was five to ten decibels louder than that inside a Command Module or Lunar Module, and Vivian was not sure she could ever get used to that.

But she quickly forgot the small stuff, because making moonfall in Nikolai Makarov's LEK Lander was one of the scariest experiences in Vivian's space career. Which, by now, was saying something.

That damned Lander just *plummeted* out of the sky. Soviet craft always did, but it was much scarier to be inside one than on the outside watching. Once they'd released themselves from Vivian's Command Module and established themselves in the LEK, Makarov's deorbit burn was brutally hard—the most G's Vivian had pulled since her Venus encounter eighteen months before—and then they were roaring down toward the lunar surface.

Vivian's understanding of the instrument panels in front of her was limited, but everything she could see confirmed they were coming in *fast*. Her one attempt to ask Makarov if he wanted her to read numbers was met by a polite but firm: "Quiet, please. Mathematics to do." And after that she left him to it and focused on breathing.

This was a Makarov she had not seen before. His left hand moved quickly across the instrument panels, while his right held firmly onto the controller. If she hadn't known better, she'd have thought he was joysticking it all the way down, but that was too complex a task for any human being; the onboard computers must be shouldering part of the burden. He looked at the guidance computer readout regularly, along with the eight-ball and the numerical indicators, occasionally glanced out of the window, and pulled and pushed and nudged and tweaked. Vivian had exactly nothing to do except look out of the windows and glance occasionally at the readout that she was fairly sure was the altimeter. The numbers seemed wrong, though, and it took Vivian much longer than it should have to realize that the dial was measuring meters, not feet.

She found herself screwing up her eyes trying to see surface features through the window. Not that there should be many: they were coming down onto one of the flattest and most featureless areas in south-central Oceanus Procellarum.

That surface was coming up toward them *fast*. Surely that fierce burst of decelerating thrust must be coming soon. She glanced at Makarov nervously—

And there it was, at seemingly the last possible moment: a strong, violent burn shoving up through her seat, and Makarov was *laughing* now, the crazy bastard. Makarov, whose demeanor was always professionally calm and sometimes appeared sleepy—even trancelike—when he was navigating, was now a new Nikolai Makarov, riding his wild LEK ever downward and still sparing the time to chortle at Vivian Carter, who was clutching her seat like a scaredy-cat teenager on her first rollercoaster ride.

The G's relented. The LEK rocked upright, and now Makarov ignored her again as he studied the surface just below his window. He shoved his craft forward with what seemed unnecessary aggression to skip them over a boulder field, their lateral movement kicking up the dust beneath them, but then brought them down mercifully slowly, to kiss the ground just as gently as Vivian had managed in her better landings.

"Kontakt," he said, cheerfully, the word sounding the same in Russian as in English.

"You lunatic," she said. "Madman!"

Makarov nodded. "Faster is better. We needed to burn as little fuel as we could, keep as much in reserve, in order to have it later. I have never come down so fast myself."

"Well, that's something. Good choice." Sure, at least she could say that now they were safely down.

"And, we made it." Makarov waved grandly. "Welcome back to the Moon, Vivian Carter!"

"You too, comrade." She shook the proffered hand, exhaled, and leaned forward to look out the window.

Oh yeah, look. There's the Moon again.

Vivian hadn't wanted to come back, but now she was *here*, sitting on the lunar surface once more, she felt a lump in her throat. It was oddly emotional to see the craggy, cut-up, grey and darker-grey and black lunar surface again, pitted with all its craters and boulders. The extremely familiar sight of the regolith, of the mare basalt stretching away into the distance, was somehow comforting. The lunar terrain was an almost … welcoming? … sight, after the sheer alienness of Venus and Mars, Phobos and Deimos, and the many months of cruising through space so far from any planet or moon.

It really was like coming home. Even though that "home", and its current occupants, were probably about to try and kill her. Again.

"You know, that was probably the first ever Moon landing by a joint US-Soviet crew," she said. Even for LGS-1, Lakontsev and Okhotina had landed on the Moon separately from Vivian and her American crewmembers and joined them in the MOLAB at Zvezda-Copernicus.

"Yes. I think so."

So, she and Makarov just made history again, in yet another small way. Though, somehow, she doubted that their current adventure would be featured in the history books. Once again, Vivian was officially off the grid.

She glanced over at Nikolai, who seemed to himself be taking this opportunity for a quiet contemplative moment. After all, he hadn't been on the Moon for five years. She gave him a couple of minutes longer, which also allowed her heart rate to return to normal, then put her hand on his arm. "Thank you," she said, although she was not entirely sure what she was thanking him for. Not killing her yet, perhaps.

"No, I thank *you*, Vivian Carter." He unfastened his safety harness. "Now, I suppose, we should begin our search."

The search for Svetlana Belyakova. Which wasn't going to be easy by any stretch of the imagination. Or particularly quick, even if it went *well*.

"Ten-four, good buddy," she said. "Let's get this show on the road."

CHAPTER 28

Marius Hills: Vivian Carter
May 2-4, 1985

HOW many times had Vivian donned a spacesuit by now? She didn't even know how to start calculating that. Surely at least two hundred times, and possibly many more. Yet this time she fumbled everything, did everything out of order, got her fingers and toes jammed into strange places, and even cut herself and drew blood once.

This is ridiculous. You're goddamned Vivian Carter. Veteran of an Earth orbiting mission and two versions of Apollo 32, with spells at Hadley and Daedalus in between. And then LGS-1, Venus, and Mars. So for the love of God, just put your freaking suit on and get out there.

And then she started again from the top, following the checklist, and put on her suit all by herself like a goddamned adult astronaut. "Once more into the breach."

She was nervous. Very nervous. Sweating, and not quite shaking. And she didn't need Amy Benson's psych skills to tell her why.

Is this one too many times to try to walk the surface?

Could Ellis Mayer beam aboard just to triple-check my suit settings and make sure I'm not just about to kill myself?

How often is too often?

The whole time she'd been on LGS-1, Vivian Carter had only once felt nervous about an EVA, just after they'd been attacked by Soviets at the South Pole and her suit had been blasted into failure. Just that one time, walking on the Moon had felt really dangerous.

Today, Vivian was under no illusions. The Moon *was* dangerous.

She did her best not to let Makarov see that she was in a funk. Maybe she succeeded.

The crunch of the regolith under her boot as she stepped off the LEK ladder was so familiar that it felt like an old friend, but now she was outside, the Moon's brown and grey surface in front of her once again seemed alien. She was viewing the Moon's surface today through eyes that had seen Venus, Mars, Phobos, and Deimos in the meantime, and traveled more miles through empty space than she really wanted to think about.

The curve of the Moon's horizon was visible, even from the ground. Fascinating, that she'd once been so used to that effect that she'd no longer noticed. Now, even after walking on Phobos, this seemed the most startling thing about the current terrain. And, closer in, the lunar surface itself: cratered and rocky, with boulders of various sizes, the larger ones generally clustered together. Craters large, small, and tiny; bending over, Vivian could see clearly the tiny pits caused by high velocity micrometeor impacts that some scientists called "zap pits," each with its own tiny, raised rim of glassy material that had once, and very briefly, been molten.

Vivian had had plenty of time on her Apollo Astarte mission to think back and do the math, and assuming she was remembering all the dates right, she'd spent a cumulative total of two hundred and eleven days on the Moon. Plenty of astronauts and cosmonauts had a higher day-count by now, but unlike most others Vivian had spent most of her Moon-time in motion, traveling from place to place. And here she was, back again for more, a glutton for punishment.

Just once, she glanced up at the Earth, that bright blue jewel in the sky. A planet that wasn't stark and actively hostile.

A planet that wasn't for her, not yet. Instead? Another lunar road trip.

Vivian sighed, checked all her gauges again out of force of habit, and kangaroo-hopped around the LEK to help Nikolai put together their transport for the journey.

The Lunokhod folded down from the outside bay of the Soviet LEK as smoothly as a NASA Lunar Rover did from a LM. It was almost as if the Soviets had been taking notes from the Americans when they designed it. Or had it been the other way around? By now, Vivian couldn't remember which country had been the first to use wheeled transport on the Moon. Too much water had flowed under the bridge since then.

Vivian leaned down as clumps of fine powder dropped out from between the unfolding chassis joints. "Hey, Nikolai, man: you're getting Deimos schmutz all over my nice clean Moon."

Apparently guessing the meaning of "schmutz" from context, Makarov nodded gravely. "This will confuse future geologists, I am sure. All right, this battery pack? Fastens with the clamps there and there. And I think you will see how to unfold the seats?"

"Pretty much." Vivian got to work, while Makarov went to another of the LEK bays and pulled out more gear: oxygen bottles, a small chest of what she took for either food or tools, and the long sausage-shaped bag that would expand to become a temporary habitat. Vivian wasn't looking forward to spending another night in inflatable digs on the Moon, but Makarov had assured her that this Soviet model was sized considerably larger than the NASA emergency unit that Vivian had hunkered down in for days, waiting for the radiation level near Hadley Plain to diminish after Yashin's bomb had obliterated it and turned it to glass.

Makarov's rover was, of course, smaller than the two Lunokhods that still appeared in Vivian's nightmares: the ones from the Soviets' first ground attack on Hadley Base, and from the hostile attack on her LGS-1 mission at the South Pole. Those had been sturdy, heavy-duty vehicles capable of carrying four to six soldiers. They'd been partially armored and couldn't be folded up in such a compact way to be transported. Instead, they were brought to the Moon in several pieces and bolted together.

Their wheels for today were more genteel, a skeletal conveyance with no armor, no guns, no signs of military application whatever. It had a shorter wheelbase than an Apollo Lunar Rover, and it was a good job Vivian had refused her crew's offer of a third team member. It was going to be a tight fit getting all their gear and spare supplies onto this.

"If you have finished, see to the antenna, next? It goes at the front, just like yours. The nuts, bolts, a wrench, in the pouch over here."

"Antenna? Are we thinking of calling anyone in particular?"

Makarov shrugged, making the movement big in the Soviet spacesuit. "I agree, it is not likely. But we should always be prepared, just in case."

They'd be preserving radio silence on the S-band that fixed front antenna worked on, but sure, it was tough to predict what might happen in the coming few days and weeks. Right now, the two of them were using the much shorter-range VHF radio in their suits, only effective over a couple of hundred miles. Vivian got to work.

The final item that Makarov loaded aboard their lunar truck, balanced precariously and tied down atop everything else, was a third Soviet spacesuit, complete with life support backpack, and an additional spare backpack for contingency. If they found Belyakova alive it was almost inconceivable that she'd lack a working Moon suit, but once again, it would be foolish not to be prepared.

And then they were ready to go. Vivian noted that, unlike US rovers which had the T-controller in between the two riders, this Lunokhod had the steering apparatus in front of the right-hand seat.

"After that landing, maybe I should drive," Vivian said. "God knows what pits or crevasses a maniac like you will put us into, skidding around at a hundred kilometers an hour."

"Ha," Makarov said, and cheerfully climbed into the driver's seat. "With all this, we shall be lucky to make twenty."

Vivian clambered up beside him. She scanned the ground around them in case there was anything they'd neglected to load, and glanced over at the LEK, sitting there like some kind of bulbous onion with legs. "God, your Soviet landing craft are just plain ugly."

"Always so impolite, you Americans." Makarov powered up the Lunokhod, and away they went.

Vivian looked back. The twin lines of their rover tracks stretched out behind them, all the way back to the LEK that just sat there out in the open, glinting in the sunlight. Today they would be leaving their spore in their wake for all to see. They had no track redaction mechanism, and no regolith weave to disguise the Soviet rover from eyes in the sky. All they could do was, rather optimistically, hope no one was looking for them. Or, at least, that any hostiles—whatever that even meant, in their current circumstances—wouldn't look in the right place just yet.

It was hard for Vivian to imagine that a MOL-mounted DORIAN optical system, or whatever the Soviet equivalent was, or even a more traditional large-frame optical camera like the type she'd originally brought up to Columbia Station from Earth, could miss them. They'd just have to hope for the best.

And this wasn't the only aspect of their adventure that was dangerously optimistic.

Nothing Vivian could do about it. She turned her attention back to the view ahead, peering into the knife-edged shadows to warn Nikolai about any boulders, surface cracks or even crater rims that he might fail to see.

Vivian knew the Moon better than just about anyone, but during those first hours driving toward the Marius Hills, it was like she was seeing it for the first time.

She hadn't forgotten the sheer grandeur of the Moon, but she certainly hadn't thought about it for a long time: the scale of its huge craters and towering mountains, its rilles sinuous and deep, the boulders and rocks large and small that were scattered in wild profusion across its surface. She *had* forgotten its sterility, and silence, and sheer lack of motion. The surface of the Moon felt unchanged, eternal. She could keep coming to the Marius Hills for a billion years, and the changes wrought by meteor impacts would still be mostly tiny and incremental.

She had also forgotten the vivid beauty of the Earth, that blue marble that held almost all human life, suspended in the sky above her like God's own nightlight. It was the only object in her sight with any vestige of real color.

To distract herself from that as they drove, she studied the subtleties of light and color on the surface: how the regolith took on that slight brownish shading when she was looking in the Sun's direction, and sometimes appeared as bright as snow in the reflected light when she looked in the opposite direction. The Moon's overwhelming palette consisted of shades of gray, naturally, but she was constantly alert for the blue-green glint of olivine, and the tan-brown echo of more iron-rich material. And, had she spotted the orange-hued soil similar to that found by Apollo 17 and others, she might even have insisted on stopping to grab a sample.

Now they were off and running, they communicated by cable, suit jack to suit jack, instead of using the radio. Even if there'd been anyone else close by and in their line of sight, they couldn't be overheard.

After six hours they started to come across landmarks that Vivian knew—or, at least, recognized from high-definition orbital photographs. She pointed. "Volcanic dome. Like a shield volcano on Earth. And another, beyond it. Here we go, this is the good stuff." A trace of sadness lurked behind the words: Vivian's earlier idealism, and those original glorious memories, had now been turned grimy by cold war and hot battles, both in orbit and down here on the lunar surface.

"These guys, the big domes: the scientists think they formed from relatively viscous lava, with a different chemical makeup from the mare basalts we've sampled in other places on the Moon."

"That is nice," Nikolai said politely.

It should have stayed pristine, she thought. *The Moon should have remained a park for all humankind.* But that wasn't what had happened, not at all.

"I expected them to be bigger," Nikolai said. "Higher, I mean. Not so flat. The tallest cannot even be four hundred meters, I think?"

"Yeah, well, they're not exactly Vesuvius, or Mount Fuji." Vivian thought back to her long-ago geology training. "And there's a giant volcano in Siberia, right? Its name sounds something like 'clutching soap'?"

"Klyuchevskaya Sopka," Makarov said. "Yes, these are not like that, either."

"You have shield volcanoes in Kamchatka, though. Anyway, these are gorgeous, the best Moon volcanos around. They're likely somewhere between three point seven and four billion years old."

"Indeed. So, we are in the right place?"

"Sure. The heading we're on is fine. These go on for quite a ways, though. We'll need to bear left a little in a few miles, I'll tell you when."

"Turn left at the corner shop, and then right at the petrol station," he said. "You cannot miss it."

Vivian grinned. "You really did watch too much television when you were Earthside. Although some of it seems to have been British."

Enough chitchat. They weren't here as tourists, or even explorers. They were getting much too casual in a terrain where enemies might come at them from any direction, and at any moment. Vivian studied the skies, then took a long, slow, sweeping scan of the landscape.

"No boogies yet?" Makarov enquired.

"That's 'bogies', and no, thank God. Not yet." She paused. "Hey, Nikolai? This is my territory. Maybe I could drive?"

"Of course." He slowed to a halt and stretched, working his shoulders and rubbing his gloved hands together as best he could. "You will find it is not comfortable, though."

She grinned. "I don't doubt that."

They crept in slowly and carefully from the side. Vivian had been told that the Marius site was unoccupied, that the NASA scientific presence had been withdrawn after the capture of Daedalus Base and the war at Zvezda-Copernicus, but they did not want any unwelcome surprises. It was always possible that the Soviets had moved in. That was why Vivian and Nikolai had chosen not to land here directly. After all this effort to get to the Moon, they'd hardly wanted to get shot out of the sky before they could even set foot back on it. But still, they saw no evidence of recent human occupation.

Soon after Vivian took over the driving, the familiar scenery opened out in front of her again, accompanied by a hint of shellshock. Had she and Terri really roared across this terrain in an armored Air Force Lunar Module, with gunners mounted on each side of them? Today they were entering the erstwhile battlefield from the southwest, but on that day back in 1983 she and Terri had flown in from the east, overshooting the ridge that hid the lava tube, and curving back around. And then she'd shot straight up in pursuit of the fleeing cryptonaut craft. After which she'd piloted the LM into the lava tube.

Into a freaking *lava tube*, for God's sake.

"I must have been stark raving mad," she said.

"Mad, because?"

She glanced at him. Even now, she had no idea how much Makarov knew about the battle that had taken place at Marius. Perhaps the details were still classified, at least from the US perspective? Vivian had no idea. "Oh, nothing."

After a while, secrecy became a way of life. Maybe she should switch to Night Corps after all this, like Terri.

Or not. Vivian Carter had been in enough danger for one lifetime.

The Marius battlefield had been cleaned up. Vivian had half expected to drive around the ridge and see Sandoval's tipped-up MOLAB still lying on its side, and bodies strewn all over the landscape. All of that had been tidied away long ago, of course. Three Night Corps Bricks and an empty Cargo Container still rested out there on the surface—two of those Bricks had been dropped in the battle, full of troops and their vehicles, and a third had arrived at a later date to bring in more crew for the site cleanup and scientific investigation—but aside from those, the lunar surface looked about as pristine as the surface normally did, and with surprisingly few wheel tracks and footprints.

"All gone," she said. "Amazing."

"It is not here?" Makarov was looking distinctly worried now.

"What? Sorry, I was just reminiscing, I guess. We can't see it yet. Look over there? That's the lava tube entrance."

He peered in the direction she was pointing. "Is it?"

Vivian looked again, and all she saw was deep shadow. She herself would never have guessed that those shadows hid a volcanic cave mouth if she hadn't already known. "Okay, wait a sec." She steered the Lunokhod to the right to approach the entrance, pulling the flashlight out of her calf pocket while she was driving. "Shine this in there."

"In where?" he said, but as soon as he fumbled the flashlight slider to turn it on, it became obvious, the roughly circular gash of the lava tube extending into the ridge. And just inside the lava tube entrance sat the monstrous cryptonaut transport. "Ah," he said in satisfaction. "It is still here after all."

"Hallelujah." Vivian moved in closer and let the Lunokhod drift to a halt, peering into Makarov's helmet. His visor was down, but by the faint status indicators that glowed inside his helmet she could see his jaw dropping in astonishment.

Eventually, he said, "It is larger than I had thought."

Vivian grinned. "Quite the sight, isn't it?"

"Yes." He looked again across the Marius site. "And there is the petrol station."

"We say 'gas' in America, Nikolai."

"And yet, your 'gas' is a liquid."

"And it's *benzin* in Russian, right? Even though gas contains no actual benzene?"

Makarov shrugged. "This is why I am a cosmonaut and not a linguist."

"Let's go check," she said. "Just for confidence."

They drove across to the fuel dump, and Vivian hopped off the Lunokhod to check the gages. Both fuel tanks were still pressurized, and as best Vivian could tell, they could have refueled four or five Lunar Modules with the Aerozine and oxidizer that remained.

The Soviet landers used the same fuel. So all they'd need to do was drive back to the LEK, hop it across the lunar surface a few dozen miles, and fill it up.

They would not do that today, but the discovery of the intact fuel depot raised their spirits. The landing had gone right, the trip to Marius had gone right, and now they'd identified the fuel that would get them off the Moon, on the first stage of their journey back to Earth.

All they needed was for that luck to last.

The cryptonaut habitat was still there too, tucked back into the lava tube, but Vivian had no urge to revisit it. For one thing it was deflated and twisted around following the long-ago US forensic search of its contents and surroundings and it would require considerable effort to restore it to habitability again. The Cargo Container was empty aside from a bunch of discarded packing materials and thermal blankets, but a search of the third Brick, the one that had served as the NASA science habitat, yielded up several trays of vacuum-sealed MREs, a stock of pressurized liquid oxygen bottles, and some water, either stashed there deliberately in case of later need, or abandoned in the evacuation because there was no space for them.

"Later need" was right now, as far as Vivian was concerned. They piled the food and oxygen up, ready to take with them.

No maps, though. Vivian had been hoping that there would be a full set of lunar charts in the Brick, to help guide them on their way. No such luck. Their one single map—which Makarov had neglected to tell her was only labeled in Cyrillic, for added difficulty points—plus an antique sextant and some good old-fashioned trigonometry: those would have to suffice for navigation.

And then it was time to face the Beast, the giant cryptonaut transport.

"Your United States chose not to take this?"

"The US has its MOLABs," Vivian said. "Much speedier than that behemoth." *And then there's the radiation danger*, she thought, but didn't say aloud.

"And yet this will go and go."

"Yup," she said. "Forever and back. Even by night."

Makarov gave a big sigh and looked around them again.

It didn't take a genius to know what he was thinking. Since the transport was still here, and showed no signs of being disturbed, it meant that Svetlana Belyakova had never been here.

"Hey." She put her gloved hand on his shoulder. "Don't be gloomy, Nikolai Ilyich. It was too much to hope that we'd find her at the first possible place. We couldn't get that lucky, right?"

"I suppose not."

"Marius was always a long shot. The other locations are much more likely."

He nodded. "And so, we are in for the long haul."

"Yes, we are."

Still, the silver lining: since Belyakova had not taken the cryptonauts' big rig, that meant that Vivian and Nikolai could use it. If it had been missing, they would have been forced to do the entire trip on the Lunokhod and put up Nikolai's habitat every night, to sleep. Secretly, Vivian almost preferred it this way. Even though they had yet to see what state the transport was in.

Makarov was still staring into the darkness. "Vivian, why would Svetlana not just hide in a lava tube?"

"In an ideal world, or ideal Moon, then sure. Benign thermal environment, screened from above ... sure. Except, in a lava tube, she isn't getting any sunlight for her solar panels. Or herself. She'd be in the dark all the time."

"So, she could go into the tube at night and not have the killing cold temperatures, and move out into the Sun during the day?"

"Except: as far as I know, here at Marius is the only place where she'd have had drive-in access to a lava tube."

He turned to look at her. "Really?"

"Yes. There are volcanic domes like these at Mairan, but those are close to the American rare earth mining operation. The best ones after that are at Gruithuisen Gamma and Delta, around thirty-five degrees north, and more at Mons Rumker. There are others at Cauchy Tau and Omega, but those are on the equator. And at Arago, and there are six domes north of Hortensius crater, but they're also equatorial and only two hundred fifty kilometers from Copernicus ..."

He waved impatiently. "Vivian, Vivian: which of these could she be at?"

"Honestly? None of them, because like I said, as far as I know there are *no* lava tubes other than here that have easy access. There are pits into possible tubes in Mare Tranquillitatis and ... I've forgotten where else. Doesn't matter. She can't just dive into those pits and survive. She can't get the Purgan into them. And, once inside, she's cut off, completely. She can't monitor radio, can't do anything. I just don't believe Svetlana would ..." Her voice caught.

"Would?"

Vivian breathed and held out her hand for a moment, mutely asking for a few seconds. At the end of that time, she said: "Entomb herself."

Makarov merely nodded. "And you would know, if another lava tube was accessible that Svetlana might use?"

"Yes. Barring some fluke, or some case where the Soviets had found one and bored out the end like they did at Marius? I would definitely know. Someone would have told me. And if not, it doesn't matter."

"It does not?"

"No. Because in addition to being very low probability, all those domed regions are so far away from one another that there's no way we could visit them all. So. Let's just forget about them."

Makarov wasn't wrong. Even the Vivian's eyes, the cryptonaut transport seemed to have grown since she had last seen it.

It also looked even odder than she'd remembered. Amazing how unwieldy space vehicles could be, either those for use between worlds or on the Moon.

It was an almost shockingly simple design, based around a big rectangular flatbed, supported by four pairs of segmented wheels on each side. At the front, high up off the surface, was a small pressurized cab. A narrow, flexible tunnel made of what looked like black plastic, linked this cab with a small square living space in the rear containing a couple of niches crammed with bunks, a small mess area, and a single toilet facility. Ten men had lived, or subsisted, in this cramped space for weeks at a time as the transport had slowly weaved its way around the Moon. This beast made a MOLAB look spacious.

The late, lamented Kevin Pope had called the cryptonaut transport "bare-bones, the absolute minimum needed for survival," and noted that the people who'd designed it clearly hadn't given a damn about the unlucky crew who'd have to drive around the lunar surface in it. That still looked like the truth, and even more so, now that Vivian herself would soon have to … drive it around on the lunar surface.

Vivian walked around it, inspecting it. She didn't exactly kick the tires, but she did carefully examine every one of its four pairs of segmented wheels to make sure they weren't too bent or damaged. They were all pitted and bashed, and the front right wheel was deformed out-of-round from some previous collision with a lunar boulder, but none of it was so bad that the vehicle couldn't move safely.

Under the rear of the flatbed beyond the wheels was a wide mechanical structure that hung almost all the way down to ground level: the track redaction device that would allow this great vehicle to obscure all signs of its passing.

And, something which made Vivian feel even less comfortable: through the small back window she could see a smallish box with radiation symbols prominently displayed on it mounted over the right rear wheel. That was the mini-reactor that powered the transport.

Yeah, the less time Vivian spent thinking about *that*, the better.

"Up we go, then."

To get up into the cab she had to climb a ten-rung vertical ladder, presumably made of aluminum. The gap between the rungs was too large for comfort, and it was almost as easy to haul herself up hand-over-hand with brute strength.

The cab had no airlock. Rather, the cab *was* the airlock. You closed the door leading into the flexible, inflatable tube that linked it to the living area to the rear of the vehicle, using a contraption that consisted of a lever plus a spinning torque transfer device. Then you pressurized the cab itself from a pair of compressed oxygen bottles mounted behind the driver's seat. The only airlock on the vehicle was to the rear of the crew compartment, allowing access out onto the flatbed.

It was … almost primitive. Because the vehicle was so goddamn large, its designers had needed to save weight wherever they could, and they certainly hadn't added any frills, bells or whistles.

At least that meant that the driving controls and instrumentation panel were straightforward, even though all the switch labels were marked with Chinese characters. After a few minutes of study, it was clear how to drive the Beast. For the few controls Vivian couldn't immediately make sense of, she could experiment later and see what happened.

Its cab was tiny. Two people *could* get in there at once, arranging themselves carefully, but they'd be constantly jostling each other. It contained a simple rover seat with an aluminum frame and webbing, not molded or designed for comfort, despite the constant long journeys this transport had needed to undertake to fulfil its missions.

Notably, the transport had no radio installed anywhere, just a wired intercom system linking the driver's cab and the crew mess area, with additional cables dangling down from the cab to the flatbed. The cryptonauts must have relied on their suits, or a portable radio system that was now gone, for any more extensive VHF or S-band communications.

"Well," Vivian said over this intercom system to Nikolai, who was back in the crew area. "I sure hope this darned thing starts."

It did.

"I think we should take this," Makarov said. "Yes?"

By now Vivian had explored the whole internal space of the transport—it hadn't taken long—and was now sweeping out the crap from its previous owners prior to loading in the food, water and oxygen. Nikolai, meanwhile, had been prospecting around to see if there was anything else useful in the vicinity.

She broke off and peered out of the portholes. "Uh, which this?"

"Perhaps you should come and see."

Simple enough, since she was still suited up. It would be a while before they'd pressurize the transport for the first time. Vivian slid through the open airlock hatch in the floor in the rear left corner of the crew area, shinned down the ladder to the ground, and made her way to where she could see Nikolai shining his flashlight around inside the lava tube.

"Oh," she said.

For a moment Vivian thought it was a Soviet flyer, like the two she'd seen before: the one that had attacked her and her LGS-1 crew at the South Pole, and the second machine that had attempted to flee by powering out of the Pit during the battle for Marius, a few months later.

But it wasn't. It was an even smaller craft, and with sleeker and smoother lines.

"It's a LESS," she said. "I've never actually seen one before."

"Less than what?"

NASA's Lunar Escape Systems craft, was a lightweight single-person 'bug,' a lander with an open cockpit. At one point the LESS had been seriously considered as a method for getting the first US astronaut down onto the lunar surface from orbit. Pete Conrad, of all people, had been a particular fan of that idea. Fortunately, NASA had thought a little bigger for its Moon landings.

At NASA's direction, Rockwell had designed the LESS to use the minimum equipment. For once, simplicity was the key design concept, not redundancy. The LESS consisted of a single seat mounted above a rocket engine, with a joystick, an eight-ball display to show orientation, and a clock, and that was it for guidance. It was designed for manual flight only, with no computer assistance. It also had a flashing light and a VHF radio beacon, to help track it. Naturally, all life support would be supplied by the astronaut's suit.

If Vivian remembered correctly, the LESS would have a launch weight of 2,300 pounds, 1,160 of which would be propellant. The loaded weight of a Lunar Module was 36,200 pounds, dry mass 10,850 pounds, more than ten times heavier. In fact, the LESS was designed to be carried in collapsed form in a Lunar Module bay, in exactly the same way as the Apollo Lunar Rovers. Even the fuel tanks were collapsible. Its rocket used the same hypergolic fuel combination as the LMs, so it could be fueled up from the usual lunar fuel dumps.

It made a good match with the Soviet big rig. Both were clunky and as simple as they could possibly be, with no creature comforts, no safety features, and no redundancy.

"I knew they'd done some aerial surveying here in the NASA follow-up studies," she said. "I didn't realize they'd used *these*. But, sure. We have no idea what's going to happen, and a big wide flatbed so … let's see about taking it with us."

And so the two of them painstakingly erected the LESS ready for flight by unfolding its landing gear and winched it aboard the transport's flatbed alongside Nikolai's Lunokhod.

Vivian sure wouldn't have wanted to land on the Moon in one of these. And flying one up off the Moon's surface, maybe even into lunar orbit, wouldn't be a whole lot better. Plus, it would only take one of them.

So, here's hoping it doesn't come to that.

After loading the LESS, the Lunokhod, and as many supplies as they could onto the flatbed, refueling and gingerly testing the LESS, equally cautiously pressurizing the transport, and stopping for a long-overdue meal, it still took Vivian another two hours to clean out its interior to the point where she was happy. Nikolai chafed at the delay—he wanted to get onto the road as soon as possible, and did not see why they couldn't clean it while they were on the move—but the smell of decay inside the vehicle was too much for Vivian, and the layers of Moon dust across the instruments in the cab and the mess area in the cramped crew quarters were clearly a health hazard. They needed to get the place as clean as possible. Plus, with only one large-scale map for navigation, Vivian would be obsessing about their location and doing a whole bunch of math while Nikolai was driving, and she could hardly imagine that Makarov would spend his downtime holystoning the galley during her shifts in the driver's seat.

Now the search could really begin.

Vivian had gone over the Marius base area as thoroughly as she could, given the time available, but had found no weapons. That was no surprise: rifles, grenades and all the rest were easily portable, and valuable. The US forces would have been sure to pack all munitions out with them when they'd moved out. But it sure would have been nice to find *something* they could defend themselves with.

Ironically, Vivian did find a core drill, left behind in the science hab. She considered taking it along for old time's sake, but, no: this last time on the Moon she had absolutely no desire to stop and take cores, and if she once again found herself in a situation where a core drill made the difference between life and death, the odds would likely be stacked against her even more heavily than they had last time around.

They had plenty of oxygen, at any rate. At almost the last minute they'd found another stockpile of full tanks back in the caves from the Night Corps and NASA occupation of the site. Oxygen was so vital that the Americans often left stashes of it in places where someone might need it, rather than shlep those bottles around with them.

And so, it was go-time. Time to set off around the Moon once again.

"Well." Vivian took a deep breath. "*Nu, poyehali.*" *Off we go, then.*

29

Lunar Surface: Vivian Carter
May 5-24, 1985

THE cryptonaut transport was unwieldy as hell, and it drove like a cow. It was hard to steer, with a several-second delay between any use of the controls and the corresponding effect on the vehicle's path across the surface, which meant that initially Vivian tended to go straight over or through obstacles rather than around them. Makarov did little better when it was his turn.

To begin with, whichever of them was taking a rest from the wheel tended to sit or lie on the floor of the cab at the driver's feet. The cab was better sprung than the rest of the vehicle. Riding in the crew quarters while they were on the road was a jolting and potentially nauseating experience.

Even when they stopped for a break, or for the night, this was hardly luxury travel. They had food trays, and water, but no water spigots, meaning that rehydrating food was often a tricky and messy business. They had an oven unit that was never quite strong enough to make the food hot. The seats were aluminum, with threadbare padding. The fold-down bunks looked more like stretchers. And a lot of their supplies were crammed into this marginal crew space as well, to avoid constantly having to go out and down to the flatbed to resupply.

All they could do was grit their teeth and stay the course long enough to swing around the Moon to where they might find Svetlana Belyakova.

Hopefully, still alive.

The Rig was not quite as good at covering its tracks as Vivian had thought, because it was so damned heavy. On mare it was fine, the smoothing-over went great. But if they went through a crater of any size, and crumbled the edge or changed its shape, there was no way the automatic redaction process could build that crater-edge back up again the way it had been. The original cryptonaut crew must have had an even more difficult job traveling around the Moon than she'd thought, having to steer clear of any distinctive looking area where they might distort the appearance of the surface enough for it to be visible from above.

And so they covered the ground, slowly but surely.

The days were exhausting, and Vivian was sleeping like the dead. One morning she awoke to discover she'd overslept by an hour and was alone in the crew mess area, and the transport wasn't moving. Part-irritated and part-concerned, she went looking for Nikolai, and eventually located him clambering around on the flatbed, apparently stringing up wires.

She pulled a headset on and pinged him over the intercom. "Nikolai, what the hell are you doing? Is something wrong?"

"Wrong, no. I am setting an antenna."

"For what, exactly? We already have more antennas than we need."

"No, this one is for short wave. Wait. Let me finish, and then we will start driving, and I will explain."

It turned out that Nikolai had calculated that, even up here on the Moon, he ought to be able to receive at least intermittent transmissions from the Voice of America, the BBC World Service, and Radio Moscow World Service. "Often, when I was younger, I would listen secretly to the Voice of America to learn what was happening with your Mercury and Gemini missions, which were not well reported in my country. Now, after all you have told me, I wish to learn more of what is happening in the Rodina, and in Europe."

Maybe it hadn't been Vivian's best idea to fill Nikolai in on the strikes, protests, and independence movements now springing up across the Warsaw Pact countries, and the measures the Soviets were taking to crack down on them. Yuri Andropov hadn't been seen in public for months, and no one really knew where the power lay in the Politburo anymore. Nikolai had had dozens of questions, none of which Vivian could answer; all she knew, she'd gleaned from the quick summaries that Mission Control Houston gave Astarte, transmissions she'd sneakily listened in on from Deliverance. Now, the inventive cosmonaut was apparently seeking his own answers.

"Great," she said. "More politics."

"So, Nikolai: what happens to you, after this?"

"After? I will go home."

"Really? Let's assume that everything all keeps going well. We get where we're going, magically find Svetlana, ferry her back to the LEK, launch ourselves into orbit and transfer back into to my Command Module—which has somehow not gone into a debilitating tumble in the meantime, stymieing us. We get back to Earth. What happens to you then? Now, you're a traitor to your country. You've abandoned your mission, gone AWOL—which means 'absent without leave'—anyway, you're basically a deserter. If you go back to the USSR, why don't the Soviets just kill you right away, or send you to a gulag somewhere?"

"You will be a deserter as well," he pointed out.

"The big difference is: I bring back two very famous cosmonauts. Who really have no choice but to defect to the United States— no, Nikolai, hear me out—you'll just have to come home with me, because there's no way in hell that you and Svetlana can go back to the Soviet Union."

"Defect?" he said in horror, as if the thought had never occurred to him.

"Uh, yes, for God's sake. Defect. Of course. *Both* of you will have to."

"We will think of something," he said. "I cannot defect. My family is there, in Russia."

"You'll think of something? Like what, exactly? A magic spell?"

"Vivian, do not worry about me. I am a friend to Raisa Gorbachev, and I have spoken with Mikhail Gorbachev himself on many occasions. You and I have spoken of this. Gorbachev is a reformer, he wants an end to the corruptions and the lying of the past ..."

"I'm sure he wants all that, and probably a pony as well, and I'm sure if you just showed up at his dacha one day he'd do his best for you and all, but ... Nikolai, you're going to have to get past the KGB and likely the whole damned Soviet army to get to him. You can't just land and say 'Take me to your leader' and expect them to salute and say, 'Sure, Nikolai, just get in this car and we'll drive you right there.'" She considered. "Okay, maybe they will tell you to get in the car, but I doubt it'll take you anywhere you want to go. Also, I doubt that even Mikhail Gorbachev is going to put his entire political career on the line to save the guy who abandoned his Mars mission or the woman who went rogue and killed her superior officers. I'm sure he has other fish to fry … I mean, matters of more importance than even you."

"We will think of something," he said doggedly. "Later. First things first."

"You're an idiot," she said.

Makarov grinned, his mouth a thin line. "I am told this often, by my wife and by Svetlana, and now by you. I am told this by my friends, and certainly by my enemies. I am coming to think that perhaps it is true."

"Mikhail …. Could you just be serious for once? This is madness."

He just sighed, and for the next few miles Vivian thought she'd decided to clam up and not talk any more. Then, his shoulders sagged. "Knowing what I now know … clearly, my country is not the place I thought it was. The lies, and the violence. The treachery. But perhaps in time, once Andropov has gone, perhaps Gorbachev can save it. He is a man of pragmatism, but also a man of vision. He believes in openness, I think he really does."

"I do like that about you," Vivian said. "That you always have faith in people. That you can look around you and see the best and not the worst. Darned if I can."

"And if I do not want to come to America, I am sure that Svetlana very much does not want to come to America. It is a greedy country, an uncaring country."

"Sometimes. But look at the one you're leaving."

He gave her a look. "That is just the leaders of now. It is not the *people*. I still have faith in the Russian people."

"Then you're a better person than I am."

He half-grinned. "Of course. I am a Soviet New Man."

"And I don't want you to become a Soviet Dead Man. Look, Nikolai: if you don't like America, then don't stay. There's a whole list of other western countries you could end up in. No one's going to lock

409

you up in the US and force you to stay. That's the thing about freedom. It means you're free."

"Free for what? Vivian, I love my country. I do not want to defect. I am not doing this to defect." He sighed. "But, I suppose, if my country is a place I cannot be for a while, and I have no choice?"

"So, you're at least not ruling it out yet?"

"I am not ruling it out." Makarov raised his gaze to look across the lunar landscape. "But I am confident we will think of something."

They navigated using Vivian's sextant, the large-scale map, and some alarmingly simple arithmetic. Nikolai made his own estimate using dead reckoning, and Vivian made hers by taking star sightings and doing trigonometry by hand. Fortunately, their estimates agreed most of the time, and there were sufficient landmarks on Nearside for them to confirm their position with ground truth.

On Farside, it got a little more complicated.

Once they navigated clear of Oceanus Procellarum, the Ocean of Storms, there were no more flat oceans or seas ahead, not for a long way. They had thousands of miles of highland territory to cover before they hit their next mare, if they hit it at all—and that sea would be one of the smaller ones. For reasons scientists still hadn't figured out, the vast majority of the basaltic mares and the Ocean of Storms were all on the Earth-facing side of the Moon.

The endless lunar highlands were anything but flat. They were bumpy and irregular most of the time, and after a few days, that bumpiness and the difficulty of avoiding boulders, craters and cracks in the lunar surface got even more tedious.

It was a long, long couple of weeks before they arrived in the vicinity of Mare Moscoviense. They'd been driving west, traveling with the Sun, meaning that the trip was just one long lunar morning. Which at least meant that the Sun was always behind them, not permanently in their eyes.

The story went that all the lunar mares were named after water features (storms, rains, vapors) or moods (tranquility, serenity, intelligence), and that the International Astronomical Union had only agreed to the name of Mare Moscoviense on the shaky ground that Moscow was a state of mind. Vivian couldn't speak to the truth of that, and of course there were other exceptions, like the Eastern Sea and the Sea of Cold, Mares Orientale and Frigoris respectively.

She did find it odd to be approaching a lunar sea named for the capital of the Soviet Union, in search of other named Soviet features, though.

After all this time, they mostly drove in silence. Generally, the one who wasn't driving would spend their time napping or doing suit maintenance, organizing supplies or tidying their living spaces. The early motion sickness that they'd both suffered had worn off, although the bumpy ride meant they always needed to be braced, or actively holding on with at least one hand. And so Vivian had plenty of time to think back to their original conversation about Svetlana's likely whereabouts, all those weeks ago in the planning stages, while she'd still been back on the Apollo Astarte.

"What did she say to you, Nikolai? Tell me everything, just as she said it. If she was trying to get a message to you, indirectly, any word or inflection might be important."

Makarov did so.

Vivian had nodded. "She was speaking to the walls. So, those must be clues, right? Naming the cosmonauts? Could that mean she's gone to Leonov's original landing site?"

Makarov had shaken his head slowly. "I do not think so. Leonov's site would be a foolish choice. It is too obvious, that Svetlana would mean such a thing. More important, that site in Mare Fecunditatis is on the equator, just as our first landing site was, Svetlana's and mine, and like those of your early Apollos." He stopped.

Vivian grinned tautly. "You can say it out loud. You have an Almaz craft in an equatorial orbit? So it would be like trying to hide in plain sight. Svetlana's not about to park on a spot where an Almaz flies directly over her every two hours."

He nodded. "And Leonov's landing site is very popular among the cosmonauts. It is photographed often from orbit. You can still see his descent stage and even the boot trail that Leonov made, walking around the craft and to Messier Crater."

"Okay, so if not Leonov's landing site ..." Vivian had grinned. "Then it's obvious where she must be. Right?"

Makarov had grinned, slyly. "Is it?"

Vivian had thought so. She really had. And so had Nikolai. They'd both independently come to the same conclusion. But here they were at Leonov Crater on Farside, and they'd found no sign of Belyakova. They'd parked the giant transport and hopped aboard the faster Lunokhod to travel the entire sixty-five mile perimeter of Leonov Crater, and then picked a path where the crater slope was shallow enough to make a vehicular trek across the center and back around.

And yet: no sign of Belyakova. Leonov Crater was pristine. They'd traveled thousands of miles across the lunar surface, only to come up empty.

So maybe Tereshkova, then? On they went, heading north two hundred miles across Mare Moscoviense to Tereshkova Crater. After the monotony of the lunar highlands it was almost a relief to switch back to the different monotony of a basalt mare.

They spent another day doing another long Lunokhod journey around the crater perimeter. Tereshkova Crater was similarly sized to Leonov, but with steeper walls. This one they did not attempt to cross. It was very clear that if Belyakova had attempted to drive a Purgan into Tereshkova Crater she'd have rolled and wrecked herself.

Nonetheless, Vivian and Nikolai both spent long minutes surveying the crater floor with binoculars. No Belyakova, no sign of any human presence whatever, past or present.

So, Korolev, then? Korolev Crater, named after Sergei Korolev, the Great Designer, the Von Braun of the Soviet Union: the man who'd build the giant N-1 rocket boosters necessary to put the Soviets on the Moon, and run the rigorous testing and astronaut preparation program necessary for them to complete that goal, way back in 1969?

But, no: Korolev Crater was twelve hundred miles away to the south ... almost on the equator. If Belyakova could not go to Leonov's original landing site, by the same logic she could not go to Korolev Crater.

"Shit. Sorry, Nikolai." Vivian sat in the still-grimy mess area on a too-small chair of aluminum and canvas, her head in her hands and her elbows on her knees, exhausted. "Sorry. I was so sure I could read her mind. But I've led you on a wild goose chase."

Makarov leaned back against the wall, staring into the space above her head. His dejection was clear, and his shoulders sagged. He looked five years older than when they'd started this quest. But, because he was Nikolai Makarov, all he said was: "You cannot blame yourself. Your ideas were reasonable and logical, and matched my own. Belyakova should have been at one of these craters." He forced a tired grin. "Svetlana, what on earth were you thinking?"

"Every day we search is one more day that Svetlana would have to survive," Vivian said. "Seriously, Nikolai, she's been out here alone for *months*. Is it really plausible that she could have survived this long? In a goddamned ... Purgan?"

"I do not know. I have never known. Only, I have hoped."

Nikolai must be exhausted, to look and sound so defeated. Vivian felt even worse.

She pulled herself upright to gaze through the tiny, grubby porthole, out over the desolate lunar surface. "I used to love the Moon," she said. "Now ... I don't know. I think maybe I hate it now. And if Svetlana really has managed to live this long, she'll be hating it too."

"Twice as much, I expect. Because her crew is half the size of ours."

Vivian didn't smile. She viscerally understood loneliness. "Sure. Alone out here with no one to talk to, and no one around for hundreds, or even thousands of miles. I do know a bit about what that's like. And to not even able to listen to ..."

She stopped.

After a few moments, Makarov glanced up at her. Now, Vivian was staring fixedly at a single point out on the landscape. Alarmed, he stood and tried to look that way, past her. "What, Vivian? What do you see?"

"Oh," she said. "Sorry, no, nothing out there. Miles of goddamned nothing. She's still not here, and neither is anybody else."

As he slumped back down, she turned to look at him, eyes glistening. "But I know where she *might* be."

"You do?" He did not sound convinced. She couldn't blame him.

"Nikolai, I'm an idiot. Sorry."

"If you, then I, too," he said, weariness in every syllable. "Idiots both. But why in particular, today?"

"Maybe we've been overthinking this. Maybe Svetlana really did want you to apologize to Leonov and the others, or maybe she initially thought she might go to Leonov or Tereshkova Craters but changed her mind. But Svetlana isn't anywhere near here, or in any particular named crater, and she never was."

"Meaning what?"

"Meaning …" She smiled and slapped him on the thigh. "Good news, comrade. We have another two thousand miles to travel."

He sighed. "What is another two thousand miles, at this point? In which direction?"

"North. All the way north."

Makarov blinked. "Are you joking?"

Vivian wanted to pace, but there wasn't enough space in the confined crew quarters to walk anywhere in a straight line. "Hear me out. Just after we'd completed the LGS-1 circumnavigation, when I was talking to Svetlana, she told me she wished she could have been to the poles as well. It sounded heartfelt. And Starman told me that Svetlana had tried to interest him in a trip to the South Pole with her, just before he left the Moon. He didn't take her up on it. By that time he was all done and needed to go home. But I'm willing to bet that if Svetlana has a truck and has to choose a destination, all else being equal, she's going to choose one of the poles."

"That is all? And so now we have to visit both poles?" Makarov just shook his head.

"I don't think so. Svetlana wouldn't have headed south. The terrain down there is God-awful and the odds of her running into Night Corps or a water-mining team of her own people would be too great— if there are still any of them down there, I don't even know. But anyway, it would be a long way.

"No, the North Pole is more likely, and not just because it's on her bucket list. At the Pole, if she positions herself in the right place she can keep the Purgan in almost constant daylight, and get enough solar power in to keep it at a moderate temperature without using too much energy. Her RTG could keep her going, but it wouldn't be pretty. And at ninety degrees north she'd be about as safe as she could be from being overflown and discovered. *Nobody* is in that extreme a polar orbit, not your people, not even Night Corps. Oh, I guess I shouldn't have told you that. Never mind, screw it."

Makarov raised his eyebrows. "If there's water at the Lunar South Pole, maybe there is water at the North Pole too?"

"Well, maybe. Though she's hardly set up to extract it effectively." Vivian stepped to the left, stepped to the right, the entire limited dancefloor available, and even so she had to be careful not to bump her head on one of the cabinets. "I dare say she *could* rig up some kind of distilling apparatus, to help eke out the water supply she took when she ran? Or a filtration system, maybe. She's quite a smarty-pants, but who knows what kind of metals or impurities might come out with the water … doesn't matter. Not the point. My original thought was that being up there would mean that she could listen in on radio transmissions and monitor communications with Earth and so maintain some idea about what's going on. That way she might get some clue of whether she might be able to come out of hiding, and where she might go. She couldn't do that as easily from anywhere on Farside. Unless she could tap into the NAVSTAR system … but it's a much shorter journey from Jura to the North Pole than to freaking Mare Moscoviense … as maybe we should have realized. Jesus Christ!" Vivian thumped the metal wall of the transport with her fist, not hard enough to break anything, just enough to burn up some of the restless energy that coursed through her.

Nikolai watched her carefully, with that air of mild bafflement he often wore when Vivian was ranting. "You are angry to have thought of this?"

"Yes, damn it. I'm ticked that I didn't think of it sooner. Even if we'd still been convinced of the Leonov/Tereshkova connection, we should have deviated to come past the pole on the way."

He looked unconvinced. "Perhaps you are now clutching at straws. Every argument you have made, you immediately then argued against. Power, water, communications, Svetlana does not *need* to be at the North Pole, Vivian. As you have just said."

Vivian sighed. "You're right. This is just another wild guess. Just because it sounds good in my head doesn't mean much anymore. I could be just as wrong about this as I was before. Realistically …" All of a sudden she felt deflated again, her conviction draining away. "She still could be just about anywhere. But, hey. If nothing else, we can visit it on our way through. We need to head back in that general direction to return to your LEK in any case, and there's no point in covering ground we've covered already."

Nikolai mimed flipping a coin, catching it, and looking at it. "North. Why not? I have never been to the North Pole."

"Don't get your hopes up," Vivian said. "It's just as boring as every-where else on the Moon."

He smiled at her. "This is not how you used to talk."

That earned him a small grin in return. "Times change. All right, look: we're both beat. Let's tidy up here and then rest for twelve hours, just sitting here in one place in peace and quiet. And then we'll talk about this again, and sanity-check ourselves. And then, unless we've had a better idea, we'll drive to the frigging North Pole and visit Santa."

He shook his head. "Santa?"

"Never mind. I just hope we finally get a gift. We've earned it."

CHAPTER 30

Lunar North Pole: Vivian Carter
May 30–June 2, 1985

AS Vivian well knew, the precise South Pole was inside Shackleton Crater, itself just inside the rim of the South Pole-Aitken basin, meaning that it was in a craggy, sloping area of permanent darkness. Thus, Vivian had never been able to stand on that exact spot. The lunar North Pole, by contrast, was in a highland region bracketed by three large, shallow craters: Peary, Hermite, and Rozhdestvenskiy, of which Peary Crater was the closest. The pole itself was thus at a relatively high elevation, meaning some areas on the outer slopes of Peary were almost permanently in sunlight.

For this leg of their pleasure cruise, Vivian spent most of her non-driving time suited up and riding on the flatbed, sometimes sitting in one of the Lunokhod seats. After all this time on the road she had tired of the cramped quarters inside the transport, along with the sour-sickly smells of mold and decay that disinfectant could not quite erase, and she could see the terrain more clearly though a suit visor than the Big Rig's thick, grimy portholes. Today she was sitting a little higher, up on the pilot's seat of the LESS, as the transport lumbered and bumped across the highlands to complete its journey to ninety degrees north.

She spotted the flag she'd planted at the North Pole from quite the distance. The American flags NASA used on the Moon these days were more rugged and enduring than the cheap hardware-store flags

417

used for the first Apollo Moon landings, and so this version of Old Glory had not faded. Its bold pattern of red, white, and blue stood out in the brilliant, oblique sunshine.

Peary Crater was some forty-five miles in diameter, with several other smaller craters embedded within it ranging from two to seventeen miles across. The smallest of these craters would be permanently shadowed, and thus potential sites for water ice. Although Vivian had barely given lunar geology a passing thought on this trip, it might be worth snagging a few samples from within those craters in areas she hadn't visited during LGS-1. Someday, with luck and if the world survived, it might matter to NASA whether there was water at the North Pole …

It was the tracks she saw first. Vivian's lunar experience gave her a keen appreciation for which surface features were natural and which were human-made, even from a distance. And although many craters were decorated with natural cracks and fissures, the wavery line a few hundred yards away that led into one of the smaller significant craters jumped out at her as unmistakably of human origin.

Of course, they'd come across human traces already: Vivian's own, and those of her LGS-1 crew, from early 1983. She could easily distinguish the tracks from the LGS MOLAB from their Lunar Rover; the MOLAB was heavier, with a wider wheelbase. She herself had driven that rover up to the Pole itself, leading the MOLAB. But neither she nor any of her crew had been as far inside Peary as the trail of boot prints she was looking at now.

"Holy *shit*." Vivian dismounted from the LESS saddle with some effort, took a running jump off the flatbed, and broke into a loping sprint, quickly outpacing it.

Her eyes followed the tracks and scanned the terrain. Boulders everywhere on that side of Peary, some of them large. And among them, a bright patch, unusually angular.

Vivian toggled her radio on, then off again, causing a double-click in her headset and Nikolai's, to get his attention. Vivian didn't want to say the words over the air until she was absolutely sure.

But, just to herself, she said: "Got her."

The row of boot prints led to a Purgan that was so bashed and battered that it looked like it had rolled down a hill, and its regolith weave was torn and hanging down from the roof in spooky strands that could have been taken for spiderwebs. Yet the vehicle itself was still in one piece.

Over the radio, she heard Makarov make some muffled exclamation in Russian as he caught sight of it himself. The cab he was riding in was mounted up higher, so he could see over Vivian and into the small crater and likely had an even better view than she did.

Then, very calmly, he said: "Wait there. I will come down."

Waiting might have been smart, but Vivian was already loping toward the Purgan. She couldn't cool her heels waiting for Makarov to suit up and join her. She had to know *now*.

As she approached, she could see the strange vehicle more clearly. It was *small*, so small, and its resemblance to a Volkswagen bus was uncanny, as if it had suddenly been transported to the wrong world. It appeared to be armored, although perhaps that was just the increased robustness and hull strength it needed to hold in atmosphere at pressure. It was colored a shade of grey that wasn't quite right for the Moon; the color match was close but no cigar as far as blending in was concerned. Vivian soon realized that this was likely because its surface paint had been discolored, bubbled and worn and faded by the continuous sunlight.

It was just as well the Purgan had been built sturdy, because it was in bad shape. Its outer panels were so heavily bashed and crumpled that it looked like this microbus had been in six different car accidents. As Vivian got closer, she saw that its wheels were larger than those of an Earth vehicle, and its clearance higher as well, to provide space for the track redaction.

"I am coming," Makarov said, and Vivian glimpsed him behind her, bouncing over the crater rim.

Then something moved inside the Purgan. A white face, unhelmeted, peered out at Vivian though what looked like a very dirty window, and then up and past her, and Vivian realized its occupant must be looking at the top of the Big Rig, which from her perspective must be visible over the crater rim.

If Vivian hadn't known who to expect, she might not have recognized Belyakova. The woman that stared out at her now was wild-haired, wild-eyed, and appeared not entirely sane. She ducked down and came up again holding some kind of pistol.

Vivian raised her hands, waving. "No, no!" Belyakova was now pointing her gun directly at Vivian through the window. If Belyakova had fired then and there, she'd likely have blown out the window and explosively decompressed her own shelter.

Perhaps realizing this, Svetlana twitched and put a hand up to her head. Placed the pistol down and pulled herself forward, lunging for the Purgan controls.

On the roof, the machine gun swiveled to point in Vivian's direction.

"Oh, God ..." Vivian stepped back, her arms now raised all the way up. "Svetlana, Svetlana! Look at my goddamned suit, turn on the freaking radio, do something smart, *anything!*"

Was there a gesture Svetlana would recognize? Any movement Vivian could make that would make it obvious who she was? Some piece of distinctive Vivian body language? She was damned if she could think of anything. "Nikolai! Do something! Make her realize it's us!"

No response or inspiration came, so Vivian dropped forward onto her knees to make herself an even less threatening target.

Belyakova would know she'd been hunted for months. And now she could see a transport peeking over the crater edge at her, a vehicle she associated only with cryptonauts. The two people she could see were dressed in a white NASA spacesuit and a red Soviet suit, a similar mix to the cryptonauts. "Shit," Vivian said. For all the weeks they'd been searching, she had never thought to consider what their approach might look like from Belyakova's perspective.

And then, Svetlana collapsed. She put up her hand again as if reaching for something that wasn't there and then crumpled and disappeared from their sight. Released, the machine gun barrel drifted lazily to the right.

"Svetlana!" Makarov was already past Vivian and running up to the Purgan. Vivian was watching the machine gun on the roof intently, hoping not to see it move again, and scanning the whole vehicle for any other threats.

Makarov called back: "I think she is unconscious."

"Great. Well, let's use the time to write her a message." Vivian hustled up to the truck. Fortunately, the Purgan window was filthy with moondust. No pen required.

She wrote backwards, mirror-style: IT'S VIVIAN AND NIKOLAI.

"She is still not moving." Nikolai had rubbed another area of the window clean and was peering in anxiously. "And she has blood on her head."

Belyakova had fallen sideways onto the Purgan floor so that her ragged blond hair obscured most of her face, and Nikolai was right, she had a patch of blood on her temple and perhaps more seeping from beneath her head.

Vivian's exhilaration at finding Belyakova had quickly given way to fear. "I don't like this, Nikolai. Not at all."

"Nor I."

"We need to get in there." She circled the Purgan, peered at its other side and rear. "This crappy piece of shit doesn't have an airlock?"

"Of course not. There is no room for one. This is a very simple vehicle."

"No kidding."

"This means we cannot get inside until Svetlana puts on her space-suit." He gestured. "Like the landers of your country and mine, and also our Soyuz and Apollo, the whole of the inside must be depressur-ized before the door can be opened. In normal use, of course, this is not a problem."

"Jeez. That's just fabulous. All right, so what the hell do we do now, in abnormal usage? What if she doesn't wake up any time soon? What if she just gave herself a concussion and is out for days?"

Nikolai pointed. "Those are the oxygen bottles, I think. That rack, mounted behind the front seats, just as in the transport. And more down there, along the floor, see? So, if we were to open the hatch, close it again, and repressurize …" He shook his head. "I would not wish to do this."

"Would not wish …? Jesus Christ, Nikolai, what are you saying? Blow the doors, jump in and repressurize? Put her through an explo-sive decompression? No way. Surely that would kill her."

"Perhaps," Nikolai said, and when Vivian gestured at him, furious, amended it to, "Very probably."

"I'm thinking 'Certainly'," Vivian said. "I've seen the *2001* movie and I don't buy it for a second. We open the hatch, all the water on the surface of her body sublimes away instantly. The pressure change likely blows out her eyeballs. As for her lungs and heart …. Hell, I'm not a doctor, I don't exactly know *what* would happen, but that's a biology experiment we are *not* going to try."

Makarov continued to stare through the Purgan window. "Then, what?"

"Right now there's only one sane thing we *can* do."

"Which is?"

"Just take it all and get going. The whole Purgan. Winch it up onto the flatbed and head out. At least put some miles under our tracks, heading back toward the LEK. Worst case, she stays put in there till we get back to Marius. Then we shove the Purgan into a Brick, seal and pressurize it, and *then* we open the goddamned door."

"That would be too many days, ten days travel time at best, I think? She cannot survive in there so long, if she remains unconscious. And all the time she is hurt, with may have other injuries that we do not yet know about."

"Right." Vivian wasn't thinking straight. Belyakova would die of thirst and hunger long before they got to Marius. They simply had no other resources to draw on, this far north. Plus, the CO_2 level in the Purgan would rise high enough to kill her, if she wasn't monitoring her air mix and regularly replacing her lithium hydroxide air scrubber. This truck was too small for anything more sophisticated in the way of air handling.

Vivian found herself rubbing her helmet as if it was her skull. "Well. First things first. Phase A accomplished. We've got what we came for, but we still can't hang around. Let's go. I'm sure she'll regain consciousness eventually. And if she doesn't come out of it in a few hours … well, let's keep thinking. For all we know she'll wake up in ten minutes and shimmy into her goddamned suit, right? And we should be bringing the Purgan along with us in any case, for whatever supplies it still has in it." *And the machine gun,* Vivian thought, but didn't say aloud. "We're obviously not leaving it behind, so let's shift our crap around to make space and get it winched aboard. *Now,* Nikolai."

With some reluctance, Makarov tore himself away from the Purgan window. "Very well. I will go and prepare the winch."

"Okay, man. I've got a Plan B. But you're not going to be thrilled with it."

Vivian heard Makarov yawn as he looked around at her. Yes, they'd been awake a long time, yet again.

The Purgan was now resting on the low flatbed. Over the past two hours they'd managed to winch it over the lip of the crater, and up and aboard the transport, without shaking it around too much. Svetlana was still lying comatose on the floor, and in her heart of hearts Vivian knew they couldn't just set off and hope for the best, with the unconscious cosmonaut being bounced and bumped and banged around as they drove. They *had* to get in there.

Which was why Vivian was—yet again—considering a half-assed, jury-rigged, slightly crazy plan.

"So, the inflatable habitat from the Lunokhod …"

"Is nowhere near big enough," Makarov said. "I have already thought of this."

"Wait, hear me out. Not big enough to get the whole Purgan in, but maybe we can duct tape the entrance snug around the Purgan hatch."

He looked at her as if she was insane. "Duct tape?"

"I know, I know. It sounds ridiculous. But put enough of it on, and it's actually good stuff. At least, for a few seconds. Here's the plan: I get into the hab with an oxygen canister, some water, and a medical kit. We tape me in there. You inflate the hab, I pressurize it internally, then I open the Purgan door and leap in. We'll likely get a bit of a pop as the pressures equalize, who knows what Svetlana's got the interior set to, but at least it shouldn't do her any serious additional damage or throw everything around. If the duct tape doesn't hold and I can't establish a stable pressure, I don't open the hatch. If it does, I'm through it and closing the hatch again, quick as a bunny. Then I see to Svetlana."

Makarov thought about it for much longer than Vivian was expecting. Maybe that was good? He might think of some gotcha that Vivian wouldn't.

Eventually, he said: "All right. We will try it. But I will be the one to go in."

"No."

"Vivian. She is my crew. And my friend."

"Yes, I know. And I'd feel the same if it was one of my people. But just this once, I'm going to play the gender card on you. Svetlana wouldn't want you to see her like this, like she must be, in there right now. Trust me. Let me go in there and fix her up. I cross-trained in medical stuff for Venus Astarte, so I have some decent first-aid chops. And then I'll help clean and tidy her up and bring her out when I can. Okay?"

Again, Makarov turned it over in his mind, blinking and not speaking. Vivian reminded herself that he was exhausted, in addition to being distraught about Belyakova's condition. It was hardly surprising if logical thought was coming slowly to him.

"Very well," he said. "We will try as you suggest."

For once, duct tape failed them, so they threw caution to the winds and used an epoxy from the Lunokhod toolkit. God only knew whether the hab would ever function again after being glued to a beat-up Purgan and then, presumably cut or ripped off it again afterward, but they were out of options.

So, they carefully glued Vivian in and waited for what seemed like an interminable amount of time for the epoxy to cure. Even while Nikolai was still inflating the hab walls, Vivian began pressurizing the inside, watching the internal pressure gauge carefully. It would be just their luck if they'd compromised the hab's integrity with all this jury-rigging.

They had not. She took the pressure up to four PSI and moved up to the back door of the Purgan.

Belyakova had not moved throughout this entire operation. She'd slid across the floor a little way while the Purgan was being winched onto the flatbed, but was still lying there in that same position, crumpled in the corner with her blood smeared across the floor.

It would be the ultimate irony if Belyakova was dead, if the shock of discovery had killed her, or the accidental fall while preparing to defend herself. Vivian tried not to think about that.

The hatch mechanism looked simple and at least the door opened inward. When pressurized, the internal pressure would form a seal and prevent it from being opened by accident, which was clearly a good thing.

Vivian cranked at the hatch, but it wouldn't budge. *Great.* She futzed with it a few minutes more before realizing it must be a pressure problem and nudged the pressure in the hab to five PSI.

That did it. The hatch opened smoothly and swung inward.

Svetlana lay there unmoving, her dirty hair covering her face, but to Vivian's relief, she could now see that the cosmonaut's chest was rising and falling.

Vivian took her own deep breath and shoved her helmet and shoulders into the Purgan.

"Well?" came Nikolai's anxious voice through her headset.

"Hold your horses, I only just got in. Svetlana is breathing, but still not moving. Let me figure this place out and then I'll get all the way in and check her out properly. I don't want to bang into something I shouldn't and create a crisis."

"Create?"

"Make things even freaking worse, is what I'm saying."

For a small space, the Purgan's interior was very efficiently packed. Vivian was surrounded by racks of food, racks of oxygen bottles, racks of water, plus various other tools and stuff packed together. It was neater and more logically arranged than it had appeared from the outside. There were two seats in the front of the Purgan, one of which Belyakova had folded up to make more space, and this was the area that showed the greatest disarray, stacked high with food trays, some of them open. The other seat, which had the steering wheel in front of it, Belyakova had reclined back as far as it would go without hitting what must be the environmental control system unit. That was clearly where she'd been sleeping.

At the rear of the Purgan, above Vivian's head in a ceiling-rack, were two Uzis with folding stocks, identical to the gun Katya had used at the South Pole years ago. Next to those was a longer-tubed weapon, most likely some kind of rocket launcher, and a sturdy case that presumably contained a couple of explosive rockets to go with it. Two handguns with extended trigger guards to allow for a spacesuited glove, and a rack of ammo lay near the floor.

For a lunar roving vehicle, the instrument boards around the cab section appeared no more complex than the dashboard in an average car on Earth. Mounted up high on the left was a rudimentary comms board, plus a temperature panel and pressure gauge. There was a tiny sink with two spigots, presumably for hot and cold water, with a small pull-out commode in a cupboard beneath it.

Somewhere there had to be an RTG to provide power for this clunky vehicle, in addition to the adjustable-angle solar panels on the roof. That radioisotope thermoelectric generator would have to be on the other side of what Vivian had to hope was a sufficient amount of shielding. Perhaps outside, underneath the chassis? But that would be an insane place to put it, given the chances of the Purgan bottoming as it went over a crater rim, or smacking into a rock or boulder. Perhaps on the roof, under the solar panels?

"I can't decide whether to be impressed or horrified," she said.

"Why? What is happening?"

"I mean the truck itself, the Purgan. It's …" Vivian shook her head. "Shit. It's well organized, but … this is no way to live."

Mainly, Vivian was amazed that Belyakova had scraped together an existence for so many months in such cramped and limiting conditions.

"That is the strength of Soviet technology," Makarov said. "It is often not beautiful, but it is sturdy and built to last."

"Okay, then," Vivian said.

She pulled herself in a little further, then tried to get up onto her knees and banged her helmet against the ceiling. "Crap."

"What is it?"

"It's a real squeeze in here. I'll need to take my helmet and gloves off before I can do anything for her. I'm guessing that when there are two prospectors in here, one must stay up-front while the other wriggles around and suits up, then they'd have to trade places, and God even knows how they do that. But right now I don't want to move Svetlana until I can check her vitals and make sure she doesn't have any bones broken and all, and the way she's lying, she's exactly in the way. Once I've convinced myself she's okay I'll try to shift her into the front seat so I can get the rest of my suit off. But … first things first, I need to close the hatch. Hang tight."

She pulled herself all the way in and twisted herself around as best she could, the stiffness of her suit fighting her all the way, then got her glove to the hatch and closed it. "Okay. Hmm." It was nothing like an Apollo or Skylab hatch, and not very much like a Soyuz hatch either. She had to poke at it a bit longer before she felt the vibration as it latched and earned her a pair of green lights above it on the ceiling. "Okay, I've got two greens. I'm hoping that's two thumbs up."

"Why two?" Nikolai said.

"You're asking me? Damned if I know."

She braced herself. Even with the sight of Svetlana breathing more or less evenly, it still took a bit of nerve to take her helmet off.

"Well, here goes nothing."

426

As her helmet came off, a wave of stale and putrid air flooded in. Vivian's first, irrational thought was that despite what she'd seen, Belyakova must have been dead for weeks. She gagged, swallowed, and then wrestled down her feelings of nausea.

It did not smell good inside in Svetlana's Purgan. It reeked of Belyakova's sweat, and it was damp, with the sweet stenches of rot and decaying food, and underlying all that were the unmistakable bass notes of badly sealed waste containers. After several lunar missions and two years aboard Apollo Astarte, Vivian had no difficulty isolating the various subtle flavors: traces of vomit, as well as urine and feces. *Dang, girlfriend.*

… But, at least you're alive. And it's a miracle that you are.

If that wasn't bad enough there was a strong smell of burning, like gunpowder, which was moondust. Some surfaces inside the Purgan had been wiped clean. Others showed a telltale layer of dust, and every joint and crevice looked gritty.

All the Apollo Lunar Modules and bases had small electric vacuum cleaners to suck up the dust. Belyakova had one too, easy to spot in the equipment rack, but it was just as easy to see that its casing was cracked. Maybe it was non-functional. Vivian was guessing that Belyakova had done her best to sweep up and bag the dust by hand, but it had been a losing battle.

"So far so good. Okay, Nikolai? I'm going to have to get out of this suit."

She double-checked the hatch and stared at its two green lights for maybe longer than she really needed to. Checked the pressure, looked at the CO_2 numbers on the environmental unit, and figured out how to pump more air into the Purgan if she needed to.

Hey, this thing's kept Svetlana alive for months, right? It's not going to suddenly break just because I'm inside of it. Right?

Unless I screw something up, of course. And what are the odds of that?

Still, taking off her suit was even more nerve-wracking than stripping down inside the transport crew cabin had been, the first time. Once again, Vivian was trusting Soviet technology with her life.

Svetlana remained unconscious, her breathing light, her pulse strong but irregular. In addition to an egg-sized lump on the back of her head and the cut on her temple that was leaking blood everywhere, it looked like she had blood in her mouth. *That* wasn't great.

"Well?" Nikolai's voice sounded anxious in Vivian's headset. Not too surprising. "How is she?"

"Alive. Probable concussion. Her arms and legs look fine, nothing broken. She has some sores and abrasions. They don't look like disease, at least I hope not. She's just more banged up than I would have supposed." By now, Vivian had prised Svetlana's jaw open. "No obstructions in her airway. There's blood around her teeth, but it doesn't look like she's bitten her tongue … oh, wait, I know what this is. Guess what?

Our girl's got scurvy."

"What is scurvy?" If anything, Makarov sounded even more anxious now.

"Relax, it's the least of her worries. Vitamin C deficiency, easiest thing in the world to fix. Our MREs include vitamin supplements, she can be over this in days once we feed her properly. She must have just been unlucky with the food selection she grabbed. Nikolai, you might just as well connect up the cables and finish lashing this thing onto the flatbed."

"But, Svetlana?"

"Is as comfortable as she can be. I'll get her into her seat and strap her into it before we start moving. And I'll also strap myself in. Should be fine."

"I would prefer to not take off the sheath at the back, only to put it back on later."

"The sheath? Oh, the inflatable. No, okay. If we can get the Purgan locked in without ripping that off, it would be better. I'll just stay in here for the time being."

Svetlana was a larger woman than Vivian, and the interior of the vehicle was cramped, so even in the lighter lunar gravity it was no mean feat to lift the cosmonaut up and arrange her in her seat. After that, Vivian located a tin of germicidal wipes and began to loosen the cosmonaut's clothing to start cleaning her up.

And that was, of course, the moment when Svetlana Belyakova regained consciousness, panicked, and began to fight her.

"Svetlana, Svetlana … *Eto ya, Vivian Carter! Ya—drug!*" *It's me, I'm a friend!*

If anything, the sound of spoken Russian made Svetlana even more agitated. Vivian switched to English. "Svetlana, take it easy, calm down. Everything is all right now. *Uspokoisa, vse v poryadke." Take it easy, calm down.*

Svetlana stared up at her in consternation, the whites of her eyes appearing to glow an uncanny, evil red, blinking furiously and still trying to push her away, but Vivian could feel the woman's weakness. She was used to the svelte, buff Svetlana. It was a shock to realize that now she could hold the cosmonaut down with one hand.

Then, finally, Svetlana managed to focus on Vivian's face and, to Vivian's surprise and embarrassment, broke down sobbing. Quickly running out of breath, Svetlana then had to heave in some ragged breaths that rattled in her throat before she could sob some more.

Vivian just held the cosmonaut while she cried. She really had no idea what else to do.

Eventually Belyakova stopped, wiped those terrible red eyes that were now even redder, and looked up at her. "Vivian Carter. What … are you doing here?"

Belyakova was injured in a dozen minor ways. Her face was puffy, and she had cuts and scratches and bruises all over her body, plus the red eyes, scratchy and irritated, from vein breakage. Just looking into them made Vivian's own eyes water in sympathy. But it could have been a whole lot worse.

"The air went out of the vehicle. Too much, too fast. Not just like a loss in pressure, but … a fleeing, a robbery." Svetlana paused, blinked. "I saw the hole in the back of the Kharkovchanka. I stared at it just a few seconds. I knew what was about to happen, and I was already moving, but, but …"

Svetlana took another deep, ragged breath and then said quietly. "The Moon came for me then, Vivian. It was empty, and choking, and dark."

Vivian shivered involuntarily, and to her surprise Svetlana reached out and took her hand, still staring ahead unblinking with those eerie red eyes. "I'm sorry," Vivian said, knowing that words could never be adequate.

"Often, I wondered what it would be like to feel the vacuum. But it was worse than I had imagined, so much worse. Before, I was always protected. I always had myself, and my suit, and people around to keep me safe from it. Until I did not."

Vivian squeezed Svetlana's hand.

"It is hard for me to find the words that are correct. But, Vivian, I felt it go. The air, and my life. Not just on my skin, but in my heart. You will think this is stupid, that I am crazy, but the Moon did not just injure me, then. It took something away from me, something I … needed. Something of value. And I do not just mean my breath."

Vivian just nodded.

"I knew my eyes were bleeding. I could see very little. I could not breathe, but remembered to blow out, squeeze my lungs clear and not try to hold my breath. I suppose my arms took over, and my legs, because I do not remember putting my suit on, there is a black gap in my mind right there, but when I next remember, I was inside it with the helmet sealed, and the pressure was coming up."

"Muscle memory."

"I was just in time to save myself. But the damage was done. Some of the pain went away, and some of the other pain became much worse. I … cannot explain it well."

Belyakova turned to focus on Vivian and looked her in the eyes for a few seconds, unblinking. Vivian squeezed her hand again. Svetlana glanced down, startled, and pushed Vivian's hand away as if it were Vivian who had instigated the contact.

But then she looked back into Vivian's face, studying her features as if searching for something. "You love the Moon, Vivian, but it is not our friend. It does not love us in return. It never has."

"I know." Vivian still felt chilled and desperately wanted to reach for Svetlana's hand again, to comfort the cosmonaut any way she could, but knew better than to try. "I'm glad you made it. I'm happy you're alive."

"Are you? Are you glad you came to find … this?" Belyakova gestured at herself.

"It's really not that bad. Once you get proper medical health …"

"You should have stayed with your ship."

"Maybe. But I'm glad I didn't. I needed to come."

Belyakova's eyes were bleak. "You should not be. We cannot escape this. They will come for us. I am sure that they are coming, even now. And they will not stop until we are dead."

That's not how we think, Vivian thought automatically. Out loud she said, "I don't believe that, Svetlana. We can do this."

"Hmm." Svetlana looked away, then, out of the window and across the Moon's bleak regolith.

It took a good forty-five minutes and a quarter box of germicidal wipes to clean Svetlana up to Vivian's satisfaction. It had been a long time since the cosmonaut had paid much attention to personal hygiene. Belyakova cooperated calmly, at the same time pragmatic and distant. Vivian then took a further twenty minutes to tidy up the inside of the Purgan, asking Svetlana questions about where to store things. Svetlana answered simply, using no more words than she had to and often merely gesturing. After recovering from her emotional outburst she appeared to have retreated deep into herself again. Perhaps her rescue didn't feel real to her yet, or she was still processing the fact that she'd been found, that she was no longer alone. Yet she was functional, her pulse and breathing seemed nominal, and she was not sweating unduly or showing signs of confusion or distress.

Vivian was worried about her but couldn't think what else she could do. Best for everyone was to get themselves back on the road.

She managed to get Belyakova back into her suit, and sealed up, and got back into her own suit, a slow and painful process in the close confines of the vehicle. She checked her own seals half a dozen times and checked Belyakova's even more. She felt shaken, as if she couldn't quite trust her own eyes and hands any more. More than anything, she did not want the darkness that Svetlana had spoken of so chillingly to come for either of them.

She depressurized the Purgan slowly and neither of their suits sprung a leak, so—again slowly and carefully—she cut them free from the habitat and guided Belyakova out, manhandled her up the ladder to the flatbed airlock, and into the Soviet transport.

"Svetlana." Makarov walked forward, arms outstretched. "I am so glad that you are alive."

"Fool!" With no warning, Belyakova launched herself at him. Vivian flinched away as she pounded on Makarov's chest with her fists, shouting at him in Russian. "Why, Nikolai? Why did you have to come? Why throw your life away for me?"

He seized her wrists, but gently, and held her away from him. If Vivian could easily subdue Belyakova in her weakened condition, Makarov had even less difficulty. "Dear Svetlana. I had to, of course. I had no choice."

"You should be at Mars! You did not have to give that up, not for me!"

"I have been to Mars," he said simply. "I have already gone, and walked on Deimos, and returned. Please sit here with me, do not tire yourself further."

Svetlana looked confused. "Already? Can it be?"

"I assure you." He smiled at her. "We can count the months later."

"But, Nikolai, Nikolai …" Belyakova slumped. "We did not both have to die."

"And perhaps we will not."

"Always hopeful, Nikolai. Always so foolishly cheerful." She shook her head. "But not this time. They will not let us live. They will find us, and they will kill us."

"Perhaps. And perhaps not."

Vivian cleared her throat. "I don't mean to intrude …"

"Then, do not." Belyakova did not even look at her.

Vivian looked at Makarov instead. "But we should get going."

He nodded. "You will take the first driving shift, perhaps?"

"Sure. If you want to stay here with Svetlana, that's fine. Let me just grab some food to take up to the cab with me."

Belyakova was quietly sobbing again, her face pushed into Makarov's chest. He was stroking her hair, rocking her gently.

Vivian swallowed. "Okay, then. Guess I'll leave you to it."

He nodded.

Impulsively, Vivian reached out to squeeze Svetlana's shoulder. "Hang in there, sweetie." She hadn't even known those words would come out until they were spoken. And this time Belyakova did not push her away, but merely placed her hand on top of Vivian's for a few seconds.

"Look after her," Vivian said, superfluously, and headed out along the tunnel to the cab, closing the hatch behind her.

Six hours later, Vivian pulled the transport to a halt and went back down into the crew quarters to use the head and make sure everything was okay.

Makarov and Belyakova had fallen asleep just like that, just like she'd last seen them. Fully dressed and curled up in each other's arms.

Wow. That was some serious lump-in-throat time. Vivian Carter was definitely a third wheel in this crew. But rather than sadness or self-pity or any real jealousy, she felt calm and comfortable.

At least I got one human thing right in my life.

They set off again, Nikolai now driving, leaving Svetlana and Vivian back in the crew space. For a while, the two women sat in silence as the rig bumped and zigzagged back and forth, as Nikolai did his best to avoid rocks and steer around craters. There was no such thing as a straight line on the Moon.

"From here we must go all the way to the Marius Hills?" Svetlana paused, and passed her hands over her eyes again, in what seemed to Vivian to be a new and disturbingly compulsive gesture. Even speaking seemed to put an intolerable stress on her.

"I wish I was joking," Vivian said. "But that's where we landed Nikolai's LEK, so that's where we need to go. The only other way off this rock are the landers at Daedalus or Jura, and we obviously can't go to either."

At the look on Belyakova's face, Vivian added gently: "Sorry. I guess there are no easy answers, not for us, not out here, not ever. But at least you'll have company along this time. And there's an end in sight. Soon, we can all go home."

"Huh." Svetlana rested her head back, already worn out by the exchange.

"You don't want to go home?"

Svetlana opened one red eye and gave Vivian a long look. "You suppose that the KGB will just let me fly home? That will never happen. Even if we complete the journey to Marius and launch off the surface, I will be dead before we can leave lunar orbit. I am quite certain."

Well, Vivian thought. *I sure hope you're wrong, because that means Nikolai and I will be dead as well.*

"They'll have to find us first," she said. "And we've seen no sign of anyone since we arrived."

"Unless they let you land, in the hope that you would lead them to me. That is possible, no?"

"Well … yes. That's possible." Which would suck, because if so, their Soviet pursuers would likely have disabled or destroyed Makarov's LEK Lander.

Svetlana reached out, and to Vivian's surprise, took her hand and clasped it. Quite tightly. "And yet: thank you for coming to find me. I am sure you did it for Nikolai, not me, but I thank you anyway. Risking your life in such a way …" She smiled wanly. "As you Americans say: 'I did not see that coming.'"

Vivian squeezed back. "But hey, guess what? I *did* do it for you, and no one else. And five years ago I could never have seen that coming, either."

"And so, here we are again. Just the three of us."

"Just the three of us. What?"

Belyakova was staring at her now, a frown on her face.

"Svetlana? Are you all right?"

The cosmonaut blinked. "I was just thinking."

"Okay. A ruble for your thoughts?"

The cosmonaut seemed to come to a decision. "In case we are killed in an hour, or in a day, there are some things that you should know. Things that, really, I should never tell you. And yet, I think I must." She sighed in frustration, perhaps at herself, and shook her head.

"Um. Am I going to like them?"

"No. I do not think so."

"Then … with all due respect, maybe don't tell me? Maybe it's not necessary. Maybe you and I are okay just the way we are. Perhaps not every secret has to be aired."

"Vivian, please be quiet. This is already difficult."

Nonplussed, Vivian nodded. "Well. Okay."

"Casey Buchanan … died at Soviet hands. His death was not natural. He was murdered by a man called Keretsky, who was my zampolit, sent to spy on me and the rest of the Soviet crew at Zvezda and ensure we behaved correctly."

The breath caught in Vivian's throat. "If this Keretsky … killed Casey, perhaps his idea of what's correct is a little wonky."

"Casey was killed with a ricin pellet. A fast-acting biological warfare pellet. The US commander of Copernicus, Grant, knows this. It was kept from the others." Belyakova turned her gaze upon Vivian. "One of the men I killed to escape was Keretsky, and because of what he did to Casey Buchanan, and some other reasons, I enjoyed doing it. I enjoyed it a great deal."

"Okay," Vivian said again.

"Also, one reason why I prevented Keretsky and Orlov from destroying the Night Corps bricks with a nuclear weapon was because … because your Peter Sandoval might have been aboard, or your Terri Brock. Were they?"

"I have no idea. Night Corps don't keep me in the loop on their deployments, and neither Peter nor Terri would ever tell me."

"And, the last? The last is that I was wrong." Belyakova paused and corrected herself. "Perhaps I was not wrong, exactly, but I was misinformed. I was lied to. The cryptonauts at the Marius base were indeed Soviet. They were not from the People's Republic of China. You were right in this. I was lied to, and I trusted my superiors, and so I told you this."

Vivian breathed deep. "Thank you. At last. I mean, at last I know for sure."

"They lied to me," Belyakova repeated.

"Yes, I get it."

"I am too trusting," Belyakova said. "It is my most serious weakness."

Svetlana said this with her face utterly composed, and Vivian had no idea whether she was being serious.

"The useful fool," she added. "That is the phrase. The useful fool."

After a pause, Vivian said: "You're going to hate me for saying this, maybe. But I think I'm glad it was the Soviets all along. We don't need two enemies on the Moon."

Then she stopped, but Belyakova grunted and completed her thought. "Because one is quite enough?"

"Something like that," Vivian said. "Sorry. So. Anyway. Do you want dinner?"

31

Daedalus Base: Katya Okhotina
May 14, 1985

"**INCOMING.**" Mila Balkina turned away from her console in the Daedalus control center, to make sure Doryagin and Okhotina were paying attention. "Do you hear me? We have a radar signal."

Doryagin was by her side in a moment. "How many? How far?"

"Three. Approaching slowly, and already low."

Doryagin turned to Okhotina. "Red alert. Bring the air defenses online. Power up the explosives along the Driver."

Ever since returning to Earth after LGS-1, Katya Okhotina had wanted to come back to the Moon. When she'd been offered the Daedalus posting, she had gratefully accepted it.

By now, she wished she had never received the assignment. The six months she'd spent trapped in the base doing the bidding of the new commander, Doryagin, and his even more obnoxious deputy, Mila Balkina, felt more like five years.

And now? All of a sudden, she might be about to find herself at ground zero of a shooting war again. And one of her first tasks might be to blow up the mass driver, so that it would not fall back into American hands. That would be a great shame.

Okhotina pulled on a headset, twisted the microphone up under her mouth, turned a knob on her communications panel to the

436

internal Soviet loop, and began to give the orders. As she did so, the loudspeakers in the control room crackled on the general Daedalus main frequency.

"Daedalus Base, this is U.N. Moon 1. We trust you have been notified of our imminent arrival—"

It was a voice Katya would recognize anywhere. She muted her comms. "That is Colonel Peter Sandoval, of the United States Night Corps."

Sandoval continued. "We will be landing to deploy, roughly fifteen minutes from now, putting down in the open area two hundred yards east of the admin buildings, on the side opposite Bright Driver. We have a Brick, plus three Lunar Modules. We request unimpeded access, and look forward to making your acquaintance."

Doryagin pressed his own button. "Nyet. Permission denied. This is Soviet territory, and you will stand away. Approach within missile range and you will be immediately destroyed."

"U.N. Moon?" Okhotina said, frowning.

Balkina waved her down. "Be quiet."

Sandoval's voice resumed. "That would be most unwise. This is a United Nations Peacekeeping force. As you must know by now, United Nations Security Council Resolution 571 was passed two weeks ago, and—"

"I know nothing of such a resolution," Doryagin said. "And you have been identified as a Night Corps operation." He turned to Okhotina. "It is Sandoval, you are sure?"

"Sandoval is Night Corps," Katya said. "Of that, at least, I am certain."

Doryagin had left the mic live. From the loudspeaker, Sandoval confirmed. "Yes. I and my colleague, Colonel Brock, have been reassigned from Night Corps, and today we are serving as technical leads for this multinational force ..." He paused. "You mean to say you haven't heard about this? You should have been informed at least ten days ago."

"He lies," Balkina said.

Again, the mics were still hot. Sandoval had heard that. "It's the truth. Uh, in that case, we'll send the text of the U.N. Resolution to the teleprinter there immediately. I advise you to contact your Mission Control center for confirmation."

Moments later the printer initialized and began to clatter. Sandoval continued. "To repeat: Colonel Brock and I are here leading a twenty-person United Nations peacekeeping force. Colonel Brock was, of course, the first American woman on the Moon, and a pilot of considerable talents, and we were selected for this mission partly due to her status as a high-visibility lunar explorer. Just as important, and as you may be aware, Night Corps is the only US organization that has the technology to land such a large number of people on the Moon, all at once. NASA has nothing like the Bricks, and doesn't have ten spare Lunar Modules just lying around waiting to be pressed into service.

"With us, we have military members from various European, African, and Asian countries, none of whom expected to be astronauts a couple months ago. You're welcome to speak with any of them."

"Are any Soviets?" Doryagin demanded, drily.

"No. The Soviet Union did sign the U.N. Resolution, but It was judged that perhaps you had enough Soviet boots on the ground at Daedalus. We do have one representative from the People's Republic of China, along with one from France, and one from the United Kingdom. Thus, once we land, every one of the permanent members of the United States Security Council will have their representatives on the Moon. We also have a member each from Madagascar, Ghana, the Congo, India, Japan, the United Arab Emirates, Canada, Trinidad and Tobago, Peru, Australia, Italy, Belgium, Thailand, Poland, and Yugoslavia." Another pause, and then Katya heard Sandoval say more quietly. "Did I miss anyone?"

"No," came a woman's voice from the background. "That's the lot."

"That is indeed Terri Brock, accompanying Sandoval," Okhotina confirmed.

Peter continued. "Plus, we have four other NASA astronauts, not Night Corps, not even US Air Force, in a supporting technical role. Given that everyone else aboard the Brick is a rookie." Sandoval cleared his throat. "Meaning no offense to them, of course."

"The Kremlin is setting them up," Brock said quietly. "Hoping they'll fire on us."

Katya muted their microphones and looked over at Doryagin and Balkina. "She may be right. We cannot discount that possibility."

"Be silent."

"Once we disembark you will see that the Peacekeepers all wear the blue United Nations patch in addition to the insignias and colors of their helmets that indicate their countries of origin. Otherwise, they will be wearing standard NASA American Apollo suits. None of the initial squad will be armed or armored. That said, you're reminded that by international law, UN Peacekeepers are permitted to use lethal force in their own defense, and in defense of civilians facing imminent threat."

Now it was Mila Balkina's turn to lean in and mute their microphones. "Night Corps tries to bamboozle us with words."

Doryagin nodded. "An American trick, to make us lay down our arms."

"I do not think so." Okhotina dropped her headset, stood and crossed the room to stand on Doryagin's other side.

Balkina eyed her. "Did we ask you? Return to your post." She pressed buttons on her console. Lights turned orange, and then red. To Doryagin, Balkina said: "Weapons systems armed. Alert the front line."

"Please." Okhotina also leaned forward, across the board. "Let me speak to Sandoval. For just one moment."

Balkina stared past Doryagin at her. "And, why? You believe them? You are taken in?"

"Thirty seconds, Comrade. That is all I ask. I know the Americans well, and I also know their tricks of old. My eyes are clear. But let us just be sure. And then you will proceed however you think appropriate."

Doryagin stared at her. Then he gestured at the button, and stood upright, despite Balkina's snort of disapproval.

Okhotina pressed-to-talk. "Peter Sandoval? My name is Katya Okhotina. Perhaps you recall me from Salyut-Lunik-A, many years ago."

"Katya? Hi. Hello, of course I remember you. Good to hear your voice."

Okhotina winced inside. Sandoval's friendly tone was doing her no favors. "Colonel Sandoval. Please understand that we have heard nothing of such a resolution, and we cannot quickly confirm your words; it will take us time to patch through to our comrades at Mission Control Moscow via our orbiting assets. And so: you need to promise me that this is true. That you are truly a United Nations force. You will need to persuade me, as well as my superiors, that this is no trick."

"Of course it's not a trick. You'll see the UN logos on the three LMs as we approach. We will not overfly Daedalus. We will land peacefully, just as stated. Three people—myself and two representatives from any of the United Nations force that I've mentioned—will come across in the first instance, unarmed, to present our bona fides."

Okhotina swallowed. "Insufficient. We are far from Earth, and un-observed. Paint is just paint. Sandoval, we do not have much time. If what you say is true, you must swear it."

"Of course I—"

"Swear it to me, now, by Vivian Carter."

"By ... for goodness sake, Katya."

"Just do it. Or stand away, and do not attempt to land here at Daedalus Base."

In the LM, Sandoval looked at Terri. "What the hell?"

"Well?" Terri gestured. "Get on with it."

Sandoval pushed-to-talk. "Katya, no bullshit. The UN Res-olution is real. This Peacekeeping force is the genuine article. I swear it by my ..." He closed his eyes. "Respect and admiration for Vivian Carter."

"Oooh," Terri murmured. "Touching. And on open loop as well."

"Can it," he said, off-mic. "Just once, okay?"

"Sorry." She touched his arm. "Wilco."

Mila snorted. "Of what value is that? What man does not lie about women?"

Katya tried to keep her voice steady. "Colonel Sandoval speaks the truth. These are Peacekeepers. We must let them in. The consequences of firing upon them would be grave."

"Nonsense," Doryagin said, but Okhotina could see that he was wavering.

"We would know," Mila insisted. "If it were true, we would have been briefed. We have communicated daily with the Rodina, and no one has spoken of this. It is a lie. A ruse."

"It is not," Katya said.

"Because you say so?"

"No. Because *he* said so."

"Step away. You talk nonsense." Doryagin pushed-to-talk. "Night Corps, disengage. Do not approach, or we will ..." His voice trailed away.

Katya Okhotina had indeed stepped back. And was now pointing a pistol at his head.

"Where did you get that?"

"Is that your most pressing question? Move away from the console. Over there, both of you."

"She is mad," Mila said to Doryagin. "Working with the Americans has made her mad. But I believe she will not shoot you."

Okhotina did not blink. "Perhaps working with the two of you has made me a little unbalanced. But this is the correct answer, Comrades. They are United Nations. Firing upon them would be a grave error."

"If they speak the truth."

"They do."

"You are sure?"

"It seems that I have risked my life upon it."

The seconds drew out. Eventually, Okhotina said: "The Peacekeepers are still awaiting your response."

"You." Mila pointed a stark finger at her. "You are finished. You are gone. A non-person. In the gulag, if you even live through today—"

Okhotina swung her pistol to cover her. "Please. Do not talk to me. Merely give the order to allow the Peacekeepers to enter Daedalus Base. After that? If I am wrong, I will hand you my gun, and you will do whatever you will do."

Doryagin shook his head. "Who is Vivian Carter, anyway?"

"Stand our troops down. Allow Sandoval's craft to land, and the US Brick."

Balkina began to move, and Katya lowered her gun to point it at the other woman's chest. A bigger target, if the woman were to leap at her. "Stop. Understand that I will have time to kill you as well as our Commander, if you attempt to disarm me. I have been well trained."

Balkina regarded her bleakly, then turned to the microphone and gave the orders to stand down.

"Very good. Now, lie down, both of you. Faces to the floor."

Even as Balkina knelt, she said: "Whatever the outcome today, you have thrown away your life. Understand this."

"We shall see." Circling the room well clear of her superiors' hands and feet, both hands on her pistol to steady it, Okhotina arrived at the communications console and pushed to talk. "Colonel Sandoval, please bring your ships in to land." She looked back and forth between

Balkina and Doryagin, and up at the door of the control room. "And please do so with all haste."

Ten minutes later the Brick landed, with its now-usual drama. Its walls did not blow outward, revealing troops. Nothing happened at all. The United Nations logo stared at them, across three hundred yards of the lunar surface.

Then the door opened slowly, and astronauts began to walk out. None carried obvious weapons, though some ported long boxes that might have contained rifles. Katya was not fooled by this; she was sure that larger weapons must be trained upon the admin building from within the Brick. What was the use of a Peacekeeping force with insufficient force to keep the peace?

Quietly, Okhotina breathed a sigh of relief.

"What do you see?" Doryagin demanded.

"Soldiers, walking. Their helmets all colored differently, but … yes, I see the United Nations symbol on their suits, all of them. Our soldiers are now walking out to greet them. Some are waving. Oh, and now the Lunar Modules are approaching, coming down from the sky. They will land within minutes."

With a loudspeaker crackle, they heard Sandoval's voice again. "Thank you, Daedalus crew. Thank you, Katya. See you in a moment. If we don't wreck this crate on the way down."

"Maybe start reading me numbers?" came Brock's impatient murmur in the background, and now Katya Okhotina smiled.

CHAPTER 32

Lunar Surface: Vivian Carter
June 5, 1985

"SORRY, goddamn it," Vivian said, as the transport lurched down into an unexpected trench and then reared up vertiginously to roll out of its other side. "Didn't see that coming. I hate Frigoris."

"I, also," Belyakova responded calmly. The cosmonaut was so far out in front that Vivian couldn't even see her, but her VHF signal had been relayed down from the makeshift radio mast they had installed above the cab the day before yesterday. Their passage across Mare Frigoris was sufficiently arduous that the only safe way to proceed was to send out a scout ahead of them to determine the best route, and break radio silence.

Most of the lunar seas were relatively benign, vast plains of dark iron-rich basalt, formed by the lava that had filled the Moon's ancient impact basins between three and four billion years ago. Generally, the seas were easier to traverse than the lunar highland regions, with fewer ridges and craters and rilles to contend with.

Not so Mare Frigoris, the Sea of Cold, the Moon's northernmost sea, an elongated sprawling mare situated at around sixty degrees north, running along the top of the Imbrium and Serenitatis Basins. Frigoris was *messy*. Churned up by ancient tectonic cracking and shifting, it was covered by thousands of features. Wrinkle ridges wormed across the surface, a hundred or more miles long and up to a thousand feet high, some of which were only tens of millions of years old. Lobate scarps due to thrust faults, one side steep and the other gently sloping, much smaller, but still a couple of hundred feet high and only a few miles long. But worse than either of these were the clusters of grabens that lined the area: small rilles with steep sides and flat floors, ranging in width and depth from a few dozen feet to a couple of hundred.

Those were the large-scale features. Then, as if the Moon operated on a fractal scale, there were smaller analogs of these formations: baby ridges and rises and undulations, with treacherous cracks in between. All of this, of course, much too small to show up on their single-sheet whole-Moon map.

On LGS-1 heading north, Carter's Convoy had crossed Frigoris at one of its narrowest points, coming off the Montes Jura highlands near Harpalus Crater and heading into the polar highlands as speedily as possible. Just that short traverse had been quite enough. On their westerly trek from Marius to Mare Moscoviense, Vivian and Nikolai hadn't needed to go anywhere near Frigoris. But now, coming south from the Pole, they'd had to skirt the whole Jura region and the northern reaches of Oceanus Procellarum, which gave them only one realistic choice: navigate the shoals of Frigoris, duck into Mare Imbrium, and head across it in a south-south-west line to curve back to Marius.

Frigoris was less than a hundred miles across, but navigating it was a bear. It was safest with all three of them on the job: Nikolai was currently in the cab, driving the transport, while Vivian bumped and swayed at almost ground level, standing on the left front area of the flatbed clutching a spar to anchor herself, and calling out what she saw. At the level of the cab the fine details of lunar relief tended to get flattened out, which mattered almost nowhere except here in Frigoris. Svetlana, ever restless, alternated her role. Right now she was scouting ahead of the big rig in the Lunokhod, scouting out what was beyond the wrinkle ridge they were currently driving alongside. Earlier in the day she had been perched precariously on the gantry structure above the cab, literally clinging to the radio mast, as even that small advantage in height paid dividends when finding a path through the regions where the scarp heights were more gentle.

After they got past what they hoped was the last of the cracks, Svetlana came back to the transport. From the cab, Nikolai lowered the flatbed ramp and the cosmonaut adeptly drove the Lunokhod up and onto its surface while the transport was still in motion. Vivian clambered down, her legs feeling like rubber from the continuous stand-and-sway of the last few hours.

The two women convened for a breather in the Purgan. Although the space was cramped with their suits on, the Purgan's suspension, combined with the natural flexing of the flatbed, made the ride in there a little more comfortable than in the rigid crew compartment above.

Belyakova pressurized the cabin and shucked her suit for long enough to use the commode, wash her face and clean up, then donned it again minus helmet and gloves. Lacking the energy to go through all that, Vivian just slid her own helmet and gloves off and lolled on the driver's seat.

Despite the Purgan's frequent purging by vacuum, when pressurized it still smelled of sweat and moondust and other lingering odors from Svetlana's long occupancy. Vivian tried not to notice. Rancid air was the least of their worries.

"Vivian?"

"Uh-huh?"

"You once told me that I never cried."

"I did?" Given the woman's obvious tiredness, Vivian was a little surprised Belyakova remembered Vivian was still here, let alone a conversation from years ago.

"Yes. I told you that your suffering at Zvezda, under Yashin: that it made me cry. I was not lying, Vivian, even though I later said that I was. I was weak, and I resisted that weakness, and then I doubly resisted it. And yet, it was true." Svetlana reached her hand forward toward her.

After a moment, Vivian took it and smiled.

Maybe Svetlana was telling the truth at last, and maybe she wasn't, but by now it hardly mattered. She obviously intended it as a peace offering, admitting weakness to a woman who had once been her enemy. Vivian would take that with all the graciousness that it had apparently been given.

"And also, you are in my seat."

They traded places, with Belyakova now taking her driver's seat while Vivian lay on the Purgan floor. After the rigors of Frigoris, the rocking of their passage back up onto the highlands was soporific, and

445

Vivian had been lulled into a light doze by the time Belyakova sat up straight, her movement shaking the vehicle. "Oh."

Instinctively, Vivian reached for her helmet. "Oh, what?"

"Here is trouble."

Reluctantly, Vivian pushed herself up to a sitting position. "What kind, this time?"

Belyakova raised binoculars to her eyes and made a minor adjustment to the focus. "The kind that comes to us. A vehicle is approaching from the west."

That got Vivian's attention. She scrabbled forward on her hands and knees and propped herself up against Belyakova. Sure enough, she could see the rooster tail of dust behind a vehicle that was heading toward them. Though it was still low to the horizon, it was blocky and looked substantial.

Belyakova passed Vivian the binoculars. "It is a Kharkovchanka."

The vehicle Makarov had described as a Soviet Moon tank? Vivian's heart sank. "Shit. I guess it was too much to hope that we'd get away with this."

"I had no belief that we would."

"Okay, but now's not quite the time for 'I told you so's.' It might have been nice to get lucky just *once*."

From his higher vantage point in the transport cab, Makarov broke in. "It is *two* Kharkovchankas."

"Yes. I see the second one now."

Vivian needed no further explanation to understand the trouble they were in. The obvious bulk and solidity of these vehicles and the speed of their approach made that clear. These were no mere Lunokhods, even of the military style that had attacked them at Hadley and the South Pole. These were MOLABs on steroids, and almost certainly armed to the teeth.

Belyakova raised her hand to the radio controls on her chest. "Soviet channel two," was all she said.

Vivian changed her radio setting to include that channel. A coarse Russian voice burst into her headset, talking quickly in accented Russian, so quickly she had trouble digging out the words. One of them may have been 'surrender,' but she was pretty sure the hostiles weren't offering to lay down their arms. Wait, had they just said Makarov's name?

Belyakova broke in, speaking in slow and clear Russian, perhaps so that Vivian could follow along. Most of it, Vivian understood. Other parts she had to guess or interpolate. "Good afternoon. This is Major-General Svetlana Belyakova. I order you to stand down and stand away. I am on [official business?] and must not be detained."

A pause, and then another stream of Russian. Whoever this guy was, he spoke in paragraphs, firehose style. This time, Vivian picked up almost none of it.

"We will not stop. We are [en route?] to a [situation?] that you do not have clearance to be [briefed?] on."

Another voice. "Major-General Belyakova. *Vot i snova vstretilis.*" *So, we meet again.*

An intake of breath from Svetlana. "Ah. Comrade Rhyzkov."

"Who's that?" Vivian said, sotto voce.

"Orlov's deputy." Belyakova's voice hardened. "I had hoped that you had died in service to the Rodina."

"Not so, despite your efforts. It appears I am stronger than you believe."

"As am I."

"Indeed. I congratulate you on your endurance. And thus, I propose a [truce between us?]. You will perhaps be aware that the situation in the Kremlin is … fluid. The new men try to betray the Rodina, spreading their lies and deceit, doubt, and uncertainty. This will not succeed. The [crackdown?] has begun. It would be wise to choose the correct side in these [turbulent?] times."

The Kharks, as Vivian already thought of them, had now divided. Still a quarter mile behind the Big Rig, their obvious intention was to flank them.

"You talk politics to me? At such a time?"

"Everything is politics, comrade. Give yourselves up, you and Major-General Makarov. You will be treated [leniently?], as [befits?] Heroes of the Soviet Union. The Rodina needs all of its heroes to [unite? stand together?] and reject the [insurrectionists?]. And, give us Vivian Carter. I believe that even now she has much to tell us."

Makarov spoke up. "Why would you believe that Vivian Carter is with us?"

"Because I am not a fool, Nikolai Ilyich. And you should not take me for one."

"Damn it," Vivian said.

"That was only a matter of time," Svetlana replied briefly.

"Well, Nikolai?" Vivian demanded over the intercom, their private channel. "Speak to me. What can we do? Is there any terrain coming up ahead that might work in our favor? Can we get back into Frigoris?"

"Perhaps. Wait a moment." They felt the truck turn to the left. *"Vyigrai mne vremya." Buy me time.*

Rhyzkov was continuing. "… and, more important than whatever secrets Carter may have in her head, she must not go home to spread her lies about us, not at such a sensitive moment in our history. I am sure, having spent time with her, you will understand this."

Belyakova turned to look sardonically at Vivian. "Oh, yes. I understand completely."

Vivian broke in again on the intercom. "Well, Nikolai, any cover?"

"Not yet. But I am convinced that Comrade Rhyzkov is not bluffing. One of his vehicles is equipped with four rooftop rockets. Whether these have nuclear or conventional warheads is impossible to tell. The other vehicle has two artillery cannons of a different style."

"And if they're nuclear?"

"If so, I would guess a yield of a few kilotons."

"Jesus Christ. So they might be pointing freaking *tactical nukes* at us?"

"It would surely explain why they are now remaining so far back." Makarov sounded calm, as if he were merely reporting on the weather, and not staring oblivion on the face.

On the Soviet channel, Belyakova was speaking. "And then what? Torture, and the gulag? We are not so naïve."

"It need not come to that. Let us make a deal. If you give up Vivian Carter to us, this will surely go some way toward atoning for your many crimes against the Rodina. If you agree to stand with us now for stability and peace, and help us condemn the breakaway movements in our republics, I would consider your actions toward General Orlov and your attack on me to be of [no importance?], and would be willing to argue for leniency. My feelings are irrelevant; the needs of the Rodina must take priority."

Makarov, on the open channel, said: "Prop up the old regime? Sell our souls to the hardliners? Never."

"Nikolai!" Svetlana snapped. "Shut up. Think what you are saying."

"Oh, I have had many years to think."

Smart, Vivian thought. *The longer they can drag this out, the more time we have to ... what? Pray for a miracle?*

Rhyzkov continued, as if Makarov had not spoken. "Or, if this is too much to ask, then just bring me Carter. I can arrange for you both to be kept from the public eye, in safety and with no retaliation. You may remain near Moscow, or any other large Soviet city of your preference. Perhaps Kiev, for Svetlana Antonovna, if that is her preference. Go to your dachas, to a well-earned retirement."

"It would be nice to go home," Svetlana said, her voice wistful but her expression steely.

"I believe you know me as an honorable man. You may take me at my word on this."

Belyakova looked at Vivian thoughtfully and pushed-to-talk. "That is a most interesting offer, Comrade, and I thank you for it. Please give us a few minutes to consider it." She cut the comms.

Vivian shook her head. "He's an honorable man?"

"Perhaps by his own reckoning."

Suddenly, Vivian pointed. "Boulder field. Two o'clock, maybe a mile away. Let's at least head for that."

"Is it?" Makarov was sitting higher than her. "Ah. I see. The shadows were ... confusing."

"Yes," Vivian said impatiently. "That's because it's a boulder field. Get us in there."

Belyakova pulled one of the Uzis down from the rack and snapped a magazine into it. Over the intercom, Makarov's voice registered alarm. "What are you doing?"

But it was Vivian who answered. "Buying us time, obviously, like you asked. Let's move."

Svetlana eyed her. "You are so sure? That amuses me."

"Come on, quit horsing around," Vivian said. "We only have minutes."

She held Svetlana's gaze. The cosmonaut looked at her and glanced up toward the transport's cab. "You two." She shook her head. "You and Nikolai, you are the goodness that I am not."

"And?"

"Take this. And one of the smaller." She thrust the Uzi into Vivian's arms, gestured toward the handguns, then turned to pull on her helmet and gloves, speaking quickly through their private channel, her words cutting through Rhyzkov's voice as he continued

449

to talk. "Nikolai, slow us down, just a little. I must leave. Vivian, please get out."

"They're saying …" Vivian was still stumbling with the Russian, while fumbling with her own glove connections. "'Surrender, come into custody, deliver up Vivian Carter to us, or die with her?'"

"Those are the main points," Nikolai said. "There is more, but it is of less subtlety."

"Vivian, you are sealed?"

Vivian did the quickest helmet and glove check ever. "Yes. What are we going to do?"

"Do?" Svetlana was flipping circuit breakers, setting switches. "We are going to war." The Purgan engine fired into life, and with a flick of another switch, all the air evacuated out of the Purgan at once, with a whoosh that quickly attenuated. Foil tray covers, papers and wipes flew.

Svetlana pushed another button, and the rear hatch of the Purgan swung open. "Out."

"Yes, ma'am." Vivian hustled through the hatch and jumped down. She teetered on the bouncing flatbed as it braked hard and veered further to the right, coming within an inch of being tossed off the side, and grabbed at one of the struts. "Dang."

The heavy cryptonaut transport had hardly shed much speed when Svetlana gunned the Purgan. It lurched off the flatbed and down onto the lunar surface, fishtailing dangerously, its left wheels bouncing high up off the regolith.

"Whoa, jeez, Svetlana," Vivian said.

"Shut up. I must concentrate." The Purgan skidded again.

"No shit." Vivian leaned her head briefly against the strut, even though it was vibrating with the stress on the transport's engines as Nikolai accelerated again. At least with those jerky, juddering movements, she couldn't tell whether her own limbs were shaking. "Crap."

"*Go*, Vivian," Svetlana snapped. "Fly."

Ahead of them the rocks were approaching, and behind them the Kharks were closing in. Vivian couldn't wait any longer. "Uh, okay. Sure thing." She braced herself against the transport's rolling motion, then ran forward and jumped, kicking herself ten feet forward and four feet up to sail over the Lunokhod and grab at the LESS. She swung, banging her right hip into the body of the craft as Nikolai swerved to avoid a boulder. "Oof, Christ."

"You are all right?" Nikolai asked anxiously.

She'd likely have twisted an ankle if her boot and suit weren't so rigid, but Vivian didn't have time to discuss it, and she was just about to do something way more dangerous. "I'm good." With a small hop and another twist she pulled herself up into the cockpit, if an aluminum seat covered with canvas, bolted onto the top of a table-like structure mounted over a rocket nozzle qualified for such a term. "I'm aboard the LESS."

The two hostile Kharkovchankas had separated now, bumping across the highland breccia toward them side by side, fifty feet apart. As with all lunar chases, the speeds were deceptive: since the horizon looked closer, they appeared to be covering ground quickly, but no vehicle could safely go above twenty miles an hour, so the Soviet advance had a steady, inexorable feel to it.

Sure enough, by now Vivian could now see that the first Kharkovchanka had an array of four missiles jutting from its roof like a crest, while the second had two rotating roof guns that resembled the Rikhters mounted on the Soviet Almaz craft, forty-pound cannons that fired half-pound explosive shells. The simple machine gun on Svetlana's Purgan could not possibly compete with the armaments on either vehicle.

"Vivian, you are sure you know what you are doing?" Nikolai persisted.

"Oh, I absolutely do not," Vivian said, strapping herself into her seat, and looping the sling of the Uzi around her neck.

Her headset crackled. Svetlana said: "Vivian. If you can save just one, save Nikolai. Leave me."

Vivian didn't grace that with a response. Given the inequality in weaponry, Vivian had little hope of saving anyone, herself included.

"I will not be taken by these men. I will die first. But," Svetlana added. "I will lead them as big a dance as I am able, before that."

"Go, girl," Vivian said, and fired up the LESS.

Beneath her the rocket ignited, jolting her upward. She eased off a bit. "Tricky. Okay, Nikolai, punch it."

She tilted the LESS back, making it rock vertiginously, and she glanced up as the superstructure of the Big Rig trundled on, revealing black sky beyond it. "Well, then," she said with a confidence she certainly wasn't feeling. "I'm off." And gunned the throttle.

She had practiced with gentle thrusts back at Marius, just enough to stir the mass of the LESS off the flatbed. The transport had been stationary at the time, and Vivian had spent just enough time and effort to convince herself that the machine was flyable, her intuition about the controls was correct, and that she could nudge the vehicle aloft, but until right now she had not put more than a few feet of space between the craft's landing pads and the flatbed of the transport.

That all changed now, as with a vibrating roar she heard and felt through her suit, the LESS flyer took off with a vengeance. In seconds she was soaring two hundred feet above the surface and still jetting backward away from Nikolai and the transport. "Holy cow!"

Neither of them answered her. Vivian attempted to stabilize her ridiculous craft's leap for the skies, glanced down to get perspective, and managed to ease the craft into something approaching a hover. As she scanned the terrain, she realized she was sinking toward it and jiggled the controls gently to left and right, as well as up, to make herself a harder target.

Svetlana had looped the Purgan away and to the left, perhaps hoping to draw one of the Kharkovchankas off. As yet, that hadn't worked. Both hostile vehicles were still barreling toward the transport. Had they even seen her leave? Vivian's mental replay, glancing at angles, showed that the Purgan had egressed the flatbed on the opposite side to the attackers. And the big boulders that dotted the landscape and the low Sun were both working in Team Vivian's favor; it was quite possible that under these conditions the Kharkovchanka drivers were focusing on the transport, and not on Vivian's erratic flight above it.

Nobody was shooting at Vivian yet. Time to take advantage of that. She eased back on one control and twisted the other, and the LESS dropped and skewed to the right, the direction in the transport's wake opposite to Belyakova's path. Vivian bit her tongue, trying not to fill the airwaves with curses while she tried to get this unruly bronco under control. It was just as well that she'd flown a whole bunch of different jets with varying capabilities and sensitivities as a young naval aviator, because it was only those instincts and her flexibility and experience that were keeping her alive right now.

But already she felt herself beginning to understand the LESS. Its controls and handling were more similar to the Flying Bedstead at Johnson than to a Lunar Module—it was dangerously responsive to the slightest twitch of her fingers—but her skills transferred. Vivian had always been a good seat-of-the-pants pilot. Which was just as well, because the next part of this was going to take cast iron balls.

She dropped even lower, alternating downward lunges with almost-panicked pulses of thrust to arrest her descent, and then gunned the LESS forward. The ground shot past beneath her, and her target Khark grew alarmingly quickly.

Too fast, too fast ... she had to nudge herself upward, stair-stepping up and gaining fifty feet at a time, and then curtsey back down again so she wasn't too high ...

The crew of Khark #1 saw her, and the rear Rikhter cannon swung in her direction ... but not up far enough. The gun had a free swivel range of three hundred sixty degrees in the horizontal plane, but didn't have the azimuthal clearance to point straight up. A design flaw they'd probably fix next time around.

The Khark #1 driver pulled his vehicle to the left, but Vivian had correctly anticipated that, and the intense plume of Vivian's rocket exhaust scoured the side and top of the vehicle. She rocked backward and then forward to spread the heat across the Kharkovchanka's roof as far as possible, resisting the insane—and suicidal—urge to just drop down and crash into the Soviet vehicle.

Vivian's craft might be small, but its rocket motor was large. Designed to propel its pilot into orbit in an emergency, it had plenty of thrust, and if Vivian remembered correctly, her rocket plume would be between three and four thousand degrees. That would be diminished a little by the bell-shaped nozzle of the rocket engine, but not enough to matter. Three thousand degrees was more than halfway to the temperature of the Sun's surface, and well above the melting points of both steel and aluminum. With luck, even a few seconds of that would do some serious damage to the cannons and the windshield.

She glanced to left and right, swayed the LESS once more as a parting blast, and then obeyed a sudden sixth sense of danger and shot away, rocketing her craft sharply upward into the sky.

The second Khark, now only a hundred yards away, had fired a missile at her. She'd glimpsed the wink of laser light scan across her visor. A laser-guided missile—which was a fine tactic for the Soviets, just so long as they could keep that laser beam focused on Vivian or her LESS for as long as the missile was in flight.

Vivian zoomed further upward, breathing shallowly to offset the sudden G-forces she was putting herself through, feinted to port, and then slewed hard to starboard and dropped. *Good luck keeping a bead drawn on me with that going on, shitheads.*

She barely even saw the missile as it shot by, her eyes focused on her instruments and the ground below, but she had definitely been fired upon and no mistake, because when she glanced over at Khark #2 only three missiles remained in its top rack.

One shot wasted. Excellent. Vivian felt a savage exultancy and looped around to the right to see what had happened to the first Kharkovchanka.

It had stopped dead. Its front window looked dark—from her current altitude Vivian couldn't tell whether it was blown out or merely blackened by her flame. The front Rikhter cannon was twisted into slag.

Of course, the second cannon now turned to threaten her. She saw the streak of tracer in the air and swerved before it could come to bear on her. Up was best direction to go to evade it, and so up she went, keeping a careful eye on Khark #2 in case it fired another missile.

But the second Kharkovchanka had chosen a different target: the lumbering Soviet transport, with Nikolai Makarov aboard, which had just reappeared from behind a house-sized boulder and appeared to be slowing to a halt.

Vivian checked her fuel. The glass was still well over half full, she could still do some damage ... but here came Svetlana's Purgan, reappearing from the left at last, bumping and rocking and rolling and accelerating in at a full fifteen miles an hour with the machine-gun on its roof spitting fire. Vivian was impressed that Belyakova could drive and shoot at the same time.

It didn't deter the crew of Khark #2. Belyakova's machine-gun fire raked the vehicle, and sparks flew, but their second missile was already away.

This one, Vivian saw clearly as it passed beneath her quick as a flash and went on to slam into the transport. Flame leaped upward, the blast of the fireball briefly obscuring the whole vehicle. "Shit!"

Khark #1 was firing on the Purgan, RIkhter shells arcing through space to skitter off its hull in a series of bright explosions. The Purgan skidded, then slewed around and rolled, bumping and bouncing across the lunar surface.

"Crap! Svetlana!"

The smoke and flame cleared freakishly quickly above Nikolai's transport. It was wrecked, its driver cabin now blown free and resting on the ground some way away from the twisted pile of steel that had once carried them across the lunar surface. It was completely destroyed. There was no chance in hell that Nikolai could have survived that.

In a matter of seconds, Vivian might have become the lone survivor of her team. If so, her only realistic course of action was fly on, and put as much distance between her and the hostile Kharks as she could. Head in the direction of Camp Jura until her fuel ran out, then ditch and hope to walk the rest of the way to the American base.

Except that … Vivian glanced at the Sun, but for the life of her, she couldn't make her internal compass behave. She had maybe a rough sense of which way to fly, but her only map—and her sextant—were in the destroyed transport.

Away-from-here was good enough for now. She'd figure out her location later.

All of these thoughts sped through her brain in a couple of seconds, while she was still gaining height and stabilizing the LESS.

Then, from the rear of the wrecked Purgan, she saw a movement.

Belyakova, easy to spot in her bright red Soviet spacesuit, had crawled out of the rear hatch and was now limping across the Moon's surface, dragging her right leg behind her, and propping a massive tube on her shoulder. It was the rocket launcher that Vivian had last seen mounted on the ceiling of the Purgan.

The crew of Khark #1 saw Belyakova at the same time. The remaining rear Rikhter gun swung around.

Again, Vivian saw that scattering sparkle of laser light. Khark #2 was drawing a bead on her LESS again.

Vivian twisted her controls savagely and dropped out of the sky. Twisted again to shove herself in Belyakova's direction—why not die together?—but she was now falling too fast and all she could do was pile on all the braking force she could, as the Moon's surface came up to meet her, and then shove forward to try to mitigate some of her downward speed.

A few moments before Vivian crashed, she realized that both of Khark #2's remaining missiles were still in place on its roof. She had probably killed herself just to avoid a beam of laser light.

Which is just bloody typical.

The ground was coming up like a freight train, but God bless this overpowered rocket and the low mass of the rest of the vehicle ... Vivian felt a couple of very long seconds of a stupidly high G force, and then she hit the ground. The landing gear of the craft crumpled beneath her. Her rocket motor, still firing even as the bell of its nozzle impacted regolith, blew back and flipped the LESS off the surface again, and Vivian, acting mostly on instinct, used that one brief instant to unfasten her lap strap. Because if she knew one thing, it was that she didn't want this goddamned LESS to end up on top of her. Its momentum would certainly crush her.

Her spacesuit became her only vehicle, and unpowered at that, as she sailed through space and then impacted the ground in a flare of agony. The Uzi, last seen looped around her neck, banged into her faceplate visor, which held despite a sickening cracking sound. And then Vivian was lying painfully on her back, twisted out of true by the bulk of her PLSS, looking straight up into the black sky and hurting like hell. But alive. For now.

"Vivian? All right?"

Belyakova's voice, the first Vivian had heard for some time. She would have liked to respond, but all the wind had been knocked out of her. Right now, Vivian couldn't even breathe. But at least she could hear her suit fans over her own gasping, so she didn't have a dead suit this time.

Methodically, fearing the worst, she tried to move her limbs. Nothing grated together, and she experienced no new stabs of immense pain. Her body must be an immense bruise, but for once she hadn't broken anything.

Finally, she took in a rasping breath. *Uh, focus.* What the hell was happening around her?

Her breathing still ragged, she managed to prop herself up on her left elbow and look out across the lunar highland plain.

The two Kharkovchankas were approaching. And fifty feet away, limping out between Vivian and the Soviet death machines, was Major-General Svetlana Belyakova, with that sinister tube resting on her shoulder that didn't look like a rocket launcher, not quite.

"Eyes closed, Vivian. Keep them closed until I say."

That could only mean one thing, and even as Vivian realized what that thing was, she tried to raise her voice in protest and only coughed and choked on her own saliva. Somewhere in all this pain and confusion she'd forgotten how to swallow.

And yet still she watched, as Belyakova professionally dropped forward onto her left knee and, with an effort, hefted the rocket launcher up level. She was aiming at the Kharkovchanka on the right, Khark #1, which was firing again, tracer and genuine explosive shells raking the lunar surface around her. The Soviet gunner was swinging it from right to left, the path of the deadly shells homing in on Belyakova.

Vivian saw the tight beam of a laser dancing on the shiny cab of Khark #1 as Belyakova fired. She watched the bright plume of the rocket speeding away from Belyakova's launcher for the briefest of instants and then threw herself back and away, multiple stabs of pain shooting through her, and closed her eyes.

The light was bright, huge, and hideous, even just reflected back from the regolith, and just too late Vivian flung up her arm over her helmet visor to try to block it. Felt her eyes watering furiously.

Shrapnel rained down upon her. Not for the first time in her life.

The second explosion came half a minute later. Vivian didn't even attempt to open her eyes in between times. By now, she knew. She just kept them closed tight, her arm still draped across her helmet.

Schrodinger's cat. One of two things was now true. Belyakova had destroyed the two Kharkovchankas, and the two women were both still alive, but without any remaining transport, stranded on the lunar surface.

Or: Belyakova had failed to destroy both, and the Soviets were about to capture or kill them.

Vivian wasn't sure which of those options she'd prefer, right now.

Another cat: Vivian was temporarily blinded, or permanently.

Everything was quiet, aside from her own breathing and the sound of the suit fans. She heard no voices over the radio, either in Russian or English, merely the hiss of static.

Reluctantly, she opened her eyes and saw nothing. It wasn't the black of the sky, the black of space. Tilting her head left and right she saw no scattered light from the lunar regolith. She saw, simply: nothing at all.

She became aware that she was lying on the Uzi, its hard, straight barrel beneath her hips. She hadn't taken the gun off her shoulder the whole time. Her only weapon in the battle had been her rocket plume.

Whereas Svetlana's had been two tactical nuclear weapons. Typical Soviet overkill.

"Vivian?"

It was Belyakova's voice.

"Here," Vivian said. "But blind. And beaten to a pulp. Probably bleeding in a few places."

"Did you say 'blind'?"

"Roger that. I can't see. I can't see." A sob squeezed itself out from between her lips.

She felt her shoulders being lifted off the regolith, from behind. "Can you sit up?"

"Ow ... maybe? The transport, Svetlana?"

"Destroyed," Belyakova said, dully. "Completely. Nikolai ... is dead, and soon we shall follow him."

"Yeah." Vivian groped, trying to reach back for Svetlana's gloved hand, but another burst of pain stopped her. "Svetlana, I'm really sorry. I know how much he meant ..."

A man's voice, dazed. "Hello?"

"Nikolai!" Svetlana screamed and let go of Vivian, dumping her unceremoniously back onto the ground. The air went out of her lungs once more, which at least prevented her from swearing, and her head banged painfully against the back of her helmet. She saw stars, and not the real kind. *Great. Thanks a lot, babe.*

Had that really been Nikolai's voice? It had sounded too deep. "Svetlana? Nikolai?"

Blind and alone. Being visually challenged *sucked*, and every muscle and joint hurt. Vivian wasn't a cryer, but right now she was sorely tempted to just give up and lose control. "For God's sake ..."

She shut up then, to focus on just breathing.

"Vivian." Makarov's voice, with an accompanying feeling of compression against her glove.

His glove, pressing against hers? Holy crap, even her individual fingers ached. "Oh, my god. *Nikolai?* You're *alive?*"

"It seems so. But I am hurt. My arm, I think it is broken."

"I'm hurt too, and I can't see … but, Nikolai, the transport? I saw it get completely torched."

"Yes, but I was not aboard it. I jammed the steering and drove the Lunokhod off it, while the big boulder blocked their view."

"Holy shit. Well. Uh, good thinking. Can you … help me stand up, at least? No, wait, not like that, don't pull me around, be gentle …. Where's Svetlana?"

"I am looking at the Purgan," Belyakova said. "It is not good."

Was anything? "The Kharks?"

"The Kharkovchankas? They are gone, destroyed. No survivors."

"With *tactical nuclear weapons*?"

"Yes. Low yield. Tuned for maximum explosive effect, minimum radiation."

Vivian heard Nikolai tutting, as if angry with a child. She said, "That's possible? The tuning?"

"They tell me so. I suppose we shall see."

"Ouch, Jesus … stop, Nikolai. I must have like a hundred cuts and bruises, this isn't going to work." Surely she could manage to stand up before she died? *Oh God.* "Are we having fun yet?"

"What?"

"I said … is the Purgan roadworthy?"

Belyakova snorted. "Not at all. It is smashed and almost flattened. It will be hard to get anything out of it."

"Okay." Vivian closed her useless eyes. "So, you're right. This is not good. Nikolai, you said your arm is broken?"

"Forearm, yes—the right. I fell out of the Lunokhod when the transport was destroyed. It is … quite painful. I may also have ribs that are broken."

"Oh, the ribs? No big deal, that happens to me all the time. Well, once." Vivian had the bizarre urge to laugh, but knew that if she started, she might not be able to stop.

"Yes … we are all of us alive, but …"

"Stuck."

"*Nam pizdetz*," Belyakova said bleakly. *We are screwed.*

"Well, at least one good thing?" Vivian said. "I'm starting to see light now, and shadows."

Slowly, so slowly, her vision returned. Not steadily, which meant that during its frequent recovery plateaus, Vivian was convinced that was all she would get. And then the temporary blindness would ease up even further, and she would be able to focus a little more clearly. Her head was starting to ache now, but hell, that was better than being totally flashblinded.

Eventually the sunlight shining off the rocks around her looked so bright that Vivian had to lower her gold visor. Relief flooded her. At least she wasn't about to die sightless.

Because they were in a fix now, and no mistake. About the only things on the "plus" side of the ledger were that all three of them were alive and together, with basic mobility, in suits that hadn't lost integrity—yet. Belyakova's right hip and leg were had been twisted, probably with serious muscle or ligament tears, and just walking was painful. Nikolai's wrist was surely broken, although by now Belyakova had strapped a long wrench from the Lunokhod's toolkit to the outside of his suit, strapping it in place with wire and plastic clips, to serve as a makeshift splint. Even at that, Nikolai's suit was so bashed up that it was a miracle that it was still in one piece. As for Vivian, now that she was less distracted by her vision, she was increasingly aware that her shoulder felt like it was on fire, which was kind of on-brand for her, and her chest and ribs were especially painful.

The Big Rig was wrecked. The Purgan was wrecked. The LESS was wrecked. Their sole means of transportation was one Lunokhod with two seats. Their only living space was a small emergency inflatable that *might* hold three, but with no assurances that its integrity had survived the damage it had taken, being epoxied to the back of the Purgan. They had four emergency oxygen bottles between the three of them—most of their supply had been stored on the transport and had gone up with it—and varying amounts of oxygen remained in their life support backpacks. And they were still a thousand miles from Marius.

"Well," Belyakova said calmly. "It is over."

"It's not over," Vivian said, and heard the hollowness in her own voice. With a little more vehemence, she looked around at the cosmonauts and repeated, "It's not over. We're still alive, aren't we?"

"For now."

Makarov was leaning on the Lunokhod. "I think … perhaps one of us could make it, based on the oxygen. But even that is not certain."

"Then go," Belyakova said. "Go, Nikolai."

He looked at her, and then at Vivian. "Perhaps. I can refuel the LEK, and return …"

"Nikolai. You are not thinking right. Vivian and I will be dead before you are halfway to your ship."

"She's right." With some effort, Vivian had eventually eased herself back up onto her feet, which felt like a considerable victory in itself. Likely one of her last. She leaned back against the Lunokhod. "We don't have enough oxygen. Not even close. And I can't fly the LEK. It's got to be one of you two."

Belyakova pointed. "Which means it is him. Nikolai has family. He must return to them. I have already been dead for months, and I have nowhere to go."

"You have a husband," Vivian said.

She snorted. "By now? I am sure that I do not."

"I will not leave without you," Nikolai said.

Belyakova snarled something at him that Vivian didn't catch. Nikolai recoiled as if he had been slapped.

"Hey, hey. Svetlana, please? We're still thinking here. What about Jura?"

"Even that is impossible. And who knows who we will meet first? Either way, they will probably kill us on sight."

"You don't know that," Vivian said.

Makarov gestured. "Climb aboard, the two of you. Vivian, you must lie on top of the supplies. It will be uncomfortable, I am sorry. Climb aboard and we will leave, all of us."

"And how fast does this go with three people?" Belyakova demanded.

"Faster than if we stand here talking …. Shit." Vivian had just realized yet another obstacle. "No map. No sextant. No star tables. They were all in the Rig. Damn." Her sense of priorities was all wrong, but nevertheless she found the loss of Kevin Pope's sextant … painful.

"Were they?" Makarov reached to the thigh pocket of his suit and pulled out the sextant. "Perhaps I am cleverer than you think." He pulled the map half-out, to show that he had that as well.

"Oh, great … That's something at least. Svetlana, Nikolai is right. We've got to try. Come on. Let's go."

Belyakova shook her head. "Go, if you wish. But it is pointless."

"*Jeez*, lady, you're a downer. Why?"

"Because," Belyakova said, "the last thing that Rhyzkov did before he died was call in aerial reinforcements."

CHAPTER 33

Lunar Surface: Vivian Carter
June 5, 1985

THAT stopped Vivian in her tracks. She blinked and found her voice. "And you only tell us this *now*?"

"Did you not hear?"

"No, guess I must have been too busy throwing myself on the ground and going blind."

Silence fell. Nikolai raised his head, and instead of staring woefully at the Lunokhod, now scanned the horizon.

"How long will it take them to get here?" Vivian demanded. Belyakova just shrugged. "Okay, so where will they be coming from? Hortensius Crater? That's south of Copernicus, right? So it'll take them a while. Uh, how long has it been?"

"If that is where they are," Nikolai said. "There are probably still Soviet forces in the Jura region."

Vivian took a breath. "Okay, I hate to ask, but … Svetlana, do you have any more rockets for that launcher?"

"No. Just those two."

"Damn." So, all they had now were the Uzis. "But for Rhyzkov's message to get through, they'd need to have had an Almaz, or whatever, above the horizon here. Do we even know for sure that the Soviets heard his Mayday?"

"I did not hear a response. But it is irrelevant. When Rhyzkov and the Kharkovchankas fail to report in, another Vympel squad will be sent to find out why."

"But that'll take longer. We need to get going, then, *right now*. The further we can get, the less chance of us being detected."

Belyakova's whole spacesuit body language radiated impatience and irritation. "Vivian. *We have no air.* Or not enough."

"And we'll worry about that later."

Makarov shook his head. "The rover will leave tracks. They will just follow us."

"So we'll just switch to manual redaction," she said.

They stared at her like she was crazy. Vivian wasn't surprised. They had a point.

Eventually Makarov said, "Brush our tracks out, ourselves, as we drive?"

"Good job there are three of us," Vivian said. "One at the wheel, and one on each side to smear out each set of tire tracks as we go, leaning over the back with dust brushes. Right side and left. Best we can, given how bashed up we all are."

Belyakova's head drooped. "Vivian. You are … insane."

"God *damn* it." That hurt a bit. Vivian knew their situation was impossible just as well as the other two did, but still. "At least let's *try*. You want to just give up and wait here to be killed or captured? *Of course,* I understand that we can't make our tracks invisible, but maybe we can make them harder to see from above … we have to do *something*. Never say die, right? Right?"

The cosmonauts looked at each other.

"We're wasting oxygen," Vivian said brutally. "Get into your damned Lunokhod and let's go."

Belyakova gave the merest shrug. "I suppose I have nothing better to do."

They had gone less than a mile when a LEK lander shot past, overflying them at an altitude of less than two thousand feet. They swore in three different languages.

"See?" Belyakova added.

"We must surrender." A tremor had entered Makarov's voice for the first time. "At least that way we will be alive."

"Not me," Vivian said. "You might be, perhaps."

The LEK had seen them. It was already beginning its turn, dropping height. Makarov slowed the Lunokhod. "Vivian, we will try to look after you. They will want you alive, so that they can question you."

"Yeah. Been there, done that. Don't want to do it again."

Belyakova shook her head. "Our game is over."

"Mine isn't." Vivian took a deep breath. "Goodbye. And good luck."

She jumped off the moving Lunokhod and staggered awkwardly to avoid falling on her face. It took a couple more steps to get her legs under her properly and then she was off, running, loping high across the lunar surface, every bounce off the ground sending stabs of pain through her ribs, her chest, her shoulder, her head, her … everything.

It was appalling how short the Moon was of serious cover when you needed it. Terrain that looked ridiculously cluttered with rocks when she was trying to drive across it at twenty miles an hour now looked flat and open … and completely goddamned unhelpful to a woman trying to run away from hostiles.

All she could do was head for Makarov's original boulder field, which was nearly a mile away. After all that arguing, they'd have been better served just staying where they were. But she also veered to the right as she ran, to look for cover anywhere closer.

Small boulders. Average craters. No rilles, damn it. After suffering the terrible terrain of Frigoris for days, now Vivian needed substantial natural features to hide among, there were almost none.

She pounded away doggedly. A glance back showed that the LEK was coming in to land a hundred yards ahead of the Lunokhod, which was now stationary, with two small spacesuited figures standing beside it.

"Jesus, people,' Vivian said. "Don't just *stand* there." What had happened to Svetlana's vow not to be taken alive?

"Go, Vivian," Makarov said. "And good luck to you as well."

And, in a quiet voice Vivian almost missed, Belyakova said, "And … I thank you."

Ah, a graben: this was more like it. Not a rille exactly; more of a long scratch in the lunar surface, barely twenty feet deep and wide, and around it some more bouldered terrain, along with some craters actually worthy of the name. Vivian jumped straight over the edge of the graben and let her momentum carry her across to land on the slope on its far side. On impact, she shouted out in pain and fell back onto her butt. Only now did it occur to her to turn off her radio so they couldn't use her transmissions to track her, even though she was no longer in their line of sight.

She was panting almost uncontrollably. Her shoulder ached like hell, and the inside of her suit smelled bad. Her stomach hurt from lack of food. And, right now, she didn't have the courage to look down at her oxygen supply. She had the feeling that was the least of her troubles.

Had the crew of the LEK seen her? Vivian needed to know. She scrabbled up the steep slope of the graben, raised her head above its rough rim, inched over to the right to put a small rock between herself and where she thought the LEK might be, and peered cautiously through eyes that still watered far too much.

Three cosmonauts had already egressed from the LEK, wearing spacesuits a subdued grey-red color easily distinguishable from the usual Soviet red. Armored, perhaps? Was that what KGB Vympel special forces wore?

Each cosmonaut held a tube in his hands, and even as she watched, one of them fired.

Makarov and Belyakova leaped, one to the left and the other to the right, as a rocket smashed into the Lunokhod, blowing it apart in a bright white explosion. The vibration rumbled under Vivian's feet just moments later.

Her friends must have hit the deck, because she couldn't see either of them, just the spray of debris that must be crashing down all around them.

She turned her radio on again. "You guys okay? If you are … come on. There's a LEK. If we can just get the better of these guys, we can take it. We need it."

Wishful thinking, she knew. Belyakova had just an Uzi, and Makarov had no weapon at all.

Neither responded, and after babbling for a few moments more, Vivian abruptly shut up. Because one of the three hostile cosmonauts had split off from the other two, and was bounding across the lunar surface, right toward her.

It had been too much to hope that they hadn't seen Vivian's run for cover. And it was also too much to hope that she would survive this day.

The other two Soviets strode across the surface toward Makarov, who was now standing up again. Belyakova was still down. She'd been closer to the Lunokhod than Nikolai. *Damn it.*

Makarov calmly stepped across to stand in front of Belyakova, shielding her with his body.

"At least *try*, okay?" Vivian begged.

And then, to add insult to injury, *another* LEK overflew her. "Damn it."

American ingenuity had allowed for two gunners, on platforms one each side of their Night Corps LMs. Apparently, the Soviets had only sprung for one, mounted on *top* of the LEK. Vivian hadn't seen anything like that before. Even as their lunar presence continued to dwindle, the Soviets kept coming up with new war machines to attempt to hold the line.

Vivian still had her Uzi, but even from this distance she could see that the gun carried by the Soviet heading her way was bigger, and his suit sturdier. Meaning she would have to plug away at his suit, pecking at it with Uzi bullets like an insistent bird, hoping to hit something vital.

His weapon would likely be much more effective against her puny NASA suit. So this couldn't come to a gunfight, or she'd lose it.

Shit.

Well. Time to move.

Vivian dropped back into the graben and ran.

CHAPTER 34

Daedalus Base: Peter Sandoval
Lunar Surface: Nikolai Makarov, Vivian Carter
June 5, 1985

STRANGE to say, but one of the things Peter Sandoval found most difficult to achieve in the Moon's one-sixth gravity was … to walk with a tray. Lunar locomotion always required a bouncing movement that made his food dishes slide in all directions. Naturally, the fact that Brock achieved this effortlessly and mostly refrained from mocking him about it made it even worse. So it was with some relief that he placed his tray of soup, meatloaf and mashed potatoes, and a slice of some random pie down on the table and slid into his chair.

Opposite him, Brock nodded. "Satisfactory touchdown achieved."

"Oh, hush."

Brock raised her eyes to look past him and frowned. "Hmm. Okhotina."

"Hello." The cosmonaut slid herself into the seat beside Sandoval without waiting to be asked and leaned in. "Something has happened. You need to know."

Brock sighed. "Every mealtime. Regular as clockwork."

Sandoval just grunted and spooned soup into his mouth.

"Something worse than usual. Professor O'Neill has sent me to tell you. He believes a nuclear weapon has been detonated on the

Moon's surface, far to the north of here. Or perhaps two, close together in time."

Sandoval coughed and almost choked. Automatically, Brock handed him a napkin. "And he sent *you* to tell us this?"

Okhotina frowned. "Yes. Why not? He wanted you to be informed, but without fuss." She glanced around the crowded cafeteria, ever watchful; the UN forces had taken Doryagin and Balkina into custody, and theoretically none of the other Soviets knew of her actions against them, but Okhotina was still wary of being seen with Americans.

"Well, get on with it, then," Brock said. "What do we know?"

"We have seismic receivers here, of course. We must constantly monitor any moonquake activity, or oscillations due to large impacts …"

Sandoval shook his head. "Wasn't I told that the Moon has only about a billionth of the seismic activity that the Earth does?"

"That is true, most events are only one or two on the Richter scale, with the largest being around four, but their effects can still be great enough to affect the pointing of the Driver—"

Brock cut in. "Moonquakes have long, slow rise times and very slow decays. The energy gets scattered and attenuated quite efficiently. So, what we're seeing from this event is different?"

"Yes. The rise time was not slow, but very sharp. Professor O'Neill says that the signal closely matches the seismic signatures from nuclear explosions on Earth, from underground and aboveground tests. Something about P-waves and S-waves …"

"I know. Save the details." Brock turned to Sandoval. "The point is that a surface nuclear explosion of any size makes the whole Moon ring like a bell. And NASA still deploys seismometers at almost every exploratory Apollo site, to help study the geological structure of the lunar interior. It's how we know the Moon has a core, mantle, and crust …"

"Terri." Sandoval made a rolling motion with his finger. *Speed it up.*

"… all of which enables us to triangulate the signal. Right, comrade?"

"Yes, correct."

"So, where did it happen? And how long ago?"

"Far to the north, and around the corner."

"Northern Nearside? We can't zero in any closer than that? It should be a simple enough calculation."

Okhotina looked irritated. "Which Professor O'Neill is doing right now. He wanted you to know immediately, to not waste time."

"Okay." Sandoval wiped his mouth. "So … your people have set off a nuke somewhere near the Pole? What the hell for?"

"You ask me?" Okhotina raised her hands. "I have no idea. I know of no Soviet activity at all so far north. And we have no nuclear weapons on the Moon."

"So you say," Sandoval said.

Terri's lips were dry. "So, a rogue group. A cryptonaut cell?"

"If this is not your people, then that is possible."

Sandoval shook his head. "It's not us. We'd know."

Brock looked at him, her face hard. "So, cryptonauts?"

"Or just ordinary Soviet military. Terri, it might not be the same people who were at the South Pole. We can't know that."

"They had no extraction plan. It *could* be the exact same group, the ones who left the bomb for Kevin. Maybe they've been here all along. Let's go find out."

"You mean, you hope it's them. So you can kill them."

"Either way, we need to know what the hell's going on." Brock glanced at the wall clock. "I can be ready to lift off in thirty minutes. Less, if I can snag another LM pilot to help me with the preflight checks."

Okhotina leaned in again. "Take me with you. Let me help."

"Out of the question," Terri said. "And, tell none of your people we're going. O'Neill shouldn't have told you any of this in the first place."

"Of course he should. And I should come with you. Do you speak Russian? I think not. If we come across other Russians, maybe I can persuade them to stand down, defuse any confrontation."

"No confrontations," Sandoval said. "We'll just go take a look. Quick in, quick out. It's not like we want to hang around in a hot zone anyway."

Brock looked at Sandoval. "We should probably lock her up until we're safely back. Mission security is already compromised."

"You can trust me," Okhotina said, her tone icy.

"Sure. Because you went around the Moon with Vivian on LGS-1?"

"And saved her life? And yours, long before?"

"Cut it out," Sandoval said. "We have no time for this. And we're not locking up anyone."

"Fine." Terri pointed at Okhotina. "But if we find out she's laid on a welcoming committee for us up there—"

Okhotina slammed her fist onto the table. "I was shot at by cryptonauts. I am *not* a cryptonaut. But *you* are very stupid."

People were turning to look now. "So much for *without fuss*," Sandoval said. "Both of you, stand down. Katya, she's right. There's no way we can take you. Sorry."

But Brock was on a roll. "So, you got shot at, then. But you also helped Doryagin maintain power here. You worked for damned Spetsgruppa Vympel for months."

Okhotina's tone was pure ice. "I did not work for them. I worked alongside, until I saw an opportunity to change the situation."

"Give me a break. That just-following-orders shit went out of fashion in 1945. You're as much of an opportunist as Belyakova."

Sandoval raised a hand. "Enough, Brock. That's an order."

Terri blinked. "Fine. Roger that. So, can I go and arm and kickstart a Lunar Module, while you go find us some accurate coordinates?"

"Sure."

Brock stomped off, her dinner abandoned. Sandoval looked at the clock and took another bite of meatloaf. "Sorry."

Okhotina just hissed out a long sigh.

"Katya … I trust you. Because Vivian trusts you."

"Thank you."

Sandoval leaned forward. "But don't make me regret that, okay?"

Okhotina shook her head in amazement. "You are as bad as she is."

"I like to think I'm not. Look, can you stand ready to be on the loop? If we do happen to need Russian language skills, or any other specialized Soviet knowledge, I'd like to be able to patch you in."

"Of course. I will be happy to."

Sandoval stood and looked at his tray regretfully, then had second thoughts and picked up his pie and a fork. "Okay. Let's go see what the Professor has got for us."

In addition to trays, Peter Sandoval also had issues with Lunar Modules. Aside from his arrival with the UN force a few weeks ago, his sole Lunar Module experiences had been to launch back into orbit in them.

He found them disconcertingly fragile. He'd almost rather land in a Brick than a LM. Then again, it just another detail, and all more or less irrelevant: he still hated everything about the Moon.

Especially flying toward the site of a nuclear explosion. But a job was a job.

To Sandoval, the Moon all looked the same, especially on Farside. Highlands, craters, and more highlands and craters. Not even any mares to speak of. Brock was reassuringly competent in a Lunar Module, though. It was the only Night Corps vehicle she flew much better than Peter Sandoval ... because Sandoval couldn't fly one at all.

He only knew they'd passed the North Pole because the Earth had reappeared in front of them, and when it did he felt a lump in his throat. God, he hated not being able to see it in the sky from Daedalus ...

More craters and highlands unrolled beneath the battle LM. They'd flown most of this trip at a height of fifteen thousand feet, but now he could tell that they were gradually losing height.

"Nearly there," she said. "Eyes peeled. Oh, look."

It turned out that the danger zone beneath them was easy to identify, even from altitude. First, because light sparkled and reflected back an unusual shade of gold-green from the Soviet LEK on the ground. Once that had drawn Sandoval's eye, it was easy to glimpse the two unnaturally similar round and bowl-like craters in the distance, each around sixty feet across, that had been carved by the nukes, before his gaze was pulled back down again by the flash of muzzle flares.

Guns were being fired on the lunar surface.

Sandoval pointed suddenly, finger straight out. "Contact. They have one in the air as well."

"Got it. Taking evasive."

It wasn't NASA or Night Corps, so it had to be Soviet. It wasn't small, so it had to be a LEK rather than an LK. And it wasn't from Daedalus, so it had to be from ... somewhere else. Meaning, at this point, they could assume it was military.

"Reminder: we're here to check out a nuking. Which means that these guys might have nukes."

"Right. So, we don't let them shoot first." She looked over at him. "Peter. DEFCON-2. Automatic escalation. Yes?"

"Wait."

Distance and height were tough for Sandoval to judge on the Moon, but he was guessing the ship was half a mile distant and maybe five thousand feet higher. It was looping around to swoop down on them.

A red light ignited on the panel right in front of Terri, flashing vigorously. In response, she put the LM into an immediate and vertiginous dive that made Sandoval wish he hadn't eaten that slice of pie after all, and then arced back up, a three-G parabolic swing, going for height. And *laughing* while she did it.

"What?" he said, when he could speak again.

"The bastards are firing at us," Brock said, viciously. "Which means we get to fire back. Right?"

Her eyes were narrowed. It wasn't hard for Sandoval to guess what was going through Brock's mind at this exact moment.

A little prayer for Kevin Pope. And a single, venomous word in addition: *Payback*.

"Do it," Sandoval said. "Fire at will."

As the two Soviets approached him, Makarov glanced up involuntarily. A third LEK? He had had no idea that there were still so many of his people on the Moon ...

No. This was American. A Lunar Module.

Behind his feet, Svetlana Belyakova lay still. But Makarov was not fooled, and the two Soviets from the LEK were wary too. Without saying a word they separated, to come around Makarov from two sides.

"Comrades," he said, his hands raised. "Let us discuss this. We all serve the Rodina, no? We are on the same side."

Neither of them answered him, just as they hadn't answered anything else he had tried to say to them.

He knew when Svetlana made her move, because the Soviets reacted immediately, and so an instant later Makarov jumped too.

Svetlana had rolled to bring up the Uzi and was now firing a spray of bullets on automatic, raking the Soviet on the left with bullets, up and down, up and down. Sparks flew as the bullets ricocheted off the soldier's helmet, radio, the oxygen tubes on his chest, and—presumably for psychological impact—his crotch. The man threw himself further left to avoid the bombardment, and Makarov leaped the same way, so that he would not block Belyakova as she turned her attention to the soldier on the right.

That man was already firing. Nikolai was unarmed. He jumped and ran, swerving as much as he could, trying to put the wreckage of the Lunokhod between himself and the cosmonauts, but deep in his heart he knew it was hopeless.

Above him, the airborne LEK and the incoming Lunar Module were also firing at each other, but Makarov hardly had time to watch the dogfight ... until the LEK exploded in midair above them, astonishingly bright.

With the destruction of the airborne LEK, the two Soviet soldiers on the ground rapidly lost interest in Makarov and Belyakova and sprinted back to their own lander. The Air Force Lunar Module was swinging around again, a little lopsided, since the remaining large missile still mounted on its port side unbalanced it. RCS firings from the thrusters atop its ascent stage worked to keep it level as it came around to threaten the LEK on the ground.

Perhaps they hoped that if they fled the scene, the LM would show them mercy. But it looked as if this wasn't on the cards.

Belyakova had stopped firing now and joined Makarov behind the cover of the wrecked Lunokhod. They saw the LM closing the distance, saw that port missile detach from the Module and drop a few feet before its rocket motor ignited. The missile came spearing in.

The LEK was a stationary target. If the LM pilot missed, he really deserved to be court martialed.

"Down!" Makarov dropped to the ground. He felt the detonation as the LEK exploded into a wreck of shrapnel, but they were far enough away that none of that shrapnel hit him. That made a change, at least.

"Svetlana?"

"Alive," she said, laconically.

He glanced up, and there was Belyakova, already pushing herself back up onto her feet and swinging the Uzi around.

"Ah," he said. The soldiers hadn't made it back to their LEK in time?

Yes, they had. In time to be destroyed with it, anyway.

Svetlana was gearing up to fire at the LM, which was now taking evasive action. Night Corps LMs might have thicker skins than the NASA versions, but that didn't mean they were impervious to automatic rifle fire.

The graben twisted and turned, but not really enough to help her. Was she running downhill, at least on the downslope of one of the Moon's many undulations? Probably. Even as Vivian thought this, she saw boulders ahead of her, littering the left-hand side of the narrow crack. Were there also boulders up top, outside the graben? There were.

She glanced back. Still no sign of the cosmonaut, although her trail of boot prints stretched out clearly behind her. No need for the guy to overexert; he could follow her at his leisure.

Well, okay. That gave her an idea. Not a great one, but the only thing she could think of. She started to run up the slope.

Even amid all this turmoil, Vivian's trained senses registered it right away when the stream of fresh oxygen coming into her helmet began to dwindle, the fans merely churning the mix that was already there. At the same time, her CO_2 level began to rise. Vivian glanced down at her gauges, swore, and reached up to flip the OPS actuator lever on her chest-mounted control unit to the ON position. Immediately, her Oxygen Purge System clicked in, behind her helmet on top of her life support backpack.

Fresh oxygen began to purr reassuringly into her suit. Just like it was supposed to. Which was great. It was always nice when life support hardware worked. But it also meant that Vivian only had thirty minutes left until she suffocated.

Somehow, she hardly cared. She hadn't expected to survive this and guess what? She wasn't going to.

Vivian set out to clamber out of the graben, puffing and wheezing and swearing as she did so. If that used up extra oxygen … well, it hardly mattered any more.

Glancing back, she caught a glimpse of dark red a couple hundred yards behind her, just as bullets started to kick up the ground around her feet, blowing out little craters and sending dust flying. Vivian felt the smack of the bullets against her boots and the backs of her calves, then achieved the crest of the graben and ran into the boulder field … the same field where the Soviet transport that had taken her halfway around the Moon had met its ignominious and explosive end.

She could see it now, a huge twisted and blackened mess barely recognizable as a wheeled flatbed any more, plus the tracks of Nikolai's Lunokhod as he'd driven it away in the nick of time.

She spared a moment to look behind her again, but the boulders still blocked her from seeing the hostile cosmonaut. That soldier's next task would be to cross the graben, running down and then up the other side, and likely proceeding cautiously, expecting an ambush. This meant that Vivian had a minute or two's grace.

She was still puffing and panting like crazy, probably burning through her precious half-hour of oxygen way too fast, but she forced herself to keep going. She had some fancy footwork to achieve, in the moments that remained before the cosmonaut gained the top of the graben and came for her.

She could no longer see the second LEK in the air. That meant it had either landed—in which case she was sunk—or it had gone ...

"Aw, *crap*."

Belatedly, Vivian had realized that both those LEKs together wouldn't have enough room aboard to take all three of them, Vivian plus Makarov and Belyakova. If the LEKs already had crews of three, even cramming one extra person into each would be iffy.

Meaning that at least one of them would have been left here on the Moon, and surely as a corpse.

So much for Nikolai's original plan to give themselves up and allow themselves to be captured. That had never been an option. The cold equations of mass and thrust prevented it.

Right now the ideal tactic would be to go to ground, to hide so convincingly that the Soviet had to give up looking for her. But that was the one thing Vivian couldn't do. It would take too long, and she'd be dead of asphyxiation long before he left. No: she had to get rid of this guy, and she likely couldn't take him out, couldn't kill him ... which meant she had to just bamboozle and outrun him, and then hope she had enough air to get her back to the others, and that they had, against all the odds, survived in the meantime.

Vivian had to stop. Had to. She just wasn't fit enough to keep running forever. She holed up behind a rock the size of a small cottage, and peered around it carefully, puffing and wheezing her way through her tiny store of remaining oxygen. Just for a few moments, to try to shift that stitch in her side and get more oxygen into her blood, before she set off again.

There he was, three hundred yards away, arriving on the scene with all the calm of a man with a full air tank and a scarily large gun. He had all the time in the world. Vivian didn't.

From his point of view, what would he see? Vivian's tracks leading to, and past, the wreckage of the Big Rig, He'd run toward the machine, giving it a wide berth in case Vivian had climbed onto it to get the drop on it, and past it.

And next he'd see her boot prints heading away, around the next boulder to the left and back toward the graben, and off he'd go in that direction.

Vivian had indeed gone back toward the graben and just over the edge, loping with some difficulty along the steep slope just below the crest for two hundred feet, before jumping out and bopping back around to her current position.

As soon as he vanished from her view, she took a deep breath and broke cover.

Back toward the LEK, and Makarov and Belyakova.

"Now what?" Brock said.

Sandoval looked at the scene below. For his own taste, he'd seen enough killing. "Two ships down. Couple of survivors over there, but they don't pose a threat. We're done here."

Bullets pinged off the outside of the LM. One of the survivors was firing at them. Brock immediately punched the LM higher. "Done, are we?"

"Yes. We'll leave them to it. Go back to Daedalus, let the Soviet authorities know that two of their folks are out on surface here, and make it their problem to come pick them up."

"Or, we could just take them out, leave a clean slate, and not tell the Soviets jack shit. You think they'd tell us, if the positions were switched?"

"No. But we're supposed to be better than them. And, take out how?" They'd had the two missiles, but no external gun platform, meaning that they couldn't chase down and shoot individual cosmonauts easily. Not without Sandoval hanging out the top of the LM with a gun ... which he absolutely was not about to do. And landing would make it two against two.

"We still have a plume," Brock said brutally. "Five gets you ten that I can nail both the bastards in one quick swoop. *Then* we'll go home."

"Terri, for Christ's sake ... we're United Nations."

"Not right now. We're Night Corps. And so was Kevin Pope."

"And we're human beings. Kill them and it's murder."

"Better than suffocating out here. I'd be doing them a favor."

"No," Sandoval said. "No more killing. No burning men to death for revenge. Just, no. And that's an order."

She exhaled, more of a hiss than a sigh. "Damn it. Sir."

"Brock?"

"Wilco." She glanced regretfully across the surface. "We don't know any more about the nukes than we did before."

Sandoval wasn't sure he cared. "Infighting. Soviet Union is going down the tubes. Same factions up here as back there, I'm betting. Not our concern."

"Okay," she said. "Let's go home … wait. What's *that*?" She rocked the LM forward.

"Brock, I'm losing patience."

"Bear with me." Brock curtseyed the LM down toward the lunar surface over yet another piece of wreckage. "Sooo … Where did the hell did they get that?"

Sandoval glanced quickly down at whatever Brock was looking at, but quickly felt nauseous and pulled his eyes away, swallowing. "Tell me."

"It's a LESS. Or was, I'm sure of it."

Sandoval shook his head, none the wiser.

"NASA flyer. Must be from Marius. That's the only place we've ever left one behind. They evacuated Marius in a hurry after Burning Night. Which explains *that* as well." Brock pointed, out the side window this time, at an even bigger bit of wreckage, out in the boulder field. "The Marius transport. The bloody cryptos went back for it. Meaning these guys *are* cryptos."

"Doesn't make any difference. And they're likely dead anyway, out here without support. And we're burning a lot of fuel just talking about this."

She waved that off. "I'm watching it. We still have enough to make Daedalus, and if we do run low, we can easily make Jura and refuel there."

"You're still not killing them," he said. "Get used to it."

"Fine," she said, and kicked up the power, putting the LM into a climb, up and away from the battle scene. "But you owe me a damned huge drink when we get back to Earth."

Vivian broke out of the boulder field, changing her running mode from a lope to a kangaroo-hop. A change was as good as a rest, right? Except it wasn't, not really; the pressures on her screaming thigh muscles were a little different, but the pains in her chest, shoulder and head were around the same, and her lungs felt like they were burning up.

The LEK was gone. Both LEKs: the one that had been in the sky, and the one on the ground. Gone. They'd left her behind.

She kept running anyway. She still had a soldier with a big gun behind her ...

... who they'd also left behind? The Soviets had really abandoned their own guy?

That hardly made sense. "Svetlana? Nikolai?"

"Vivian?" Svetlana's voice, though Vivian couldn't see her.

"Yes, yes!" Then came a sudden, new pain in her head, and Vivian knew well what that meant.

The oxygen pressure in her suit was dropping, and fast. Her time was almost up.

"I'm going to need a buddy air-hose," she said. "So I sure hope you've got one handy."

Brock pointed. "There! Did you see that? Wasn't that an Apollo suit?"

"Brock ..."

"I'm serious."

He peered in the direction she was pointing. "I don't see anything."

"Not Soviet, anyway. It wasn't red."

"Their Krechet suits aren't red," Sandoval said.

"And their Kretchets have a hard aluminum torso. They look completely different."

He shook his head. "Fuel?"

She glanced down. "Damn it. Getting borderline for Daedalus. But we're still fine for Jura, or even Marius or Kepler. Peter, I know what I saw."

"Okay," he said. "Okay. But if you're—"

"No." Brock released the controls briefly to hold up her hand. "Whatever you're about to say ... don't."

Vivian looked back over her shoulder at her nemesis, plugging away behind her. Not firing at her, though, not yet. Maybe he was a little freaked out himself to see that he'd apparently been abandoned by his buddies. Or maybe he just wanted to save ammo by getting closer.

He was four hundred feet behind her. She was three hundred feet from a pile of scrap metal that might have once been the Lunokhod, plus a whole lot of other debris. Had the ground LEK exploded? Whatever action she'd missed out here, it must have been really something.

Now she could see Nikolai Makarov, and even better, she could glimpse him screwing a connector into the array on the front of his suit and holding a short tube. All she had to do was get to him.

Belyakova had her Uzi up and pointing past Vivian at the guy chasing her. Not firing, not yet … and then she raised her head and jerked the Uzi up.

Vivian glanced upward and saw a battle LM swooping down on her. "Holy shit!"

Then she coughed. She should really stop talking. But she couldn't.

Belyakova fired up at it.

"Svetlana, what the hell! Stop, stop!" Vivian shouted, and fortunately the cosmonaut did.

Vivian switched frequencies. "Night Corps, Vivian Carter. Hi. This is Vivian Carter, US Navy and NASA, with … some high-ranking friends. Do you read me?"

She switched frequencies. "Night Corps LM, this is Vivian Carter, come in?"

Nothing but static on the line. "For God's *sake*."

She switched to Soviet frequencies. "Night Corps LM, this is Vivian Carter … Night Corps, this is Vivian, hold your fire …" And so on. The problem was that there were so many damned frequencies; by now NASA, the Air Force, Night Corps, and the various Soviet factions made extensive use of the available VHF bandpass for surface operations.

Then she started to cough, and her head threatened to explode. She didn't have much time …

"Dark red suit," Sandoval said. "That one's Vympel."

"And chasing an Apollo astronaut. Now can I kill him?"

"Fine. It's on your conscience, not mine."

"On my what, now?" Brock dropped the LM out of the sky.

Vivian fell forward onto her knees, gasping for breath, and looked around just as the Night Corps LM did its low pass. Very low. The Vympel guy was now ducking and weaving back and forth, well aware of his peril, and shooting upward at the LM, but its pilot knew what he was about. The Red soldier didn't have a chance.

The plume hit the KGB Vympel soldier and turned him into a flaming torch. *Crispy cosmonaut*, Vivian thought, her dark humor attempting to push away the horror of it, but she had little air left to speak. She was involuntarily breathing faster and faster, quick gasps, as her body tried to find oxygen, any oxygen, anywhere. She tried to flex her suit, to move around any gas that might have pooled anywhere else in the system. Woozily, she could see that Makarov was running forward toward her. Belyakova was walking more steadily, her Uzi up on her shoulder and ready to fire.

The LM hit the ground in what must have been a damned hard landing just fifty feet behind her, both hatches already open. A Night Corps astronaut popped out of the top like a jack-in-the-box, while another shimmied out of the front hatch and leaped down onto the lunar surface.

Both started firing past her at Makarov and Belyakova, Makarov threw himself flat. Belyakova fired back.

"Svetlana, stop shooting, Jesus …"

"If they do, then perhaps I will."

Vivian twisted the radio comms dial on her chest, searching the frequencies … and now, at last, she heard another woman's voice through her headset. "… the guy on the left. I'll take the bitch with the gun."

"*Terri?*"

Gasping, pushing back the waves of dizziness that threatened to rob her of all consciousness, Vivian stood and raised both her arms. From somewhere, she found her voice. "Terri? Hold your fire. Right now. Please."

Brock kept firing. Vivian took what passed for a gasping breath and stepped forward, thrusting herself into the line of fire between Brock and Belyakova. Bullets raked the front of her suit before Brock stopped firing abruptly and put up her gun. "*Damn* it!"

Mercifully, Belyakova stopped firing too.

"Terri, Terri, it's me, Vivian, for the love of God. Don't shoot them."

"Tell the Soviet to put her gun down. And put your gun down."

In all this, Vivian had forgotten she was still carrying her useless Uzi. She unlooped it and threw it away, then pointed at Makarov. "I ... need him. Need his air." Without waiting for a response, she switched frequencies again. "Nikolai ... air."

He walked forward, hands up, and kneeled by her side. She fumbled for the umbilical but he brushed her gloved hands aside and made the connection himself.

Oxygen gushed in. She sucked it down eagerly. Coughed, inhaled again.

Buddy system. Now, she was sharing Nikolai's air, for as long as it lasted.

Brock was moving closer, her gun still trained on them. The other soldier had leaped down from the top hatch and was following, walking to the side so that he had a clear shot at the Soviets if he needed to fire.

"Okay," Brock said. "Who the hell are you? What's going on?"

"I'm Vivian, I told you. Vivian Carter."

"Bullshit. Carter's a billion miles away."

Over the crackly radio, Vivian might not have recognized Terri's voice if she hadn't already known who it was. "Slight exaggeration, babe. I'm right here in front of you."

Brock came to within ten feet and leaned just a little closer to read her name tag. "Simmons."

Exasperation flooded her. "You want to write our goddamn book all by yourself? Fine, kill my ass. But have fun explaining it to NASA."

"There's a Laura Simmons on Astarte," said the other guy. "Is this her? Or just her suit?"

"Damn it all," said Terri Brock. "How ...?"

Vivian's mouth dropped open. She felt like she'd been punched in the gut. "Is that ... *Peter Sandoval?* My God ... *You* sure as hell shouldn't be on the Moon."

"Neither should you," he said.

Peter Sandoval. Here on the Moon. Right in front of her, all of a sudden, and completely unexpected. Vivian's legs threatened to give way.

"What?" Brock shook her head in frustration. "Vivian *Carter?* Really? What the actual *hell?*"

"It's nuts, I know. I'll give you that."

481

"And who are *they*?"

"Oh, these guys? You wouldn't believe me if I told you. Hang on a moment. Let me get us all on the same frequency. And stop pointing those damned guns at us, okay?"

Belyakova had summoned their rescuers by nuking her enemies. That was almost amusing.

Half an hour later, they'd pretty much gotten everything straight. Vivian and her cosmonauts were sitting or lying on the regolith, all plugged into the LM's oxygen and cooling water supply by umbilical. Terri was still holding her gun and speaking with that clipped voice that meant she was angry. Why, Vivian couldn't quite fathom. Was she pissed off that she couldn't kill Makarov and Belyakova? Mad at Vivian for leaving her ship, for being here?

Vivian was still shaking. She'd thought they were all dead, the three of them. She'd even come to terms with it. Now, it appeared she'd have to go on living for a while longer, because she'd been rescued by two of her favorite people in the world … even if they had briefly tried to kill her first. She had whiplash.

And Peter was here, so that was messing with her head on a completely different axis. She tried to pull herself together. "Okay, guys. So, what now?"

"We airlift you all back to Daedalus," Sandoval said. Was there also a tremor in his voice that hadn't been there before Vivian identified herself? She couldn't quite tell. "Somehow. Since we have three extra bodies we'll need to call in another LM. Ours is a bit low on gas. Then, once we have you there with the UN group, we'll figure out how to get you back to Earth—to the US—securely."

"Daedalus," Terri said thoughtfully.

"We cannot be safe at Daedalus Base," Svetlana said. "Nikolai and I? We are now enemies …" She paused, swallowed down her emotion. "We are now enemies of the state. We cannot walk into a den of lions."

"Daedalus Base is under UN Peacekeeping jurisdiction," Sandoval said. "It's a safe zone."

"I wish I could believe that," Vivian said. "But Svetlana is right. There are still too many Soviets there. It's a bad idea. We need to skip that step and just get these two back to the US as soon as we possibly can."

"There can still be Vympel groups anywhere," Makarov said. "Getting their orders direct from the hardliners back in the Kremlin who have nothing left to lose."

"Plus, we need to keep all of this quiet," Terri said. "With something this big? The defection of the two most famous cosmonauts in Soviet history?"

Belyakova closed her eyes. "Please. Do not say 'defection.' I am not a defector."

"Call it whatever you damned well like," Terri said.

Vivian shook her head. "Terri, jeez—lay off her."

Makarov looked thoughtful. "Gagarin, Leonov: these men are better known than I, of that I am sure."

"Guys, come on, good grief," Vivian said. "Look, Terri's right. I hate it, but she is. There's no way we can take these two to Daedalus. Svetlana disobeyed orders and killed her superior officers, and Nikolai is effectively a deserter. By Soviet lights, they're criminals and fugitives."

Belyakova gave a little groan. Vivian reached over and patted her arm. "Sorry, babe. But you are. So as soon as we arrive at Daedalus, the Soviets will demand we hand them over. And if we refuse …"

Terri nodded. "If we refuse, we get stuck in an extradition mess that will overshadow everything else the UN is trying to do at Daedalus. Diplomatically speaking, we'd be tossing a bull into a china shop. And that's not even mentioning the physical risk to the cosmonauts and Vivian. Unless we keep them under twenty-four-hour lock and key, some KGB goon can fire a ricin pellet into any of them, at any time."

"They can't go to Daedalus," Vivian said. "I can't go to Daedalus. There's no point going anywhere else on the Moon, except back to the LEK and off the surface as quickly as possible."

"Yes," Belyakova murmured. "Yes."

Sandoval was looking back and forth between them in irritation. "I'm glad you're all in agreement about ignoring our chain of command. That's refreshing. But this isn't our decision to make. We need to report in and run it up the chain."

"No," said Vivian. "Peter … You really don't."

He stared at her for a moment, and then said: "Vivian, the three of you may have burned your bridges, but Terri and I haven't. We do this, we get court martialed."

"Doubt it," Vivian said. "If we can get these two back to the US safely, I think that would actually be quite the career coup for you, once word gets out."

Sandoval leaned forward. "You don't get it. I want you and your Soviet friends safe, and as soon as possible. Obviously. But I also want to keep my damned career."

"And you can have all that," Vivian said. "It's just a matter of timing, right? When you came to Hadley in charge of Apollo Rescue One, you had complete operational authority. At Daedalus, you trumped Johnston's chain of command and stopped him from reporting to Cheyenne, because the urgency of the situation demanded it. This is the same. Operational authority, and a decision that needs to be made fast."

"Except that then I had a letter from the President granting me that authority. This time, I don't."

Vivian waved her gloved hands. "Details."

"This time we're leading a UN delegation. We're not supposed to even *be* Night Corps for the purposes of this deployment."

"Even better, right? Then it's a humanitarian decision. Sure, the moment you've got us on our way you can make a full report up through Night Corps channels. We'll need to be in touch with either Cheyenne or NASA for the trans-Earth injection burn and cruise phase anyway. Because, although in principle I could calculate my own course back to Earth and half-ass my way through splashdown, I'd *really* rather have a competent flight dynamics team working the numbers, plus a recovery crew on station to pick us up when we arrive."

Terri nodded. "NASA, then. Cheyenne could get the job done if there was no other option, but the Air Force doesn't speak Apollo. Our computer systems, deorbits and splashdowns use a whole different lexicon, trust me. But the way to get this done is still through Night Corps: we can get a secure line set up to the NASA flight controllers and all, and get them to handpick a small, secure, top-clearance team of trusted folks to get you home. That minimizes the chance of all this leaking out."

"Okay, sure," Vivian said. "I guess."

Terri grinned tightly at the doubtful expression on Vivian's face. "Leave the cloak and dagger stuff to us, Viv. That's kind of why we exist. For now, deriving your Deliverance ephemeris is all you need to do. We'll get the other pieces of this into play."

"Roger that." Vivian looked back at Sandoval. "So, boss. You ready to make the decision? We really need to be getting this show on the road."

Sandoval shook his head. "How? Even if I agree to this, we still have the problem of getting you all back to Marius with only one LM."

"Oh, that? Piece of cake," Terri said, and they all turned to look at her.

"You can seriously hop us all back to Marius in *one* LM?" Vivian said, incredulous. "You, me, Peter, Nikolai, Svetlana? Five people in a Lunar Module?"

"It won't be pretty. And you can't all be *in*. At least one of you will need to sit outside."

As Vivian blinked and looked across at the LM, Makarov finally stirred himself to speak. "Are you joking? Or not joking?"

"Not joking. That LM has the same engine as the one Vivian and I flew into the Marius battle, which had two pilots, two gunners, and some heavy ordnance. We fired both the missiles on this one, saving your asses. So we can lift the weight of five, even with the fuel we have, but there's no way in hell all five will fit inside. Not if I need to still be able to see and operate the instruments."

Vivian frowned. "But, your LM doesn't have the gunner positions. So, no outside seating."

"Meaning we'll need to strap someone onto the egress platform, or the back of the craft. Vivian, stop looking at me like that. How the hell else is this going to work? You know how cramped LMs are. I can't ferry you across the Moon one person at a time."

"Hmm," Vivian said.

"And, not to be facetious, but there's a rule against allowing Soviets aboard US landers."

Makarov nodded sagely. "And no Americans inside Soviet landers. We have this rule as well."

"Oh my God." Belyakova put her head into her hands. "*Uzhas.*"

"Nightmare," Vivian translated for the Americans' benefit, and then patted Belyakova's arm. "Don't worry. Terri's messing with you. Neither of you are flying outside. I am."

"No way in hell," Sandoval said immediately. "Are you insane?"

"I wish people would stop asking me that … but, listen. Terri has to fly this bus. I haven't flown a LM for over two years, so she's obviously the pilot. And, frankly, I don't trust her not to just drop one of my Soviets from a great height."

Terri half-grinned. "You think I'd do that?"

"I'm so tired right now that I don't even know. But I can't rule it out. And we can't put Peter out there. He needs to be in there keeping an eye on the Soviets, while you're doing the flying. So, it's me. Try not to kill me."

Terri nodded. "Okay, fine. If you were inside, you'd just back-seat-drive me anyway. And the boss would give me all kinds of flak if I killed you. And, just so we're all clear, you're only volunteering for this because you think the view from out there is going to be really cool."

"Well," Vivian said. "There's that, of course. But, hey, whatever you do: don't drop the descent stage, okay?"

Peter went pale behind his visor, but at least Terri laughed at last, and some of the tension left her voice.

Terri was right. The view was amazing.

Terrifying. But amazing.

CHAPTER 35

Marius Base, and Cislunar Space: Vivian Carter
June 6-7, 1985

FOR Vivian Carter, it seemed that all roads led to Marius. Because here she was again.

For her Apollo 32 mission, Marius had been the road charted and planned for, but not initially traveled. The Cold War had intervened and exposed Vivian to a number of traumatic experiences before she finally got to do her original exploratory mission in the Marius Hills in early March of 1980, three months late.

Her next conflict with the Soviets had brought her to Marius again in 1983, this time in late March.

Science had brought her here, and war. And now, her mission of mercy, in May-June of 1985. But this must surely be the last time. Right?

Seeing the entire Marius Hills scenery laid out beneath her, and coming down upon it from a parabolic hop that had taken them several tens of miles above the surface, was an incredible experience. At the Marius longitude it was a day and a half before lunar sunset, and so the solar incidence angle was ideal for bringing the surface features into sharp relief. No narrow windows obscured her view, and she didn't have to concentrate on piloting. For once she could just be a tourist, and gape like a kid at the vista of ridges and valleys and volcanic domes spread out beneath her.

The landing itself was hair-raising. LMs came down slowly, but strapped outside it as she was the ground did seem to be lurching up at her pretty fast, and once they got within a hundred and fifty feet of the surface, the spraying of dust from the blast of the LM's plume was alarming. The plume deflectors protected Vivian from any substantial reflected heat from the surface in those moments, though her suit did register a brief temperature increase.

She had no idea where the ground was anymore. All she could see was dust, rattling off her helmet visor. Then came the bang of contact, transmitted up through the landing gear and the platform beneath her. It felt much harder than it had when she'd been standing in the LM, with her legs as additional shock absorbers.

But they were down, and the dust dropped, and the heat dissipated, and for a few moments of complete silence Vivian Carter was alone and at rest, with nothing to do but feast her eyes on the panorama of the Marius Hills, while the rest of the crew completed the shutdown procedures, disentangled themselves, and prepared to disembark.

After that, it was all business for a while. Getting herself unfastened from the platform so everyone else could get past her and onto the surface. Pressurizing the most robust-looking of the Bricks that still lay outside the lava tube. Doing a much better job of putting Nikolai's arm into a splint. Cleaning the corrosive dust off their suits and the inside of the Brick and then breaking into some of the leftover MREs to get some food inside themselves. After that, the Soviets went to their bunks, and the three Americans got some more time to chat and get themselves organized.

Almost all business, anyway. Once they were all out of their suits Vivian got to see Peter and Terri for real, for the first time in years. Terri had been helping Vivian off with her suit, so it was her who Vivian hugged first. For all of Terri's earlier seething anger, she did cling onto Vivian just as hard as Vivian was hugging her.

And then Peter was next in line, and when they hugged each other, Vivian couldn't tell which of them was shaking more.

Then they separated, both cleared their throats, and with wry glances turned away to get on with the matters at hand.

* * *

"Okay, we're all set," Peter said. "I talked to Night Corps and, after all that drama, they're oddly okay with the plan. They were damned surprised, I have to say. But, turns out any opportunity to steal a march on the Reds is looking good to my management these days. They're on the case, working to pull the strings with NASA and get you your help to for your return. And, hopefully, all this stays under the Soviet radar."

"Great," Vivian said.

"Besides, the Soviet Politburo is *busy*, right now. Their empire is crumbling around them. Separation movements in various countries, and protests in all the major cities of the USSR. Still no word of where the hell Andropov is. Some people are even saying we might be looking at the end of the Soviet Union, as we know it. The old guard are fighting a rearguard action, trying to hold the central core together: Russia, Ukraine, the other adjacent republics. How much attention they're paying to space is anyone's guess."

"Huh," Vivian said. "Unexpected."

"Is it?" Terri grinned.

"And a surprise bonus." Sandoval looked so happy that Vivian had a fair guess at what he was going to say, before he even said it. "We get to go home, too. We've been recalled early, Terri and me. Since we're already on the move, it hardly makes sense to go back to Daedalus, tell a bunch of lies about where we've been and what we've been doing, only to then ship out in a week anyways. Daedalus is stable. They don't need to feed us anymore."

Wow. That was great. But … "How are you getting back?" Vivian asked. "And don't say you want to put five people in Deliverance, because that would be crazy talk."

"God, no. They're sending us a Blue Gemini."

"*Sending?*" Vivian shook her head. "You dark space guys. You just have spare ships lying around?"

"Uh, yes. Some, at least."

"There's a reason our budget is classified," Brock said.

"So, where's this Blue Gemini now?"

"MOL-B, in high halo."

"The same MOL-B that I went to? It's still there?"

"Well, for some values of 'there'—it's in the same weird orbit, anyway. It's not the same physical vessel—the hardware's been replaced a couple times. But the MOL operating in high halo is always called MOL-B."

"And your Gemini is coming under ... what, remote control? Automatic pilot?"

"Yes," Terri said. "That second one."

Vivian shook her head. "Fine. What *else* don't I know about what you guys are getting up to, on and around the Moon?"

"We could tell you," Terri said, deadpan. "But then we'd have to ... well, you know how *that* phrase ends."

"Okay, sleepy-head, your bird just went over."

Vivian opened an eye. It was Terri, of course, standing at the door of the small bunkroom that Vivian had commandeered and looking down into the cot she was snoozing on, fully dressed.

Vivian rubbed her eyes, shifted position, and stretched cautiously. Yes, she still hurt in two dozen places, but it was manageable. "Good to know. Thanks."

Better than good, of course. No reason why Deliverance shouldn't still be there, patiently orbiting the Moon and waiting for her. The onboard orbital maintenance software was designed to detect any unexpected variance to its altitude or bearing and correct for it automatically; the Moon had mass concentrations beneath its surface that perturbed orbits and could, in time, erode them completely. But it was nice to confirm that Astarte's old CM-2 hadn't suffered some sort of anomaly, and that no hostiles had blown it out of the sky.

"So," Terri went on, "I've programmed the LM's comms system to watch out for it on the next pass, and any subsequent passes. Record the exact times of acquisition and loss of signal, plus its bearing and range-rate and all. Two or three of those and we should have the ephemeris nailed. Night Corps magic. You're welcome."

"Boundless gratitude, I'm sure," Vivian said sardonically. That was, of course, a straightforward calculation she could have done herself in about five minutes, and Terri knew it.

"So, next up: I'm going to drive our Soviet cousins out to retrieve Makarov's LEK, in our rover. I'll load them aboard it and watch them take off, then come back overland. They'll put down next to the LM, and once I get back we'll see about getting both ships fueled up. And then we can start shaking the dust of this rock off our boots and getting home."

Terri waited expectantly. "Great," Vivian said. "Thanks."

Patiently, Terri explained. "Sooo that means we'll be out of here for several hours. Six or maybe seven, I'm guessing, when all's said and done. You and Peter will be fine minding the store here while we're gone, yes?"

"Oh," Vivian said. "Oh! Me and …?" She coughed, trying to cover a sudden uncharacteristic surge of embarrassment. "I guess. I'm sure we'll cope."

"I'm sure, too." Terri smiled sweetly. "Again, you're welcome. You guys be good, you hear?"

"Roger that. Uh, where's Peter now, exactly?"

"Well, not that I've looked with my own eyes, but I believe he might be in the shower."

"You guys." Vivian shook her head. "This is a total setup, right?"

"Purely acting on my own initiative. It wasn't Peter's idea, sad to say. Anyways, gotta go."

As she turned away, Vivian called, "Hey, Ter'? You're not just taking this opportunity to kill off my Soviets, right? Because that would just be rude."

Terri stopped and considered. "Hey, there's a thought … Nah. I'll keep 'em safe. I mean, not that I care, but your boy scout would have me drummed out of the Corps if I let anything happen to them."

"Thanks. Love you, Terri."

Brock grinned again. "Aw, don't get sappy now. At least, not with me."

Vivian put her hand up to her eyes. "Could you manage to make this any more embarrassing?"

"I'm sure I'll find a way. Byeee!"

"So, you remember how at Hadley Base we had that joke about everyone leaving us alone together?"

Sandoval sat back from his computer terminal and smiled at her. "Sure."

It was the first time she'd seen that smile from Peter in person for nearly three years—that warm and affectionate smile that he never used on duty. And right now those three years seemed like a scarily long time. All of a sudden, her skin felt very warm all over.

"Well, um," she said, kind of lamely. "I guess it's just happened again."

"Guess it has."

She tried to lock eyes with him, but couldn't quite do it. "I mean, if you're busy …"

"No, it's pretty much a waiting game for now. Want to talk for a while?" He glanced around. "Not here. This is too business-like."

Vivian swallowed. "Somewhere more cozy, maybe?"

He looked quizzical. "This is a Brick. Absolutely the wrong kind of cozy."

"Let's give it a try, anyway. Back to my place?"

As they walked into Vivian's sleeping quarters and he pushed the door closed behind them, it suddenly felt overwhelming.

"Peter …" He was *here*, right next to her after all this time, all those solitary cycles of the Sun with no human contact beyond the casual brushes of crew in weightlessness moving past one another. It was a lot to take in. And all at once Vivian wanted to cry, except that wasn't what she'd thought she wanted at all.

And maybe Peter felt the same. He just put his arms around her, both still standing up just inside the door, and they stood there for a few moments in silence.

Eventually Vivian wiped her eyes on the chest of his jumpsuit and looked up at him, and his eyes were glistening as well. "It's okay," he said. "Uh. Is it okay?"

"I think maybe it is. At last." She sighed, breathing him in. "It's just been a while."

He gave a short laugh. "You're not kidding."

"And we're both still alive."

"Sure. For now."

She poked him. "Buzzkill."

"I just mean that I'm trying not to take anything for granted anymore."

"Fair." She hugged him, hard. Never wanted to let him go. "Very fair, to be honest."

Another awkward silence, before he took a deep breath. "So. You're leaving the Moon for the last time. And heading back to Earth with Soviets. Who ever saw that coming?"

"And you're heading back to Earth with Terri Brock, in a teeny tiny Blue Gemini." She tried to grin, to keep it light. "Good luck with that."

"Maybe you and Terri should trade places," he said.

"Best not." Vivian snuggled into him. "First up, I've been in a Blue Gemini, and there isn't anywhere near the amount of space we'd need.

And I have a feeling that after a three-day trip back to Earth in one I'd never be able to bend my arms and legs again."

"I'm not looking forward to it myself. Except the part where I'm leaving the Moon behind me forever."

"And, if I came with you, that leaves Terri to nursemaid the Soviets, and … she might kill them. Unless Belyakova killed her first." She grinned up at him, feeling the tension begin to ease at last. "Plus, Terri isn't a Command Module Pilot. Not that I am, but I've been studying. And, let's be honest: in the Gem we'd be so into each other's business that we'd screw something up and never get back to Earth. I *really* need to concentrate over the next week. Because this is going to suck."

Peter nodded and began to absently stroke her hair, which she discovered she liked. "It'll be okay. And after that?"

"After that, I'll be home. Back on Earth. With you."

He grinned at that. "So Earth is home, now?"

"Yes, it is. At last."

"And you're quite sure about that?"

"Yes. This time, I'm sure. It had to take … however long it needed to take. But now, I'm ready for Earth." She took a deep breath and forced herself to look up and meet his eye, at last. "I'm ready for you, Peter. If you still …" She swallowed.

"Just so you know, I won't hold you to that until it really happens."

"What, you don't trust me?"

"I don't know anything," he admitted. "To be honest, I do feel like I need to be cautious. After all this? Who else has lives like ours?"

"Everyone's life is different, I guess."

"And up here in space you and I are one thing, and then when we go back down to Earth it somehow turns into something else."

"And that was me last time," Vivian said, very seriously. "Peter, that was all me. You were just the same, and I was a huge mess. And, I'm really sorry about that, but … it really just had to happen. I had to sort myself out, and I *had* to do LGS-1 and I *had* to do Apollo Venus Astarte. And I don't regret them. It was what I was meant to do."

"Yes, it was. And now?"

"Now I'm meant to go home," she said. "I'm done. I've had the Moon, and the planets, and … I've had friends at last, real friends, and now it's time to go home."

Peter looked amused. "You talk like you're dying."

"Not dying. Just rebooting. Can we sit down?"

"Of course." They perched on the bed, and she slipped her hand into his. "Okay, fine, so once we get back to Earth ... what do you do? I mean, apart from be with me, and ... and what else?"

"The next generation," Vivian said. "Not kids—not kids of my own. I still think that would be one hell of a gamble after all the radiation I've sucked into my body over the years. And, Peter, we have to be real about the consequences of that. I might not live to be ninety-six. For space reasons."

"I'll take however many years we end up having. So, what about 'the next generation'?"

"Of astronauts. I have a lot of experience, now. Maybe I can help the next batch of astronauts to not screw up quite as badly as I did, from time to time. Maybe I can teach them. NASA has a lot going on and maybe we might have even more in the future. We can have Mars. We can have Venus. We can keep going, and we should. And for that, we need people who've been there, and done a bunch of stuff wrong, and occasionally figured out how to do things right. And that's me. And that's what's next."

"Sounds great," he said. "And I'll be there with you, if you want me. Most of the time, anyway."

"I think I've heard this one before. You're going to give up space altogether. Stay on Earth and be an airline pilot, or some shit."

Peter grinned. "No. I'm smarter now. I know I can't do that. Space is still my life, but not *this* space, not the Moon. This is your territory—or was. Earth orbit, looking down on the planet, keeping everyone safe? That's my world. I mean, literally. You can have the whole damned solar system. I just want the Earth."

She leaned against him. He felt very warm and solid. "And you'll keep it safe."

"To the best of my ability. But that means I might be gone a while, from time to time."

"Gone?" Vivian made wide eyes. "From me? In space?"

"Weird, I know."

"Well, turnabout is fair play, I guess."

He began to rub her back, squeezed her a little harder. Vivian shivered and didn't respond, and he hugged her tighter and then loosened up quickly and said, "Is this okay?"

"Yes," she said. "That is definitely okay. I just need to take this slow. Sorry."

"That's fine with me. I understand that you're regularly working on a months-long timescale these days."

She grinned. "Jerk."

"Vivian Carter. Space explorer."

"That's me. And ..." She allowed her fingers to graze his knee. "If it's okay with you, I'm going to go exploring, right now."

His breath caught for a moment. "Okay."

She touched his chest experimentally and then began to undo the buttons of his jumpsuit. "Bear with me. I'm still having trouble believing you're here."

"Vivian, if you don't want to ... you know, that's okay. We still have time. On Earth."

As more buttons came undone, Vivian felt herself begin to relax, and with that relaxation came a feeling of inner warmth and certainty. She smiled at him, an open smile, a cheeky smile. "Sure. But if we never do it up here, we'll always wish we had. Right?"

"I love you," he said, and now his hands began to move as well, stroking, caressing, unbuttoning.

"I love you too," she said. "I really do. Now, come here. Lay down. And please take this thing off me."

Their trip back to lunar orbit in the Night Corps LM was straightforward. Vivian and Terri between them aligned the guidance and navigation system and worked the liftoff Pre-Advisory Data and prelaunch checklist. Then Terri launched them off the Moon, with Vivian calling numbers and Sandoval behind them, perched on top of the ascent engine cover with his legs crammed uncomfortably into the instrument bay.

Five minutes later, the LEK launched in their wake, chasing them up into the sky. After that, Terri and Nikolai put their heads together over the radio to finalize the approach and rendezvous with Deliverance, while Peter and Vivian tried to chase down some of the free lunar dust and Mylar fragments and other debris that was now floating around the cabin in their new weightlessness. For once, Vivian was content to not be doing her own piloting. She'd have enough of that to do over the coming few days. Right now, she could do with the break.

Another bonus: once they matched orbits and were on the final approach to CSM-2 they found they'd got lucky, because the Command and Service Module was hardly tumbling at all. Vivian was greatly relieved. "Thank God. That'll be an easy spacewalk at least, to go grab it and neutralize that roll."

"Spacewalk?" Terri's eyes twinkled. "We can do better than that. Watch and marvel."

She reached over to another console and typed some numbers. Looked out of the window professionally. Then pressed a button and, almost instantaneously, Vivian saw the small plumes of opposing RCS thrusters on Deliverance firing to slow its tumble. "Oh hey, look what I just did."

"Terri, what the *hell*? You just hacked into my *ship*?"

"Sure looks like it." Terri pulsed the thrusters again on CSM-2 until it was stationary in space and then started juggling with its attitude relative to their Lunar Module.

Sandoval was grinning as well. Vivian looked back and forth between them, exasperated. "You guys ... that's a dangerous power to have. If you can do that to my craft, and the Soviets figure out how it's done, *they* could hack into our Apollos and fly them from outside just as easily."

"Good job the Soviets don't know about it, then," Peter said sardonically.

Over the radio, Nikolai chuckled. "Of course, we have had that capability with our own Soyuz craft and landers for a lot of time, almost since our first landing on the Moon. But I suspect you could never duplicate it, and have an American craft control a Soyuz. It is complicated."

"It is, actually," Terri said. "So, not much danger there."

CSM-2 was now head-on to them. Terri relinquished the controls with a flourish. "*Et voila*. Let's go dock with your ride home."

And so, another uncanny constellation assembled in lunar orbit. A Night Corps Lunar Module, beginning to look a little the worse for wear, mated up to a NASA Command and Service Module, which was itself connected by a short makeshift aluminum truss to a Soviet LEK Lander, with an Air Force Blue Gemini soon to come. Four craft for five people, although no single vehicle had enough space for all of them.

By the time the Soviets had arrived and completed the docking maneuver, Belyakova was on the edge of collapsing with exhaustion, and Makarov was not a great deal better, blinking and bumping into everything. The two chose to remain aboard the LEK to get some sleep. Neither of them had a role in preparing the Command Module or Blue Gemini for their return-to-Earth cruises in any case. Toward the end of Deliverance's journey, Vivian would require help from one or other of the Soviets in working the checklists in the usual call-and-response mode, checking her switch settings and reading numbers to her, but neither of them were in any shape to think about that right now, and they'd have three days to train up for that on the cruise back to Earth.

"Well," Vivian said, and took a deep breath. "Time to call home, I guess."

"My God, Vivian. My God!"

"Oh, hi, Ellis," she said, mock casually. "Long time no hear."

Ellis was staring at her wide-eyed through the camera, as if he could scarcely believe what he was seeing. Now he shook his head. "You are freaking unbelievable."

"Thanks. I think. I'm guessing you've been brought up to speed on my recent activities?"

"Yes. And now we have to get you and your, uh, cargo safely back home. And there are going to be some interesting wrinkles with that. For one, inserting you seamlessly back into your Apollo Astarte crew, once you all get back to Earth."

Vivian shook her head. "How d'you mean? Astarte must have gotten back to Earth, what, a month ago?"

"No. You didn't know?"

In an instant, her heart froze. "What? Oh God ... Ellis, what the hell happened? *Is everyone okay?*" While thinking, *If they all died, there's no way it's not my fault.*

"Oh, everyone's fine, no problems ... all of them. Astarte and its crew are in fine shape. NASA just made a late-breaking decision to reshape their trajectory home."

"To what? Reshape how?"

"It was Dave Horn's idea. Rather than continue on their existing path, once you left, they decided to make an early deceleration burn, to reduce the speed they'd be carrying when they arrived back in cislunar space. The NERVA had gotten them up to such a clip that if the deceleration burn failed to come off flawlessly, they'd be in trouble. By slowing earlier and coming in at a steadier pace it retired a lot of risk and enabled them to do a much smaller Earth orbital insertion burn. And NASA went for that and agreed that establishing the feasibility of a smooth Earth-orbit injection burn on the return was a valuable test for future interplanetary missions. At the cost of a few weeks of extra mission time, of course."

Vivian gaped. "My crew agreed to extend their mission even *longer*?"

"It was unanimous. They'd all agreed on it even before Horn broached the idea with NASA management."

"Holy cow."

Unbelievable. Her crew had deliberately plotted to postpone their arrival back on Earth. To make their long mission even longer. And they'd made that sacrifice solely to cover for Vivian, to help her and her cosmonauts, although that additional risk reduction surely didn't hurt.

"That's amazing. Even Josh Rawlings signed off on that? And Rudy?"

"I told you; it was unanimous. Not that a crew's a real democracy. As captain of Astarte, Rawlings could have vetoed. Horn could obviously have vetoed. In fact, my impression is that they'd decided that they'd only do it if everyone agreed."

"Wow. I owe those guys a *lot* of beers. So where's Astarte right now?"

"They entered Earth orbit three days ago. And now they're stalling with another weeklong delay until splashdown while they put all the Astarte systems to bed and pack everything up."

"Which they don't need, because they could have been doing that in the extra month they gave themselves." Then again, Vivian thought, most of the scientists had been pitching for a few days of Earth-orbit rubbernecking anyway.

"Maybe. But, you know the drill. Best to be prudent and not rush things. Safety is our number one priority. That's the public story, anyway."

"Amazing," Vivian said again.

"Somehow, you have friends," Ellis said, deadpan. "Go figure."

All Vivian could do was keep shaking her head.

Ellis continued. "So. Once they splash down, we'll insert you back into the crew with a bit of sleight of hand. Shouldn't be too hard, no one televises crew retrievals after splashdown any more. We'll just fly you onto the aircraft carrier to join in for the first shots of the crew's return, and that'll be that."

"A *lot* of beers," Vivian said.

"Anyway, all that's for much later. First up, we need to get you home safely. And I'm sorry to break this to you, but the CIA has credible intel that the Soviets haven't given this up yet. They'll still be gunning for you, or more specifically for your cargo. Which means …" he took a deep breath. "Your return to Earth is going to be a little more complicated than you might have imagined."

36

Cislunar Space: Vivian Carter
June 8-10, 1985

IT was done. The Soviets were safely installed in Vivian's Command Module, Deliverance, having made the complicated spacewalk across from Makarov's LEK. This had been made even more challenging by the injuries the two Soviets had suffered on the surface. Just getting themselves back into their suits had taken close to an hour. The depressurization of the LEK, the transfer across to the Command Module, and the dance required to get all three of them inside it in their bulky spacesuits while the Night Corps pair sheltered in the LM had taken another hour. Their last act before closing the CM hatch had been to transfer to umbilicals again for their oxygen, and jettison Vivian's PLSS and Nikolai and Svetlana's equivalent Soviet backpacks. Vivian had pushed them out into space, and closed and dogged the hatch on them, rather finally. Another piece of redundancy, gone by the wayside. If any of them needed a life support backpack again, they'd just be shit out of luck.

And so now it was almost time. Three more orbits of the Moon, and then it would be go-time.

During those six hours, Vivian spent almost none of her spare time looking down at the lunar surface, and almost all of it looking back towards Earth.

They'd already cut the Soviet LEK loose and separated from it with a small delta-V maneuver. An hour from now the Blue Gemini would arrive, with a booster attached to give it sufficient thrust for the trans-Earth injection burn. Peter and Terri would cross into the Lunar Module, and power it up again for its next journey. They'd separate it from the CSM, and then the two Night Corps astronauts would depressurize and transfer over to their Blue Gemini for the voyage home. They'd fire up that big-ass booster and be on their way, getting a healthy lead on Vivian and her crew. After which, their LM would automatic-pilot itself back to MOL-B for reuse in some future Night Corps operation.

Right now, the Soviets were strapped into couches in the Command Module, Nikolai in the middle and Svetlana on the right. These days the cosmonauts seemed to be in an almost catatonic state of internal reflection. Vivian could hardly blame them, but she'd need to work on them a bit on the journey home.

But that could wait. The clock was ticking, and Vivian wanted to make the best use of the time available. Dressed in tee shirt and shorts in the warmth of the LM, she and Terri had just finished tidying it up to make room for Vivian's Moon suit and the Soviet suits—they would not be needing those any more either, and space inside the Command Module was a premium, so they could be sent off in the LM.

After a brief strategy discussion, Terri had just shoved off back through the tunnel into the CM, and for a few brief moments, Vivian was alone.

She looked around. This would probably be her last moment of solitude for many days. Her last alone-time in space, and soon she'd be exiting from a Lunar Module for the last time in her career.

Pity it couldn't have been Athena, her Apollo 32 Lunar Module, but Athena was long gone.

She patted the wall. "It's been real," she said. "Thanks."

Peter Sandoval slid through the tunnel. "Terri said you wanted a word?"

Vivian grinned. Some things were even better than solitude.

She reached up past him and closed the hatch. He raised his eyebrows. "Change of plan?"

"Sort of. I told Terri three was a crowd. You know how we girls like to gossip."

501

"What?"

"We've got some schedule slack, waiting for the Earth to turn, right?"

"Well, sure."

"So I asked Terri whether we could … maybe we should … get this LM to ourselves for a while. For humanitarian purposes?"

He grinned. "And she said?"

"She said, 'Get a room, you two,' and I said 'uh, yeah, that's kind of the idea.'"

Vivian reached out her arms, and he floated forward into them. "And then she said, 'Try not to bang into any of the instrument panels while you're …' Gee, Peter, are you *blushing*?"

"I'm just thinking of the ribbing I'm going to get from Terri for three and a half days in a very small Blue Gemini …"

"That is absolutely not what you should be thinking about right now."

"You're right." He scooped her up and held her, and they rolled backward slowly in space, just holding each other. "So, in one-sixth G, and now again in zero G?"

"Got to have *all* the experiences. Make all the history we can. That's kind of my job. Spacewoman. History-maker."

"Is this one going to end up in the mission report?"

"Yes. And also in the New York Times. Above the fold. With pictures."

"Well, then, better show them your good side. May I?" He started to slide her shorts off, and then they bumped up against the instrument panel on the port side and he laughed. "Jesus. We're really going to do it in a Lunar Module?"

"Better than trying it outside." She finished unbuttoning his jumpsuit and slid it off his shoulders. "Hey, Peter, you know what?"

"What?"

"Let's stop talking."

Two hours later, Peter was resting up in the Command Module, grabbing one last meal with Makarov and Belyakova. Which left Vivian and Terri, belatedly stashing the suits and other excess items in the Lunar Module.

"So, how was it?" Terri murmured. "Sex in zero G? Come on, girl. Dish."

Vivian grinned. "More difficult than you probably imagine. Especially since, well; I have bruises in all kinds of inconvenient places."

"But you both showed initiative, I bet. Kind of a trademark you both have."

"Why, yes, we did."

Terri shook her head, still grinning. "You do realize that I'm never going to let either of you forget this?"

Vivian smiled back. "I'm counting on it."

"And you're really not going to tell me anything else? Come on, are we girlfriends or what?"

"Terri. Peter's your boss. Just to name one of ten different reasons."

"Not for long, I'm betting. Because I really think I'm overdue for a freaking promotion. Plus, all Peter wants to do is go around and around and around the Earth and, well ..." She gestured. "I kinda like to go further afield."

"In that case ..." Vivian leaned forward until her lips almost touched Terri's ear. "It was great," she whispered. Then she leaned back, her expression mischievous. "And for any more than that, I guess you'll need to read our book."

"Ha." Terri sobered. "So, different topic. And forgive me for asking?"

"Uh-oh. Serious talk? Okay, what's on your mind?"

"Are you *sure*, Viv? About going back to Earth and staying back on Earth? Because it's a big change. And all joking aside ... no offense—and I'm just saying—but I really don't want Peter to get hurt again."

Vivian nodded. "And thanks for having his back. But ..." She paused. "He won't be. At least, not by me. I swear it by my ... respect and admiration for Peter Sandoval. And for you."

Brock cringed. "Yikes. Peter told you about that?"

"He sure did. Another good reason why I can never go back to Daedalus Base."

"Right. Because between them, Katya and the UN team have told pretty much everyone by now."

"Ouch. Does Peter know that?"

"I don't think so. Strictly behind-the-hand giggling, as far as I can tell."

"Phew. Anyway. Rest assured, Peter is safe with me. I'm going back to Earth and staying there."

"If you say so."

Vivian considered. "All right. Bear with me, here. A couple of years ago, I had a conversation with Svetlana about dreams, and it turns out we're both the same in that regard. We both have dreams of flight, of space. Of things we want. That's where our dream-heads are, apparently.

"But over the last couple years that's all changed, for me. Now, I dream of Earth. I dream of the beach, the forest, the city. I even dream of the mall. I dream of being there. What I want now is on Earth. I'm done with space. I'm certain. Not a doubt in my mind."

"Okay. Good to know." Terri's eyes glinted. "So, what you're saying is, you dream of Peter?"

"Sometimes. And whatever your next question is about that, I'm not answering it."

Terri laughed. "Okay."

Impulsively, Vivian reached out. "So we're good? Despite my unfashionable friendship with evil Red Commie bastards?"

"You and me? Sure. We were always good, even when I was being a bitch."

"It was just because you cared, right?"

"Something like that. And despite your awful taste in friends."

Vivian just looked at her. "Well, you said it."

Terri grinned and bumped her shoulder. "See you on Earth, babe."

"Yep. See you there. Now, let's get this shit squared away so *we* can eat."

Swinging around into the Moon's shadow for the last time was bittersweet for Vivian. Poignant, and just a little nervy.

They'd be in trouble if the SPS engine at the other end of the Service Module failed to fire. They had no backup for that. The SPS had been out in the cryogenic cold of space for close to two years. It had fired up readily enough when Vivian had used it to leave Apollo Astarte, and again to inject CM-1 into lunar orbit. With luck, the engine had one more flawless firing left in it: the Trans-Earth Injection burn. If that went well enough, any subsequent course correction burns they'd need to steer them into the reentry corridor could be done with the RCS thrusters alone.

After living in the doubly-and sometimes triply-redundant environment of Astarte for so long, this last act felt very much like walking a tightrope without a net.

The TEI burn would take place on the Moon's far side. Not really a problem, in the sense that they were mostly maintaining radio silence anyway. It did mean they'd need to verify their own position. This meant a lot of math for Vivian. In fact, she'd likely be doing math most of the time she wasn't eating, sleeping, or taking care of her two charges.

Sleeping. Hah. As if.

"Fire in the hole," she said, at the appropriate moment. And pressed PROCEED.

This was the toughest burn they'd done so far, in terms of acceleration, taking them up to a full g for a sustained period—something none of the three of them had experienced for a long time.

The TEI burn was two and a half minutes long. It felt like ten.

But Vivian's first major burn as a Command Module Pilot went fine, completely nominally. And then they were on their way home.

"Mission Control, Deliverance, how do you read?"

Acquisition of signal came at exactly the predicted time, which was comforting. In came Ellis's voice: "Deliverance, eh?"

"Catchy, huh? Every Command Module needs a name. I kind of like it. Burn appeared nominal, but I'd like confirmation."

"Fine. Reading you five by five, Deliverance. Stand by on FIDO confirmation."

"Deliverance, standing by."

All parameters were indeed nominal. The CM's speed was well above the one point five miles per second it needed to exceed the Moon's escape velocity, and its trajectory was picture-perfect. Deliverance had begun its long fall back to Earth.

Although it was a view that dozens of astronauts had seen by now, Vivian still set up the mapping camera to photograph the Moon as it receded behind them, ever further into the blackness of space. "Goodnight, Moon," she murmured.

And then, after an almost monosyllabic exchange with her two passengers, Vivian pulled herself into her sleeping bag in the lower equipment bay for ten hours of well-needed rest.

"Welcome to the equigravisphere," Vivian said, fourteen hours after the TEI burn, and eyed her two crewmates. "Did you feel the bump as we crossed over?"

"The …" Nikolai struggled with it for a while and then gave up. "I am sorry, what has just happened?"

"We just went through the point of gravitational equality. We're now back in the Earth's sphere of gravitational influence. Which also means we're moving very slowly, right now. We'll accelerate from here on in as the Earth really gets a grip on us."

Seasoned cosmonauts knew all this, of course, but Vivian needed to engage them in conversation somehow.

"Ah. And so now you change this vehicle's frame of reference to Earth's, now, as we do, yes?"

"My next job."

"And … the bump?"

"Old NASA joke. Back in the early days the NASA controllers used to kid with the press that the crew could feel a bump as they went over the hill."

Nikolai smiled. Svetlana merely looked out of the window, uninterested.

"Just another two hundred thousand miles and fifty-four hours to go, then," she said, and Nikolai nodded politely.

This was going *great*.

Normally, the three-person NASA crew would share the work of maintaining the Command Module during its three-day journey back to Earth. As Vivian was the only seasoned NASA pro aboard Deliverance, most of the work fell to her, even though both Nikolai and Svetlana would quickly come to her assistance if there were items she needed a hand with, or help working through a checklist.

For all that, there wasn't a huge amount to do. They had no experiments to run or observations to make, no film cassettes or other equipment to retrieve from the Service Module's external compartments. By and large, Vivian's jobs were routine: purging fuel cells, recharging batteries, and changing out lithium hydroxide canisters to ensure their air remained breathable. They all needed to exercise regularly, of course, although the role of exercise taskmaster sat uneasily on Vivian's shoulders. The Soviets simply didn't have the energy to exert to the levels she would have liked to see.

Vivian also regularly realigned the guidance platform and performed astronomical observations to double-check their state vector.

Mission Control, of course, supplied a more accurate vector that they derived from radio tracking, but Vivian wanted to ensure that she maintained her ability to do this. In principle, it was possible for the CMP to navigate them safely home without any input from Houston. She had no intention of doing so, but certainly wanted to make sure she could, if the need arose. Plus, it gave her an excuse to use Kevin's sextant in space a few more times.

Shortly before the halfway point, Vivian did a nine-second course correction burn to tweak them into the correct flight path for splash-down. As it turned out, that was the only correction she had to make until she was almost up against the Earth's atmosphere.

Not too shabby, she thought, *considering this isn't even my real job.*

From Earth, Ellis Mayer grinned at her. "So, I have a special guest who'd like to speak to you. I'm going to go split-screen so that you can see both of us. Hold on a second."

"Okay," she said, adjusting her headset and glancing across at her cosmonauts, who were deep in a conversation of their own. And then the screen shimmered and Dave Horn's face appeared on half of it. "Oh, hi! It's an Apollo 32 reunion! How's it going?"

"Oh, you know," Horn grinned. "It's going. I'm well ready to go down to the ground, though."

"Tell me about it. You're still on Astarte?"

He tilted the camera and there it was, the Astarte foredeck. "Stiiill here. Along with Laura and Rudy. The others went home a few hours ago; Josh, Marco, Amy."

"Damn, but I miss those guys. And you. We're going to have the best barbecue Houston has ever seen once I'm back. And all the beer's on me."

"Looking forward to it."

"Do I get an invite?" Ellis said, just a bit plaintively.

"You sure do. Honorary member. And we'll need someone to turn the steaks and carry out the trash."

"Oh, great," he said. "Thanks. So, getting down to business, I figured you'd both want to hear this. Some real interesting stuff is coming down the pike."

Ellis didn't look alarmed. Vivian shook her head in pretended bafflement. "Surely you're not saying there's some *good* news? Can't be."

"And yet. We already knew our star was riding high at NASA, but apparently it's infectious. We're finally making headway in Congress, and with the man in the street."

"Wow," she said. "Pigs *can* fly."

"The good ratings we got for Phobos and the Soviet encounter are still holding up. Seeing US and Soviet astronauts celebrating so calmly together, halfway across the solar system, is making people at home ask why we can't all get along on the home planet."

"Kumbaya," she said. "Good question, though."

"We've dropped down another DEFCON, and those atomic scientist dweebs have backed off the Doomsday Clock to five minutes to midnight."

"We have a whole five minutes, now? That's great."

"Anyway, I was talking about NASA, and the short version is that the President and Congress are now all keen to put together a dedicated manned mission to Mars. And this time, go all the way down to the surface. The money isn't in the budget yet—that will be for the next Appropriations Bill, next fiscal year—but it already has a lot of steam behind it.

"Not everyone is on the same page—the largest faction in the House wants it to be an all-American effort, for NASA to beat the Reds to Mars and then declare the Space Race over, in our favor. Then there's a sizeable minority that want to capitalize on the recently-demonstrated fact that astronauts and cosmonauts can get along just fine when the politicians get out of the way—so hats off to you and Nikolai and everyone else on that score. The chances of putting a joint trip together seem iffy, given the turmoil in the Soviet Union, but you never can tell. And then there are the grumpy Gus's who can only talk about the inner cities and such. But with George H. W. Bush on our side, the momentum is definitely swinging our way."

Vivian's eyebrows were raised, all the way up. "Wow."

Dave said: "It helps that the NERVA was such a success in punching us out of Mars orbit and into a great trajectory home. The Administrator has quickly capitalized on that. NERVA is now proven technology for Mars, at TRL-9, so that's a great help."

TRL: Technology Readiness Level. Nine was the highest value, meaning that that the NERVA was now officially fully tested and spaceflight qualified. "Well," Vivian said, "In that case, I guess it's a good job we didn't all perish in a radioactive inferno. But I hope they'll still test it a bit more before relying on it as the main propulsion system. I'm worried we made it look easy."

"Easy." Ellis shook his head. "Man, if you'd been in all the meetings about it that I've been in …"

"I don't think they're about to rely on it as the sole rocket motor for Apollo Ares," Horn said. "They'll still take chemical rocket motors as bolt-ons. Maybe the same kind of Centaur boosters we're using."

"Apollo Ares," Vivian said. "It already has a name? Apollo rises again."

"Plus, there's Europe and China to consider," Ellis said. "The Europeans are about to man-rate their Ariane rocket, and you already know that the Chinese are in Earth orbit in their own space station. Having beaten the Soviets, no one in the US wants to then cede leadership to the Chinese or the Europeans."

Ellis sat back. "So, yes. This is for real. People are talking about the rejuvenation of the space program. Not that any of us ever thought it was moribund. Folks have been predicting its demise for some time, but now … everything is looking brighter again."

"I really thought this was the end," Horn said, very seriously. "I thought we'd be NASA's last shout. That everything would just trail off, or we'd be forced into starting up the Shuttle program and flying around in our own back yard for a few decades."

"There's still Bright Driver to support," Vivian said.

"Sure, and that's one of the other pieces of the puzzle. They're talking about opening that up to ESA collaboration. And then there's the water at the poles. And I don't have to tell you that even the ordinary regolith is forty percent oxygen, twenty percent silicon, plus a bunch of titanium and even some iron. Useful stuff. And the rare earth elements. We're only finding them in small amounts, it's not exactly a huge bonanza, but it's sure helping with the balance sheet."

"Eventually we'll be able to mine helium-3," Dave said. "That will be even more lucrative."

"Well, maybe." Ellis looked unconvinced. "That would be a whole lot more steps up the ladder. But at least we're *on* the ladder now; the Moon is much cheaper than it was, and if the Moon is cheaper that means Mars is cheaper too. It all makes for a much more convincing package, as far as Congress is concerned."

"I used to hate the politics," Vivian said. "Still do, I guess. But it's all part of the math. And if we do the math right, everyone wins. The politicians, the scientists. NASA. And the public, whether they realize it or not, and not just the American public. Everybody wins."

"Everybody?" Dave said.

"Everybody," Vivian said firmly. She stared him down, a slight smile on her face, and added, "I will not be taking further questions at this time."

"Fair enough, Commander."

Once she'd signed off, Vivian took off her headset to discover her Soviets still deep in their conversation.

"We have not *invaded* these countries," Belyakova was saying stubbornly. "Entering Afghanistan was our internationalist duty. And in Poland and East Germany, we were invited by our socialist brethren. They needed help. The Rodina is there to provide such help to our satellite states."

"You're hopeless," Vivian said. "Your country hates you, and yet you're still defending it."

"My country does not hate me. And, please, but this is not your conversation."

"You're right, sorry. Happy to butt out."

"I think the time is over, when we can control the Warsaw Pact countries," Makarov said. "And I think this is what Gorbachev believes. Once, they were assets to our national security. Now, they are burdens. We cannot always send in troops every time to crack down on every protest and factory occupation. We need a new way. Otherwise, such countries will drag down the rest of the Union with them."

"Ridiculous," Svetlana said.

He sighed. "Even in your state, and in mine ... there have been strikes by machinists in Leningrad, in Russia. The dock workers in Odessa are joining with their brethren in Poland, in Gdanzk, in striking. It can happen inside the Soviet Union as well, Svetlana."

"Of course it can happen. And it can be stamped out. Men will bluster and then order will be restored." At the look on Makarov's face, Belyakova relented, just a little. She put her hand on his arm. "Nikolai ... you cannot pin all your hopes on Mikhail Gorbachev. It is a dream, and he is just one man, and misguided. One man who wants more discussion in the press, of matters that should not be spoken of, matters of history that would weaken our country ..."

Vivian put her headset back on, dialed up some music, and took out Kevin Pope's sextant to make a few star measurements.

Later, after they ate, Vivian took a deep breath. "So, Nikolai? Svetlana? I'm afraid there's something I haven't told you yet."

Belyakova shook her head. "Always, there is something."

"Yes, always there is. I was pushing this conversation off, because the plan might have changed in the meantime; Houston might have been able to come up with a different solution, or whatever. But, I guess they haven't. So: it concerns our prime landing site."

Makarov nodded. "The North Pacific, close to Hawaii?"

"Yes, that's what we've been saying over the loops. That's our story, in case the Soviets ... uh, your people have cracked NASA's secure radio. Night Corps transmissions use a much deeper level of encryption, but the NASA equipment hasn't kept pace, especially the equipment in this Command Module, which is three or four years old, now. So ever since we lost the LM I've had to obfuscate. Mislead."

Makarov blinked. "Not the North Pacific, then?"

"No. Usual for the exploratory missions is to splash down near Hawaii. Obviously we have naval facilities there, plus a big mass of empty ocean in case of contingency ... which NASA has rarely need-ed. But that's too dangerous this time.

"Hawaii is weird territory, right? US waters and airspace only extend for twelve nautical miles offshore, and outside that it's international waters ... and international airspace, which means that the US has no power or justification to keep Soviet military jets out of it. As it happens, your Air Force jets poke at that exclusion zone on a regular basis.

"Your normal MiG-25 Foxbats can operate up to about a hundred thousand feet, right? Twenty miles high. Possibly higher if they're stripped down, but we know they can achieve a hundred thousand loaded, meaning with full ordnance." Vivian looked at the guarded expressions on their faces. "You don't need to confirm that; it's in the open literature. You built it to go after our Lockheed U-2 aircraft, after all. But your MiG-105 spaceplane takes that aggressive capability up to *two hundred fifty miles* that we can confirm, and with the right booster underneath it, there's no reason why it can't go just as high as they want. And so that's a problem for us—and by 'us' I now mean the three of us, right here."

"Yes," Belyakova said quietly. "Our MiG-105 can easily operate at a much greater altitude than you have just stated."

"Great." Vivian swallowed. "And, you already know that we'll be traveling two thousand kilometers eastward from our point of atmospheric entry—which is at about four hundred thousand feet—to our landing position. Twelve hundred and forty miles. Right?"

Makarov nodded. "Of course. Which means what?"

"Which means that the US military needs to maintain active control of that whole air corridor in order to keep us safe, with enough visibility to respond promptly to threats in any part of it."

"Vivian," Belyakova said, her weariness clear in every syllable. "Please just tell us."

"Sorry. Almost there. You also know that the US Air Force launches from Vandenberg Air Force Base in California? Including its X-22C spaceplane?"

"Of course," Belyakova said automatically, but Nikolai's expression was becoming increasingly perturbed.

"The Dyna-Soar is limited in how far west it can fly at extreme altitudes from a Vandenberg launch. East of Vandenberg, no problem, but west is tough.

"So. Our current trajectory takes us to a regular splashdown point near Hawaii, on the side of the Earth facing away from the Moon. Anyone tracking us—meaning your people—will see that trajectory. But, real soon now we'll be doing a burn to change that and lengthen our incoming arc to take us around a further quarter of the Earth's circumference before we come in. We're not splashing down in the North Pacific. In fact, there won't be a splash at all."

Makarov blinked, and if anything, just looked even more tired. "Landfall?"

"Bingo. It's my honor to inform you that Deliverance will end its mission by coming down to Earth smack in the middle of West Texas, USA."

CHAPTER 37

Inbound to Earth: Vivian Carter
June 10-11, 1985

VIVIAN had been expecting instant pandemonium in the cabin. Instead, she got a dazed silence.

Eventually, Nikolai broke it. "But your Command Modules are not designed for this."

"That's sort of true, and sort of not. Throughout our space program, water landings have been preferred. Softer landing. Less danger for civilians. But there's no hard-and-fast reason this beast can't land on actual land, just like your Soviet vehicles do at the end of their missions.

"NASA did a field study impact-testing full-scale models and actual Command Module test rigs, way back in 1972, titled 'Apollo Command Module Land-Impact Tests.' Its authors concluded that they'd expect extensive structural damage, but the crew themselves would risk only minor injuries in most scenarios."

"Most scenarios," Belyakova echoed, still sounding stunned.

"Intriguing." Nikolai leaned forward. "When we land our Soyuz craft, we have a retro rocket that fires less than a meter above the surface of the Earth to reduce the descent speed from twenty-four feet per second to five or six feet per second. But you have no such system on Deliverance."

Vivian did the math. "So, from sixteen miles per hour to three or four mph? Okay. That's terrific. We won't be that lucky. Assuming all three parachutes deploy, we'll hit the deck at twenty-eight feet per second, or twenty miles per hour. If we lose one parachute, like Apollo 15 did, that only goes up to thirty-two feet per second, twenty-two miles per hour. Which is survivable, according to everything we know ... Nikolai, what are you doing?"

Characteristically, the cosmonaut had swung himself through a hundred and eighty degrees and was now peering at the mechanism beneath the couch that Belyakova was occupying. "Our couches are designed to collapse on impact. Are these?"

"They are," Vivian said. "Well, first of all, the CM structure itself will absorb a lot of the impact energy. The ribs at the 'toe' of the Command Module, down there, are designed to crush in impact, to absorb some of the force. But the couches, yes. They're suspended on struts to absorb the impact. See, here? This is the side strut support, attached here with a ball-and-socket-mounted shoe ..."

"That?" Nikolai said, appalled. "Oh dear."

From above them, Svetlana gave what could only be described as a whimper.

"Guys, guys. Even our sea landings can be pretty rough. Everything depends on how the Command Module is swinging when it hits the water, and whether the swell is moving up or down at the time. Apollo 12 came in really hard. Gene Cernan said Apollo 10 hit the water like a grand piano. Apollo astronauts regularly get cuts and bruises during the water impact." Makarov looked at her. "And we, by contrast, will be coming down on an absolutely flat and grassy surface? Gentle, forgiving mud, perhaps? And not on a road or somebody's house?"

"Not much mud in Texas this time of year," Vivian said. "But the area we're coming down is sometimes called the Big Empty. For real, because the population density is so low. Look, our splashdown accuracies are typically about three miles, and for this Houston has chosen us a big, wide patch of flat desert with almost no habitations. A few low hills. Desert shrubs, cacti. That's as good as you're ever going to get in the continental US."

Makarov gave up his inspection of the couch. "But, beyond Texas there is the whole Gulf of Mexico we might have used ..."

"And that was exactly my first question," Vivian said. "And then they showed me a satellite map of the commercial shipping density in the Gulf. And that was just the big ships, not the smaller stuff, tourist boats, fishing boats, whatever. It's one of the busiest maritime areas in the world. Sure, we might be able to clear out a patch of sea large enough to ditch in without landing on someone's deck, but the area immediately adjacent would be hopelessly insecure. Think how easily a surface-to-air missile could take us out while we're dangling under the parachutes: from a sub, or a Soviet spy ship masquerading as a cargo vessel, perhaps flying a Finnish or Norwegian flag. Which your guys do all the time, by the way. Not to mention that Soviet ships travel quite openly to Cuba, and around it. And then they told me the predicted tropical storm activity in the region and the typical swell in the Gulf in June—three to eleven feet, with a wind of fifteen knots—and I said, sure, fine, I'll take Texas."

While Vivian spoke, Svetlana had been scrutinizing her expression and body language. Now she said to Makarov, in Russian: "She is putting the best face on it that she can. But even herself, she is not convinced. Vivian is worried about this plan."

"*Ti prava*," Vivian said. *You're absolutely right.* "I'd be lying if I said I wasn't apprehensive. But this is our best shot. It's what we're doing."

Belyakova shrugged and switched back to English as well. "And, anyway: before we can land, we have to survive possible attacks by our own people, and the upper atmosphere."

"There you go, comrade," Vivian said. "Looking on the bright side, like you always do. First things first, eh?"

Deliverance hurtled towards Earth at twenty-five thousand miles an hour. Five hours from now their flight would be over, one way or another.

They would not be going into orbit around the Earth. Like almost all Apollo craft returning from the Moon they'd go straight into reentry and splashdown from a running start.

After separating from the Service Module, the cone-shaped Command Module would carry on into the atmosphere with its human crew. It would enter the atmosphere blunt end first, compressing the ever-thickening air beneath them into a shock wave that would build to a temperature of three thousand degrees Celsius.

515

Protecting them from this devastating blast was a heatshield made of honeycombed steel and fiberglass. The several hundred thousand cells in this honeycomb were filled with an epoxy resin. The maximum thickness of the shield, the aft section directly above the shock wave, was less than three inches thick; the conical upper parts of the Command Module were shielded with a mere one to one and a half inches of shielding.

It didn't seem like much, though in reality the heatshield was engineered with a substantial margin of safety.

On its way down through the atmospheric column, the Command Module was designed to lean to one side in an aerodynamically stable attitude, due to a deliberately offset center of gravity. This allowed the Command Module Pilot, and her computer, a small amount of flying control.

Surviving reentry critically depended on the entry angle of the spacecraft into the atmosphere. Even at the perfect entry angle of six point five degrees, the crew would experience a bruising six gees of deceleration. Steeper, meaning seven point five degrees or greater, and the dramatically increased heat and G-forces would incinerate or crush them. Too shallow, even an extra degree the other way, and the spacecraft might not shed sufficient velocity to be captured by the Earth's atmosphere, and punch back out into space and into a heliocentric orbit, dooming the crew more slowly.

NASA hadn't yet lost a crew during reentry. Vivian would do everything in her power to avoid making that kind of spaceflight history today.

Deliverance was projected to make landfall in West Texas at almost exactly eight o'clock pm, local time. Sunset was at 8:47pm. They would enter the Earth's atmosphere streaking eastward at almost twenty-four thousand miles an hour, with the Sun behind them in the west, and their landing site dead ahead of them.

For reentry, Vivian put herself in the left-hand seat, as Commander. Ideally, she'd have wanted Makarov in the center seat, but his broken wrist seriously inhibited his usefulness. So she'd have to settle for Belyakova assisting her from the center, with Makarov on the right.

And for that, she'd need to buck her crewmate up a bit. Vivian glanced over, noting Svetlana's slight frown. "Hey. We've got this, between us. You know that, right?"

Svetlana surveyed the array of instrument panels before her, and the Earth still growing beneath them. "Of course," she said dourly. "How hard can it be?"

Very hard, Vivian thought, but did not say. Just because no Apollo crew had burned up in the atmosphere before, there were no guarantees. This Command Module had been subject to years of deep-space soak, and even more seriously, it had been abandoned in lunar orbit for weeks with no internal temperature stabilization or systems monitoring. Anything could happen.

But we don't think like that.

So, Vivian forced a devil-may-care grin. "Right. So, here goes. Women against nature, am I right?"

Svetlana just looked at Vivian like she was crazy.

"Fine. I'll need your help, you know, from time to time, so we don't turn into a fireball."

"If you wish. I do take direction well."

Vivian peered sideways at her. "That's a joke, right?"

"Yes, of course."

"But you *did* once say you were willing for me to be the commander."

It took Belyakova a moment to remember. "That was to Mars. Hypothetically. Not for … this."

"Still. You should be careful what you wish for."

Vivian turned her attention to the board, started closing circuits.

Belyakova cleared her throat. "You have done this before, yes? Piloted a reentry into Earth's atmosphere?"

Vivian was surprised neither of them had asked until now. "Me? As an actual Command Module Pilot, sitting in the command seat? Nope. Never."

Belyakova's frown became a little deeper.

"I've watched twice, though."

The Soviet gave her the slightest of nods and turned her attention back to the checklist.

Did Svetlana look … scared?

Vivian couldn't fault her. She herself would have been very weirded out to be reentering the atmosphere in a Soyuz, especially with an inexperienced cosmonaut at the helm.

None of them were wearing pressure suits. If they suffered any type of loss of integrity, or other failure, it would be a Criticality One event, and the suits wouldn't help them.

Suited up or not, they'd die quickly. And without the suits they'd probably perish so fast that they might not even be aware of the glitch that killed them. So, that was *good*, right?

At 3:24pm, with four and a half hours to go, and still 63,000 kilometers out, Vivian received her last PAD—the set of numbers with Pre-Advisory Data—and read them into her guidance computer, with Svetlana sanity-checking her.

"Conditions in the recovery area continue to be good," Ellis said. "A few clouds at two thousand feet, scattered, some high cloud, again scattered, visibility ten-plus miles. Winds a little high, now eighteen to twenty knots out of the west, occasional higher gusts. Sorry about that."

"Hmm. Roger that."

"Texas law enforcement is being fully briefed, including all regional city PDs, county sheriff's offices, the Highway Patrol, Ranger Division, and Parks and Wildlife. Between NASA and the cops, you'll likely see a lot of helicopters and flashing lights when you come down. Don't be alarmed, they're all there for your safety, to secure the perimeter and retrieve you ASAP. There'll also be a covert military presence that I'm not supposed to talk about on the loop."

"Exciting stuff."

"You should certainly be making the evening news in Abilene, let's put it that way."

Makarov put his head in his hands. Vivian frowned. "Tell me again how this squares with keeping my presence there a secret? And doubly so for my cargo?"

"They'll do their damnedest to make sure your *faces* don't make the news. That's why we're doing it this way. Job One for the cops is to keep the news media at a distance. They're being told it's a matter of utmost national security. But it's kind of hard to conceal a flaming meteor the size of Deliverance, blazing a two-thousand-kilometer long trail close to sunset."

"So, you're just going to plead national security and hope that works?"

"Not much else we can do."

"Conspiracy theorists are going to have a field day with this, like, forever." Vivian glanced at the clock. "Anyway, roger that. Moving on …"

At 4:46pm, Vivian performed her last midcourse correction—a gentle nine-second burn to nudge Deliverance into the optimum trajectory for reentry. So far, so good.

After this their activities became an efficient blur, and Vivian was too busy to think too much. She was conducting extensive and almost continuous checks of their power, environmental, and propulsion systems. Testing the EMS, Entry Monitor System, that would guide them through reentry, confirming and reconfirming that they were still on the right path. And even with those, Vivian still made a few extra navigational sightings with the Command Module's sextant just to convince them all …

"Water," said Makarov.

Vivian glanced upward where he was pointing. Sure enough, the area all around the top hatch was wet. "It's cooling in here. Water is condensating out of our air."

Svetlana shook her head, muttering in Russian.

"Not too much critical wiring up there," Vivian added.

"Not too much?"

Did Belyakova *have* to keep repeating everything she said? "And very little we can do about it, Svetlana. Eyes back on the checklist."

Belyakova just gave her a look and they went back to work.

As the last hour loomed, they stowed away every loose or potentially loose item they could find. The last thing they needed was to be struck by anything that came adrift under a six-G acceleration, especially if it was pointy.

At 7:10pm, with fifty minutes to go, they turned off the CM thruster heaters, checked the batteries, and checked the pyros that would separate them from the Service Module. They primed the Command Module's Reaction Control System for action—the thrusters that they'd been using throughout the mission so far were located on the

Service Module. They set off pyros to open valves and pressurize the CM's fuel and oxidizer tanks for those thrusters. Again: so far, so good.

At 7:15pm, Vivian prepared to switch back to VHF for the landing. They'd be tossing the high-gain antenna away when they separated with the Service Module, and they'd be below the horizons of the main S-band stations on Earth anyway. VHF would serve them just fine from here on in.

The Entry Monitoring System was on the control panel right in front of her, and she would be laser-focused on it for most of the remaining descent. Its first display showed a graph of their deceleration against their velocity. From this, she would be able to immediately tell whether they were coming in too steeply, two shallowly, or just right. Below that, she could read off the remaining range to crunchdown point in nautical miles. The third display provided her roll stability information, showing her the attitude and the direction of the CM's lift vector. Now, she prepped the EMS for action by entering the newly updated starting conditions for reentry ...

"You are falling behind the checklist," Svetlana said.

"I know, damn it," Vivian muttered. "Next?"

"Command Module RCS test."

"RCS test, roger." Vivian switched the thruster power to the CM, quickly pulsed each thruster, returned attitude control to the Service Module. "Confirm, Command Module RCS is nominal."

At 7:24pm, three minutes later than scheduled, they began shutting down the Service Module's oxygen, fuel cells, and radio system in preparation for jettisoning it.

"Doublecheck me on these circuit breakers," Vivian said. "No, faster ... damn it, never mind. I'm going to P62." P62 was the computer program that would handle their separation with the Service Module.

"Vivian ..."

Despite the remorselessly ticking clock, Vivian took two extra seconds to scan the displays and gut-check herself. *Fine. Nominal.* She pressed PROCEED.

"Vivian, you have a hostile incoming."

For a moment, distracted by carrying out her seventeen-minute-to-go horizon check, Ellis's words didn't register. "Horizon check thirty-one point eight degrees. Guidance and Navigation seems nominal. Say again about—hostiles?"

"You have a MiG-105 incoming. Soviet spaceplane. Likely rocket armed."

"Shit, *now*? You've got to be kidding me. This far up?"

Deliverance was coming in toward the atmosphere at twenty-four thousand miles an hour. Then again, how fast were ICBMs going when the passed their course midpoint? Fifteen thousand miles an hour?

"We are dead," Belyakova said, with utter composure.

"Shut *up*." Vivian was getting nothing more from the ground. Houston wasn't Cheyenne. They were probably scrambling. "Houston, Deliverance. Ellis! What the hell are we supposed to do?"

But she already knew the answer: nothing. She could change Deliverance's attitude, but she couldn't make even minor course changes at this point, and she certainly couldn't take any kind of evasive action. Not with the tunnel of death coming up.

But if she didn't proceed with getting rid of the damned Service Module and expose their heatshield, like *right now*, they'd tumble into the atmosphere and die in a ball of fire regardless of what the MiG did.

Perhaps that was the point? Were the Soviets hoping that the mere presence of the fearsome MiG-105 would be enough to make her panic and screw up? Really, anything Vivian did would risk jeopardizing that forty-mile-wide entrance corridor, or that precious six point five degree entry angle.

So, it was brutally simple. They were out of time. It didn't matter where the goddamned MiG-105 was. All Vivian could do was *ignore the bastard*.

"Overriding." Vivian applied power to her logic circuits and armed the pyros. Once the system armed, she flipped up the metal cover that guarded the switch that would initiate separation.

Ellis came back, sounding very calm, which likely meant he was screaming inside. "The MiG will likely be on you within a minute. It's hard to translate the tracking numbers we're seeing from the Air Force. That's all I can tell you."

"Sure, whatever," Vivian said. The timer was running to trigger the RCS separation jets on the Service Module. The fuel cells that would fire the pyros were still live. That, at least, was good. "SM separation initiated."

In the Service Module, explosive charges fired, ripping out the cables between the two modules. Another pyro initiated a guillotine to sever the cables and plumbing tubes. Tension ties released, and strong mechanical springs shoved the modules apart. Now the SM's controller automatically fired its jets on a timed sequence, rapidly increasing its separation from the Command Module. "Boom," she said. "Anchors away."

"What?" Ellis said. "Say again?"

"We have a good sep. Realigning for atmospheric entry. Anything new on my hostile?"

"It's right on you."

"Well, that sucks." Vivian checked pressures, safed the system that had just fired the pyros, and checked her batteries. Yawed the CM around on its axis by forty-five degrees. "Coming in blunt end first," she said and pressed PROCEED on the guidance computer to bring in the autopilot for P63. "Here we damned well go ..."

"The MiG has fired a missile," Ellis said abruptly.

"Shit," she said. "Well, bye, man. Love to you and the family."

"At your speed it's a Hail Mary play," Ellis said. "We're guessing—"

Vivian interrupted. "Never tell me the odds." And then thought, bizarrely, *Did I really just quote freaking Star Wars? After all this?*

What an epitaph that would make. Vivian Carter's last words: *Never tell me the odds.*

Makarov suddenly cried out, and Belyakova *screamed*, a sound Vivian had never heard from the cosmonaut before. The bright flare from outside the window pulled her gaze, and she found herself looking into a scene of complete obliteration, debris flying everywhere at speeds almost too fast to see.

Next second, the Command Module was battered with chunks of shrapnel, the impacts throwing them around in their couches, a sudden din of clunks and thuds and bangs, ten or twenty different noises all compressed into a short but very loud interval ... and then it was over.

The Command Module was rolling again. The computer was confused. Makarov had banged his head against the hull next to him, and Belyakova was inexplicably reaching above her head, moaning, "*Hai yomu grez ...*" which Vivian only knew meant *god damn it* or something similar because her Russian instructor had taught her a bunch of Ukrainian epithets.

"For God's sake …" Vivian stabbed buttons to override the computer, to grab back control and spin the Command Module around and regain the right attitude for reentry, with the heatshield forward and with their heads down, looking back the way they'd come, without consciously thinking about it at all.

"Vivian! Astarte CM, this is Houston. Please respond."

"Somebody?" Vivian demanded. "Busy here." They were only minutes away from Entry Interface, minutes from atmosphere, and one of her cosmonauts was bleeding copiously while the other one keened. "Svetlana! Help me!"

Belyakova blinked, stopped wailing and leaned forward. Pushing-to-talk, she said with a calmness completely at odds with her behavior just seconds ago: "Houston, Deliverance. The Service Module has been destroyed by a Soviet missile. A heat-seeking missile, perhaps, which chose the wrong target. We have been bombarded with its debris, but Vivian has regained control of our vehicle."

"Roger that." Ellis sounded more shaken than Belyakova.

Control, sure. The real question was: had those impacts pushed them out of the corridor? Vivian couldn't tell, not straight away. She'd need to wait for realtime data to appear on her EMS before she could gauge their gradient. And the EMS wouldn't fire up until they passed Entry Interface.

"Shit," she said.

Ready or not, they were going in.

CHAPTER 38

Reentry: Vivian Carter
June 11, 1985

THERE could be no aborting now, no go-arounds, no do-overs. They no longer had the Service Module, with its power and oxygen supplies. They only had consumables for a few hours now. Any delay in returning to Earth would be fatal. Not that any of that mattered, because they no longer had a rocket motor capable of preventing their reentry.

Get me down. I want to be down. I am so done with this crap. Get me down.

7:46pm. Altitude, 400,000 feet. Entry interface into the Earth's atmosphere. Any moment now the superheated air in front of the spacecraft would become ionized, blocking all radio transmission. They'd enter communications blackout and stay in it for the next four minutes or more.

"For God's sake, Svetlana. Try to do something about Nikolai's blood."

Svetlana looked at the wispy red cloud that surrounded Makarov's head, and got to work with a cloth.

A light on Vivian's console lit up. *Hello, there's the atmosphere. Right on time.* That light meant that the ship's accelerometers were now measuring 0.05G of drag.

524

The life-giving atmosphere of Earth. But, just like the Moon, the Earth's atmosphere was not their friend. At least, not right now.

That G-force was going to go a lot higher. Very soon, and very quickly. But at least in the meantime Vivian would be getting EMS data. At the 0.05G mark the computer system had automatically kicked them into P64, the program that—in theory—would ensure they slowed down sufficiently to remain in the atmosphere.

Outside, and streaming behind them, the shocked and heated air was already glowing a delicate orange. Vivian felt the beginning pressure of the seat against her back and butt, was aware of her feet drifting down toward the floor of the Command Module, of Belyakova's hair beginning to settle toward her shoulders …

Cold water cascaded down on them. All that condensate that had been building up in the apex of the Command Module had been released by gravity to spray across them all. None of them even mentioned it.

As the Command Module dug into the tenuous gases of the upper atmosphere, the compression shock wave was growing beneath the heatshield. The friction generated a temperature extreme enough to envelope the craft in a sheath of ionized plasma.

"G's, Svet," Vivian said. "Tell me G's."

God, she could feel the force of gravity building without needing to be told.

"Point three, point five … point eight … one. Rising."

Rising *fast*. Still less than one Earth gravity, but the dramatic ramp-up was already giving Vivian's ribs and shoulder hell. All her old injuries were coming back to say hello.

"Cabin temperature up two degrees," said Makarov.

"Already? God damn it."

The shaking was already worse than Vivian remembered from her last two reentries. And here came the light show. Tenuous at first, mere hints of red and orange, it quickly flared up to become a plume scarily reminiscent of a Lunar Module rocket firing.

It lengthened, became a comet tail, a tunnel. Not just red-orange-yellow now, but a range of colors appearing around the edges of the plume: blue-greens with touches of violet, almost lavender. Trails of incandescent white and yellow streamed behind them. Deliverance was inside a blowtorch now, at the center of a ball of white and purple flame, a blazing river that they couldn't escape.

Vivian braced, almost unblinking, and then forced herself to relax as the killing pressure built up on her chest, her hips, her whole body. Svetlana had now stopped reading G's, choked off by the pressure herself, but the gauge was clear enough: five G's now, edging up over six, and still increasing.

Once, Vivian would have been able to take this, back when she lived full-time in Earth gravity and habitually endured high-G turns as a fighter pilot. But she'd been away from such intense accelerations for a long time and was already beginning to get tunnel vision. She chuffed, short breaths which were the only way she could even keep breathing, and tried not to look at the clock, because she didn't want to see just how little time had passed, how much more of torment was left to go.

The Command Module rolled as the computer tried to reduce the G-forces on them. Vivian tore her eyes from the inferno reaching up behind them and studied the readouts on her EMS. If the computer were to screw this up, she would need to override it and take manual control—somehow.

Okay. Okay. The ship was doing what it was supposed to do: keeping the lift vector down, making sure they continued to decelerate, easing their angle through the atmosphere. The G's gradually eased to four and stabilized there.

"Is this … normal?" Makarov was having trouble breathing, but managed to rock his head sideways to indicate the window. "The pieces coming off."

He was right. Sparks were flying past Makarov's window, and the occasional large chunk of something. A piece of aluminized Kapton foil insulation fluttered up and briefly, incongruously, stuck to the window before being whipped away. More sparks then, and a flutter of a dozen or so smaller pieces.

"No," Vivian croaked. It was all she could find to say. She couldn't remember Minerva shedding any debris at all during the Apollo 32 reentry. Same for the unnamed Command Module from her rookie mission, a routine Earth-orbital supply run.

The temperature was up ten degrees inside the CM now.

Vivian looked back at her EMS system. "We just dropped below … critical velocity," she said. This crazy ride had at least slowed them to the point where there was no longer a danger they'd zoom back out of the atmosphere. Some good news at last.

The G's started to build up again. The computer rolled the craft dizzyingly, trying to control the lift vector, but with little effect.

"Take ... over," Belyakova said. "This ... will kill us."

Back to six G's. And rising. *Jesus Christ.*

Vivian really didn't want to take the controls. Didn't want to try to deadstick this beast down. She hadn't done anywhere near the number of simulations necessary to give her that kind of confidence.

But if she didn't take over by the time it got to seven G's, she never would.

"Wait," she croaked. "Wait."

They swung again, tossing them all sideways. Makarov cried out, a wounded-bear sound that cut through Vivian's ears.

The G's began to ease again. *Thank God.*

"Off target, now," she said. "Ten, fifteen miles long."

She paused, exhausted, as the CM thrashed around her some more and the G's came down to three point five, and then managed to add, "It ... should use the lift vector to pull us shorter but ... it can't. We're ..." She coughed, out of air.

To her surprise, Svetlana put her hand on Vivian's arm. It felt like a lead weight, almost cutting off her circulation. "Do not talk. We understand. We came in shallow by a quarter degree, and then ... corrected ... but, with the G's ..."

"Yes." Given the choice between landing accurately and crushing the crew, or abandoning the programmed landing coordinates and allowing them to survive, the onboard computer had chosen wisely. "Good girl."

"Uh?"

"I meant ... Deliverance."

Once their velocity dropped below a thousand feet per second, the P67 program switched the display so that it showed their latitude, longitude, and distance to crunchdown point. That distance was now registering as eighteen miles off target. Vivian had no map of Texas and was unable to guess what difference eighteen miles might make. She'd just have to put her faith on the scale of the Big Empty.

As they were now falling vertically, Vivian disengaged the stabilization and control program. The blowtorch inferno that had sheathed them had now faded away. The sky above them was morphing slowly from blue-black to a lighter blue.

Even though the highest G's were behind them, Vivian was still having difficulty breathing. Deliverance hadn't disintegrated around them. They hadn't died in a raging inferno. But they weren't out of the woods yet.

The air outside was now dense enough for the altimeter in the cabin to give accurate readings. They watched, spellbound, as the numbers spun backward.

"Checklist?"

"ELS logic on," Svetlana said.

"Okay. ELS logic on."

"ELS to auto."

"Auto on."

At thirty-three thousand feet, Vivian had just turned on the Earth landing system. Another computer program would now use their height, barometric measurements and timers to deploy the parachutes.

They were plummeting toward the ground. Vivian had spent a lot of time over the past years in free fall, but this time was very different. Beneath them was an unforgiving patch of very hard desert. One way or another, they'd be impacting it very soon.

Svetlana was still following the checklist. "Sequence Pyro two, to arm."

"Pyro to arm," Vivian concurred. "Standing by."

When they reached twenty-four thousand feet, still dropping at five hundred feet per second … nothing happened.

"Shit." Vivian scanned the board. "Apex cover didn't disengage."

"What?"

Vivian's hands danced over the control. "That pyro we just armed should have blown the apex cover off."

"Yes?"

"And if we don't get rid of it, we have no parachutes."

Power to the system was nominal. It *should* have blown. Sensor problem? Hopefully.

Vivian flipped the cover off another guarded button and pressed it. "Manual deploy. Yes!"

Away went the apex cover, shoved off by gas pistons and then snatched up and separated from the Command Module by its own small dedicated parachute.

"One, two ..."

One point six seconds after the apex cover disengaged the drogue parachutes were supposed to deploy automatically. They hadn't, but Vivian was already flipping up covers. "Manually deploying drogues."

"There they go!" Makarov shouted.

The two drogues had released.

"Oh my God," Svetlana said. "Oh my God."

The sky around them was now completely blue. Off to the west, the Sun was lowering in the sky. Beneath them, presumably, was the ground. Vivian wasn't about to look down. Not right now. She was watching the altimeter.

"Deliverance, Houston. Do you read?"

"Ellis, Vivian. Hi, we're still here."

"We have visual on you from the chase planes, seeing two good drogues."

"Sure. Stand by ..."

At ten thousand feet, the three main parachutes were supposed to deploy automatically. Vivian had no faith that they would. Her hand hovered over the switch to override the system and deploy them manually.

The drogue chutes disappeared, parting company with the Command Module. For two seconds they were back in free fall.

Bang! Three mortars fired in pyro packages just a few feet above them. Three parachutes billowed out above them. Main chute deployment had happened automatically after all.

"Son of a gun," Vivian said. "There's just no calling this, is there?"

The mains deployed reefed, meaning that a line prevented them from fully unfurling for ten seconds, reducing the shock to the craft. Vivian counted out loud, trying not to sound as anxious as she was.

More pyros fired at the ten-second mark to break the reefing. The parachutes, three beautiful red and white canopies, billowed open above them.

"Houston, Deliverance," Vivian said. "We have three good mains."

"Roger that," Ellis said, back to his usual calm professionalism. "Recovery One reports he now has a visual on you." Their primary recovery helicopter.

"That sky," Makarov said quietly. "That blue sky."

Svetlana was crying silently. Vivian squeezed her shoulder, a little awkwardly, and cleared her throat. "And no one else came to shoot at us."

"Oh, someone did." Ellis was just as calm as when he'd been reading the weather forecast a few hours earlier. "A second MiG-105 was sent to intercept you at a hundred fifty thousand feet. But he got chased off by a pair of Air Force X-22C's. You were in blackout—there was no way to inform you."

"Oh," Vivian said. "Well. Good. I'm glad we didn't know that at the time. Better the devil you only find out about afterwards, am I right?"

Ellis chuckled. "I'm being advised by the room around me that I should say 'no one messes with Texas' at this point."

"Sure enough," Vivian said, "and thank you, Texas," even though the Dyna-Soars would have launched from Vandenberg in California. "And, Houston, on that note: what's my local windspeed, and what's directly beneath me right now?"

After the massive speeds at which Vivian had careered around the solar system, it was almost amusing to be worrying about whether a twenty, thirty, or forty-mile-per-hour impact speed would be capable of killing or maiming her and her crew.

"Up to twenty knots and still gusting," Ellis said. "And, mostly desert-like. You're coming down in Irion County, Texas, on the Edwards Plateau."

"Okay, nice," Vivian said. "Never heard of it."

"That's kind of the idea. The whole county only has about thirteen hundred people in it. It's pretty much all savanna, not much farming, basically prairie grass with a few trees, and mercifully far from any major rivers or canyons. But try not to go too much further east, you hear?"

"Sure," Vivian said. "I'll get right on that."

"Trees?" Makarov said. "What trees?"

Vivian ignored him. "So, nowhere near a major city, I take it?"

"Your nearest big city is Odessa, and that's the best part of a hundred fifty miles away."

Svetlana twitched. Vivian said: "Not *that* Odessa. We have one too." To Ellis, she said, "Nearest highway? Roads?"

"Damned if I know. I-10, maybe? But you're nowhere near that. Just crappy little country roads where you are."

"And, how far are we from Houston? Just out of interest."

"Four hundred miles or so."

That would have to do. Vivian disengaged with her CAPCOM and looked across at her cosmonaut colleagues. Both their faces were pale and drawn. Vivian's likely didn't look any better. She was definitely feeling the strain of the steady one G they were now feeling ... and would presumably be feeling now for the rest of her life. Vivian's spacefaring days were over.

She'd get used to Earth gravity again, she was sure. How long it would take, and whether she'd have any long-term ill effects, she had no idea.

"Couple of minutes to the ground," she said.

Neither of them answered her, so she did a quick board check and looked around the cabin. When they hit the deck, there was another good chance stuff might break loose and cascade down around them. When Apollo 12 splashed down, Lunar Module Pilot Alan Bean had been conked on the head by a falling camera, knocking him out briefly and requiring stitches. Even then he'd been lucky: he could have been even more seriously injured or even killed. Vivian had done her utmost to make sure that everything was stowed or fastened while they were still inbound for Earth, but she was now double-checking, alert for anything that might have shifted position or be hanging down now that they were back in gravity. There was nothing she could see ... but maybe they should have kept their helmets out and available as head protection anyway?

As they drifted downward, Deliverance was not level with the ground. Its parachute system was designed to suspend it at around twenty-seven degrees to the horizontal with the main hatch uppermost. This spread the impact well when landing on water, allowing the CM to flop and pivot. Vivian would be "interested" to see how well that worked on land.

"Brace for impact," she said. "Stay alert, watch for falling objects."

Belyakova looked up in alarm. Makarov merely nodded.

"Look on the bright side," Vivian said. "At least we won't get seasick."

Here goes nothing, she thought.

* * *

8:01pm: Crunchdown.

They landed with a hefty crash. To say the least.

And then they bounced and scraped against the ground with a shriek of metal against rock.

"Nikolai! Circuit breakers! Jesus Chr—" The spacecraft smashed back down to the ground, again with that unearthly screeching. This time, Vivian's couch gave all the way, its struts breaking, and she and the whole structure fell back several inches.

"Sorry, sorry, sorry …" Nikolai shook his head to clear it and peered at the control panels.

Belyakova pointed calmly. "There."

Makarov closed the two circuit breakers beside him, so that power could reach the pyros in the parachute installation above them. As soon as she had power, Vivian threw the switch. The squibs detonated above them, and guillotines cut the parachutes free from the spacecraft.

At last, Deliverance came to a halt on its side, nose down, heat-shield up.

Vivian dangled from her restraint straps, head down, body at a forty-five degree angle to the gravity that was now steadily and infuriatingly dragging her downward. She had feared that the Command Module's offset center of gravity would pull the ship around so that its forward hatch faced the ground, but some rocks or other impediments had clearly prevented that. With luck, and provided they were careful where they put their weight, they should be able to get out.

Half-deafened by the clatter of their landing, Vivian only now realized that Ellis was hailing her, anxiously asking her status. She pushed-to-talk, her arm still feeling like a lead weight.

"Houston, Minerva … uh, I mean, Deliverance. We're okay. All three of us fine, banged up but functional. Powering down the Command Module now, then we'll go off comms and open up. We need to get the hell out of here."

"Roger that, Deliverance. Help should be with you soon."

In a water splashdown, Vivian and her crew would have spent a leisurely twenty minutes righting the CM's attitude, if necessary, and then waiting for Navy SEAL frogmen to apply a flotation collar to the craft. The SEALs would have helped the crew out one by one into a life raft, and then used a recovery basket to winch them up into the Recovery One helicopter. On land, none of that was necessary.

Vivian wanted nothing more than to get out. For one thing, the Command Module still had toxic thruster propellants aboard in its RCS system. They'd had no opportunity to vent them, not coming down over land. So far Vivian smelled nothing, but this was still a risk she'd prefer to avoid.

She busied herself charging up the gas-powered hatch counterbalance. Under Earth gravity the hatch door was heavy, especially in their weakened condition. To assist the crew, the hatch had a counterbalance arrangement powered by compressed air.

As she hit the switch, Svetlana reached down to the calf pocket of her jump suit ... and pulled out a pistol.

Vivian froze. "Uh, Svetlana. You're not going to need that."

"No." Svetlana held it out to Vivian, with a hand that shook and soon wilted under gravity. "Please, I want you to take it, so that I do nothing stupid." Her voice was quavering.

Vivian gently plucked it out of the cosmonaut's hand, checked the safety, and filed it away in a cabinet behind her. "Svetlana ... please, Svetlana, look at me. It's going to be all right."

"No," Belyakova said. "It is not."

"I'm going to look after you—make sure you and Nikolai are all right. Trust me."

"No. You will go back to your crew. We know this, you have said so."

"Well, yes, I'll have to, for a while. For the cameras. But I'll come right back. I promise."

Svetlana just shook her head.

"Look, let's just get you both out of here. Hang on. Nikolai, you okay?"

Makarov released his restraining straps and lowered himself gingerly onto what was now the floor of the Command Module, taking care not to bang either his arm or his head. "Yes."

Vivian turned back to the door mechanism and began to open the hatch, but even with the counterbalance assist it still took both of them, Vivian and Svetlana, to get it fully open.

Texas air spilled in. It was eighty degrees and humid outside Deliverance on this June evening, and yet the air still smelled sweet and somehow clean.

The air of Earth.

* * *

Vivian clambered up and out. As Commander she would have liked to be last to leave the ship, but this was her country.

Plus, if anyone was going to shoot at them, Vivian didn't want her Soviets to be in the firing line.

She managed to keep her determination long enough to slide down the outside of the still-warm Command Module and then ran out of strength and crumpled to the ground, nauseous.

The landscape around her was gently undulating, bleak, and huge. Prairie grass seemed to extend to the horizon, and the horizon was a *long* way away by lunar or Phobos standards. Despite Makarov's fears, there were no trees anywhere near them, presumably because there were no rivers. On the horizon she could see a low line of hills, glowing golden in the setting Sun.

The Sun .... Seen through the Earth's thick atmosphere, it looked alarmingly faint and diffuse. Lots of stuff to get used to, back here.

Vivian took another breath. Everything still ached, and her head felt like it weighed a hundred pounds.

"Help me." Svetlana sat with one leg out of the hatch, the other still inside, balancing precariously.

From the outside, the Command Module looked ridiculously small. "Uh ... I'll try. How's Nikolai?"

Makarov's face peered out of the hatch behind Svetlana. "Alive, I suppose?"

"Welcome to the United States of America. What d'you think so far?"

Makarov looked around, his eyes as bleak as the landscape. "It looks more like Siberia than I expected."

"A little warm for Siberia, no?"

He raised his eyebrows. "Siberia is not always cold."

"It gets better," she said.

"I will trust you, Vivian Carter."

"Good. I'm," she swallowed, "worthy of your trust. I think. At least, I'll try."

Far away, on what was presumably a distant road, she could now see police lights flashing red and blue. And now, Svetlana pointed. "Helicopters. And more."

Helicopters were indeed approaching them, some from the northwest, others from the east.

"The air here is nice, at least. And the breeze on my face …" Svetlana looked away.

"Hang in there, girlfriend."

The helicopters grew in size alarmingly quickly, but then held their distance.

"*Six* helicopters?" Makarov said.

"Aha," Vivian said. "And there's the land contingent."

Jeeps were bouncing across the desert, taking up positions several hundred yards away, marking the four points of the compass. Behind them, and proceeding more sedately, were two vehicles Vivian couldn't identify, but which could only be armored personnel carriers of some kind. She'd known that the Texas Highway Patrol owned some, for border work, but had never seen one before.

Holy shit, she thought. *This is what Ellis meant by a covert military presence?*

Out loud, she said: "I sure hope all these people are on our side."

She had intended it as a joke, but it didn't come out of her mouth sounding like one.

Belyakova was looking around with considerable trepidation. "Do you think …" She tailed off and looked up at the Command Module hatch, perhaps regretting giving up her gun.

"No, I was kidding, sorry. These are the good guys."

"The good guys," Belyakova said flatly.

"Sure. That one, the Bell 206 helicopter that says Texas DPS, that means Department of Public Safety, so it's the Texas Rangers. The real ones, not the baseball team … never mind. Those two smaller ones on the perimeter are normal police helicopters. The two black helicopters flanking us, I really have no idea. But hey, no one's shooting at anyone else … so they're just here for your protection. And mine. See how important you are?"

"Okay. Okay. That big one coming in now? Nice and low? That's a Sikorsky SH-3 Sea King, which is kind of ironic since we're on land … but that's the helicopter NASA uses for splashdown recoveries. That must be our Recovery One."

Nikolai landed beside her in the grass, but his legs wouldn't support him and he tumbled, catching himself with his good arm on the side of the CM and lowering himself to the ground next to Vivian.

Svetlana, resolute, stood firm but swayed, her hand on Nikolai's shoulder. Tears were falling down her cheeks. "I do not want to be here."

"Have faith. This is the safest place for you right now."

"It does not look safe."

"Not right now, I'll grant you that."

"Surrounded by my enemies."

Belyakova still looked completely miserable. Vivian braced herself and stood, sliding her shoulder up the side of the Command Module to steady herself. "Hey. Hey. Come here, okay?"

And Svetlana did. Vivian put her arms around her, squeezed her.

The police helicopters were small, the type generally used to monitor traffic, only capable of carrying three people. The Recovery One Sikorsky was huge by comparison, with a four-person crew but capable of carrying twenty-eight soldiers beside. It was variously used for search and rescue, anti-submarine warfare, and a Marine Corps Sea King, operating as Marine One, was used to carry the President. It was a majestic beast.

Now it landed some two hundred feet away. Soldiers jumped down and stepped to right and left, scanning the horizon. Considering how deserted the terrain around them was, this felt like security theater to Vivian, but she wasn't complaining. She'd been shot at quite enough over the past six years.

A team of half a dozen men and women deplaned next. Clearly a medical unit, they were weighted down with medical kits, a stretcher and two folding chairs, and blankets …

"Jesus Christ," she breathed.

Peter Sandoval had jumped out of the Sea King immediately following the medics, and now strode across the grasslands toward her, easily outpacing them. Behind him and to the left, Terri Brock half-walked and half-jogged to keep up with him, her gaze sweeping back and forth across the grasslands in the light of the setting Sun.

They must have been flown straight here after their own splashdown in the Blue Gemini. Irrationally, Vivian found herself hoping they'd at least had time to get a few hours' sleep and take showers.

Peter was walking determinedly, striding fast but not about to break into a run. Broad-shouldered, square-jawed, and handsome.

He looked great.

"Hot *damn*," Vivian said.

Makarov eyed her, uncertain. "Bad?"

"No, no." She squeezed his hand. "Very good. Very, very good. It's all fine, Nikolai. Everything's going to be all right. For all of us. I promise."

Vivian would have liked to run to Peter, but that wasn't in the cards. She had no power in her legs. It was all she could do to prop herself up straight in Earth gravity, and that was only possible because she could lean on Svetlana and Nikolai in this bizarre mutually supporting spacefarer triangle.

Sandoval arrived and threw his arms around her. Belyakova wobbled, and Vivian reached out a hand to steady her. "Hi there …. Oh, boy, be careful. We're all a bit puny right now."

The medics were unfolding chairs, bringing out stethoscopes, all the usual. "Uh, Peter—let the doctors in."

It was all a bit dizzying. More people surrounded Vivian right now than she'd seen for *years*.

The doctors helped them away—so that the NASA techs could get to the Command Module—and sat them in chairs in a line, with Vivian in the middle, Svetlana to her left and Nikolai to her right. Terri Brock came to stand behind her and rested her hands on Vivian's shoulders.

"So," Peter said. "You're home."

"Yes, I am. Absolutely."

"I hope so." He nudged her. "And, look." He pointed to the east.

Vivian followed his pointing finger. "Nice. Yeah. Look at that, right?" She reached out for Svetlana and squeezed her hand. "Hey, space sister. Look up."

Far away, over the plains to the east, the Moon was rising.

ACKNOWLEDGEMENTS

As the tale of Vivian Carter and Apollo Rising comes to a close, I'm delighted to give thanks once again to my agent Caitlin Blasdell, of Liza Dawson Associates in New York, and to all of the fine crew at CAEZIK SF & Fantasy: Lezli Robyn (stalwart editor), Alicia Cay (copyedits and proofs), Christina P. Myrvold (eye-catching cover art), Leylya Udimamedova (meticulous front matter schematics), and of course CAEZIK's valiant captain, publisher Shahid Mahmud. Additional hearty thanks go to Karen Smale and Kelly Dwyer for careful beta-reads; Alex Shvartsman and Tetyana Royzman for help with Russian and Ukrainian translations, phrases, and cultural references; Kevin Ikenberry, for advice on authentic military jargon; and Brad Aiken, for input on medical matters. The blame for any errors or oddities that may remain in the text rests solely with me.

DRAMATIS PERSONAE

Americans

Astronauts, Apollo Venus Astarte:

Vivian Carter—Commander (also: Apollo 32 CDR)
Dave Horn—Lead Pilot (also: Apollo 32 CMP)
Josh Rawlings—Astarte Skylab Systems 21 CMP
Marco Dardenas—Command Module Pilot 27 CMP
Amy Benson—Mission Specialist: Medicine, Health & Safety
Rudy Frank—Mission Specialist: Solar Physics
Greg Heinz—Mission Specialist, Planetary Science: Venus
Laura Simmons—Mission Specialist, Planetary Science: Mars

Astronauts, US-Copernicus:

Ryan "Starman" Jones—Outgoing Base Commander (also: Apollo 22 LMP)
Daniel Grant—Deputy, then Base Commander (also: Apollo 38 CDR)
Feye Gisemba—Incoming Base Commander (also: Apollo 29 CMP)
Casey Buchanan—Associate Commander (also: Apollo 21 LMP)

Other NASA Astronauts:

Christian Vasquez—Astronaut; Geologist (also: Apollo 26 LMP)
Jon Evans—Astronaut; Geologist
Karl Johnstone—Commander, Daedalus Base
Gerard O'Neill—L5 Project Scientist, Daedalus Base
Ellis Mayer—CAPCOM, Mission Control (also: Apollo 32 LMP)
Bill Dobbs—Astronaut, Geologist (also: Apollo 26 CDR)

Astronauts, Night Corps:

Peter Sandoval—Commander
Terri Brock—Flight Engineer (also: Apollo 25 LMP)
Kevin Pope—Flight Engineer
Jose Rodriguez—Flight Engineer
Krantzen—Flight Engineer
Doyle—Pilot
"Major Alpha"—Commander, Kepler Base

Soviets

Cosmonauts, Zvezda Base:

Nikolai (Ilyich) Makarov—Cosmonaut (also: Soyuz TS-1)
Svetlana (Antonovna) Belyakova—Commander, Zvezda Base
(Also: Soyuz TS-1)
Yelena (Dubovna) Rudenko—Deputy Commander, then Commander,
Zvezda Base
Konstantin (Borisovich) Keretsky—Zampolit, Zvezda Base
General Arkadi Orlov—Commander, Zvezda Base

Cosmonauts, Daedalus Base:

Vasili (Yurievich) Doryagin—Commander
Mila Balkina—Deputy Commander
Katya (Valeryevna) Okhotina—Cosmonaut, Mission Engineer
(Also: Soyuz TS-5)

Cosmonauts, TMK-Mars:

Vitaliy Petrushenko, flight engineer
Igor Kaleri, flight engineer
Fyodor Terekhin, cosmonaut-scientist

Other Named Soviets:

Alexei (Arkhipovich) Leonov—Cosmonaut
Valentina (Vladimirovna) Tereshkova—Cosmonaut
Sergei (Pavlovich) Korolev—Engineer; The Great Designer
Dmitri (Mariyevich) Vlasav—Flight Engineer
Colonel Anton Rhyzkov—Deputy Commander, KGB Vympel

TECHNICAL AND POLITICAL BACKGROUND

Spoilers follow! If you just flicked back here without reading *Burning Night* in its entirety … you might want to do that first.

Politics of the Soviet Union

In the timeline you're reading this book in, Soviet leader Yuri Andropov died of kidney failure in Moscow Central Clinical Hospital on February 9, 1984, at the age of 69, and was succeeded as General Secretary of the Communist Party of the Soviet Union by Konstantin Chernenko. Gorbachev and other reformers were indeed protegés of Andropov, and it was certainly Andropov's intent that Gorbachev should succeed him. Others in the Politburo were not so sure, and eventually awarded the position to Chernenko, who was even older than Andropov and already in failing health, but at least provided some kind of a buffer and breathing space before the reformers were eventually able to come to the fore. Chernenko lasted until March 10, 1985, at which point he was succeeded by Mikhail Gorbachev, and the rest is history. (Well, it's all history, of course.)

In Vivian Carter's timeline Andropov took power in February 1980, not waiting for Brezhnev to die of old age in November 1982 but edging him out after the debacles of the Soviet invasions of Afghanistan and Pakistan, and of various unacceptable activities by Soviet agents on and above the surface of the Moon, for which Brezhnev became the scapegoat. Thus invigorated, Andropov was much busier much earlier, which was advantageous for his health.

Despite the differences in these leadership dates, it seems likely that a number of pivotal events in late 1983 would have played out similarly in both timelines, and these are of course the succession of political and military near-disasters that Peter Sandoval briefs Vivian on, shortly after her successful Venus flyby.

If anything, the Soviets' paranoid(?) belief that the US might be planning a preemptive nuclear strike upon them might have been even stronger in the world of *Apollo Rising*. Gromyko and Ustinov, and other members of Andropov's inner circle, would have been the same in both universes; the buildup of intermediate-range ballistic missiles on both sides of the Iron Curtain could well have been the same, and a Soviet Union that had effectively come out on top in the Vietnam conflict might be inclined to more decisive action in attempting to crush strike action and independence movements in its satellite countries. That greater repression backfired, causing those independence movements to flare up even more dramatically. Combine that with the economic stress on the USSR caused by massive spending on space infrastructure on top of the exhaustion of the early-1980s oil boom, and it's a recipe for disaster for the Soviet empire.

The Soviet "Seven Days to the River Rhine" plan for a "limited" World War III nuclear exchange in the European theater was quite real, and originally developed as early as the mid-1960s. In our timeline it was made public by the Polish defense minister in 2005, long after the fall of the USSR.

Oh, and the Soviet MiG-105 was also a real project. Development began in 1965, and eight suborbital flight tests occurred between 1976 and 1978. If it had become fully operational in the 1980s a booster aircraft would have carried the spaceplane up to a high altitude, whereupon it would detach and fire up its own engines to enter orbit. Post-mission, the craft would reenter to glide back down to Earth, landing on a conventional runway. In our world, the work on the MiG-105 was canceled in favor of the Buran mission, but then again, Buran was a response to the NASA's Space Shuttle program, which is not considered a viable option in Vivian Carter's universe (see the Technical and Political Background Appendix in *Radiant Sky* for a refresher on that).

Venus Flyby, and Beyond

Some readers might think it's a stretch to suggest that the human eye could see features on the surface of Venus through its notoriously thick atmosphere, but, surprise, surprise: on the night side of the planet, this is actually possible. My main scientific reference for this is: *Parker Solar Probe Imaging of the Night Side of Venus*, Brian E. Wood et al. (2021), Geophysical Research Letters, 48, https://doi.org/10.1029/2021GL096302 .

Other information about the changing face of Venus between day and night in various wavelengths can be found in: *Venus looks different from day to night across wavelengths: morphology from Akatsuki multi-spectral images*, Sanjay S. Limaye et al. (2018), in *Earth, Planets and Space*, https://doi.org/10.1186/s40623-018-0789-5 .

In other places during the Venus Flyby chapters I freely borrowed from the Venus Pioneer missions in our timeline for the technical capabilities and derived science carried out by the Apollo Venus Astarte mission.

Sometimes the high and low amounts of thrust it can take to get from place to place within the inner solar system can seem counterintuitive, but all the burns required in *Burning Night* were as accurate as I could make them. For those interested in delving into the numbers, if you Google "Solar system delta-V map" you'll find several graphical representations from reliable sources. After checking it carefully, the one I found easiest to use is at

https://upload.wikimedia.org/wikipedia/commons/9/93/Solar_system_delta_v_map.svg .

Lunar Radio?

The always-ingenious Nikolai Makarov strings a shortwave antenna across his vehicle so that he can listen to shortwave broadcasts from Earth, particularly the terrestrial Voice of America and BBC World Service, to educate himself on what's happening back in is home country. While it's true that the Earth's ionosphere refracts high frequency (or shortwave) radio waves back toward the surface, which is why shortwave is so good for transmitting long distances, the process isn't completely efficient, and in fact it's entirely possible for shortwave broadcasts from Earth to be picked up on the lunar nearside, given an appropriate antenna and receiver. For the nuts and bolts of this, take a look at *How to Dx Earth Radio from Outer Space* by Glen Hauser, in the magazine *Popular Electronics*, April 1977, pp.37-40.

Mare Frigoris

It might seem odd that the Moon's Mare Frigoris would be such a pain in the neck to navigate across, given how smooth and boring many of the Moon's other seas are, but this also seems to be true. For all the science-y details, see *Evidence for Recent and Ancient Faulting at Mare Frigoris and Implications for Lunar Tectonic Evolution*, Nathan R. Williams et al. (2019), *Icarus* 325, 151-161. For a slightly more accessible treatment, try *Study Finds New Wrinkles on Earth's Moon*, a NASA press release from 2019, available online at the time of writing at https://www. nasa.gov/missions/lro/study-finds-new-wrinkles-on-earths-moon/ .

For those interested, a great introduction to the lunar volcanic domes mentioned in the text, including those at Marius, Hortensius, and so on, can be found at:

https://skyandtelescope.org/observing/a-little-guide-to-lunar-domes/ .

Landing on Land

And, regarding the feasibility of dropping an Apollo Command Module onto solid ground for a "crunchdown" rather than the usual healthy splash, the study Vivian describes to her Soviet friends is real: *Apollo Command Module Land-Impact Tests*, J.E. McCullough and J.F. Lands, Jr. NASA Technical Note TN D-6979, October 1972. See also a related publication: *Apollo Experience Report—Earth Landing System*, Robert B. West, NASA Technical Note TN D-7437, October 1973. Both are publicly available online from the NASA Technical Reports Server https://ntrs.nasa.gov .

BIBLIOGRAPHY

In addition to the books mentioned in the bibliographies for Hot Moon and Radiant Sky, many of which I reread while writing Burning Night, I found the following books and materials useful:

Aldrin, Buzz, and Wayne Warger, Return to Earth, Random House, 1973.

David, Leonard, Moon Rush: The New Space Race, National Geographic, 2019.

Gorbachev, Mikhail, Perestroika, HarperCollins, 1987.

Orloff, Richard W., Apollo by the Numbers: A Statistical Reference, NASA History Division, NASA SP-2000-4029.

Saunders, Andy, Apollo Remastered: The Ultimate Photographic Record, Black Dog & Leventhal, 2022.

Swedin, Eric G., When Angels Wept: A What-If History of the Cuban Missile Crisis, Potomac Books, 2010.

Swedin, Eric G., Survive the Bomb: The Radioactive Citizen's Guide to Nuclear Survival, Zenith Press, 2011.

www.ingramcontent.com/pod-product-compliance
Lightning Source LLC
Jackson TN
JSHW021928141225
95594JS00001B/1